A Testament of Spears

J.W. Tate

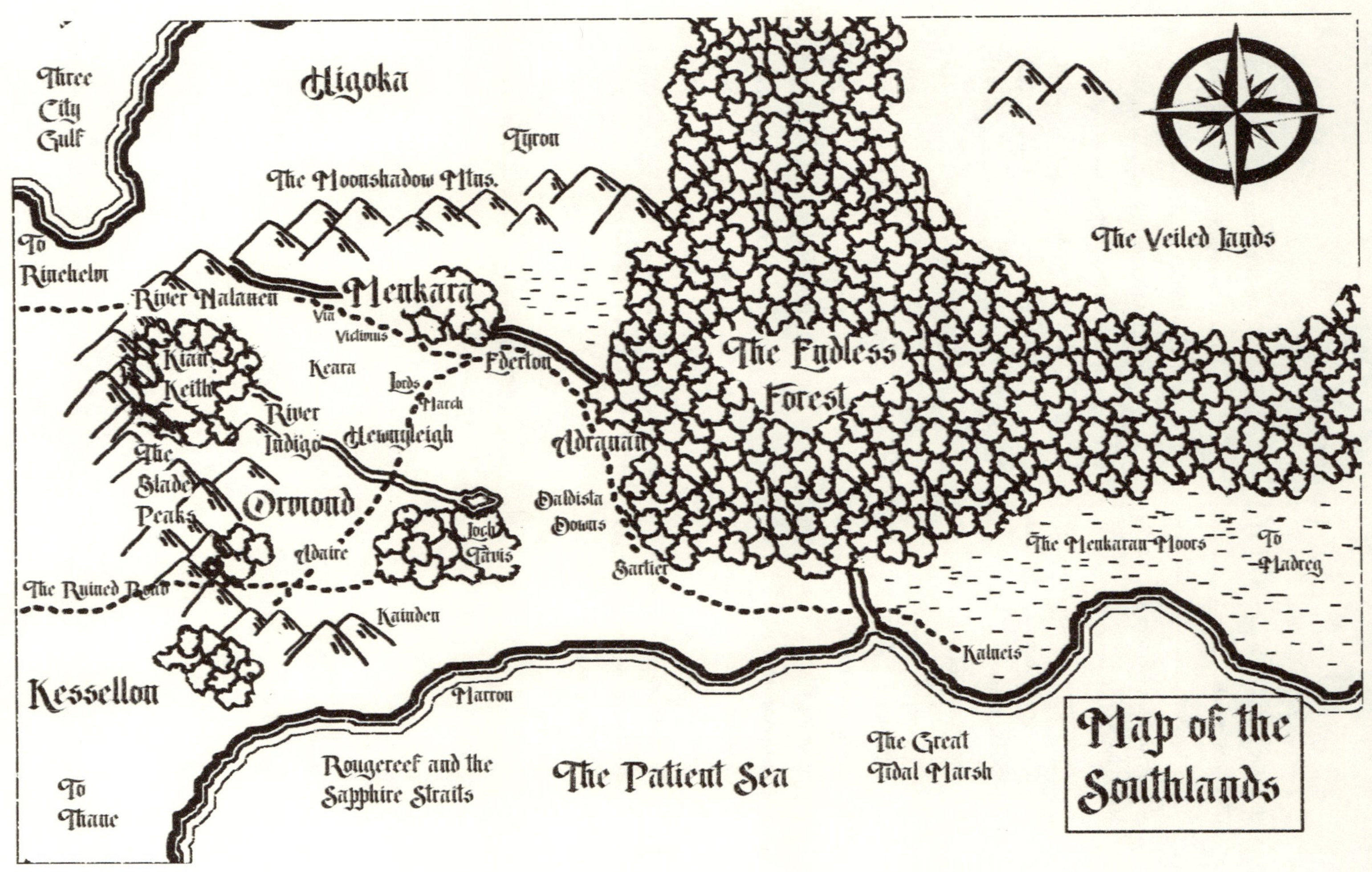

Map of the Southlands
The Veiled Lands
The Endless Forest
The Menkaran Moors
To Fladrey
Kalueis
The Great Tidal Marsh
The Patient Sea
Rougereef and the Sapphire Straits
Three City Gulf
To Runehelm
Aligoka
The Moonshadow Mtns.
Tyron
River Nalanen
Menkara
Via
Victimus
Ederton
Keara
Lords
March
River Indigo
Hewmyleigh
Abranan
Daldista Downs
Sartier
Kian
Keith
The Blade Peaks
Ormond
Adaire
Loch Jarvis
Kainden
Marrou
The Ruined Road
Kessellon
To Thane

Table Of Contents

Prologue..............................5

1. The Grigor..............................11
2. TheStrangers..............................17
3. In the Dark..............................24
4. Dreams and Promises..............................32
5. Allhallows..............................36
6. Night Terrors..............................46
7. The Sound of Chains..............................51
8. Beyond Balfour..............................58
9. The Tell-tale Tell..............................65
10. Fear..............................70
11. Reverence..............................80
12. The Endeavor Begins..............................90
13. Hewnyleigh..............................100
14. An Unexpected Reunion..............................108
15. The Pledging..............................115
16. Reflections..............................127
17. Relics of War..............................136
18. The Flooded Fortress..............................145
19. Guardians of the Breach..............................150
20. Into the Dark..............................157
21. Broken Words..............................165
22. The Swordsman..............................176
23. A Declaration..............................180
24. Ederton..............................189
25. An Earned Respite..............................196
26. Curious Sights..............................202
27. Moving On..............................208
28. Imposition..............................215
29. Strangers..............................221
30. The Salt Fair..............................236
31. Of Magic..............................243
32. Assumed Fangs..............................252
33. Frozen in Flight..............................258
34. Homecoming..............................265
35. Crossroads..............................273
36. Blood and Stone..............................286
37. A Lament for the Questing Beast..............................290
38. The Darkest Night..............................293
39. The Bonemother's Heir..............................297
Epilogue..............................309
Glossary..............................311

Prologue

The Dao Vae believed that the Arid Lotus only grew in the most desolate of places. This much he knew from his time with them. They were gone now, like so many of the others--like everything would be, eventually, but he would keep his memory of them with him always, and he hoped that in the end it would make all the difference.

Even through the gentler light of an evening sun and the smoked glass goggles Merris had made for him, the unrelenting glare of it all still dazed him, the towering crystal blades and snow-white sand blinding him like glare from a thousand tiny mirrors.

The Glass Desert. The stories were true. Other stories: of pockets of fiery slag, of wind storms that could mill steel like flour from wheat berries—and even worse, stirred in his mind, but the King Once and Future banished them all, steeling himself with the gravity of his purpose here.

He slid gently from his horse. These dunes were too precarious to rely on the surefootedness of hooves encumbered with a rider, divine hooves or no. It was perilous only for himself, of course; Enbarr was unmoved as always, offering not so much as a squint, seemingly unbothered by the sight of it; Immortal beings of the somesuch place outside the Realm of the Real were divorced from such trifling notions as searing hot pain or the threat of being impaled by spear-sized shards of glass. He envied them.

He didn't even have to take the reins for it to follow him, for with but a thought, Enbarr— or Devdatta as he was called in ages past, heard him and obeyed; it was the most immediate and noticeable advantage of having their wills entangled by the Magic of the Geas.

He adjusted the sword slung across his back, The Binding Blade, The Sword in the Mirror, twisting round the old woolen flannel he'd found in his things with which he fashioned its makeshift sheath. It, and the small silver cauldron which accompanied it, had been jostled loose upon his last miscalculated step across the Great Isthmus. After adjusting them both with a sigh he led on. Behind him was the last Crossroads he could sense, the last time he could take respite in the Otherworld, and he knew there was no turning back now, though he never would...this was the culminating task of a hundred lifetimes, and he would see it through, *then the False Flame would be gone forever.*

He'd once, in simpler times, in his youth, spent the majority of a day watching the journey of a caterpillar as it embarked on its traipsing exodus from one side of a corn field to the other. At first it occurred to him that the reason the memory had come to him was that he envied the fruitive results of the thing's endeavor; it was no doubt wrought from some inner spirit of enthusiasm that he could only wish to match. Then the accompanying thought came which refuted it: the caterpillar well could've been just as bored to undertake his journey as he was back then to undertake the task of watching it all the livelong day for lack of something better to do. The caterpillar, after all, (as far as his expertise in the understanding of caterpillar-reckoning went) had no aim or purpose to his trek. It had no call to adventure, no rhyme or other reason to journey but to go. When the King came to this conclusion it forced him to then concede that it was <u>this,</u> not his own slow-going, not his own wavering morale that he resented, but <u>this</u>: the carefree, unchased caterpillar itself; the unrealized fear and anxiety in it that needn't ever be allayed or otherwise dispelled, the dread that, whether for the simple lack of understanding to be found in its tiny mind or otherwise, had never been stirred in it. He envied the mind that saw the at-handedness of time to alot all the livelong day to the observation of a caterpillar's crawl. He envied the lack of purpose itself, that they themselves at that time had no good need for one, nor understood or had the capacity to care how important it is (surely) to have one.

The ground crackled beneath his close-toed caligae shoes, the glass-razors pulverized by hobnailed Solaristine soles (yet another one of the great Merris's sparks of forethought).

He descended one of the many dunes to come. At the first, when he almost slid and skewered himself in the moonslight, he mulled over the prospect of using that most holy sword of ages 'cross his back as a walking stick to steady his footing. Still, unshaken, he fought his way over it.

Then the next. Then the next, until the astrums filled the skies, and before he knew it he could see his breath. Sweat soaked the insides of the white linens which blanketed him from head to toe, but he felt it fleeing fast, as the chill started to grip him even now. It had helped deflect the sun a little, for what it was worth, but would serve poorly to keep him warm when the sun finally fully succumbed to the engulfing maw of night.

He sat with Enbarr on the most hospitable patch of ground they could find. Shielded by high dunes on all sides, from the folds of his clothes he produced a hefty bronze idol, and placed it on the ground before him, and with folded hands closed his eyes and was silent.

The item in question was very old. This was good. It meant that, while its Form had depreciated, its Nature had remained the same. What's more, it contained Salamandras, the Subtle Air of Flame, meaning it had even more potential for his purposes--if one believed such things.

Such could be said of old things, that they held Magic, especially if cleaved to dearly and for long enough; he'd come to learn that the Dao Vae and their descendants in the Veiled Lands burned old items such as this in temple rituals for this very reason, for fear that the objects could grow dangerous, even come to life. This statue could be Worked for sure, and easily, as it was both very old *and* very dear to him, qualities Thaumaturgy both valued.

He recited the True Name of the goddess it represented, using the words of All Creation to seal the item and rend the statue from itself, one from another, before he recalled the Seithr, the motions and gestures with which one could evoke the Spell.

He pictured the intricate circles of the Great Work in his mind needed to break the bonds of its physical state, the movements of his Seithr recreating them in four dimensions. These movements allowed him to recall the words in the Tongue of Shadows—for Anwyn, as it was called, slipped from the mind forever upon reaching one's ears unless thus reinforced. When he finished, with an energetic 'whoosh' the bronze statue ignited, an effigy now in Magic flame that roared like a bonfire with no conceivable fuel.

It would burn for weeks if he'd let it, and disintegrate into literal nothingness in so doing, but though it was harder to stop it than to start it he would see to that not happening; he'd promised to return it someday.

With that he sat the cauldron down upon the fire. This was perhaps the most crucial tool in his arsenal to see to his survival. A simple cookpot this was not; The Cauldron Chalice could give a man anything asked of it. It could grow to any size (it was once even mistaken for an ocean), or even not look like a cauldron at all. It could feed armies. It could bring the dead back to life (if the dead wanted that for some reason) and even grant immortality if he'd wanted it (though he wouldn't wish that on his worst enemy). No, after fumbling for a small mess tool he whispered a prayer, kissed his fingers, and touched the Cauldron of All Wants, as such imparting to it his wish: his mother's spaghetti casserole, piping hot.

He slept little, despite Enbarr's vigilant gaze to guard him, knowing that entities that existed before this world wanted to spill his blood for what he was trying to do, coupled with the uncomfortable cold even in the fire of the statue and the fact that the sand shifted unnaturally, making the ear-piercing 'crack' of breaking glass every time he was almost sleep, it was difficult.

The ground also rumbled throughout the night. It was not anything he'd anticipated or heard of being a phenomenon in the White Sands, but it almost seemed like the dunes slowly rolled like the tide of a great ocean. It unnerved him for some reason he could not place.

Before he knew it, dawn was on its way. Restlessly he decided to perhaps make some more headway before he would have to take shelter of the day. He quenched the Spell he'd pronounced upon the statue with a piece of himself, allowing it to resume normality, and pocketing it and putting away the Cauldron he headed on.

This was about the only time he could gain ground, he was told, in the hour or so it took the Moon of Days to swallow the sun at dusk and usher in the night, or just before it fled in the morning, only there would it be not too hot, not too cold. Finally reaching the peak of the next dune, he fought the steam and bewildering mirages for his quarry. Nothing. He expected as such. He crossed half a dozen more heaping hills of sand in the sun's corona. The other moons haloed the horizon, their blue and amber light throwing a violet blanket over the landscape, bringing with it a twinkling luster to the sand that reminded him of a winter's night back home.

He knew he was probably going too far, doing too much. Several times he had filled the Cauldron with ice cold water; it had started heating up again, and the sun was mostly still hidden. His plan was that he would hide in the nearest valley, and bury himself in the sand, wrapping the cauldron in his white linens to reflect the sun and use it as a shelter, wishing for ice shavings if he must--at least he hoped it would work.

But the plan was again delayed. Scurrying over one last dune, he stopped dead in the halflight, in awe of what stood before him. Stark black, and enormous even at a distance, its dark spires stretched upward like a great hand clawing at the heavens, there it stood: Ezaiadus, the living fortress.

He didn't know he would have to draw so close to it. He'd heard of it, of course, heard of the prison made closest to the indomitable flame of the unmoving, unyielding sun. It was the only gesture the Formerians could muster to stifle Sluagh Gora's power. It was futile in the end, of course, as now it served only as his stronghold and place for the thing to torture its previous captors.

Then Enbarr turned the king's head for him. Movement.

In single file they danced, their long shadows cast by nothing. They were the sluagh, the prisoner's servants, the hoary host of the King of Shades. They normally dwelt in the Deep, far away from cleansing light. He'd seen them there many times, but here, brazen enough to be caught in daylight with no place to hide...cavorting to the raucous tumult of dinless drums, frolicing to unheard melodies played on unseen horns...

He could see that the precession was only just passing them. Leading them was the silhouette of a solid shape, a person. In a few moments it would intersect where the young King was going and draw near.

It was riding a dromedary, cooling itself with a fan, wafting the flowery smell of exotic perfumes into the stale air.

"You. I know you." it wasn't the most elegant way to start a conversation, but the utter disbelief begged it of him. "You're Grimory. Pimonia." it came out almost like an accusation.

It was difficult to tell if Grimory was male or female. He'd heard Malacasta once call him 'he', but Pimonia, or Grimory--he was never sure which, was quite obviously not. 'He' wore a king's crown tightly around his otherwise bare midriff, which would seem somehow impossible to fit over his…buxomness. Otherwise he would appear as any other albeit attractive woman, save for a lithy tufted red tail that peeked from above his silk sarouel that always whipped about like it had a mind of its own, and the pair of faintly-glowing golden eyes that judged everything with equal disdain.

He wore an article called a heraldrix, a garment consisting of a pair of long sleeves connected by a protracted length of cloth. The swath between the sleeves was worn in various styles and colors. In ancient times it was called a Bahuvastra Sudre, where those colors and style denoted one's Tradition and level of skill. It was worn by the well-to-do nowadays, even viewed as posh, its esoteric meaning forgotten; Pimonia would've fit right walking around in any metropolis on Morida. But his was black, and meant black, worn crossed around the neck and down the back. It had probably been Transmuted, like most worn by the skillful were, sublimated to deflect or absorb harmful Spells.

Pimonia squinted, blocking the sunlight with a fan he incessantly had been known to hold, even in the snowy chambers of the Winter Queen.

"Oh, you." Pimonia sighed. "Again. It's always you. It always ever was always you, if there ever were a you to begin with."

"You were sentenced beneath the ice at the World's Heart, Forgotten." he reminded the demon.

"Me? Ha!" he guffawed "And Forgotten?! Never, thanks to you!"

"But how did you escape the Rathlands?"

"Escape? Te-hee! I was never the queen's captive, oh So Dreamed! I was her <u>advisor.</u> She followed my advice, so….here we are!" Pimonia's voice was effeminate and meek, with a certain hoarseness to it, giving it a tinkling sound like clinking champagne glasses. "I should thank you for freeing us." he said. The twisted tongues and minds of Immortal things always left him struggling to decipher their motivations; he wasn't sure whether he was being sincere or sarcastic. "Oh, you Hyu'manii with your bottomless lusts, so busy squiggling around like that, hither and thither. You never even realized you were unbinding us!" That made it apparent; he'd forgotten that Pimonia never missed a chance to deride those he perceived to be beneath him.

"You're welcome." said the king.

"Especially you, oathbreaker. You've served us best of all. In the end it was impossible to keep your vow. Wasn't it? Inevitable, no matter what words you invoked, what intentions you had: you couldn't save the Matron of Frosts from her suffering in the end. Now you see the futility of this world."

He grinned. "Here's your reward. You still have that odd shaped body, the squiggly one. I will relieve you of it." he splayed out his hands, and the shadows slithered and swarmed. They would rend him to nothingness, much like the bronze statue, he knew. It was their purpose.

A dozen shapeless nightmares from beyond the comprehension of the mind cloyed at him. He clasped the sword in his hand, and its light, bright enough to pierce the dazzling day even where they stood, subsumed them, banishing them before he'd even shown its foible.

"You misunderstand. I have not given up. I never will."

"You promise?" He snickered. "So the rumors are true, eh? You have Claimh Solais. Have you come to give it back to him? He may still let you enjoy a few more trips around this place if you did, before he returns it to oblivion."

"Back…to him?"

"The Binding Blade was <u>his</u> first." he explained. "You've no idea, do you?" he feigned being appalled at the stupidity of the man. The ground shifted beneath their feet for a moment, making the both of them shuffle to find footing, but Pimonia dismissed it. "It wasn't always like this, you know. In the beginning there was no One and the Other. No death, no time. Then She got involved, wanting to 'go there' and 'do that', and going on and on about this invention of hers called boredom."

"Selean."

" 'The Great Goddess.' " Now that one was slathered in enough sarcasm to be understood. "You know, it takes nothing to create a place like this, this All Creation, from within the Sea of Milk. I'm not impressed."

"I'll stop you, for her."

"Oh hushaby, Hyu'manii scum!" the Forgotten's face twisted in disgust. "Before you were born, He was! And will be when you're gone. He is eternal, and you, you are tiny. What measure of hope do you have against the always? You could live a billion lifetimes for all we care, gather all the knowledge your little mind can handle and compared to eternity all of those years would still equal precisely zero." The demon pinched a clump of sand from the King's shoulder, grinding it between his fingers. "To Him, YOU never happened at all. You are nothing!" he punctuated it, flapping the fan closed and turning up his nose. "Don't know why I'm even bandying words with you anyway, I've a world to crush." He then proceeded to brush and straighten the young man's shawl judgmentally.

"She has forgiven me. Your queen."

"She has?"

"Yes."

"You're lying."

"I swear it."

"Well, we all know the fat lot of good your word is."

The king took a step forward, himself brushing the comment away like dust. He looked him in the eye. "You know what that means."

"W-What? Pray tell." The king could see a concern on the demon's face that neither of his veils could hide.

"Her heart is safe from the likes of you."

"Ha." the laugh was doubtless meant to sound snarky and confident, but was executed as a nervous croak. "Means nothing. Nothing at all. Nothing means anything at all, for any of you."

"You keep saying that. But, you thanked me for saving you. Were I 'nothing' then I wouldn't have been able to do it. If I am nothing, then nothing matters."

"Right. It does."

"You mean doesn't."

Pimonia's eyes narrowed. He had talked to enough of these types of creatures to know that they always seemed to need the last word, especially him. "Beg pardon?"

"Nothing matters. You're right."

His eyes were stoked embers. " 'Nothing' as in the lexical notion of the absence of a thing, or 'nothing' as in the primordial everlasting abyss of unfathomable dimension into which you—and all things, must invariably fall?"

The King Once and Future shrugged, you could almost see the smile on his face through the cloth over it.

Pimonia's face twisted with agitation, "Pish-posh, you're one to talk of mincing words. The one trying to kill Death."

"Nothing lasts forever."

"True." Pimonia smiled. "It does. You'll see, soon enough."

"<u>Nothing</u> lasts forever."

Pimonia let out a feral growl of consternation that broke the facade of his femininity, then promptly departed.

The sun peeked out from above the moon now, the way its first rays pelted at him like a forge fire or the hammer, he wasn't sure which. Pimonia spoke of him and his host as being an inexorable, indomitable, inevitable power which none could repel or resist, yet his shades bothered the man no more. Though, again, such was the ways of Immortals; he'd wager equally Pimonia's motive being some convoluted yet infinity well thought-out machination (possibly centuries in the making), being genuinely fearful, or being unable to view the king as much more a threat than one would an ant. He looked about, befuddled. The terrain had changed again. Shifted. The castle could no longer be seen. He knew it was not likely enchanted with such Magics as to do so, Enbarr could see through illusions, and only the Endless Forest had such Otherworldly effects as to physically distort the world itself--this was something else entirely. Then it all came to him. Breath. It was breath that moved the world in the night for him, the breath of great a beast, one so immense that an army might march upon its back--that he may walk upon it for a full day unawares. Just then, it began to lift its unfathomably enormous head. The ground breathed.

He knew this creature now and had since forgotten it, having been told so long ago. Still it helped none at all; he couldn't even see the beast; <u>he </u>was an ant whom it had paid no mind until now, he was the caterpillar, who had no means of knowing that the shade was not some cloud or other natural event, but the eye of an observer falling upon him. It was everywhere. It <u>was</u> everywhere.

Eternities of dust and sand rolled away from the beast, that it might glare at the impertinent speck astride its back. Yes, breath it had been all along, breath, and the King knew the creature would not suffer to see him still drawing his.

Chapter 1
The Grigor

"...Past's long shadow stretches over the Last City, where he stands all day until the sun sets and he reveals his purpose as a messenger of woe. He tells the people that his master, Death Himself, would soon come to claim them. The people panic and try to leave, but Past will not let them; all night he looms over them, watching.

Now, Death can only come out at night, for only those in darkness can one fall prey to his powers, but Past says that for the people of Shamba'ala night is eternal, for his enormity blots out the sun. The faithful will not accept it, and rally themselves to climb the hill where every day they paid homage to Anan unabated, and at the first light of dawn a fire from the heavens, a great bird, wreathed in flame as bright as Past was dark appeared before them. A terrible battle occurred, a battle that destroyed the Last City as they toppled from the mountain, and Past, knowing the truth: that no night could last forever, retreated to safety, but a great stone had fallen and crushed the..."

Laina's mouth slammed shut as if she might be able to gobble back up her words if she'd done it fast enough, when the bellowing beckon of Bearch Buckroy came from the cracked double doors leading outside. "Adi! Stop lolly-gaggin' and get on your shift!"

"I'm so sorry. Again." She said. "You always get me talking when you speak of those dreams you have." She took up the mug from which he'd drunk his cider.

"No worries. If there were no time for fun or flights of fancy..." The young man smiled, politely trailing off.

She'd once told him that her people came from the east, across the great waters, fleeing from the clutches of Death (Himself), and led by a goddess who took the form of a great bird of fire. She even bore a mark on her cheek, a feather, a sign which branded her as her devotee. The mark never came off, no matter how it was washed.

It was hard to swallow, done so by most with more than a few grains of salt. Such stories abound in myth, of course, like those of the Veiled Lands or the Tuathan Fae or even his own people. He could see the value in telling such tales, in illustrating the tenacity and indomitability of a culture by providing such a pedigree to their past, such an impossible feat, but though Adimus had never seen the ocean himself, even <u>he</u> knew better than to believe them. *No one crossed the ocean.*

"Hurry along." she waved him out, returning the expression in kind. Reluctantly he lurched to his feet, stretching dejectedly.

Adimus always enjoyed her stories though, that, while far-fetched always seemed to have a strange ring of truth about them that he knew his ears couldn't quite follow or his mind dare not lead him to; he'd be remiss to admit he always liked stories like that.

The boy proudly donned his outfit, these, the special regalia and munitions of the Grigor: he pleated his great plaid of green and black and deftly lashed it around his waist, pinning it at the shoulder with a brooch upon which dangled a small crude stone talisman of a man with a single eye. He tugged his hair out from under it, sure to rough it back into the wild lime-bleached mane it was-- it always helped him look the part, and added some much needed height to boot. He then picked up his targe, wood and leather backed, lined with comfy fur and bearing a blazon of the great white stag on a field of sable and vert. He lashed on his leather vambraces, and sheathed his bronze dirk and skean dhu (boot knife), He then shouldered his sounding horn, the horn of Teutates. Last, not least, he took up the old iron broadsword they passed between them on shift (only slightly rusty and even more slightly sharp) before he was out the door.

The brisk air immediately slapped him in the face; it was going to be a long night. Rouge leaves glowed like embers, the kindling of autumn's hearth. Where they had fallen to lay bare their maple and oak boughs, several of the larger farmsteads could be seen, their squares of worked land stretching far off into the distance.

That was Balfour village proper, Bearach had reasoned, *"the houses were closest together here, too close together and within sight of each other to be in danger."* he'd said. Including their house. With a quick breath as if before a plunge he stepped onto the path that took him beyond, away from said safety.

It was called the Beat, a colloquial name taken from the grassy runs which served as the property lines between the plots of farmland. It was also the namesake of the lodge in its center as well from whence he came: The Green Beat. Maev was referring to a beetroot, of course, as evinced by the etched sign above the door depicting one...she always thought the name was clever, despite the misspelling (none save Adimus ever seemed to notice at any rate).

His path would take him in a large circle tracing the outermost of these runs on the edge of the village, a journey that took the boy nearly two hours. It was a boring task, most would say. On most occasions Adimus actually enjoyed it, soaking in the scenery and clearing his mind. On most occasions. He'd usually not much else to do anyway; there was always plenty of time to waste in Balfour. <u>On most occasions.</u>

There was also a footpath through the old woods he followed. It was beaten into existence almost exclusively by the feet of the Grigors; he and Bearach and Eichgun and all the others in generations before them.

It gave him a little solace; nothing ill had befallen any of the previous of them since the time of the war nearly two centuries ago, and before then it was men, not Nissies or Red Caps or the Tuatha. Even at that, people were but a shadow of a threat, for besides the occasional squabbles of politics inland, as he understood it, the country was at peace. These things he told himself. Still, the nights were cold of late, and the shadows long, and he had to fight himself from running.

He crested the hill behind the Beat, marking the end of his view of the place and the end of eyesight and aid for a while on. He stopped for a moment to catch his breath and sheath his anxiety, rubbing his sweaty palms on his thighs. He gazed upon the lake in the gully and Blaise's Parish beyond, visible only from here.

He wondered where he was, the Shepherd of the temple, whether he lurked nearby, what he would be able to say to him to evade and just do his job. Now that was unsettling enough a thought of its own to begin with...he thought not to think of it, which, as he would well know, was impossible.

This was not what pushed chill into his bones besides. Not this night.

The setting sun flickered like a candle being slowly drowned by its own wax. It was to be a well-lit night at least. The moons shown brightly in the sky. Nights as these were as twilight, and he'd always heard that the worst of monsters feared such times. It would be long into it before he would be finished, especially if he didn't start. Adimus held his lantern tightly, and with much effort forced his legs to move forward.

It had to be bandits, Bearach said, perhaps from the Ruined Road. But Adimus knew the truth. He'd heard from his uncle Anwell. Niall had told him a much darker story of what happened that night, and while Anwell was always one for spinning a yarn--especially around Allhallows Night--he didn't think he would turn such a thing into an anecdote.

Yes, it well could've just been bandits or other such hooligans and not goblyns, simply imitating their behaviors to cover their tracks: stringing up people's dogs, tearing up books, breaking mirrors and windows, spilling troughs and buckets and other man-made vessels. But...

From the hilltop between the trees he could still see into the valley where the charred bones of the old house stood.

The smell of smoke still lingered in the air near old Niall Anstead's farm, even though it had been three days; it was a deep burning fire that left its marks on more than just the man's home.

Leaves rustled and winds whistled, an incessant wall of noise that could mask any foe's approach, fictional or not. The youth struggled to push the thoughts to the back of his mind and keep his senses with himself and not with his nightmare daydream. Still, they drifted to the blackest corners, whispering portents of a thousand dire fates and worries to him, what dangers might befall him, his frail sister, his even frailer grandfather.

He finally reached the final run, and the old inn came into view once again. He let out a relieved sigh; he could now see the Green Beat across the creek, and his house just a stone's throw up the hill behind it.

He stopped for a moment to catch his breath again when he reached the road that intersected the path of the Beat, leaning a moment to dry his brow against the large rock at the intersection.

Setting foot onto the stone pavement felt good after a night of marching on the rugged trails.

The road had been here long before the village ever stood, laid here by a conquering army long ago, level and flat in defiance of the bounding mountains, cut with a precision and laid by a method no mason in the south could match even now. In its day, before the collapse of the mountainside, it held its trajectory unimpeded westward for a hundred leagues. Why, it cut even through the very rock in places as to not deviate. But for this statue.

For this statue, it gave way with a wide berth. Adimus looked up at it perched atop the stone. The figure of the cloven-hoofed horned man must have invoked some measure of fear or reverence in those soldiers to warrant such, Adimus was sure, but neither he, nor anyone there could tell him which, much less why.

There were many things like that in Balfour, things that, like the figure itself, stood lost to time. The very post of Grigor was said to be like that; the Grigors, or the Watchers, as they were sometimes called, had been around for at least that long, and again, like the statue, for whom offerings were still left, many obeisances still paid, and respect still given. Still they needed no reason to honor the Grigors, for void of reason the meaning still remained. The mystical-sounding names of his accouterments and the heavy-handedness of the ceremonies surrounding their march was like a talisman to the people of the small village that warded against the darkness. He'd always felt like he was an actor in a play, leader of a gallant one-man parade, or like some Ormondian bard portraying one of the great heroes of the epics, like Prasclia the Thrice Slain or Belegarm the Blithe. He was an actor only, and he knew it, not that it mattered.

He wasn't for being a Grigor now. No, tonight the call of the evening made him shrink even more, and no amount of obligation could push his shoulders back or straighten his neck; if there <u>were</u> purpose to the Watchers, he may well know it soon enough, whether he wanted to or not.

The march ended across the square, passing the great thing and overlooking the edge of the plateau upon which the village sat. The road ended abruptly with some of its disheveled stones hanging over the sharp edge of the cliffside where the road had crumbled--the kingdom that united the world had been great, but the gods that dwelt in the mountain had been greater.

The new path into the village from the Ruined Road began here, a swooping slope down the hillside to the road below that served as the only entrance into the village from the entire plateau.

Beside it was Brian the Blacksmith's house, whereupon reaching he would ring the iron bell that sat outside it, marking the completion of his march.

Just then, just as it was in sight, he heard a voice. It startled him, naturally, but not so much as when he identified from whom it had come.

"Adimus!" It was Tolten Blaise. It had come from the porch of the Beat. "I got something to say to you..." He said with a crooked finger.

Age and a malady of the bones always kept the man leaning heavy on the crook Niall had whittled just for him. The hurried way he ambulated down the long hill toward the Watcher showed well his urgency, quickening the boy's dread even more. It reminded him of one of the many nightmares he'd had, the kind where he is being chased but his legs won't move. He tried to yammer an excuse to try and leave as he approached, something like 'I've got to ring this bell' or 'I left the kettle on.' 'My dog just died.' nothing came out.

"Good evening, pardoner."

The old man heaved with strain, doubled in exasperation to keep up with him, but no less hastened by the subject matter. "It's a fine night. A fine night. Walk with me, Watcher." It was a sweetly stated sentiment for a compulsory act, and he could feel the scolding looming, like the venomous snakes which he handled in his Almsday ceremonies, poised to strike.

"They got into the cloister out back." He said plainly. The Grigor had heard about it already, but he feigned ignorance to hear the man tell the tale himself: that all of his ledgers and notes had been torn to shreds. What's more, one of the graves there on the property had been forcibly exhumed, and the bones stolen, and writing on several gravestones had been vandalized, gruesome details Meav had left out. The boy rubbed his nose. "Father thinks it is bandits masquerading as Nis. What do you think, shepherd?"

The Watcher had managed to reach the end of his Precession, the bell at the edge of town, before the rebuke began. "You tell me! It is your job to suss out! And it couldn't be done sooner. But...there are more pressing matters, now." He gave Adimus a stern eye, "Grigor Buckroy, Meav tells me you're listening to those Mansii stories again."

He knew it wasn't true. Meav would never gossip such a thing, much less to the pardoner, much less to get the boy in trouble. But Adimus was always bad at hiding the truth, and the old man knew that merely hinting at it was enough for cracks to show. Adimus scratched at his head nervously, a habit he'd picked up when at first the limestone with which it was dyed bothered him.

The man scowled. "I've said it and I'll say it again but not thrice: dabbling with falsehoods, even in passing fancy, strays the mind from Purpose!" He said. "Buckroys be Named," he cursed. "you and your ilk have caused enough trouble...that it was your pa that failed to see those flames the night they happened...No doubt the blindness was...spiritual in nature." His face grew dower. "Wrought of wavering rectitude in the precepts at the very least, indeed. At the very least. Still I pray for you, still I pray." He added the part at the end, though it did little to hide his castigations.

"Beg pardon, shepherd, but you feel that <u>this</u>, that me talking to Miss Akima, is more important than what's happening here? Now?"

"A weak mind is a tool for Fae trickery. What your eyes for the material world cannot tell that <u>these</u> eyes can, is that it well could be those transgressions that brought this ill moon over us! The transgressions of you and your father both."

The boy managed a jovial grin. "My father has little to do with my penchant for enjoying the fictions of other cultures, now, pardoner. And before you make the assertion that clearly your face says is brewing, he's not any interest in taking up another wife, and hasn't shown the slightest interest in miss Akima--were the former the case he'd be at the door of your Meav, and you know that."

The candidness with which he spoke jarred the man back to sobriety. "Aye, still, he and your grandfather..."

"What? Traveled?!"

"Yes, precisely! You must be lucid to what you could bring back with you, be wary of that to which that carnel eye is blind! Those Menkarans worship the heathen Fae as gods too! As did your mother, doubtless…The Eye of Crom Cruach sees right into your bones, boy." he said ster. "Sees what makes your heart move. Does yours move for Purpose, or for those stories?" his eyes narrowed. "Or for the harlot what tells 'em?"

Adimus consciously fought to unclench his fist. Instead he maneuvered to invoke pity, as that usually worked. "I don't remember much about my mother." He lowered his head solemnly. Tolten raised a brow but gave no response. "It is divine providence surely, shepherd, that she died before she had a chance to fill my head with those lies."

"Blessed be." He bowed his head, the sarcasm lost on him. He put a hand on the Watcher's shoulder. "But be not sorrowful. Your mother has returned to rest, no doubt, to be with those who came before in peace."

"Despite being a heathen worshiper of the Tuathan gods?"

That noticeably knocked the wind out of his sails, which manifested much as a sigh. "Look boy." he then said. Blaise pointed out over the vale, to the great gorge and the land beyond, far off in the distance. "You see that out there? You know, well as I, that all the village is built upon a mountainside. Now, my boy, it looks flat, but if one but journeys hither or thither they'll simply find it not so." His allowing the boy to come here before his rant seemed intentional now, for it was the only vantage point in all of Balfour from which one could see over the mountain. He raised a bent scholarly finger. "Nor is the world itself flat, though it may at first glance appear to be so. The elders tell us this, and to a learned man it is incontrovertible." Adimus lowered his head.

"I know the world isn't flat…" Adimus scuffed at the dirt with the toes of his boot.

The shepherd drove his point home with a wagging finger. "Well, just the same, there are plenty of things in this world that seem not to be so that are, <u>but</u> so many more are there that are that aren't so…" it was a dense statement, clearly. The pardoner gave him a moment to digest it before looking sideways at him, fondly. "You oughtn't rely on your own reasoning to figure out the world, boy. Hubris and vainglory <u>that</u> is, and the way of the heathens! This world is bigger than you, and man's proclivity for sin and invention bigger still! It's only by the endeavor of the ancestors, and the Graces of gods that man has found Truth. Grace and Endeavor…." he eyed him critically. "Numitorum says that you, you Adimus, are the gatekeeper to the dwelling of your spirit! If you allow such things--such foolishness to be permitted, if you let it in…" he pointed a crooked finger. Adimus knew the 'dwelling' he alluded to from having it pounded into him dozens of times. "This is the true test of a Watcher, boy. Vigilance! In hand! Heart! Head! " with a gnarled brow he thumped his own head with his finger to drive it home. He straightened, as best his hunch would allow.

He looked out at the lay of the land below. There, the Ruined Road, and beside it…

The lake had erupted from the ground overnight, they'd said, a calamity that threw down houses, even hewed the very stone from the tor, sending a mountain's worth of rock cascading into the chasm of Pangor Vale. Ever thereafter the pristine lake sat, the very summit of the highest mountain of the Blade Peaks buried in its depths.

It was the stirring of the Formerians, the children of Crom Cruach, deep within the earth, that caused such catastrophes, everyone knew that. Pardoner Tolten taught that such disasters only befell those, only occurred when such things were forgotten.

Tolten didn't ask to be led back to the parish, instead leaving the boy to stand and give thought to the words he just heard. And there, on the cliffside, it was exactly what he did.

The mountain's peak still disturbed the surface of its waters as a tiny protrusion of stone. This cap was once the summit of a great mountain, but was now but a tiny island. Loch Herespil it was called, and while the ramifications of its creation were monstrous ideas about which to daydream, it seemed as nothing compared to the thought of the bloody ceremonies held on nights like this upon the rock in days gone by; when the High Shepherd of the Druids, keeper of the ways of Illea, had always made sure the giants <u>were</u> remembered, by performing acts no one could ever forget. Worse that it is tempered by a truth deeper still: these things were necessary. *'The Bound King is unblinking, even in his slumber, and throws down mountains even in his sleep.'*

But all that was set aside. Instead, his eyes locked on the bottom of the gorge. All else fell away, his skin felt numb, and his mouth ran dry. *Torches.*

Chapter 2
The Strangers

He struggled to take a breath deep enough to sound the horn.

A thousand times he'd rehearsed scenes in his mind about what he might do if the village were under attack. They always ended with him being the hero, but now he'd found himself a fool for not considering the other outcome. Finally mustering every ounce of his courage, he lifted the instrument to his lips, and with a chest filling like a bellows sounded the proper tones from memory. The rhythm of the sounds were distinct and known by all, warning of danger, to make preparations for it, to bar doors and brandish blades if need be, to gather the horses and ride.

"Put it away, fool boy." He gave a start when he heard the female voice above and behind him, atop the blacksmith's roof. Faster than he could fumble his sword from its sheath and wheel around, he heard another, even closer. "See?" This one was a man's.

A black cloak drifted before him. It had defeated his vision, and he gave little thought why: unwavering in the night air, it draped around the gaunt figure disturbed only by its owner's sway in its otherworldly dance, and seemed to thwart any light that might betray it; its furls as untouched by it as its folds.

"Told you we'd scare the daylights out of them."

The man's warm face somewhat disarmed him. Giving the boy a quick smile as his ghostly hand appeared from the folds of his garb to tip his funny-looking hat to him.

"Adi!" Now he really felt panic, as he couldn't help but wince. "Make way, foolish boy, we got company!" He was really getting tired of being called a fool.

"Bahh…" Tolten's grumble could be heard in the distance.

After a few moments of frustration at the boy's apparent paralysis, the Pardoner started up the hill on his own at a markedly hurried pace. Adimus was somewhat relieved.

The man oddly seemed to notice it too, as his chuckle seemed to show. Then with a spin that showed practice he whipped off the cloak. He watched as what had been a second earlier black as night turn to a respectable bright red. Adimus couldn't help but stare blankly at it. "He's already tending to us, thank you very much!" He said, throwing it into the boy's arms with a wry wink. "Tell them I sent you." he whispered. He followed the man's glance toward the caravan behind him.

It was all that the gentleman said to the boy. The voice yelling at him was the reeve's, and the comment could have very well saved him some guff, but before the boy could dispel his astonishment enough to utter a 'thank you' the man was also strolling away at a pace.

With that, he'd started to flip the cloak onto his shoulder, until he noticed the heaviness in his hand. He lifted the cloth to reveal the coins that had been neatly stacked in them. Both.

Then a faint sound from the rooftop above him snapped him out of it. Adimus began to glance up only to feel a shadow pass over his head, then hear the soft landing of feet plopping down behind the stranger some half a dozen paces beyond the eaves of the building; it was a leap no person he ever met could have cleared by a long shot. The Grigor looked to see who, or rather what, it was, but before he could he felt the man playfully sat his hat atop the boy's head and blinded him. He only had the chance to see that gentleman's back as he shuffled away with the other figure, who hurried off as well, swaddling the muddy hooded robe it wore and whispering something to him in a tongue he'd never heard before--in a displeased tone that overcame <u>any</u> language barrier.

The young man had stood stilt-legged but for a moment at these revelations, but it was just enough time to be bowled over by yet another person in a hurry.

"Ack!" The woman yelped. "Watch where you're going!" It was hard enough to bare the boy to the ground, as if whoever it was hadn't seen him at all.

Her dejected tone was somewhat muffled inside in the young man's ears when, after rebounding, he gazed upon the woman. He was unsure of what part left him speechless. Her adornments, the myriad bracelets, necklaces, rings, sashes and charms clasped in her fiery red curls, shells or coins or lustrous strung stones of aqua and amaranth and goldenrod. Perhaps it was the leather cuirass she wore, worked explicitly to fit her quite obviously feminine figure-which she wore with the bust bare, or her unbefitting baggy trousers and riding boots, or perhaps it was the notion that any of this disarray could possibly draw eyes from her porcelain face and emerald eyes.

"...What?" she said, not helping but notice his lingering.

Adimus tried to stammer up an apology, and almost prided himself in that he could, but when an expectant eye under rustled brow fell upon him and her outstretched hand beckoned, he decided helping her to her feet was courageous enough for him at the moment. She was perhaps only a few years older than he, but the way she held herself was mature and distinguished, with an air of confidence that asserted her seniority, an air that made him, and probably anyone else, feel that if forced to address her, they should undeniably do so only as 'my lady'. She pushed her curved sword down with her palm to free it from tangling her legs when he offered the hand, and took only a moment to look him in the eye and give an obliging (and perhaps apologetic) smile before hurrying off as she was. He could feel his face flush in the cold autumn air.

Making sure he'd actually stand aside for whatever traffic might be next, he hurriedly nabbed up the rest of the strewn coins. He was forced to dismiss the thought that his haul seemed markedly lighter, that perhaps he had missed a few, when the next of it, a horse-drawn wagon came through—he would look early tomorrow, perhaps.

The driver of the carriage he at first mistook for a bear, as he was wearing the furs of one, and could impersonate one for size easily. Beneath it he wore a shirt of bronze chain links. It must have cost a fortune, much more because fitting him for it would've been the cost of two—he made Brian look small. His hair was short and cropped, like a Kesselloni soldier and few others. "Hail, Watcher." He nodded his salute with a dismissive tone that belied that he was thinking of a nice way of saying 'outta my way'. At least *he* was attempting to be polite.

The youth timidly stepped forward "I was sent by..." he then realized he didn't get the man's name. He glanced up at the man's tall, brimmed hat atop his head, to which the man replied with the simple shake of his head and point of his thumb to the back of the wagon.

He waited for the hooded wagon to gait past him. He could see the wagon's faintly lit insides. He attempted to hop in, but it was going rather fast. The shadowy occupant holding the lantern offered a hand. Adimus grabbed it.

Crash! The lamp shattered on the ground when the man reached for something on the table. Everything went dark; thankfully the base hadn't shattered. After a moment it was reignited by the man from a source of flame which Adimus had no explanation for, that simply leapt to life from a stick of wood out of nowhere.

"Umm, umm, hello?" he yammered after an odd moment of silence. The man simply looked down at his hand with an unreadable expression. He wore spectacles to correct his vision, rectangular and silver-framed, a luxury none other than the reeve ever hoped to afford, along with a gown of robes of a vibrant shade of cerulean he'd never seen in a garment before. His pecan hair was also not long—though framed his face well, it was not the look of a local. Finally, the man looked back up at him with a critical look in his eye. "...Who are you?" It was an uncouth way of being asked to introduce himself, coming from someone so helpful just seconds before. But when the boy looked upon him he could see a plain sort of shock on his face, as if he'd been startled.

Adimus awkwardly pressed on. "I was sent-"

"What in Lyr's Name! Regil!" came a voice from around the front-end veil of the wagon. Opening it there stood a long-faced, tired-looking man. "Oh, Juminion, my apologies." The man said, peeking behind the curtain of the carriage. His eyes darted about until they fell on the boy.

"No, mine." the man said. "Please, allow me to pay for it." He said, putting on a pair of snow white gloves from his pocket in a way that Adimus could only construe that touching him had somehow made him unclean; Adimus found himself looking down at his person--to ensure he maybe hadn't fallen in manure or something.

"No, no. Your services have been indispensable during this trip. If anything I should foot more of the bill than I have. Especially for what you did back there. But don't hold me to that." he chuckled at his own joke. Noticing he was the only one, he cleared his throat and looked up to the boy.

It was like he wasn't even there. "I...I was sent..." Adimus started, but drifted off when the look on the man's face showed he more than understood.

"Name that Argent!" he cursed. "Every time it comes to stabling the horses or unpacking, or doing any form of labor he finds a way out of it." he said. "What did he pay you?" He finally addressed the boy.

"N-not much." Adimus immediately regretted his thoughtless choice of words; he didn't know whether to tell or not, so he said the first words he could blow passed his lips. He did that a lot.

The man simply guffawed. "No doubt he could afford it, whatever the cost." he brushed the comment aside. Adimus could feel the tinge of jealousy. "Named Whispermonger. You should've partnered with him, Alfred, whoever he is." he added, again patting the robed man on the shoulder. "Well then," he said giddily, looking at the boy and rubbing his hands together, "start by picking up this glass, then when you are done with that, untack the horses, and then..."

* * * * *

Their leader's name was Baron Torrin von Krasad, a wealthy nobleman from the west. Adimus had learned this from the man's talkative associate, Regil.

Regil was a warrior from the capital of the once Great Kingdom, and was hired as a bodyguard for the road. He spoke of his days fighting in the arena--and of the Labyrinth City, to the gaping-jawed youths and adults alike. His stories may have been interesting after a fashion, but when the boy was singled out for his position and questioned about his experience in battles things got awkward, and Laina, the treasure she was, spirited him away from it, but not before blathers of a "friendly sparring match" came up.

It had been far worse than bandits or even monsters for sure: guests. And strangers at that.

Adimus caught his breath in the common room with the other regulars. He never thought that he'd have to resort to such drastic measures, but there was nowhere else to go. He could hide in Laina's room (she wouldn't mind it), were it not for the questioning eyes of the ever vigilant patrons, the same curmudgeonly old codgers that now passed their same myopic judgements on these new folk.

He'd usually be home by now, and everyone else long before that, but apparently Adimus's horn was a wakeup call that summoned every villager out of the woodwork to gawk and stare and gossip. No, instead he sat doodling on his wax tablet.

"I think they're outlaws. Escapees from Brigden. There's an astrolabe in their effects. That Regil chap looks like a quarryman, and that lady has the tricorne of a cap'n." said Anwell.

"An ocean captain? And a girl at that? Ha! Surely you can do better. They're defectors from the war up north if they are anything. They've a Sum Seer with them." Said Regby Goddard.

"Sum Seer? What's a Sum Seer?"

"A wizard."

"Wizards?! Hah! At least I'm not dragging fables and Faerie tales into my guess."

"So it is a guess."

"He's a Magus."

"All'khemist, he's a Thaumaturgist." another chimed in.

"You don't even know what that means!"

Adimus himself had been pestered several times now, much to the boy's frustration, and the fruitlessness of their questioning had stopped them from speculation or the outright invention of dramas involving the new strangers none at all. As such, he'd managed to learn from interpolation that Krasad and company were made all the more suspicious by, in fact, giving nothing at all for them to gossip about: Krasad had told no one anything; nothing of whence they'd come, where they were going, or why they were going to or coming from anywhere to begin with.

The boy gave a sigh. He wished to go home. His father and the reeve were having a meeting--it was about their new guests. *Hopefully.*

They couldn't disturb the peace too much, the Grigor reasoned, or else Tolten would eject them from the village--and the reeve would allow it, as a concession to an angry mob that with a few words could be stirred to violence if the priest of Illea so wanted. Adimus shared this sentiment with the villagers, usually. Strangers always made him nervous, and every stranger that visited Balfour, save for perhaps Laina, was exhausting.

"They were supposed to leave tomorrow, but I heard Luloch telling the driver that if they stayed for the next two days they could do so, room and board for free, no questions asked." said Anwell Buckroy.

They all shot glances toward the closed doors of the meeting hall, wherein they all spoke.

"That's awfully presumptuous of him." said Maev.

"Who does he think he is anyway?" said Regby. "The chief Watcher needs to mind his station."

"Prudent, I'd say. With what's going on." Anwell argued.

"You're more a fool than a fuller, Anwell. Or bloody mad. Seems to run in the family..." he said, taking a drink of ale to punctuate the insult. "We can handle our own business well enough. Why, I'll put an arrow right through the eyes of those bandits meself."

Anwell shook his head. "Bandits..." Anwell snorted. "Best hope I'm just mad."

Uncle Anwell, well at least who he'd learned to call uncle, was the resident skeptic. He was a retired fuller and sheep herder, a little too old yet a bit too eager to give his farm to his heirs so he could spend his twilight gossiping and drinking.

Adimus stretched. "The reeve has neither the resources nor provisions to alot for their board. It'll never happen." He was beginning to get frustrated himself. "-That's what he said." He said, hopping up for just a moment to put the tablet by the fire so that the beeswax would melt and he could start again. He added that last part quickly; he had accidentally sounded learned, a little too authoritative. He'd always watched the words Luloch taught him, his family received enough derision as it was when he wasn't considered pretentious.

His own eloquence aside, he could remember the number of times since his childhood that the village had visitors, and could count them on one hand, and each time they were met with suspicion. He didn't know if it were the simple xenophobia talking, but it was said that The Ruined Road was most certainly not the safest or easiest way to cross the mountains, that those who came this way did so to avoid the more patrolled and controlled northern passage. Laina was met with the same distrust when she came.

"Still. We could sure do with some strangers parting with coin though, if our larders can manage. They want me to shoe their with iron." bellowed Brian the Blacksmith to a few gasps.

He'd apparently mustered up the courage to finally talk. Before Brian could still be seen staring silently into his drink--he had no business being here so late, he just didn't want to go home. Some still giggled with glee, and still others jeered with jealousy at what had happened to the man earlier. The girl that had come with them had shown herself to fancy the man. She sang like a nightingale to him and danced like a bird of paradise. She was quite talented, versed in "sea shanties" and the like, which the bar-folk enjoyed, as well as a few classical ones, even belting out a few verses from the Cantos of the Thrice Slain King. And he rather enjoyed being serenaded by her, watching her sultry figure with discerning eyes--that is, until his wife showed up, whereby the girl promptly left (albeit with a full belly and a more than a few drinks in her gullet, all compliments of Brian's purse).

Laina giggled, sharing a knowing smile. "He wants them to stay for Ellyllon, surely. For High Samhain's Night." she said, setting down a sloshing bucket of hot water. Then she gave a thought "Wait until the shepherd hears about it." she said to Maev.

"Heathen money's still money. That's what I'll be tellin' him." Maev joked back.

Laina's pause was perhaps to tone down the pace-and thus the volume- of the conversation. "I hear they're already spending." she nudged Adimus. "The one upstairs gave him and me quite a decent gratuity."

"The bard?" said Meav.

"Wait. He's a bard?" Even Adimus chimed in at that. *Now there was someone who could tell a story.*

"A real one, Adi. Bowen trained." Said Anwell, bringing the probate conversation public. "Not some minstrel or jack that uses the name, a genuine Whispermonger, they say, from right here in the provinces." Adimus could hear the stools sliding around, and feel the eyes on him.

"Haha! You think a <u>proper</u> Whispermonger would boast that he were one?!" Regby antagonized him again.

"Never mind that." bellowed Brian, now in on it. It seemed they were all still listening now. "...Well, Buckroy, How much did they give you?"

It took a moment for Adimus to realize they were talking to him, longer than the boy realized it should have for some reason. Adimus pulled the coins from his pocket, almost as if presenting evidence; he almost couldn't believe it himself. Maev's wide eyes darted about the table as he tallied the little coins of turquoise and jasper "Three favor and six." she managed to pull the slack from her jaw enough to say.

"He gave me four stripes just to draw him a hot bath." Laina said, drawing up her sleeve to reveal them strung on her bracelet. With a smile she began to waltz up the stairs with the bucket of water, all but swooning.

Suddenly he became conscious about the grime between his fingers, and the stickiness of his skin. *A hot bath. That would be great.* It was something he wished his family could afford for him more often.

Adimus started to pocket his change when he heard the dejected sigh and growl above him.

He could tell exactly who it was, as could everyone else. She was in nothing but a silken sheet. "Psst. You!" She whispered loudly. It took Adimus an even longer moment this time to realize that she was talking to him as well.

He didn't want to make eye contact. He quickly looked away; perhaps she, and in turn the situation, might go away if he ignored it, but when she swiftly stomped down the stairs past poor Laina and right up to his table and slapped it. "I need you." All was silent with the exception of his heavy breath and a stifled chuckle from Anwell. She grabbed his hand this time, pulling him to his feet. "Now." she growled, jerking him out of his chair from behind the table, sending a blood-curdling scrape across the wood floor. He recoiled nervously, and she gave a conniving smile meant only for her before turning back up the stairs, looking on at his audience. Adimus glanced about for a moment to confirm the fear in his mind that everyone was indeed watching this whole event transpire.

Her soggy footprints stained the varnished oak staircase. He noticed this because he kept his eyes to the floor the whole way up the stairs.

Rather than the loft being an open area, it was separated by a thin wall which created a shallow hallway, made even more shallow by the piles of chests and crates that filled it. Awkwardly he brushed past her.

Adimus passed the door to the room where Torrin, Regil, and the spectacled man stayed, then Argent (who had a room all his own) where she stopped just before hers. She waved him past.

"...That case. There." She pointed at the very corner of a chest at the bottom of a towering pile of bags and chests that had been heaved on top of it. "I need it dug out." she explained. "Because someone stole my clothes!" she yelled, perhaps loud enough for the perceived culprit to hear. Caddy-corner cases padded with saddlebags towered above his head, crowned by a precariously perched rundlet of leaking spirits, probably whiskey judging from the smell. Adimus had brought this luggage up from the carriage himself, and didn't remember placing it as such. He himself would have a hard time lifting it above his head, but by mustering his strength and patience he undid the terrible mess over the span of the next minutes, and fetched the case for her; the biggest, heaviest, and most awkward one of the bunch. She stood with arms crossed again, waiting. The stance she bore was perhaps out of modesty, Adimus had thought, as between having just apparently bathed the sheet was drenched and clung heavily to her, but when she pressed against him to hurriedly squeeze through the cramped doorway before he's made it through himself he realized that such concepts must have been foreign to her.

The amenities at the Green Beat were by no means fancy, and such luxuries as silk sheets would not in a millennium be found here. He wondered who would bring a silk sheet with them for traveling, but shook the thought from his head to steady himself for the task at hand, which would no doubt take mindfulness if he were to survive the night.

What the Green Beat did have was space. It was by far the largest building in the village, having both an upstairs and a basement. It had actually been a small moat house belonging to the reeve's ancestors, spanning back centuries, but the man had already moved on to claim a larger estate, and knowing an opportunity when he saw one sold it to the pardoner, who gave it to Maev. The upstairs area had been a defensive feature (it was Adimus's business to know such things), an arcade for archers to fire down the hill, but when they renovated it for her he added a kitchen on the base floor and a set of rooms that would replace the loft windows upstairs from that, turning the floor into the common room. This left it with several private rooms for guests, a luxurious feature for an inn even in big cities.

He finished pulling it into her room, as she'd instructed. He sat the chest down, and wiped his brow. The sweat was not from exertion.

She looked over her shoulder and down the hall before coming in, then shut the curtain behind the both of them. Adimus dumbfoundedly thought to excuse himself, but found that he couldn't make the noises with his throat needed to articulate the thought; he thought back fondly to the time he blew his horn in the face of (at the time what was) inconceivable danger, a fond memory indeed.

She walked up to it and knelt. The chest was curiously sealed with a palm-sized pad-lock, to which she produced a dagger she'd kept somehow hidden in the fold of the sheet and a crook of iron from within the locks of her hair and proceeded to jimmy the lock clear with a skilled twist of the wrist.

Adimus's eyes widened even more when she opened it and a tiny little person sprung from its depths. "Tirlag, you filthy breather! I'll scalp you!"

The girl slammed the chest shut again nervously, "Ha, ha." she shot Adimus an awkward smile to hide her surprise, the muffled voice still spitting curses. When they'd stopped, she cracked the chest and lent down to whisper something in a language he didn't understand. Whatever she'd said, it placated the thing. Tirlag—that was her name, opened the chest, now more confidently, clearing her throat expectantly.

Slowly the tiny figure stood. She was only a thigh's height. Her hair was made of locks of verdant vines and scarlet blossoms. Were it not for arms and legs and tiny fingers, Adimus might have mistaken her for floral arrangement, but the eyes embedded in her fleshy green face were like any other person's he'd ever seen, albeit bigger and bluer and farmore filled with curiosity as they darted about, despite at the moment appearing cross. She was clad in a hempen robe and iron chains which dangled from her wrists, which were perched angrily on her hips. "A week." was all she said.

"Three days." The lady replied.

"I could feel the sunlight through the cracks! One week!" It said. The lady hushed at her-at least Adimus supposed it was a 'her'.

"There was a village! And we were stopped by the Order of Jasmine!" the lady explained. "It was a good thing I hadn't taken you back out yet!" Tirlag tried to explain.

"You could've just called me your slave."

"Not in Menkara! Your people are free here."

"Backward Hyu'mans--make up your minds. I'd rather go by myself. Better off in the wilds with Nissies and Shades than dealing with you savages!"

"You wouldn't even know where we were going if it weren't for *this* savage!" she pointed a thumb at herself for emphasis. "You little...hob!"

The creature gasped and looked Tirlag up and down, then her tiny face twisted with even more outrage. "You were just opening the chest to get your britches!" she realized. Having read the look on her tiny face Tirlag quickly reached in to grab the garment upon which it stood. "No!" the creature snatched it from her hands and clammed herself back in the chest when the girl grasped at it.

It took her wedging the dagger between the opening and twisting it to, then squeezing her fingers in and prying before it relented. "I can't believe you!" it cried.

She still clasped the garment in a death grip. Tirlag stopped for a moment, and lent in with a solemn look in her eye. "Delaney. I'm so sorry. I didn't mean to-" The 'to' came through gritted teeth. She started to tug at it again, hoping that she had loosened her grip. She hadn't.

"Your honeyed-tongue won't work on me, sweetie!" it hissed. Tirlag pulled again, hard enough to lift the little thing off the floor. "You...forgot...about...me!" She yelled, holding fervently on as she attempted to flap the creature off it. "And what's worse, I <u>know</u> you don't care at all! You could've let me out!"

"That wouldn't have worked, they're hunting your kind—!." She tried to explain, but the thing was hearing nothing of it.

Finally, with an audible rip, they came free. Tirlag looked down at the torn fabric, face frozen in shock, far too concerned to notice the brisk breeze that brushed her bare skin now that the creature had run off with her sheet. Adimus, of course, had been looking on at the sight the entire time. He tried to stammer a word of discretion, he really, truly did.

"Wait. Who is that!?" he was cut off by the squat creature mirthfully swaddled in the swath of linen, who had easily (he'd hate to admit) managed to sidle up to him out of his view.

Tirlag spun the sheet out of the creature's hand. "That's-" she paused just a moment to rewrap herself, which lended a dramatic pause to her pronunciation."...Our accomplice."

Chapter 3
In the Dark

He felt as would a victim to a robbery, or perhaps a hostage, skulking about in the dark well after decent hours on the orders of a complete stranger. Whichever it was, when she told him to stand and keep watch as the plant creature, clenching a sheet-dagger in her teeth, hopped up into the wagon, he helplessly obeyed.

He <u>was</u> more afraid of what Bearach or Eichgun might do to him. But there was no escape. There, thus standing, worry-wracked, the sound of footsteps echoed from up the hall. "Adi?" the sound was like scraping of nails on a chalkboard.
Adimus winced when his sister shuffled into the room. He quickly tried to fake nonchalance, leaning against some nearby barrels "Adi," she said, "are you still moving stuff for them?" She rubbed her eyes with the baggy long-sleeved shirt she always wore, his shirt. She appeared disheveled--a bit more so than usual, her matted gobs of hair down over eyes—she'd been sleeping in one of the chairs of the common room.

"I am." Adimus had hesitated only a moment before answering, making it seem perhaps more believable. Maybe saying the first thing that came to mind <u>was</u> how you became a good liar-- as long as the first thing was the wrong thing--or by a liar's measure the right thing.

Dyrshul yawned. "I want to go home." She slumped over the casks with him. There was a long pause as if she'd doze off.
Adimus unnaturally held his breath to hide his panic. "What are they talking about in there?" he puffed finally, when he could no longer.

A noise clattered behind him. Sweat beaded on his forehead, but Dyrshul paid the racket no mind; thankfully she dismissed it as belonging to the horses. "It's the same. Only worse." she dismissively waved her hand. "Dad seems to think that they are smugglers, and that the merchant's lying about really being a lord. The reeve thinks so too, but paw-paw seems to only want to talk about his dreams." Adimus shook his head. "He even thinks that they should take up swords with the Watchers to guard the town in case something bad happens."

"I doubt Eek would be fond of that." he snickered despite himself. "...Reeve breathing down our neck the whole time, as if this already isn't trying enough."

"Did you hear what happened to Eichgun?" she perked up at the name.

But Adimus clung on to what she'd said. "Wait...they <u>are</u> staying?"

Dyrshul, her head plopped down, nodding into the barrel. "Well. That friendly man with the glasses said yes, and the merchant said he had nowhere to be in a hurry."

An audible 'thunk' came from the wagon. It jumped him to, "Well," he said. "I guess I need to go see if Laina needs help dressing cots!" He marched for the door.

Dyrshul's glazed amber eyes suddenly became much more astute. She put her arms up to bar his path. "Laina says you're getting paid to do all this."

"...She did?" Before the question could come out she felt at his wrists, and when that failed swatted at his pockets until she found the change.

"Aha!" she jerked the coins away from him. She gasped in awe.

"You...know...!" he said calmly, then abruptly snatched them back. "Laina might give you a little something if you want to help her." he said. She glowered skeptically. "If she doesn't, then <u>I</u> will. How does that sound?" She stood a moment staring at the handful of stones. "Here." he feigned a growl of disgust as he flipped one of the discs of jasper at her.

He'd thought it may have seemed a little too suspicious--his charity, but with her eyes alight she said little else and he was able to coax her out the door. *She's always been a bit more the naive one* he mused, until he remembered what <u>he</u> had just been duped into.

After the coast was clear a great rattling noise came from inside the carriage. "Well?" the little creature crawled out from under it--she'd simply ducked beneath the carriage when she heard the voice, and she was so small no one was the wiser.

There was a clash, then what he could swear sounded like a 'quack'. Delaney made a strange soothing noise with her mouth, an attempt to calm whatever was inside. It was followed by some more rattling, almost like that of a cage, and Tirlag's growl "It's chained around the Named axel!"

"Well, can't you pick the lock?"

"I can't get my hand 'round it, there's not enough room." There was the distinct sound of her kicking it.

"You scared her!"

"Maybe you could do it, you've got tiny hands."

"I can't pick locks."

"Sure you can. I'll think about it really hard, and you'll read my mind."

"That's not how it works!" Delaney protested--it sounded like it wasn't the first time they'd had the conversation.

"Then we're stuck. For now." She came out.

"We <u>will</u> need it before we are on our way." Said Delaney. "I can lead you, but I have to know where we're going."

"He must keep the key on him." Tirlag hissed. "...You know, we <u>could</u> leave tonight if we had it. Just us." Adimus wondered if he was being included in the conversation, and why he wanted to be.

"Well, I for one am not picking his pocket to end up a toad, or worse!" the little one said. "Your selfishness is going to get us both killed!"

"I...don't think I should be here..." He finally mustered the courage to say.

"It's okay. I don't need you anymore." Was all she said, them both saundering past him. Delaney muttering something about 'seeing her' and 'she's lonely.'

Adimus, feeling both oddly regretful, yet relieved, turned to leave.

"Ha! Another puppet for her to play with. Another dupe." The voice had come from above. It was the same voice he'd heard atop Brian's roof earlier. A thousand thoughts rushed through his mind. *Am I caught? Is this thing, whatever it is, one of the merchant's guards? What would grandfather say?*

Adimus spun around when the voice whispered from behind him. A pair of green slitted eyes glowed in the darkness, piercing right into him. They were accompanied by the grin of a toothy maw "Aren't you going to run?" it said.

"No." His lies had worked so far, after all, he was on a roll, though his legs had already started betraying him, sidling toward the door, seemingly on their own.

The eyes drew closer. In the faint light of the lantern he could make out the dark cloak again, but the face showed nothing save the eyes, as if the insides held perhaps nothing. "Why not? You could make it back to safety in enough time to create an alibi for yourself, surely. After all, whose words would carry more weight: a guard from one's own home town, or a bunch of thieving interlopers?" Adimus nervously reached a left hand down to steady his sword-sheath; a knee-jerk reflex he never knew he had. He wasn't wearing a sword of course. "Though, she is a manipulative one, just look at you."

"I know." The helpful tone disarmed the figure for a moment. He also felt a little judgmental for saying it, as if perhaps he'd not given her the benefit of the doubt, but he wasn't going to defend her honor--whatever the six foot tall bestial thing said, for the purposes of this conversation, was true. Or maybe it really was right, and he was telling the truth and he didn't want to admit it to himself.

Adimus knew what he was dealing with was not a person like he or anyone else had come to know them, and that the creature's choice of words were quite deliberate. "Tell me, why did you follow her then?"

"...What?" He had forgotten.

"If you know she was manipulating you, then why do you let her?" the voice sounded impatient. "Given that I trust your answer."

"I-I, "

With that the figure stepped fully into the light, dropping the hood of her cloak.

What stood before him was an ebony-furred creature. Its physique was clearly enough like that of his; it had arms and legs and stood upright, yet its face was like that of a cat, whiskers tufted ears, fangs and all. It disarmed him for a moment, but not as much as it appeared she'd hoped.

She analyzed him. "You <u>are</u> afraid. But, you are startled, not frightened. You are not a good liar yourself, but, despite claiming to know it yourself, you enjoy being in the company of them." she perched her head. "Curious."

"...What's curious about it?" He was stalling, trying to think of something. When he couldn't, he said "You are a Cessairian, one of the Nis. I know of your kind. Maybe--maybe I was playing along. To find out what they were doing."

"No. And an Ormandian who claims to know of my kind? Very curious." Was all she said of it, then she rounded the corner to the wagon Tirlag had just been plundering through. Adimus followed to see her tending a bird in a cage. She produced a tiny key unlocking it. She picked it up, soothing it as she did. It <u>was</u> a duck. Adimus's head cocked itself sideways against his will at seeing it.

"Who are you, then?" he called after the surprise had worn off.

"...Why haven't you left yet?" sneering, she replied.

"Curiosity." he answered, against his better judgment; though the language of lying seemed foreign to his tongue, it always seemed to speak snarkiness fluently, and it wasn't the first time he had placed himself in trouble because of it.

She stopped for a moment, perhaps taken aback, those eerie eyes analyzing him like a piece of meat again. "Alara la Piscici de Madari, of the Mosi Tala." Silence. "Cait shii'. You people call us cait shii'. Yes, a Cessairian. Though not a Nis, I am unaffiliated." she relented.

"And you are...?"

"Adimus Buckroy. The Watcher." He thought to include his title, but didn't think it wise to alert her that he was an authority figure, *as if the Balfourian post of Watcher might be taken seriously by such a scary thing.*

"Good." She stepped out cradling a bird. From the ire in her predator eyes he suddenly regretted being so curious. "Watch to your heart's desire. I surely have." She said with a sadistic grin. "And I will tell no one what I have seen: that you are in fact a naive little twit of a boy after more the affections of girls than evil Fae that go bump in the night–or whatever your backwater little town tasks you with, if you promise to tell no one about anything that you have watched here tonight." With the menacing glance she gave him he couldn't help but find the arrangement more agreeable. "Good night." She grinned as he left.

He tried not to scramble for the door too quickly, and it took all his will power not to run. All the while the Cait Shii talking to the bird curiously. "If you can hear me, you know I'm watching you." She spoke to it. "I'll always be waiting in your shadows. Test me, I beg for it."

* * * * *

Adimus stumbled into the common room. After he had calmed down, he slowly began to realize he was beyond knackered.

The room was only sparsely populated now. Moyra was there, berating the blacksmith. Moyra, the man's wife, stood only waist high to Brian--the giant he was, but could make him, and easily any other man, feel quite the mouse when it came to it. And it had tonight; the blacksmith had no business being out this late, he just didn't want to go home, and Adimus now felt kinship with the man.

Niall was also there. Meav, of course, had opened a room for him, free of charge, to stay until springtime and they could rebuild the house.

It was an old house, one of the only ones said to have survived the lake burst of Loch Herespil. But with even this there was plenty more that could not be replaced. He'd lost his hound in the fire as well, and all of the beautiful wittlings he'd spent so much time on, and all the rest of his livelihood. The old man swaddled himself in a blanket near the hearth, staring into the distance despondently. Adimus thought to say something to him, as he had every time since then, when he'd seen him exactly like this, but could never think of exactly what to say.

Laina cleaned up glasses nearby, she herself looking the worse for wear, half-listening to the scolding with an amused smirk, seemingly happy that she was not the object of the women's ire for once.

Typically it was she Brian would be given guff for flirting with. Most did; her bronze skin, honey eyes, dark lips, and exotic accent were far more alluring than the erudite xenophobes of the hills would like to admit. Laina had simply happened upon the village one day a few years ago, and before anyone could say anything there she'd stayed. With the snap of her fingers Meav invited her in and set her to wait on patrons and cook, and that was that; her exuberance and caring demeanor was a rainbow in a world of gray, naturally meaning that more than once the women of the village went out of their way to find issue with her. The patrons were always fascinated by the stories she told, of giant creatures that roamed the Maritian plains, of strange ruins and stranger natives--of the Fae Kind. That's where he had learned of that Alara thing back there. Still, most of what she told them were simple anecdotes, not like the tales she told Adimus; stories in a discreet hushed tone, of great miracles and ancient rites and blessings the Goddess had bestowed upon her people by following The Law.

"Where is Dyrshul?" The Watcher asked her.

"They've started home already." she didn't look up at him. "They asked where you had went. I
could not answer them." she snipped.

He would sneak out the back, as the reeve or even Tolten could be lurking in the front. In so doing he passed Anwell, who was standing there with Regby. "Boy, come look!" he whispered.

It took the boy a few moments to process what the man was showing him. He recognized the collection of mugs, steins, glasses, as from behind the bar in disarray at the man's feet, all spilled. Anwell had filled them all up with water it seemed, and placed them all about the banister and on the floor of the porch, of this he was sure. "See? See, boy! You'd best ready that Cold Iron sword of yours." he put a finger to his nose. "Goblyns."

"Uncle..." Adimus raised an eyebrow, were he actually blood related to the man he would say he got his 'tell' for being a bad liar from him.

"I know, not funny." he slumped. "Not for you, anyway, but for me? Ha! You should've seen ole' Regby's face. And your sister!"

Adimus simply shook his head at the old man's orchestration. *Ever the trickster.* But it was telling: Regby and anyone else of interest had already left, and it was only when the boy and his sword had decided to leave on his own that Anwell finally departed, and very near behind him when he did.

* * * * *

Adimus awoke in the early morning to tend to the chickens for eggs and their milking goat, Bessie. Morning chores such as these always took around an hour, whereupon he would bathe in the stream out back. He did this, almost without fail, no matter how cold it got, and today it was exceptionally chilly. Nevertheless, when he was finished he always came beneath the quiet eaves of the porch, dusting off and cleaning the whittled alter beneath its small tea table and placing it atop it.

He pulled from his sporran a small saucer-like cup, pulled from the clay of the vale and baked and fashioned by his very own hand. With it he gave offerings of milk to the small stone statue he carried, setting it atop the table and offering a prayer in Old Daldistan.

All in the village had such a cup; some were fancy, covered with masterfully textured knotwork patterns or meticulously painted. An honored few, such as the reeve, used a hand-sized seashell. The boy had never seen such a thing before seeing it, knowing only the small elktoes and other such shellfish that inhabited the streams of Suul Vale in the springtime, but the reeve told him that it had come from the ocean to the south, where the creatures that lived in the great water grew so as to match its vastness; greater still was the Pardoner's sacred shell, said to have been plucked long ago from the waters of the underworld in which the gods themselves slept.

It was a daily rite, the Slaking, the tradition of the people of the mountains to give offering to the deities, to be done at dusk or dawn. He never knew what the prayer meant, only that it had to be said, like all other aspects of the Slaking they were instrumental, crucial.

He was told that the prayer was to honor the Formerians: Cailleach, the Great Hag, Conand of the Unbending Knee, Aarianrhod of the Stirring Stars, Tethra, Seer of Dreams. He knew little more than their names, and could pick them out in the prayer—Pardoner said that to speak on them too much would draw attention away from the goal of it, for first and foremost, the prayer was to the Grand Idol, of whom the others were but subordinates.

Having concluded his morning ritual, he finished grooming himself, shook off his gruesome tiredness, grabbed a tea biscuit to tide himself over, and donned his gear.

Once a season the reeve and his local council met at the Green Beat to deliver edicts, address grievances and complaints, and catch up on general goings on in Balfour. Everyone attends these meetings, even the children, usually bored to tears at the ceremonious babbling and hollow domestic politics. The village held this meeting, simply called the Meet, and by those standards this one was a few days early. Though it was to be expected, tomorrow was Ellylon, Allhallows, Festival of Lanterns. Adimus couldn't help but feel like some exhibit at a menagerie as he stood quoetly alongside the counsel at it commenced.

The strangers sat only a few paces from Adimus, safely placing him between they and the reeve. Tirlag wore the baby blue fru-fru dress Adimus had helped her fetch the night before, though she wore it in a most peculiar way, to put it modestly. It had torn just below the thigh, and she'd simply finished the tear. The dress had long sleeves, also, so she'd tore those out as well to match, and accented the look of it with a leather corset, a matching pair of dainty ballroom dancing shoes, and a pair of knee-high men's stockings--atop all of gaudy rings and bobbles and Argent's chapeau, which she insisted brought the whole ensemble together. The seething outrage of all the other women at the Meet was a palpable fume. In her hand was a prissy fan she waved about as she mockingly jeered at them with her exceptionally dolled-up face.

Adimus stood with Bearach. Alara stood beside both, obviously because she was considered Fae Kind and people were afraid of her, also because she refused to put down her arms.

The proceedings began: Regby Goddard has a grievance against his neighbor Deverall. He'd found a clod of dirt belonging to Devrall's farm on his property. One of the reeve's councilors witnessed the alleged infraction on the day of its occurrence, and upon giving testimony to the reeve, Deverall is fined the amount of two Favor.

Anwell, local wooler and spinner of more than one kind of yarn he was, had come to demand his sheers back from neighbor Regby Goddard, who borrowed them to cut his son's hair and never gave them back.

"I gave 'em to *your* boy to give back! I can't help it if he's a Named nitwit!" he argues.

Anwell jumps to his feet, and Bearach jumps to intercept before the Reeve with a gesture of warning halts him. "Is this true, Ailen?"

"I never seen them sheers, save for when I seen him using them to trim the fencebush outside his house!"

There was a moment of consideration, "Very well. Adi--Adimus, I place you in charge of this task. Grigor Adimus, by the will of the council you will be granted hospitalities by Regby Goddard, that you may investigate the matter with impunity." Adimus's father Bearach cracked a smile. He gave a wry glower back. "If the accusation be proven by evidence, Regby you shall be found guilty of perjury before these proceedings and shall pay the wer or forfeit your life." He gravely responded.

The strangers had spoke through the whole of the proceedings, discarding looks of shock, disgust, and downright horror from all of the other participants, but this exchange Adimus was privy to in the silence. "Forfeit his life? That's excessive, don't you think?" the one they all called Alfred quietly mused.

"...What's a 'wer'?" Tirlag said in a jarringly loud tone.

"It's the measure of a man. One's worth to the community." Argent replied in a hushed tone, a que that Tirlag would continue to ignore throughout the evening. The latter never happened, nor had he ever heard of it happening. A Balfourian peasant held little value anyway, he'd heard, the 'wer' amounting to little more than a few years of extra taxes to be given to the village, often over the course of years. Adimus might have told him, if not for the stifling silence his elders and station and (everyone else now) demanded.

"That a person's worth could be monetized. Disgusting..." Delaney said.

"Watch your tongue, servant!" Tirlag rapped her in the back of her head with her fan. They playfully exchanged a glower.

 Meanwhile, the reeve calls for a count of votes on whether to commission new horseshoes for the Watcher's only horse, and to appeal to clan Dwyer for the issuance for Adimus a horse of his own. Reluctantly the majority agree, echoing sentiments that the mobility and speed of the Watchers may be crucial in light of the goings on. Brian, acting as official local smith and ferrier is charged with the work, much to his excitement, for there has been little need for him in a while.

Brina Lathern addresses the council and villagers, requesting help for tomorrow's Ellylon. She suggests the help of the children, to which the townsfolk agree, erupting the room in a chorus of joyous cheers from the little ones. Dyrshul had outgrown such things obviously, from the look of relief about her face when no one acknowledged that she would be participating. Adimus ruefully glared at Dyrshul, who sat nearby, enjoying her comfy chair, having to do nothing—not now, and apparently not later as well.

The Watcher rocked back and forth on the soles of his boots. The proceedings took several hours, and despite that it was only midday his feet had already become tired. He was forced to rise early and perform a march that wasn't his, filling in for ol' Eichgun, and to rub it in he'd been told to get used to it for the foreseeable future.
Eichgun had apparently banged himself up pretty badly when he fell from his loft. Not surprising, and not actually the first time he had missed his shift before; Eichgun, as Meav could tell you, despite being a fierce friend to everyone, was a notorious drunk.

"Are there any more grievances..." Cayden began "or articles of discussion before we set about addressing the concern which the council, and I say everyone present wishes to speak on?"

There was silence. "Very well then. Now for the order of business which you all know ought to be addressed."

Niall's farmstead had been razed to the ground. By someone unknown to the village-- there was no sugar-coating it.

A parade of villagers would recite for them all of the anecdotes Adimus had heard in the past few days, the things that had set him on edge: spooked cattle and horses being restless, a dug up grave, animals that usually flee in fear at the sound of footsteps wandering into town and gawking about as if watching. And then there was Niall's dog. It was found on the corner of his property, right beside the Beat, by none other than Adimus himself. Its head had been smashed in. Adimus prayed that he would not have to stand in front of them all and recount the gory tale. Thankfully he never was.

"Graces are upon us in our hour of need. We have the privilege of welcoming one who may be able to shed light on all of this." He said, with as much pride as he could muster given the grim subject. Only a few looked confused; apparently this was already old news. "Alfred Juminion III, Lapidarian of the Holy Trust. A Sum Seer." He announced, and the spectacled man stood and bowed. In his hands he held a staff, which he handed to the boy to hold.

The thing was unlike that which he'd ever seen. The haft of it appeared to be made of stone; a black and green marble perhaps, though he wielded it with ease. The upper third was worked with gold that looked like licking flames, inset with some sort of crescent-shaped clasp composed from a red and black metal, which was jointed and connected in two places to be manipulated like a vice--it reminded him of an old set of calipers Regby had. The black and green metal appeared again, emerging from the flames, grazing the tips of the crescent before ending in a sharp point. A ring of stark white and gleaming gold, beginning amidst the flames before the crescent and ending near the pointed tip of the haft, set with a socket to pivot and spin freely around them all.

The villagers muttered amongst themselves. "Bearach. Present the first article to the Seer." he motioned. Adimus was at a loss as to what was going on, he thought that perhaps he should have been listening in on their conversations last night instead of skulking about, he thought to himself.

"First." He said. "At the request of the council we wish to offer a test to the Seer, to allay any doubts as to the authenticity of your status and to the accuracy of your Readings." He said to Alfred.

"Of course." He answered softly.

Bearach stepped forward and handed to him the first item: a coin.

"What's going on?" he decided to whisper to his father when he stepped back in line.

"He's a Faeth. A seer of omens." Bearach answered back, in an unsure tone as if he himself were just passing it along.

"We will start with this coin. Who here has held it?"

Delicately he removed his pair of white velvet gloves, then took the coin in his hands. He paused for a moment with an unreadable look on his face, and closed his eyes."It smells of smoke and sweat. It was given to the village blacksmith." He studied the rectangular shard of jade. "It was found on the ground and given to you by none other than the one you trust as a Bard of Bowen with whom I travel."

Brian the Blacksmith, with the lungs from his barrel-chest bellowed "You found it, thank the Ollatharii!"

Inexplicably Tirlag swatted at her pockets in panic (or where her pockets would've been), then she shot a smiling Argent a spiteful glare no one else meant to see. Adimus was instructed to give it back to the bard. "<u>Trust</u> as a Bard of Bowen?' " he seethed under his breath. "Thanks, kid."

"To whom does this book belong?" The reeve continued.

Adimus watched as the soft-spoken man held the book, eyes shut. He ran his fingers down it, as one would when examining some alien object for the first time, then flipped its pages. Adimus already knew whose it was.

"Hmm..." he delicately closed it. "I get the strong impression that it belongs to a person from afar. The person who came about it perhaps had not had it very long? They could have gotten from a merchant. Or a trader, because it does not belong to a southlander. It most definitely was held by someone with the smell of grass in their hair. A Mansii." He said finally as if coming to some conclusion.

Adimus handed the book back to Laina, who clasped it almost as if hiding her shame. He didn't have to look, it was a romantic Torantii novella she'd collected, one of several she'd been seen peeking at under tables when she thought no one was watching. He had to give a wide-eyed shrug to repel her accusative stare when he returned it to her, *'it wasn't me.'* he was saying with his face.

"Then, at last, this." Cayden said, handing him a charred walking stick.

The knubby blackwood cane was Niall's, Adimus knew. He made them as a hobby which in turn had become a small side-business for him. When Bearach produced it and handed it over to the spectacled man, the room fell into dead silence once again. The old man, hidden in the crowd by anyone who didn't know it to be him, watched intently.

Adimus watched as the soft-spoken man gripped the cane, eyes shut.

Just then the sturdy wooden door was slung open. "Councilmen!" a voice interceded. "Councilmen! I have a grievance!" The reeve continued unimpeded, for a moment, attempting to ignore the lithy, gnarled little man that had just barged in. Though few probably could. Strange charms and talismans made seemingly from odd-shaped twigs and twine dangle from pins from under his periwinkle cloak. Knots tied into eccentric patterns dangled from his ardent head, adorned with sprigs of herbs and a berries. His hair was wild matted locks from a lifetime of ornamental liming. The hunkered old man was garbed with the green and black tartan of a Grigor, though his cloak clasp bore and owl's talons, grasping a band of leather knots that resembled and eight-spoked wheek. It matched the 'stunning piece' that Adimus heard Argent remark about which sat atop his head, which could only be described as the stuffed corpse of an owl somehow fashioned into a hat.

Adimus hid his face, looking down at his younger sister in shame; the same look he gave her when she'd gotten herself into trouble and there was nothing he could do to help her. Dyrshul looked straight ahead, eyes widened; the same look she gave when they both got into trouble and were interrogated and she held her tongue to absolve herself of being co-conspirator.

After a few moments of muttering curses and realizing that he was not going to go away. "I admire your...fervor, Luloch, and once again we appreciate your concern for your fellow villagers, but-"
Luloch attempted to interrupt him again before he could finish, "But this, this here is but the beginning of it. It is as the crow of a cock! We've but a single season left, if it isn't addressed now--." but Cayden's commanding voice hushed him.

"But, just as we discussed and upon which we even voted, prior." he motions to the throng, "Of which you speak cannot be done. It is a pure matter of coin. We just cannot afford years of debt at the hands of the lords of Ormond for this... scarecrow. Now, if you please, we are set out today to deal with these problems right before us, the ones not literally dreamed up." The man turned and tried to continue.
The reeve then motioned the Watchers to escort him out.
"Well, Adi that's our cue." Bearach growled.

But the old man's rant continued. "Your timid tongue and pandering before the Steward Princes shall be the doom of your countrymen!" he said, emphasizing his words by stamping his cane. "And the lives of their children! And yours! Scarecrow!? Speak to me of such when the birds of carrion roost upon your tatterdemalion remains hanging in the field for the sport of the Unslaked and their masters, reeve of Macmearion! Sluagh Oiche is coming!" he continued. Looks of outrage and even horror beam out from the faces of the crowd. "Charnel ash shall yet feed the first seeds of spring! And short arms and deep pockets is no excuse, McConell!" Luloch Buckroy pointed his gnarled old cane at the man, no less itself a shillelagh of blackthorn that Niall had made for him. Bearach reluctantly stepped in front of him.

"Out of my way, boy!" he tried to push him aside with his cane. The old man tried to resist and Bearach, and batting away the man's feeble affront, pulled him out the door kicking and screaming. "The Darkest Night is coming, and you'll beg for death before the end!"

<u>*Chapter 4*</u>
Dreams and Promises

Large, white puffs of willow and dandelion blanketed the ground like snow, blowing along with the occasional stray leaf in the inexplicably warm breeze that often filled this valley. Lantern Beetles–fist-sized insects that invaded such valleys in midsummer, still flooded the cozy grove with their green light, and thumb-sized grasshoppers scattered to the air whensoever one might graze their eating place. It was still warm, unseasonably so, which, according to the old man could only mean one thing: it was going to be a rough winter.

A wall of such rattles and buzzes blotted out all beyond this grove; the moons and stars easily available to be gazed upon from atop the large stone in its center were their only guests.

Adimus watched Luloch do as he always did–standing silently at the rock's zenith, admiring the view as he filled the strange divet in the stone with water. It was an ancient place, he'd explained, older than even the lake. The ancestors had made this stone an altar upon which to pay homage to the Teg Flaith, the spirit which held Dominion over the forests of Balfour. The bowl was for them by the Flaith, they'd said, and, by the grace of the lord god of the clans, the flower petals and leaves which he had carefully selected to float atop it, when given as offering to the spirit, drifted in a pattern that would foretell the portents for the coming year, among many other things.

Ever since Adimus had come to stay at Balfour with the Buckroy family, Luloch would come to this spot on the same day each year, just before the festival.

Poplar crackled from their cook fire, throwing sparks into the dusk-laden air, Dyrshul was off chasing a sparrow that always seemed to be just out of her reach, as if it delighted in teasing her, her face covered in molasses, an ingredient that between Luloch and she hardly made it into the supper pot.

"Hah, Boy?"

"Stop." Adimus deflected the stick that poked at his ribs. Bearach came in again, unfazed. He batted at it again. *Bonk.* "Whacha gonna do, eh? Whacha gon' do?"

Adimus nabbed the end of it, having been thus challenged. It was a game they always played: take a sturdy stick, around a foot long. Each person grips the end of it, and attempts to get it out of the other person's hand, with no other touching allowed.

"Ack!" He finally relented after a good five minutes of it. His forearm burned like fire. In his youth the boy thought it was a game--and it was; many a win came when the opponent couldn't catch their breath from laughing, but he didn't realize until later that it was also an important exercise that taught of distance, footwork, and leverage, and strengthened the chief muscles needed for wielding a sword. He'd only been able to best him a few good times, and only fairly recently.

He could also beat Eichgun on most occasions. His old man said it was because he was getting stronger. He never wanted to believe it, and always felt as if Bearach were just getting older–though it should be noted that Luloch could still beat any one of them unless he was challenged more than once, and only then was it the tiredness that accompanied his age that defeated him, tenacious codger he was; Luloch had been a Grigor as well once.

"Shouldn't we be going?" Adimus hid the worry in his voice well, but not well enough for his family to not see through it. At that Bearach gave a phlegmy snort of exasperation and went to tend the fire.

"Afraid of the Pardoner?" the old man said, finally frustrated enough to break his concentration.

"No." he scratched at his head.

His grandpa was not the first or only person to come up here. *Cover your mirrors before dousing your candles. Never count the attendees of a funeral procession. Always wave at a magpie, always bow at a crow, at a raven's gaze hide your hands, or all your secrets he'll know.* Those beliefs never died; to those few who kept the tradition, it was just another thing you did.

And Luloch did those things a lot, regardless of whether he ought to, one to have old book hid under the floorboards beneath the rug in the living room, along with several whittled contraband devices: scepters, wands, dousing rods, tiny sticks carved with runes for casting fortunes, tinctures and suspensions to heal sickness or ward against hexes or misfortune. *Trees are sacred and not what they seem. Burn pine, sage, or jasmine to keep away evil spirits, use the smoke of ash to carry prayers to the gods and confound the working of the evil eye, use hazel sticks and you will* always *find water, and no matter what you do,* never *, ever, cut down a hawthorne.'*

Today he carried a brand of elder. "It is looming." Luloch glumly said, sobering them both when he turned to them. "All running down. Time, getting away from me. Can't you feel it in the air?" He tapped the remnants of his pipe out on the ground. "You know...the Grigors of old knew the Ways of Working, knew the All'khemy. Had the power of the Quality to defend the village against such darkened times. Wish we had such..."

No, he wasn't afraid of the pardoner. Not for himself, anyway. He put his hands on his hips defensively. "I've asked Tolten about this, grandfather," (during these times he is addressed as grandfather, not pawpaw) "He says you are a dabbler, playing with a fire that may well consume us all if you keep poking at it." he jabbed at the air with the stick. "That the Forgotten deceive men with the power Spells grant. That it must have been one of them whom our tribe paid tribute to."

The man's wrinkly face twisted in shock. "You told on me?!" he accused. He opened his mouth with a stutter of disbelief. Suddenly he looked around. "Does he know we are here?"

"You never told me not to." he quickly defended. "You-you spoke with authority, I thought he might divulge something helpful on the matter."

At that the old man's terseness dispersed like a cloud passing beneath the sun; the look never held well or for very long on his face anyway. Adimus explained, "I was only trying to help. I didn't tell him of <u>this</u> place, no. Though all the same, we probably shouldn't linger here. If he found out..."

"Well, you seem more than a fair bit charmed by that lass at the inn. I see your eyes go all starry when she talks of it, the great Works of times before."

Adimus knew at that point that he had caught wind of something too, from the Pardoner. He couldn't come up with a response. The old man shook his cane. "It's a tool lad, just like that sword. Just a tool. One he may regret disarming us of it before the end." he huffed, using the cane now to pull himself to his feet.

"Magic and its ilk are the dominion of the demons men worship in the Grand Idol's stead. He said that in order to even wield it one must swear to one of them."

"He would." he guffawed. "It was his grandfather what took our words from us, after his pilgrimage to The Grey Cities. The chronicles that hid the Magic, he has, somewhere down on that lake! Burnt to cinders as an offering for all we know! Order of Jasmine he was, and made it well known to everyone." he huffed. "You'll never know the truth if you don't see both the one side and the other."

Then gave the boy a wry sideways grin. "You know, that man that travels with them, that Alfred. He's a wizard, a Sum Seer."

"Then <u>they</u> had better leave as soon as possible, before Tolten catches wind of it. Just like we should hope he doesn't catch wind of our being here..."

Finally, feeling his way down off the rock with his cane like some blind beggar, having thus the time to clear his head, Luloch came up beside the boy. "I know. I know." he coddled. "For what it's worth, I must apologize, for this, and my for my froth-mouthed jabbering at the Meet, my boy. I know you, of all people, don't want to draw attention to yourself." Luloch said. He'd not been asked to apologize, nor had Adimus given any indication that he'd been even bothered by it; he knew Luloch was not one prone to such outburst, this was true, but he could tell the guilt weighed heavily on the old man's mind, so heavily in fact that it drove him to apologize, another thing he was quite not prone to doing– the last two days had been full of firsts. The old man continued, as with a grunt he took his final steps off the thing, easing himself down with his shillelagh, "It's just that, you know just as I the dire consequences we face. If only I could tell them without betraying you and Dyshul and the rest of this family." he sighed, adjusting his glasses for a moment, and gazed up at the boy, this young man that now towered over him, "Have <u>you</u> had any more dreams, Adi?"

Bearach's eyes now glowered off into the darkness from beneath a furrowed brow, hand on the pommel the broadsword, his terse lips concealed beneath his fiery beard. The old man's word had stolen his whimsy.

"Yes." He replied. He gave a few moments to think and reflect. Luloch wasn't just asking if he'd had any more dreams, Adimus knew by the old man's bated breath of what he truly asked. This was a secret that he'd been told never to keep from him. Everyone had called them dreams, despite the fact they even seemed to occur in the day time, or anytime Adimus began to think about this strange feeling he would get, mostly when he was bored, in which case people simply accused him of having an overactive imagination. The boy closed his eyes. "It's sunset. I'm gazing out onto an empty field of rolling wildflowers and barley grain from...my room. I see a tower off in the distance, impossibly far away and yet still visible, glowing as it catches the fading light of day. It stretches from the roots of the world off into the firmament. I'd hurt my neck to try and see its top. Another moon glows above, lighting a yard of shorn green grass outside my window sill. All glows here--lit in inviting rainbows of color that twinkle in mist or upon the cobblestones in rain. It's mid-summer, Crea, sweltering, yet it is not hot at all, I'm actually quite cool. I see a beautiful lady with golden hair, braided in the back. I'm sitting in my room while she serves me food made of snow."

"...I see." Was what Luloch almost always said. There was a long silence. He looked at him meaningfully. "There is portent in these dreams, Adimus. Just as my dreams of the wolf vex me." He put his hands behind his back, a habit he always showed when embarrassed, as if he were hiding his feelings behind himself. "I believe you, know that. Whether they be memories of a life forgotten, or simple flights of fancy, doesn't matter. No matter what Tolten says of dabblers and lost ways and heathenry. Whatever they may be, they mean something, and we're going to find out what it is."

It was as conflicted an opinion as anyone else had ever given him. He was beginning to wonder if he'd ever really know what they were.

The visions were vivid, almost like real life, and while most of them were simply mundane occurrences such as this one, some of them were wildly fantastic in nature. Both the mundane and the wild ones always captivated Laina, who told him that his imagination was very vivid and that he should become an artist, especially whenever he would sketch them in charcoal or carve them with his tablet for her. Adimus always amused the notion with her, masking his real feelings about the experiences.

"What has gotten to you, old man?" Bearach then moaned. "First you lose your mind with the council, as if that helps..." He made sure Dyshul wasn't listening, "...our situation." it was in a much lower register. "And now you're spouting off all heart-felt at the boy. And what's more, you encourage this nonsensical talk he croaks from his wattle." He strided up the old man and put a hand on his shoulder, trying to ease him along. "Give it a rest. You've done enough to embarrass us today."

"Let go of me!" He swung his cane at the lug. "What I'm saying to Adimus is important.

Now *you* give it a rest!"

"You know lad," he continued on with what he was saying. "I think you should know that regardless of where these dreams may lead you, that you should know that you have a family right here with us, Adimus. And I'm sure Bearach would say much the same, had he the wherewithal to be a man." With that he turned and left.

Bearach blew raspberries as the curmudgeon walked past him. "It's not in what you say-- It's what you do. He knows that." He looked at Adimus. "Some things needn't be said. Right, lad?" He thwacked him on the shoulder, and turned to leave with him, hurrying Dyrshul along. "Action always gets the better of words." He looked at them critically. "If you two don't stop it with this I'll prove it--cause no amount of words will do to describe what my fist is going to do to your faces."

As they began to leave, Bearach picked up the cooking pot and poured out the remainder of the sweet beans. When the old man was far enough away for his comfort he pulled him aside. "Adimus. I know I make light of it, but you know that if anyone knows it is I: it is hard to call for help when sworn to silence." he dusted off his hands. "It's a curse. I don't want that for you." he spoke in a quiet tone. "Just do what he says. I think everything's going to turn out alright. I do." The look of strain upon his face was more unnerving than any scowl he'd ever seen the man make, indeed, this was hard for him, and Adimus was left wondering there in the hanging dusklight what had warranted it.

The warmth had finally broken, like a flourishing crescendo that marked summer's end before the day bowed and the curtain of night was pulled. A cold autumnal wind whipped around him as if to usher him along, and as the rest of them trailed off into the dark, like a leaf tossed in the torrid tempest he could do naught but abide, helpless before its pull.

Chapter 5
Allhallow's

In a clear green glen upon Walpurga's Vale there lived a flock of sheep, and among the sheep there lived a little lamb. So beautiful this lamb was, so precious, that this story is about her. Her father was the Golden Ram who'd fought a dragon. Honorable and valiant was he, and the ovine he had chosen to be her sheeply bride was the fairest ewe of all the flocks of the land of Morida.

Now, she had been barren, this ewe, but promised to the Ollatharii that if she but had but a single baby lamb she would protect and nurture it with all of her will and heart, and give the most luxurious wool, and offerings and song and prayer to them for the rest of her days. And, as it is in these days, for those who believe it, the gods reciprocated and granted it. In fact, this little lamb was the first of many, many more, for the Goddess blessed this ewe with such fertility that all the lambs in all the pastures in all the land descend from this one, which the farmers call Mother Ewe.

But this first lamb, Leana, was special: her hair was fiery gold and her eyes blue and innocent, but what's more is that she was taught by her father of the greed of dragons, and from her mother the importance of keeping her word. This story is about her.

One day the old farmer who took care of the sheep fell ill, and so he could not care for her. It was one of those fine days on the plains of the dale when Albrastricano, the Silver Wolf, the ol' trickster, came to lurk in the eaves and rushes of the old wood. Now, this was before the days of the Thrice Slain King, before Perun of Mathendon and his axe of silver, so without a shred of fear in his heart he skulked the glens until he's found a choice one in which to hide, then every day went about the business of haunting the shadows of the hills of Pangor and Blade, scouring the downs for the weakest, the sickest, and the smallest upon which to dine. Then, Albrastricano--we all know he can speak to animals--had learned from a wildcat of the deeds of these two great sheep. So one day, lo and behold, when Mother Ewe was giving her prayers in the grotto near the place where the lamb played, the Silver Wolf, drawing a thick fog over the vale with his Magic, snatched up the little lamb.

"I've not come to eat you, little one." He told her, sweetly, when he'd spirited away to the foul cave. And he was sincere, for eating the little lamb was not his aim. You see, Albrastricano, the beast, was prideful and vain, and had clamored for a long time to feast on the flesh of a creature as mighty as one what might slay a dragon. Such a deed would be quite the boast, and make his two brothers much envious of him for sure.

"Fear not." he said to her. "Explain to your father that I wish to exchange your life for his own and I will spare you."

The little lamb shuddered. Her legs quivered and strained to stay aright, yet still they did, and head held high she spoke to the great wolf. "You wouldn't be afraid he would kill you, Mr. Wolf? My father has slain a dragon, and many other great beasts of the world of whom you would be their lesser."

"Lesser? You are a fool, same as he, and your answer shows it so. Honor is a fool's mark, and quite valiant is he indeed. He will sacrifice himself willingly if he swears to forfeit his life for yours, and will come to my lair gladly to see it fulfilled. Go now and you will be rewarded dearly by keeping yours."

The lamb looked him in the eye, "No, I have learned from my great father, of the avarice and great greed of dragons. It would be greedy of me to want <u>my</u> life more than another's."

"You would wish to be eaten in his stead then, little one?"

The lamb shook her head. "I did not say that. I wish for nothing, but I would honor my father's teachings just the same to be humble and not expect rewards for what I am; I am no dragon."

The wolf, cunning as ever, redoubled. "I have heard of the story of your mother," he said, "that she praised the Goddess every day for giving birth to you. This is how I caught you. I do not want you, you are such a small meal, I want your mother then. Go and get her, and I shall spare your life."

But she refused again. "I will not."

"But she has made the promise, she has agreed to pay the price. A mother always protects her child. She is willing! You will do her a great honor by allowing her to die to save you, for she will have fulfilled her purpose. I am simply the hand of the Goddess come to see it fulfilled this day! How else would I know this?"

The little lamb replied, "I doubt no more than you that she would come and trade her life for my own in an instant, but what better given than one's solemn word in all earnestness, such a pure gift as one's word should be honored in kind, not besmirched, if everyone lived by their word there would be no wolves like you. No, that choice is in my hands. If you are the Goddess's messenger then surely nothing should stop you, yet here I am. No: <u>I</u> am the Grace of the Goddess who protects her devotee."

"Are you not afraid that I will kill you?"

"Of course I am afraid, I am a lamb and you are a wolf. That part is natural."

"Yet you do not act upon it. That part is not. It will hurt greatly when my teeth sink into you, and I will not do it quickly." The wolf growled in consternation.

"Perhaps if you yourself were as valiant and brave as my father and as honorable to your word as my mother you would've gotten a meal tonight."

The Wolf's pride, great pride was wounded at the attack. "I am every bit as valiant <u>and</u> as *brave!"*

"Then prove it. Tell me you've kept your word, that you will be as faithful and honest as they, that this world shall not lose another good life, that the daughters of Many Faces does not churn another good soul into stardust!"

"I do. And I shall. You play a good game, little one. You leave me no choice, I suppose I will have to eat you, then." he finally said.

But the lamb smiled, and let out a baying snicker in spite of herself. "But you said you haven't come here to eat me."

The wolf flailed in anger, for he knew he had lost. "For all my bluster of the folly of virtue, eating you now is as unfulfilling as a moonless howl." He said, then knelt before the lamb, in defeat.

Still today some hear him howl in lament from pangs of hunger, and whether to simply allow others to tell this tale of the surviving little lamb to simply boast of his augustness (old braggart that he is), or, like his Dreamspeaker children, believe: that he truly did know then that pride without honor is so empty and hollow a sensibility that even his stomach might well pity it, none can tell. And for what is said of the Silver Wolf, what more could be, of the lamb that tamed him with temperance and faith, void of wish or fear of fate, who so made such a villain virtuous?
The little lamb returned home into her father and mother's loving arms that evening, and was content, as she was and would ever be, for the rest of her days.

* * * * *

Many gathered in the town square to watch the bard tell his story and observe the Grigors as they pranced their horses down the promenade in show of their vigilance.

It was just Adimus and Bearach; Luloch was too old and Eichgun, Adimus had heard, had taken a fall.

The recent events had left want for any manner of lightheartedness or frivolity, and so the holiday was all the warmer. Everyone had shown for the occasion--as they normally did (there was not much to do elsewhere anyway). Though it itself was filled with an air of fearfulness, a dreary, dreadful holiday with dark roots, it itself disguised, it was welcomed.

The holiday, Ellylon, had scarcely been a day to be taken lightly by others. It was the last night of the Saohin Moon, a most frightful night, a night when it is said the Curtain between this world and the Otherworld was lifted, and the Fae, on their way to the eternal lands of Mag Mell no doubt, terrorized and accosted mortals.

In times past this patrol would've been of the utmost importance, Cayden would always explain, if only to set the tone of unease that elevated the exhilarating festivities; nowadays the march was little more than a vehicle around which to frame it. Though the rest of the year they had but one old draft horse to share between them, during Ellylon horses were commissioned to all the Grigors and the guards.

The statue around which they rode them had always been there, even the road itself was built after it, or 'terminus post quim' Cayden MacConell would've said (he was always eager to flaunt his upbringing in Hewnyleigh). It had always baffled Adimus, this cloven-hooved giant. It had been tradition that it was an image of Conand the Formerian, Successor of Balros, he to whom if the ancestors had paid homage the mountain would've never fallen. Lichen clung to his stone face. Atop his great head was a pair of ram horns, one of which had been broken. Crumpled with pain he clasped a spear, propping himself on it like a crutch. The spear was made of what appeared to be white marble, with a metal head that withstood all elements, and to this day was gleamed as if polished and was sharp to the touch--more than a few children had thrown apples at it to confirm this, Adimus included. Several broken shafts protruded from his chest made of actual wood, buried deep in the statue somehow. The Precession always rounded it a number of five times before coming to a stop and dispersing on this night, marking the beginning of the festivities, and that is precisely what they did.

"Watch where you're going for Thrice's sake!" Tirlag exclaimed when Adimus's horse nearly bowled her over. Adimus had not been given one officially, as the reeve had not commissioned a new one to the Watchers in some years, Lord Pembroke of Adaire had delivered one personally for the occasion on loan. Adimus was a clod on one no matter its temperament or training.

It was her fault. She was, after all, standing in the middle of the street during a parade. He apologized just the same, the cait shii's emasculating words from the other night echoing in his head the whole time. Just as the first day they met, Adimus observed that she had a penchant for bumbling--moreover, it seemed to be a certain stare that the girl often had, off into the distance, as if she were either far too involved in what was going on to have the mindfulness to note the fact that she even had a body, or quite the opposite a genuine lack of caring so great that it paralyzed her. He could never tell which it was, but wagered she was doing what had really caused him to not see her in the first place: gawking.

On this day, town elders would tell frightening stories and act out mummer's plays, unsavory tales meant to spook the young ones, always played to the hilt to suspend disbelief. He'd hoped to see the Bard do one himself, but the Whispermonger, for reasons that escaped him, had decided to tell his strange tale, of the lamb and the wolf, to the children.

Adimus could only reason that it had to do with the presence of the Pardoner, but this tale, mentioning the Goddess and the Ollatharii, would do little to avert the priest's ire had he heard it. Adimus therefore found himself nervously peering over shoulders while up on his horse, looking for a miter or cudgel, feeling as if he himself might get in trouble just for listening to it.

Adimus was off his horse the moment he was able to be, if only to avoid further collisions. Grown-ups led children with carving turnips and pumpkins with malicious faces to be lit by candlelight. The sentiment after which the holiday is named, these Ellyllon, or Faerie lights, were always (allegedly) seen in places where the One World and the Other met. Accompanied by kindred stories like Jack o' the Lantern and The Will o' the Wisps, tales of such lights were in no short measure.

Laina was one amongst such grown ups, laughing right along in merriment. Thankfully, she had averted the rueful gazes of the townsfolk when she had first come here by choosing to partake in traditions like these willingly. Quite willingly, in fact. She was always interested in learning about other people's beliefs, and when she could follow headlong with them. She even practiced Slaking, awakening in plain view and practicing it, and gathering at the parish temple to learn from the Pardoner in plain sight of the others. No one is sure what would have happened had she not done this, but Adimus for one was glad that she was so pliant in her faith. Thus she affirmed the tenants of their beliefs, taking on the identity of a devout follower of Illea without renouncing or forsaking her own. This, at first, forced Adimus to deduce that she was of poor faith when it came to her own religion, but she still continued all of her own ritual in tandem with theirs, and followed the strictures and tenants of her own faith even-handedly and with the same transparency to all, that with the exuberance with which she illumined anyone who wished to hear of her culture would tell anyone who saw that it just wasn't so; none, not even Pardoner Tolten could argue with her who seemed to see such things as one would a dance and she merely a lover of music.

She was dressed as a Dearg Dhul, with a pale face and darkened eyes and sharp teeth; she'd always called them Vampyres, though he'd never heard the name before that. Suddenly Adimus felt a little self-conscious; he wasn't dressed as anything. He went to go and talk to her but was interrupted, as it were.

"Soul Cakes! Soul Cakes! Give us tasty Soul Cakes! Teehee!" He could tell who it was if only because it was the strangest costume. She brandished her hands full of food at him. She carried on "We walk the mists in hoary bands to return from whence we came, taking along with us the Damned and hunting Hyu'man game! If you cross us we'll cast a Spell or kill you just the same! Now give us tasty soul cakes or *your* soul we will claim! Mwahaha!" She'd apparently *not* outgrown this part of it.

"Where did you get those?" In times past this question would've been tinged with jealousy, but he was surprised at how stern and mature-sounding it came out.
Undeterred she continued her taunt "Why? Want one?"

"No—Dyrshul." He snapped, in his best authoritative-sounding voice. "You need to stay with everyone else until we *all* go guising." Dyrshul lifted the tip of the giant paper mache nose that she wore over her entire head to reveal her face through the nostril to take a huge bite of cake. The nose had little beady eyes at the top of it. He didn't ask. It wasn't that if duty hadn't tied his ankles in earlier days he wouldn't have bounded off with her. But now, especially now, he had to be big brother, and wished, just once, that of all the costumes in town, the Buckroys were not always the strangest.

Children dressed as Goblyns--or what they would imagine were Goblyns, with green or brown or orange paint on their faces, or Merrows, with covered rakes on their heads that resembled fish frills. A gaggle of them formed the Wild Hunt, sporting horses made from broomsticks. A pair of them huddled in a conglomerate to make the uncatchable leopard-spotted Questing Beast, a while another pair pantomimed being the gory Nuckelavee.

Still several more wore pointed ears made of bands of dried grass--they were Tuatha. One with them, all green and crowned with stick antlers carrying his father's bow was the Erlking, lord of the seasons. The little girl wearing a veil and dressed all in white: she was a Bean Shii, specifically Myrra, the washer woman. There was an old nursery rhyme about her that even he knew by heart: *'Old and pale, withered and frail, she sits before the ford. Mortals dare not deign to look upon, her washing with her board. Keening in mourning 'neath her veil she cleans the dead's attire. One day she'll wail for you as well, Myrra o' the Misty Mire.'*

Two of them paraded nearby with simple hempen mill bags over their head with holes for eyes, wearing filthy clothes, one carrying a big stick and the other a shovel. Still others had sticks and flowers in their hair; they were Urisks like Delaney, several of them were the Blossom Bride, villain and enchantress of many a tale. A few attempted to depict the statue around which they pranced, with woven horns like it had, and many more Adimus couldn't identify at all.

There were activities and games for the children: bobbing for apples, catch the cat, carve the pumpkins, toss the black hat. There were adult games as well: there was a growing contest for biggest pumpkin, a wood axe hurling competition (Brian always won that) and an archery tournament (Eichgun normally would have easily won that, but with him out of commission it was a real nail biter). Adimus was horrible at all three, and it left him wondering if he should find Dyrshul under the guise of chaperoning her just to find somewhere to belong. He was particularly bad at archery, and there were more than enough holes in side of the Green Beat to prove it--he had neither the strength in his fingers to pull the string and hold it long enough to aim, nor the instinct or coordination to simply pluck it and let the arrow fly like Eichgun did--Eek always told him that as he grew he'd have the frame for it, and to pick the method most natural to him accordingly.

By the time he'd gotten the chance to speak with Laina again she would be gone, having packed up the Beat's kitchen utensils and going to put them up for the night. They turned to slowly watch the parade wind down. Adimus stared blankly, off into the distance. The evening was a dull haze, accented by moments of raging impatience. When night finally had come and all the lanterns were made, the 'guising' would begin, where the children would receive small cakes and pies door to door as the procession led them through the Beat, led by the Reeve on his new white horse tied with a pair of deer antlers. Adimus helped Bearach hand out the stack of bags, most nothing more than pillow cases, with which they would store the night's haul.

"Just because we're on horses doesn't mean you have to be on one. Go and enjoy yourself." Bearach protested to Argent, his muffled voice bellowing from inside his prop armor. He fumbled to get back on his horse, half blind from peeking through eye-holes. He was a Dullahan, complete with a carved pumpkin under his arm in lieu of a head. Argent replied something along the lines that it was his duty to be ready should he be needed.

The horses which the Watchers rode, were arguably better suited to plowing fields, and McConell's youthful stallion ran circles around them. He wore a bright blue cloak with gold embroidery billowed majestically as his nimble horse pranced. It was white on the inside, contrasting his striking black coat. He had a gleaming bronze hand axe at his side. He also carried a small silvery shield with him, bearing a quartered blazon of the same colors as the outside of his cloak, with a boar's head in the center, which he displayed proudly on his arm.

Pulling up the rear was Count Thadeus Pembroke himself. He was the Ankou, as he always was, with a wide-brimmed buckled hat covering his unscary bald head and a high collared coat that covered his only slightly scary sideburns, with his horses and buggy painted all black and tied with rattling chains. Volunteers pounded against the inside of the carriage and screamed and moaned like those he captured to carry off to the land of the dead (if they were, in fact, really uncaring and about the whole prospect and a little too tired to boot). Every once in a while (to accent the true horror of it) he would do his best scary laugh "Ohohohoho!" and brandish a scythe at the crowd.

Brian clad himself in hooded robes that made him look like a giant with a hunch, and used a bull's eye lantern to make himself King of the Baleful Eye, Balros himself. The burning gaze projected from the guise would illuminate the evening as they went on as he led the kids to the different houses, would, that is, until a man came to impede them.

"What is this?! Blasphemy!" Tolten decried. "You've now grown so bold in your Hubris to dare to dress as The Bound King? Calling up the Named One!" He cursed. *Crom Cruach. Ol' Evil Eye.* "You feign in jest, but he watches. Better pray and give penance for all our sakes!"

"Oh come now, Pardoner." Brian said, fearless enough to object, but not too fearless enough as to not use the man's title. "I will simply pray: 'Parthos, god of light and mercy, protect me from my own irreverence, for I dared portray your worst enemy in a childish light.' "

To see Brian, of all people, jeering at the Pardoner would be telling to anyone who knew him, for Brian was typically a meek man for his stature.

"May your ignorance stay hidden in the mists of this life, damned in two faiths! You blaspheme the Ollathar's name as well! Bah! Worshippers of the Gentle Folk, they all have you tricked!" he looked at them all judgmentally. "Heed, the Lord of the Baleful Eye is the Parthos Ollathar's will given Form! *'The god of Many Shapes sculpted him in his image from the deepest stone, and gave his final life's blood to him, that he keep man aright.* Keep us safe forevermore, for vile and deceiving is the heart of man!' "

"...Tolten, this is not the time for proselytization and castigation!" Luloch Buckroy rebuked him, emerging from the crowd, standing brazen, the tip of his cane hard on the ground as if to bar him. "At least I aired my grievances at the proper time and place!"

"Time?! You, Luloch, should know it! What time do we have? The Wild Hunt's hounds clamour to gnash at your entails, to lap them up like a Longnight feast! The Ankou's chariot wheels, even now, make their preparations to grind our bones to dust like a millstone! Far too long we have celebrated this 'holy day' as a sterile day for heedless revelry! And we pay for it! Crom Cruach demands sacrifice, and it shall be done, and it shall heed not timeliness! This is the way. This is the time. Luloch Buckroy! Slake His thirst, avert the Fearful Eye, before it falls upon us!" He shook his shillelagh at him. "If you worried about your Sluagh Oiche you know what ought be done!"

Some people sighed, some wondered what 'proselytization' meant, but a few (more than Adimus and Laina had ever been comfortable with) looked on with a frankly unnerving kindred resolve as he spoke. An understandably concerned look fell upon the travelers' faces. The reeve's as well. He started to raise his voice, but Argent cut in. He put his arm about the man.

"Now Pardoner, that was a good mum, but perhaps it's subject matter a bit too scary for the children, eh? Let's adjourn to the tavern, I've some important news for you from the Circle at Bowen..."

"How many more loons must we suffer before the day is done?" The reeve finally sighed, away from the ears of the priest and Luloch.

Adimus patted one of the children on the head. "Carry on now, he's just tryin' to scare because its Allhallow's Night. Like Dyrshul did when she said she saw the Raven Man." he chuckled as best he could.

"Right. The raven man." The reeve strained a grin.

It was best that he distanced himself from that story, even Dyrshul would agree. That was a debacle that he, and apparently everyone else in the village, remembered so fondly so that it became eponymous--ask anyone in the village and they'd tell you about the Raven Man that haunted the hills, only ever seen by the girl--it had made an even bigger wedge in trying to fit in than them actually trying to fit in.

It took only about as long as the interruption for it to be forgotten. Children ran up and down the street gathered in their little groups, as Adimus walked amongst them, nostalgically reminiscing on how he used to be Dyrshul's age. He used to visit The Green Beat, back when it was just the reeve's house to get the first of the staghorn-glazed green apple tarts. That was before the reeve's lord became the ruling house of Ormond. His new house was much more luxurious. *What does he give out nowadays, I wonder?* He couldn't help but muse. He paced the streets, all but forgetting the troubles at hand. Hours passed, and the night had seemed to come to a close (as much as the reeve had doubted it) without further incident. Under the golden crown of the devouring moon Adimus came to a child crying beside a barn.

He'd suspected the routine: someone had bullied him, or stolen his candy, or played a prank on him. Several children stood nearby, looking on at him and talking amongst themselves, either witnesses or perpetrators, Adimus assumed. "Chains! Oooooh!" One of the kids moaned, shaking the clattering brass links in his face, that is until he saw the Watcher and hurried over to the rest, hiding the evidence behind his back. "What's going on here?" Adimus asked.

They all looked at each other, as if agreeing to speak up. "He's telling fibs." An older boy then stammered. It was Regby's son, Ailen, dressed as a Greenman with his face painted and staghorns of sumac in his (notably uneven and lop-sided) hair.

"No I wasn't!" the boy turned and yelled back at them, his face and eyes beet red. Adimus had begun to espouse the virtues of appreciating a spooky tale or two and perhaps even commend the boy for being so good at telling one so skillfully that it obviously got under the skin of someone several years his senior, when he noticed who it was. "Killien?" he said, and with that he briskly came to him. The kids scattered. It was Eichgun's youngest one. Adimus had been there to watch his first steps, baby-sitting him on occasion, and had carried him piggyback on many a day in summers past besides. It was more than a little upsetting to see him this distraught. He did not have the look of a child frustrated at being bullied, or scorned at not fitting in, and definitely not for attention seeking; this was the cry of a child that cried because he just couldn't help it. This was different. "What happened?" he knew it was more than just this. "Tell me."

"Why? You'll laugh at me too! All the grown-ups do!" he exclaimed before storming off toward the Green Beat. Adimus tried to stop him, but the boy disappeared into the crowd.

Adimus turned to see Dyrshul standing there with her helmet off. She had apparently watched the whole time. "You didn't know?" She spoke quietly despite being in a crowd. Adimus drew closer to hear. "He's been saying things. Strange things." She began, they stepped aside to let Bearach and a crowd of other adults by, the Precession was moving.

"What do you mean?" They walked along behind as she spoke.

"Well, it's about his father. He claims it was something he said." Adimus knew. "He forbids Killien to go near the barn." She said.

"The barn where Eichgun fell?"

Dyshul nodded. "He says there is something in there. He says he didn't fall." she said soberly. "He was pushed."

"Pushed? By whom?" Adimus, didn't have to hide his intelligence with bad grammar to Dyrshul. Dyrshul just shrugged, before she left him to stew with it as she hurried up to the front to get more sweets when she'd noticed that the crowd had stopped.

"No one will mourn your death! "Ohohohoho!" Lord Pembroke yelled at the little girl. Standing and brandishing his scythe at her.

"Poor sod." Argent said, sidling up beside Adimus. "He has no idea the trouble all of you are in." He was sure Argent meant the trouble of the burning barn and the like, but his words came out like a judge's sentence. Observing his unease he circled the boy almost as if to stoke it. "Hahaha! Just kidding. Or am I? Haha!"

But it was obvious even to an outsider. While Eichgun and all the children played, oblivious, adults wore masks of their own, which hid the furrow in their brows and quiver in their lips.

He tried to peek above the crowd to spy the porch of The Beat off in the distance, and maybe catch Killien, when he saw Luloch on the porch, far away from the festivities speaking with Alfred. And then Alfred's eyes locked uncannily with his the instant he had looked, as though piercing even the darkness, making the boy shrink.

"Remember, boy. Not a word." Tirlag whispered as she wheeled around him, then spun back around to smile and take a bite of a cake, pacing backwards to eye him as she disappeared into the throng. She was holding the hand of a little person one might mistake for a child wearing a pillowcase over its head, who with a sadistic giggle made a gesture as of one slitting a throat.

His gaze then fell on the dark cloaked figure, the Cait Shii', who had been silently observing him. It was dark enough now that it could walk about freely and most would assume she was a woman disguised as a monster and not the other way around.

He was hyperventilating. "Are you okay?" Dyrshul asked. He didn't answer, instead wiping his sweaty palms on his thighs. His head was spinning. Thunder rolled in the distance as if to speak on his behalf. "Are you alright, boy?" echoed Bearach, peeking his head out of his costume. Seeing this, Dyrshul tried to hand him a cake, only to realize that her hand was empty.

"Adimus!" It was Tolten. He didn't know how he'd gotten there, how the bard had let him escape. He was nursing a plate of baked goods. "I got something to say to you..."

"Adimus!"

The Grigor, thus overwhelmed, scrambled up the hill toward the house. But he was blocked by a sight. *Kids being rowdy. Great.* This time, there were three of them. There Ailen stood again. *He's a troublemaker this year, I'll not hold back on him this time.*

Ailen and his friends from earlier stood before with two other kids this time, the one with the hempen mill sack over its heads and another wearing a pumpkin. They were fighting over a stack of candy, the biggest of the three pulling against the other two. Adimus was fed up with the day "Alright now, stop it! Break it up! Ailen!" he yelled. Ailen looked at him, stunned. It was then he realized it was Ailen fighting over his own bag and the other two trying to take it. "You two, drop the bag!" The pumpkin-headed figure looked over his shoulder, and then from his raggedy shirt he drew a rusty knife. Adimus, in shock and hopeful disbelief and confusion, froze. The Watcher could only watch. *Some cruel joke? Some prank?* Before Ailen could even see or Adimus do anything about it he lunged at the boy. Blood soiled the bag and Ailen, his face twisted in horror, stumbled backwards, then crumpled over a nearby cart full of pumpkins. The blood trailed from Ailens's mouth.

Adimus turned. "Put the knife down!" He ordered, as if insanity might listen to reason. Of course it didn't. He carried only a dirk of his own. *What do I do? Use my blade on a child?* Gripped with unsurety, he embraced his shield, took stance and drew near.

He remembered his training well, even now when he'd always wondered if he might fumble, hopefully, the long hours of drills and training his father had given him seemed to make it reflex—if he had to do it consciously he knew he was in for it. Silence spread throughout the crowd, just as it was now beginning to realize what had happened.

All of them were watching, in fact, save the two children, who ignored him, seeming to grapple with each other over the hemp bag they had just mugged Ailen for.

He watched as they continued to fight over the flailing and swishing the blade through the air. Finally the other let go and pulled out a bludgeon and started swinging as well. "No! Let him have the bag!" he didn't even know to whom he was speaking. And then the club landed a blow across the head. Adimus had no idea what to do now.

Where the pumpkin had split there was no child at all. Its beady red eyes fell on him, though the cracked visage and its needle-toothed grin shined ear-to-ear as if it had just told a joke that only it got. A long, pointy, green ear, all chewed up with scars, popped out from the crack.

"Goblyn!" Someone cried.

Adimus thought to reach down for the sword only to realize that Bearach had it, but even as he did the creature took off bounding up to the rooftop with blinding speed. There he lept to the rooftop of the next nearest house and up over into the woods. Adimus looked down at the weapon: it was one of Niall's. It too took off toward the woods. Gasps rippled through the gathering. The already lifeless corpse of the youth lay at his feet. Then the first person to get to the child, a concerned-looking mother, knelt down and removed the sack from its face, no doubt to see whose child it was, and only to realize it too was no child at all. He quickly looked behind him to see Dyrshul, eyes wide in the nostril of her costume and Bearach standing behind her.

Luloch came down from the porch, leaning hard on his cane, and Laina outpacing him. They were both silent. "Take her inside." Bearach ordered. Luloch obeyed. It took him a moment before he realized he should address the whole crowd to do just the same. "Everyone inside your homes!" he said. A moment later the warning bell rang and the Horn of Tuetates blew.

Luloch looked up at Laina, and with a nod she picked up the limp child and blood poured from his mouth when she did. "Upstairs, Laina." Luloch followed her inside, a grave look on his face. Alfred was behind them, his expression of concern mixed with resolve showing behind his lenses. Argent pulled up behind him, the reins of Adimus's loaner horse in his hands. Adimus hesitantly hopped onto it. He gave a wry smile. Lightning struck. "Are you ready?"

Chapter 6
Night Terrors

The cold air burned his rasping lungs as he made his way to the wood path of the Precession that encircled the village. He knew this plot well. This swath of forest that sat on the cusp of the wildland that led up into the mountains belonged to Brian the Blacksmith, and was used to fuel his furnaces. He and Dyrshul had played in them often; today, it was of help. It was these woods into which the Goblyn had fled. He wondered what sacred hedge or quarry, what tree or clearing of his childhood they had come to infest, to desecrate.

He clasped the iron sword.

It was Cold Iron. Iron was hard enough to come by, fetching a high price when and where it could be found (Brian was rationed it from the reeve in special portions he had to keep track of) but this tool, this instrument of the Grigor, was a product of high All'Khemy from the age of the Great Kingdom, and had been handed down through the generations to the captain. It was perhaps the most valuable commodity in all the village. "Here. Take it with you, but remember: never touch the blade." It was what he and Dyrshul were always told, and he'd never even laid hands on it until this whole thing had started, and despite riding with the boy tonight he never asked for it back, instead choosing an axe to wield; now he knew that the night's feeling of dread was well warranted.

Argent hushed Tirlag, "Shh!" who was loudly humming a tune despite it all. She, Argent, and Delaney and Bearach had all come on commandeered horses. Alfred and Alara remained on the other side, in case the creature sought to return to the village.

The forest swaddled them in darkness. "Delaney." Tirlag said after a moment. "Do you see anything?" She'd suddenly decided to be helpful.

Delaney removed the pillow case from her head. Her beady little eyes scanned the darkness, her tiny fingers holding a tiny bow with a tiny arrow.

Argent leaned in, "She can see heat. She's a-"

"An animaflora." Adimus answered. He'd remembered Laina telling him about them, now that he'd had a little time to think. "A brownie."

"A sterile observation followed by a racial slur...perfect. Suppose that makes you a mammalian bumpkin." Tirlag scoffed.

Argent defended, speaking to Delaney, "Forgive him, he lacks the couth and sensibilities of <u>your</u> choice of company." he glanced over his shoulder at Tirlag. "They are Urisks. Gnemedians. You know? Hobs."

Argent ducked; he'd immediately been silenced by the whistle of the arrow coming from her direction that just barely missed his head.

"Call this one a hob one more time and she'll use your bones for fertilizer." Delaney growled through gritted teeth.

"Hob is far too impersonal," Tirlag shrugged. "Just call this one what it is: a bitch-!" Tirlag might have continued if not for the sharp jab in the ribs.

"Gnemedians?"

"A child of Gnemed. Yes. "Argent strained, reaching up into the tree into which his hat had been stapled. "Why are you all dressed up anyway?" Argent then asked her. "Your kind walk freely here."

A giggle erupted from Tirlag's covered mouth, as if she just couldn't contain it. She showed him the sack full of candy.

"You've the mind of a goblyn, my dear. You must be so proud." Argent returned fire, "Maybe you can help us find them." just before snatching it from her and digging through it himself.

Delaney, her face becoming more and more twisted with frustration over the last several moments finally jumped down from the horse. This stifled them. They watched as she silently crept off into the darkness.

The wind rustled through the trees, nipping at the chilling sweat on Adimus's face. The blue and red moons in the sky tinged the night with a glaze of violet. They stood there for quite a while, or what seemed like quite a while, until Tirlag suddenly spoke up. "There are three of them."

Bearach had a totally confused look on his face, and with a raised finger started again to question but before he could Argent ordered him. "Escort Tirlag to the others, please. Let her inform the Seer of this." Begrudgingly the pair of them sped off.

Argent looked down at the bag of candy, and then back up toward Tirlag, and then gave an unreadably devilish grin. He hopped down from his horse and peaked off into the brush ahead. With a practiced spin he whipped off his cloak. "Are you good with that sword, young man?" he asked off-handedly, shaking the garment. Adimus couldn't even answer, for the breath was taken right out of him as he witnessed before his very eyes the cloak changing colors again, now from gold-embroidered scarlet to white-Iced baby blue. He slung the shield along his back, higher than Adimus would think comfortable before putting it on. "How about sneaking, are you any good at that?"

"No."

"Then keep a few steps behind. Only a few, hear me?"

"But, I am the only one wearing any manner of armor." Adimus argued, somehow surprised that now that he knew the danger to be real he now volunteered such a thing, but Argent had already disappeared headlong into the brush before he'd even finished.

It may have become a game of cat and mouse if it wasn't for his familiarity, as they trotted over stumps and dodge brambles in the dancing moonslight. Like this they wound their way through the wood, Argent's light-footed feet evading the dried leaf or stray twig that might betray them, until finally the Grigor found him planted against a tree, placing his fingers on his lips.
Faintly, Adimus could hear the tiny growling voices, and off several paces, beneath the boughs of an old hickory, he saw the wild things.

One of them was the one he'd chased. Having removed his pumpkin, Adimus could see his pushed in nose like that of a bat, his needle sharp teeth and his red eyes which glowed like candles in the moonlight. He was gangly, and perhaps only thigh-high, with longer arms than he put on when wearing the children's clothing. The old working gloves he used to disguise his long, three fingered claws lay haphazard on the ground, thrown off in a frenzy that he might viscerally feel his way through the bag he'd stolen, and slavering at the cloth-wrapped pie he'd pulled from it, let out a growl the largest one grabbed it.

Goblyns were creatures born from the souls of children whom the Fae god Mac Ollamian lured away to the Otherworld. There they are transmogrified into foul beasts, mockeries of the temperament and selfishness and ignorant cruelty children can sometimes be known for. That was the story Regby and Luloch always told, anyway.

This other one was horribly disfigured, like a wax sculpture marred by a fire, or an angry squash that had been left in the sun for too long, with black greasy-looking little eyes plugged into it with which to jeer and a sparsely toothed mouth carved with which to jape. At its side, tucked into a ragged belt was a broken half-pair of shears, its handle wrapped in cloth.

The third had a beak like that of a hawk, the rest of its body was pink-skinned like a newborn mouse. Its one eye in the direct center of its head was intently fixed upon the bag, its lizard tail flicking with anticipation despite having his hand slapped away by the big one again and again.

He could hear them vaguely, arguing in chunky warbles and yelps that he imagined, somehow, must be a language. The beat of Adimus's heart thrummed deafeningly in his ear, loud enough to make him expect to be caught by virtue of it alone, only outdone by his need to breathe; he fought it, if only so that he might hear something, knowing even himself that it was bad policy when trying to be quiet.

He looked back at Argent, who simply gave him a roguish wink and put up the hood of his cloak. When he did the Watcher had to blink and ensure that the moonlight were not playing tricks on him, for, right before his eyes, Argent's face changed, now what stood before him was a wrinkled, haggard, hunchback (from the shield) old crone.

He took Tirlag's bag of candy in hand. *"Hayden!"* he yelled, in a shrill and feeble voice *"Hayden! Where in All Creation are you!?"* as he turned and hobbled right into the midst of them. It took Adimus a few moments for his mind to register it, as strange as it was, that Argent was speaking in a different language, a language he'd never heard before, not only this, but what seemed stranger still was the fact that the boy could understand it. *"Oh, there you are!"* He addressed the biggest one in the foreign tongue. *"What are ya doing way off out here anyweh? Don't y'know there are Goblyns about? We need to hurry along to the Dougall's before she's out of the those sweet apple tarts and honey cakes."* The green one growled and the squash-faced one appeared on the cusp of protest before *"Oh, here's yer bag. But I'm takin' this piece for ma' trouble."* He took a wrapped piece of hard candy, one of Luloch's licorice chews, before having the sack of goodies snatched from his hand almost before he could offer it. Adimus perhaps would be panicking, millions of thoughts racing in his mind as he grasped at what to do, but he just couldn't look away. The creatures immediately started fighting over the bag, each pawing at it trying to get hands down in it. *"Oh, are these your friends? Look at these costumes, oh, how creative! What are your names?"*

"Hay-den." the green one started to say before the squash-faced one shot him a dirty look.

"Dooogals." the other parroted.

"Boi'Bocan." The one-eyed one said.

"Very good. Are they coming along too?"

They each looked at one another, then nodded, when "she", having fumbled with the piece of candy, dropped it on the ground. "Oops. *I invoke thy Name and implore, Boi'Bocan, as that which ensnares thee, captures thee, enchants and enraptures thee, quickens thee to the Lands of Death, as I am its master and a friend unto thee. I invoke thy Name and implore."* The Goblyns appeared confused at the strange thing he'd said, rightfully so. Eve Boi'Bocan, who innocuously picked up the treat without mention; he gazed at it with an intent as singular as the eye with which he did.

Licking his beak with a forked tongue he began to tear at the wrapper, salivating. *"Boi'Bocan,"* Argent said again as one might scold a child. *"Give it here."* Trembling, almost as if fighting an invisible force, the creature handed it to her with a remorseful eye. Dexterously, the bard, unwrapped it and popped into her mouth like flipping a coin, *"Boi'Bocan,"* the Bard said once more in his real voice, tossing the wrapper over his shoulders and dusting his nimble hands off on his cloak. *"Subdue your friends."*

Seeing through the ruse the squash-faced one drew his weapon, and without question or choice Boi'Bocan lept onto him. Still the creature lurched forward at Argent and caught him in the thigh with it, "Ergh!" he winced. Adimus, giving it no more thought perhaps than Boi'Bocan, drew his sword to come to his aid, but the green one cut him off. It brandished its dagger, still bloody, looking at him with the same crooked glee that he did with the candy treats as he whipped it about in the air. It charged. Adimus braced. The tiny arrow it had found in its neck, was only drawn to his attention only after the creature had stopped to pick at it, whereupon it crumpled to the ground. Adimus wasted no time leaping over it to get to Argent, who struggled with the big one.

Adimus hesitated at just what to do, the thing relentlessly flailed, its belligerence only rivaled by its speed with the razor sharp blade, the other creature clinging to its back all the while. Argent wedged the great hickory between them, doing his best to evade. Just then, as finally it had feinted the bard to get a clear swing at him, Adimus's eyes were drawn to a faint white glow beyond the treeline. The creature dropped the shears without a second thought, it seemed, gnashing its teeth as it covered its ears. Adimus could hear it too, though apparently not as loudly as the creature; a warbling din that permeated his mind, followed by a heat that seemed to emanate from nowhere. The light burned the creature, scalding its skin, marring it with coal-black streaks. *"Boi'Bocan, come here!"* Argent quickly yelled when he noticed that the Goblyn was being subjected to same malady. Skin flaked off in wisps that incinerated in mid air, fire erupted from tears in its flesh, its eyes and mouth. Adimus watched the creature immolate from flesh to bone, and bone then to dust.

The light went out, and there Alfred stood holding the staff. Laina, Bearch, Rigel, Tirlag, and Luloch, stood with him. With an audible 'tink' he removed a clear crystal from the staff's clasp and quickly put it in his pocket. "Is everyone alright?"

Argent whipped off the hood of his cloak. The illusion was gone, and Argent's face was back to normal. No one had seen it, presumably, save Alfred, who'd looked for some reason like he'd just seen a ghost as his eyes fell open Argent, then to the magic garment, confusion, shock and concern unhidden. "Yea-I'm fine." Argent said, as if nothing had happened, gripping his leg. He snatched the pillow case from the ground where it had fallen, dumped it out and began tying the wound.

Delaney jumped down beside him. "Breather! That's what you get for trying to do it all yourself!" she exclaimed. She sneered at Adimus, "You're welcome."

Cautiously the others drew together to look at the Goblyn Boi'Bocan. "Don't worry. I have control of him."

"How?" Bearach questioned, but Argent was already talking to the creature again. This time Adimus couldn't understand what he was saying, as he spoke in yet another tongue. Calmly removing one of his gloves, Alfred produced from his pocket a delicately ornate silver ring, which he then placed on his finger.

"He speaks its True Name, and knows the words to command it." said Adimus, as bewildered at his verbalization of it as when he first saw it.

"He speaks Dhuun." Alara shuddered in wonder.

"And Puck." The bard added in the midst of his conversation with the thing. "See? Aren't I useful?"

They spoke for a few moments. "He's asking them if there are any more." Alfred narrated, Argent shot him a quick eye of disgust. "He says there are three." He asks this one not completely unlike the one the Goblyns had spoken, without the grunts and hisses. Cleaned up the language sounded quite pleasant, flowing and complex. "But...He asked why they'd decided to burn the farm and string up the cat. He says he was told to."

"By whom?" Tirlag asked.

The bard had started to whisper to the Goblyn again in that voice. Only Adimus was close enough to hear *"Boi'Bocan, you will follow what path the Longing takes in you, with the others in the wood, to the Land Beyond the Mists this night, and harm no one. I release thee, now go forth, free."* and with that Boi'Bocan scampered off never to be seen again.

"The bigger one." he answered in normal tongue, dusting his hands off concededly "Not that one, I asked." He pointed to the pile of ash. "Big. And hairy this one was, he said."

Luloch's voice came from the darkness.

"And toothy and tall, behind the doors and under the bed..."

"...What is it, grandfather?" Adimus asked.

"Why, it's the Boogeyman, Adimus."

Chapter 7
The Sound of Chains

Pembroke was more than obliged to allow the continued confiscation of one of his precious horses. Though Adimus fought to wrestle the tiredness out of it, those who followed him now: this time Laina, Alfred, and Argent, had a hard time keeping up with him. Adimus knew too well why Laina had decided to follow, as she'd had a chance to speak with Killien directly when he'd come running into the Green Beat, and though neither of them could exactly guess why the Seer and the bard had come along, they couldn't help but feel that they too understood. This time no thoughts entered his mind about whether his actions were heroic, whether this was his heretofore aspired-to shining moment; he grasped the reins until his knuckles were white.

They crossed the bridge, and hardly tying the reins he ran to the door. A round, soft-faced lady opened it, holding a bowl of cookies; Brina had been expecting children. "Adimus!"

"...Umm." He was a bit taken aback at her nonchalant demeanor; maybe he wasn't on the right track at all. "Can we come in?"

Argent removed his hat for the lady with a silent bow.

She looked warmly at Laina, then behind her at Alfred with a somewhat concerned look on her face. "Of course." She opened the door for them, and took their coats. "Is this about the Sum Seer coming to speak to Eichgun?" she asked.

"Not exactly-." Adimus said.

"Yes." said Alfred.

The squeaky staircase leading to their bedroom upstairs was blockaded by Killien, tears cleaning trails on his dirty face. The boy looked more than a little relieved to see Adimus as he ran upstairs. "Papa, Papa! Your friends are here."

Eichgun was a grizzled fellow, calloused by long years of toil on the farm and being a guardsman to boot. As they rounded the corner Adimus, seeing him lying helpless, his stubbled face doing little to hide his sunken cheekbones and sullen eyes, filled him with a dread for which he was not prepared. "...Eek?" He greeted him.

"Adi?" He'd been snoozing, only just roused by Killien. "And the bar wench! Both!" He joked. "Haha, it's my lucky day!" He suddenly clammed up when he saw the stranger come in behind her.

"Who's this?" he asked Brina quietly.

"A Faeth, eh?" he echoed back. "Here to see little old me?" he looked critically at them. "More like to question me." he said. Then his boy ran in. He strained a smile and looked back at them. "Well, begone, I've no time for it."

Laina sat down on the edge of the bed. "Oh you must be so busy, with being broken and bedridden and all." Laina mused, poking at the bandaged leg. He couldn't hide his wincing.

"We're actually here because of him." Adimus nodded toward the boy. "About what Killien is saying."

Killien cowered at the mention of his name, Laina comforted him. "You're in no trouble."

Eek sat up with a groan. Even in bed the man's size could be felt. He wasn't big and brutish like Bearach, moreover he was exceptionally tall and stringy. He was no push over though, all tough muscle and sinew, strong enough to sling the boy around when they wrestled or weasel out of any attempt to pin him; what Adimus grappled with now was what manner of creature could have managed to do that to him.

Alfred immediately jumped to it. "Tell me about the night of your fall."

"And you know better than to lie." Brina Lathern warned, and hands on hips, nodding at the Sum Seer; she had suspicions of his forthrightness as well, apparently.

Eichgun gave a deep, heavy sigh. "It was last week." he began. "I was up in the loft at dusk, pitching hay for the horses." he started. He took another breath. "I jabbed my fork into to the pile." He fought a stammer "And it made a noise. Horrible noise." His eyes went vagrant. His hands tried to express its enormity. "It was, it was, big. And hairy." Adimus repeated the rhyme in his head. Eichgun's eyes widened. "Its eyes...It made a roar that..." he didn't finish. "All I remember when I hit the ground was the sound of chains coming toward me.

"Chains?" Alfred and Laina both shot.

"Jangling chains." Adimus answered them. "Killien's heard them too, hasn't he?"

Eek gave a silent nod.

"He won't sleep in his room anymore." Miss Lathern explained.

"It had glowing eyes and a ball of flame in its hands. Scorched me." He pulled down the front of his overalls and showed them the burns on his chest. "He shoved me. My leg slipped through the ladder and snapped. I clawed my way out into the sunlight. It didn't want to follow me there. It only stood, snarling until my wife came. And then it was gone."
"It fears light, could it be...a Shade?" Said Laina.

"No." Argent shook his head. "Shades are not Nis. And mortals don't get touched by the Sluagh and live." He solemnly replied. "No. Sounds like a bugbear."

"What's that?"

"A Nis Shii, and a nasty one at that. An Effigy Wraith. Bogeyman, wickerman. Has as many names as it does accompanying tale."

"True. Not this long at least, and there's no sign of Dissolution." said Alfred.

Still they examined the spot on his chest, just in case, as Shades apparently left marks.

Adimus turned to look at Killien's room across the hall. The door was open, and across the bed there was a window. Adimus left the conversation, which paused in his absence. There the child stood, eyes vagrant, lip quivering as he stared off into the darkness. Pacing up to it Adimus gazed out to see, unsettlingly close, the barn and open doors to the loft. Candlelight.

"...Adimus?" Laina looked at him questioningly. Adimus said nothing. He looked down at the quivering boy, then turned back down the stairs.

* * * * *

They had sent for the old man the moment everything had happened, but he'd never come.

He wasn't sure what he could even help with, but surely it would be something. After all, he held the powers of the Seven Golden Veils, miraculous powers granted to him through his great faith. Adimus had seen some of them first hand.

With the words from the man's tongue he'd seen food that had not been offered to the god go rancid, as in the case of Meav at the opening day celebratory feast when the Beat first opened...

Once, he accompanied the Pardoner to search for the Lake of Sacred Stone hidden deep in the mountains, the stone from which the greatest of idols were made.

A snow squall befell them and they became hopelessly lost. Eventually they came to an old oak in a lonely grove. The Shepherd instructed him to climb it. The Watcher was thinking he would be using it as a vantage point to spot a way out, but when he got to the top he was instead instructed to climb about on it and cut off the longest of the branches with his hatchet. When they had all been shorn to his liking, the Pardoner gathered up a few of them and, far away from the tree, using red charcloth from a sacred fire he sparked a flame to them. From the smoke emerged a spectral hound. It moved and behaved as any living thing would, but its eyes glew like embers, and its bark was as the crackling of a hearth. Leaving the flame burning but safely sequestered, the Magic held until they were home, whereupon the hound returned back into the wood.

The boy found the spot the next year, stumbling upon it on one of his long patrols with Bearach, and the oak itself had been burned to blackened coals inside and out by the power of the Magic.

All he could do is seek solace in his faith, that perhaps <u>he</u> were worthy enough to be protected so. He was doing right, after all. Doing his duty to the village. Being the Watcher. He never imagined himself saying it. "If only he were here..." Adimus muttered to himself.

Had the lantern only been a bit brighter, and not stained with the soot of a generation's use he may have been able to see up into the partially open shutter. He'd asked for Eichgun's hooded one that shed reflected light, but he hadn't seen it since that day. In fact, several things had been missing from the house that went unaccounted for, Brina had said. A scary thought, Adimus admitted, that whatever it was may have been skulking about inside the house.

Light flickered in the shadows of the deep claw marks that marred the wall all the way up to the window of the loft above. He came around to the front side of it, and setting the lantern down he pulled free the large cross bar that held the doors together, and laid it on the ground with a loud 'thunk'; Eichgun hadn't kept it locked to keep livestock in or out, because he'd removed them all from the barn in the past week just the same.

With one deep breath he went on. The sudden cracking lurch of the door and the croak of the rusty hinges was more than enough to let anyone know he was coming, so he figured he'd announce himself. "...Hello?" His voice rattled the bones of the building in a loud echo. He took a few steps in, lantern in one hand, sword in the other. Deep inside atop the loft he could see the faint flickers of candlelight.

"Are you really going to face this thing alone?" He hadn't heard Laina tip-toeing up behind him, it nearly made his feet leave the ground.

Neither Argent nor Alfred would come. "Let's not be hasty. It is safe enough here until daybreak." the Sum Seer warned. And Argent echoed the sentiment happily.

He didn't feel the need to explain. <u>He</u> was the one who had seen the flames devouring Niall's house. He didn't expect outsiders passing through to care or mind anyway for their safety. What's more, he had to suspect that the sword gave him the courage and solace to move forward, itself a talisman to him as much as the Watcher was to the village--it was made to slay such creatures.

"Yes. I am." It sounded like a confession of guilt.

Without another word Laina rolled up her sleeves and picked up a pitchfork. With begrudging hesitance, he relented, and handed her his dirk, which she tucked in her sleeve.

He cast light on the lumps of shadow within the animal stalls, all empty save for their tying ropes and troughs. Then he came to the ladder for the loft. He gazed down at it. It splintered into pieces. He feigned to imagine such a thing, something able to rend wood to shivers as one would paper.

A musky smell, like rust and rotten greenery and wet burning leaves filled the damp air, but not a noise was heard beyond their own footprints, not even a field mouse dared come near. The wind blew in a draft from the open double doors, rustling the straw and spitting stray leaves, and pushing upon the shutters, opening them even so slightly more and bathing the insides with moonlight. Adimus looked down to examine the busted up old ladder, still on the ground from where Eek had tumbled, and then as of the wafting of some great cloud which covered the sky a shadow loomed from above. Chains rattled in the darkness.

The boy's first impression of it was that of an immense furry hulk of a creature. As it drew near though he saw it in truth, that it was more composed than covered, not with fur, but foliage: straw and moss and sinewy vines and ivy, matted and spun together and held by a spiral of braided brass chain. The thing shifted and moved when it stood, and saw that it was stuffed with debris: a carved handle from a wheelbarrow that showed Niall's hallmark and craftsmanship, one that he was positive used to sit at the edge of the old man's property, the bones of the robbed graveyard that rattled and clunked as it roiled, the skull of the poor man forming a portion of its shoulder. It towered over him, easily twice his height.

Saucer sized holes like bird's nest cradled the two dripping candles within that made up its eyes. From those lights stark Otherworldly shadows, too deep for their own possibility, sprang to life and moved and flitted like living things wherever its glance fell.

The glowing eyes fell upon *him*. "What's this? A courageous little man? A Fool?" it bellowed in a deep, rumbling murmur. "Selfsame!" It spoke from a maw fashioned from a hard rake for gardening and razor sharp thorns. Its nose was a spinning wheel.

The boy brandished the sword, though he had no need to, as the thing was already looking at it.

"Cold Iron?! A rich fool, who thinks it can defeat fear with weapons. Tell me, what makes it think is a match for the Wurrychul?"

"I…I don't. I'm performing my charge. I'll not allow you to hurt anyone else." He fought to say.

"Then misplaced pride shall be its doom!" Black smoke roiled from the burning tips of his eye sockets as its brow furrowed. The light shown within glowed from what perhaps would be its nose, ears and mouth, and cinders linger about it though no spark caught. "And make no mistake, this night it shall know pain! Fear!" It pointed at him with an index finger made of a scythe blade from a hand made of snips and cleavers. The other hand gripped the edge of the loft angrily: five stubby digits consisted of burning candlesticks which leaked onto the floor below as its fiery fingertips sparked against the wood. Chains slithered from the loft. "Deluded Cessair child, I am a creature of Shade! A sluagh! Do you not know death when you see it?!" Adimus took a guarded stance. Laina stood close, brandishing her broomstick. The wind blew once more, the doors slammed shut, pulled by the clanking irons. With the swoop of its hand the barn became a blazing inferno of burning straw and timber "Your soul will be mine!"

A Shade?! Bound King, have mercy! The mere mention of the word sent his logical mind into throes of terror, overriding any rationalization that would identify it for the ruse it was. Adimus disregarded the expertise of his compatriots in that moment in favor of utter panic.

Then it was on him. The sheer immensity of the creature and the force with which it lept upon the boy bore him helplessly to the ground. Planks of wood came crashing down around him, splintering as the chains snapped them. The crushing weight of the beast pinned his legs motionless. He couldn't breathe.

His sword had done nothing even though he'd tried to catch it mid-flight. Wax salivated from its grinning maw. "Fear me!" It growled, and held its flaming hand over the boy. Candlewax dripped onto his cheek. Then it paused, only a moment, for inextricably the fire of the candles began to leap up its hand. Adimus never questioned this, or gave pause, using the moment to try and shake free.

The flame caught on the hay and straw, and in seconds a blaze had been started in the room. Laina saw an opportunity to strike. "Yahh!" She stabbed at the creature, who dismissively lifted its other hand, five lengths of chain which unfurled in a whipping spiral and engulfed her with a force so great that it tore the feeble weapon to splinters. Wrapped and held aloft, she squirmed for but a moment before the creature slammed her to the ground, and wound her up tight like a spider saving a meal. Adimus tried in vain to reach a blow around it, but its girth thwarted any meaningful exchange, as he could but swat air.

"Contemplate death." It growled quietly. "Know true terror!"

Adimus *was* thinking on it. This was it.

He hadn't known why there had been this churning madness in him, what manner of primordial urge that had dwelt deep within him to go and confront the creature himself. He hadn't the time to think about it, this push, whether it was out of curiosity, of altruism, or because he simply wanted the night to be over, just not like this.

"That's right, squirm, pitiful thing-erk!" The last syllable came out as of a gag and the knife penetrated the back of its head and out its mouth. Fire and smoke lept from the wound, as it spun around to see the face of the cait'shii staring back at him. It held some manner of wand that next he pointed at the creature. A deafening roar let loose from it that tore through the creature, toppling it.

She tossed the boards aside and reached out to help Adimus to his feet, her own feet came out from under her, as a whipping chain jerked her too to the ground; the creature was still very much alive. This time Adimus's sword struck true, a desperate full-bodied slash across the creature's mid section. Sparks flew from the friction of the chains, and again fire and smoke roiled from the wound.

"See?" The cat quipped. "Curious." It let out a shriek and grabbed the rafters with its chains to pull itself skyward, then with a heave it bolted through the open window and out into the night.

Adimus hadn't seen that the creature had caught Laina. A cry, "Help!" and an outstretched hand and Laina too was gone.

Adimus ran to the door. It was jarred. He could hear the little giggles of the goblyns from outside. Flames licked the roof of the building filling it as they stood trapped, thick black smoke choking and blinding them.

"What do we do!?" the boy said. Thankfully the cat was already on it. Grabbing one of the tying ropes and holding it with his teeth, with a hop accented by claws clinging on wood she lept to the loft and lowered down the rope. Adimus scurried, giving no thought at all to having never actually climbed one, his heightened senses and panic carrying him. He doesn't even remember the descent, which came as a fall-tumble-rappel onto cold hard ground; he hit it running, choking back coughs from the smoke. The boy stabbed his sword into the ground to keep upright. He came to a large wheat field on the edge of the property. He waded on, following the smashed flat trail that the large creature had left. He could hear the mumbles of people behind him calling. The others he turned but for a moment to check on the safety of the others and found himself side-swiped.

The goblyn lept at him from the brush with a yell of fury, its heretofore unaccounted for shovel swinging at his head. Adimus shoved at the thing with his shield when a shillelagh caught the creature mid-stomach and sent it on its backside. "Go Adimus! "Don't be afraid!" Luloch ordered when the thing skittered off faster than the old man's legs could take him. Pointing, he could make out Alfred and Bearach running toward them from the Latherns' yard, and see Brina and Killien on the porch. He pressed on.

The dark environs of the forest blinded him just as before. Adimus swatted at brambles in his path, and spun as he tripped over obstacles in his haste. He knew where he was, not far from the village proper. His memories guided him along, bolstering his speed.

It was an old rock quarry from his childhood that he desecrated, in a grove of elms, there he could see the glint of his candlelight eyes. Finally, he'd caught up with it, only that it had taken the time to scurry up a tree with its living chains. The Grigor slowed his step, biding the moment to catch his breath and possibly break the rhythm of the pursuit; he had thought the thing to be waiting to pounce down upon him from above like before, but the being again touched ground quicker than the boy could grasp his true intent. Coming into the clearing into which had followed, he saw Laina dangling from her heels, over the jagged rock.

"Come close and she dies!" the creature warned, the chains of its sprawling hand holding her aloft.

None of the fire and fight had left Laina though, as she adjusted her neck and in a strained voice taunted "You are the one who is afraid, creature. Not he. Not I."

At this the creature let out a roar of consternation. Smoke billowed from its eye holes and mouth. It pulled at the chains to hoist her up further.

When he was finished Adimus looked into Laina's eyes. He expected to see fear or panic, but instead her face showed terse determination and rectitude. "Adimus...no night lasts forever."

He knew Laina probably better than anyone in the village. What's more, he knew her heart--that she would do anything to protect them-to protect him, and so he knew what her wishes would be. But Laina also knew him as well. *No. She wouldn't ask me to do this. To let her die, even if it saves these people. Does she really think that much of me? Does she really think I could bear such a burden?*

The creature laughed at the boy's hesitance. "I've won!" The Wickerman courtled.

Then it came to the boy. He spoke out loud the epiphany. "It doesn't matter." It cut the creature's laughter short. "I won't do it. She won't do it, and most of all *you*. You won't do it." His blade enunciating his point. "Because then there would be nothing between me and my blade."

They stood with Laina, arms outstretched. *She would be safe.*

His eyes narrowed. "You are bigger and fiercer than I, for sure. There would be no need for you to fight like this unless...unless you were the one scared." he said. And with that he fell into stance, the plough, one of several Bearach had taught him. "So, let her down and face me. You'll not be able to put up a good fight so wound up."

Its eyes narrowed, burning the tips of its sockets. Then, defeated, in answer it did lower her down. "It sees much." The Bugbear said. "Thinks it sees all, but it does not even see itself! Wrong! Wrong about everything! It is Cessair, it is Hyu'man! It is no Immortal Fae. A mere mortal fed on lies, sweet lies to instill that sense of duty, sense of pride it has, its faith! No life awaits it beyond the veil of death when its blood is spent! The stars weep not for it! Like the stone it worships, to earth it is and to it you shall return, then all goes black!"

Adimus's blood ran cold. The beast cackled.

Its fiery fingertips roared its malice. Flames gouted from its mouth "Now there is nothing between you and the endless silence."

The cold autumn wind blew. Between the treeline he saw the tiny lamplights of the village far below, tiny shadows dancing in the windows, children eating candy. Cold iron glinted in the moonlight. He looked over at Laina. *No.*

"...Come." the creature's words made him question his own. Adimus brandished his sword again at the beast. He cloaked his ceaseless shuddering with his shield well enough; he'd been a good liar, maybe he'd even convinced himself; he'd never felt so frightened.

He buried it deep nonetheless, and charged.

It wasn't the sword that had made him brave, that pulled his legs forward in this moment, it was simply the house behind him, wherein terror had shown on a little boy's face. This monster had invaded his home, all of his childhood, and it would stop tonight.

The creature took a step back. "No!"

Adimus gained ground on it, sword pointed and tucked behind the targe, as Eichgun had taught him. "Yahh!" But the blow never landed; it never needed to.

Fire shot up from its sockets, crawling down its arm. "No!!" Its eyes became blazing fountains. It stopped Adimus dead in his tracks; he could do nothing but watch. Fire roared from its mouth as the creature erupted into a plume of smoke and cinder. The chains themselves now seemed to burn it. They that bound the mound of foliage now started unwinding it, as one running from oneself; spinning and spinning until it tore apart. Only refuse and smoldering scrap remained.

Adimus jerked at the hand that met his shoulder. Luloch had stepped up behind them. "It's in the hand--not the head, boy, where fearlessness lies. The will that moves them just the same, even when the heart flutters and the legs shake." he said, staring into the now still wreck.

"Big and hairy, and toothy and tall
Behind the door, under the bed
Gangly and jangly, the Bugbear sees all
Beyond where the candlelight sheds

A tree in a window, a face in stray clothes
Night's fancy and neck hairs on end,
Farther than mind reaches, past 'no one knows',
There dancing in blazes it lets

Big and hairy and toothy and tall,
On phantoms and nonsense it's fed
Gangly and jangly, the Bugbear sees all
The fears that you choose to abet."

Chapter 8
Beyond Balfour

The Pardoner tottered astride his horse, still noticeably disturbed by hearing what the night had held, steadying it in the midst of the square as he addressed the crowd as an authority on the whole matter, despite having not actually been there. Even in such pressing affairs as this he had found time to put on his miter and robe and even powder his face to look more presentable. Adimus wasn't sure of what he spoke, but it seemed accusative; his sunken face and demeaning disposition twisting as his pale lips yammered and green eyes darted like some lizard.
It seemed to affect the townsfolk little, as Killien stood there with his father, speaking on what had happened, amidst a sea of teary eyed and elated witnesses.

"What do you think he's saying?" Adimus whispered even though it was just them.

"Be still!" The old man snapped, tugging the boy's peeking head toward him for now a third time as he straightened the young man's tartan, a parent dressing his child.
Still he gawked. After such a gaping wound and all that blood, the fact that Eek was up and about and talking at all seemed impossible to the boy, yet there he stood Tolten would said it was a miracle, he would guess, a grace from the old god, for his devotion—Eichgun always was first in line and first to speak at temple functions.
Nearly all of them stood to hear what the Pardoner Tolten Blaise had to say, save for Adimus, Bearach, Luloch, and Dyrshul, who stood peeking out of the den window of their house atop the hill.

A thick haze of smoke permeated the den, between the puffing of nervous pipes, the burning of a hastily stoked cooking fire, and subsequent burnt breakfast that had come from it. Such noisome odors always gave the boy a headache.

Adimus had pondered the need for such a hearty meal, cooked hours before the sun rose, but now it was quite clear. He was sweating from it, being wrapped in his thick wools and long sleeves, the large ruck sack slung across his back slipping from the unease with which it laid across his shoulder blade. Bearach had strapped it with a belt at his hips to distribute the weight but it wasn't helping.
It dawned on him when he'd found the rug beneath the rocking chair had been disturbed, and a hempen pouch of talismans prepared for him: A charred rowan wand with a handle made from the leather of a cow who died of old age, adorned with a tassel of blackbird feathers. A laquer-smelling potion of charcoal, meadowsweet and yarrow, with several unidentifiable notes of an animal nature, acorns from the tree outside, suspended in a tincture of powdered salamander floating above the pulled teeth of a white horse who had been struck by lightning--It was an upsetting accident for the Cayden, who owned the young colt, a tragedy of course, but Luloch acted as if he'd won the lottery that day.
Someone rapped loudly on the door. "Anwell!" Luloch opened it, grabbed the old man and pulled him into the room. He started to slam the door shut behind him. "Tolten's looking for you!" It was common practice for the brothers to scream at each other as they were both a little hard of hearing, but this one was out of imperativeness.

Luloch's face twisted, a wrinkled bag of disappointment, outrage, and solemnity all tied up with angst. He nodded "I know it...I know it." He looked over at the boy. "We'd best not keep them waiting, he might get suspicious..." He didn't need to make an excuse, Adimus understood.

Luloch put his hands behind his back, as he always did. He walked over to him and looked him up and down, examining what he wore, he gave another nod of approval. "You'll do fine." The man gave him a pat on the arm and then he was off. Bearach had fled off out back before the exchange had even happened. Adimus was sure he'd say he was getting his horse ready, but it was really to hide his face.

Adimus stared absently at the map that hung framed on the wall beside the hearth. He got it the time they visited the big city up north in Menkara, where they mass-printed such things on a press; it took so long to get there, to Ederton, and he saw so many things, but the map was so limited, showing just the corner-of-a-corner of the world, and that, even then, Balfour was of such insignificance that it wasn't on the map at all.

Anwell sat down in Luloch's old rocking chair beside the fire. "So...How's your Pa taking the news?"

"Well..." Was all Adimus said. He always hated those kinds of questions, the ones that were almost rhetorical but carried some expectation of being answered.

Anwell sort of caught the inkling of frustration in the boy's voice, but ignored it, he never never could tell when anyone was uncomfortable, as anyone privy to his dirty jokes could tell you. "So, this Faeth's going to take you under his wing, eh?"

"I hope." The lies came out perfectly now, though this lie did seem to share a ring of truth about it, from what Luloch had told him. "And Argent says I am going to be able to speak to the Stewards of the Clans about...you know." He gestured toward the old man.
Adimus watched as the old man hobbled down the hill to meet with the priest, trying not to let himself feel mournful. There were always moments in his past where, even though he didn't realize it at the time, it would mean far more to him later, and he always remembered them whether he wanted to or not. He wondered if this were one of these moments.

It was apparent that Anwell was just making idle chit-chat until he could segue into more serious matters. "You know, the Pardoner thinks that the Bag-bug..the bea...that creature, was Named. Conjured. By a witch. Said that's how they're most often made. He's calling for the Princely Stewards to summon the Order of Jasmine. And that's the least of it." He shook his head.

No one answered him. It made Adimus worry all the more.

"We're ready." Bearach's voice broke the awkward silence.

"Well," the man gave a smile. "Good luck." Anwell stood. "And travel safe now." he added, poking him in the breastbone. "The Ruined Road is a dangerous place."

Dyrshul ran and gave him a hug as soon as he opened the door. "Where are you going?" Her muffled voice sobbed within his coat.

"I...I don't know."

"Don't forget, Pa said to take the sword." she reached for it on the mantelpiece. Adimus had protested, knowing well now more than ever that they might need it, but they insisted. Luloch slapped her hand, though not maliciously. "How many times have I told you not to touch that?!" There were many.

Bearach handed it to him. "You got the coins I gave you?" Adimus nodded. "Your waterskin and your wits?" the man asked. "Of course." He beamed at the boy for just a moment. "Don't worry, son. The smoke'll clear and you'll be back before you know it." Bearach always called him son, even when there was no one around. "You'll be back in time for Longnight presents and eggnog."

He had almost walked out the door, when he felt the bejeweled statue dangling from his brooch and remembered. "I must Slake before leaving."

"Of course, of course child." Said Luloch. He looked at Bearach, who quickly cleared a table, mostly by knocking its contents on the floor. "Come now. I've already milk prepared." Luloch handed him a cup. Missing a conspicuous amount from it, he glanced up to see the old man's milk mustache. "You're not supposed to drink it before it is offered!" he shuddered.

He wiped his face with his sleeve. "I was just tasting it. To ensure that it was a worthy offering. I'd heard Bessie got into Niall's onions the other day."

Nabbing the mug from his hand he quickly said the prayer, and jettisoning the beverage out the window, was out the door. Before he knew it he too was swept away down the hill. Alara and Argent both stood outside to escort him.

Curious to their whispering, the boy, of course, listened in. "...Did she threaten to curse us if she did not come?" Alara said to the bard.

"That's bigotous hogwash." Argent scolded. Adimus pondered only a moment of whom they were speaking, for when they turned a corner there she stood.

The pack at Laina's side was hers, the one she'd entered the village with so long ago, the bow and quiver of arrows she carried were not.

Alara's arms crossed with impatience at the slowness of the proceedings as they passed the crowd, herself glancing over her shoulder to see the caravan making its way over, and Tolten outpacing it. "We need to hurry." both her and Laina said in tandem, a worried look on their faces. Finally they'd started to move, and Tolten was snared by Luloch, no doubt on purpose.

"Don't you worry about the pardoner." Argent assured him when they'd trailed behind the others. "I've spoken to Lord Pembroke. If he so much as looks at your family wrong while you're gone he'll be wheeled off to Cairnfang before he can blink." He knew something, more than he let on, something he shouldn't. Adimus fought his raised eyebrow.

Eichgun Lathern himself was in his yard as they passed his house. He waved and smiled exuberantly as they walked.

Adimus felt like a peeping tom, but he'd seen Laina from atop his hill visiting them just before dawn, he guessed to make sure they were okay. Miraculously he too seemed much more than able to get around. He was glad to see him on the mend so. *At least they will be safe without me.*

Even the uneven dirt path which led from behind the boy's house to the back of the Green Beat felt wrong, as it always circled the other way when he marched. The jarring footfalls and rocks made his head throb and his already weary feet ache.

Alfred, Tirlag and all the others were there waiting for him.

"Welcome aboard, emissary of Balfour." Torrin tipped his hat.

Thadeus Pembroke himself stood talking to Torrin von Krasad holding the reins of a horse. It was the horse from the night before. Off-handedly he passed the reins to the boy. "Aethan is his name." said Lord Pembroke. "Keep him well."

Argent handed him a small leather envelope from his breast pocket, branded with a seal of griffon holding a key in its mouth "Here is his license--you'll need that."

Adimus brow curled until he saw the small bag of coins at the man's side, covered in squirrel fur.

He shot a stare back, aimed at the top of the hill. Bearach held a beaming folded-armed look of pride that could dispel any useful protest. Dyrshul jumped, waving with both arms. The scowl melted into a smile in spite of it all. This was the moment. He looked back, regretfully.

"Thank you, Milord." If Adimus had learned two things in the hills of Ormond, it was the importance of honorifics, and to not besmirch a gift; life was sometimes harsh in the hills, and if anyone gave anything to another it was out of the purest kindness of their heart, and it had better be cherished. Adimus cherished it all.

* * * * *

Broad and forgiving, yet steep and treacherous where it gave, the road which descended from the hills of Balfour was just the first of the uneasy terrain between here and the Daldista Plateau, heart of Ormond. The road had been used to move an entire army in ages past, yet year after year the had become more swallowed up by nature, eroded by rainfall, covered by mudslides and caved-in openings of old caverns and aquifers. This was made known, as but a few hours in and the journey had already come to a screeching halt, where an old tree had fallen.
It was alive when it had--the roots still partly clung to the ground before it; it was now dried and leafless, a mute testament to how little The Ruined Road was traveled, much less kept.

Not even Lord Pembroke went this way when he would come to Balfour, though his hometown was closer heading this way. Instead he made for Pardoner's Pass, a longer yet better guarded passage which led to the other side of Macmearion county, and much more easily to Adaire. Adimus felt it was perhaps a case of special pleading on the boy's part, and he felt a little at fault as he stood there in the road, staring at the old thing. Everyone gathered around in the interim, the first time they'd actually gone to take a breather, as they watched Pembroke's guard Ambrose (one of the volunteer 'lost souls' from the night before) and Rigel hack at the obstacle with their camp axes.

Laina stood too, hands on her hip, all the while still glancing back toward home as if perhaps Tolten might suddenly materialize from around the bend—Adimus didn't have to ask why she'd come along.

Finally, perhaps if only to give herself something to do, she hopped into the wagon and popped open the large chest of provisions Maev had given her and started going through them.

Adimus too, paced restlessly. "You are sad." Alfred said, glancing up at the boy after a moment, after Laina had left. He was sitting cross-legged on the edge of the wagon with a rather large tome in his lap. "Do not worry about that man, the Illean priest." again was said, this time by the wizard. "I have signed an affidavit that should corroborate your family's innocence."

"He is sad! The legendary powers of a Faeth." The Argent guffawed " 'Lo as his mystic insight pierces the veils of the mind that lie beyond the perception of mere mortals!" The Bard never seemed to run out of energy, restlessly pacing between all of them, contributing quips to every conversation at every pass.

Alfred dismissed the comment as he watched him scamper off when it was made known he wasn't welcome.

"You'll get to see them again. Don't worry." the Seer assured him.

"Is that a premonition?" Laina's voice echoed from inside the carriage. She pulled out a potato with a questioning look.

"An educated guess. As soon as they uncover the actual reason all of this happened, you'll be able to return."

Adimus couldn't help but look concerned. He hadn't thought of it until this moment.

"What *is* the actual reason?"

Alfred didn't look up. "...This Darkest Night business your grandfather keeps talking about, no doubt."

Sluagh Oiche. That was his true business, to find help.

"It will get worse, pawpaw says. That this was just the beginning." He'd really hoped they disregarded his family's preferred term of endearment for the old man, but Alfred said nothing, only watching his response, with a scrutiny that made him even more uncomfortable; he couldn't shake the nagging suspicion that the answer the man gave was a test.

"...Who knew even tiny hamlets like that had such politics?" Alara said to Krasad. Apparently everyone had heard, thankfully.

The bard interrupted again. "Well, ladies and gentlemen, I have good news and bad news." He took off his hat solemnly. "The bad news is that it's going to take the rest of the evening to clear the way." He gave an awkward pause, no one was biting. "The good news is that we'll have plenty of firewood." He frowned when the delivery fell flat, flopping his hat back on with disgust.

With a sigh Alfred put his hands on his knees and rose to stretch. Then, as if just remembering, he turned and pulled something from his satchel. "Here, I borrowed this from you. Hoped you wouldn't notice."

It was his tablet, and the small larger bag with all his wooden styluses. "Thank you!" Adimus had never even thought about it in the rush, but he was glad it came with him.

As the day wound down Alara and Tirlag (it was her turn, they said) unpacked the tent in which the count and the merchant lord slept. It was indeed crowded in either wagon, and not everyone would've fit. Moreover, it was a place in which Thadeus and the noble spoke dire business in hushed whispers, to which outsider ears dare not be privy.

To Delaney's delight they removed the small bird from its cage. The Gnemedian played with it; picking it up and tossing it into the air, letting it flap its wings. She giggled and snorted as it followed her along and she threw bread crumbs at it. Tirlag and Alfred watched her interactions with it, both with an inexplicable look of interest on their faces.

"What's with the duck the wizard keeps?" Adimus overheard Argent asking Alara. "Is it an Implement of Magic?"

"Yes. It's a Magic duck."

"...Like a witch's familiar?"

"Yes. A familiar spirit." Tirlag answered for her, she'd overheard too apparently. "Shows his divine dominion and esoteric mastery of...bread." she grinned a grin of such disdain that it frightened the bard away again.

Soon, campfires dotted the hill of the Ruined Road: the lords and Ambros had their longfire where they cooked mutton (Anwell's, had he seen it butchered Adimus would've known its name) and drank from a keg of Tawny Lass, Maev's signature brew. Alara had a meager yet functional cooking fire, and the adventurers had the one which they sat about, which Adimus and Laina had helped build.

As night settled in, Delaney coddled the bird to sleep, holding it in her tiny arms. In an almost whispered tone she sang to it.

Adimus sat only close enough to hear. Her voice was unlike anything she'd ever heard before. It was as if several voices came out at once, her having complete control of each of them, harmonizing them into a haunting melody. The words the choir sang Adimus didn't understand, but he'd never heard anything so beautiful. When the bird was finally asleep, Alara was sure to take it and put it back in its cage.

Aethan was up too, tied to a nearby maple with the other horses save one, munching on barley wheat (Bearach had purchased feed for it as well). Alara circled the camp by the firelight with the other horse from the wagon. It was still painted as a skeleton, and scared the wits out of Tirlag on the first pass much to the cat's amusement.

Adimus had come to know that the old, decrepit one, the one that most often held up the whole group, was Argent's. It was a Dwyer mule, of a breed and stock so poor that it held its own colloquialisms, infamous for being frail and scrawny; historically, possibly more of them have been eaten than ever put to good use.

It had been Alfred's suggestion to delegate a watch, a fact which made everyone a little uneasy. Adimus had insisted he take it from Alara to share the burden, who took the three longest shifts, but she proudly declined.

Tirlag and Delaney whispered secrets astride a plunky log, glancing glares hotter than the burning coals beside which they sat when anyone who came too close. Alfred read by the firelight, with a quill and ink and parchment nearby. He took notes every few moments, scribbling down something on a piece of parchment which he had lying atop yet another book.

Laina stood, munching on a few peanuts while she waited. It hadn't occurred to him until then, *bar food makes decent trail rations.* Adimus cracked a few of his own, throwing the shells in the fire. He silently thanked Maev in his head again, as he had several times that evening; it could've well been nothing if she hadn't snuck it in Torrin's bags before departure that morning. His stomach was curtling, as he hadn't eaten since this whole thing started.

Quietly he sat and drew patterns with his tablet, trying to keep his mind quiet, having removed his plaid to sit on and later use as a blanket. The hissing and cracking of the fire helped; the pops and wafting sparks from the poplar always reminded him of the fireworks he'd seen in Ederton and the fragrant smoke of the burning poplar that made him miss sitting by his hearth at home, in winter while he sketched. Laina sat by the fire as well, watching their pewter pot of potatoes boil.

She hadn't talked since everyone had come around, if he could only manage to stick around prying ears for the entire trip he'd be in the clear. But sometimes, he knew, silence was more telling than words.

"It's a fair night."

"Mmm." She nodded.

"Where are we going?" he said finally.

"I don't know." Laina answered after a moment. "Where does this road go?"

Adimus weighed again whether it was another one of those rhetorical questions, whether she was being sarcastic, or whether she was simply asking. Then, warmly handing him the bag of peanuts with a smile of revealing mischief and excitement, he knew.

"To Kainden. Or Adaire and Hewnyleigh." he answered not helping but giggle.

"Kainden is your capital, right?"

"I...think." Adimus was a little ashamed that he wasn't sure; he was supposed to be a citizen of Ormond, after all.

"It is." Alara startled them, slinking out of the darkness, way closer than he thought anyone was. "You need only ask."

"...What?" he said.

"Where you are going." Argent replied in a song-songy voice as he danced just beyond the fire's light. He flourished his special cloak, this time turning it a dark black.

Alfred glanced up at the bard and his cloak, his unreadable glare masked by the fire light reflecting in his spectacles.

Alara sat down beside the boy. The unease was palpable.

"...Where *are* we going?" the boy repeated.

He flourished his midnight cloak over the fire. Alfred looked up at the bard with a questioning face. He examined his cloak again. "You need to tell me how you are able to do that." the Seer demanded.

"Dance?" he gave a deep facetious bow and in jest offered a hand to the Seer.

"That cloak." Alfred rebounded, unflinching.

"I tell you what I know if you tell me what you know." he addressed the Seer, continuing with the buffoonery.

The Seer's eyes narrowed. "Concerning?"

"The Spear of Fate."

Alfred chuckled under his breath, but it was enough to make him take his eyes off his book. Alara's unblinking golden eyes stared at him now through the darkness.

"It's a Daldistan legend," he answered. "and you are a bard of Bowen no less. You know more about it than I, I imagine." Alfred gave a flustered glance up to Tirlag and Delaney, who in return shot him a worried look, until their eyes wandered up to Adimus watching the exchange. Their teeth gleamed in the firelight like bloody knives as they smiled back at him.

"Fair enough. " The bard pouted turning to the boy. "Hewnyleigh." he answered. "We are going to Hewnyleigh."

"Hewnyleigh?" Laina said. "Why?"

"I don't know." he proudly professed as he spun on one foot. "Do *you* know?" He pointed at the spectacled man. "Almighty Seer?" he jeered before sauntering off into the darkness when the man said nothing.

Laina checked on the food again, then grabbed it with the sleeve of her baggy beige robe. "Here." She put the small pot in between them.

"Thanks."

She had a simple tea cup she'd taken from the tavern with which she'd begun to pull a portion out for herself. Adimus had not much more to bother with, an old wooden tankard, and his Skea Dhu to stab at them.

Finally, Alfred snorted in agitation, and, shutting his book tellingly hard, retreated into the wagon.

Adimus unrolled his ruck-sack, which also served as his bed, and sat down. He was no stranger to sleeping outdoors, and it felt good to get off his feet.

They ate quietly. Laina had passed out on a down pillow before his food had even stopped steaming. Adimus, poor Adimus, would remain awake for many hours more, contemplating on all that had happened, wondering and worrying until he felt sick. *What did Luloch mean the other day? What does an Imperial Seer want with me? Will paw-paw and dad and Dyrshul be okay? What are we going to do now? Where am I going?*

He mused about how he could face down a terrible monster the day before, only to be paralyzed with fear now. *Having no control. That's the real paralytic.*

He would only find relief in the wee hours of the morning when in a lapse of conscious vigilance and not without defiance, the stamping feet of time's unyielding march his lullaby, he succumbed to exhaustion.

Chapter 9
A Tell-Tale Tell

Laina arose first with her stole, a blazing vibrant length of cloth the fuchsia-scarlet color of the fiery sky of a lazy sunset in silk. Beneath the crescent moon's red arc of dawn she donned it, bowing before it as she covered all but her eyes in reverence. She did this each morning without fail, as sure as a cock's crow; 'a man could time his kettle to it', Luloch had once remarked.

Even when she wasn't wearing this length of cloth like this she still had it on her, usually in a more peculiar way, tied around her neck like a choker, the double spiral down her right arm to her wrist. She explained that it was a reminder to keep the Law, like it, with her at all times, in mind, speech, and action. Some days she would conceal her face with it all day, and remain silent in contemplation, and explained that not only this, that even those days were just the beginning, and as time went on she strived to conceal her face more and more.

If, by chance the sunrise was obscured, then she also carried with her a bronze statue which served as a proxy. She gave worship and offerings to it as well, offering up the prettiest flowers, and incense when she could manage it, though her supply had long dried up, as such commodities were goods with which only the parish on the hill were supplied.

Here, in the quiet of the morning she uttered her prayers in prostration, and danced a curious twisting beat to a rhyme in time to them, one that concerned not just the flightness of feet but the movement and position of her hands, which she held in sacred signs upon certain soundings. None had seen it this dawn save Adimus, who was awake against his will.

Slowly, he watched others arise, and though it seemed like hours, very soon they were up and on their way.

The wheels of the wagons lurched and slammed loudly on the pavement as they rolled over the white cobblestones of the path upheaved by nature's course. Adimus grabbed his head. "Ugh." as he rode his horse down the path in a kind of slump.

Finally they stopped for a break to feed and rest them up. Seeing the pain the boy was in Laina gave him a potion. "Take it."

Adimus protested, but to no avail. "I'll buy another from him when we come back." It was one of his grandpa's: a tincture of powdered willow bark and wild ginseng. Luloch often sold it and several other such herbal remedies to Maev for her to stock at the Beat, oftentimes trading for nic or anything baked and sweet, and Laina collected such queer colloquialisms in her travels as souvenirs; her words soothed her more than any potion ever could. *When we come back.*

The gentle exchange was all but drowned out by the pontifications of one Torrin von Krasad. Over the last two days, the fellow had jabbered lord Pembroke's ear off about the prospects of a meeting of the minds between him and the nobility in charge, with "prosperity for all" in mind. He'd come to the southlands with a mission of great import, after all, of which it sounded he was now candid about now that he had someone of equal import to himself to confide in. Whatever it was, Adimus learned that the march through the Ruined Roads had been out of necessity, that the company not risk the kingdom of Kessellon finding out.

He and Alara did carry with him a new and strange substance, a 'marvel of khemetastry' they called it.

When alight this powdery substance burned violently with great heat and at speed.

Adimus had heard of it from Laina. Bruana, it was named. "The vouxites shared their secret with the people of Pangor Tor, and if the lords of Ormond are interested in hearing what we have to offer we will share it with you—to sweeten the pot so to say." he'd told them.

"Only the weapons, mind you, not the powder itself." he was sure to clarify. "For it was upon a Geas that the makers are sworn to secrecy as to the bruana's making." the merchant explained.

"He just wants to profit off selling the ammunition from now until the Epochellipse." Argent snorted. He was sour at his failed attempts to eavesdrop, rounded back to make commentary with the others not involved when they started to march again, Adimus included; as much as they didn't seem to want Kessellon to know their reasons for being here, they didn't seem to want poor Argent know about it either, for whenever he would inconspicuously drift conspicuously close they clammed up about it.

He started to go on about how it wasn't as simple as that, that there was a very stringent system of licenses that Para'voux levied against the people of Torant for its use or some such, but Adimus ignored it. "What's a Geas?" The boy asked.

At that the bard puffed up, seeming to get some wind back in his sails, "A Geas, young Watcher, is a Spell of both forbiddance and compulsion. A binding incantation that none who are the subjected to--voluntarily or not--can willfully break." he sure to say the second part more loudly.

"Like what you did to the goblyn the other night."

From his look of surprise it appeared that he'd assumed he'd used words too big for the boy to understand. "Sort of." he shrugged.

"...The Fae are bound by strange rules. Most of them." Alfred continued to explain, coming out from the wagon to watch. "Sometimes all you have to do is know them."

Argent continued, "The Seelie fae. Courtly fae, follow them, but despite what they lead you to think they are a minority." explained the bard. "As for the rest? Cunning, esoteric study, and good old fashion bargaining with them."

"Bargain with a fae." Ambrose scoffed. "Dabbling with devilry, that is." he shook his head.

"You have to know their True Names, is that correct?" said Alfred.

"Yes. Knowing it you can command them, bind them, even call them to your side with the right Spell."

Ambrose looked sideways at him. "The Pardoner there seems to think that that Totem Wraith, that Bugbear or whatever you people called it, was conjured: 'Called to someone's side'." Ambrose looked at them judgmentally. "He suspects there's a changling among the villagers. Only explanation, really, 'less there's a sourcerer is our midst."

"-So," Argent butted in, after he was well sure Ambrose had broken earshot. "You say you are an Imperial Seer. Do you come from Shambaya?"

"Why do you ask?" said the Seer, who gave him a discerning look.

Argent simpered widely. "Well. Laina, you're a Mansii. You come from the lands to the north. She tells me she missed it dearly sometimes. 'Twould be pleasant to have someone with which to reminisce."

Alfred looked up at him, his spectacles masking his expression again, then after a moment, after looking over his shoulder to check for prying eyes, he answered. "I'm not from Histban. I'm not an Imperial. I was simply taught by one." he clarified.

"Taught? Is there a school to learn what you do?" Whatever game they had continued to play, Argent seemed to have won, as Laina was now engaged. "We have such powers of prophecy as well as many others found amongst the Mansii, but women are *born* with the gift. We do not teach."

"One can be born with the power to Read?" Alfred asked.

She only shrugged.

His demeanor noticeably relaxed when he saw that she wasn't prying, the topic had caught both of their interest. "I don't know about prophecy, or whether my family even bore such a gift, I don't remember much of them, but Psychometry can be taught to anyone."

"Psychometry?" Laina said.

"What I did to your book at the Reeve's Meet." at that the priestess's eyes shot to the ground in embarrassment. "And the coin Tirlag pilfered from the blacksmith. I can tell where they've been, who they've belonged to. What has been done with them, to them...sometimes even around them. *Everything* has a history."

"You didn't know your family." Adimus said. Suddenly he himself was caught up in the conversation.

Finally, with a whistle and a gesture from Pembroke, Ambrose broke to the fore. "Figured we'd change the subject on him." Argent leaned in and said to the Grigor with a nudge when he did.

"Thanks." the boy managed to utter. Under normal circumstances Adimus would've been again delightfully bewildered, how everything that came out of the bard's mouth at any given time seemed to serve at least three different purposes, but Adimus was too busy himself being delightfully bewildered by the stupidity of his own words.

"It was a trivial comment that no one would catch, save an orphan himself. Yes." said Alfred.

"Adimus isn't an orphan!" Laina interjected.

As soon as it had come out Adimus started sweating; his curiosity was steering him right where he didn't want to go. Perhaps it was paranoia, but Adimus imagined the man's smile manufactured, that now those judging eyes fell on <u>him</u>.

Just then, thankfully, the deafening tone of the cait'shii's weapon shattered the silence. Everyone looked to see. It was the strange wand she'd used on the Bugbear. With more than a little frustration on her face, possibly fighting the urge to demonstrate on Torrin himself, she'd pointed it at a stump and with the familiar deafening crack blew the thing to splinters.

Alfred suddenly got an uncharacteristically giddy look on his face. "The cait'shii is using the pistil!" he announced. Curious, he and Argent both scampered off.

✱✱✱✱✱

That evening they broke for camp, then came the moment the boy had secretly put off.

He had done it several times before, when on the road with his father on the larger monthly patrols that came always when the Moon of Omens fell dark. Dread filled him, and nervousness, but he would calm his nerves for the sake of a steady hand, concentrating on the courageousness of his ancestors and his own willingness to give; it was to be done, for blood and milk were the only suitable libations. Better his own, he supposed, than that of another's.

He took the skean dhu from his sock, and bowed his head with a sigh, and rolling up his sleeve spilled his own blood into the offering cup. When he was finished Laina stood there, watching. She said nothing, but he was certain there was something behind the solid of the even expression she kept as she gathered her bedroll, one that he knew must have taken conscious effort.

It wasn't until they'd come to pitch up their tents again and Laina and Adimus had already cooked their meal, this time boiled peanuts, that the Seer was drawn out of his hole. It was to watch another show this time.

The clouds that blanketed the sky above diffused the glow of the moons, drawing the night in like a curtain, and as it did the steep hill upon which they sat seemed steeper and steeper, until at dusk they sat on the road between an endless climb and a bottomless abyss. In a carrying tone of gravitas the Bard regaled the two lords:

"The tales of old would say Menkara was not as it is today, but was once it was another way, not roaming bands and conquering clans, Lathnia, it was named, ruled by a man who ruled the land with his wise, wise ways. Well upon his throne in what is now the Drowned Lands, alone." he began. *"He befriended the giant race of yore, who traded in their golden ore, to unite the clans of the Nalanen and open his nation's door. Quarrels endured before Epochellipse unfurled and unknotted before showers of gold begotten betwixt Neldina's Spires and nixxed the futile folly of the haughty bands unworthy of such gifts."*

"It would be a grave mistake..." Pulling off his cloak in the same quick spin as he always did, he held it before them, and was sure to shoot Alfred a glance as he did it. Again it turned the vibrant red and gold he most often wore, but as the shadows danced from the flames in the folds of it they began to move in shadowy shapes that acted out the story as it unfolded. Everyone had assumed up to this point that this had all been a bit of local color for Torrin's ears, that perhaps something about the folklore of this foreign land had piqued the merchant's interest, but this was not the case. Alfred stood beside the wagon while Argent shot smug glances at him all the while; that was the real show. *"All the masses gathered, and the people clamored, to swear their fealty to his banner in the most ardent manner. His territory grew and grew with time, this monster he had made, unto the nation that he had wrought he had become a slave. His means and riches so thin it begins that the hand stretched so far be bitten, if there is one thing true said or written it is that you cannot please them all, the same men into his halls he'd let, these clansmen cross and fierce you bet, for swearing to a man they'd had never met they ushered in his fall...the murderous masses amassing mounted without so much an asking a terrible instance of lost innocence passing when their axeheads they did whet. And took his head from his neck."* Adimus watched the macabre scene play out as the shadows danced.

"His weary son worries warranted, wasting wit wondering why the wily warriors of woe would wonder why they went without, and so stood the prince who took his place, and quelled the pounding at the gate, he mustered his men and once again the savages they did rout, yet perplexed on throne he pondered the fate of his forsaken father, and whether his might be the same when a traveler he met."

"Tell me your name" he demanded but the stranger upon his spear lent, standing said, quick as wit 'You bed what you abet. For loyalty, like respect is earned, for we among the Fae, judge by acts and not by right whom we should obey. Nay, how dare you stand and demand that upon my knee I should bend and pay tribute to a man if I know even naught his name.' he bowed. 'So. Good. Day."

"The prince instead of taking his head apologized to him and said, 'You are right about this life, this rule of shame, how could one swear to a sire if he does not even know his name? Take this burden from me please, I do not know my way. Kian the Ancient bowed his head at this

unworthy prize and laughed 'Nay, you shall remain a king this day.' he said, a glimmer in his eyes. "Look." And then he wrote the words for all men to abide, risking almost certain death for this gift he did betide, for Fae tell that from verse did All Creation form, forbidden it was for the Tuatha to draw the written form. The prince then read it verse by verse, and in reading this he understood: that a man's reach should only stretch how far his praise is heard."

Argent paused, and broke his rhythm to elaborate. *"The kingdom thus was split into two provinces, Lathnia and Ormond. The prince would rule Lathnia, the land of his forefathers, and later be called Menka'aran, the people of the Goddess A'aran, but this other land in the mountain highlands would need a new king."*

"He asked again, just rule these men that I no longer see, for their needs are great and are not met by the unworthy likes of me. Kian refused again, "Perhaps one day I shall return and all your men I'll lead, but today you are a king, just let me take my leave." he broke again as purport. "He went on his way. We know now of course that he went off to fight in the Catha Moytura, the war against the Formerians, and kingless, the western reaches of the land beyond the mountains were taken by Mathendon, the first king of Kessellon. But both of those are tales for another night." They all agreed, some in moaning begrudgement. "A steward the prince placed in his stead in hopes that he return. He ruled along the new lordship with the lessons he had learned. Until one day the steward died much to his dismay, again the land saw turmoil, again began the fray. The king fed up had had enough he'd let the clans then meet. 'You want to fight, then here's a tourney in which you can compete.' The clans obliged, in their eyes the crown of this new land, a fire in their bellies, a weapon for each hand. Until came a warrior from afar Kian's begotten son, the Nameless Boy of legend, countless in deeds done. The thrice-Geased nameless son of Ethne and the Magic it belied had laid low the Black King of the Baleful Eye. No one dare contest the man who slew his kin and king, to purge the lands of his darkened rule and the chaos it did bring. He held aloft a spear of dread, and gravenly he said. 'I bear this spear at Kian's behest for he my father is dead. Gae Bolga is its name, Bane of the Eye, and whosoever comes against it surely will die. But strength is not a virtue, and bravery's no match for wit, for no better by they does one wield a scepter than by any other gift. Instead I pay it to you in turn, to be wielded and remain, in his stead as your new crown, that may its possessor reign. The Tuatha shall hide it in your land, that not only the brave, but the kindly, timid, wise or the cunning may still yet play at this game. And so set out the lords of Ormond, were called to glory and fame, to rule the land of a king of who, to this day, none remember a name."

Chapter 10
Fear

Craggy reddish stone surrounded them. There, in a fork in the road, a roughly hewn alcove was carved in which a large figure loomed. It stood barrel chested, holding a great axe with menace in its eyes.

It had a snout and tusks like a warthog, and cloven hooves. It appeared perhaps to be female beneath its bulky armor. Whatever it was, it was savage, fierce, its face of fearful malice forever frozen, its wagon-wheel sized axehead poised to smash Into oblivion anyone who passed over the gap in the stones.

"What are these things?" Alfred asked.

At its feet were strewn offerings of fruit now rotten, and coins, and on its tusks were wilted garlands of flowers.

"There was one in his village as well." Laina observed.

Indeed, it did seem to be a depiction of the same creature, cloven hooves and all, save that this one had pig-like features instead of sheep-like.

"An idol. To the Bolg." said Tirlag, "That's what I read in an old book my dad gave me."

"You read?" quipped Argent. "It's 'Fir Bolg'. The giants from last night's story."

"No, just Bolg." She shook her head. She seemed frustrated. "There are different kinds of these statues, this one appears to have been made to honor the Orculli...Now the one back at the village, that was a Fir Bolg."

"Jidovi. Or Blajini, the Kindly Ones. These idols are plentiful in the lands we came from as well." added Laina.

"The Jentiliak." Said Alara. "In Torant they are called this." he explained her outburst. "We have ones like this as well."

Adimus repeated the rhyme he'd heard many times in his youth:

> *"Each in turn, with great care paid*
> *Set before them, preordained*
> *By sculptor revealed, evinced by Fate*
> *To destined Purpose, each were made:*
> *The Fir Bolg taught us how to sow, that we forsake our savagery,*
> *The Glastigs revealed the stars above, that we may map the seas,*
> *The Fir Domnan built works of stone, that our cities stand the ages,*
> *The Gailion showed us how to write, to fill the prayer book's pages,*
> *The Orculli fought against the dark, keeping safe our Forms frail*
> *And the Formerians, greatest, rebuke the ungrateful, who in ignorance fail."*

"This is what Illea teaches." he explained, when everyone was left staring at him. He scratched at his nose awkwardly.

"It's more than that," Thadeus answered. "She is a divine intercessor, defender of the breach, a vessel who one day shall be filled with life and vigor and the prayers of the desperate in our hour of need."

"This idol shall come to life and move?" Tolten, now curious, chimed in.

The lord nodded.

Adimus muttered, half to himself. "Sluagh Oiche is one desperate time if ever there were one..."

Argent snarled in frustration, then turned his head to explain to anyone who'd bother to listen who wasn't more knowledgeable than he. " '...*And so the god plucked the giants from the earth and with his blood gave them life, and they made for us all the splendid cities of old, and taught man the ways of planting, and the stars and the changing of the seasons.*' "

"...Then what happened to them? Are they not around any more?"

"They killed each other. That's what we're told." said Alara.

"I've heard they all went to sleep." Said Adimus. "Slumbering literally beneath our feet as the land itself."

"Sounds like a pleasant way to put dying to me." Tirlag snickered.

The bard ignored her. "I don't think you understand the literality of what I just said, merry Buckroy." his face grew grim. "These <u>are</u> the Bolg, born from the blood of the god of many shapes. That blood now spilled, they rest as the stone from which they were made." Adimus went numb. The bard continued, "That statue in the square, my boy, is no statue at all, and neither is this one."

"In all my life I have never heard this." Thadeus harrumphed. "By what fireside in what backwater hamlet have you heard that one, eh?" he half-heartedly chuckled. "Sounds like some Buckroy nonsense to me!" he japed. "No offense." he addressed the boy.

But the Grigor was no longer listening, instead staring down the thing, locked in its stone gaze.

Thadeus Pembroke superstitiously walked up to it and kissed his hand and touched its feet. "Well I for one, shall adhere to the tradition of the ancestors. I pray for safe passage." He said, and muttered something in old Daldistan. The whole show smacked of pretentious upstaging on his part.

"On the morrow." Krasad unceremoniously announced at that, bringing the procession to a halt. "We camp here tonight."

"Look!" Delaney cried. And she tossed it into the air, it fluttered its wings a few times, bearing itself aloft for a few short moments.

Tirlag cheered. "Yeah, she's a keeper then!"

"Won't be long now."

"Yep."

Alara, Alfred, and Torrin, (who was curiously as far away from the statue as he could get). All shared the sentiment "Have you thought of a name yet?"

She shook her head.

"Innana." Laina said. "The name of my goddess."

"No..."

"Gravy Boat." Tirlag chortled.

"No!" She shielded the bird from her.

"Penelope." Said Rigel.

"I like that." Alara agreed.

"Finola." the urisk finally decided.

"Finola it is." Alfred smiled.

Ambrose would explain later that it was customary to sleep in the shadow of the great statue; the silent guardian warded against the intrusion of monsters and 'fought 'gainst evil'.

No monster came, but thunder woke them several times that night, flashing across the snarling face of the beastly figure and leaping the Grigor's heart into a fluttered panic, even though it was but an omen of the wet day that was in store for them.

The rain fell in sheets the next morning, pounding against the inside of the wagon.

Adimus, in the wee hours awoke to provide his offering for the day ahead. The only other awake was Laina.

"I noticed that you did not Slake after we left yesterday." he said to her.

"This is true."

"Come on. I can help you, if you'd like."

"No, thank you."

"Nonsense. It doesn't hurt. I will be gentle with it."

"It's a generous offer, but I don't want you to cut my arm, Adimus. Please."

Furrows of water swirled across the sunken spots in the path, cascading over the road down the steep hills in tiny waterfalls as the downpour pelted them. Wind tore at the freshly turned leaves of nearby trees, plucking them from their homes prematurely, and blustered against the canvas of the wagon as if it were a kite. They passed a swollen creek over an old rickety bridge, and a standing puddle nearly knee deep, a large rut hewn from similar years of such rain which chose to run under the road. There, beyond, two large, winged, female figures loomed on ornamented pedestals, clenching swords to their armored chests. The middle between their crossing wings and the points of the swords from their folded crumbling arms formed an archway, and beyond it a darkened doorway.

"More Bolg statues?" complained Regil.

"I don't think so..." answered the bard.

"...What is this place, then?" asked Alara. She, Argent, Tirlag and Laina stood beneath the wings to keep themselves dry. Adimus looked up at the one he stood beneath, with a crack down its cheek funneling water as if it were crying.

"A decent shelter, I'd say." Argent threw up his hands.

The carriage and horses finally came to a stop. Thadeus stood forebodingly. "We're not going in there." he said.

"It'll only be for long enough to get the chill out of our bones."

"What kind of bard are you, boy? There are restless spirits in there, you should know that." he paused, that the Bard might wrest his sanity and agree. When he didn't he drove it home. "The dead of the dale are not wont to be disturbed."

Adimus stared into the uneasy shadows that filled its gaping mouth.

"Of course I know. About this place." the ruffled.

Tirlag's mocking giggle rebounded on the stone.

"Spirits? Perhaps. But benevolent ones. A place of repose for the heroes of Slaine who fell despite the blessing of immortality given them by the Ollatharii. It is guarded by these statues, sentinels..." He looked up and down at them "Legend has it that when the armies of Kessellon marched to Kainden they could not enter this place, for they were followers of Illea, that only true believers in the Goddess Aaran and the Triumvirate could enter this holy place."

"Followers of the heathen tuathan gods?" said Thadeus. "Rather not."

Tirlag's eyes narrowed after a moment of listening to this. "If they are immortal then how could they be buried?"

"Buried?" He tisked. "Dear child, I mean no slight to you and your vocabulary. I said tomb, I mean cenotaph." He wiped his nose to hide his face.

"Ceno...taph?" Tirlag rolled the word in her mouth in wonder.

"Means there's no one in here." he shrugged.

The corsair hid a wry grin behind his back. Alfred peeked his head out. "Fascinating. Do go on." Alfred goaded him.

Adimus thought Tirlag was about to pass out from stifling her snickers.

"Yes. Go on, master storyteller." Alara chimed in.

"Why yes." He rebounded effortlessly. "How could I explain to you miracles of the immortal warriors of Slaine? By expounding upon the divine secrets all night? How about we just go in and let the eyes feast."

"You mentioned spirits, but how can it be haunted if there is no one there? And who would do the haunting since you say they are immortal?" Laina hid her knowing smirk as well now.

"It's also said to contain riches." he threw up his hands and silent surrender, "trophies won by the princes of Slaine within its walls, forever protected against the religion of the god kings. Well... it did, I'm assuming. You all have probably collected them, am I right? That Tolten chap has no doubt procured them for his temple's reliquary. Or more likely to destroy on an alter as offering to the teachings of Illea."

"Riches?" The face of Pembroke, shown to be gullible on many an occasion, was unshakable in his daftness.

"Perhaps it's all poppycock. Nonetheless," he said taking a cautious few steps beyond the arches. "Ah, see? We are worthy. Why don't we go have a look-see?"

Everyone naturally doubted the truth of his word, still the boy caught Tirlag reaching out and touching one of the statues to test it as they moved forward. Alfred lent him his lantern, which the bard placed at the end of a long forked stick, and with much the same caution hesitantly stepped inside.

His voice echoed after a moment. "All is calm." He handed the apparatus to Alfred "Now." He said rubbing his hands together briskly. "Let us get some firewood."

Adimus crept in behind them. There was a fissure in the domed ceiling, and ivy grew through it as if nature itself had stuck its arms in to pull it open and have a peek. It also let in a diffused glow, not quite enough to see by on an overcast day, along with a spattering of rain water on stone, which pattered in echoing drops upon the floor far below.

Ambrose and Rigel brought down the remnants of an old tree, and splitting it laid it beside the door. Pembroke and Torrin took to the task of tying the horses down to the statues outside, while the rest piled in. Argent paced confidently behind all of them, hands on hips, proudly overseeing, and Tirlag playfully sat her hat on Delaney's head and rang her hair out like a rag. Alfred, having thus retrieved his lantern, walked off into the darkness. The light shined upon what could've possibly been old benches, all lop-sided, covered with cakey moss. Large, ruddy mushrooms hid in the corners of disintegrated trappings. The whole room, in fact, was covered with an old grime, as if a flood ages past had once swallowed up the whole scene. Glove off, the Seer ran his hand across the walls, eyes closed.

Many small alcoves sat in the room's walls. With them were tiny gods, many of which he'd never seen: a figure shrouded with layers of old hempen hoods and clothing, now matted and tattered to rot and moss. A woman with wings like the figures outside, but with three eyes, along with long pointed ears like a tuathan and a doe's tail.

Still other smaller ones Adimus did recognize. Some from the collection of curious books Luloch held: the figure with a distinct arm made from silver (which Tirlag picked at until she was told to stop) was Nuada, king of the Tuatha. The one with the green skin and the noose around his neck was Aoi mac Ollamain, or Gyllion as he was colloquially called—and the pile of small hyu'man vertebrae and knucklebones layed before him in offering was less morbid than they appeared once one knew of him. And the lady with the cow-horns was Brigid, whom the menkarans adored, though the small ceremonial fire set before her had doubtless not been lit for an age, and no hearth fire had been kindled to life from it in quite some time.

Others were straight from the Pardoner's abbey. There was Taranis, god of storm and gale, whose club was thunder as he pounded the ceiling of the sky, and whose ax was lightning that cleaved the trees in twain.

Statues set in large alcoves gleamed in the lamplight: a one-eyed, bull-horned man holding a spear. A youthful, hooded one holding a cauldron, and an older, weary one, wearing an ornate wreath of holly and leaning mirthfully upon a white staff. They were only perhaps Delaney's size, and the pedestals atop which they each stood brought them to eye-level, but the detail in them, even showing after years of rot and weathering, made them seem alive. Several more which the light did not catch sat it in the silence of millenia.

"They are the Triumvirate." Tirlag's wonderingly extolled.

Adimus looks up at the three figures in a new light. The bard nodded in agreement, "Correct. The Ollatharii, chief gods of the Tuatha. <u>The Three Who are One</u>."

"Many Shapes and the Goddess, do they not have names?" Laina asked.

"They do, but one should not invoke them in vain, out of respect." replied Argent.

"What are they?" she then asked.

Tirlag, of all people, chimed in. "The one with the cauldron they call Lyr, I think. Keeper of the Crossroads where beyond the dead rest. There were an old salt, superstitious type what muttered prayers midships whenever we were in a bad storm, or on a happening he saw as an ill portent."

The bard looked somewhat taken aback. Then Alara followed up. "Parthos, Oathen, Lord of Beasts." she pointed to Many Shapes. "He is in our stories."
But stood a moment, but no sooner than Alfred's lamp drew near to them were their attention drawn to the far back of the room.

This one was larger than real life; she was two of Ambrose easily, but its imposing majesty made her seem even more grand, standing on the dais she was nearly the height of the temple, what's more, her immense three-fold pair of wings stretched nearly the entire corridor, trailing off beyond the edge of the feeble light of the Seer's lantern...sapphire, emerald and ruby were her three eyes. Her long hair of shimmering silver sprawled out from her head in all directions as if frozen in a buffeting wind, stretched upon some great golden radiant-spoked wheel. In one hand she held what seemed to be a silver rope and in the other her hand touched a large needle, bright red paint denoting blooded still untouched by the elements made a single dot on her outstretched finger. It was a large spinning wheel, even the boy knew that.

Above her head was a triquetra, a symbol of three arcs interlaced, forming three points where they touched like a triangle; even concealed from him, Adimus had seen the symbol of the three crescents many times, if only in the knotwork patterns he liked to emulate when he drew.

Argent's torchlight flickered across the busy walls behind the figure. An ornate relief stretched the full span of it, depicting a tale. "What is all this?" Adimus, squeaked in nearly inaudible whisper.

"These gods seem quite different to the ones up on the hill." Torrin commented, daring to peek in when he heard the 'oohs' and 'ahhs'. "Or anything I've ever encountered back home." Argent motioned to the first of them. "What do you think, Adimus? This is a glimpse of the gods of old, before the coming of the Great Kingdom and Illea."

They were exquisite in detail, covered in knotwork illumination and filigree that, even crumbling and covered in mold and lichen, evoked the devotion its creator held. It took the lot of them a few moments to discern that the bard actually seemed to know what he was saying and not just making it up for show, showing each for the merchant lord with his torch and narrating what it showed, starting with a god sitting upon a great flower ascending from the water.

"What's with the flower?" Asked Alfred. "I've seen the imagery before."

"The Arid Lotus, Vimana. Its meaning is mostly lost to time since Kessellon's arrival here," he explained, Adimus sensed that the word 'arrival' was a euphemism. "But the Bowen sages believe it represents the god's mastery over both worlds: this world and the Otherworld."

The bard narrated per usual: "Upon the Catalystum, and the separation of the One and the Other, when all things were made separate, the world we know now is a torrid wasteland where nothing grows, for its heart has been stolen by the Sluagh, creatures of shadow and shade. Many Shapes descends, awakened from his celestial slumber upon the Ocean Cosmic. Called upon by his brothers to see the fulfillment of all righteousness, he lays low a great three-headed beast of darkness, a dragon, guardian of the prison of stone and ice, Am Carrig, whereupon the goddess is kept. The world floods, and washes away the host of the great King of Shades."

Naturally captivated beyond all reason, Adimus hung on his every word. He continued.

"The weight of the great beast crushed the goddess beneath the vast and virgin ocean. Parthos Many Shapes swims to the bottom to save her, but to no avail. That was when, seeing the hero on the point of drowning, the spirit of the Goddess willed the seafoam to coalesce into the form of a great mare, that he might live. When he awoke, in his hands was a seed. Enraged, he diced the creature to pieces in anger. Its body became the continents, its heads became the three moons. His fury became the rainclouds that poured forth all sweet waters, and his tears filled the Well of Slaine. But when he was through, he saw that, quickened by his heat, the seed had grown. It became a mighty oak, the first tree. It was named Kalpavriksha, the Tree of Ages. Its immensity reached the firmament, its branches breaching the veil that separated the two realms. This became the night sky we see today. From this tree and the starlight, the other gods came, the first of the gods, who are called the Partholonians, for they were, in turn, as his children."

The cat chimed in, "We have a very similar telling in our myths. The pisici of Madari say we came from the mare in the story.

"Cats were all born from horses?" Tirlag snorted at the absurdity.

She ignored her dig. "All the Cessair. That includes the Hyumanii." Tirlag's laugh was stifled by sudden interest. Alara elaborated, wresting the narrative fron the bard. It was the loudest Adimus had ever heard her. "The mare which saved Parthos fed upon the fruits of the tree. Soon, the seeds of the fruit would grow in her belly, swelling as though heavy with child. She would give birth to the Wild One, lord of offerings, of the underworld, of forests, but died in the process.

He would create the animals of the world from the bark of the tree which he would hunt for pleasure, the horse, first and foremost, to honor his mother, the Cessair lastly, as he honed his skill and longed for further challenge."

"...This god have a name?"

"Karna Nos. We have a lot of stories about him. About how he married the Formerian Winter Queen and bore a lineage of gods all their own, who mingled with the Partholonians and became the matriarchs of the clans of the Cessair. I see them here: Taranis, Teutates…but nothing of him. Strange."

But Adimus was a muffle in the mind of Adimus, who now stood flat-footed, drawn away by an striking image just beyond the torchlight

The bard took notice.

"The Landless Princes, emerging from the ocean after the catastrophe. They come to live atop Migdal Bivel, a great tower at the center of the world. The Formerians. Their king, Balros, observes all." He looked at it, and the fiery figure beneath it. "Ol' Crom." He jeered.

Adimus stared at the stone depiction of the tower. Suddenly his heart began to race. He didn't know why, but in his mind he could see it. Perhaps it was a flight of fancy, or the Bard's ability to whisk away the mind, or something more, but he saw it; an unnatural streak of gold ascending high, high into the dizzying sky; this was in his dreams, he knew it.

"These are not the gods of Ormond. Of the Daldistans." Thadeus warned. Best be on our way now, the rain is breaking.

"You are correct." Said Argent goading, as he had with his story on Allhallows. "They are those of The Lathnim, last of the Cessair people who are indigenous to this land. Closer than any other of the Hyu'manii, they were, to the Tuatha. In the days before the Epochellipse they walked with the children of Oathen." Adimus caught the petulant gleam in the storyteller's eyes, like those he had when he'd told the story of the lamb on Allhallow's "But, this temple was made _by_ the Daldistans, the people of the Great Kingdom. So charmed were they by these people and their ways that they defended them when the time came." He looked back at the stone fondly.

"And their forebears were gifted with immortality because of it. At Slaine." added Alara. "The court of the Gentry always rewards loyalty."

"Now," he said, knowing he'd been beckoned to continue, "The two brothers came to his aid: Many Names," he pointed to one of the brothers, an old bearded man holding a scroll and quill, "lifted the four corners of the world into the sky. His other brother, Many Faces, blessed with a Cauldron which can give life…" he pointed to the younger one holding said cauldron.

"He has one eye." Laina was obviously curious, interrupted for the same reasons Adimus was (though he'd never admit it.

Tirlag added what she'd heard to the story. "In Thane, his eye became the sun…"

Adimus had stopped listening at this point, mystified by the depiction of the tower. *The Tower at the Center of the World.* He'd never heard about it from any of the tales Tolten told. *But he had seen it.*

Then he jumped to at the Seer's exclamation.

"This is marvelous." The Seer exclaimed. He gasped as he touched the rope. "This is real silver! Spun into twine!" He stood for a few moment more, bedazzled. "These people were masters of All'khemy!"

"That wheel… it looks like…" He said to himself, stroking his chin and pacing around it, then taking his glove off he reached out and touched it. Curiosity, then shock, then amazement flashed across his face choreographed by his eyebrows which went one up then both. "There's something beneath the floor. Here!" He said stomping his foot, he felt it with his hand, then setting the lantern down to mark his place with a brisk pace (taking care not to slip) he hurried for the door, majestic eyebrows full of endeavor and purpose.

"Not the most elegant of solutions..." Argent came, heaving in his arms a large rock from outside. *'Slam!'*

The small crack in the tile shown, then he shoved his quarter staff in and levered the tile free.

Metal coins, silver and gold jewelry encrusted with gems, and a large silver chalice. Tirlag had made giddy noises as she nabbed it from its resting place. They all reveled and self-congratulated as Adimus watched on.

In the flicker of the lamplight and the glinting silver, the echoes and the cheering, the boy had thought his mind had been playing tricks on him at first, when he saw the nearby shadow shift. He glanced back for but a moment, looking for verification that he was not insane. He had, after all, just had one of his visions, one of his strange moments that made him question everything.

Everyone was busy, even Laina, who was meticulously arranging the wood for the fire.

Then he looked back. A pair of red piercing eyes fell upon him. A loud rumbling growl emanated from within, as if the building itself growled.

The beast stepped forward. On all fours stood nearly as tall as a man at the shoulder. If the goddess's eyes were ruby, sapphire and emerald, he was perhaps made of jet, for no light touched or betrayed a shape save for its silhouette, that of a large hound, which Adimus saw only moments before it came at them.

Adimus wasn't sure if everyone scrambled or stood, but he took a few steps back and drew his sword just the same.

"Barghest!" Pembroke's voice called from outside.

The creature let out a blood freezing howl, the whole foundations trembled before it, bits of dust fell from the ceiling as if the structure itself protested in defiance of their presence.

Then it charged. Someone grabbed him by the sleeve. "Outside!" they yelled, pulling at him. Argent had come back with the lantern. There was something strange about the way it undulated in the lamplight, leaping from the intervening shadows as it lurched forward, Adimus put his shield out to stave off the creature but it made no difference.

Adimus was frozen in shock. He knew that the creature had not come close enough to sink his teeth into him, but still he had him. Through his shield and even incomprehensibly through his very clothes the creature sank its teeth into his arm and pulled. Adimus pulled back as the creature tried to pull him off into the darkness, his feet slipping in the muck. Argent dropped the lantern to use both hands and when he did Adimus saw it, as the creature moved unnaturally. He watched as the dark creature latched onto his shadow.

"No!" Adimus let out a cry and dropped his targe. There were no bite marks. There was no blood, but still the pain came, like ice cold water was being pumped into his veins. The numbing pain crawled up his arm. Finally, when nearly enough pressure had built that it nearly lifted him off the ground suddenly there was a jerk. He was free, but only because the beast had taken something from him. They scurried for the door, the creature nipping at them. Argent clutched the boy in a tumble roll, crashing down the stairs. They looked up as the creature stopped in the doorway, just beyond the light of the door.

"A Barghest!" Argent confirmed, panting. "That's a Barghest."

"A what?" asked Tirlag, in between catching her breath.

"A Church Grimm."

He jumped up. "Come men." he began ordering, as if he said any authority to do so. He ran over to the horses and started untying them.

Adimus sat there the rain pouring down his face. He looked down at his right arm, lying limp at his side. He dropped his sword with an audible clang, which he'd grasped with white knuckles (thankfully it hadn't hurt anyone). He couldn't feel it. He couldn't move it. In a panic with his other hand he scooped it up.

"Adimus!" Laina ran to him. She looked at his arm, that he couldn't help but cradle.

She pulled up the sleeve. Adimus gasped. It was stark pale, like moonlight upon snow. Lord Pembroke drew near, and Laina obstructed his view. "Hide it for now." she whispered, flashing a serious look and pulling his sleeve back down.

"Are you alright, boy?" Pembroke asked.

"I-I'm fine." He struggled to get up, floundering again when he thoughtlessly tried to use it.

It was like it wasn't even his arm anymore, that whatever warm quality had animated it, given it life, was gone now. In fact, he was certain of it. He'd stood and lingered several minutes on as everyone gathered their supplies again, listening to the thing gnawing, lapping and grinding its teeth on bones of his real arm.

Argent popped in the carriage. "Alright?" he said. Adimus nodded quickly as he'd learned one should when lying. "Fool boy." he tisked loudly. "That foolhardiness will be the death of you yet." He drew nearer, that no one could hear. "I'm sorry, Adimus." It was a graven, serious look that he had yet to see, even when the goblyns appeared, and that alone set the boy on edge.

Am I?

The rain had stopped, much to Argent's chagrin. Now there was no reason to go in. Adimus never went back out, but sat on the chest of Maev's goods and mostly concealing his face with the wagon shroud watched them work. Laina had not come back to check on him, but looked back nervously at him frequently, as if called to some task she couldn't get away from.

He saw Argent whispering to Alfred and pointing in his direction, and the concern on their faces.

Alfred had hatched an idea in the meantime. He watched as he felt around the edges of the structure, brushing at old creepers and lichen, and feeling around on each block of stone until. "I've found it." He said.

Tirlag stood nearby with a shovel, and below the block where he'd pointed started digging. Sweat beaded upon her already drenched head. The hole got bigger and bigger until they stood knee deep in the muddy clay, Tirlag's temper seeming shorter and shorter as they went. The red eyes pierced the shade once again. Everyone gasped. "He cannot harm us out here, keep digging!" Argent ordered. The bard's words carried no weight now, nonetheless they hurried on, albeit with skeptic glances over the shoulder.

Finally there was a surprised stop, Adimus watched the silent charade of giddy dances as she plucked out what appeared to be a bone. A few minutes passed, and they assembled the crumbling skeleton of some huge dog one by one on a splayed spare linen from the wagon, then gently they bundled it up and placed out in an esoteric circle Alfred had drawn in a spot in the mud with a simple stick. "Well. Speak a prayer, someone, because I don't know any." Rigel admitted. Pembroke slunk up to peek at it.

They all looked at one another as if they'd forgotten their own names. The bard stepped forward and stammered a few bars of something in another language. Nothing happened. Pembroke said something, Rigel figured he'd give it a shot and even Tirlag, clenching her hat to her chest muttered what could've well been a sentiment of goodwill.

The barghest watched them from the threshold of its lair, looking on threateningly, yet it never passed into the light. If a hound could laugh it did, and Adimus grasped at his sword the entire time, his hair on end.

The Sum Seer held up the silver chalice, spoke a few words and sat the chalice down. Blue flames engulfed it, and he filled it with water from his waterskin, and the flames licked up to wick onto its surface to settle there. Then with a few more words he poured the water into the bones and they ignited like spilled grease.

Hellish blue sparks and a black smoke bellowed from its maw which roiled and spun to smother what little other light there was left to be seen. Haunting shapes moved in the tenebrous fume, spears and swords and shields; the tiny motes fell upon them, eyes of warriors roused in silent tumult.

Laina lent down and picked up the shovel and walked off. Adimus peaked his head out to watch her search the treeline. Finally she'd found what she was looking for. She started digging in the small clearing nearby before an old hawthorn tree. Others started to come. "Bring me the bones." she demanded. She sweated and panted and when her exhaustion slowed her Alara took the shovel and dug deep into the ground. They placed the bones in it and filled it in. Laina produced several items from her personal effects. She placed a chain of iron upon it and leaning down spoke a prayer in her language, and anointed the remnants with ashes, and sprinkled upon it dried jasmine.

They looked from afar what Adimus saw up close. The creature was dismayed. The smoke and hoary flame continued to billow from it, though this time it had eyes of worry, as if it just couldn't stop. Its eyes shut one last time as its insides poured out, churning in the winds above until subsumed in the vastness of the pure air until it dissolved into nothing.

Chapter 11
Reverence

With the rain mostly subsided, they had found a clearing, some distance away, in which to set up camp.

Adimus sat inside the wagon. "I've a terrible headache." he'd told them again; it worked well, since it had been established that he suffered from them, if only that it made him seem like a complainer.

He wasn't exactly lying, as again he hadn't gotten any sleep, but the physical pain was dulled by the distractions of his gnawing worry.

Laina had come in to check on him. The arm was pale and numb, and so she bandaged him and gave him a potion to help him sleep. "You will be alright. You must tell no one." She warned, just before he dozed off, no doubt from the exhaustion. When he'd awoken, his fingernails had turned a bluish black. But what was more, far more startling was that when he shined the lantern on it, no shadow fell. He didn't know what she meant to say now, he could see the concern on her face, yet she said nothing. This was Almsday, the day where she wore her veil all day. She would not eat today, or show her face, and would not be heard speaking, other than muttered prayers in recitation under her breath.

Adimus, when he was younger, would visit her at The Beat anyway on those days. He fondly remembered following her around, if only to entertain her or raise her spirits, as he reasoned it must be boring or lonely to spend all day in solitude, and he could see by the smiles that touched even her eyes that she did enjoy it. As he grew older though he came to respect and even understand such times, which spoke to him across the lines of religion. And Meav had grown much the same way, assigning her menial chores in the back that day at first, saying that she ought to enjoy her day off and not be tied down by such things, but came to make it the day of reflection it was meant to be soon thereafter--he just wished with all his heart that it wasn't this one.

He had looked at his shadow while the sun still shown, saw that something wasn't right; nothing about it could be right. All the boy could repeat in his mind were the words he'd always heard *'Mortals don't get touched by Shades and live.'* The chill allowed him to wear his great kilt in a tossed hood style without a second glance, allowing him to conceal it and cradle it as would one with a sling.

Swirls of vibrant red and deep green and bright yellow leaves danced in the path that led down in the town of Adaire the following day, stark against the white and black brick paving stones and houses that dotted the main street. It was much larger than Balfour, but could barely be worthy of the title of 'town'. Adimus marveled at faces that seemed all-too-familiar. This town had a Niall, and an Anwell, a Brian too. Most hurried through the streets, as if the rain had made them all late for some life-or-death task, paying no mind to the carriages as they went about their daily do.

Strange ornaments adorned the white wattle and daub houses. In windows and chimneys and on walls and doors these talismans sat in mute vigilance where strung, mounted or dangled. Elaborate criss-crossed tangles of mystic branches, wicker worked, barred some of the portals entirely, while black iron shutters barred the windows of the more well-to-do, bells of black iron, sprigs of holly, vials of white sand or oceanic salt, pairs of open scissors, horse shoes, half-burned plugs of sage or dried jasmine flower. Alara with a quick prompt from Argent piled into the wagon with Delaney, sure to hide her face deep in her hood.

"Briskly." Argent warned the others.

Lord Pembroke greeted several people as he came into town, all platitudes until one stood before him astride a horse.

"Weylan." Pembroke saluted him.

He was a proper city guard. The brooch of his family, worn above his iron chainmail unblemished, shown upon his livery with neither stain nor crease: the boar's head on white and blue, crest of clan Pembroke. The chopped, smooth look of his sideburns and his well-groomed toss of hair showed that appearances were important in his station. It gave him an air of authority that transcended the meager stature that seemed to plague his family.

"Welcome back, uncle." He said. How mannerly.

He stood. "This is Baron Torrin von Krasad and company. My traveling companions. They are to be treated with the utmost hospitality."

Weylan gave a flustered look, "If you'd told me you were going to take the Ruined Road we'd have sent a contingent of guards." Resting a hand on a polished sword hilt with a black leather glove he commented. "It's a miracle you weren't killed by bandits. Or worse. Found some more Nis hiding in the barrows."

"Truly?" Thadeus stammered. "We encountered a Grimm."

"What?!"

"We're unhurt." He assured him. "It was my own folly and fault." He strained a chuckle, hitching up his pants. "Did give us quite the scare though, all in all." He looked at everyone behind him, who shared the same strained sentiment, all except Adimus. "Besides, I had Ambrose with me."

"Ambrose." He acknowledged him with a nod.

"Milord." He saluted.

"We will follow up with a patrol. I am glad you're well." Was all he said of it.

"So, never you mind. How are your wardens?"

"One fallen. Otherwise it was a victory. We've overcome the bulk of them, routed them back to the hills. We've subdued a shy half dozen of them."

"Subdued?" Thadeus scoffed. "Why not let the little buggers meet their end with cold iron and be done with it?"

"That's not how it works, uncle. If they be cessairian Tala fleeing the Empire's Magustrate we'll have to do politics with the Menkarans. And, Crom guide us, if they are Seelie we may incite a war. No uncle, Mac Dougall is with them on their way to Cairnfang as we speak."

Shades were a laughing matter, but mention of this man's name had apparently soured his face back to seriousness. "Cadifor? He..he came through here?" he stammered.

"...Yes, but you were away. Enjoying cakes." He gave a playful wink, and with a couple more glances and a salute he left them. The comments were pure levity and facetiousness and had no malice in them. "He and his conscriptors. Again." He elaborated, "Only the Baleful knows why; not a worthy footman to be found in all of Macmearion."

"So we've bandits *and* stray Nis within our borders?"

The man shook his head "Most come from without, crossing the Ruined Road. I have by the authority of house Foxwell that it is so."

"Indeed." Argent simply nodded along.

"Knaves and vagrants from the contested lands on the northern border." Weylan explained. "All the more reason to use more discretion, uncle. Pardoner's Path is much more well guarded."

Argent chimed in. "Why would Torant not give them asylum? Rougehastier and Foxwell have sworn fealty to the Lord Protector, by now they should have a voice in the privy council, no doubt from some well-fed statesmen that can air their grievances."

Weylan sighed. "Lots of goings on in Torant too these days. The noble houses squabble worse than the Ormandians."

Thadeus concurred, "Only the fear of imperial encroachment keeps those two-faced blaggards decent." He glanced back at Krasad, who gave no response.

The Whispermonger, again, seemed to agree. "Doubtless."

"Tell me, who is this man of Ormond who has such ears for the machinations of kings and rulers?"

At that Weylan dismounted and strode up to greet them.

"Little, save fear, keeps a man decent at all nowadays. Dark times." The minstrel introduced himself, dismounting to meet him. " Argent, a bard of Bowen.

Taking off his black leather glove, Weylan shook their hands warmly, each in turn starting with his, until he came to Adimus.

"What's this? A Grigor?" he remarked. "Then you <u>were</u> in safe hands after all. Well met." He reached out a hand.

"And you." The boy replied in the smoothest voice he could feign.

He raised his left hand, of course, which led to an awkward exchange where Weylan hastily leant his gloved hand to meet it. He gracefully covered the awkwardness, "Left-hander, eh? Puts a man on his feet in combat. I should like a spar sometime." he smiled, trying to put him at ease.

Finally he came to the Baron himself. "Milord, we are honored." Torrin took the invitation gracefully.

Thadeus patted Adimus on the shoulder as he passed, following his nephew. "You see, lad. There's much work that needs doing by our lordships nowadays." It was meant as an excuse and apology to Luloch, the Grigor knew, but he was more concerned at the fact that he didn't feel the pat.

Argent took his hat off, and continued his reasoning. "Pembroke is the clan that enforces the edicts of the stewardship...as I understand it. Why, milord, if I may, do you take it upon yourself to fight brigands and the like?"

"Much has changed in the years you were gone, Whispermonger." Said Thadeus.

"But Mac Dougall holds our army, the army of the king, that much has not changed." Argent responded. "Last I checked he had men to spare. Foreign invaders or simple ruffians, surely they could spare a few bannermen to ease your burden."

"Oh, his conscriptors have subjugated half the county and made them ready to ride, all at the Council of the Kingship's command."

Argent's eyes widened in shock. "Dark times indeed, that Menkara would allow Mac Dougall to muster a force in their borders. And a shame you must pick up the slack in their stead. And here I was, trying to witness to you for the Grigor and his mission..."

"Come again?" Said Weylan.

"This brother-in-arms seeks assistance with the Aes Shii, with the Fae, himself." He pointed at Adimus.

Weylan looked to his uncle questioningly.

"We enforce the local laws as well now, not just in our own county but abroad. We are the Royal Constabulary of the Stewards now." His sincere eyes fell on Adimus. "Sorry lad, I just can't."

"But wasn't that the charge of clan Casey?"

Adimus zoned out. His teeth chattered uncontrollably. He was certain he was beginning to lose sight in his eye.

"As I have said, Whispermonger, much has changed."

"Hmph." His look was one that Adimus read as disconcertedness that quickly melted into delight. "No worries. So, an official keeper of the peace, eh? Can't think of a clan more deserving. Come on then, let's toast to this new revelation." He put his hands on both of their shoulders.

The place even had a Green Beat, the boy had found, albeit much larger and more extravagant, if a little less well named. Nestled atop the cresting hill opposite whence they'd come, it served as a civic building and alehouse and tavern just the same, Stackstone Lodge was its name.

By dim beaming sunlight they'd all gathered around the communal longfire in the center of the room, to tear at spatchcocked chickens cooked between the stacked planes of granite, and drink flaggards of stout.

Adimus sat all to himself in the corner, clawing at the wooden table with his fingernails in mad anxiety.

He overheard a conversation the bard made with the common folk, of a ruckus from a cait shii' who attempted to rob the general store through the back window and was caught by one of Weylan's men, after that, Alara came to sit with him.

Finally, Argent, too, joined them. "Not a normal everyday occurrence, but less than fortuitous for us." He spoke to her without bringing attention. "We'd best be going as soon as possible."

"Why should you give mind when we leave?" Tirlag said, elbows on the table, straddling the stool, eyes on the massive leg of fowl she held. It had come out rather defensively. "Argent, *bard of Bowen*." it was slathered in mockery, "You don't have to leave with us."

"Yes, minstrel, you needn't be so hasty." Thadeus had overheard them. "Stay with us, tell us your tales, regale us with your songs, I'll give you special accommodation and all the drink you can survive." He laughed at himself.

"It's a generous offer, truly. But one I must regretfully decline. You see, we must away to Hewnyleigh, before the inns are well and full." The lord gave a questioning look. The bard continued, "We've many ears to harken and many heartstrings to pull for our Pledging."

He almost choked. "Pledging?"

"Surely you haven't forgotten."

The man finished his drink quickly. "Goodness. Ten years do go by." He pulled the handkerchief from his pocket to dab the sweat from his head. "Weylan!"

"I'll be attending. I've already made the provisions." groaned his nephew. "My lord will be...indisposed."

He glanced at them all with darting eyes. "Good. Very good." He harrumphed.

Argent leered at Tirlag, but was courtly just the same. "You've been known to say that you are from Marron, correct?" he responded, after a moment when Thadeus was distracted with his nephew. Tirlag grunted. He continued "I've been there. A reasonable bunch, sailors. They will take any help they can get. Invite any manner of Gentryman or Fair Folk aboard if they have sea legs. But

I don't think you know what one would fancy of an imperial, a cait'shii, and a free urisk this far inland. Especially ones so secretive." He was sure to glance at Alfred to ensure he took no offense.

"I think it's unfair to say such things about the Ormondians." Ambrose piped up. Everyone froze. "Why, my uncle lives in Tavishire and used to keep a Killmoulis in his home. Fed him bread. Was right nice to him and he was nice back. The thing cobbled his shoes, fixed his door, cleaned the house." the conversation trailed off when everyone appeared less than interested. "Besides, you saw how Count Pembroke enjoyed Ellyllon! He reveres such tradition." He finished his tankard of ale.

Alfred sat and watched, sipping his tea. Adimus could tell he had something to say but he bided his time.

Argent dismissed him. "Fear and reverence," he pled now to the reasoning of Alfred "they are selfsame, friend: both born from ignorance. Do you think he'd laugh and carry on if it were the Great Hunt on Allhallows? If he were the sport of the spirits that fly and hunt men for pleasure?"

Laina suddenly spoke "No. One always fears the unknown. The difference between fear and reverence is whether one simply recognizes something as unknown, or honors it for being unknowable." It was the first time Adimus had ever seen her break her silence. There was something different about her voice. She smiled comfortingly at Adimus.

"Be that as I may, I warn you all to make haste just the same." the Bard said, ignoring her clear missing of the point. To punctuate he got up and left. Alfred followed.

The Grigor looked at Laina, whose eyes widened. Trying to hide the shake in his legs, he stood "I think he is right." he said. Tirlag glanced at him from her food. Adimus continued, "I know no one has asked me, but we should leave. My mission is dire as well."

"You're right. No one asked you." Tirlag said. Laina twisted her face in disgust.

There was silence until Rigel finished his plate, then got up to retire. He glanced sideways, and spoke only after Argent had sauntered off. "I still stand by my decision. I think his political knowledge could be an asset when it's time to decide." It took Adimus a moment to realize they were talking about him.

Then, when he was sure he was gone, Tirlag chimed back in. "I think he is simply trying to make himself *seem* helpful." The bard strung his lips like a bow ready to fire, but Tirlag cut him off. "But he's not. Besides, already got one extra aboard by your graces." She answered, looking at Adimus. She snarfed down some food. "Go ahead and invite the whole Named city, why don't you?" Her eyes shot curiously up to the boy as she stood. She grinned, whether it was a mocking or sincere expression Adimus wasn't sure. "I voted that we be rid of you. To continue alone on your little quest." She shrugged, then shot a sultry grin. "No hard feelings."

Adimus felt faint, but the room read it wrong.

Argent lept to, and whispered something in the wizard's ear. His eyes widened.

"Is it the fear or the reverence that keeps his tongue so stiff?" bemused Alara guffawed when she saw the look on the boy's face, at what she thought was his response to Tirlag's teasing.

"...We're leaving. Before the catchpole takes the thief to Hewnyleigh and we're forced to meet him roadside. We need to make up time anyway." Said Alfred.

Tirlag stopped with a sigh, before directing herself instead to the stable.

"My words instill both." Alfred smirked back at them, and he got up as well.

"Adimus. You come with me." Alfred gestured with a nod that beckoned him to follow.

He found himself in one of the vacant back rooms.

"In here." he beckoned.

The Seer shined his lamp unhooded. It blinded him. He heard the Seer's voice. "You were bitten." A small part of the boy was relieved at the acknowledgement. But the man's voice was even, unreadable, unaesthetic, like a man trying to steel himself from some trauma. "Show me."

He hesitated, the Seer looked into his eyes. "Be brave, Adimus."

Adimus volunteered it: it had been hidden long enough.

The Faeth picked up the arm, Adimus only knew because he saw it in his hands. He adjusted his glasses, fogged from the beading sweat of worry. "Well?" The bard pled. They doused the lantern. Their figures were looming shadows.

"He is in Dissolution. His Nature and Form are separating." It took him a moment to reason that no one knew what he meant, and it seemed all the worse to him to explain in non-sterile terms. "The wound will spread, like an infection no one can see or cure, until he becomes one of them." He adjusted his glasses awkwardly. "The rate of this process seems to be determined by the type of Shade, but eventually." He had neither the heart--nor the need to--finish his thought.

A new numbness befell Adimus, one that he could not be sure was real as a symptom, but felt real enough to make everything else unreal. "I'm sorry." the boy kept muttering. "I'm sorry. I let it in...I let it in."

They ignored him. "Is it..? Can...can it be cut off? Is there an apothecary, a barber that can help?" Adimus asked.

But Alfred said nothing. Then Laina peeked her head around the corner. She too said nothing, but her eyes warned: *'You will say nothing of this.'*

"How long?" Argent asked.

"It's hard to tell at this rate."

"What do we do?" The bard answered for the boy, before he could even utter the words himself.

Alfred silently stood and left the room. Argent lingered for a while, he could only see his silhouette in the darkness, its shoulders buckling from the weight.

* * * * *

It took a lot of convincing to push Torrin and the others out the door, but promises that there were bigger fish to fry finally got through to him. "Lord Cadifor McDougall is there, and Ross of Ward, and all of clan Mathune. All hold powerful seats on the Council of Princely Stewards." Was all Argent had to tell him, but promises of the wealth to be found in the windfall he would receive from the party's 'excavation' helped too.

Whether they would regret it or not they could never tell, in some serendipitous twist, as if the gods themselves played some great caprice, it poured rain even more so now than the day before.

Adimus reasoned to himself that it was the wrath of the same gods coming down on them; he shivered all the more in the freezing downpour. There was no room for both he and the provisions they'd gathered, and so the boy was now shunted out along with Laina. She'd had to help him get on his horse. Rigel and Argent rode further up ahead. The sky had darkened first from rain, then from night.

Laina straddled the horse and sat behind him, her arms around him shielding him from the buffeting winds with the hems of her robes. She was warm. He forgave her for her silence. He looked down when he felt something bristled on his leg. She held his hollow hand.

The road to Hewnyleigh made the Ruined Road perhaps a bit of hyperbole. The Lord's March led from Adaire to Hewnyleigh, and was little more than a wide muddy trail.

Regil had went about the order of finding a level and dry spot for Torrin's tent. Alfred sat around the lantern, looking over some old rolled up vellum manuscripts. Alara circled Krasad's wagon like a vulture turned sentinel. Trickles could be heard in the dark as the rain spattered nearly an hour after they'd come to a stop.

Finally, upon the rain ceasing, before everyone else decided to peek their heads out, Laina jumped down from the horse. "It's time. Let's go."

She took the boy's hand (his good one) and helped him from the horse. "Where--?" he tried to say, but she hushed him. With wide, determined strides, her robe pulled up in her other hand, they plodded through damp foliage, their breath shown hard as they awayed into the night air.

She lead them down a steep embankment, slippery and difficult, with loose clods of sliding sod and snagging roots beyond the treeline. Adimus watched all remnants of the wagon and horses and everyone disappeared. And then they walked some more. They came to a small copse of trees, its floor clear and its footing steady.

"Ancient." She commented upon the copse of stifling pines, the looming hutch of trees shielding all below them from the intrusion of the sun's scrutiny until all smothered. She put her hand upon one of them. "Providence. Just as our many whispers hide secrets from unworthy ears, Adimus, they shall hide my actions from ignorant eyes. The Airs in your body must be called back."

"The what?"

"The Airs." she said, almost sounding frustrated. "Your arm is dead. Gone is the fire that brings it warmth, the Earth that keeps it from rotting, the Water that keeps it from becoming stiff, and the Ether, the space between through which sensation is felt. They each leave at varying times upon death. But it is only the providence of the gods that tethers the soul to the body..." she explained. Finally they reached their destination.

Trickles of water tinkled as the rain settled and dripped cold onto his head. There they stopped. He could hardly see. "What-what are we doing?" he said.

She turned to him. Slowly, deliberately, she removed the shawl from her neck. "You must never tell anyone? Understand?" she said, shaking a finger at him. "You are so lucky." he smiled.

He didn't answer, and she knew he didn't have to. Her eyes softened, and in this tender softness there was a glow. She placed something in his numb hands. It was the fangs from the skeleton they had buried. Adimus thought his mind played tricks on him. Her hand was warm. *Warm.* It took him a minute to fathom it. He looked up in astonishment. She began speaking. He didn't know what language it was or what she said, but it didn't matter. The symbol upon her cheek lit up like some hot brand, her eyes smoldered like the coals of a fire at the hearth on a cold night at home. She finished the prayers. A golden effulgence emanated from her mouth like flames. The warmth from it infected his hand, and then his whole body. As he looked at her he saw the glow completely enveloping her. The droplets scattered rays like embers and burned to steam where they fell too close. "There is a third mind one has, that the bard did not mention: when the unknown is brought before the one who is convinced he *already* knows. Ignorance." The voice she spoke was both hers and someone else's. "The mystical is always secret, never known. One must revere through faith alone. But for you Adimus, behold." it muddled his mind, as the robe of flame came, as from an infinitude away, far beyond her, called forth by her lips.

It suddenly clicked in the boy's mind. "Ailen. And Eichgun!" he gasped. She placed a finger over his lip and looked into his eyes. Then they saw something over his shoulder.

Adimus's eyes followed. The twinkle of little eyes reflected in the glow.

There the little urisk stood, arms folded. Like a flame doused, the glow faded away and was dispersed.

"Now what in All Creation was that!?" it said.

"Heathen Mansii Magic, I'd wager." Tirlag's voice came as she appeared from behind a tree holding a candelabra. Behind her was the urisk. "Though I've been from the Gulf of Three Cities to the Patient Sea and never seen anything like <u>that</u>."

Laina's eyes narrowed. The girl gave that same unknowable smirk. *'Fear.' It was undoubtedly fear.* "What should we do with them, eh?" she asked her little accomplice.

Tension filled the air and Adimus snapped. The words just came out. "If you say a word about this I'll tell everyone about you! How you tried to betray them back in Balfour and leave!"

Her eye widened for only a second. "Ohh! Bold you are, like Alara says, Watcher. All blustery and cross! It's kind of...titillating. Puts wind in my sails, haha!" Then she gave a mirthfully flirtatious grin, and watched him blush again. It broke just as quickly. "I don't suppose there'd be any reason to do so, anyway. There's no reward to gain." She shrugged. Then looked at Laina critically. "Now this gift of yours..."

"It is not for the eyes of fools!" Laina said, reflexively pulling the boy away from the girl.

"Are you going to curse me, Mansii witch?"

"That's bigotous hogwash." Delaney scolded.

"Not that I believe that necessarily, but you're not helping yourself very much." She replied, hand on her hip, thumb on her sword. They locked gazes for quite some time. Finally she relaxed. "I'll just call it a bird in the hand, love. I'm saying there'd be less than a good reason for me to tell, and I'm sure there'd be more than a good reason for you *not* to tell, right?"

Laina said nothing.

"Right...?"

"What is she talking about, Adimus?" Laina questioned.

"Let's just kill 'em!" Delaney snapped.

Tirlag let out a dainty gasp. She swatted her with her hat. "See, you don't think these kind of things through! We'd have no alibi, and where would we hide the bodies? For shame! You uncouth little savage!"

She looked at them and shrugged, "I was just saying what <u>she</u> was thinking."

"If you could really read my mind right now you wouldn't be in arm's reach, hob."

* * * * *

Argent struggled with flint and steel and a bundle of tinder in the damp. "Name it all for Thrice's sake!" he finally threw the bundle down. It landed right into a puddle, which didn't help. "Where's that candelabra?" He threw them down. "You!" he pointed at Alfred. "Use that thing you had the other night. The staff...thing."

He was sitting on the edge of the covered wagon, casually examining a pile of notes.

"It's not to be used for foolishness." The Sum Seer replied. If Laina had heard it she would have perhaps fallen in love.

"How is it to be used, then?" he shot back.

He lifted his head from his notes after he'd finished a few more sentences, only because he could feel the burning gaze upon him. "Not lightly."

"Why?"

"I don't think you know what this 'thing' is exactly."

"Try me."

Alfred lifted his head again and examined the joker for a few moments, weighing some unknown variable in his head. Then he smiled. "You're a scholar, same as I. I can appreciate your thirst for knowledge. Tell me what you know and I'll see if you're correct. Go on, now."

"It's a Vesican Harp." he announced. "Also called a Holy Distaff. An imperial marvel. They call upon the the power of Thaumaturgy to create, destroy or transform according to your proclamations."

"Proclamation?"

"Yes. It does what you tell it to do." the bard answered. Alfred's smile grew as the Bard talked, a smug sneer of victory.

Alfred pulled a rolled up leather bag from the pocket of his robe. "Proclamations."

Argent stood for a moment, looking quite confused.

"What are those?"

"As you said. Proclamations. Graces and Spells in crystalline form, would be an easy way to describe them." He unrolled the bag. Inside were tiny shards of crystal of different size and luster. "There are thirteen known such. I have only five of them."

"...But how?"

His smile fell. "That I'm not quite sure of. I've never seen one made, but I do know that they are imprinted by some other form of device."

"Imprinted. Like a printing press?"

"Cymatic conduction. I don't quite understand it myself, but yes, it imprints the sound. Albeit imprecisely."

The Seer rolled the bag back up and put it in his pocket. The Bard's face twisted half awe and half stricken fear. "The voices of angels in a stone."

Alfred reached again into his pocket, this time pulling one of the tiny twigs from it, like the one he'd lit the lamp with when Adimus and he had first met. "I just don't think this situation requires the will of the gods." he lent down, striking it. The tinder caught perfectly.

"So, now perhaps you can clarify something for me." Alfred started to say. "Now that cloak--"

"Aha ha! It <u>was</u> a trick!" Argent exclaimed. "I'll not tell you 'till you tell me what I asked." Alfred tried to hide his guilt as best he could. Then Argent looked at him, and he himself judged some such variables. "Why are you so interested in this cloak anyway?"

"Just academic curiosity." He took off his white glove. "Let me just-!"

"Oh nononono!" Argent swatted at him. The Seer lept. "No!" Argent took off running around the wagon. Papers rained down from the sky in delicate swirls and right into the mud as the Seer took off after him.

Adimus came up just as it had started, and couldn't help but chuckle in spite of himself, both at the humor of the situation and out of elation to be able to laugh at such things at all again. The boy looked down at the pile of papers, all now caked with mud. He started to gather them up, with his fresh new hand, until his eye caught a particular drawing; a faceted pillar of crystal. He whispered the page's title under his breath. "The Stone of Kings."

Argent tumble-rolled over both horses still tied to the wagon. Alfred took the long way around, giving the Bard ample time to get away, but when started to bolt his feet slipped, causing him to have to scurry once again to get away from him.

"It's important to me, alright?!" Alfred huffed, starting to tire. They were both drenched now.

"You know what's important to me? Piles of jade! Lordship! Glory to last the ages!"

He turned to run, but Tirlag had just come from the bushes. Adimus hadn't seen whether it had been on purpose or not, and he would dismiss neither, but either way the Bard tumbled into her and Alfred saw his opportunity. He leapt on the Bard. Argent tried to get away, putting a muddy hand in the Seer's face. They rolled in the muck. They were both covered now.

Adimus quickly tried to snatch up more papers before they rolled over them, until he grabbed what appear to be a crinkled old map. Tirlag immediately walked over to him. "Give me that!" She snatched it from his hand and gave it to Delaney, then walked up to the both of them.

"Ack!" they said in unison as they grabbed them both by the ear.

"Inside. Now."

Chapter 12
The Endeavor Begins

"Pull in that boom line, sailors!" Captain MacCayden yelled, the frustration for his crew's lack of enthusiasm plain in his voice.

Tirlag had been working non-stop for days. *This's for the dogs,* she guffed under her breath, tugging at the lines with what appeared to Captain MacCayden to be spirited fervor, but was really anger.

"Don't worry..." Kirkwell assured her, seeing the exasperated face. "It's almost over."

"Can't wait..." she huffed, knotting the Cormorant's huge sail arm to the main mast and wiping the sweat from her brow. It was more an affirmation of finality, she knew; a reminder that her days as a shiphand would be finished soon altogether.

With a jarring slam the ship's anchor snagged taught. "Here we are, boys! Thane!" The captain sounded, in a tone that sounded like even he too was relieved. "Prepare to disembark!" he shouted. "Drop the plank, Arden!" He ordered the first mate, her tall lanky bean-pole of a brother, who merely passed the captain's orders to the rest of the crew while never doing any real work himself.

Arden always took great joy in spouting orders to others, especially Tirlag, which is why captain Mac Cayden chose him as second in command, she figured, even if his sadistic love to watch people squirm beneath him was mistaken for the inborn qualities of a leader.

"Bring up the cargo!" he yelled to the loose hands on deck, which meant Kirkwell and Tirlag and a small handful of other crew members.

"Start with the passenger goods." ordered quartermaster Walker galloping down the stairs as best he could with his limp, to the lower deck. Silently he motioned to Tirlag and Kirkwell to follow him.

Tirlag shook her head. It wasn't over yet.

Kirkwell swung wide the doors which comprised the passenger's quarters with a yaen and a stretch. It was really the garrison, which had really just been a pantry, but the captain had ensured that the Baron had been given every accommodation. It didn't bother Tirlag any; she didn't sleep in the space as the men anyway, which had well gotten under the skin of the others.

Wiping the morning sleep from her eyes (she had yet to do so), Tirlag clopped into the room, to see and cringe at the sight of the stagnant water that stood in it.

"Silver Hand!" Walker cursed. Tirlag jumped at the sudden outburst. "What in All Creation happened here!?"

Then the putrid smell wafted under her nostrils, and he didn't have to ask what he was talking about. It made her lip curl and his already nauseatingly hungry stomach even sicker. Walker held his dew rags over his face.

"What is that rank--!" Kirkwell started, wandering into him, but was stifled with shock.

"Tirlag, it's a wonder we didn't sink! Or at least run aground!" the quartermaster leered at them, who all gave him guilty faces, "When was the last time this bilge was flushed?" he griped. Tirlag grumbled, yet another of a long list of chores. "You'd best thank Lyr's Graces that it's Thane and not Madreg." Everyone looked puzzled, save Tirlag. Madreg was in the shallows. "Bennon, run the screw pump!" he ordered finally. "Aroun, Glib, try to start wheeling out those barrels." he groaned. "Karris, clear the halls. Tirlag, Kirkwell, come with me..." he moaned, putting the colorful rags back on his head before walking back outside. "I want all the cargo brought topside by the time we set anchor."

They had come down here for the barrels. Some were rum and grog, some fine wine from Dechamp province, to be sold while in port, and still others belonged to their guests.

He turned to Tirlag and Kirkwell with a sly look and a mischievous nod as she came back, who shook his head when she'd seen that he'd lifted one of the expensive bottles of brandy in one of the cases and deftly stuffed it in his pants "He won't miss it."

Tirlag and her father and her brothers had met Torrin Von Krasad in Torant, yet another country that was forged in the fires of the war. He'd come from an island off the western coast. This island (he had told them) was a prison colony, a place to exile the political conspirators and rabble rousers who had threatened to subvert the throne. Torrin's twice great uncle was descended from one such noble family. He was locked away there for many years for suspicions of one such conspiracy, only to be celebrated as a hero once the country's affairs had been settled, and he was freed back to the mainland and re-issued his title to boot. Tirlag didn't really understand all of it.

"...There's plenty to do down here." frowned Kirkwell, handing Tirlag a lantern from one of the hooks on the wall.

The lower deck was cramped but Tirlag was well used to cramped, living most of her life in a fishing boat with twenty other men.

"Blimey! I can't bear much more of this..." Walker protested, standing on one of the Baron's kegs they were supposed to be hauling up above. "Just think though." He pulled a stick of pan from his pocket. He squished it up, grinding it between his teeth. Tirlag had always found it disgusting. "But just think." Walker started again pushing the gob to the side of his cheek. "Pretty soon, the only thing that will be fuller than our coffers is our bellies!" he gave a wild eyed grin.

It was a nasty habit, chewing pan; he'd gotten it in the Gulf of Three Cities in the north, he'd said. It was a Veiled Lander pastime, and how he kept getting ahold of it was a mystery—but a lot of ports in the provinces, as well as Madreg catered to such novel vices nowadays.

"I'd have to say this one was the most uncomfortable trips I've ever been on." Kirkwell complained.

"Tirlag, he always bellyache like this? My condolences." Walker joked. He spit on the floor. "So, where do the Fates take you after this, young lady?"

She raised a brow, it was not often he bothered to feign concern for her, "Inland." She tersely replied.

"...'Tis a shame you'll be leaving us. Would've just started to be fun!" he said, obviously trying to hide behind the remark that he was going to miss him using the insincere-sounding comment. There was a quiet pause, then he leaped from his perch and dusted off his hands.

"So you say this Kazren fellow," Kirkwell thought he'd ask since they were on the subject, it had been digging at him for a long time. "Does he owe you a favor or...?"

"I know something he don't know I know. He'll listen to us." Was all he said. She knew why he was skeptical. Suddenly the vigor for work had come upon him. "What say we finish this, handsomely!" he said, taking off his shirt and picking up one of the kegs, a sudden renewed (and transparent) resolve.

Walker was an experienced salt--a rare trait aboard the Cormorant. He had been given authority due to this experience. That and, he was a man, Tirlag would be quick to point out. He <u>said</u> he even used to have his own ship until it was captured by pirates, but Walker said lots of things. One of the newest of which was his promise to Kirkwell, (and anyone else who would listen).

Bennon was the other experienced salt. He was there to meet them on the stairs and unload. Bennon was in his forties at least, she'd wager but he could still press a hogshead over his own and think nothing of it. He had also sailed the waters of He had an ink tapping, it began at his leathery neck and its tail ran to the base of his skull, hugging his right shoulder blade and spiraling all the way down to rest its head in his hand. Its forked tongue licked his palm. The serpent's back was covered in writings in a language that none of them could identify. He said he'd gotten it too in the Veiled Lands. Kirkwell told her the meaning of the markings he had seen in his life, and none of them were pleasant. He called it an Ink Tapping, and it was mainly used in the foreign lands to brand criminals. There, a serpent branded one as a murderer, but he was quick to point out that this particular one didn't mean that. *'Of course.'*

They couldn't say much of it, it was his connections with Kyogode that gave them their pay day.

They'd met him in Madreg, through her uncle who'd worked in the military. He was a smuggler, and her uncle the young officer whose captain took bribes to ensure the safe passage of the goods. Any real money to be made was taken by the middlemen, shrewd Jin and their southside cartels, but this year's haul of untaxed tea and Nic was a much needed boost to their coin purses that none would protest.

Trade with the Jin themselves was a commodity--the entire reason Menkara dared build a city in the Drowned Lands, the foul moors to the east beset by dark Fae Magic.

"Did his answer allay your fears, my dear brother?" Tirlag snorted, once he was far enough away.

"Any man would keep his secrets among thieves and smugglers. Can't say I blame him." he parried.

Tirlag, like he, had thought it was a mad fever dream of his, or maybe another one of his stories. He was a colorful fellow, and could spin quite a tale. She'd found early on that old wive's tales were more for old salts around a pint than old wives around a knitting circle. True or not and nevertheless these stories granted him a measure of repute, and an air of charisma and mystique that caught the ear of many of Mac Cayden's crew, much to his consternation.

It was a dire and dangerous undertaking which Tirlag and they discussed. Walker had gone on for several moons about a job that would pay so well that he'd need a crew for his new ship. He pitched it to people he took a shine to, including Tirlag. She wouldn't hear of it, Kirkwell on the other hand...

She picked one of the barrels and started back up, and Kirkwell followed "I'd be surprised if anything came of it. All bluster, that one. I suppose he'll have you hunting for that floating palace he's always talking about after this, or that lost city he found that one time and could never find again because of the moon not being right or some such. You can follow him to the ends of the world for all I care."

"And of you and this spear business? What better job prospects, following rumors of whispers! At least Walker has the foggiest idea of where what he's looking for actually is."

"Yes he does. Right under the Steward Prince's noses, Kirkwell! That's what worries me. And when *I* say swiping something is risky--especially when it's from rich folks--you should take my word for it."

"...Then, sister, think nothing will come of it." he shrugged, rounding the stairs and realizing they had company. She just rolled her eyes. He always had to get the last word in.

The baron's bodyguard simply nodded as she passed him, careful to avoid direct eye contact. He was always bashful around her. *'I bet he fancies me.'*

Alara the cait shii' brushed past her. "Good morning." She smiled. *The only nice one of the bunch. And a former navy officer from Torant to boot. Useful and mannerly, and she has a ton of stories, that is, if you can get her to talk.*

Then there was the Baron. His head was beaten red, the look upon his face defeated, his originally auburn facial hair (which Tirlag was surprised to find he even had) now bleached with splotchy white bright with sun spots and made him look aged far beyond his years. She could tell that this had been the longest trip Baron Torrin von Krasad had ever ensured.

"Good day, madam." he said briskly as he took the bags from her. It was all she even got from him anymore. She giggled in spite of herself.

She had tried to even fathom what all the fuss was about; she'd never even heard the man's surname before, though she'd never really had ears for history, but she'd heard he was a swath gentleman, some lord from Milliard, one of the wealthier provinces in Torant.

Trying to sell her off was always his first go-to order of business whenever her father saw coin, and this had been no exception. *'The catch of a lifetime'*, he had called him. Tirlag scoffed at the notion everytime, and this one too was no exception. It was always a contest of wills; her father never had the gall to force her to marry even though he knew she would if he willed it, and she knew this well, and always made it well known her disinterest in a suitor, especially in front of such discerning parties.

She'd almost convinced herself that it was a good idea; he wasn't completely uncomely though he was a bit older, and not by any means poor, the two qualities her father had most touted about, but these were not why she refused--several moons aboard a wave-tossed ship and none could tell poor from rich, handsome from homely. No, the dubious company he kept alongside whispered secrets. That was the reason she told him that she was not interested. After several weeks aboard the ship her father had noticed it too. He'd caught wind of something, something that had made the entire forty-two day journey to Thane a silent affair. He hadn't spoken of marriage again. Unbeknownst to him it was the same wind that had been put in the sails of the girl to do some dubious things of her own.

And then came the spectacled man. The imperial. He said nothing as he passed her, as he nearly always did, but shot her a rather pleasant smile today on passing, something she'd most definitely not been used to. *He must be all chummy because he's finally getting off this ship.* She rationalized. *Or...I bet he fancies me too.* She beamed bashfully at the thought in spite of herself, glancing down to see if maybe she'd done anything different today. He'd had an awkward conversation with her father as well about Tirlag's interest in marriage, and how hard times were as her father always expressed, but then she swept it aside when the thought came: *Or maybe he knows...* she inadvertently leered back at him at the thought, making the man drop his warm demeanor awkwardly when saw it.

The larder was located in the cargo hold, of all places, and there was a small portal for a dumbwaiter which used to lead to the tiny galley on deck. When the ship had been 'repurposed' for its business needs, it called for the use of this storage room as a new cramped sleeping quarters for the crew. The dumbwaiter had been cleared from it but it was never really secured or boarded up; it was no wider than a man, but Tirlag was no man. She'd spent her whole life slinking between it, hiding in it, playing in it and sneaking food to others on occasion, usually her brothers.

She had taken extra precautions to ensure her discretion: tucked her breeches into her soft boots and removed jewelry and the like. She'd wrapped her chest tight with bandages and had even made sure not to eat and to sweat well with chores during the day as to make sure she could still fit.

It was the perfect night, a hot summer rain pounded on the planks, a storm not so hard that it tossed the ship, but just hard enough to pad her feet. Still, every uncontrolled breath, every slight creak, every wispy flutter of the candle she held set her on end--even the rubbing of her clothes around the edges of the portal sounded grating as she slowly lowered the first leg almost in a handstand. Her second leg perched on the inside of the chamber about halfway up she used for leverage, slowly rolled on the palms of her hands to work her way in backwards until the first foot touched bottom. Using the leg to pivot, she held her body until she was completely turned around backwards, so as to be facing the tiny exit to the lift on the bottom. She then placed the second foot down and bending at the knee and undulating like an eel arched her back acutely. A few deep sawing breaths then one final exhale she closed her eyes and shut the intrusive thoughts from her mind.

It had been a few years, but she knew the movement from memory, it had gotten a bit more complex and what others might call difficult, but the gentle slope of making such incremental adjustments made this contortionist maneuver a mundanity to her. But this time it was different: This was at the risk of far more than the half-amused tongue lashing.

The suspense made her struggle to not draw breath, as slowly she went through the motions, as if she could. That had been the easy part. Trickier was getting out on the other side without being seen. It was a lengthy process, that required her to, after clearing the door panel, ensuring that it didn't creak, she feed one foot out and with one leg knock-kneed, with ankle and foot flat on the floor, and the other bent in a crouch she would clear her head and torso before finally standing up. She'd carried stuff down here before but never a live flame. She was glad she also tied her hair back or else her head may have been on fire. The worst part is that it left her completely vulnerable, her face staring flat at the floor and unable to see whatever or whomever might be waiting on the other side.

She opened her eyes. There they were, laying in the men's cots. She took a slow breath through her nostrils and fought what was now a giddiness. She looked down at all the prospects. The bag of coins and cards with which the lord gambled Shadows with the men, a small pouch containing strange crystals that belonged to the spectacled man, his strange looking ring that he sometimes wore. *Better not. Steady now.* She had to tell herself.

She knew every joist on the keel and just where to step so as to not squeak. Two long strides and she stood before the Seer's chest. She bent down like a cat ready to pounce. A hairpin for the teeth and a lithy stiletto for the torsion and the padlock sprung free. Then she remembered there was one thing that had slipped her mind. *'It's a new chest. It should open smooth.'* Still she was hesitant, knowing the damage salty air can reap in even the shortest amount of time. Just then there was a rumble of thunder. She tossed it open. It had. Made a horrible cracking noise. She looked about making sure none had roused, then, with a sigh between gritted teeth, she quietly removed the chest's contents, taking special care to take note of where they went and in which order until she had found it: the old leather-bound black book. She sat it aside.

He had always been jotting down something, whether it be notes, stray thoughts, correspondence or actual record-keeping, but it was one particular conversation they'd had, in hushed whispers, that Torrin showed the Seer this book of bound loose pages.

She grinned triumphantly.

The climb back up was a breeze, as after dousing the candle she could slide up and grab the loop of dangling rope that still hung in the shaft and pull herself back up to spring in a backward somersault back into her room. And there she had sat and read the document

She blew raspberries now as she sat it back in the chest when loading their stuff to disembark. *'To write so much he sure says much of nothing.'*

She wagered that it was some sort of cypher or script of some kind, as she'd seen a few in her time, but all the notes the man had scribbled in the margins of the letters were incomprehensible. She kicked herself for not expecting it. Still she gleaned what little she begged to know from them. Enough to know what they were searching for, and that they were more than competent at finding it. *Gae Bolg. The Spear of Fate.*

Karris frantically lept atop the bowsprit to catch the first glimpse of land he'd seen in nearly a moon. Tirlag had to admit, though the city wasn't much to look at, it was a sight for sore eyes, and even he put down his load to stare at the picturesque city glimmering in the rays of the morning.

Karris caressed the face of the decorative marble statue below. "It's been a long time coming," he said, and at first everyone thought he was talking about the landing. "But, it's time that we part...You've just grown too cold and hardened and weathered is all." he said looking down to the lady statue with her hand stretched skyward. Bennon and Aron burst into laughter. "I know...I know...it's okay. Shh..." he hushed it with his finger. Even Arden cracked a grin. Many bowsprits had such carvings of such angels, Faeri'vahar or Vaharii they were sometimes called, said to ward off evil spirits and usher a safe journey. Most of them were depictions of men, but this was one of the very few feminine figures amongst them. *'Maybe this is why there isn't.'* Karris, as well as many other homesick seadogs, oggled it ceaselessly in the absence of the real thing. And her as well she'd come to realize in the last year.

"Ahh, yes! That is nice!" Even Bennon admitted, setting foot on the solid ground past the dock.

Kirkwell feverishly pushed to be the next one off, when "Where do you think you're going? You're not done yet!" Arden pertly remarked to them, looking down at the large bags and crates that had just finished being loaded up from the hold expectantly. "You are to help Baron Krasad."

"Come on." Kirkwell encouraged, "We'll share the load. You won't have to make two trips."

The unloading of all the Baron's goods then the polite request of her father to help them to an inn. Tirlag, Bennon, Rigel, Kirkwell, and Karris carried their myriad supplies, strangely very little of which seemed to be mercantile goods.

It was an across town trek to the outskirts; the environs where horses and carriages could be bought in which to place their wares. The journey took several hours. Finally, by mid-evening, they joined the others.

Tirlag stumbled and strained to keep from tumbling over by the time they had finished making the long arduous trek. "Come on." Blake patted him on the back. "Just imagine that first bite of lamb and that first sip of ale." said Karris.

"Spirits and ale are for the heathens. Good luck finding a bar here." Bennon frowned. "You'll not find ale for a hundred miles." The look of panic that came across his stubbled face was priceless. He had just been teasing.

"Coffee?" said the spectacled man, picking up his chest and setting it in the wagon.

"You mean this whole town's dry?" The look on the sailor's face was priceless. Bennon couldn't take it any longer. "Hahaha!" Karris was still a greenhorn, and Bennon always went out of the way to give him a hard time of it.

It wasn't unheard of to find a dry town in the provinces or in the reformed Kessellon, many of the governors of the privy council ascribed to the Old Way, and always made sure everyone knew it.

Everyone had ignored the Seer's comment except Tirlag, who when not help but to glance sideways at the man caught him still smiling at her before he marched off and out the door. *'Creepy.'*

"Don't worry." Kirkwell chuckled. "We'll get you soused and slurring in no time." and with that he spun. "Milord, any more requests before we--?"

"You may leave. Good day, sirs, and many happy returns." the man uttered earnestly and without hesitance.

Tirlag dug her heels into the road to keep up, but fell behind nonetheless, after all, she had been up all night. Then she saw the spectacled man. *'Where's he going?'*

She really didn't know why she'd decided to stalk him, Thane was a confusing place and easy to get lost in because everything looked the same, and a few times herself she'd thought she'd lost him in the dusk-lit busy streets, but she couldn't help but notice the man's stride; his determined gait, the rushed ambulations of a person late for something.

He was up to something.

She peeked at the sign from around the corner of the establishment she'd heard hum enter. *'The Goodly Cup'* she slowly peeked around the corner to the glass windows of the establishment. *'A coffee house.'* She peered inside a little further, looking for him. She'd lost sight. *'Drat'.* She would have to get closer to the door to get a vantage. She crouched low near the door, and speed him again, watched as he spoke to a maid who sat him down at a table with two chairs. After a collected moment he pulled the book from his pocket. He took it and a small rolled up scroll and sat it on the table. *'I knew it!'* This is the break she was looking for, she thought.

Walker and her old brothers had taught her many useful skills. How to sneak, how to fight, even how to pick locks, but not how to read lips. *'I just need to get in somehow.'* Then he got up. *'What's he doing? Setting up for another dubious meeting, no doubt.'*

The shock of it sent her off kilter and she fumbled at what to do, but before she could the door opened and his soft voice came. "Aren't you going to come in?"

Tirlag was shocked that not only had she been caught red-handed, but now she sat before her accuser in discourse.

"You know," he said, politely pulling out her chair for her. "I knew you'd peeked at the book before I even opened the chest." he sat down himself. "It's a special gift I have."

"You didn't invite me here to tell me that." she hid her shock and shame behind indignation. "And, of course you do." She sprung. "You invited me to make a deal right? You want to pay me a little quiet money, right? Because the Lords of Ormond or the King of Kessellon finds out about what you're doing, you and the Baron might as well crawl in your graves."

He seemed amused at the threat. There was an awkward silence, himself grinning in contentment at watching her squirm as the maid came back with cups and a pot, and slowly poured their drink. She thought she had asked at one point if she liked cream, to which Tirlag blinked three times.

He continued after she'd left. "My apologies, I don't think I've introduced myself properly." He jerked into a stand, bumping the table and causing the chair to loudly skitter. "Alfred Juminion III, at your service." He bowed and put out a hand. They did a strange ballet of one trying to greet with a courtly kiss and the other giving a hearty shake, climaxing in knocking over the decanter of cream Tirlag hadn't asked for. "A pleasure. And you are?"

"Tirlag Mac Cayden."

"Good." He quickly unrolled the scroll and took out his quill. "Now how do you spell that?"

"What is that?"

"Your agreement." he explained.

"You inlanders and your laws, you think a piece of paper's going to scare me?"

"Entice." was all he retorted with. He handed her the paper.

Tirlag stared at it blankly. "I'm not a lawyer, I don't speak High Daldistan."

Alfred turned the paper around. "Apologies. Again. Allow me to translate. Ahem:

I, Alfred Juminion III, hereby defer and relinquish <u>all</u> due earnings, monetary or otherwise, gained by myself on behalf of Eastward Endeavor Company Ltd., to Tirlag Mac Cayden henceforth, in accordance with and as addendum to article 38 of the charter agreement signed the 13th of Satiom, year 1702 A.E. by Baron Torrin Von Krasad De Greseus Le Mer and Company, for such a time up to and including the finding, procuration, arbitration and dispersal of the spear 'Gae Bolg' herein invoked as referring to quatraine 23 of the Kainden Codex, and all other articles of historical or cultural significance or otherwise requisitioned during the venture outlined in said charter in exchange for the services and conditions warranted herein: All room and board shall be paid out of pocket. Attendance is required for the duration of the work. Call to aid in defense from threats (brigands, Faekind, Shadespawn, or otherwise) when requested, and full discretion and secrecy as to the scope and nature of the work defined in article 38 mentioned above; full and due effort and companionship in accordance to the scope of the work aforementioned shall hence be provided.

"Wait...companionship?"

He handed the paper back to her. "Just sign and acknowledge." he said, putting the cap back on the pen.

"Like...a mistress?" she gulped.

The man's face turned beet red, "No. No no..." he stammered. "<u>In accordance to the scope of the work.</u> A companion. During the adventure." he chuckled nervously. "Apologies." He yammered a third time, nervously tugging at his white gloves.

Then the gravity of it settled on her, then so did the disbelief. "...Why me?" she finally said. "And why would you give <u>everything</u> away? Is this some kind of con?"

"What I seek I cannot take, and no amount of jade can buy or sell." He enigmatically explained. "I shan't be needing my share of the wealth in this endeavor. And your family does, as I understand it."

Tirlag's shaking hand splattered coffee as she struggled to bring it to her lips. She set down the cup soberly. She remembered she didn't like coffee.

* * * * *

Tirlag once again dug her heels into the pavement to try and gain some traction. Her legs still felt like jelly, and being exhausted didn't help. She had forgotten about the ballast. Her worst fears were realized as she approached the dock where the Cormorant made berth, and saw the lonely figure resting beside the plank.

"Knackered, are we?" spake her father, leaning on the bulwark enjoying a pipe as he watched her drag herself up. She said nothing. She saw the handle of the mop leaning against the banister and the bucket between the slats.

The evening sun threw deep shadows in the creases of his face. If anyone was tired it was he. He wasn't as old as his face shown, but he was haggard, his wrinkles not from age, but from a lifetime of sun upon it, evinced by folds around his eyes as if he were permanently squinting at it. It made her wonder if one day she might look that way as well.

His shining eyes fell upon her from beneath the shade of his tricorne hat. "Must be all those late nights you've been up studying." Suddenly she went stiff as a board. "You could've simply asked me you know." he finally added, after being sure to watch her squirm a bit.

"They're looking for Gae Bolg." She said, it came out like they were white knights and she was some starry eyed maiden in distress.

"You know, maybe you shouldn't marry him after all."

"Oh, but father, he's ever so dashing. Handsome. Rich." she glibly retorted.

His face grew grim like an approaching storm in a clear blue sky, when her smile didn't fade. "You'll not be going with him." He was the only one who always saw right through her.

"Are you going to have the same talk with Kirkwell when we get back home? He's got a wild hare up his arse as well." She misdirected, a cunning feint.

"I'll deal with him when it's time." he dismissed it, his sun-bleached mustache bristling like some crawling caterpillar as he puffed on his nic, eyeing her with a stern seriousness. He kicked the bucket toward her. "We set sail tomorrow. Need to make good time before The Moon of Seasons heads above that horizon, else we'll never make it through Rouge Reef. Remember last year, we don't want a repeat." he leaned against the banister again. He smiled. "I'd rather face down a white squall in a paddleboat than deal with your mother this time."

She hid her smile with a gaze upon the immense azure moon cresting in the distance. He was right, more than likely, but she'd die before letting on.

"We could've made it last year." she said. "That's the problem, you never take any risks, you always play it safe." A feeling glissade to draw her opponent out.

"Aye, perhaps. If it were my hide alone, it may be a different story. But it's not, is it?" He set his tricorne hat on her head with a warm smile. "Besides. Got you and the boys to worrying about. And my crew. Each of them have family as well. When you're the captain, Tirlag, it's not just about you." he disengaged.

"Everything worth doing warrants risk. Why-we sail in the Named Treadless Sea for our meager take." she left the 'for Thrice's sake' part out, as Kirkwell always did when around him. "You saw it fit to jump from fishing to smuggling right under the noses of the Emerald Contingent! Of what manner of safety do you speak, dear father, when your men now risk Cairnfang for want of extra coin?" Her lunge came a bit more feeble, as she knew she hadn't the proper footing, she had after all just called it meager, and though it wasn't honest work, everyone knew that but it beat eeking out a living as a fisherman, having to compete in the few calm coastal waters and crowded bays or tread already unsafe seas during storm season. But she pressed on "Walker's idea I might add. But now that he wants to steal your boy away for an even bigger catch! He's a man of ill advice and discretion." she redoubled.

"You remember how hard it was before? You think I want to put them in danger any more than they already are?" he sidestepped. "Your dad's not got many more good ship-standing years in him. I gave these men and your old man the opportunity to feed their families and retire early." he countered.

"That's exactly my point. An early retirement. You don't think the reward of finding the Kainspear is worth the risk of not having me aboard?" she said, dodging in quartata.

"They're chasing a bedtime story!" he reposted.

"I beg to differ." She crossed her arms. "I saw the letters. That Low-loyl..." She tripped.

"Lowyln of Dougall." he mockingly disarmed her.

"-That *general* fellow had it." She tried to get up.

"I've heard that before too, in all my years." He said. "It was a rallying cry to bolster the people to fight! 'Behold the one true king, Lord Saint Lowyllyn, come to lead you from tyranny, Bane of the Eye in his hand, Claimh Solias 'cross his back, waters of Slaine in his belly, the white stag betwixt his legs and the Goddess's Heart nestled in his arse cheeks!' Stories say he slew a dragon before that! Oh, that and--oh yes, that he was immortal, so there's that...Tirlag, I need you here. Playing it safe with me." He'd run her through.

"...Father." She smiled.

Chapter 13
Hewnyleigh

"Lord Saint Lowyln Mac Dougall not only had the spear, he kept it safe, having been given it by the giants for defending their homes in the time prior. He was afraid to show it on the field for the very same fears you mention. He hid it in the fortress, ready to stand and become the king of this newly freed nation--until that is, he died in the Battle of Pangor Vale, just shy of the day of the miracle at Slaine, they say." Alfred's face flickered by the shadows of the lamp he'd set on a keg between them.

Tirlag summarized. "All his men scarpered when he did. *No one* ever found it." She was caught looking down at the tricorne she often wore with a strange fondness. She put it back on her head.

"So how does a marronian sailor and a gnemedian fit into the picture?" asked Argent.

"Well, her abilities will be of use here. The urisk knows where this place is." said Alfred. Delaney waved as if being acknowledged for the first time. "Or she will, better than us. Tirlag..." he raised an eyebrow "Found my employ because she was nosy and persistent, same as you."

"I have my uses." Tirlag huffed. "If only to reduce the total homeliness of this miserable lot."

Laina shook her head at the comment and continued. "So this man wants to be the king? In Ormond? A foreigner? Surely the island sun has baked his brain."

"He wants to be rich. Me too." Tirlag said soberly; to her it was no laughing matter.

"Well, that explains why he wants me to take him on a meet-and-greet." said Argent. "He wants to sell the spear off to the highest bidder..."

"He asked you do this already?"

Argent shrugged, "He hasn't said it directly, but he keeps probing me and suggesting that I will stay. No doubt he wasn't set on paying me for it." Then he rubbed his hands together, "but it seems I've remedied that." He cracked his fingers. "Ha! To hitch a ride with the finders of the sacred spear...who could hope for better luck? And you'll thank fate as well for it, mark me words." He extended his hand to the wizard.

"So...what *were* you doing roadside in the middle of nowhere, anyway?" Alfred eyed him suspiciously.

Argent yammered, grasped for something to say, perhaps for the first time ever, Adimus thought. He was cut off. "It doesn't matter now." said Tirlag.

She plucked her dagger from her bosom. "We need a navigator and he knows the waters we tread." She looked at the bard. "It was my idea to invite you in. Because <u>he</u> didn't trust you. See? <u>Useful</u>." She crossed her arms. "The voice of reason between us, I am." She beamed.

"You are now making the offer less enticing, dear." Argent quipped.

She ignored him. "My offer to you is the same as your offer to me. We give no quarter to traitors or fools. You leave your past, you keep your bond, you take your share." She pointed to Laina and Adimus with it. "All of you." She plunged the dagger into the keg dramatically. The lantern clattered to the ground. Alfred picked it up with a dejected sigh. "Sorry." she whispered. "But what about Torrin? Shouldn't he be the one treating with me?" the Bard asked.

The three looked at each other. "You are a calculated risk." Alfred explained. "If you can garner a better deal than Baron Krasad can land then we will present it to him and demand a higher margin of the difference. If not, *we* shall take on the contractual burden of suffering the loss, as we will be splitting <u>our</u> take with you, not his. You will be...our contracted advisor."

"You have faith in me." Argent gasped.

Laina looked at Adimus with a 'why not'. "Very well then." then, without so much as a wince she pulled out the mess knife from her belt and proceeded to slice her hand with it "I give in tribute the Matchless Gift to the stone, sweeter than honey upon the tongues of the gods, I give of blood mine own--!"

"What are you doing?!" Alfred said, face as pale as a sheet. "Give me that!" he grabbed the knife from her hand and slapped it back to Tirlag, who now had the priestess's blood on her. He pulled a handful of scrolls out of his pocket, trying to shake the disbelief out of his head. He handed her a cloth from his pocket to clean up the mess. "Here." he unrolled them. "Crazy Mansii..."

The three of them looked at it.

"Eastward Endeavor?"

"It's a company I've chartered. I supposed it was as good a name as any."
The bard explained it to them as they went on, "Your penmanship is atrocious, my friend." he squinted, straining out the words until he got to: "*...and full discretion and secrecy as to the scope and nature of the work defined in article 38 mentioned above; full and due effort and...*" he squinted "*...general associativity? In accordance to the scope of the work aforementioned?*' " The bard scratched his head as he read it aloud. "*...Not familiar with the phrasing--.*"

"Are you signing it or not?" Alfred snapped. He handed Argent his pen. He stared at it blankly on making his mark until Laina snatched it so that she too could sign. She, of course dropped the pen twice trying to do so, and managed to bleed on not only on it, but on the feeble scratch she had made (between that and earlier catching the boy playing with his own shadow by the lamplight the Grigor was prepared to tell the Bard that they had snuck off to drink if he asked, and was fairly confident he'd buy it). Adimus's eyes widened, rather impressed with the way it moved and swished so effortlessly, the ink eagerly sealing the page.

* * * * *

In perhaps only the echoed memories of his dreams Adimus had ponderously marveled upon phantoms of such mind-boggling scope and vastness. It had always been something woeful, some awful and awesome thing that chased him through his nightmare, or sat forebodingly on some horizon paying him no mind, being some force of nature whose threat to him was the mere misfortune of being in its presence--he'd once seen a tornado that was such a thing, with Bearach on one of their broader walkabouts: small against the distant horizons of the horse plains past the Ruined Road. Trying to fathom its size to be seen from so far yet be so large always stirred primordial terror in him, so much so that even afterwards he had gripping nightmares of it at least once a season, but on waking such feverish fancies were always dispelled. But not today. The boy stood in admonishing solace and despair: a city. Hewnyleigh.

Its claustrophobic streets provided insulation from the true nature of its unthinkable architecture and the sheer amount of people who lived here, which was of little comfort to the boy.

Where these jettys relented, clearing their view around monuments, fountains, parks and squares a better view could be taken in. More than once he bumped into someone, often another awe-struck kindred spirit, as he took in the vertigo-inducing tangle of walks and the building-laden horizon; buildings stacked on buildings stacked on buildings, all gathering in competition to be the closest to where he stood, no matter where he was, it seemed.

And the people, all the people.

Folks dressed more primly here, often proudly sporting kilts of their clans, sure the colors were as vibrant as their knee high socks were white, carrying canes and puffing sophisticatedly on pipes full of expensive nic. Ladies wore eresaids, and parted and embroidered gowns and bodices, velveteen caps with veils, rouge, and beautiful necklaces of jade and bronze, bejeweled with tourmalines or garnets.

Built on an agreeable patch of green at the base of the Daldista Plateau, almost equidistant from four of the five major cities in Menkara, Hewnyleigh was a meeting grounds both for the the clans and the minds of academics throughout the south, argent had told him.

White brick paved the main thoroughfares, upkept well by cleaners of offal and other waste, mostly younger, and mostly wearing red and gold livery. When pressed, Argent explained. "The Servants of the City. Tuition is often paid in service here. Nowadays. After the slave prohibition." He heard Delaney vocalize a growl after the last part.

Gargantuan cathedrals of white stone towered over tightly packed shops and establishments, pressing against them with wrought iron fences as if to hedge them away from the ample yards they possessed. Glass windows filled with coats and shoes and jewelry lined the streets.

Statues of unrecognizable armored knights, and scholars reading books and the divine imagery of the Menkarans dotted nearly every square.

Finally, after hours of meandering its corridors, on the northern gates they came to a large cavernous building.

It was a squat, one story affair, but the inordinate amount of real estate that it and its yards took up showed plainly in a place of such sparse space that it was of great importance. The whole place was built on crenelated stone, like a fixture of the wall that surrounded the city, and all seemed to spread out or led to it. Adimus gazed at the resplendent crest above the portcullis that served as its entrance. It was Ravenhound. Even Adimus had heard of it, the meeting grounds of the Steward Princes, forbidden from the acts of bloodshed by the laws of the king of old. He was surprised to find that this is where they would stay.

A gnemedian stableman saw to their horses. Servants wearing the city's livery helped them unpack, and soon Adimus found himself treated to hot food and an even hotter bath, and a restful night upon canvased mahogany, perfumed black satin and goose down. But it was all a ruse, the leisure and joy of simply another color of the rainbow of sensations and stimulations that came with the city. Pulled into the harsh sunlight early the next morning, with warning that he'd better have prepared himself in his best clothes, he was thrust back out into the harsh daylight and blaring noise.

Beneath its sturdy arches, the full blazons of the clans of Ormond stood woven in glorious tapestry. Argent introduced them. An eye amongst thorns in white and green cut per pale down the middle. *Dougall*. A prancing horse of vert and azure, as if he stood in a green field. *Casey*. A griffon on silver and sable carrying a key. *Dwyer*. An eight spoked wheel on purple, surrounded by flames. *Ward*. But two hung from oriflammes flanking the door for all who came in to see: a white wolf rampant on a field of gules and gold, and a raven perching on a gnarled oak branch on sable and violet. *Bran and Mathune.*

One in particular, the wheel, Adimus caught Alfred pausing at when he might think none were looking.

A man carrying a stack of books passed them. "Hello, Alfred." he said.

"Do I know you?" the Sum Seer answered.

"Shh!" Argent nudged him.

The quiet halls into which they'd come echoed at their footfalls. Dark stone at their feet muted the scenery as columns of sunshine lit the long tables and chairs and spines of dusty tomes lining immense shelves. It felt like a museum. In it the people scarcely peppered about the myriad seats sat quietly and read. This was the Bowen Archive: the repository of the ancient knowledge of the Lathnians.

Smoke wafted from a stray pipe, steam from tea. The only sound to be heard, aside from the occasional stray cough, was that of a father quietly teaching his son a recitation in old Daldistan.

Argent embarrassingly skidded past all of that and spirited them away to their room, a short little thing perhaps slightly larger than lord Pembroke's cloak room. It was fitting, all the silence, as after an unsettlingly hushed few moments of settling their gear and straightening themselves with all the glee of a funerary usher Argent gestured them on, beyond the spiraling staircases flanking the large archway leading to into stark sunlight.

There, the city walls sat behind them, and a massive stone mound sat before them, and in between them, framed in the blackness of the mound's yawning entrance, was a courtyard. In its center a white-barked tree stood, slightly grotesque in the way it had grown with disregard and abandon in the light with which it was fed, gnarled with age and perhaps a bit malnourishment, and guarded by a circle of engraved stones, and beneath the tree sat an old man atop a modest throne, his gloved hand resting upon the pommel of a downturned sword, its tip planted in the dirt.

His scalp was balding, what remained of his long silver hair draped around his face like an open curtain, held in place by a silver circlet. His broad mustache hid his terse lips as he gazed upon the men standing before him. Another man stood at his side, his hand also resting on a sword on his hip the likes of which Adimus had never seen, his thick hair, like red clay, pulled back to clear and make way for the gazing of his stern eyes. He, like the one seated, carried a sword, though its bowed shaped was unlike anything Adimus had ever seen.

One of the men before them stood in chains and rags. He was haggard, dirty, and unshaven. The other who stood with him was quite the opposite. He wore a blue, high collared tail-coat, his long hair slicked back behind ears. Those ears were not those of a Kind Adimus hadn't seen but a scant few times, they were lithy, pointed, and long, protruding even several inches above the crown of his head. He was a Tuatha. Adimus only knew because he had spied a few in Ederton and Luloch pointed them out, like a shooting star or a rainbow, like an event one might scarcely see again.

He could tell not only by the ears (though some other types of fae did have those ears he'd heard) but by the alien way his hair moved. He couldn't explain the phenomena by any means; he'd heard it recounted a myriad of ways and never knew what it meant. He heard it described as if they were underwater, as if it were alive, even writhing like snakes. Putting it in his own words he would liken it to being blown by an unseen wind.

He wore gloves a bit similar to Alfred's, and cradled a cudgel-like rod beneath his arm. "...on behalf of the Erlking, in accordance with the treaty set forth by Argetlam and King Mathendon I, I hereby formally request due asylum until a member of the Seelie Court can make arrangements to provide representation in these Hyu'man lands."

The old man leaned back in his chair. He'd noticed Argent and the others come in, but broke no eye contact. Argent slunk off to the side where several others stood, and with the sweep of his arm begged the same of Adimus and the others.

The seated man rocked forward in his chair. "Tell me, fae, what is your name?"

"...I am The Valeyard, milord."

"Well, 'The Valeyard'." He openly jested. "Why does this man need representation?"

The tuathan nodded, hands joined in front of him at the waste in a most courtly manner. "Why, to accommodate his need to establish his case against the accusation."

"The law he broke wasn't a fae law. We are talking about murder."

Argent, along with Adimus found himself squinting to get a better look at the man, who had not even ears to make him unremarkable.

The dapper one who called himself Valyard stifled a giggle. "Of course we are. And once his case is established if he is found guilty the court itself will take on responsibility for his actions and pay the Wer of the slain."

"The problem is this man is not one of you."

Argent whispered over top of the conversation. "Lord Cadifor of Dougall is one of the Immortals of Slaine."

"Oh I assure you, *milord,*" it was slathered in contempt "he is." he turned to the accused, putting fingers in his hair as if examining a dog. Then he took the rod and jammed it against the man's skin, which sizzled and smoked and made a horrible ringing noise. The man stymied a cry of pain. "See?"
At that Tirlag tugged on Argent's sleeve, a startled reflex.

"He was one of *my* people!" The white-haired man rumbled.

"-And I assured you, you will be duly compensat-"

"Him!" The man roared. He stood to his feet. "*He* was one of *us*!" He pointed his sword at him. "Who spent his whole life living and doing what ought be done of a man of Ormond! He is beholden to *our* laws, not yours!"

The seated man pointed the sword at the accused.

"Harken to me. You shall speak the truth for I, wielder of Gram, will it!" He proclaimed.

"*Gram.*" Argent whispered with giddy awe.

"Now answer me, did you kill the boy and his son?"

The large man's lip quivered. "I did."

"Why?"

"Because he found out about me."

"And what reason warranted such an act? Why were they not privileged to know?"

The Tuatha fumbled and tried to stand between them. "Milord, this is unlawful-" he tried to urge, but he continued to speak.

"...Because...Because my wife and child can never know."

The Valeyard lowered his head.

Cadifor lowered the sword. "They can never know what I am." the man repeated. "Please, milord, I beg you. May no harm come to them."

"You have my word." he said. "And they will never know unless you will it be said."

The man wiped his eyes of tears, then the lord turned to him. "Stand ready. Man of Ormond." The prisoner nodded then stood proudly. The Tuathan's malcontent was plain upon his face.

"I sentence you to the punishment handed down by my forefathers."

"I invoke the Dominion of the Vahar of the Second Wheel, purveyors and keepers of the virility from which all seeds grow and spring and lifeblood of all creatures between the Vales of Ormond. I banish you to the Deep!" The runes in the stones began to shine. "I speak the names of Dian and Tial, and Mathien the First So Named, who by their sacred Geas protect and keep all in their lands who champion the Words of Ethne. In their name, depart this place!"

Just then the sun paled, as if an eclipse or cloud of ill omen had fallen upon it. The ground shook, and the earth split forth with lashing chains. They grabbed the man like the lashing of a whip. The autumn air stilled to permit the sound to permit the horrid sound of growls and the gnashing of teeth. Adimus cowered at the sound; perhaps he alone was intimate enough with it to know what it was. Church Grim. No. Several of them. They yowled and bayed, like pups awaiting scraps.

The man spun to try and run--he'd said he was prepared when nothing could prepare him. Adimus's eyes locked gazes with his for a moment, as the chains began to pull taught. Acrid smoke billowed from his searing flesh as his fear-stricken face locked eyes with the boy.

A moment later and he would be gone, leaving only tracks in the dirt where he'd tried in vain to claw his way out, the only evidence he'd been there at all. The Valeyard, a disappointed look about his face said nothing, turned slightly, then with an aloof expression paced off into...nothing. Adimus even looked around, as if his eyes were tricking him in the distress of it all, but the man had literally vanished.

Himself noticeably affected by the ordeal, the older man stood. He took a moment to clean the tip of his blade. Finally he glanced upward, as if just remembering Argent and rest.

He turned to return to his chair. "Bring forth the accused." it came out as a flustered sigh.

"No, Milord." the servant said. "These folk are here to see you."

"I'll speak to them the night of the Pledging." He waved dismissively.

"...Very well." he began to motion them toward the door.

"Lord Cadifor, the Demimortal, the Unavailed, Hero of Slaine, all hail!" he gave a dramatic stooping bow. The man on the seat saw immediately through it, and with the wave of his hand dismissed all the foolishness. "On with it, Mathune!"

"Ahem, then, if I may." Argent sidestepped the servant. "Fortuitous that you mention my surname, as it is why I am here, summoned on behalf of the Clan of the Wolf itself."

"...Is that so?" he said. Then pointed the sword at him. "Is that so!?"

"It is."

"Oh. Well." He shrugged, sheathing the sword and shaking his hand. "Apologies." Chuckled. "Well met, well met."

"We have come to you today with a grave warning from the people of Balfour, a small village on the border of Kessellon."

"I know of Balfour." he sounded as if he were patronized.

Alfred's face twisted in curiosity.

"First, my lord, if I might introduce you to my compatriots." The Bard said. He presented them each in turn with flattering titles. *'Grigor Adimus Buckroy, Son of Bearach, Junior Prilate and Emissary of the Fraternity of the Watchers.'* He called Adimus.

"Yes, yes, may we? Today? What does the reeve of Adaire want, and what has it to do with clan Mathune?"

"They have sent this young lad to speak on their behalf." He patted him on the shoulder, the last pat being a shove him forward and before the man who had just called upon the ground to swallow someone whole.

Needless to say Adimus hesitated. He just tried his best to keep his breath in his lungs and his heart in his chest. He told him of what the man spoke, of his dreams in the night.

"Sluagh Oiche..."

It was the first time the words had ever left anyone's mouth in a tone of validation.

"The Night of the Shades is a time of danger for all of us." It was strange hearing him say it, and a bit worrisome. "The Darkest Night is always dreadful. Every generation it comes, I've seen many. For those unwary it leaves only sorrow in its wake. Build a bright fire indoors, invite in no strangers, look out of no windows, cover your mirrors and you shall be safe. What makes Sluagh Oiche in Balfour any different?"

"I believe his dreams to be a portent." Argent replied. "A warning, pronounced by a Druid."

Druid?

"Truly?" he roused. "A druid? In Balfour?"

"It is true, he speaks Dhuun. He also knows some about the ways of Thaumaturgy, and perhaps can even pronounce Xanthic Spells by sight."

"What is his name?"

"Luloch Buckroy."

Adimus blinked. Argent continued.

"There hasn't been a true druid in Ormond since the time of the Daldistans."

"Perhaps I misspeak. I suspect he has at least had past relations, of one sort or another, with the Fae. It is the only other explanation. He speaks to the animals. They tell him that the Winter Queen makes ready for war. He has had many dreams about it as well."

But as it came out of the man's mouth the lord was already beginning to uproar with laughter. It penetrated the stone beyond, and perhaps even the bard's resolve, such that, for a moment, Adimus thought he might have seen the minstrel's facade break. "You speak as a man of knowledge, bard." the lord said, "But I know you to be nothing more than a Whispermonger. You don't think I know who you are, even with that mangy pelt on?"

But the man seemed more amused than anything. Argent, understandably, remained silent. "Your kind perverts the knowledge of Artur Bowen to play the same debased game as your selfsame illiterate kinsmen. For shame, William!" His face, thankfully, softened after a moment. "You needn't spin tales to add gravitas to your claim. You should be more cautious. Especially when the one you lie to can force the truth out of you, and punish you for it, at that."

"Please, McDougall. It is true." Argent wiped the sweat from his brow with a hand made steady with marked concentration.

"The Unseelie seek to wage war, eh? In Balfour..." his skepticism was still apparent..

"I was bidden by the reeve of Adaire to tell you. Well, he was loath to do so; for even such superstitious and backward people it is an extraordinary claim to try and believe, as the both of us can see. But *I*, a bard of Bowen," he gave another reassuring smile. "know the signs. The man knows what he speaks."

"No doubt. And you, boy! You are kin to this *great prophet*?"

"Y-yes, my lord. He is my...elder." Adimus said.

"Who is your mother and father?"

"I..I." He glanced around, everyone was looking at each other.

Again his anger kindled. "Named Whispermonger! You may well have just invited a changeling spy into our midst! Did you, in your omniscience, foresee that, <u>bard of Bowen</u>?!"

"Why would they warn us and then send a spy?" the bard spat. It was a risky move, the minstrel no doubt realized after Cadifor took stance and his retainer bore down on them all, that he, with unshaken bravado, had reached over Adimus's shoulder and drew the boy's sword from his belt. The lord's retainer held his sword halfway out of his scabbard when the bard touched it to the boy's cheek.

"See?" the bard said, pleased as punch, then with still a little too much carelessness than the boy should like, he hurled it at the man.

He effortlessly caught it. "This is cold iron." Cadifor beamed in awe. Even the retainer seemed to peek over the lord's shoulder.

"An heirloom of the Great Kingdom, no doubt." he nodded; Argent's pride would see him win the crowd, even if it killed them this much Adimus knew too well.

"Very well. He is not Fae. But he could still be a spy. That, <u>my</u> sword shall answer." and with that Cadifor pointed the blade at the Grigor, and spoke the words he'd recited from before.

The man uttered then, "Adimus, are you hiding something from us?"

His eyes widened with worry. They shot over to Laina, who in response winced and clasped his hand despite their gaze.

He couldn't help it, it was as if the words themselves were being sucked out of his mouth. "Yes."

"Who are your mother and father?!"

"I do not know."

The boy failed to hide his look of utter shock. He'd tried to lie, tried to tell them what he'd told everyone, that it was Bearach, but it was as if the words were siphoned from his mouth without his consent. He attempted to protest, but when he did he fell into an inexplicable panic. Somehow--he didn't know how, but somehow he felt as if the sword would most definitely slay him if he didn't speak promptly and true, as if it were a snake poised to strike; it was the first time he'd ever admitted this secret to anyone, and upon the pull of the unaccountable feeling he had done so gladly.

"Tell us what you choose to conceal."

"...My sister and I are foundlings."

"Elaborate. Who found you? Where were you found?"

"Luloch. In the forest outside of Balfour."

They were all looking at each other. There was nothing he could do but watch his life laid bare.

"Do you still think he is a changeling?" Said Argent.

"What is your earliest memory?"

"Darkness. Caves. I see by the light of the pretty flowers. Then Dyrshul...my sister is there. We travel toward the light, I lead her from the wooden road. She wants to run, so I clear her way. Then the forest. This I have told you. Nothing more."

Cadifor looked judgingly at Argent, then, as if lost in thought, replaced his sword.

"Leave me, I must think on this. All of it."

They promptly did.

Chapter 14
An Unexpected Reunion

"So what's on today, Adimus?" Said Argent, undoubtedly inquiring about the food again.

The accommodations of Ravenhound made The Green Beat seem quaint and plain. Though it wasn't Meav's food, he complained not at all at the on-demand fair available (and neither did Argent), and though sleep was scarce these days, the fresh linens and soft down pillows soothed just the same.

"Not sure." he grumbled, doodling on his tablet.

"I'll get us something." He nodded. Rubbing his hands together.

Adimus glanced up for but a moment, to glare at the back of the pandering princling, when someone strolled before him.

The flowery fragrance she wore already imposed itself upon his senses before his eyes even registered the figure. She was distinctly beautiful, memorably beautiful, when finally they did.

Her pleasing face was sensibly powdered and rouged, eyes darkened, lips reddened. She wore a necklace to match the barrette, but aside from this the rest of her was perfectly terrestrial: cloth chausess stuffed into riding boots, and a green men's doublet.

Her quaff of fiery hair would've brushed her knees, but, as it was, made a voluminous cascade down her back. Unlike Tirlag's, wild and course, hers was straight and smooth, save for the few curls that haloed her face. They were purposefully selected to do so, hanging with intent from the gemstone-inlaid barrette that crowned them.

It left Adimus suddenly feeling wanting when her eyes fell upon him, cognizant of his every flaw. *His hair was an ungroomed mop.*

"Is that your shield?" She asked.

"...Yes." Adimus shifted nervously in his seat. *His fingernails were dirty.*

"I'd not seen that blazon in escutcheon for an age. " She remarked.

He had absolutely no idea what that meant. "Oh? Well. Me too. I know, right? Haha." *His clothes were dirty too.*

Her brow twisted in confusion, but she was, unsurprisingly, graciously above addressing his ignorance. "Hail the House of Eochide, hail the house of the last king of the Fir Bolg. Oinde."

"What?" He hoped it was enough to stir her into an explanation, as he could only assume it was some expression in another language that everyone was familiar with but him, that he had fallen so deep into a foreign situation as to be irretrievably lost–that, *and his breath stank, undoubtedly*.

"My name. It is Oinde, milord." She giggled, undoubtedly reading this dumbfoundedness on his face.

"A-Adimus." *She'd explained because his face was frozen with stupidity; his face was stupid.*

"Nice to meet you, Adimus." She stuck out her hand.

Adimus kissed it. He'd heard that was what was to be done. He felt immediate doubt at its correctness, and in his self-audit assessed that he hadn't stood. *He should've stood.* It sent him into a sort of lurching spasm that shook the table.

She replied with a kind giggle. "I would sit, if it pleases you."

"I-of course." *His hands were sweaty, leaving noticeable stains on the table.*

"And...much more for you, should you choose."

Adimus fought the widening in his eyes; he would've reasoned this struggle as the basis for his red cheeks, if he could've seen them.

"Well? What do you think of the prospect?" she smiled.

"I..I."

"I, for one, am titillated by it." Argent chimed in. He pushed a plate in front of the boy with a wide grin.

She gave a low curtsy and yet another coy giggle.

"*Lord* Adimus, might I share a word?" He asked with hollow candor, glancing across the table for her equally disingenuous approval.

But Adimus smirked. "Of course, *Lord* Mathune."

"Lord Mathune? Pleased to make your acquaintance as well." She rose and offered her hand.

The bard kissed it proper with a bow, and, brushing away Adimus's caprice with the smugness in his reply lent in to the Grigor's ear. "<u>She's talking about the Pledging, you fat-headed git!</u>"

"...Oh. Oh!" He rocked in his chair. He looked back at her trying to hide the pooling of sweat on his brow as brushing his hair out of his face.

"I think they are a great selection. Of candidates."

"I doubt not their competence. Just the blood in their veins." She said.

"I agree." Argent replied for him. "A lot of meddling from entities with their own agendas. And fewer native than not nowadays, which says much." He picked up a life and fork and started sawing at his food.

Adimus nodded in a hollow stare, not yet truly in the conversation. He elbowed his plate of food by accident, not realizing the bard had sat it there for him: ham and eggs.

"There are several strangers in our midst." She continued. "Imposters."

"Truly?" He agaped.

"Foreigners." She harrumphed.

They glanced around the table. There was an awkward silence. "Tell me. How do you feel about their encroachment on <u>our</u> traditions?"

"We have gone for centuries without finding the Spear. I see no harm in letting others continue not finding it." Adimus answered, pleased as punch he got a whole sentence out in one breath.

She smiled. "Well put, milord, I suppose." She spun in her chair, glanced over her shoulder at the other patrons. "But do you think they have our interests at heart?" "There is a defected Imperial Seer pledging. You think <u>he</u> has the fate of our country at heart?"

"It shouldn't matter, as long as one of our kinsmen sit atop the throne. The clans that sponsor them will always be the ultimate benefactor, that much has never changed." he answered. He took a swig, and paused "Imperial Seer, though." Argent looked at Adimus and back to the girl, his face growing dark "That would be troubling now." his eyed lock with hers with fawning attentiveness. "Where did you hear that?"

"The Bowen college is all aflutter about it. And General Dougall has let it slip to the court."

"And what <u>does</u> Sir Cadifor think?"

She put a knowing finger to her nose. "Can't be too sure, but he is meeting in the spring to discuss a campaign to repel the Histban and reverse the Maritian occupancy, so what do you think yourself, milord?"

"That if they can find the spear, and they deliver, then it's all the same for us. Right?" Adimus tried to butt in.

Argent nodded, noshing on his food. "I think... That they would be more clandestine and secretive about it, you know? They wouldn't go traipsing into the noble court and announcing themselves, surely."

"Unless there was something that only the nobility could give them. Something they wanted."

Argent wiped his mouth. Now he did look worried, and he wasn't just feigning it. "Like... what?"

She gave them a graven eye, and again, glanced about for eavesdroppers leaned in, and they with her.

"Land."

"...Land?"

"Yes. Already Ederton is aflood with them, the Merchant Lords, their guards, their servants. The Free City is free no longer. They are a staging ground for an invasion force; but that's the kind of fear they wish to instill. Enough to plant paranoia among the nobility—it's a wicked game they play, and it won't matter if there's strategic value to the swath of land the Seer might end up getting (though it'll be along the Nalanen, just you see) it's enough to sow seeds of doubt in whosoever claims the Spear and the kingship, crippling the already heady relations with Menkara and weakening the southlands for a final blow."

Adimus and Argent both scratch their heads. "That's a keen observation." The bard said. "However..." he reasoned. "I think it warrants the snatching up of the Seer up as a pledger as soon as possible, by a reputable name. That would be the only way to ensure his loyalty and disarm any such assertions."

"I hope my words haven't excluded me from either of your thoughts." she looked up worryingly.

"Never." he gave a warm grin.

"If I pledge to you, what will we receive?"

Argent beamed at the boy. "Yes, Sir Buckroy, what is your offering to this fair dame?" Adimus lowered his eyes to the table in locked panic. Argent chided, nudging him with an elbow. "A seat at your side, perhaps?"

The maiden looked on soberly.

"Oinde!" a man's voice called out to her, and just as suddenly as she had appeared she had fled, with bows and "excuse me's" and "pleasure to meet you's."
Adimus was so thankful.

"Well, that was strange." Argent poked at him.

"Not so much as you might think. She was rumor-mongering. Digging. Assessing her competition. I saw the signs. Mark my words, she's a snake."

"How's that so, then? She thought I was a lord."

He tisked haughtily. Adimus didn't need to hear the words that might accompany his skeptical snoot. "At any rate, best to mention as little about us as possible in the coming days."

With that he adjusted his chair to sit more comfortably, sprawling over where she had sat. He nursed a stein of fancy lambics.

After a few moment the Grigor went back to drawing, sure to let his food get cold and the troubadour looked on.

Seeing this, finally the bard confided. "You know, I didn't want to say anything, but I'm glad that bite didn't kill you. Maybe it's a blessing. A sign." he said. He didn't have to add the context. *No one gets touched by a Shade and lives.*

"You know signs well, don't you?" the Grigor replied, not looking up. "...Like my grandpa being able to speak to birds and such."

"What are you getting at?"

"Nothing. <u>William</u>." he said. He glance up at him.

With that, William Mathune shrugged, and leaning back in his chair stuck his hand in his pocket.

It was then, in the lull, and as if to mock him, that Tirlag and Delaney, appeared.

"*Argent*." It sounded weird and strangely formal on her tongue. She and Delaney glanced at each other, as if to ensure they were in accord. "So, Delaney and I were talking about your conversation with that Cadifor chap. You said you spoke on behalf of...who was it?" She looked to her friend, who whispered in her ear. "Mathune." She giggled. "The Clan of the Wolf, the clan who owns this city." She put her hand on her hip. "What does that mean?" She said innocently. The bard raised a finger to reply but before he could she was sure to add. "We don't think you'd lie to someone like that."

Argent then glanced around warily. He motioned them to draw close "Alright. Keep this between yourselves, and especially from the Seer." He said. "I <u>am</u> part of Mathune." Tirlag's eyes lit up for a moment. "Just a humble envoy, mind you, but no less working on their behalf." he was quick to add. "My job was to oversee potential prospects for the Hunt, to report back with my findings." He quickly finished his drink, slamming it on the table "It would appear I've found quite the one." he smiled proudly. "You see? Actually in the crew who finds the Spear is going to make me a very rich man...a sort of an insider investment, really."

"So..." she spent a moment taking it in. "What do you think you can get us?"

"We'll see. We'll see." he said, then curiously he hopped up and reached his hand in his pocket. "But in the meantime, allow yourself to revel in some of the amenities granted being friends with a lordly diplomat." he produced a handful of papers.

"An estate auction?" Tirlag's face curled in confusion.

"The fellow whose lot in the Cache of Kainden is being cleared. Merris, was his name. Not a noble, mind you, but a Thaumaturge.

"The Cache of Kainden, you say?" Alfred startled them. It was as if the words had summoned him. Or perhaps they had all been listening. Adimus hoped not.

Argent nodded.

"A rich bloke then, I take it, to have his own lot in the most heavily guarded vault in all the land." Tirlag's dourness had suddenly dissolved. "Alfred, I move that Eastward Endeavor attends this auction. It would do well to help get us fraternized with our hosts." she grinned.

"Vultures picking at the carcass of one of their own." Alfred rubbed his chin.

"Much better: well-to-do vultures. Come on, what do you say?"

* * * * *

Whether it was a gesture of final comradery, an apology of sorts for hiding his true identity, or perhaps simply a way to get everyone's mind off of their current status, the bard had cordially invited them to the estate auction of the late Merris Xanthos La Magie.

It was hosted not far from the hall, in an adjacent theater. That late afternoon, they arrived, and after they'd all settled in, Alfred came to Adimus and handed him a pocket full of coin. "We liquidated our findings at the tomb. Argent found it important that you get a share. Not that you wouldn't, you're one of us now." He tried to cheer him up.

Adimus's jaw dropped when he looked down at what he saw: one coin, a bar of lapis lazuli, was a full season's work in Balfour. He'd only ever seen them a couple of times, when the reeve acted as money changer to them. The two jade pieces and the favor and stripes that accompanied it was enough half again as much. He would pocket it, and ponder a means of receipt to ensure keeping it safe from Tirlag.

The articles gathered from the vaults below Kainden had belonged to the man, and between this and the fact that he was not a lord of Ormond, but a Sourcerer and collector of the arcane and occult, the Faeth's interest was piqued.

Folk from far and wide and elsewhere attended. There was another Cait Shii there. This one with grey and tabby mottled fur and attended by Hyu'man foot servants and was referred to as 'the Duchess'. A Gnemedian envoy and his entourage also attended, wearing the tabard of the white stag, a symbol Adimus recognized from old tales he's been told as the blazon of the Erlking himself. He giddily wanted to ask if that were the case, but the unapproachable demeanor was enough answer for him, and everyone else seemed to share the sentiment. *Surely they were.*

The auction was beset with colorful hyu'mans as well. People in vibrant plaids from a dozen different clan's peoples, Toranti nobleman wearing white wigs and poet shirts and swallowtail coats, Shambayan Merchant Lords wearing turbans sporting bejeweled beards.

For whatever reason (perhaps because he had been recognized on sight earlier), Argent used the cloak to wear a different face today, one with which none were yet familiar, a rather snooty-looking mustachioed debonair-type persona.

Tirlag stylishly fanned herself with her signaling fan, wafting a new exotic perfume she'd bought and teasingly flaunting her new lacy bustier and all its contents for the blue-blooded congress; she herself were on sale to the highest bidder, it seemed. They both had moved on, Argent hardly staying seated, and when he did it wasn't in his seat, hopping from spot to spot gabbing insincerely to anyone who looked important.

Alfred grumbled about their lack of privacy.

They sat near the back, it was the least crowded there. There sat only two others: a man in a fuschia robe and a girl with short black hair reading a book.

"Good evening." The man began, during a lull in the host's proceedings. "I don't believe we've met." He invariably said before Alfred could even reply.

"Hello." Alfred gurgled, having to ungrit his teeth to do so.

"Reis Valkeir, a pleasure, surely." the man was unshaken. "Are you friends of Merris?"

"Were." the wizard replied.

"I see. He was always a bit abrasive." he stroked his beard. "Then, it's hard to believe we've not met then...are you from Paravoux?"

"Sorry. I was correcting you. You meant '<u>were</u> we friends of Merris?' Estate auction and all..." Alfred supposed it was a bit rude. "Apologies." he said with a sigh. "No, I never knew the man. We are simply here to purchase." Then he pointed toward the auctioneer, hoping it was enough to turn the man's head back to where it ought to be.

"Hello." The girl that sat beside him greeted, finally lifting her head from the heady tomb she was engrossed in. He gave an unusually warm smile to Alfred despite his impertinence. She glanced down at his hand then turned back around. "Forgive my uncle," she turned back around for a moment to Alfred's relief. "It's just that ring on your finger. Merris too carried such a band upon his." She explained, turning back around.

Alfred's brow raised against its will.

Alfred wore the ring worriedly nowadays--it provided him a measure of comfort, it seemed.

"Wait...Mister Valkeir? Adimus cut in.

The man turned. "Adi?!" His face melted to fondness, and he leapt to his feet. "My, look at you, you've become a man!" He gave a sturdy handshake that let his age show none. "That lime mane...you're a Watcher! Congratulations, congratulations! No wonder I didn't recognize you!"

"They know one another?" Argent twirled his mustache, addressing whomever would gossip.

By grace their loudness was met with derision from the rest of the assembly, allowing the withdrawal to not look so clumsy. "Nice seeing you."

Alfred too slinked back into his chair, perhaps wondering if he had just been the butt of a joke that apparently only they had gotten. Surely, after the whole of sitting through the proceedings he had started to wonder, if like the exchange with the man in front of him, if it all were a joke, some elaborate prank among the aristocracy with an eccentric punchline that somehow escaped him.

Old clothes. A collection of various small amateur wood carvings and paintings. Some copper and brass jewelry. A wardrobe full of frankly silly-looking hats. Dried tree leaves of various kinds. A bright yellow cloak. A waist-high translucent glass amphorae full of Hyu'man teeth. An old spyglass, astrolabe, a compass. Some old ornaments: statues, figurines, specimens in a bottle and other knick-knacks.

What was more, the bids were at one jade increments, an amount on par with a week's wage wage, ensuring that unless there was wide and mutual disinterest in the item in question Adimus couldn't afford any of it.

They watched as piece by piece the estate was sold. "You didn't find anything of interest?" The girl tried to hold a conversation when the auction concluded, speaking to anyone who would reply. They sat to the side in shame, watching the rich march row by row with their hauls.

"Too much." Adimus guffawed. He felt Argent's sharp elbow.

"Too much for too little." said Argent, twirling his illusory mustache in his fingers.

"The only 'too little' that statement shows is one's level education in Thaumaturgy and Sourcery." she eyed him. Argent cowered in spite of himself.The old man awkwardly stepped in. "So. Adimus. How is Luloch and Dyrshul?"

"Doing well, nowadays."

His attempt at being intentionally short had failed. The man looked at him judgingly. "Even with the...complexities of it all coming to light?"

Adimus's astonishment at the not only man's knowledge, but his candidness showed that he perhaps expected a little discretion, but the man afforded him none.

"How do you know about Dyrshul and Adimus?" Alfred came forward with the question. The Grigor's heart jumped.

"You mean "<u>what</u> do I know." the man mocked, then put a wry finger to his nose. They locked gazes for an unreasonable amount of time. "Enough." he said, then his face softened. "Enough to know that there's no need to worry. He's neither a Devil nor a Fae."

"Mister Valkeir, I wasn't being forthright. Grandfather's having dreams."

"Dreams? Like yours?"

Adimus lowered his head in reflective withdrawal. "No." he replied. "He dreams of ice and snow and wolves. And shadows so deep that no light touches them."Reis stared at him blankly, aloofly. "Sluagh Oiche, sir, the Night of the Shades." He felt the need to elaborate.

"That is on the calendar this year. Lots of strange astrological phenomena this year..."

"...Do you think you could help us?"

"Curious. We will surely have to talk of this over tea." was all he said. "So. Where will *you* be heading from here?"

"We're going to go find the..."

"Ale house." Tirlag kicked him in the back of the heel. "To drink away our memory of this farse."

"Actually..." the man stroked his beard glance back at the girl.

"Here." She came forward with a book.

"The costs were steep." she flippantly agreed. "But it was expected that the great Merris's name alone precluded affordability. But not without reason." she smiled. "I want you to have this, Alfred." she explained. "A consolation."

It was *Words Set in Stone: The Writings of the Ancients*. The auctioneer showcased the hefty tome earlier by showing some of its writings, full of elaborate pictograms and confusing cartouches.

He adjusted his glasses awkwardly. "I...I can't."

"I bought it for you. From one savant to another. I insist." she said. She fell in with the old man to leave, leaving it in his hands. "Should you wish to return it, find me." she shot a tiny smile, meant just for him. "Goodbye, Alfred."

Chapter 15
The Pledging

The wispy smell of pipe smoke, born of the nervous puffing of perusers and the heedless habits of contemplative codgers, permeated the walls of the Bowen Archives permanently.

It seemed to infect every page in every book of the great library. Adimus both hated and secretly loved this smell, that though it often bothered him with nausea and headaches on more trying days, it always reminded him of home.

Towering shelves spanned the cavernous split between the first and second floors, slanted and staggered to alot for the maximum sunlight for viewers from the great glass-domed ceiling both floors shared. There, basking in the sun, were neatly organized books and alcoved walls full of scrolls where many a private hutch and chair or longtable sat to be shared. But this was a facade: these were not the real archives.

All the writings that sat on the shelves were either copies of manuscripts stored elsewhere or public records of little importance. This was not the true Bowen Archives. That was in the wings, where neither sunlight nor smoke could damage what its precious pages held. The two walks into which the second floor was divided lead to wings of the building heretofore off limits to <u>most</u> visitors, but, thanks to the generous pulling of strings by Argent, there Alfred and Adimus meandered halls where none save the bards of Bowen and the cloistered monks of this place were invited to tread.

It was in one of these four wings that the Grigor stood, huffing, arms filled with heavy books and loose parchment and the burn of exhaustion.

Conversely, this place was filled with the smell of ink and crisp autumnal air (as fresh as a city's got).

Teams of scribes worked here. More commonly referenced manuscripts, ones often thumbed through by visitors (mainly law books) were produced on a series of dies much like a wax seal, but using ink, using a contraption Adimus had never seen before. There was an entire wing dedicated to this.

The large chamber in the eastern hall in which they now stood was very different. Here, the words of old were painstakingly transcribed by the monks of Dwyer.

The man behind the desk where they waited wore a green tailcoat that billowed and rocked in rhyme with the hanging unfurled scrolls that hung drying in rows behind him like the curtains of some royal reception hall, and as if the heavy glasses he wore weighed his head down too much to lift his chin, his eyes never lifted from the page as they approached.

"Excuse me." The faeth startled him. "Are you the head scribe?"

He gave a sudden lurch from the high chair upon which he sat, quickly adjusting the powdered wig that had jostled loose when he did. "...Master Juminion?"

"Yes?" the man blinked. "You were informed of my request for commission?"

He simply stood, smiling with the toothy grin of wooden teeth.

Alfred glanced back at the boy as if to validate to him the appropriateness of his reaction to the strangeness of the man's behavior.

The man furrowed his brow in offense. "Oh come now, friend. It's not been that long has it?"

"Beg pardon?"

"It's me! Marius!" he asserted, by Alfred had nothing but a blank stare to give him. "I was an apprentice when last we met." he added.

Alfred, and in true fashion with everything Adimus knew about Alfred Juminion, replied. "I wish...a reproduction be made of these."

"What are you building this time, eh?"

Finally, given no other choice, he engaged. "I feel you have mistaken me for someone else, good sir." he straightened his garb awkwardly. "Now, I have the pages marked in this one, to here. I shall need these bound as a separate volume. Simple cord binding will do. And these I need on vellum."

"Very well, sir." The man looked put out.

Adimus looked down at a few of them as he handed them over. "*Thaumaturgy and the Great Work. Scholomanca's Libram: A Compilation of Practical Gladr. Imps and Foci, Volume II.*" he wondered at them.

"...Do you know what those mean?" The Seer asked, looking sideways at him.

"I hate to admit, I haven't the foggiest."

"So tell me..." Alfred started, adjusting his glasses. "This Reis fellow. How does your family know him?"

"I never really was sure." The Grigor admitted with a shrug. "He's some kind of lord or something. I was told not to mention anything about him to anyone at the time."

"Hmm."

There was a long silence. "What *are* these books about?" was what Adimus decided to break it.

"You'll find out soon enough. " the man answered. "<u>If</u> you are to travel with us you must grow your skill. Anything that you can add to your repertoire to help the company ought to be made available. You may read these at your leisure and absorb what you can, then, when you are ready, you can begin learning."

"...Thank you for the offer." was all he said.

"You do have a rudimentary knowledge of the concepts, I take it. Like the seven cycles of the Great Work? The difference between Incantations and Invocations and the like?"

"I can't say I have."

"Well, you have to start somewhere." he tried to sound cheerful.

He faced forward. "But surely if you are a friend to Mister Valkeir and that girl you overheard something."

Adimus sensed the transparency of his motives, still he answered honestly. "I don't remember much. I mean, he had a library full of books, and would appear to study such things, and grandpa would talk to him about the faeries and about Magic, but never anything I could understand and with no manner of technical expertise that I was witness to. And that Charleze girl wasn't around when I was there!"

Alfred recoiled; he hadn't expected it to come out as if he were defending himself from an accusation, but prodded on. "She wasn't?"

Adimus reinforced it with the shake of his head. Alfred looked more and puzzled as the conversation went wrong. "Master Faeth." he addressed. "What is your concern with them?"

"You'll call me Al." he demanded, and was right back to the subject. "...Do you not think I should be?"

"They always seemed like nice people to me. Charleze even bought you that book."

"Sure enough. But it doesn't dispel my upset in the slightest." A look of dread and concern fell upon his face.

"What do you mean?"

He produced the book from his satchel to the confused boy, and inside showed him the pages, within a notation had been made.

"*When you're ready Alfred, let us meet, at 21 Midnight street.*"

Adimus expected some manner of suspicion from the Seer. Some missed detail that might reveal some truth they had somehow divined the nature of their mission. That they had been found out. Some story regarding a ghost from his past, but when he spoke the phrase he would be embarrassed that he had missed it entirely, and even more disconcerted by it.

"Adimus, I never gave them my name."

"...That's odd." He said.

"Very. But what is more odd is you."

"Come again?" Adimus tried to hide his concern.

"Well. I must know my pupil. I want you to tell me your story."

"You are a Seer, you seem to know much about me as it is. It is why you brought me along."

"I want to hear it from your mouth." he replied. "Knowing facts is one thing, understanding them is another. Now, please." It came out in a demanding tone, one that Adimus felt implored to address.

Adimus took a deep sigh, and began.

Adimus had been party to a secret that his family kept for many years, one that ever since the time when he'd been brought into the family seven years ago he'd been sworn never to mention. This truth, even to Laina, he had not spoken, whom even he knew would never tell.

It always sounded strange to his ears calling Bearach 'father' or 'pa' even, but he'd had to do so to keep up appearances; even Luloch's own brother wasn't in on the secrets they all shared. It was a lie so intimate and integral to the family that it held more detail that even the truth, meticulously crafted to be found inscrutable by even the likes of Tolten and the reeve: it took three years to construct, and even involved traveling cross-country to stay in Ederton under the pretense that Bearach had been offered a job by the constabulary of the city.

Anwell, like the rest of the village, had been told this story on many occasions; that Adimus had come to them as the son from a young widow's previous marriage. Bearach had fallen in love with the woman, with her golden brown hair and her eyes blue and crisp like a chilly spring frost. They'd met over the High Bridge, Bearach saving her from a shambayan pickpocket; the previous husband had died of the Thanic Plague, of course, and once she and Bearach were wed, she too fortuitously died giving birth to Dyrshul. She'd grown up in Ormond, and her father, a trader and redsmith, had come all the way up to Ederton in the Daldista Highlands to serve the great Merchant Lords of the north, and she'd wound up their indentured servant (this added a xenophobic flair to the story).

Their exchanges were well documented in Bearach's mind and could be recounted ad nauseam if need be--the story was well constructed, which had always given the boy a measure of relief, as both Adimus and Dyrshul's real past was much stranger, and far less believable than *any* lie. They had planned to make a life together, until, that is, she had died in labor giving birth to Dyrshul. He did give a good with encouragement from Luloch, stays a couple years(this part allotted for Dyrshul's age, which actually still appears a little too young in the account) but alas, unable to bare the weight of his post and haunted by his memories of the place he returned to Balfour with the two kids in tow.

In truth, Adimus had no past to speak of that he could recall, the words forced from his mouth by this Cadifor was the harsh truth. His earliest memory is standing in that grove, Dyrshul in his arms. This was the unbelievable truth, the dangerous truth. Adimus and Luloch and Bearach, with the help of the man they had met at the auction, spent years pouring through books, trying to glean what they could of the mystic ways of the fae from the huge library in his possession, the nature of the Otherworld, and many other avenues of learning, any of which that might shed light on the experience. All they found were stories of changelings, or accounts of people being spirited away to the land of the faeries but who remembered everything still. This all, The Watcher told the man, who replied with but contemplative silence.

* * * * *

The rooms overlooking the main thoroughfare would overfill in the coming days in preparation for the Pledger's Rite, where the lords of Ormond and the Daldista Vale would recognize the valor and diligence of their champions who, year after year, embark on the sacred hunt for the Spear, Alfred and all among them.

The first of them came in a parade of veiled wagons, their shining buckled boots made only to touch the cobbled stonework landing of the great hall as not to get soiled. "It was a different kind of costume party than Allhallows, where the monsters disguise themselves as people instead." Argent explained.

Draping mink-fur trimmed cloaks hid ornate vambraces tucked in velvet sleeves. Men wore full war regalia, clad in polished armor, fitted and filigreed. Women wore garish hats and pleated corsets with skirts like circus tents.

Adimus hunched in his chair, hoping not to be seen. Alfred had told him that had they 'a little more liquid assets' (money) they would very much have liked to buy him new garb for the affair. Adimus thought little of the prospect overall, having to wear tailored clothing, but now realized that he brought more attention to himself without it; the boy's clothes–for all the sense of awe it inspired in Balfour, was tattered rags before this assembly.

"William Mathune! My boy!" the earl of Tavishire addressed the bard giving him an embrace. "How's the road fair for thee, Whispermonger? Prince Souteneur is hounding me about that cloak! No pun intended, haha. Says if you don't have it back by Midsummer he'll never introduce you to that Duchess. You know, the pretty one from the banquet in Malstat?" from the first time Argent was speechless, the tension was palpable.

"I...am far from unwell, uncle Horus." The man's name came out a confession. Adimus was surprised that Tirlag's gaze could not literally bore through the back of the bard's head when the man said it.

Horus perked up proudly. "Getting along, getting along. He, uh." The man drew closer to him. "He got to meet with the Tala."

"Truly?" Argent stroked his goatee.

"The man nodded. "The sanziana have sent him back, with a message for one of our dignitaries. I await the news."

The bard quickly and quietly muttered something in Old Daldistan language again. Whatever it was Horus fell silent.

Adimus sat beside Tirlag, who held her jaw so tight he thought he could hear teeth cracking--either that or it was her knuckles. "Mathune...!" She growled.

They themselves were preparing for a banquet, having been run out of the common room to make way for large tables and many chairs, silverware and porcelain dinner plates. Soon they allowed the people arrayed outside to pour in, and hors d'oeuvres for those uncouth enough to take them begin to sill from the kitchens: deviled eggs and heavily salted and cured meats, fried or pickled sweetbreads and haggis served on wafers made from broomcorn. Colorful vegetables steamed in the heat of their own juices and served from large ash-encrusted pumpkins, treasures dug up from the ceremonial bonfire that took place earlier that evening, privy to the dancing and singing and the discreet drinking of less sophisticated drinks—an event far more full of life and telling that the boy and the crew had apparently missed.

People had begun taking up seats informally. Adimus played a seating game, trying to find the meridian between not sitting so close to Krasad as to make him look bad while sitting just close enough that he might be mistaken for a part of his foreign entourage, while also trying to stay away from Argent, who hobb-knobbed and carried on with the south's Great Clans like it was just another picnic and Alfred, whom the nobles would invariably address at some point in the night since that was the whole point of them being there. This put him fittingly between Laina and Tirlag.

Adimus hung his hat of the prim and proper nonsense early in the evening, giving in to stuffing his face with these exotic things he'd probably never see again. He had plenty of company at least, as more than once the crew snagged Delaney to tell them exactly which of the dishes they sampled that she could lift from the kitchen to bring to them directly, or better yet, lift out the back for the journey later.

Then unceremoniously the main courses were served alongside the rest: rotisserie cooked Maritian Veldtfowl prepared with thyme, lemongrass and staghorn sumac. Tomatos florentine, served with toasted sourdough. Cold Joun Vene, a sparkling white wine, served with Mont Pangor cheese--the boy understood both to be rare, from a specific vineyards and pastures on specific hills belonging to specific families in specific counties of Torant.

Adimus glanced over at Alara, angry that he hadn't thought about her until now--she had an empty chair in every direction around her. He thought to go sit with her to keep her company if it wouldn't cause too much of a scene, and suddenly became uncomfortably self aware, not only of the prejudice and resulted in the empty table, but the social pressure that ensured its continuance. There was nothing he could do about it, after all, nor was he solely accountable. He hadn't been called upon, nor had anyone else volunteered. Besides, she was Fae Kind, by axiom to not be trusted. He didn't want to draw attention to himself anyway, or, perhaps most regrettably, implicate affiliation with her for fear that it would tarnish the rapport they'd set out to build; he'd never given thought about how the faceless glances of dispassionate strangers could stifle simple decency so.

"How is the food here, Baron?" Horus asked Torrin.

"Just like back home." he replied.

"I guess there's no salt there either. " Tirlag nudged Adimus with her elbow. It was slathered in sarcasm by its tone, but still was a little too loud for Adimus's comfort, and Alfred, as the subsequent sound of his boot colliding with her shin under the table would inform her.

She'd had Delaney snag the malt vinegar from the kitchen, which she poured over most every dish she ate until anyone facing her was forced to contend with a roiling pungent fume. He would think it a tactic of hers to avoid having to feign niceties, would had he not seen her realize this and desperately attempt countermeasures against it (in vain), noshing on spearmint and dousing herself with her perfume after the meal when no one was looking.

"All of this meal comes from the homeland." The fiery haired bearded man across from him bade. "This is a meal of the Daldistans, of our ancestors. Of course it is familiar, we are, after all, of the same blood."

He was from a clan known as Casey. Bevin was his name.

"...I never noticed until now! You are Mansii. Fascinating!" another of them said.

He sat at Alfred's left side, much to the Sum Seer's dismay, as Adimus had learned he was of the clan Alfred despised.

Argent introduced them "Laina, this is Lord Ross of Ward. The Ward clan is heralded as purveyors and protectors of the ancient lore of the Cessair, those who had lived in the mountains in ages past, and a grand master of the Southlander religion."

"Oh really?" she sounded ecstatic. "It is a pleasure to meet you."

"Likewise, my dear. And keeper and curator of the Cache of Kainden." He added at the end. "Let's not forget that." It suddenly added a formal subtext to the affair. They'd thought the conversation to be over, then she said "I have come to learn much of your culture as well, staying here.

"That is good."

"Actually, Lord Ward, I have a curious question."

"Regarding...?"

"The Formerians." he answered.

Argent's eyes widened, and he hid worry with a napkin, feigning embarrassment at a full mouth.

"Really? Such an interesting subject. And an elusive one. It even stumps us some time." he paused for a few moments. "Well, go on."

"Mister Ward, how is it that your god Many Shapes made Formerians to fight against the Formorians? Which of the two came first?"

"Apologies." Argent began to intercede, but Ross dismissed him with the wave of a hand.

"My, no." Ross wiped his mouth. "It is a very good one. Very observant." he glanced about, reading the room. He drew near. "It is an esoteric truth, and one I do not wish to bore our company to sleep with at the dinner table. I will expound upon it later on, surely. I'll ensure you learn its way." he smiled. "Tell me, my dear," he said after a few more moments. "Is it true that the Mansii memorize all of their history instead of keeping it in writing?" he said after taking a rehearsed bite as to add pacing to his transparent apple-polishing.

"That is not quite the case." she politely explained. "We are not like the Tuatha, who commit word for word to memory. But we do have an oral tradition, some common shared stories."

"You do not have them set in verse? Interesting."

"It is."

"I would bet." He mulled over the prospect over the next few bites. "Tell me. How do your people ensure that the facts don't change?"

"What do you mean?"

"Like the Whisper Game." he said. She looked confused. He gave an assuring smile. "Always a charming, if quant, activity that pops up at these gatherings. One speaks a phrase into the ear of another, and he to another, and so on, until the last person professes to the first what was said."

"You mean to say 'how do we judge the fidelity of the stories we tell against the ones our ancestors told?'"

"Precisely." Ross nodded.

"We don't." She said proudly, she gave him a few moments to let it sink in. "I have been told that in these lands this detail makes my religion somehow lesser to yours. Are you meaning to say that this is not the case? That your faith is not much the same? Is that not why the inconsistencies persist?"

"Why, not at all." He replied. She raised a skeptic brow, but his bluster remained unassailable and steadfast. "Quite the contrary. As I have said, Lady Laina. I shall this explain later."

Argent glowered at the priestess at her clear misstep. Adimus now wished he'd chosen to move.

"She is a Mansii witch." Weylan Pembroke chortled. "Whatever it is, we'd better deliver or her heathen gods will curse us. Fictitious gods or no." Said Weylan Pembroke.

"So, what is it you will be Pledging for this night, my dear?" Ross said though, seemingly unbothered.

Tirlag on the other hand, was unflappable, and even a bit amused by the sight, she leaned over Adimus's lap, reeking of vinegar, to whisper in Laina's ear. "You've found our 'in'! Threaten them into giving us a better deal."

Ross Ward chimed in "Heathen? Bigotous hogwash! There is no such thing. She follows a god of conscience, same as we, I am sure. Not the woeful Devils of these backwards hillfolk." It was obviously a jab at him concealed by gracious ignorance. "That's who you should watch out for."

"Speak what you will of the Mansii gods, Sir Ward, but do not speak ill of the Formerians, lest they hear you." Said his uncle, Thadeus Pembrooke.

"Yes, Lord Ross, I beg of you, forgive my cousin's ignorance or you invite ill-tidings over these proceedings." Said Gavin.

Ross gave a sigh. "And so that it was in the days of old that fear ruled over us. Sacrifices were necessary in those days. The folk worshiped the Devils, who clamored for blood sacrifice. That is All'Khemy speaking, child, as it is written in the Great Works that change cannot occur of itself; it must be moved from the outside." he was talking to Alfred, who hid his sneer with a drink of wine. "And as such the gods in those days were moved by blood. This was the way of the world, that boons were withheld. Crops would not grow, nor livestock give new young without such due recompense. Illness ran rampant, and death would come without giving back, would such sacrifices not be made. But that is not the way of the Ollatharii who cleansed this world. Now all of this is freely given us. We were given the Bolg to teach us the secrets of the gods, medicine to heal sickness, how to grow crops ourselves, and raise the sheep. The Partholonian gods are moved by deeds. Deeds of selflessness, deeds in faith, deeds of sacrifice not of others but of self. Those who do are granted Graces. They are gods of conscience, and of free will, and, as Cadifor can attest, their rewards are great. This 'Crom Cruach' as they call him is one such god, should they see it. Not a god to be feared, but revered."

"Ha, yes. We've little left of such traditions, save for this feast." said Bevin Casey. "A last supper for these adventurers, a lord's feast to pay respects for these brave souls, few of whom will return." he looked at the myriad folk of his table and rose, along with his glass. "To the brave Pledgers of this year's Huntingtide. May you bring glory to us all."

Adimus almost choked. He'd never thought much about it. The wild untamed frontiers was often the aim of these crusades, where beasts he'd only ever heard of in fables or campfire tales might lurk. Beasts just like the Barghest or the Bugbear--and those were ones they'd encountered here at home. He shot a glance to Laina, who was sitting closest. She seemed unconcerned.

"It is so in my faith as well," she continued with the conversation. "We live by the Graces of the gods! We in Shambaya simply call this The Law. You do not speak like other Southlanders, Ross of Ward."

"That is the answer to your question, Lady Laina. 'How', you ask? One has always wondered such a thing. Several of my peers are of the opinion that it is a narrative device, an homage if you will, that marks the Formerians as being equal to the new gods, and beholden by the new covenant."

"And what do you say?"

"Saying such things undermines the literality of the subject; as a practitioner of this faith and not just a scholar I must protest. These gods of fear and reverence aren't just figurative. Me? I know the truth."

"What is it, then?"

He glanced around, at what Laina would have to assume was at his present company. "The spear you search for? Its truth is his truth." He gave her a courteous nod. "As I say, I must divulge it at another time. We will speak again soon." he assured her.
"Except maybe with the eloquence and penchant for deception befitting a man of your influence." Alfred raised a glass to him.

"I-I do not know, master Faeth, what I have said or done to offend, but I wish you well on your adventure and luck on your Pledging." he raised a glass to him as well, before swiftly returning to carousing.

"So my dear, let's return to the more civil conversation. Why are you here?"

"Oh, I'm with him." She admitted, apparently regrettably.

"What is his goal for the pledge?"

Alfred feigned not listening at first, until Argent whispered to him, forcing himself into the conversation, finally, when he realized all the eyes were upon him. "Access to the Cache of Kainden." he said.

"What for?"

Argent covered for him. "Full access. Our choice of the riches contained therein."

"I wasn't aware you were in their company as well, master bard. I'm sure you'll be indispensable in that regard." He who'd been known as Argent just moments ago almost choked on his food.

"Why, with your education, William," he used the name with deliberate enunciation "you'd have your pick of the litter." Alfred seemed unphased. "Well." Ross said after a moment. "You know Ward is charged with the curation of the relics of the vault." he said nonchalantly, picking at his food. "We would be the final arbiter in their relinquishment."

All the eyes of the Endeavor were on him, save Alfred, who unreadably paused, politely dabbing his mouth as if, like he always seemed to, he somehow knew what was to come next.

"What, praytell, do you and your friends here have your eye on that would be worth more than Kainspear itself and the kingship over all the Southlands besides?" No one answered. "No matter." Ross said. "Whatever it is, I'm sure it can be more than arranged. If you so wish it, Clan Ward gives you their endorsement."

Alfred got up from the table. "Excuse me." and left. He didn't return until well after the last plate had been taken up.

"That was rude." Laina lashed at him.

"And you are gullible. His niceties are not literal either. He appeals to you to get to me, that's all."

"If this is what you think." she shrugged--Alfred didn't have to be a great seer to read her frustration.

It had been hours and Argent had just disappeared. As the evening after the banquet dragged on the hall was cleared by the servants to allow a reception area, the tables pushed to the walls and covered in drinks and desserts.

Adimus watched as they all, women included, took part in a throwing contest, hurling curled hatchets at what appeared to be a replica of some great throne with a bird on it, trying their best to hit the head. He sat intently and watched at a table near Pembroke and company.

"'Tis a shame, cousin, that your sire chooses that knave over you as his personal guard." they were jeering at Caleb. "Being a retainer to an Immortal seems like an awfully easy job."

"He's a competent one though, I've heard." said Ambrose. "It's a job of skill and prestige, not lightly assigned. And I've heard he is peerless in combat."

"He wouldn't survive a scrap with a real Southlander." Said Weylan, "Him *or* that mongrel blade of his."

"Fancy a drink sir?" Delaney asked with a curtsy, holding a serving tray.

"...A splinter-laden old tankard of ale served on a silver platter? Fits this place's notions of nobility quite fairly, don't you think?" Torrin said to Alara. They'd decided to come and stand by the boy, for familiarity's sake, he supposed.

"That one offered me sheep." The merchant lord smirked for just a moment before hiding his face with embarrassment; one could tell he'd had a few of those tankards himself.

"How about you, pipsqueak?" The urisk jeered at Adimus, but before he could reply a rogue hand snatched it.

Tirlag banged the mug down on the platter. "Well?" She said, wiping her mouth on the perfumed handkerchief she'd carried about all night, flirtatiously wafting at every man's nose that evening.

Delaney wore a children's dress they'd bought at a tailor down the street just that evening. She (tellingly) blended in well with the nobles' brownie serving staff, but he didn't need the mystic insight of a gnemedian to know she was still seething about the whole thing.

Adimus had learned much through his extrapolation of the evening. Casey and Bran were disenfranchised, no longer officially clans, but invited anyway. Dwyer was the law-makers and record-keepers of the clans, though nowadays more concerned with charters and trade, having absorbed the duties of the two aforementioned clans, horse breeders and scribes respectively.

If Dywer was the writer of the laws, Pembroke was its enforcer, discharging the executive duties of the governing body to the counties and collecting, (that's actually what Thadeus was doing in Balfour, his yearly round in the village just so happening to correlate with his favorite holiday).

Dougall, of course, was in charge of Ormond's military in regards to foreign threat--if there were any one person Adimus himself wished to appeal to, it was him. He thought about approaching Cadifor, but he would have rather fought the Barghest again.

"One from the guest audience is demanding lordship and land." The little spy said.

"What of it...are they getting it!?" Torrin cried.

"Lordship?" Tirlag grinned to herself, nodding in agreement with the musings in her head. "I was expecting gold and jewels but I could make due with becoming a dame over my own...small village. Province. Principality." She giggled, playfully batting the handkerchief in the boy's nose.

They all jumped at Alfred's voice. "Why stop there? Why not take the Named Spear for yourself and become the new queen?" he was obviously joking but the twinkle in Tirlag's eyes showed that she really didn't get it.

Alfred walked over to a brandy glass lying on a table. He picked it up. "Clan Collins promises 5000 pieces of jade." Alfred told Torrin.

"For Gae Bolg? The Spear of Fate? Grown by a god and wielded by The Nameless Boy?"

"Pittance!" Tirlag hooted. She may have been drunk.

"Still, that's not bad right?" said Adimus. "It's enough for all of us to buy farms and live the rest of our lives in peace."

"Farms!? Keep your peace, farmboy, and I'll keep mine: a piece of the world, that is, harhar!" In fact Adimus was sure of it now.

"Here," said Alfred, placing the glass on the platter. "Go and collect the others."

"You're not the boss of me!" she said, then he noticed eyes on her. "Yes, milord." Adimus had never seen an angry curtsy before.

Eventually Delaney returned with the glasses.

Alfred picked up another glass with his bare hands and looked at it.

It was the first time Adimus noticed that he hadn't been wearing his gloves at all this evening.

Alfred chuckled, a joke he kept all to himself. He glanced over his shoulder at a nobleman wearing a cloak, who waved. A few moments elapsed. "Pembroke offers us ownership of Balfour." he said matter of factly.

Torrin groaned. He glanced down at the boy "No offense."

As he grabbed the next one, then the next one though Adimus watched his smile dissolve into an unreadable soberness that did not return that evening.

Before too long a small crowd had amassed outside the iron gate. The boy thought at first to alert the servants to let them in, but it was made obvious that their presence had been acknowledged.

It wasn't until the echoing toll of the Bells of Bowen rang through the streets that the gates were pulled. There was a marked change in the air of the room then, and in these moments the servants brought each of the nobility a bundle of sashes bearing the mark and color of their respective houses, and they all gathered to this side or that to clear and make way for these strange new attendees, while a pair of Gnemedian ushers guided them in.

Some were dressed in mere peasants garb, others wore more lordly fair. They held gleaming arms, the only he'd seen here tonight besides Gram, which apparently never left Cadifor's side.

Adimus didn't realize until this moment that he had been an honored guest here all along, as were the others, and would've been barred from the festivities just like these ones until this moment when the first of them stepped forward and began speaking their pledge; *maybe Argent had been useful after all.*

"The Black Brigand you may call me, for as the Ancient One you will know not my True Name." The black Cait Shii eyed them sternly. "Mine is to treat with House Dwyer in hopes of finding a cure for my sister, upon whom has befallen a great affliction. I boast many skills, not the least of which is tracking and survival in these wilds..."

There was a moment of silence. "It has been many years since a Fae offered themselves to the pledge.", spoke Therissa Dwyer, who had only just finished adjusting her large powdered wig after their name had been mentioned when all of their eyes fell upon her. "The Spear of Fate is a relic of your kin, and if this realm sees fit for it to be found by any among you it by all graces should be you." several scoffed in protest at the notion, she continued nonetheless. "We of Clan Dwyer therefore accept your pledge, and henceforth provide our blessings in this most sacred task. May the virtue of the kings of old guide your feet." A servant presented him with a sash of green and gold, which he tied around his waist before them before joining the throng.

Adimus turned at a whisper to see Argent, again seemingly appearing out of nowhere.

"We've little time to negotiate, I'll need an answer now." He said to the concerned wizard.

"None of them offer what I want."

"Then perhaps consider, if I may be so bold, what the company wants."

He sighed and shook his head, conflicted. He looked up at him after a moment "What would you have me do? Besides handing it over to your family?"

William lowered his head. Alfred sat the bard's beer stein before him for emphasis. William redoubled. "Swear to McDougall."

"What kind of game are you playing? What manner of threat or leverage does his clan have on yours?"

"None. I swear it."

Alfred glared deeply at him--Adimus imagined he wished people were as easy to Read as objects.

"What of yours?"

"What has my own family to offer me that I don't already have?" He shrugged.

"Why should I believe anything you say?"

William pursed his lips, and for the very first time that the boy had seen, he had nothing to say.

Malkin of Bran, another of the nobles houses, along with Oinde from the other day, and a crow which perched gently upon his shoulder. His clothes, bright yellow enshrined in black, matched the feathered chapeau he wore, which he did not graciously remove like everyone else gathered. "To return honor to my family. I pledge to mine own name." was all he said. He did not mingle, but left with his companion so a pale horse soon after he spoke.

"Your indecisiveness is going to lead us into ruin. We'll end up with nothing. Strike now, Sum Seer." William warned. "At whatsoever you choose."

"Caleb Knolls, Ederton. Servant of the Sword. " Adimus recognized him as the man who stood with Cadifor when they first met, the one the Pembroke's had mentioned. Argent shook his head and threw up his arms. " I will claim the Spear to honor the memory of my master, Aritoshi Tetsuyo of the Veiled Lands," the warrior said. "and bring glory to his name by spreading the teachings of his way of life. My blade, Caladbolg, has felled many foes, and was given to me by he." He drew the strange-looking blade and kneeled, prostrating himself, holding it up as if giving it in offering-- Adi could hear the cousins snicker. "Smithing was my trade before he came, and I vow to learn the secrets of its craftsmanship, that our new nation--and its new liege shall prosper. It shall serve the House of Dougall well." It only took Cadifor's nod for them to acknowledge him, and his men presented him with a sash of white and red.

William threw up his hands. Sweat started to bead on the Sum Seer's forehead.

The next adventurer came, and. clan Mathune answered. "We will give you all the land from Adaire to Balfour to share amongst yourselves." Said Horus.

"They do offer land!" Tirlag whispered, before being stifled again by Alfred for a second time this evening.

They each spoke some variation of this: Beaumont and his company Chancey Coalfax, All'Khemist and noble in his own right and The Stalker, a Sanziana, a being with strange angular features not unlike those of a Hyu'man save for long, pointed ears and a strange head wrap. They wished for lordship and land (and must have been of whom they'd spoken when Delaney had eavesdropped). "I shall give you the king's portion of the Cache of Kainden, as in within our power, with your choice of the possessions therein." Clan Ward answered. Alfred could feel Ross's eyes in him the entire transaction.

Eastward Endeavor all turned and looked at Argent when he motioned rather frantically, and with an inquisitive look cut his way back through the throng as another stern upright gentleman stood before the assembly and gave his graces. They would be next. "What did you decide?" he huffed, finally getting within whispering distance.

"We will not be the champion of Ross Ward." Alfred sternly said.

"-But he offered everything you want! Access to the cache! The King-" he lowered his voice when the Faeth's eyes fell on him. "The Kingstone." he finished in a whispering whimper.

It was just then the ushers appeared, and before the boy could reason what was happening all of them were standing before the assembly.

Alfred spoke. "We abjure from favoritism or favor from any clan." The crowd gasped, so loudly he had to wait until it died to continue, "We choose to embark on our own."

It hadn't gone over well. The wizard adjusted his glasses and took a breath.

"What is the meaning of this?" One bellowed.

Argent quickly stepped in before him, though not sparing a dejected glance at his difficult business partner "Words are useless." Adimus wasn't sure if he were making it better or worse.

"What we seek…" he masked his loss of words with dramatic pause and sweeping gesture "Is the restoration of this kingdom. To see the days of a true king rule with dignity and justice not seen since the days of Mathendon." They all looked at each other. "What we do is the simplest of favors: we shall allow this. It will be the actions of lesser or greater men that come after that which shall bless or doom this country. I therefore place this task in your hands. We pledge to find the Spear of Fate, and wear no colors in so doing." He explained. "And perhaps, as Sir Ward so eloquently put it, we shall seek the rewards for us that mere mortals shall not give." he looked at him to show sincerity, however feigned. "May therefore our Endeavor be our offering, that in the spirit of Kian the *true* colors and caliber of this worthy kingdom be shown. And be blessed by the gods in so doing, if only in so you will then open your hearts to us thereby. "

It left a stale silence in the air, that as they made their prompt retreat from the sight seemed to linger like a darkness. When they'd made it out of earshot. "What was that?!"

Alfred let him fume for a few moments, loosing the straps on one of Torrin's horses. "You were right in your speech: none were worthy. All of them pandered, all of them feigned."

"What is this? Suddenly now you're concerned with this? I could've told you these things before, and spared you the targets on our backs! Ross had *everything* you wanted and more!"

"I'm sorry, Torrin." He was now ignoring the bard. He was putting a saddle on the steed.

"…<u>This</u> is the place you leave me? I think I'd rather go home."

"It had to be done Torrin. I hope you understand. As he said, 'words are useless'. We'll show them the Spear first. "

"Then you'll get what *you* want?" Torrin didn't sound happy. "What about me, Sum Seer? Eh? What about what I want?" It was the first time the Merchant Lord had used that tone with him.

Tirlag nonchalantly sidled out of the wagon with the cage under her arm, shooting a knowing grin to Delaney when amidst the chaos no one protested.

He climbed onto the horse. "It is all just a bunch of silly games, isn't it?" he replied after a moment. "Out there, as well as in here. You knew there was a risk of gaining absolutely nothing from this when you got involved. The hunt for the Spear is a fool's errand, it's alway been said. You should worry about whether it can be found, or even if it *actually exists* at all, foremost, and this is your point of contention?" He answered.

"But I know it exists--we know it exists!" Torrin replied.

Torrin had not much to say after that, and neither did Alfred in return, besides a formal goodbye to him, and soon after they were abruptly on the road again.

"Alara, remember your promise to me. Remember, and do what must be done should it come to it." Was all he said, which was replied with Alfred's rueful glance.

* * * * *

"You know, I saved our hide back there." Argent finally broke the silence, pacing his horse up beside the Seer.

He never made eye contact. "I know. And you did a tremendous job using that cloak. I saw you trying to start a bidding war on our behalf."

"You as well, master Seer. I expected you to notice no less."

Alfred smiled. "No doubt you believe it. You even went so far as to narrate into your wine glasses." He chuckled. "In all seriousness." he continued after a moment. "You have paid for your services, bard of Bowen."

"That's the nicest thing you've ever said to me." He mused. "I am suspicious."

"Pandering and feigning." Delaney heckled.

"I..." He stopped his horse. "I've let my personal desires jeopardize the adventure. I forfeit my position as arbiter in the Company's affairs, and should you choose to disband I will absolve you all of your contracts."

Tirlag's horse veered past them. Alara's wheeled around her. Tirlag hid her gesture with a mirthful smile.

"We are all heading the same direction. Let us adjourn and discuss later. After we are safe." Said the Cait Shii.

In the midnight hush they passed through the city. The chilling cold whipped in the hollowed tunnel of a road beneath the jetted buildings, lit by glass-covered lamps, disturbed only enough to cast unnerving shadows as they wound the quiet streets. Adimus had expected them to be stopped, if only by the gatekeeper on the way out of the city, but they were given only pleasant goodbyes.

Chapter 16
Reflections

The Watcher had not slept. Neither had Alfred. In the early hours of the morning before anyone awoke and before the sun came he'd found himself looking over at the wizard, still sitting up in thought, his eyes baggy with fret and exhaustion, and seeing he too was awake in the wee hours a simple sideways glance he beckoned "Follow me."

Even without sleep the Faeth moved inexorably, unwaveringly, as if drawn by some compulsion beyond his control, and Adimus followed him, stumbling in the darkness. It was well an hour's walk away from where they'd slept, when they'd come to the old orphanage. It was occupied now, sold as a manor house, rebuilt with a resplendent pillared porch and painted violet and gold. The Seer's head drooped in despair when he saw it.

"I'm sorry." Adimus empathized on seeing it.

"Clan Bran. Might have known." Alfred observed the raven crest on the door. "I should've hoped to see it again."

"Maybe he knows of this Mister Riverstone you spoke of. We could ask them." He normally wouldn't be so bold as to place himself in direct social interactions, and with a noble no less, but with Alfred's concern for him he felt the call of needed reciprocity.

The Seer knew what a sacrifice it was, kindred introvert he was. "Very thoughtful, but no. It was just an afterthought, not really why I came." He backed away a few steps, and sidling behind one of the stone gate posts and ensuring the coast was clear he began to walk the property line.

"Master Faeth, pardon my questioning, but, what <u>are</u> we doing?" He was given no answer, and he dared not speak louder. Lights shown within the window of the bottom floor, and silhouettes of people dining. "A wooden fence once sat here." It was now a sturdy stone one. After a few moments of searching the man lent down to it, one of the wood planks, thrown over the hill and buried in greenery now. He solemnly put his hand on it, hiding sentiments as wiping sweat with his sleeve, and perhaps tears with the adjusting of his glasses. "Come." After a silent moment they continued. They came to a small gully that trailed down the hill. "Here." The wizard said confidently, and in the fading light they trekked down. Clingy moss and sticky brush made the going an ordeal. When they were finally at the bottom, there beside a trickling brook sat the bones of an old quaint house.

Moss clung to its caving roof, and its porch sat kiltered from its wavering foundation. Hesitantly he crept up, for though it was unquestionably abandoned, even still the wizard shown a strange hesitancy, as if sneaking up on some wild thing. Slowly he pushed to half-open door and gazed in, and his expression softened to morose self-reflection, "No...I thought not." He muttered to himself when he realized it so.

Adimus followed. In the hush the dust stirred, and through the dirt-smeared glass the evening light illuminated the living room. "This is where I learned." He said, half to himself. He strode in, touching the desk. He wandered into the study. There sat a bookshelf. He touched the empty spots where the books sat.

He looked at him fondly. "Teacher was a demanding one, but the fruits were many."

"What was his name?" Adimus inquired.

"Just that. Teacher. He never gave me his real name."

"Was he Fae?" the boy asked.

"No, and that is a misconception, as I understand it." he seemed flustered at the question, as if it were certainly not his first time answering it, no softened his voice at the end. "Mr. Riverstone was Tuathan," he explained "and did not have a mystical sounding title instead of a name." Finally, he shrugged. "Furthermore, you don't remember your parent's names, do you? It was well enough; it would've been replaced as easily with 'father' or the like. I was a child."

"I don't even remember my parent's faces…" Adimus tried to relate.

Alfred, sat down in the creaky chair and cradling his fingers in thought. He eyes the boy soberly, "My parents, Adimus, were killed. At the hands of Clan Ward."

"That's horrible." Adimus gasped.

"Again, I was young. Too young to remember much of it." He explained. "And I turned out well enough, thanks to Teacher." But he drew near. "It is only the years with them of which I was robbed that I lament." He rocked in his chair, put out by the squeaking noise it now made. Adimus said nothing. Alfred elaborated. "Surely, you know what I mean more than most. No matter how sweet those fruits, I would trade it all for those days that Ross Ward and his men have robbed of me." Now he was silent.

"I wouldn't." Said Adimus.

What if I could trade my dreams for reality?

Adimus leaned forward, eyes vagrant with contemplation on his words. Alfred obviously hadn't expected the boy to have thought it through so thoroughly, but of course he had. "I know my mother and father only through my dreams, Alfred. And like they, any moments I've thought myself to have lost from them is just as much a product of my imagination." He looked up at him "I don't know what was--would've been, in this imagined world, this world of dreams and shadows; who would know it the better one? Bearach and Luloch care dearly for me. I would like to *imagine* I wouldn't trade my heroes for ghosts. Even if I could…"

"Thank you for being curt with me, but…" Alfred curled his mouth at the prospect, showing judgment and dismissal at the sentiment, taking a deep breath. Finally, the wizard leaned forward in his chair, and eyed the boy critically. "The man that lived here found me, chose me, took me in, dusted me off, and taught me…taught me what you will learn, same as I: with this knowledge there shall be nothing restrained from you that you have *imagined* to do." He stood soberly. "Are you ready?"

Adimus blinked. He was quite unsure. "Luloch said as such. That you wished to teach me Magic."

"You do not wish it." he read the look on his face.

"It is against the Old Ways."

"I am aware. I only offer it, should you decide that it is needed."

"I appreciate it. It will never be."

He leaned forward, soberly. "Adimus." He began. "I am trying to help you as best I can. Help because you will realize before it's too late that these lords and noble have not a care for those who offer nothing." He began thinking out loud. "What you carry in that purse…your grandfather knows much in the way of preparing votive items and Implements. It could be an immense asset in your fight, even with no army."

The Grigor looked ahead blankly. *That old junk?*

"You don't have to answer now, but it could be possible, that if no one else will help you but you. Will your faith alone suffice?"

He stood and stretched, finally perhaps relaxing his guard now that he was confident they were alone. He wandered into the small kitchen and threw open to larders and pantries to look. "He did not leave in a hurry." he said to himself; it took Adimus a minute to realize he was talking about Teacher again. Then on to one of two small bedrooms. There was a cot there.

"Rory!" He ran to the dresser whereupon sitting alone was a stuffed bear, ragged from years of being played with, now dusty from years of not being. With a fond grin the wizard picked it up and shoved it into his pocket. There was nothing else to be found here, as the dresser and the wardrobe, like the pantry, were empty. A small study sat adjacent, host to the fireplace that it and the kitchen both shared opposites of, a blackboard, some bookshelves and a writing desk. Across was another room with a bed. *Teacher's room.*

Alfred strolled up to the bookshelf with purpose, laying a hand on it, closing his eyes. After a long moment his shoulders slumped, and he again plopped down on the furniture, this time a nicely patterned velveteen chair.

"So, how adroit <u>is</u> this power you have?" Adimus asked. "Can you read the books on the shelves without opening them?"

He snorted. "Even *I'm* not that good...!" He started to say, then gasped in epiphany. "Actually, I Read nothing."

"Hmm?"

"Nothing." He verbalized again.

"It...must be some form of trick. Some heretofore unrevealed power that he has hidden from me." He looked back at Adimus. "I've seen it before, it would seem. I can't Read him taking these books, or the books themselves for that matter. The bookshelf doesn't recall."

It was a weird way to word it, referring to the bookcase as one would a person, it made Adimus wonder even more about the true nature of the power.

Adimus pointed at the shelf, at the dust, or rather the lack of it. "These books were taken recently."

Alfred slumped in the chair again for just a moment before suddenly lurching up to look at the Grigor. "Wait. Recently?"

Alfred fumbled for his lamp and lit it with one of those twigs. Suddenly with new eyes they gazed at the floor. Footprints.

"Men's boots, it looks like." said Adimus.

With that Alfred would run to the door, almost as if expecting to see him still on the porch, all he would find is cold wind and a stormy dawn.

* * * * *

"Tirlag and her brothers met us in Torant. It's another country like yours, forged in the fires of the war. We'd come from an island off the western coast. An old prison colony, a place to exile political conspirators and rabble rousers who, at the time, threatened to subvert the throne of The Great King." Alara explained. "Torrin's twice great uncle was descended from one such family, locked away there for many years for suspicions of such conspiracy."

"The 'suspicion' part was the only thing what kept them alive, far as the Seer explained." said Tirlag. "But when the power changed hands, they were celebrated as war heroes and freed back to the mainland. That's when those suspicions were confirmed."

Alara gave a fangy grin. "He had letters, correspondence with the generals who fought in the Secession War. They speak of a hidden fortification, Lowylyn's base of operations during the conflict."

The bard's eyes narrowed skeptically. "Who's to say that that old Queen Githa didn't take it for herself then, to keep the Ormondians from having a standard to rally behind, eh? What if it's in some other blue-blood's trophy room in Malstat, or leaning atop the Alkonost in Brousse--or in the vaults of the Seat of the Sacrosanct?"

"A Seer." Alfred's expression was downright fox-like, he and Adimus appearing just from earshot as they strode up. "The parchment itself was written after the conflict. It was evidence enough for me: he did have the spear, and hid it. I was able to supply Torrin with the details of where. At the reasonable cost of taking on a partner, of course."

"Where were you just now?"

"Making plans."

No one questioned. "So Torrin's right: you really do know that it exists." Argent continued.

"Well." Said Tirlag. "Isn't that nice?" she jeered. "It was the same sales pitch I'd heard too."

"Tell me." Alfred inquired soberly. "Have you made your decision? Do you wish to disband, or do you want for me to leave?" It sounded like a clumsy, unelegent question, but its directness was intentional, a means to hamper her verbal maneuverability.

But the girl simply shrugged. "Why would I want to leave? You've promised me everything. And we filed the statement with the Consortium back at Thane, so it's binding now, as I was sure to have done for this lot when we stopped." he gestured to Laina and Argent.

"Wait. Everything?" Said Alara's ears shot up curiously.

Alfred said nothing.

Argent chimed in. "I tried to reason out his intentions myself, and got more and more lost. I thought perhaps he fancied the notion that he could do better with the bargaining with the Spear in hand. But then, he promised away all that he possesses to this one, even before we started, so who knows." he pointed with his thumb. "My new best friend." he tried to put an arm around her, but all it did was expose his ribs to her fist.

"His motives are suspect." Said Alara. "But I have no horse in this race save for actually finding the named thing. I for one choose to continue."

"He could be a spy from Histban. He also has that Harp thing that melts people." Said Delaney. "Who's to say you don't just use us the way Argent used that goblyn in Balfour, and kill us all once he finds it. You Breathers <u>are</u> a vile lot."

"What Alara really needs to be asking your partner's surrogate is: *'what is the Stone of Kings?'*" said the Bard "Whatever it is he values it above all else, even our mission."

"Including the welfare of his relations with business partners." Tirlag jabbed. "I mean, look at him. He's not asking if he's coming with us. No, it's the other way around."

"...Then you are staying?"

"Yes. We are." Argent spoke for everyone, being sure to gain accord as he did. None objected.

"Even though we risk gaining nothing?" Alfred reiterated.

"No." Laina, of all people, interjected, jumping to her feet with fervor. "What Ross of Ward says, Alfred, is true. Argent's words as well, whether he meant them or not; if the gods are indeed good, if the world is indeed just, then we've nothing to fear. Righteousness and its fruits do not go unrewarded: let the power I wield by the Graces of Ananya be testament to it. It is The Law. I have faith in this, with all my heart." she clasped her hand to her chest. "Lead on."

"You just want the answer to your question." Argent chuckled.

"The road ahead is very dangerous. I've done all the convincing I could to this one that we *should* all stay together." Said Delaney, gesturing to Tirlag; it wasn't like her to have such a serious demeanor. "Kain Keith is not a place to venture alone."

"*That* is our destination?" said Argent, who apparently knew just enough to sound worried.

"Tell them. Tell them what you saw." Said Alara.

"...It is a hazy vision, hidden in the mists of generations." he prefaced "A great four-legged beast." he said. "It stands upon and guards The Bane of the Eye. It is his lure, his snare. It salivates in anticipation, devouring all who seek it, resting beneath its immense foot, a thorn in the lion's paw."

Tirlag said soberly. "You didn't tell me that part."

Alara grinned. "What's wrong? Don't want to go double-or-nothing anymore?"
"It looks like we are either way."

They traveled yet another day, down a rough dirt road long past the small fork that had led to the orphanage. The road became even more rocky and disheveled, filled with ruts covered in broken boardwalk and a pair of rickety bridges that they crossed only one at a time, and were brave for daring to do. Not much came from the mouths of them, not even the minstrel's.
All day, the words of the Seer wore on Adimus. On the other end of the second bridge they'd crossed, they made camp again.
Adimus could see the whites of everyone's eyes in the firelight as well. He couldn't help it anymore, he voiced their concerns "Could it be a...dragon?"

Half of them chuckled, the other half gave skeptical looks.

Then Alfred said soberly. "We are seeking artifacts from far before the time of even the Silver King. We can't dismiss the possibility."

Tirlag had apparently been pondering it too. "To think we might find the Spear only to see it in the hoard of Gandereba of the Yellow Heel or one of the children of Azi Stramos himself."

"Cadifor McDougal slew the only dragon that had ever terrorized the Southlands. 500 years ago." Argent shook his head.

"500 years..." Laina echoed, staring into the fire.

"So it is true. Cadifor is an Immortal." Said Adimus.

"He is Fae Kind?" Alara asked.

"No." The bard simply replied, but with an eyebrow he stood. "Alara..." he started, scratching his head to wrack his brain for the words.

"You are Fae...are you Immortal?"

"I don't believe it." She scowled. "The Tuatha espouse such nonsense along with their elitist notions that we are inferior creatures to they. We are simply ignorant to the divine truth, and that's why we are how we are."

"But you can't refute that they seem forever young."

"You fill one with holes, they die as surely as any other." Was all she said.

"What about the Otherworld?" Delaney chimed in. "Doesn't it have the power that gives them life? That's what my Elder explained to me."

"I see nothing out of the ordinary." she shrugged. "The light leaves their eyes just the same, like any creature that ever was."

A chill went down Adimus's spine, and not just from the gruesome comment.

"Longevity is not immortality, it seems." Answered Alfred, adjusting his glasses. "As for the latter, I'm not sure there is such a thing." He added flippantly.

Laina added, "Longevity is not immortality, but body is not soul." She explained. "In my faith, after the airs leave the body the spirit wanders, like our journey here to this land we will be guided by the light of the Great Goddess again, this time to the land of the Numinous, of the everlasting, just as surely as the Fae do."

"What if you refuse, like Adimus here? He doesn't believe in your goddess." Argent poked at him, ever joyful to stir the pot.

"Then they do not reach the land of the Numinous. They fall down into the earth. Into the Deep. Into Hell."

The Grigor felt the need to defend. "<u>We</u> are told that the Numinous <u>is</u> below us." They all looked on in curiosity, "It is true! All life springs from under our feet. All of our ancestors are down there, buried under the ground. We face tests, guarded by the foul shades, but, there is a world down there, of light and life beyond, from which all green things grow, and if we are strong, if we avert the gaze of the Baleful Eye, we attain it."

"Plants do not grow without light." Laina shot back.

"And the Kesselloni believed you are placed in a big cauldron and churned into stardust or some such—they can't all be true." Tirlag rubbed her nose.

"Well, that was an enlightening conversation. Let us be done with it before it causes even more reasons for us to hate one another." The sentiment seemed shared, as with that, Argent had ended it.

The night before was a partial night, where the full effect of it had been muted by its brevity and all the worry, dread and strife, but now, here, Adimus discovered all over again now how much he hated camping. It was never comfortable, always too hot or too cold, everything invariably wound up covered in dirt. He could feel every rock and root poking him beneath his bedroll. At least Laina had wherewithal to snag some of the leftover food from the kitchens while everyone argued. She handed him a dinner roll in the dark and shared a knowing smile with him. At least he had someone to identify with him to ground him. Then there was the gnawing of the conversation. And, most of all, Dyrshul

It would be a long night.

Everyone seemed to sleep easy atop the cold ground that night, save him. He wasn't sure how long he had laid there pretending to do so in the hopes that he actually could.

"Why aren't you doing that thing with your eyes that everyone else does?" It was Delaney.

"Excuse me?"

Her beady eyes glistened in the firelight at him.

"Sleeping. That's the word. You don't do that--sleep, I mean." Delaney said. She was sitting right in front of him and he hadn't realized it. "You didn't sleep well at the Ravenhound much either, and now you won't sleep out here."

"How do you know I don't sleep?"

Her beady eyes glistened in the firelight. "I watch you."

"...Well, that doesn't help." He said, rolling back over.

There was a long, awkward moment of silence. He turned back around, now not helping but feeling her eyes on him. "You don't sleep either, then." It came out like a question.

"Nope." she declared. "We do get tired, and need to root ourselves." It was a strange way of wording it to be sure. She gestured with a nod down to her feet planted firmly in the ground to illustrate. "Daytime is best for it, for us. But you Breathers insist on doing all your doings when the sun is out."

"Interesting."

"Withdraw, that's what we call it: Withdrawing. Like you." She said.

Adimus lifted a brow. "Why are you so concerned?"

"Want to talk about it?"

Adimus was more than a little skeptical. "You actually care how I feel?"

"I mean, yeah." she said, wiping her nose awkwardly. "Why can't you sleep?" she said.

Adimus was quiet for a moment, he looked at each of them in their bunks to ensure they were all asleep.

It wasn't the only reason he couldn't sleep, but it was the only one he dared to verbalize. "That man. In that place where we met Cadifor."

"Cairnfang." she corrected. "That guy in the courtyard?" she sounded confused. "Yeah. Why?"

"...I dunno." There was a long silence. He thought about the man. The look on his face was enough to keep him awake without the added worry. "Me and my sister. We're foundlings." it sounded odd to him, finally saying it to someone voluntarily.

"I heard that part...And?"

"He's worrying that he is Fae Kind again." Alfred sat up. From the look in his weary eyes he hadn't slept much either.

"No. Actually not." Delaney answered him. "It's his sister he's worried about. But..." she turned back to the boy, "If you are not Fae then it should proceed that she is not as well." said Delaney. "She is your sister...That *is* how Breather stuff works, right?"

"It is." replied Alfred.

"You know, it is because she is beginning to bond with you that she talks." It had awoken Tirlag. "Your not sleeping bothers you, and what bothers you bothers her." she grumbled. She raised her head to deliver a scowl. "Don't worry--it is not a genuine concern. She is only worried about she herself continuing to be restless because you are, I'm sure." with that she shoved the nice pillow she'd stolen from the Hall over her head with a muffled curse.

Delaney huffed.

"Not true, Hyu'man." she said to Adimus, blinking her blue eyes. "You also feel like you don't belong. You also long for a past that isn't there, to know your true parentage." The boy said nothing.

"Not as much as you might think." Alfred adjusted the glasses that were still on his head.

She continued. "All the same. Then, for whoever needs to hear it: you must not let such things define you." she paused, weighing whether she should continue "We never know our mother and father."

An airborne boot nearly found its way across his head. "Oy, shut it!"

Delaney tisked and continued. "<u>We</u> are divided into septs, and when a sept's numbers dwindle the elders arrange the other septs to...act as donors. For the tribe. They do the Mergence, make new urisks, and go back to their tribe, never to meet again."

"The Mergence?"

"Reproduce." Alfred answered. "A strange and sterile way of going about it, no doubt."

Alfred adjusted his glasses (he hadn't remembered to take them off.)

"We view yours as uncouth and messy." she said. "Our Animae, of course, are made from amongst our own through the natural course of things."

Alfred twisted his face in curiosity, and dodged a pillow that came flying at it, followed by something of which could be discerned as a stream of expletives.

She continued "Shivers—whatever it is you Breathers call them." Adimus and Alfred looked to each other for clarification, but each found but another dumbfounded face staring back at them. "The point is, I will never know my parents, nor would it have really mattered if I had." Deleney whispered. The boys looked at each other, confused. "I will be who I am, regardless."

Adimus gave a vindicated grin to the Seer.

"Which sept are you anyway?" asked Alfred, after a few moments.

"Mealae."

"*The slave sept*." he said, ominously. "So, your sept bonds with people too. I understand now."

She nodded. "Animals, though there isn't really a difference." She shrugged. She seemed to be answering a different question, perhaps addressing something they'd spoken of before that the boy wasn't privy to.

"Adimus." Alfred's tone then shifted. "So. You remember nothing at all? From before."

"What do you mean?"

"When he found you, how old would you have been?"

"Twelve or thirteen." he wagered. This part always scared him.

"Then Dyrshul would've been pretty young." he responded. Adimus was a bit taken aback that she knew his sister's name so well. But he knew the question coming next was worse. "But you, you would've been old enough to remember, correct?" Adimus nodded. "And yet you know nothing?"

"...I get strange sensations sometimes. Like, I'm supposed to be somewhere or I forgot something important and I can't remember what. I chalk it up to anxiety, but I also have dreams. Strange dreams."

It was something only Luloch had ever heard from him. "...I see."

There was a long silence.

"That's why you really took me along, right?" Adimus finally mustered the courage to ask.

"We are much the same. Only, my parents are not separated from me by knowledge or distance." he stated. His visage softened. "You may have a whole past and future unbeknownst to you. One we may discover, together, in time. Here. " he produced something from his pocket, which he tossed him. "At least, I want you to try this." The Sum Seer said. It was a simple coin of turquoise. "The Lapidaries worked alongside the Order of Jasmine, the enforcers of Illea. You may not wish to practice Magic, but surely you wouldn't be adverse to mastering <u>this</u> age-old tradition."

At this Adimus's eyes lit up. The thought hadn't occurred to him until then. This was permitted Magic, Magic that he could learn. "You're going to teach me?" To which the man nodded. "Do you think I can?"

With a nod he began. The exercise he taught to him, he explained, was the preliminary step to being able to perform psychometry, that is, the Reading of items and materials, attaining the knowledge of what they were made of, what acts they had committed, even what they had witnessed. He showed him a mental exercise designed to clear his mind and quiet his mind.

"Your focus should be on the coin. The coin alone exists, nothing else. You can do this by meditating upon its qualities: feeling its weight in your hand, the texture in the furls and cracks and impurities, how its luster catches the eye. If ever your mind strays from it, you must willfully, consciously right it, return it straight away." That was the beginning. It was a slow process, he explained, but once finished, much like a wild horse being trained to obey a master, the senses can be brought under the control of the mind, and the Work of Reading could begin.

Complete and utter attention and concentration on the coin. An exercise it was. He tried until the wee hours of the morning, just staring at the coin, until his mind exhausted itself and, struggling to stay awake even a moment more.

Chapter 17
Relics of War

The small town of Keara on the cusp of Kain Keith was not much to speak of in comparison with Hewnyleigh. Balfour was perched on the frontier, the wildlands between The Great Kingdom and the Barrier Peaks, and like Balfour, it too was unused since the days of the reclaiming of the Via Victimus, a much wider and well-guarded means of travel through the Southlands and beyond. A few towns such as these made their living harvesting timber or breeding livestock. Keara seemed to have neither of these. They did have a modern apothecary shop with the witty namesake "Kary's" after its owner, Kary Coalfax, with several curious Vouxitian wares found nowhere else in Menkara as well as some very good candy (he bought some licorice to bring to his grandfather when he returned). There was also a modest jeweler who knew Alfred and Alara. There was an ancient circle of standing stones, a bowyer of legendary repute, a local taxidermist with a museum of odd creatures and a general store fraught with supplies for the cold mountains. Adimus knew little of these however; what he *did* know is that their Inn was called Eichgun's Rest, and had a life-sized, ornate draft horse whittling on its front porch, and they offered hot baths for 3 stripes. After practicing the Sum Seer's exercise stone, trying to get one last wink of sleep, he visited the general store with the rest of them. Delaney purchased a long spindle of rope and several torches and waterskins from the general store as well as "Breather food": bread, hard cheese and pemmican. She packed it all in two large rucksacks that she gave Argent and Adimus to carry--Tirlag reasoned it was the people she liked least.

The Watcher thus embarked.

Adimus lamented having personally been given a horse by the reeve only to have to leave it behind. The forest of Kian Keith was a ceaseless mangled mess of dried ferns, briars and shrubs. Torrin's carriage could have never traversed it. Not even their horses were taken, Alfred having paid for their stabling for a time.

"Even the trees are giant." William observed. Delaney pointed out the rings of some of them, that were ancient even before they were shorn from their roots.

They blockaded the path through the woods, a morass of fallen timber that formed a labyrinth that funneled them along a wide avenue with many odd angles, branching paths and double backs. Delaney took the fore for the most part, outpaced by Alara, who bounded amongst the trees.

The giants who'd made this maze had been done so as a deterrent against the Hyu'manii who'd encroached on their homes in the mountains, according to the bard. Made to be highly defensible, it melded the natural terrain, the barricading trees and the occasional stone wall to create a gauntlet that a giant could easily circumvent where a short-legged Kindred could not.

Tirlag produced the cage and unlocked it with the key she had finally been given. She delicately popped it open.

Finola was hardly a baby any more, having quite the spurt over the two moons since Balfour. It was definitely a duck, they'd determined, his down feathers finally molting and his beak turning that distinctive orange.

"Do you think it will work?" asked Argent. Tirlag looked at him, and tickled the birds back and watch Delaney absently scratch her own. "Hehe, yep."

With some coaxing the bird took off. "It's a technique that has been practiced since the War of the Leaves." William explained. "The Blossom Bride hunted the Tuatha of the House of Euscias at night using owls. I suppose it will work just the same."

Alfred, in an obviously rehearsed course of events, gave the urisk a book and a piece of charcoal, and opened it for her to a blank page.

Delaney sat cross legged, her eyes closed. Over the next few minutes she scratched down what at first appeared as simple lines, but over the next minutes became a series of shapes. Every few moments she'd glance at it, correcting any errors made with the placement of her hand.

Finally she opened her eyes, and looked down at the drawing.

She'd drawn the way forward, and it seemed to match perfectly, they found after the first few turns.

"The forest welcomes us. This is good." They'd no idea by what criteria she measured, but it sounded comforting. This time Delaney would supply the answers, if she so chose. "Follow me." she beckoned.

Dead brush and brambles covered in thorns and stickers withered by the lateness of the year. Argent was scratched by Fencebush growing wild, and spent hours thereafter letting everyone know about it. Alara joked that he could be used for bait to catch a mountain lion or a bear, the way he bayed like a wounded animal.

"Adimus was touched by a Shade and didn't complain this much." Said Tirlag.

The fact that now they could laugh about it gave the boy some relief, it reminded him that it was now the past, it couldn't hurt him anymore.

"Not Shade. Shadespawn." Said Laina. "There *is* a difference." she elaborated. "It had a form, however wispy it was. Were it a true Shade, one of the Sluagh, he might not have been so lucky. Still, I could call down the primordial fire of divinity that created the world for you too, to heal your boo-boo."

Tirlag chuckled.

"Not necessary." The bard glowered.

A dry, musky smell channeled through the tunnel, a concentrated dose of autumn, full of the odors of dying things.

"No chance of seeing one those in here, eh? A Shade?" Argent nervously said; it would be fitting that it was him who would ask, no doubt half-expecting some sort of cosmic recompense.

"Hope not." Was all Delaney could offer. "It's not like the Endless Forest if that's what you mean." she added.

"Thankfully not, else we'd never get out, regardless of encountering a Shade." Said Tirlag.

"Surely you don't believe what they say." Alara argued. "It's not really bespelled."

"I've heard all kinds of stories in my travels, love. And never doubt one of them, it's how you get killed." Her eyes went vagrant in thought. "No. You've got to respect them, like a snake: best to always assume fangs." Tirlag glanced up at her. "Besides, I've seen the lands to the east for myself. Seen what blights Fae Magic can bring to bear on the prideful."

"...The moors cursed with eternal rain?"

She nodded. "Aye."

Adimus had heard about the forest of which he spoke: a great, rolling, copse as far as the eye could see that the Tuatha called their home, and its Magic that gave the lands beyond it their name. He supposed she was right.

Many of the trees dripped with the moss and lichen and dead ivies that seemed to cake and coat everything in sight. Consumed by the thicket, the endlessness of the outside world was strangled by the vegetation. Adimus's first impression of the forest was that of the normal woodlands found in his home in Balfour, those he used to play in as a child. Then as they traveled on he realized he was perversely wrong. Tall dead ferns that if uncurled would tower over his head come to his waste stood like undisturbed clay sculptures. Dried vines laced vaulting canopies, meshed so thick it made what seemed like a roof, making it all the more like an exclusive scene made just for their eyes. It made Alfred stop reading. Despite this, beautiful wild flowers, late blooming, only recently tinged with the rusting wilt, grew in the logs and on the mossy floors.

Pollen of late blooming goldenrod and the like or spores of mold that linger in the air of autumn's dawn joined the lingering freshly disturbed dust motes in the shafts of sunlight let in. Leaves still sprinkled from trees, the only sound that could be heard. They landed in undisturbed banks like snow drifts if bright yellow and scarlet, verifying to Alara that no large animals seemed to have passed through recently.

"Except us, just now." Tirlag ominously joked. Alara had anticipated deer, out for rutting, and had her wand readied for them, but nothing of the sort; rather it was the insulating nature of the maze or something more sinister: a deafening, alien silence that befell the place.

They discovered a nest of Hyu'man remains, remnants of some forgotten skirmish, naught but a few tattered rags, almost turned to soil, some stray arrows and the bones themselves their only clues. They found it only when Adimus tripped over a bronze helmet.

He'd worn a bronze armet with an ornate face guard that looked like a fearsome face (that might have looked nice in a museum if the boy hadn't crushed it). "This one was a Daldistan warrior." Argent pontificated. They found his sword nearby, and a shield and lancea, which disintegrated when touched. The sword, corroded with verdigris, was stuck inside its sheath. They took it with them.

They traveled for hours in the winding brush. Even though the trees made clear the way forward, the forest itself had continued to grow, placing trees in the way, or brush so thick as to be nearly impassable. Several times they had to climb their way over and rethink the solution to the maze.

Then they came to a small clearing sequestered deep in the maze, at what Delaney would reckon was the halfway point. It was only sparse with trees, mostly saplings, and pastel roses grew in patches, each colored their own. The days were growing shorter and colder as Macha drifted toward its meridian, covering the sun for longer, so they'd decided to make camp there, having clean lines of sight on all approaches, when one of them came upon it. It stood perhaps twice the size of the tallest of them.

He held a hammer with a head the size of a brandy cask in a stance as if to swing wide in an arc, his ruby eyes full of ire. His head was as that of a bull, as was his appearance from the torso down, from what they could tell from his tail and backwards bent legs. The rest off him, up too perhaps his thighs were sunk in the soft dirt, as the material that comprised his form was rather heavy.

"Gold!" Cried Tirlag.

"What is it?"

"Some sort of local god, perhaps?" Said Alara.

"There's always so many gods…" Alfred huffed.

"The god of these woods, no doubt." Said Laina.

"One of yours?" Argent said to Laina, pointing.

"I've never seen such a thing." Said Laina, ignoring the facetiousness in lieu of the awe invoked in such a thing.

"He is not one of the Daldistan ones. He fits no description of a Vatra or Pan or Erlking that the Tuatha revere."

Argent declared with a questionable scholarly surety.

"It's not spent gold, either, it's the real thing." Alfred commented, touching it with a bare hand.

" 'Spent' Gold?" " Laina echoed questioningly.

"He means Denatured gold. All'khemical slag. Worth less than the dirt its sunk in." Argent answered for him.

Adimus could only look on in awe; he had only once or twice seen gold, and that was at a museum in Ederton, but he knew enough to know that even a lump of it could make a man rich. He'd heard.

"Let's just pack it up and leave this forsaken place! Retire as kings." said Tirlag, almost drooling as she said it.

"I mean, I'd wager we've come further than most have in ages, but something bothers me about the fact that it's undisturbed." Alfred stated.

"Maybe we should sacrifice the bird to it." Tirlag picked, just to see Delaney's expression.

"I'm not the superstitious type." Said Argent. "But after last time..."

Alara looked at Tirlag and they both nodded and said in unison. "Assume fangs."

"Don't disturb it." Said Alfred. In fact, I think one of us should keep an eye on it tonight." Alfred said, concerned look on his face.

"Adimus." Alfred pulled him over in an aside, shortly after they'd started to set camp. "Those trinkets your grandfather gave to you." he sheepishly began. "If you've little use of them, I may have. Could I coax a few from you? To study?"

Adimus was surprised at his own reluctance to do so, and chalked it up to sentimentality, but banishing the thought from his mind, having them would only tempt him to use them, after all, he relented. "You are right, I have no use for them."

It didn't help, the presence of the great thing looming over them; it made sure Adimus knew wouldn't sleep. He sat up the tent and bedrolls, just the same.

He'd noticed he'd been given a bit of a break since they'd found out about the incident, even seeing Argent jump in and volunteer to carry firewood for him. When he'd finally finished, he saw Laina sitting by the fire. Alara was scouting, Argent and Alfred and Tirlag went about searching for wood. Delaney sat with eyes closed--she'd decided to send the bird out scouting a few more times that evening, just to make sure the coast was clear.

There, in lack of earshot and the time to repose, Adimus took a deep breath and prepared himself.

It had taken weeks to formulate the words, days to decide that they should be spoken, and hours conjuring the courage to do so. "Laina." he started with a deep breath to still his nerves. "I just want to say thank you."

The vessel in which she prepared the meal had grown gradually bigger--what had at first been the simple cook pot from the Beat had become the larger one from Argent's mess kit, when after tasting one of her stews he began asking for a portion himself and even contributing to its ingredients. Now it was a roiling cauldron Laina stirred, procured by the Company. She sat by it, grinding some dried thyme with a mortar and pestle.

"You are most welcome, Adimus. I know that it was hard to say."

The subtleties of what it meant weighed far more on the boy than even he thought it ought to, and from her appreciative smile she understood. Still it threw him off-guard. "What do you mean?"

"Well, I could not help but mull over the consequences of that action myself. Even afterwards the shadow of the thought haunted me that you somehow resented it." she stoked the fire, never glancing up as she said it.

"...Why would I resent you saving me?"

She stirred the pot with a huge ladle--another commissary of the Endeavor. "It occurred to me that perhaps you might think it better to face non-existence than to stray in the principles of your faith, being healed with mansii Magic."

"Do you want me to be ungrateful? Because I can be." he tried his hand at some levity.

"I didn't mean it as an insult." she quickly added. "I simply meant that all things considered, I should have thought to ask."

Suddenly those words were as a mirror shown upon him. He looked at the ground. "I'm glad you didn't, because you'd think the lesser of me." he tried to joke. "Shadespawn..." he shivered. "When faced with the prospect of oblivion I fear my notions of virtue waver a bit."

"Only a bit?" She giggled. "Then it is a shame I didn't ask, to spare me from such a worry that I'd done it against your wishes." she joked, shrugging. "But alas, I was too selfish to ask your permission. I wanted you safe, even if it would have been against your will. I _am_ glad you are thankful, and I do not judge your choice either way--I am simply glad to see you well."

She leaned in, whispering as if it were a secret "If it helps, I did ask Eichgun, and Ailean, and his parents; and they all gladly took my help."

"That's good, I suppose..." it sounded strained, though he didn't mean it to (even though it was).

She called him on it. "You are shocked that so many others waver in their faith?"

Adimus sat for a moment in thought. "It isn't that." Laina observed.

She stood and looked down at him critically. "You feel undeserving of that life. That somehow I have trapped you." she explained. "That in a sort of contradictory way that you have been both saved and defiled but the god of another; you are grateful for the life you have been given, but feel that with it you can never be deserving of it. You have failed in the eyes of your god, and for you there is no worse a fate."

He soberly stared into the flame. "...Sometimes no. Thankfully." he admitted in defeat. Her insight was devastating. Again, he half-joked. "It is true what they say: sometimes there are some fates worse than death."

Then she smiled. "Such paradox is the nature of Grace. As for me? I choose my goddess over your god only because of the power it grants me, power to help the ones I care about. I revere and love her for what she gives me. The power to save you. All you need do is simply live, Adimus, and I will accept it as sacrament." then she kindly dusted off her hands and poured him a bowl.

* * * * *

Nothing had happened. "This place is getting to us. That's all." Tirlag assured the boy the following day. "Stirring up fancies of spooks and spectres." It sounded more like her assuring herself, he suspected, uncharacteristic as it was (she also had noticeable bags under her eyes). "We'll get it on the way back." She winked at him.

The tree barrier had blocked the wind, that coupled with a hot fire concealed well the fact that it was cold enough to snow, and they could tell by the whipping branches above them it was a blustery day.

It had come quickly, almost as if the forest itself didn't wish them to proceed. It would be the first snow of the season, but with its sheer volume it seemed to stick just the same, in the dropping temperature of evening.

Alara was scouting as usual, her fur leaving her unbothered by the snow's presence; she was perhaps even giddy about it, as it made a perfect medium for tracking.

But what she'd found left her perplexed, and noticeably distraught. She even made the bard and the boy come and look.

It was a footprint. A Hyu'man footprint. Bare ones. In the snow. She tracked them, but they had come at the beginning of the snow, and by the end they were covered. No new ones could be found.

"Strange. Very strange." It was surely a muted expression to publicly illustrate his aloofness, as he had done time and time again, but no amount of acting could hide his unnerved expression.

"What do you think, Watcher? Simple Fae mischief?"

"There are no need for shoes in the Otherworld."

Argent swallowed his concern as best he could.

Adimus continued, "The most powerful of Fae come and go as they please from the Otherworld, the meadows beyond Mag Mell out of reach of living mortals. Scouts for the Wild Hunt most likely." Adimus supposed he would make a good bard himself--he too had no clue what he was talking about. He thought to admit this to him, until he realized how good it felt good seeing William's eyes so fraught with self-concern.

The weather forced them to retire early, not more than a mile from the strange things.

It was at a particular spot on the map, a cul-de-sac with a large pine tree that they figured might prove a good shelter.

Adimus sat under a lean-to he'd made of his great kilt with a simple rope strung between two branches, braced against the one entry point for the wind. He'd used tiny stones to make anchor points like little toggles in the plaid, to prevent having to damage the garment by threading the rope through it. It was one of the first things his pa had taught him, on one of their first patrols while they were out camping. He was shocked that everyone seemed so impressed by it, and was pleased as punch to, for once, be seen as clever.

"You pack everything in that rolled up blanket don't you?" Argent observed.

"It's a plaid. I bet your backpack doesn't do this." he pointed up with his thumb.

He'd put the coin the Seer had given him on a hempen cord, around and through its hole, so he could wear it around his neck; it kept him from losing it along with his other pocket change. "The senses should be brought under the control of the mind, the mind should be chastised to be brought under control of the will of the intelligence, which you must understand is separate to the mind. Firmly, but do not dwell upon it, or the mind will stray to thoughts of guilt, which is just another trap. You must relax, but don't think about relaxing or you will tense up." Alfred instructed him as he began his quieting exercise.

The boy stared into it. It was easier said than done.

"Silver Hand! Was that in your hair?!" Tirlag hyperventilated when the urisk playfully let the huge spindly spider crawl back up her arm.

"It keeps the other bugs away. You know, the ones that eat plants. Wanna hold him?" She nabbed it again when it tried to run back up her arm, putting it back into her hand to show it off before cackling and chasing her around the camp with it.

Adimus rested on his back, his leg crossed one over the other, and staring at the coin began again.

"You know he only told you that to put you to sleep." Delaney commented at him, before glancing over at Alfred to see if it had gotten a rise out of him, but he was doing exercises of his own, face was planted in one book archive books.

"Were that true, you've broken the illusion and now it will never work. So he'll be up again tonight, and so will you! Nice going." Said Tirlag.

"Don't listen to them, my boy. This is precisely how a Sum Seer trains, I watched them in Hewnyleigh. Keep at it." He glanced back at the genuine article, whose face was buried in a book "Why, I knew a practitioner, best in the business, who trained by burning himself with a hot poker to the nipple each time his mind strayed."

Tirlag chimed in, pulling a stick from the fire. "Need an assistant?"

"Don't let them distract you." Said Alara.

"Aren't you distracting him by telling him that?" Laina joined in. The Cait Shii rolled her glowing eyes in defeat.

"Nay, Adimus, you must hone your concentration to the exclusion of all else." Said the bard. The entire time he spoke he watched Delaney, "It may take weeks, even years, before you gain mastery over this most esoteric of paths," Her hands cupped, tiny tip-toe by tiny tip-toe, "but one day, one shining day, you will attain the unerring steadfast concentration of a Seer. " she dumped her friend on Alfred's head. He'd never seen the Faeth speak language so colorful.

* * * * *

The following day when they awoke they find snow shin deep. They thanked Delaney for her thoughtful preparations, as she had been sure to buy wool socks, scarfs, and coats for them with Alfred's provisional money he'd gotten from Torrin.

They sought to catch up from their early rest, Adimus snacked on an apple as they went. Alfred read his torn pages. Tirlag bantered loudly with Laina. Argent sang:

"A fair young lass of the Karanash, taken both to there and hither, taken by the whispering wipperwills and flowers that bloom in winter. Ohhhhh--O'er endless sky and golden green that autumn never withered, she'd taken to the beauty of the land of the Blue River."

It was a day of many shadows, where the light played its tricks pitching and swaying them, throwing and scattering them into contorted diffusions as the wind billowed and blew. There they stood silently in the falling snow, the maidens. Their skin was pale and their hair was dark, and they gave not even a hot breath to belie their presence, not even moving until the first of them were upon them. They would be given no warning, as the things had no tracks; their barefoot footprints were long covered up from the long night they had waited in ambush for them.

It was here they had hid, standing in the nude, statuesque figures tef pallid beauty. When the gaze of one fell upon Adimus he could not help but feel allured, as if there were no rhyme or reason, no need for the grasping of logical straws how it was that she stood disrobed unabashed in the chilling snow. There was only fascination.

The noises they made were like the blithe giggles of damsels walking the promenade at court, with all the calculating and practiced intent of a predator. The lurid figures encroached in alien unison and were upon them with thorny clawed fingers and needle-teeth behind luscious lips. They were upon them before they could blink.

"Get back!" Argent snapped to as it swatted at him.

Adimus jumped back. It was barely enough. He scooped the loop of the shield strap and snatched the brace just in time to bring it up and buttress himself. When he did he shoved her back and by that time he had worked his sword free from the frost, landing a slice into its arm when she slashed at him with her thorny claws. In a strange sort of regret he gritted his teeth more than it did, though it did little to it. He could smell her alluring fragrance, like the sweetest flowers, but the sappy monstrous ichor that dripped from the wound snapped him out of it.

"Are they Fae?!" Argent gasped.

"Redcaps?" Alfred asked.

"Huldrafolk!" Delaney yelled.

Tirlag called out as she found her back against a tree.

"Ahh!" One of them clawed into Argent, leaving trails of bright crimson in the snow.

The loud crack of the All'Khemist's Wand come be heard, tearing one that came at Alara into splinters.

The thing came at Adimus again.

"Damnation!" Tirlag snarled, using the back of her cutlass to try and pin the monster back. Then a pale blue light blinded the both of them.

Adimus saw, for just a moment, the pickled acorn and it flew from the wizard's hand. Adimus could hear Alfred's words in the clear of it all.

The words made perfect sense to the boy when he spoke; it was like the recitation of some great truth or sudden illumination of a riddle being solved in his mind. Then it vanished as if it never were.

Where the acorn landed came a blinding light and a flash of thunder. The heavenly bolt of lightning that streaked from the sky blew the enemy to splinters, and left in its wake only a glowing pile of embers.

The third one was killed by Delaney herself, who took a hatchet to its leg to fell it and barbarically chopped it in the face until it quit moving, appearing to gather a strange satisfaction from it when she did.

She stood, disregarding everyone's look, covered in the ichor. Argent heaved, checking the wound. Laina came to his aid. Delaney closed her eyes in the stillness. Tirlag, frustrated with the whole ordeal, finished what she started, freeing herself.

"A Spell." Adimus said, looking at the Seer. "That was a Spell."

"That was Thaumaturgy. Your grandfather's doing." He said, matter of factly. " He is an exemplary Druid. Too bad he's been stifled by that Tolten Blaise fellow." he cleaned the fog from his glasses.

He wasn't even done talking and Delaney took off.

"Wait!" Alara tried to protest, "There might be more." she ignored her. Alara helped Argent onto her horse to ensure that they followed behind. They realized a short while later that she was not leading them down the path she had instructed.

Turning the next few bends, they found themselves standing before an immense shadowy tree.

Its branches were covered in black leaves, and a tarry ichor hung about it. A pungent scent wafted from it. Once titillating, it was now an overpowering, sickening fume.

Large black swollen fruits, like overly ripe plums, hung from its boughs. One lie on the ground before them. Delaney walked over to it and kicked it. With a loud 'pop' the fruit burst, shriveling and contorting, where in an instant turned itself inside out like popping corn. Arms and legs, then a torso and a head formed of its innards. The only sign it had ever been a fruit in a tree and not a fully matured beautiful adult female was a hollow orifice in its back, left from the tucking of its squishy outsides inward. Then before Adimus could even process it the creature rasped to life like a newborn being slapped. Delaney interrupted the process with her axe.

"What is this?" asked Tirlag, a visible crack in the veneer of her apathy plainly showing, clearly concerned at her companion's upset.

"Nariphon." she explained. "A relic of the Bride's war on her maker and all of his Kind." she went on. "It has now lost its purpose and only seeks only to feed."

She looked over at the Sum Seer, but had no need--he was already lighting a torch with one of his twigs.

Adimus jumped when the creature Delaney had just slain unnaturally lurched as the tree was sat ablaze, its detached head contorting in fear.

Blood-curtling screams and screeches resonated from the fruits. Soon they would fall to the ground in the burning, bursting when they did. Delaney ended each in turn.

The harrowing event took most of the evening. And Adimus found himself sitting, staring into the lifeless eyes of the burning dolls.

Chapter 18
The Flooded Fortress

They were hewn from blocks of stone, each big enough themselves to fit the Green Beat inside of and then some. They even stymied the majesty of the mountain beside which it sat, making them appear as but gentle hills in their presence. Standing in relief against the colorful trees it made to appear as shrubs, the great pillars were seen three days ahead. Slowly they had watched them draw near, disappearing from sight as they meandered through clearings, closer and closer until finally they had reached the mouth of the maze at the mountain's root.

They conjoined in gentle vaulting arches, coupling in one long line almost like a bridge. There were four in succession--no doubt mind boggling spans from each other--but from this distance the whole of it could be seen as one connected piece.

Earlier in the day Alara had scrambled restless among the canopy. All morning she could be found holding her ears to the ground, to rocks, to trees. There was a noise she had heard. No one else could hear it, though she claimed that she herself couldn't cease in doing so, noticeably distraught by its presence. She could only conclude that the sound was beneath their feet. The ground rumbled, thrummed from deep within. The growl of the beast; all seemed to resonate to its din.

A thick mist hung around it, veiling its details and forcing the perfume of rain water into their nostrils. This mist was a spray, they would find, and only then, when they'd drawn closer to it, would its true nature and purpose be revealed, as catching the morning light, sending a soaring rainbow across the sky above them, the massive falls greeted them.

The torrent of water which issued from the mouth of the great beast could fill Loch Sul in an instant, the Watcher wagered looking wayward at it, and the massive pressure of it as it tumbled thousands of feet to the ground below one would by all measure split the mountain in two and spill an ocean onto the forest floor besides, but for a shallow fissure at its base, a modest ravine weathered by the water, there was no disturbance, leaving the ultimate fate of the deluge it would invariably be the mother of nowhere to be seen.

"What is it?" Argent had asked.

He now appended his question as they drew nearer to it its size became apparent, as it remained small and in the distance for far too long. "*How* is it...?"

"It's an aqueduct." The epiphany had struck the wizard. "To carry water. It's an aqueduct--well, a broken one."

"Built by whom?" asked Laina.

"Jantiliak. Has to be." said Alara.

"The giants within the mountain." Adimus chimed in authoritatively and was ignored.

"Delaney. Lead us down there." he pointed to the valley below.

"There?" She said. "Finola says it's this way." she pointed to the left. "Gordona fortress."

Alfred said, staring down at the map. His gloves were off, and he thumbed at his ring "You are correct." he said after a moment. "Lead on."

Most wouldn't have even noticed the fortress as anything more than rough shapes against the stone of the structure, but Finola had seen, and thus so had they.

"See, I knew you were useful." Tirlag jested.

The path she led followed around the valley, and itself conjoined with the mountain path beside it, a tell that even a military force could not find a direct way to approach such a beast.

The steepness of the path up the mountain broke the treeline, and for the first evening they took respite with plenty of visibility from the shining moons and open space to give warning, and to show well the hazardous path ahead. Blade Peak. Not so tall as to be topped with snow, yet indomitable nonetheless, a sheer shaft of stone that sang praise to the talent of its namer. It was said of the Daldistans that it was only when the mountains bowed to them that they could avail them and journey eastward to the lands beyond. He'd only the authority of his elders to interpret this. *Formerians. It has to be.* Of what truth there was to this Adimus could never be sure: whether it was reference to the presence of some spirit that dwelt within them, some metaphor for surefootedness and patience that none in the present crew seemed to possess, or something else entirely he perhaps would never know; he just hoped that, whatever it was, it was with them.

The next day, they tested it.

There were days of endless summer whereupon Adimus and his sister would dare to find the biggest tree just for the thrill of climbing it, but here, exposed to the thin air of prevailing winter, able to find no landings or place of respite, no handholds along the stone, being hustled along by others more brave (or worse, less brave) he found no joy.

This mountain and its surrounding brethren served well as a barrier to the encroachment of The Great Kingdom upon the Lathnians, and now he saw why.

"Githa's army would've used these hills to follow the forest's edge to the river Nalanen, where they could evade the maze of the forest. Where they had planned to build a bridge to cross the great river, but would never get the chance." Argent had explained.

"Because of Lord Saint Lowelyn and his men."

"It would've been an impressive feat of revenge had she succeeded." Tirlag commented.

"Such was her countenance."

"There was really no reason to fight at this point, except out of anger. But Githa, as we all know, was want for sanity and forgiveness, and so her men rode. She would extinguish every last one of them, Lathnian and Daldistan alike, for their treachery. Stories say that is when the Fae appeared, and finding favor in these lords aided in their defense, even so far as choosing the most valiant among the warlords to join their ranks as Immortals, that the Bloody Queen could never extinguish their light."

"There are lots of stories like that." Tirlag commented. "I hear them at sea—the Fae appearing before the worthy in a time of need."

"If anyone deserved it it was him. That dragon he slew was the original good deed that impressed the Gentle Folk in the first place." Argent gushed admiration. "Cadifor McDougall dies from neither age nor ailment. He is the eldest patron of any clan, and they say he is peerless in combat."

They took a moment to process it. "A well that makes those who drink from it immortal." mused Tirlag.

"Long-lived." Alfred sourly corrected.

Tirlag ignored him. "Why aren't we all looking for that?"

"Fair point." the bard replied. "But, no one knows where it is. The Spear on the other hand is just up this hill here. Right, Alfred?"

"It is supposed to be *in* the forest here too somewhere, they say." said Alfred.

Tirlag spun around, still hung up on the subject. "Lowelyn drank from it. And Lowelyn possessed the spear." She said. "You could use your...that...touchy thing."

He smiled and adjusted his glasses. "One step at a time." was all he said.

"Where's Lowelyn, then?" It begged the question from Laina's after thinking the narrative through, even amidst her struggle.

"Full of holes, eyes glazed over." Tirlag japed.

"Hope so."

Adimus consoled Laina, who openly cried at one point, when pitons and tackle had to be introduced, when what little man-made path had one lie had now itself fled in fear.

From here there was no more sure footing, and the party would eschew their heavier packs in sacrifice to sure footing and agility.

There, there, nestled at the crossroads between mountaineer and billy goat the teetering fortress stood, emerging from the mist beyond: Gordona.

It itself was massive, and it took an hour still before they arrived at its gates.

The large iron portcullis that would once bar an army from passage could now barely thwart a stern kick from a bookworm, much less one so well motivated, and when Alfred in his excitement used his priceless staff as a crowbar to lever the latticing open it crumbled into useless rusty chunks, as did the rest of the party's doubts to his feelings of certainty that none had tread this road in search of the spear before.

They cautiously plowed ahead, past the looming arcades of the inner wall where arrows and spears in their time would've stopped them, and into a rampart-surrounded courtyard.

On the other side was an opening that would funnel them left into the mountain, were it not collapsed into useless rubble.

"So the secret of its unobtrusiveness is caverns. Makes sense." Argent professed aloud, after they traversed the rocky path to find a hollow alcove of unworked stone.

There the path branched to the right again and to a set of stairs on their left. Rats hugged the walls, scurrying from the torchlight, which Adimus's eyes followed up to the morbid sight of several desiccated cadavers.

It shouldn't have come as a surprise, the fortress, after all, had fallen, still Alfred paced up and examined them and summoning the courage to draw nearer the boy could see why.

People shorn in twain. Mail and shield, cuirass and helm, lay split like wood logs, the limbs and heads and torsos to which they were attached all disparate from one another, strewn about like Longnight wrapping paper.

"What could've done this?" Tirlag muttered. "...the 'beast' ?" muttered Tirlag, hiding her concern.

"No." he dismissed.

Perplexity shown on the Sum Seer's face as he laid his hand upon a soldier's helm. "A..an accident?"

"...Whoopsy?" Tirlag joked at the absurdity.

"Umm...come again?" The bard said.

"I get a feeling. An impression." he said, grasping for words that might help him make sense of it all. "Like a wildfire, or a rockslide. A tornado. A man ran over by a carriage but the driver was unaware. Was no ill intent. No hand. No will that moved it. An accident."

Alara cautiously slinked up to them and began to feel around at the walls, ever so gently. "I've seen traps in Kessellonii fortifications. Using the Vouxite knowledge of the Physica. Mechanical ones. Triggered with springs and gears." She continued for a few moments while everyone in unison slowly backed away. "Hmph. Nothing." Argent drew near, squinting in morbid interest, "I guess." she smiled at the Bard.

It did not take long for them to find the answer to their query.

The room it stood in was some twenty paces across. It appeared to have been perhaps several partitioned rooms now turned to rubble, as was the mostly destroyed second floor, making a single tall ceiling. There, tangled in a mess of vines and crawling moss, the bronze-like statue still shined in the rays of sunlight dappling through the cracks in the ceiling with the marbled iridescent sheen of blemished bronze.

It stood perhaps a full person taller than Adimus. Wide gashes marred the floor, the ceiling, and the threshold that led to the room and in its hands-- all four of them--and the malefactors which had wrought the destruction, four axes with heads the size of wagon wheels, gleamed in the shadows still, made of a metal with which Adimus was wholly unfamiliar, one that did not show not the mercies of tarnish or rust or dullness.

"Now that is new." Alara marveled.

"What is it?" asked Laina.

"A symbol of the might and splendor of the line of Mathendon and his Great Kingdom. It was said that the Silver King could bring life to metal and stone..." he said. "It's a Labori."

The grim tone his voice held would urge caution to be sure, the boy thought, but Adimus had never seen the eyes of a moth up close before it flew into a flame, and was hence surprised when the bard drifted into the room toward it.

No sooner than he had the noise came: a loud popping and sputtering, jumbles of gearworks crunching as they articulated beneath the molded frame of its body, cracking off the dust of a hundred years as it leapt back to life almost as if in mid-swing, straight at the bard.

"Gahhh!" Screeching sparks of double tandem axes skidding off of the floor.

Whaammm! The blade collided with the stone in the doorway. The whole structure shook. Dust and debris jostled loose from the ceiling at the blow. All Adimus could see was the billowing of a red cloak followed by a cloud of dust. Then the bard came tumbling out, thankfully whole and intact.

He coughed once and dusted himself off. "Is that your accident, Alfred?! It couldn't just be your happy tornado or the murderous wagon driver?!"

The thing had stopped moving, just as quickly as it had started.

Adimus had his shield up, not that it would've saved him, the thought occurred to him as he gazed upon the finger deep gash it had taken from the stone.

"It's guarding the room." The bard said, turning on his heel and looking at the thing.

"How do you know that?!" Said Tirlag.

"Well, either that or that swing *really* knackered it and it's adjourning for some tea before it commences to murder us all."

"Use the Vesican Harp." Alara implored.

"It only Dissolutes non-votive Forms..." he defeatedly eschewed the parlance when her eyes glazed over. "It won't work. But..."

Tirlag huffed and turned, "Well lads, it's been a pleasure. I reckon you can all tag along with me on the way back too. Need something to laugh at." She started back down the hall until she was jolted into turning around again when the curious Cait Shii peeked into the room only to bring it back to life for a heart-stopping moment, "Ahh!", and immediately reversed her decision when the sputtering started again.

Alfred perched his chin with a gloved hand. He pined at the passage at the other end of the room, the only way in. He looked down at Delaney, who turned her head to notice only after a nudge from William.

"How nimble are you?" he asked.

"Me? Haha."

"It didn't attack the rats." Alfred professed.

"If I had to venture a guess, I would say that chasing after every moving thing would be a horrible flaw."

"...How small can it see?" Alara pondered.

Delaney closed her teeny eyes and stuck her hand into the room. Then her foot. She opened them. Slowly she crept past the threshold.

There was an admittedly long silence as they stared at it, ready to jump; Adimus thought She made her way to the passage. Tirlag squeed. "Now go, go find the spear! Go, go, go!"

Alfred looked sideways at her. "Good, now come back." She listened to him.

He sat down straddled and began to rummage through his brown satchel. He produced a large folded sheet and unfolded it. It appeared to be made of a golden foil, and etched on it was a strange circle covered in ornate writing and symbols. He stood and rummaged through his pocket for the leather band of crystals for his Vesican Harp, and with it an old golden coin and a vial of liquid.

Chapter 19
Guardians of the Breach

Its inhuman face, a simple armored visor, almost seemed to belie some sapience. She could swear it was watching her through its darkened eyeholes.

The little gnemedian froze for a moment when the awkward staff in her hand clanged against its leg.

"A bit to the left!" she heard Tirlag cry. She sneered at her, sticking out her tongue before unfolding the All'Khemical writing. She dusted off the area as he had instructed, laying the etching face down, then unsurely she took a few steps back and lifted the staff, pointing it toward the drawing. She held the latch-like trigger he'd shown her, and the familiar sound came from it: the horrible invasive rattling that caused everything in the world to vibrate. Then *'Zap!'* the fiery light came. It left the paper foil glowing and filled the air with a smell like effervescent sulfur. Delaney opened her eyes again, which she'd closed partly to keep from being blinded, but mostly out of sheer terror at what she had just been forced to do. Still, glancing up, she saw that the thing did not move, so she walked over and picked up the foil as instructed. Beneath it, just as he'd said was a darkened outline of the drawing burned into the floor.

He produced a gleaming gold coin from his pocket, and spoke to it.

"Where did you get that?" Tirlag's eyes gleamed. He didn't answer, instead he whispered a few fleeting words of arcane power into it and flipped it to her.

"Place the coin in the exact center of it." The Seer called. She did. "Now uncork the vial and place a single drop on the coin." She did. "Now run!" She did.

Worry grew on her face when she realized at what speed and breadth the long-legged man's command had meant, for her tiny legs couldn't keep up. The etching glew for only a moment with a growing intense light before the interceding blast shattered the silence, engulfing the passage and reverberating into deafness. Rocks and debris scattered like shot, zinging past their heads with deadly force. Capstones and arches whole were thrown to the ground as the corridor itself all but crumbled.

When the dust settled the metal creature lay sprawled across the stone. Where its legs might have been now was now molten void of sprewing gears and collateral. It still flailed in a futile attempt at ambulation.

"After you." he gestured to Argent.

The bard jumped as to his surprise the thing lurched back to life even after all of that, but mustering his courage he sidled his way across the room, the machine flailing at him all the while. Next came Tirlag. Then Alfred.

"Energetic chrysopoeia." Alfred beamed with a grin as if telling a joke no one else got, looking at it in her hand, when with a darting juke the girl reached in and nabbed the coin, then with a dejected growl she flipped it back at him when she realized that what she had was now just worthless lead.

"They weren't very smart. I'm not sure if I mentioned that." Argent observed, as the Labori flailed helplessly at them.

"Oh right. Insult it while it's still in earshot." she chided. Then, almost as if it *had* heard, and to the shock of all it dug its axe into the floor and with it starting pulling itself nearer.

"Adimus! Laina! Quick!" Alfred screamed.

By the time they had all realized what was happening the creature pulled itself close enough to take a swing at them.

Adimus froze. The reason would come to him later, that he'd hesitated to ensure Laina went first, ensuring her safety. He didn't wasn't sure he believed it though.

She cleaved to the wall in an unsure scurry. He could see the reflection in her wide eyes of the axes as they drew within inches of her, close enough for the wind of it to touch her hair. Still she sidled to safety.

"Come!" Laina implored of him.

It had drawn nearer. Argent stepped forward to draw an attack from it, using his cloak like a matador.

"Go!" the Cait Shii yelled, who was waiting to ensure his safety.

The next few moments were a blur that somehow still seemed to take forever. The boy lept forward. It was too late for hugging the wall to provide any safety. The Labori's swing would've cleaved him in two if it were head on, and may well have claimed his arm were it not for the reflexive posture Bearach had taught him. He took the blow across his shield. He supposed the blow of it fortuitously knocked the boy clear of its arm reach and (mostly) safe across the other side. His shield lay in splinters, both in the floor and dangling from his bleeding arm.

Once they were all safely across, only the silent peace which had befallen the room for hundreds of years before their arrival remained, the Labori moved no more.

Long hallways of rough stone branched to the left and right.

It was pitch black until the bard once again lit his torch--he'd left the other one in the room with the Labori still burning, and he wasn't going to go get it.

"The bulk of the fort is likely this way." Argent motioned to the right."

"Then we need to clean up our backsides." said Tirlag crassly. They got the point, though, deciding to try the left side hall.

They were lured by the glow of misty sunlight, where they saw a long arcade of fashioned arrow slits which ran parallel to the oncoming road, and climbed the debris of the crumpled crenulations and rickety ramparts to find a set of stairs leading to the inner walls above, its sturdy oaken doored permanently waterlogged and swollen open where it was propped.

Water spilled into every crack and crevice from overhead, trickling along the walls and staining the white limestone with swirls of red from rust and green from slippery algae. Centuries of water eased the pliant stones, pushing them into smooth warped shapes that reminded the Grigor of melting candle wax.

The deep rumble of the waterfall was all that could be heard. Its head far above its foot somewhere deep below, resonating in the walls of the whole thing like the roar of some beast. Inside the room old tapestries hung covering large cracks and fissures. Water trickled in behind them, leaving little rivers and puddles on the floor. The stone here was pitched this way and that, the whole crooked structure offset from its footers and foundations.

Beyond this door was nothing.

What may have been down the passage none could never tell, as but a few paces beyond, the journey ended.

The Endeavor, bewildered to a loss for words, for the first time spied the empty chasm into which the waters above flowed.

The pressure of ages had worn the very mountainside beneath it, opening wide the crevasse which devoured even the very stone upon which the old fortress stood.

All disappeared into the dizzying cleft and into whatever abyss lay beyond it.

The air made the Grigor's chest ache and his bones chill, a cold mist that tickled his throat. The selfsame miasma scattered what little light there was to be had into a haze, concealing even further the precarious footing.

"Damn...nation!!" Tirlag exclaimed at the top of her lungs when she twisted her ankle and took a tumble, attempting to stop herself by jabbing her scabbard into Argent's leg.

"Well if anything's here it knows we are now." He huffed. "Are you alright?" He did have genuine concern in his voice, if only because such an injury could be a horrible bother and stall them greatly.

She took a couple of steps. "The legs of a named landlubber, that's what this adventure has given me. Let's get on with it." She puffed up and continued. Adimus could tell she was hiding how much it had hurt.

They doubled back, and soon found passage to the inner chambers and keep, climbing along the walls and up the tower that served as the antechamber that led to it.

The innards of the tower had descended from the top with uncareful stairs when it had been made, spiraling anti-clockwise to thwart the right-handedness of typical attackers, but what remained was an empty shaft, kiltered and pitched like some unholy helter-skelter. They would need to use ropes to descend it safely (much to Laina's dismay).

Slowly, they repelled onto the rubble below. The dust on the floor there had turned into a cakey grime, spill-in from the above. Finally, as the last of them dropped, Alara halted them from entrance.

"There are tracks here. Recent." the Cait Shii knelt down. She pointed out the tiny Hyu'man-like footprints to them.

"Goblyns?" Adimus asked.

"Perhaps." she said.

"Wonderful." Argent shook his head, still winded from the last threat. "How many?"

"Half dozen or so. At least."

"Great." Tirlag repeated. "It is infested. Who's to say that the spear hasn't been gone for ages? Used by some little Nissie as a skewer to cook horse meat or something?"

"I doubt it." Alara objected, to her surprise. "Even Goblyns and the like have masters, usually, and war with each other. If one found such a Sublimated weapon of Magic and Grace it would have made it into the hands of something greater, and the world of the Fae would know it when it made its presence known."

A sturdy wooden door sat behind them.

"Let us hope, Cait Shii." said Argent with a shrug.

After debate on whether they should continue and perhaps find and engage the critters or hold up for the night, Adimus and Argent went above and found some green wood--stray branches that had grown over the rampart, and mixing it with the splinters of an old wooden table and chairs they barred the doors and lit a fire. "It would be best to fight them on our terms, if need be, for a change." Argent remarked.

A short run of stairs at the bottom were still intact, and, after barricading the door with heavy debris, there they holed up, bows and swords at hand.

The chill of the night crept in from the open slits in the walls, and the cracks in the walls left open drafts.

They each took turns keeping watch. Alfred, then Alara, then begrudgingly Tirlag. They'd agreed to rotate this day to day from here on in; Adimus would take tomorrow night.

Delaney cleaned and bandaged the Grigor's arm, much to his surprise. He would (attempt to) sleep in the deep hours of the night on the uncomfortable stairs like most of them did to avoid the muck, cradling his sword and fighting the draft from above (the door was now the campfire).

The thought of goblyns (of all things) reminded him of his last days in Balfour. He missed it. Missed his home, beset by cloudy pipe smoke and strange fumes of boiling potions and incense. The semi-frequent hot bath at the Green Beat. Most of all he missed not having to worry about so much that he couldn't sleep and his stomach soured. He found himself worriedly peeking every few moments, awaiting the next fresh threat to come bursting through the doors.

The following day they began the removal of the rocks. It wasn't too far into the chore that Argent turned to the Seer "Why don't you use the Distaff for this?"

"No."

"We will be tired long before the day even begins."

"I said no."

"Surely this is not a frivolous cause. It'll take us half the day to get through this door."

"And you are wasting breath and time better used clearing it."

"...It's because it uses gold, right? I will gladly pay. Silver Hand! Is it not worth it?"

"It...doesn't work on stone, alright?!"

The bard laughed with an uproarious catharsis that rebounded off the walls. He stifled himself only when everyone glared.

It would be that the door wasn't locked or barred at all, and short of being swollen into their frame by the moisture, opened with little effort.

The halls beyond were long and meandering, natural, apparent in that they were not the result of any mortal planning. They conjoined with more domestic areas, like a barracks, an armory, a mess hall. Each one they scoured and found nothing. The journey was punctuated by long double-backs and chambers made to funnel enemies into pincering engagements from multiple sides, making them all the more cautious with the unseen threat possibly lurking around every corner.

Delaney scouted ahead and made sure these rooms were clear long before they arrived. Adimus learned that she could wander around in the pitch black just fine. She explained that urisks had a preternatural sense that helped them find warmth and sunlight, and between that and an innate sense of other living creatures she needed no light at all to 'see'.

This was good news, as, while Alara was the only other who did not need so much light to navigate, goblyns did neither, he was told, but the Gnemedian needed none at all.

The fortress within was immense, and the going slow, as they waited for her to scout every room before they could see it themselves. Eventually they'd crawled their way past the fortifications and to the kitchens and other common rooms--finally gone were the long, undulating hallways. They found a cellar with overturned barrels of beer and amphorae of moldy grain that had been pushed over and disturbed. "More tracks." Alara alerted them, though it wasn't needed.

And then...she didn't come back.

"What in Lyr's name is taking her so long?" Tirlag tried not to sound worried.

They had waited for a long while, longer than any of them were comfortable with, and with each minute their hearts beat faster. Finally, Alara looked back to Alfred, and with an approving nod, disappeared into the darkness. Adimus wrung his sword guard worriedly with both hands, wiping the sweat from it. Alfred turned on the apparatus, which made its horrible noise, though none protested--if she were in danger it was already too late for them to worry about it.

"Forward." Alfred commanded sternly. He'd not sounded so sure about anything thus far.

Then Alara reappeared, silent as death. Her face was unreadable, but she urged the boy and Argent to come forward. She already had an arrow knocked.

Adimus was only nominally good at pad-footing or being any sort of sneaky, really only touting enough skill in it insofar as being able to get a good scare out of Dyrshul when they played hide and seek. Argent, as expected, was a feather wafting in the breeze. They both came to the corner, where beyond there seemed but blinding darkness. He could see the shii's glinting eyes shooting at him from the black. He wasn't well at reading them, but they didn't seem worried. He could feel her hand pushing on his sword in a gesture to put it away. Then they heard Delaney's giggle from down the hall.

"I...don't know. I don't know what you're trying to tell me. What?" her disembodied voice said. Slowly they all entered the small room she was in, Argent's torch letting in the needed light.

"No, no they're friends. It's okay." she said to the shadowy figures who cowered in the corner.

The creatures before them stood about as tall as the urisk did. Clad in dark clothes, they were difficult to see. Adimus realized he didn't in fact put his sword away, so in a gesture of good faith he sat it on the ground. Slowly she coaxed them forward. "See?"

The figure slowly crept up to them and gestured something with its hands, holding out one of them.

What sat upon what would've been the head of the figure could scarcely be described as anything short of an immense nose.

Adimus giggled in spite of himself. "Well I'll be named, they are real!" He exclaimed to himself.

"It's a Killmoulis." said Argent.

The creatures looked at them with their little beady eyes.

The thing pulled the ski dhu from Adimus's belt. It startled everyone until they realized he was just examining it. He then pulled something from his pack.

"Mushrooms?"

Another stepped forward, then another. All with curious looks in their beady eyes. They poked and prodded at Adimus and Argent like they'd never encountered something so strange. Two of them picked up Argent's cloak and splayed it like a curtain. Argent allowed it, with a twisted inquisitive brow.

One drew near Adimus. It recoiled. It was unmistakable that its eyes caught the glint of his blade. "Hide your sword, and don't let them touch it." Alara warned.

One turned to another, and, twisting its gnarly fingers to express some signal, all began to scurry backwards into the small entrance from which they had come.

"Wait!" cried Delaney. "Come back! It's okay!"

Quickly she ran over to Adimus and, climbing him like a pole, reached into his pack. Then bolted back toward the entrance. "Wait!"

A few more minutes elapsed. Again the urisk had disappeared. By that time Laina, Tirlag, and Alfred entered the room, all confused looks on their faces. "What's all this?" Spat Tirlag, doing well to hide her concern.

Alara hissed dejectedly and went looking for her again, this time motioning for them to keep up.

"Bless my peduncle, you can understand us!" Adimus heard the voice speaking to the urisk as he approached.

"Hardly. This tongue is barbaric, hardly more grunts and groans." Adimus blockaded the others from entering, stopped in his tracks at what he saw. It was a talking black bird.

"A crow?!" said Tirlag.

"A Pangoran thick-billed raven." Alfred muttered to himself.

"Admit it, not the strangest thing we've seen so far." Argent bumped past him. "Hello there." he saluted, tipping his hat. "My name is Argent, what's yours?"

It shuffled across the handle of the oven door atop which it perched. "Al'Kasar." the thing took a moment to straighten a stray feather. "Not the best of names, I know, but it is the one my master chose."

"Your master. Then you are a pet. Who is your master, Al'kaiser."

"Pet. That's an interesting word." Was all he said. "But pitiably the most concise in this mongrel tongue of yours."

"Pretentious little thing." Alfred remarked.

"Pretension implies a desire to impress. I, Hyu'man, do not care what you think."

"So your master is not a Hyu'man, I take it?"

"Dear me, no."

"If you are a watchman you're doing a poor job." Argent replied.

"Or we are about to get ambushed." Alara darted her head to every dark corner.

"Who are you all? Why are you here? Who is <u>your</u> master?" He echoed.

The bard looked at Alfred as if asking permission. Adimus could see the apprehension in the Seer's eyes when he replied. "We are here on a quest."

"Ah, now I can't tell if you are being intentionally vague or lack the words required to express your savage selves. Surely I must assume the latter, as I have answered truthfully and to the best of my knowledge thus far."

"You've not told us who your master is."

"But I have told you what he isn't, which is the same should you listen. I've been as concise as you have. Apologies, I thought perhaps it was another limitation of your language; leave it to the near-sightedness of cessair language to label a noun that which should be a verb, and get flustered when it escapes their ability to conceive."

"See, Adimus? These Fae are nothing more than deceit beneath arrogance." Said Alfred.

"Bloody self-important parrot." Tirlag cursed.

Argent ignored him "I'm not sure what you mean...We are searching for <u>the</u> spear: Gungunta, Gae Bolg." He put his hands on his hips. "I have been concise, now you should be."

"The persona my 'master' expresses himself as at this time does not wished to be named." He cocked his head. "But. If you must have a word, your kind will call him Mal...CAW!" it was cut short. The creature that tackled it seemed to appear from out of nowhere.

"You blathering fool!"

"It won't matter if he's not alive to hear it!" the raven cried.

The creature relented. It stood and shook itself off.

It was slender black house cat. After a moment hopped up onto the stove in the ravens stead.

"Fluffykins?!" the name sounded strange coming from the Seer's lips. "Is that you?!"

"Beg pardon?" the cat said. "Who are you?"

"It's me! Alfred!" It was jarring seeing his veneer of stuffiness and professionalism be forgotten in his enthusiasm. "Teacher?! Is he here?"

"I...don't know you." the cat said cautiously. "My name is Elaith."

Adimus hadn't even realized Alara had eased Tirlag, Alfred and Laina into the room.

Delaney climbed up the boy again and grabbed something from his pack. It was bread. She chuckled as she watched one of the Fae creatures stuff it up his nose.

"Come now, don't play. Tell me what you've been up to?" insisted Alfred.

"Well, I suppose, not being this Fluffykins. Quite busy at it, in fact." he quipped.

"And I am forced now to assume there is more than one talking black cat in Morida. Fascinating." he himself would be unable to tell whether the statement he'd just uttered were sarcasm or not. "...Guess they all have talking cats." he said to himself.

"Uncanny." was all he said.

The cat said something to the cat in a language with which Adimus was altogether unfamiliar. The raven replied with an inflection of defeat.

The raven shoved him aside, and with a sigh he spoke. "I shall speak on your terms, without evasive words or reservation. I shall speak plainly..."
Elaith shoved him out of the way. "Missing. Missing is what he is."

"Your Familiar is missing." Alfred adjusted his glasses.
Argent looked at him in confusion.

Al'kaiser's feathers puffed up. "Yes! I've heard this word. Yes, that will do. We are Familiar, I am his and he is mine." He explained. "Bounder. We call him Bounder."

"Now, see? He does have a name!" said the bard. "If you hadn't made a fool of us we may have never known." he said, brushing himself off.

Raven eyes lacked the expressiveness to show the contempt that clearly slathered his voice. "You put up quite a fight."

Elaith groaned, and spoke over them.

"He told us to stay here and watch the entrance," he said. "He hasn't returned. It's been nearly two days."

"...Where did he go?" Asked Adimus, finally catching up.

At that the cat motioned. They cautiously followed.

In an inconspicuous solaire, amidst displaced waterlogged furniture and the rolled up rug that concealed it, was an opened hefty hatch.

They peered in.

"Tell me, Al'Kasar." Laina said. The adeptness in which used his name showed plainly that she had been listening acutely yet remaining silent until now.

"Why have you and your friend not come down here to look for him? You're both small and undoubtedly stealthy. Were you afraid?" She sounded obviously skeptical.

"We Promised." said Elaith.

Laina paused at the strange answer to give it thought. "Promised? I am sure you wouldn't mind if you broke the promise if he were in danger."

"An oath. A Pooka Promise." explained Argent.

"Correct." The bird said reluctantly, swatting at the cat again in a worried manner.

The space opened up into a gaping passage. Cold air whirled and beat at the torch. There, chiseled stairs descented far beyond the torch's light to the maw below.

Chapter 20
Into the Dark

The first few runs of the stairs that spirited them down from the upper chambers were tiny–they were made cramped and claustrophobic as to be unobtrusive to any who might notice it as more than a chimney shaft or latrine chute, but, reaching the terminal bedrock of the mountain, far below the foundations, the crew of the Endeavor had found themselves traversing a seemingly endless series of descending steps into a ceaseless cavern.

They followed Argent, the volunteer, reluctantly. The stairs they descended were narrow and uneven, with nothing at all to impede a plummet into whatever abyss lay below.

The silence of baited breath was deafening. Finally, Tirlag, after catching hers upon the first short landing they'd found, far beyond the heightened earshot of any animal, piped up. "Now, we know this not to be a trap...how?"

Argent answered. "Well, thankfully, our antagonist is quite toothless. Courtly Fae cannot lie to the Cessair." said the bard. "They are bound by Magic as to be unable. Well--" he paused. "A spoken falsehood. They can still lie by omission or if another stricture of the Code supersedes or demands it of them."

Adimus wasn't much listening, he was busy trying not to die--he'd always been afraid of heights.

"Code?" Tirlag bit.

"The Code of the Kind." said Argent.

"How do you know he has sworn?" Questioned Alara.

"The Bran family are all sworn."

"What do you mean by 'sworn'?" Tirlag asked.

"To the Oath of Covenant. It is a geas to which all fae of the Seelie Court swear." Argent explained. "A set of laws by which they must all abide."

"Laws? Ha! Shackles." spat Alara. "That they may rule over us with no fear of scrutiny or revolt."

"You did not commit this swearing?" asked Laina after a few moments of silence.

"They tried to get me to for a time. The hyu'manii <u>and</u> the gentry both." she explained. "In Torant the hyu'manii are fearful of us to the point that they have their own law: no Unsworn fae may walk freely in the cities of the west. When they found out I wasn't, I was arrested and taken to Brigden."

"The prison island." It came out as pitiable. Tirlag apparently knew the name well.

"Correct. Mister Krasad had me freed."

"And you swore indenturement to him." Argent deduced.

Alara nodded. "Until such a time as the Spear is found, or one year and one day from my oath, whichever comes first."

"Not a bad deal for freedom." said Argent.

"I intend to stay here when this is all over. There are no such laws in Menkara." she said. "It is nice here, barring some of the more backward folk."

"...So we have you for how long?" asked Argent.

"Four Moons and three days. Then, heavens help you, you are on your own." Her facetious grin could be heard in her voice.

"We'll find it before then." said Alfred. "We'll find it before dawn. I know it." he added encouragingly.

"Anyway, I'd heard of a noble house who learned they had Fae blood among them, and as a show of appeasement to the people they took the seelie oaths." Argent explained.

Finally, Delaney, who had reluctantly followed after saying goodbye to her new friends, spoke after a few more moments. "They were strange, the Killmouli."

The phrase almost evoked a snicker from them. "You don't say? " said Tirlag.

"No. The way they acted, and maybe thought. Strange," she said, almost to herself. She paused, thinking. "It was almost like they'd never seen Hyu'manii before. Or bread. Or colorful clothes."

The precession stopped, and so did Adimus's heart for a second when near-sighted Alfred came bumbling into him.

Argent had stopped dead before them, as if the very revelation that bade him go no further. "This is how they got in here. This passage leads to The Deep."

"Why would anyone knowingly make a passage that leads to The Deep?" said Alfred. "This is probably some hidden route of escape for Lowelyn's men."

He didn't answer.

"The Deep is real?" Tirlag gulped. "It's a real place?"

"Very."

"My Pa used to tell me stories when I was a girl." she said. "Monsters that pulled entire ships under by their chains for dropping anchor into their domain. A fish that could fit a galleon in its mouth." she spoke to Adimus. "That's the underworld you are describing, doubtless."

Adimus just nodded along to the conversation. He would've perhaps chimed in were he not preoccupied with the stairs. Mention how the gods slept in the Deep, how the dead come to rest there when they die.

"Our people have stories of a great sea beast who accosted us on our journey across the ocean to Morida. It swallowed a whole fleet of ships, and made the seas boil." added Laina.

"It's a vast ocean--an ocean beneath the ocean. Covered in islands." Tirlag continued.

"Can we stop talking about monsters?" Delaney tried to protest, but was ignored.

"I've never heard that." said the bard. "I've always been told that it was an endless labyrinth of caverns. That it was the home of the Formerians who survived the Epochellipse, and that's the least of such." he continued.

The stairs had led them hundreds of feet downward. And still they walked, down, down. The Grigor's legs were numb, and each arduous step made him fear that his legs might give out from under him.

"Crom and his brethren rest there too. In the undermounds." said Adimus, trying perhaps only to distract himself. "M-my grandpa told me that. It's not in the Numitorum, but it makes sense." he felt he had to explain to lend credence to his being in the conversation at all.

"The Rathlands." Alara clarified. "The fae live there as well. That's where you go if you break fae law. A prison of darkness. Forever."

"...If fae cannot break their geases, then how can a fae break the law of the fae?" Asked Laina.

Alara simply shrugged. "I don't know how it works. Don't want to know."

"Neither do I." Argent agreed.

There was a long silence, then the Grigor asked. "...Are there flowers that grow in the Deep?"

"What? Why would...?" Argent did nothing to hide the perceived absurdity of such a question.

"...Nevermind."

Finally they made it to the bottom. Adimus doubled over. His calves burned, and sweat, despite the cold, beaded on him leaving him in shivers.

They were left in a hollow cavern, their torchlight stretching in all directions with no indication of its breadth. The only hint to its size was the echo; every shift and step reverberated in the dark.

They quietly debated what to do next, wrapping themselves tightly in their cloaks, huddling and warming themselves.

Calling for him in the dark would attract too much attention, as such, Alara and Delaney were dispatched to lookabout.

Adimus would wager that the day was drawing to a close, though he'd no way of telling aside from the fatigue and malaise that had crept over the whole of them.

Over the last hour or so Argent had made preparations for what might be considered a camp. They found broken barrels, three quarters on the way to becoming soil, with which they made a smoky fire. By that time, the two would return empty handed.

"It will take all of us days to search this place." Alara hung her head.

"It'll take me two myself to muster up the strength to climb back up those stairs." Argent tried to joke.

"Maybe he is still down here searching as well. For Gae Bolg." Tirlag answered.

* * * * *

Adimus opened his eyes. The fire was out. It took him a moment and several blinks to register the importance of these facts and reconcile them.

"Well, it's dawn. Where's the spear Alfred?" Argent teased.

However dim, ambient daylight struck the cavern, and in the hush and grogginess of the morning they gathered their things and headed on.

It wasn't before too long that he saw it. The ravine below, which Delaney and Alara had retracted, made a natural footpath, and seemed to be the only reasonable way forward, and there, at its base, a single shaft of light penetrated from the stalactite-covered ceiling high, high above. Snow tinkled in through the opening, marking a roof well more than a hundred feet above them.

Where the gorge had begun was where the light entered, between the craggy seams of two enormous slabs of rock that seemed to be made of a different type of stone as the cavern; one grey, hard and harshly geometric, contrasting the rest of the cavern's the smooth rolling limestone.

Adimus's legs bounced as he walked, and were tight and sore; he held a new appreciation for simply having to walk all day. Finally, reaching the end of the gorge, in the moisture where the groundwater had settled was a run of caked sediment, and there, tracks.

"A..a.hare?" The normally stealthy Cait Shii's voice rebounded on the stone in the throes of such bewilderment.

"Well, of course he is." Said Argent, to the confusion of everyone.

They followed, until they too ended on the hard rocks some thousand paces on. The roaring din of water invaded their ears; it distorted their idea of space, both being very loud and sounding far off.

They approached the epicenter upon which the alien stone hung, the spot where it stood directly overhead.

"A city? Is that a city?" Tirlag vocalized, giving a name to how strange the concept was.

Crumbled remnants of masonry carpeted the floor below, with more joining them, as from time to time one could hear the clatter of the falling stonework, vibrating free from the constant resonance of the waterfall against the stone.

"Upside down? And on the ceiling?" Alara questioned the nonsensical notion even as she said it.

Before them just ahead was a piece of debris that itself could have been the Green Beat, but by its shape was but a miniscule piece of a larger structure. It was the balcony of some solair within a palace, or the decorative walls of a castle. Would that it were not ruined by time, the detail in the graceful patterns of knotwork that adorned its cap would've shown a level of skill and devotion to detail a sculptor of the modern world could only hope to achieve, yet what traces, what shadow left which clung to it still impressed.

Adimus stared at it for a long moment, mesmerized.

Argent's awe-struck head never turned terrestrial. "This could only be." he professed, pausing as if having to pick up jaw to enunciate. "Tripura."

"What a huh?" Tirlag heckled.

"The four corners of the map in the story, that the gods raised." said Argent. "Of them, three fell." he closed his eyes and recited from memory."

To rend the golden tower twain, plucked they fell upon the plain: Findias, Morias, Gorias; of old were their names, offered were they to end the Black King's reign.

Just as he had finished, a strange gust of wind caught them. It was strong, almost enough to press them back.

When it was over, they all stood there, confused.

There was something amiss by it, stranger than even its presence out of the blue. He had thought it at first to be his imagination, and as strange as it was, he was remiss to mention it, hoping someone else would say something, and perhaps be able to articulate better what he had just felt.

"The wind, just now. My cloak did not billow upon it." said the bard.

"My torch did not flicker." said Laina.

"It cut straight through me. Straight through my wools." Adimus finally added.

"A work of Magic? Perhaps?" Alara pondered aloud.

"There were many Spells pronounced in those days. One long forgotten." said Argent, usurping knowledge. "Doubtless their echoes still hang in the air."

It was a hollow explanation, and helped little, but in light of no recourse it was enough for them to shrug and move on...

"...They were cast down. And fell here?" Tirlag grasped for clarification as they trailblazed the dim maze. Argent nodded.

"This knowledge alone could be priceless. I wonder what else is here?" Tirlag drooled, glancing down at what appeared to be a broken brazier.

"A curious place for the resting place of this spear." said Laina.

"Or a fitting one." Alfred pointed out. "The four treasures belonged to the four cities. This would be Gorias, if I had to guess."

Now they could see more clearly. Whereupon the ceiling sloped at an unnatural angle, like a rolling hill in the sky, structures of stone dangled like stalactites. Strange monolithic portaled structures like houses, grown rather than carved, smooth rather than harsh; they reminded the Grigor of the shells of sea snails he'd seen once when a merchant from Marron passed through town. If the windows were windows and doors were doors, the needle-tip ramparts of their tower-tops were taller than the blue oaks of Sul Vale, and the broad ones were bigger than the Ravenhound besides.

The flora that clung to its surface were of the like of which Adimus had never been acquainted. Glints of twinkling light like a calm sky at heavy with dusk twinkled from the deciduous leaves which clung to their alabaster trunks, in defiance of the lack of light or water to sustain them through the eons.

Coiling braids of ivy clung to some of the structures, crowned with flowers whose heads were as blown glass, scattering and refracting scintillating rainbow patterns on the white stone-paved streets below above.

Largest of all, cascading in curtains from the ceiling hundreds of feet above and touching the ground below in some places, were gangly yellow roots like golden yarn, which protruded out from everywhere in the structure, from popped paving stones to rooftops. Though the eye could not tell from direct observance, as if, somehow, the roots held some faint golden incandescence which the air, though they themselves did not.

It wasn't too long before she would order Argent to cut swaths of them with which to start a fire--an order that for once he obeyed without contest, when offered the choice between fire-building and scouting.

Nearby a reverse fountain swayed, wound and hanging intact from the roots. Atop the kilter spout was the visage of the bearded horned god. Ground water trickled across it, dripping from his eyes and mouth, and from the great gash in his wrist.

'Many Shapes' Adimus's mind stirred.

"We camp here." Said Alara, finding a small hutch nearby, formed from another looming piece of masonry which had fallen, and shrouded by the roots.

Adimus took a few moments to drink down his waterskin and refill it at the font, as the others were. Then he took a few moments, thinking no one to be watching, he nabbed a piece of parchment from his sack and a bit of charcoal with which to stoop and rub some of the knotwork etchings he'd found on the walls of where they camped. "You can do that after." Tirlag insisted. "We're going to need a strong back and some rough hands for carrying." Was all she said to Delaney, almost as if the boy were a tool to be used.

"What do you mean?"

"There has got to be something of value here. Plenty of somethings, I'd wager. Come on." She grabbed his hand and pulled.

"No." he snatched it back, dropping the charcoal. He heard it bounce somewhere beyond the firelight when it fell. He sighed, "We'll need to make a trip back here on the way back through anyway. I'm tired."

Argent hid his smirk of pride.

"We'll share half." She plead.

"It's not yours to share, remember?" said Argent, unrolling his bedroll. "It's everyone's anyway. Per the contract."

Tirlag knelt to meet him eye to eye. "Look where you are, Adimus." she gestured with her arm. "The ancient ruins of a lost people. What legacy they might have left. What's more," she shifted when his face didn't change. "What if <u>we</u> find the spear? Then we can leave this awful place." (Suddenly it was awful), "Please?"

The boy sighed. It was her enthusiasm, the starry twinkle in her eye like an excited puppy--an excitement that he knew to be genuine even if what she said wasn't, that made him move.

"Don't go far." Was all Alfred said, not even looking up from his notes.

She didn't listen, as soon the light of the fire could not be seen, as almost entranced, under some Spell herself, the girl led wherever her feet dared take her.

Before long they passed by the large structure overhead, heretofore obscured.

Figures bearing heavenly weapons stood guard round it. Some had multiple arms with which to do so. They wore garlands of painted flowers, or skulls. Some were red, or blue, or green, with horns, or pointed ears or tails. Some had multiple faces, or the visages of animals, or sometimes no discernable face of all; a blank canvas upon which the worshiper might attribute the impressions of their mind's eye.

From afar, the grand citadel above that sat in its center appeared miniscule and impossibly busy. Would that it were not a colossal wreck left to time, the detail of the thousand gods that adorned its cap would've shown a level of skill and devotion to detail a sculptor of the modern world could only hope to achieve, yet what traces, what shadow left which clung to it still impressed.

Tirlag wasn't even looking at it. "Damnation! Where are all the people who lived here!?" She growled.

"You would be disappointed to know if they all evacuated and were safe?" chided Delaney.

"Of course not." it hardly sounded convincing. "There are no bones, no nothing! Did they have to take everything with them as well? So selfish!"

An old goblet, worn with verdigris. A flat disc of stone about the size of a saucer, covered in ornate knotwork. What looked like an ancient brooch missing its clasp (its insets where once gems were inlaid was empty) was all they had found in the hour or more they'd spent wandering the cave.

"For Thrice's sake!" she cursed, after scouring what had appeared to be a fallen house in which she found only wooden objects which turned to soily dust when picked up.

Adimus's arms were well tired, and he could feel the chill on his nose and fingertips which he couldn't warm. Still her fever led them.

Two halves of another Fir Bolg statue lent against a large crest stone of the cave.

"There!" said the urisk, pointing to a twinkling spot in the debris.

Tirlag scurried toward it. "Yes!" she jaw dropped in disbelief as picked up and scraped the caked soil off the gemstone.

Adimus could see its reflection glimmering in her eyes. Quickly she scanned them with her torch.

"Adimus!" it was probably the first time she'd said his name.

Her face frozen in sudden dawning dread she stood looking down at the footprint.

A simple rabbit's this was not. It was the print of some beast. A hoofprint the size of a dinner plate, of a cloven hoof of a creature whose a gait two paces astride.

"We…We should get back." She said soberly.

And that was what they did—or were, until it fell upon them again. The breeze.

They stopped, before a veil of glowing roots. They writhed as if alive before the vitality within the air, shifting and swaying to reveal beyond them a glow the color of gold.

"Do be a dear." Tirlag motioned, trying in vain to hide her timidness.

He needn't reply. Adimus reached out to begin brushing the roots aside for her. They moved. They moved without him touching them. He recoiled.

"Well?" She apparently didn't see it, still scanning the darkness for the roaming beast.

Memories of the Huldra raced into his mind, and whether this thing was some sort of carnivorous plant monster too. He pointed to them and began to vocalize what had just happened, *'they moved'*, but before his lips even parted they themselves did, like a veil, to reveal what lie beyond.

"How did you…?" She started to ask, but then the golden glow caught her eyes as it did his.

It was a warming, welcoming, glow. The boy couldn't explain it, but it reminded him of Laina that day, the day he was healed. He cautiously stepped forward. The wind blew again touching their flesh, this time like a breeze: it had come from this.

"What is that?" Tirlag stepped forward. When she reached for it the roots shifted as if to oblige her request to take it. A golden orb. It was smooth and round, and was difficult to hold under the arm, as he found, and she decided to forget most of their heftier hauls in favor of it so that he could carry it.

It got Alfred's attention; he and everyone else were standing long before they arrived back at camp, seeing it's unnatural light from afar. Adimus immediately handed it to him. "What is it?"

He closed his eyes as he always did.

Alfred hesitated for a moment, reining in his giddy anticipation. "It--it's alive." he said. "Perhaps."

He opened his eyes and began examining it a bit more conventionally.

"I don't understand." he said. "I am getting impressions like last time."

"Perhaps the items here are too old for you." Argent stated.

"…When I traveled to Thane I held a coin passed from the hand of the Gold King himself, taken from the coffers of the Thrice Slain monarch of Agrathea, after the Epochellipse and the fall of The Kingdom Once and Future. Through its eyes I saw the face of Mathendon II, son of Perun Silveraxe, demigod and patriarch and first king of Kessellon." he half-boasted. "I doubt it."

"On with it then." Argent said, sounding a little frustrated.

His eyes tightened, straining, as if all his thought was being bent toward simply enduring it. "It knows that I am. Its eyes are bigger than my memory, and so in its mercy it tells me as I remember it."

"What…what does that mean?" said Tirlag.

Again he spoke in a broken stream of consciousness as the imagery came to him. "The effulgence of the stars in all their forms, the breath of the primordial from which all souls emerge, on wings soaring the skies never and forever more."

"What is it?" asked Adimus.

He let go, as if it needed to be away from him, almost throwing the thing, Tirlag caught the precious thing like a baby.

"The heart of a dragon."

Chapter 21
Broken Words

They slept little, taking only a few meager, vigilantly overseen hours before they doused their warming fire, and quickly moved on.

Adimus kept the treasure they'd found wrapped deeply in his rucksack, as the glow of it would be a beckon from whatever was indeed out there. They'd doused their torches too for much the same reason instead opting to navigate via the sunlight shearing in above their heads.

Adimus watched them clamor about what it might be, upon seeing the tracks. *Formerian. Div. Shadespawn.*; "The great four-legged beast",

By mid-morning they'd found more tracks, albeit a few of them in the sod and moss. Soon the floor became hard and barren and again they disappeared, the cave was tightening, and it seemed more and more a possibility that wherever the beast was, that was where they were going.

Narrowing into a chasm like an underground canyon, the cave funneled them even closer to the roots of the mountain, to the large, fast-moving underground river that was the consequence of the great falls.

Finally, along its banks they decided to break.

Alara paced about. "Surely if he were alive he would have made it down here." he spoke, mostly to herself. "There are not many other places he could go."

Then she stopped. Without saying a word she grabbed the nearest person, Laina and pointed at the ground.

The large print in the mud near the bank. This one was fresh, and led dead into the water.

Alara was already gone before the first words were muttered, following a road only she could see. The look on her face when she looked back at them silenced them. With naught but the hushed sounds of drawing blades, they followed.

* * * * *

It was a peculiar sight.

Nestled in a crag in the rock away from line of sight, there sat a small fire, gold coins, strange bobbles, jewelry, weapons and hides, and along-side it, captured in a cage made of bones and leather straps, was he, the hare.

"Well, hello there." Argent echoed the sentiment from when he'd met the raven.

"Shh! Go away! Can't you see I'm busy?!" They were all shocked when it responded, flicking back its ears in irritation.

They all looked at each other. "Busy? Being caged?" Argent rebutted.

"Who are you? More Pledgers? No. I'm serious. I was here first."

"What is it blabbering on about?" said Tirlag.

"What is the creature that captured it?" Alfred whispered, ever the one to push silliness aside. "Him." he corrected. "Captured him. Ask him." he gestured.

"An Orculli." it answered. He disregarded their blank expressions; rabbits apparently had impeccable hearing.

"We were...we were sent from above by Fluffik--I mean Elaith, and Al'Kaisar." stammered Alfred, trying to keep his composure.

"Well, tell them I'm fine and begone."

"Well, thank you!" Laina said it as if it were a curse.

"It's a lobster cage." Tirlag observed. Her face became one of unreadable concern "Wait, did you say Orculli?" she said.

"Too late."

The water rippled and stirred. "Quickly, come!" said Alfred. Adimus didn't know what he meant, as he motioned to gather them all together.

Then he spoke again, those strange words that Adimus both knew but were gone by the time he sought to remember.

And then their eyes fell upon the creature. The ripples in torchlight disturbed the water as its head peaked above the surface silently. Glowing red eyes met with them. Tusks, a snout, bulging muscles, cloven-hoofs. It stood perhaps twice as tall as Argent, the tallest of them. Kelp and algae covered its matted dripping hair, and barnacles clung to its green skin.

Water trickled as it lumbered forward and It drew its weapon, a mace with a head the size of one of Niall's pumpkins. It sat down the large net full of items it carried.

"Who's there?" Its gurgly voice rumbled. It sped at them, quite easier than they could have ever expected. "What's this, more pilferers?! Robber crabs!" He cursed, and let out a resounding roar. "Shellhearts!? I am Neroth of the Red Stripe!" He introduced himself, to their astonishment. "Stone take you, the Turning will be yours this day!"

Then he rushed them. Tirlag ran. Argent tossed on his cloak, which turned pitch black and disappeared into the darkness. Alara drew her sword and wand. Adimus froze. Delaney hid behind Adimus. Laina grabbed his arm and dragged him aside. Alfred didn't move. He reached into his pocket, and removed a ringed finger from it, then closed his eyes and finished the Spell he had been speaking the entire time.

The creature swung at him. "Rrrragh!" the crushing blow fell right upon the man, crushing his skull, buckling him like a snapping twig, laying him low beneath the massive thing, at least that's what Adimus could've swore he saw, he even remembered seeing the shattered glasses fall at his feet, but there stood Alfred, behind the beast; then like some foreboding thought or vivid daydream it was gone from his mind, and he'd never remember what he never remembered.

The Orculli stood for a moment scratching his head, then after a moment slung his mace back over his back.

He grumbled to himself a bit, and shambled around with a vagrant look, as of someone who'd just woken up from a vivid dream only to realize it wasn't real, or someone who'd entered a room and forgotten why. He ambulated over to the sack, hesitantly picking it up and dragging it to the rest of his horde, the bunny included.

"What do we do?" Laina whispered. Adimus slowly stepped backward, but his foot slipped on Argent cloak. They all froze this time.

"Who's there?" said the giant pig-beast.

It turned to them. They'd been seen. "What's this, more pilferers?!" He cursed, and let out a resounding roar. "Robber crabs! Shellhearts! I am Neroth of the Red Stripe!" He introduced himself, to their astonishment. "Stone take you, the Turning will be yours this day!"

"Not again!" Tirlag squeaked.

Alfred stamped over to them while he was saying it, his face more one of frustration than concern.

"Rrrragh!"

Alfred pulled the bard's cloak over them like a curtain. Adimus ducked in panic until he realized that...nothing happened. He peaked over the cloak, and there the Orculli stood, sorting his haul. The crew cautiously reappeared.

He looked over to Alfred, who gave a wry wink.

He then mouthed to Tirlag *Get it.*" he gestured toward the cage. She had landed upon the pile of the thing's luggage, blending in with the busy looking piles of loot, the creature's back turned to it.

Nervously she lifted it, as silently as she could manage. She almost seemed to vibrate with her fluttering heartbeat tearing at her as she forced herself not to breathe. She jittered past the giant, almost getting swatted by its whipping tail as she passed.

It didn't take long before they had journeyed back to the crevasse from whence they'd come, where Alara and Delaney (too stealthy to have had the privilege of being seen) were waiting for them.

Well on they backtracked, until they found themselves at the pillar of light.

"You can stop here." the hare said begrudgingly. "Orcs are blind in the sunlight." he explained. "Let me out." he then commanded.

They observed as when unlatching the cage the hare emerged and in a puff of glowing golden mist he became the familiar man they expected.

"I suppose you expect a thank you." the man huffed. "Though you've ruined my plan." he said, dusting himself off.

"You're a Pooka." Argent presumptuously pointed out.

"And a powerful Sourcerer; inheritor of a dozen Cunnings, and tenfold Graces that whisper to me from within the Polyphony, that hunger to exist bespoke. Shall I oblige them?" he looked longways upon the Seer. Then his face softened. "Malkin of Bran." he introduced, tipping his hat, which seemed to appear from out of nowhere just a second earlier. "But you know that." he smiled. "You know who I am, you know that you are but a stone's throw from Gae Bolg, and yet seek to help me just the same? You are not like I've been told Hyu'manii would be. Especially Pledgers." He admitted. "Fascinating."

"So, you were trying to be caught."

"He is looking for the same thing I am. That we all are. And he has an advantage."

"And what is that?" Tirlag asked.

"He is Orculli. He has been drawn here by the smell of it." he shrugged.

"...Smell it?" she questioned, but he didn't answer.

He paced up to the riverbank, and stared upon its surface feverishly. "It is in the water." he glanced back at them. "He smells it in the water." he stroked his chin. "If only I'd befriended that merrow back in Kalneis."

Slowly, Alfred drew near. He removed his glove. He touched its surface. His eyes lit up, and he glanced back at the passage from whence they'd just come. "Of course!"

Tirlag stepped forward" what is it?"

"Could you see what I see, Tirlag you would weep..."

"The treasure." Argent explained. "It's down there."

"The ruins must have all gotten washed away by the falls." Adimus explained chipperly. Perhaps she would finally have an answer to her question the other night."

She hung her head solemnly, but Alfred looked all the more resolved. "Then it is here."

* * * * *

It was hours before they mustered enough courage to check on the Orculli, this time from above the chasm.

In the interim, Malkin showed them the passages he and his unwilling stooge had explored, and the ones that he himself suspected led elsewhere.

Bran was one of the clans of Ormond, Adimus had learned from the bard. They had once been tasked with diplomatic matters and trade, and they used to be keepers of the archives at Hewnyleigh along with Mathune. They were ousted and ostracized when it was found that the widowed matron of the clan had married a changeling, that along with their ties to the royal family of Kessellon cast suspicion on their motives. Her offspring, such as Malkin himself, that was his 'disgrace.'

He, like the man in Hewnyleigh, learned this in adolescence. In darker times would've been executed, but after a period of threats and disownment suffered simple derision and shame over the affair. But there in his youth he'd learned the truth of himself. Adimus envied him.

He never answered how he (unlike every other generation who came before him) also knew the resting place of the spear, but none of them could protest; they wouldn't tell him how they knew either, and none asked directly.

"I am confused." Laina piped up. Tirlag growled in consternation. "Your cat and raven, are they people too?" Several of them gathered closer, apparently she was not the only person with that question.

"Well, they are as much cats and ravens as I am a person." he cryptically answered. "Oh, you mean can they change into kindred forms? No."

"Do you do so by way of Magic? Is there some Spell to it?"

Malkin blinked, then gave a satisfied smirk. "I understand what you mean only because I've spent most of my life speaking to hyu'mans. There is no 'spell', yet what you call Magic is simply the truth of Nature. There are plenty of things that you hyu'mans do that call upon the same mystic power….you act out Spells every day without knowing." They fell silent in their bepuzzlement. He looked back at Alfred. "It <u>was</u> a clever use of the Aurum Agri, back there, by the way. With the orc. And your use of Anwyn. Well done." he said. "Your cadence was a bit off though, your Seithr doesn't quite match your Gladr. It shows a lapse of rigor."

"It was <u>perfectly</u> executed." Alfred said defensively.

"Perhaps in regards to you, but not the Agri. You couldn't hear it by the ear, but believe me, I know it was there. Not 'know', no, but know, no?" he bemused, really only to himself.

"So...you are a Sourcerer." he answered.

"I listen to the Agri, but no, I just hear it, and it sounds wrong. I'm telling you for your benefit. Bad things can happen to you mortals when the Work is wrong. The Spell can rebound, using your own calcinates to fuel it if you're not careful. You could end up a lithaugurized masicot, or worse."

"The Aurum Agri is hokey mysticism, as is lithaugury and all the other 'bad things' practitioners warn others of to keep dabblers from dabbling!"

"Confound it all, would they shut up?!" Tirlag whispered to whomever would listen.

The rest of them stood on edge as they made friendly banter in the echoing cavern with a twelve foot tall angry giant about, but the seer could not help it--he was compelled. "Who was your master?"

"Master." He read the man's face, "You mean like a teacher? Of sourcery—?"

"Ahh-!"

Their idle talk had disarmed them again, as they rounded a corner to gaze upon the sight now before them. Their weapons were half-drawn before noticing there was no threat, though perturbed still they were at such a sight, where upon the floor the carcass of some great serpentine creature lay toppled, splayed and flayed into pieces.

Tirlag squeaked.

"Dragon!" Argent cried in reflexive warning before he noticed how dead the creature was.

Alara knelt to look down at the creature's head, which was several paces removed from its body. "It was..."

Adimus peeked out of curiosity, though admittedly feeling queasy about the nightmarish sight. The head alone was nearly the size of the boy, its fanged jaws big enough to bite him in half.

It's great reptilian eyes glazed

Its sickly yellow slitted eyes seemed to glow in the contrast of its jet-hued scales. It had long, pointy horns that pointed forward much like a bull, and the tongue which dangled from its mouth was forked. He also mustered a look at the body as Alfred snatched Argent's torch and walked up to examine it. It well could have straddled both banks with its girth. He gazed upon its long, undulating body, with clawed hands and feet; he remembered back to the stories he'd been told from Luloch as a child, of Gandareba of the Yellow Heel, of the demonic Azi Rao, or of Coarthanach, the dragon of the moors. Still, there it lay on the cavern floor, lifeless; a feat so great as to be enshrined in storybooks to tell children by the fireplace after supper.

Alfred, again, touched it with an ungloved hand.

"Magic, no doubt. Thaumaturgy. <u>Powerful</u> thaumaturgy." Malkin said. Alfred turned and looked at him.

"What could do this?" Argent said, the worry in his voice alone distilled his concern to them all. *'What could do that to us?'*

No blood touched the floor or walls, as whatever carved its head from its neck wound appeared to have cauterized it with an intense heat.

They took from it what was demanded by the seer: ampules of blood, a fang or two, scales from its thick hide (with much effort), and, steeling their mettle, moved on, further, further up the bank, toward the sound of the growing noise.

Dust still lingered in the air, that, coupled with an obscuring haze made the terrain confusing to navigate. Were it not for the sensation of Tirlag's hand grasping his arm until it bled he wouldn't have been sure he was still alive.

Light consumed them. The pallid, suffused daylight of the open sky high above blinded their sun-starved eyes. Alight below them was a craterous void where the fortress once stood. Their ears rang. Everyone had to strain to keep up with the flight-footed seer, who as if possessed made his way, sometimes stumbling over his own feet, down to the shores until he was out of everyone's sight.

The surrounding basin in which the falls emptied were as candle wax, limestone having been pounded by the immense force of the falls for hundreds of years, yet there at its bottom was a single pedestal of heart stone, a crystalline granite untouched upon which stood one of the great four pillars of the bolg-built aquaphor.

There standing was Alfred, looking down at a spot on the ground.

It was a sigil, not entirely unlike the one he had made the urisk draw, though this one several paces across.

"He was here." He gasped to himself.

He leaned down to pick up an object nearby: a rope made from a golden twine. He began thumbing through the torn old papers in his pack until he came across a drawing that much resembled the thing they looked at.

He looked closely, as if reading what it said, then a look of excitement came across his face.

There, behind the waterfall, the true shape of the pillar which held the gigantic structure above it at lady lay bare before them.

One might think that it hovered in the air as of by magic some six feet above the ground, as the small slivers intact of stone at its base would never have been enough to hold it aright, but when Adimus peaked his head in to see the Seer standing there, he witnessed the amazing truth.

Perfectly balanced to hold the incomprehensible weight of the stone above it effortlessly for centuries, without bow or bend in head or haft or handle, there it stood.

"Behold, Gae Bolg. The Spear of Fate." Said Malkin.

It was the very spear itself, that held it in place. Its haft was of simple ash, yet, as if the feat were not enough, dispelling any doubt that this was an object of Magic, a Sublime Work, were the streams of blood, unmistakably blood, which issued from its jagged ebony blade of a head, shunted and channeled away by the living wrap on its haft, a wrap of trellising mistletoe which grew and fruited even in utter darkness, and which adorned the head's cross guard of three sharp curved bones. Those bones were the ribs, arrayed like the sacred triquetra, barbed and inverted to repel outward.

Adimus noticed the ichor which issues from it beneath his foot. It puddled beneath there, the coppery stench of it filling the crevice, staining the insides a mottled auburn.

"You do not act surprised. You expected it to be as such." said Laina to Malkin.

All of them stood at the entrance, agape at the sight.

Alara let out a groan of utter defeat.

"This. This is horrifying." Said Argent. "Diabolical."

"But how...?" Delaney stammered.

"A trap, centuries in the making." Malkin courtled.

"The pillar itself was wearing away at the damage." Adimus observed.

"Lowelyn must have had the mind of a Nis." commented Argent. "No offense..."

But the pooka just shook his head, "Lowelyn never laid a hand upon it. He did not do this. He only ever knew of the spear's resting place, and sought to keep it safe."

"...Then this is a test of the devising of Kain himself." Argent postulated.

"Yes. The Ancient One." suddenly Malkin's voice sobered, only a moment out of reverence. "Fitting: the Spear of Fate." he said, "The spear that sees to your mortal fate should you dare take it." he guffawed.

"You are glad at this?" asked Laina.

"Well, what are you waiting for? Go get it." Tirlag egged Alfred. Adimus figured she could not do much save channel her fury and disappointment into vitriolic quips.

"Very well, then, but you'll have to follow me." he joked, straightening his glasses with a snide grin.

With that he threw the golden rope down, and began to tie one end to its base.

"Adimus, give me your shield, I will need it for the Spell." The Grigor relinquished it without question. He walked out and up to the glyph upon the ground. "All of you, stand here." he came to the center of it.

Just then in total dismay, they, being so mystified by both the spectacle and the ecstasy of the revelation of the Sublime weapon, they were startled when behind them came: "Shellhearts!? I am Neroth of the Red Stripe!" He introduced himself, to their astonishment. "Stone take you, the Turning will be yours this day!"

"Quickly now!" Alfred yelled. "The center, now!" The creature charged.

The wizard pointed his Vescican Harp at the floor, completing the single missing rune, which as of the turning of a key caused the circle to flicker to life. The writing began to exude a golden incandescence, as if its radiance were found somewhere deep in the rock, only brought forth by the Sum Seer's will. That strange feeling came over them again, that a wind which left all but their inner being untouched had swept over them.

The creature charged, his colossal mace swung for Adimus's head. Adimus tried to scurry but the Sum Seer grabbed him by the arm.

With eyes big as saucers they looked to the half-mad unreadable man, who took the line. "Pull!"

Thankfully, in that moment it was not only Adimus who had faith in him. He could not really tell it in that moment, he only knew that his strength alone could never been enough to dislodge it.

Tink.

The first large stone which crumbled from the awesome thing came from above, and would've crushed the lot of them with impunity, the clouding mist averting any attempt to see and evade the rain of destruction. Instead there was a loud crack and a hum, and a crackle of blue energy and the refractions of such against a field of energy, and when the creature swung his mace he met with it too.

The crashing din of tons of stone deafened them, but of the chaos of the world around them crumbling they were sterile observers; as the entire fortress fell around them not even the dust that settled afterward reached the hems of their clothes.

When it was finished, the sky was open above them. The Orc lay upon the ground, fatally pinned by the stone that was once held by the spear. Still it spoke, "Bwahaha! That was a good one!" It said. "I'll get you a good one next time!" it said gleefully, even as it choked to death on its own blood. Then the creature's features froze in a permanent grimace as they watched over the next moment as first its face, then its body petrified, turning to darkened stone before crumbling under the weight above it with a loud crack.

Laina tugged at her robe that seemed caught just beyond the bubble, and she realized had been sheared at the end, as if by invisible scissors.

Everyone else was still frozen in abject panic and disbelief. "Very good." Said the Sum Seer. He passed through the field as if it weren't even there. "See? The field only bars non-living things from entry." he said, matter-of-factly.

"Like massive grizzly clubs, thankfully." Argent gulped, looking down at the orc mace, adjusting his shirt collar to feign coolness about the whole thing before going to look for his hat. "It begs the question, what is the rope made of?"

"How is that for fate?" he mocked the pooka, reeling in the mighty artifact as if it were a fish. "Very fortunate." He huffed, stepping cautiously out of the field only after several others had. He paced up to the orc. "For us. For him, not so much. Poor fellow." He leant down and touched what appeared to be the shattered face of the thing.

"Whatever it was, it was left for us. By my Teacher." Alfred continued his boast, but the pooka wasn't listening.

"You mourn your enemy? Wretched thing." Tirlag's twisted face asked.

"Yes. Of course. He faces non-existence."

Something about that phrase, rang in Adimus's ears, and left a tickle in his brain that could only be scratched with answers. "Non-existence? You mean he's mortal. Like you."

"More than that. He is Bolgkind. Only oblivion awaits those who haven't the Blood to stir them. According to them, like the Cessair, all shall be black, forevermore."

"The Cessair? Like us?"

"Carved from wood, instead of stone, but just the same. Yes. Inanimate things given life by Grace alone, having no intrinsic Nature of their own that life ought to fill them."

When the whites of the boy's eyes became white enough for him to notice his misstep, he recanted. "Apologies. It is what I learned that the Bolg say about you. My mouth gets the best of me sometimes. Makes me say things I don't mean." Was all he said of it.

That same cord and Delaney's rope proved indispensable in crawling their way out of the newly shorn canyon. As they climbed, Alfred spoke.

"Now, you must answer <u>my</u> questions." It was strange seeing this treasure, this ultimate symbol of all they had strived for, cast aside in conversation so easily, but it was obvious that the question irked him like a splinter. "Who are you, really?"

"I...I don't...?"

"That Spell is only known to the one who taught me. He mastered its use during his time with me--I helped him with it. One of eighteen I received from him." It was unlike him to not have answers, his stammering sounded foreign in his mouth. "This, your cat--the talking cat. And the headless drake." He panted as he pulled. "Most never think of it, but a corpse is an inanimate object as well. I Read it. It was felled by my master. It is not—<u>cannot</u> be a coincidence."

When they reached the top, pulling the Spear with the cord like a fish being reeled and catching their breath, when a bird came fluttering down to join the pooka. It was Al'Kaisar, and in his beak was Elaith. Malkin smiled, seemingly unsurprised, and continued, "It wasn't a coincidence. It was Fate. You said so yourself." he simply said. "In all sincerity, Hyu'man, I do not know of what you speak. I am in the service of the fae court, bound to them by geas, <u>and</u> my family, only insofar as the geas allows. I can serve no others. You Hyu'manii have ensured that this is so."

Alfred untied the Spear, and gazed upon it with a delighted sigh. Malkin's eyes locked on it, staring in awe. Finally, he himself sighed. His was in defeat. "Speaking of which..." Malkin said. He removed his hat. "The Endeavor is victorious. The spear is yours." he declared. He looked over the man's shoulder at the boy. "I suppose I get a 'seat at your side', eh, *Lord* Adimus?" Adimus looked at him confused.

Al'Kaisar addressed his master quietly. "Mother will be most displeased." he seemingly warned.

"Quiet!" Malkin hushed, brushing the bird with his foot. He continued. "I know it is not my place to ask it of you--you already have saved me once today. But I beseech you for this one final favor." He waited for them all to gather around. "Let its grace be upon me."
They stood there for a few awkward moments. "What say you?" he said again.
Argent spoke up, "What does he mean?"

"Use the Spear. Absolve me of my oaths with it."

"I don't understand." This time it was Alfred.

"Of course you don't." He cynically huffed through his nose. "Far be it from those who seek a Sublime object of legend to actually know what it does." He looked around jokingly, the bird and cat apparently his audience. He finally shrugged. "To be fair, it is a more obscure property of the thing, a little known consequence of the Magics sealed within it. Not even the Court knows about it." He gazed at the object fondly, touching the bloody tip. "The Spear--and the spear alone, has the power to forgive the transgression of oath breakers. With this treasure of the Tuatha, I can be free." He looked at them all. "You only need say the words."

"You do ask much." Argent answered. "Geases are unbreakable." he looked for Alfred to share his outrage, but the wizard was deep in thought. "Even if it could...Cross the Seelie Court? I think not."

He rubbed his fingers together, finally wiping the ichor of the spear's blade on his pant leg. "Freedom. From my Name. From all that I am: the politics, the struggles, the strife...it is unbearable to be so, under the thumb of another. You of all people, Mathune, should appreciate the goal." he pleaded. He looked to the Grigor. "I was being literal, you see, about my mouth saying what it wills sometimes—it is difficult to hold your tongue when it isn't even yours to hold."

Argent shot back. "I thought your goal was to claim the spear to restore the honor of your family? Sworn fae cannot speak falsely."

Malkin hid an embarrassed grin with his hand. "...I was going to avoid mentioning that for the sake of upholding our truce and appear more generous, but yes: I swore to see it returned by my family. I'm not sure what the powers of the geas would judge, but I feel I may be bidden to take it from you by force to fulfill them." He shrugged. "I would be powerless to stop it."

Adimus found his knuckles clenching, and fought the urge to preemptively draw his sword.

The bard's eyes narrowed, and he himself took up a cautious stance. "I always thought geases compelled the afflicted to act. You would <u>know</u> if you were required to do it."

He paced, "You are in part right. It is a deep call. An all-consuming desire all at once mixed with an unaccountable sense of fear and aversion, like a morsel on the tongue of a man dying of starvation, or the need to withdraw one's hand from a nest of venomous snakes. Such is the geas, greatest of poisons. But this world is large, and one can be enchanted by strong delusion, lulled into false senses of security, ensnared by madness to think that the morsel would be better saved for worse days, or that the snakes may not be venomous."

"I don't believe you."

"I cannot speak falsely." he spat back at him. "I wouldn't mean to do it, of course." he gave them a decisive stare. "I would be...very sorry."

Suddenly Alara stepped forward. "We will permit it. We will oblige your favor." Said Alara. They exchanged an empathetic gaze.

"We will?" Questioned Argent.

The bard, perhaps for the first time Adimus had ever witnessed, was silent.

"This spear can <u>undo</u> a geas?" said Alfred.

"I. Cannot. Speak. Falsely."

Alfred looked down at the cat one last time. Then back at him. "Tell me what to do." Said Alfred.

He motioned to William. "<u>He</u> must be the one to do it."

"My hands will not be on this." said William. "The fae court would have my head!"

"No one shall know…" Malkin assured. "I swear."

"How can you know that?! You should know more than most what led us here!" he pointed at Alfred. "A simple touch would betray me. No, Alfred, if you choose this, it is your deed."

"He cannot. He doesn't know the tongue of Dhuun. And none can recite the tongue without knowledge of it."

Alfred held the spear aloft. "I have ordered William to do this, as per our contract. What blame is to be had of it is mine."

"This <u>wasn't</u> in the contract." William objected.

"I have spoken it into the item. Anyone who would do a Reading with it now would know that these words were spoken."

Malkin curtly looked at the bard, "What will it take? If you so wish I will make new geases with you. I will relinquish any right to the spear, swear to do you no harm, whatever you wish."

With a hesitant sigh, William took the Spear.

Malkin instructed him. He held it as told, pointing the tip at him. Over the next few moments, he showed him, and he repeated:

I invoke the Velskanda, bite of the bitter Flame of Falsehood, swayings upon its ponderous pole, gambit of the gods, the blood from stone, these the words of Gae Bolg:

He said something beyond that, reciting words written upon the head of the spear. As he did, it glowed, and went he finished a light issued from the spear's tip, piercing the pooka's chest. Adimus could swear afterwards he knew what they had said, but never could remember the words that meant it, meant that Malkin was free.

Lykil, young soul. I expunge his word. Pardon what of him is still yet undone! Free him of his oaths proclaimed atop the mountains of Gunge arisen, his Covenant of the Highest Grace, absolved, may he go forth, forgiven!

Malkin bowed, and said thereafter, in exchange. "I will accept that the Spear of Fate, Gae Bolg, is your charge. I will not pursue, I will not harm, I will not betray. I will tell no one, lest it be your will. Then he too spoke the language:

To this I forswear my will to abstain, that I shall not unduly refrain, the coming to pass of all you shall gain, being that which ye are and desire.

The pooka spoke in yet another foreign tongue. "*Ghiana. Un dat!*" The creature's claws on wiry green hickory sinew cut into him.

With that he swooped his ears back and placed his hat on his head. "Be well." and with a final nod turned to leave. It was at that moment, caught in the momentum of all that had transpired, that they did not perceive the movements of the creature who had been standing with them. From Adimus's periphery it had appeared to have just been an old mossy stump.

Wiry vines were its muscle and sinew, and leaves branches protruded from its form like the spines and horns of some beast. The thing stood some eight feet tall. It reminded him of the Bugbear in a way, or perhaps Delaney, but massive.

It made no hostile movement, instead retrieving a parcel from a nearby hutch in a tree and joined the pooka. As it turned, the boy saw it, a basket-like cocoon of live woven greenery, within which was a beautiful red maiden, her eyes shut as if in a deep sleep. It was the one who'd accompanied him during his Pledging, he knew it.

"Whatsoever's fate you choose of it, Hyu'man, by all means choose well, with more studious care than you use to draw your conclusions about me. We will <u>all</u> be watching." he warned, then with the tip of his hat he resumed his animal form, and being scooped up by the creature along with the rest of them they were gone.

Chapter 22
The Swordsman

It was only a few steps outside of the palisade walls of Keara proper, in the quiet shanty environs, that the bandits were upon them.

Argent whispered a curse to the pooka under his breath-- convinced beyond doubt that he had betrayed them.

Cold rain pattered the quiet streets of the burrough as people in their nearby houses looked on at the scene.

"We know you have it, the holy spear. Relinquish Velskanda or perish!" Said Chauncey Coalfax, the man from the Pledging, the man in the blue Heraldrix.

Argent had muttered some somesuch about whether they thought it were wise to accost an individual who wielded the same spear that had felled a god, but as it were, all wrapped up in bandage and linens to keep it from bleeding everywhere it wasn't a confident one. It didn't seem to take, he figured (like Chauncey Coalfax obviously did) that a keenly pointed All'khemist's wand would put a swift end to any funny business--divine in origin or not.

"Ross of Ward moves swiftly." Alfred bellowed to Bevin Pembroke, who'd only revealed himself after the situation was well in hand.

"A cutting accusation." He replied "It would not stave the bloodshed of the day to deduce that." He gestured to one of his men. "Remove that staff from him."

Adimus felt sickened; he didn't know which it was: that they had been fooled, or the realization that one so seemingly cordial and kind, kin of Thadeus no less, was in truth callow and callous, and hid it so naturally.

He'd banded with Beaumont, Chancey Coalfax and company, and a several others, who traveled with livery and colored tartans of their post as wardens, much like the Watchers, but today they donned the armor and weapons of a makeshift militiaman over them.

They spread out, edging in to encircle them.

Just then a voice cut through the cacophony keen as a blade, with enough steel, authority, and promise of threat to bring them to a stand still. "Disperse now, all of you." It said. The boy spun around to see the lone swordsman striding up.

An exotic-looking wide-brimmed hat concealed his face.

"And just who might you be?" Called Bevin Pembrooke.

"Caleb Knolls is my name, Servant of Caladbolg." he said, proudly removing it.

"Ah, you. Caleb, you are a lowly servant of a lowly house on a lowly hill." professed Pembroke. "They were not sponsored by Cadifor, I implore you, knave, stand aside."

"I will not."

"I don't believe he understands. I'm not surprised." he said to his men. "We are acting on behalf of the clans, same as you." he gestured with his pistil. "<u>They</u> are not. They are quarry." he said.

"I do not act on my lord's behalf, but for my own sake. You speak of quarries like you're a hunter. Then, where is your sportsmanship? Your actions sully your name, the name of your family, your country, and the family and country to whom you pledged. " he said. "I will give you a chance to redeem yourself from this course of action: face me in single combat and I will ensure you have an honorable death."

"It is the Pledger's duty to claim the Kainspear for the glory of our great nation. You should be the one to talk." said Bevin. "Spouting sanctimonious about station, all the while pirouetting around with that queer Jin blade on your side. And you call yourself a countryman?" he tisked. "Shoot him." he commanded.

The thunderous din of the wand erupted from the silence. Sparks flew from the blade, which they never saw, for the moment it was drawn and the man's closed on him it was already over. He stood many paces away, still the All'khemist, having missed had no time to replenish the weapon and jettisoned it only to draw another one, which may have found its mark if the blade hadn't cleaved through both it and its wielder in one stroke. Blood sprayed across the swordsman's face. Gasps and screams erupted from the crowd.

It halted the bandits' approach, even if only because of the spectacle of the whole thing. It was enough time for him to wheel around and engage the next closest.

Adimus drew his blade. It was the first time he had to do so on another person, another Hyu'man. He'd never given it thought until that moment. He froze. Thankfully, so did his adversary. There he looked into the man's scared eyes, and felt the same stammering hesitance, making it all the worse. But he wouldn't have to; whether it was the fear that the swordsman brought to him or the man's own squeamishness at killing another person the moment's pause was enough for the swordsman to cut in between them, the bandit's natural cowering giving the swordsman room to engage. He allowed the man but a moment to square up, but no more before he slew him. Beaumont's huge shadow fell over them as he got off his horse. Nothing was said as he drew his axe. Caleb gave a grin which morbidly framed his blood-soaked face along with a nod as the man drew his axe, not one born of wanton bloodshed, but a warm smile of appreciation, which was perhaps a little more chilling. They rushed at one another. The brawny man came down with it with might and surety, but the swordsman had broken the rhythm of his stride, feigning a lack of speed in his approach only to burst forward at the last second after his opponent had committed to the swing, angling his body only just enough to avoid it but not enough to break his momentum. Instead he barrelled headlong into and beyond the strike, with a speed combining the step, the lunge of his legs, the twist of his torso, the closing in of his long arms, and the leverage and length of his curved sword given full range of motion to swing from behind the man's axehead after the attack had missed. Adimus's eyes forced themselves shut. One of the men with him vomited at the sight.

"Take up your sword, Bevin." was all he said, eye of the storm amidst the carnage.

The Earl of Tavishire stood back. "Well, defend me!" he becried.

They sheepishly started to close in again, when Alara stepped up to him, weapons drawn to head them off. She looked at the rest of the crew.

Adimus only had to stand guard along with them thankfully, parrying a few half-hearted swings jabbing a few thrusts of his own until the swordsman had made it to the man.

"We yield. We plead for clemency, and in exchange we will advocate for your lord's ascension." he yelled to his men as Caleb began toward him. "Put down your weapons!" he yelled to his men when he did not stop. "I am unarmed. You can't slay a man unarmed." Still he came. "I am your lord's cousin! We surrender!" He fell to his knees and prostrated himself "Please y-!"

The breath from his lungs failed to vocalize the plea with his head rolling away from them and onto the muddy pavement.

The rain left tiny rivers of red as it washed over them. The small garrison dispersed quietly without contest, all the while eyeing the mad swordsman in fear that he would come after them as well. The swordsman calmly wiped the blood from his blade with a handkerchief, and skillfully sheathed his blade.

"Tirlag!" Delaney screamed. "Tirlag is hurt!" She ran around the carriage in a frantic search. The others followed.

There she sat, under the enemy's wagon, hutched behind the wheel, cradling a wound in her side. A felled man lay before her.

"Peekaboo." She managed a grin at the urisk.

"...Tirlag?"

She said nothing. She'd used her handkerchief to try and stop the bleeding, but it ran from inside her cuirass and down her pants and up her sleeve. It was everywhere. Like a scared animal they coaxed her out, Argent and Adimus both pulled her to her feet.

Laina came up and looked at them. "Get us as far away from here as we can go, as fast as we can do it." she said. "Now." She turned to Tirlag. "Where's the one that hurt you?"

Tirlag stared at her blankly. "What, are you going to scold him? Wag a finger at him, smack him on the wrist? He's dead, love. Me too, probably. It figures."

"I need you to listen to me. Where was he?" she reiterated.

Tirlag pointed to the crumpled man on the other side of the wagon wheel. "Adimus." Was all she said. He didn't have to be told. He hoisted her up.

They fled the city. "Finally useful, aren't you, farm boy?" she still joked. "All those years pitching hay bales." she playfully felt the muscles in his arm. "That arm healed up real good, dinnit?"

Argent looked around at all the people staring. "You don't have to tell me twice."

"I will make my statement to the city guard. Her Magic is strong. Do as she says." he swordsman said.

"Thank you, Servant Caleb." Said Argent.

Laina scrambled about in the mud, and picked up the dagger, the culprit's weapon. The girl's blood was still on it.

When they'd made it far enough he helped her up onto Aethan, who never bucked or protested. "He's a good boy." Tirlag observed. "People don't give horses enough credit."

"Will you talk through your funeral as well?" Laina cut, giving her several unwelcomed looks.

"I was trying to keep my mind off it."

"Well, shut up for a minute. Please? Hold her hands." She gave the boy his second order, which he followed, only slightly more hesitantly.

She started to protest, but Laina halted the horse, and removing her shawl with a quick kiss and stuffing it into the spot between her robe gave her a look that silenced her.

She held up the dagger. That glow was about her again. At her first word the dagger lept alight. She spoke in that same voice, the one that permeated their minds clear as day yet was a mere whisper.

"Phoenix Flame, I invoke thee, heed my wishes, mote it be. This knife is the fire, sacrificial flame, your sacrament: deeds done in fervent faith. With these words in prayer I quench Fate's thirst. I give you them all...make right these wicked Works! "

She plunged the dagger back into the wound. Tirlag squirmed, but it was too late. The dagger erupted into nothingness in her hand, and she was left staring down at...nothing. The wound had been erased, unwound from this world.

"How did you do that?!" Alfred stood agape.

"Wha-! It's gone! Laina!"

"I did nothing, wizard." Said Laina. "The graces of my Goddess answered." Immediately she put the shawl back around her neck.

"I was told by my master of your kind." The swordsman said. "You are Magenta Sudre. A Magus. That was Magic."

She didn't answer, she didn't still seem to want to. She finished tying the stole around her face, then bowed her head, though not to them. Obscured by the cold rain, they gripped their weapon upon hearing the galloping horse approach.

It was Caleb. "Is she well?"

"Like it never happened." she said.

He simply nodded, and was on to the matter at hand. "Is it true then, Lord Mathune? The Spear is found?"

Chapter 23
A Declaration

It was another few hours before they were all allowed to go along their way. They stayed while the town guard took statements from several witnesses, but they all seemed to at least know Caleb, if not personally then of him, and he and his authority allowed the Endeavor company a measure of discretion when they were questioned.

When asked why he beheaded the man he said *'to keep the honor of Bevin Pembrooke.'* It was an odd thing to say.

They dare not enter back into the city, even though by that time the rain had turned to snow and they were soaked to the bone. The news would be out after all, as all the bystanders heard the man's cry. *'Relinquish the Spear or perish.'*

Adimus praised his wool cloak, which had kept him dry and warm for the most part.

"Again, I thank you." Argent echoed after it had quieted down a bit. He had told the wandering swordsman about the fortress and the resting place of the Spear, "The Fae, Malkin, Lowelyn, even Kain himself was right; men are not to be trusted with it. It was hidden for a reason. It will not be dragons or traps or Orcs or the Labori that would defeat the Endeavor, but the hearts of wicked men."

"I will see to it that this does not happen." said Caleb Knolls.

"Why?" asked Tirlag. "And what if your lord stands to gain nothing from it? What if it does not wind up in his hands?"

"...How did you know we would be here?" Alfred asked, more pertinently..

"He seeks favor for Cadifor McDougall, gallantly swooping in to save us." Argent sneered.

The swordsman bowed his head. "You will not believe me." He said. "It is alright. To answer your question, Faeth, it is to deliver a message personally to one in your employ. Tirlag McCayden. Thankfully she lives. Thank you, Magus." he nodded toward Laina, who hesitantly acknowledged.

Caleb looked down at her.

"...Huh?" Slowly she sat up. "What? Me?"

"I regret to inform you that your brother has been incarcerated."

She laid her head back down. There was a long silence. "...And?"

"You are the only family member inland we were able to reach. Your mother and father are out to sea, as it were."

"...And?"

"He requested bail."

"Ha!"

"...You don't seem surprised."

"Only one question. Was a man named Walker arrested alongside him?"

"Not to my knowledge."

"Just wondering. I decline."

"He is being held in Adranan awaiting his fate. He is to be sentenced to Cairnfang. You are not concerned as to the conditions for his freedom?"

"He had it coming to him. Let him stew for a while." She crossed her arms. They were silent for a moment. "Cairnfang, you say?" She could only feign so much apathy.

"It is how my lord knows of it."

"And he has the authority to order his release, I take it?"

"He does."

"In exchange for what, one sacred treasure of the Tuatha?"

"Tirlag!" Argent scolded her. "He saved our life."

"*She* saved my life!" she pointed at the priestess.

The swordsman said nothing of it. "We will not be able to weather the night in this cold." His pace quickened, and they followed. Just beyond the precipice of freezing, the muggy night air seemed to soak them from within, the culprit evinced in misty vapor seen on the streaming nostrils of their horses, and felt on their skin, wet from sweat and rain with a sickening damp. The wind seemed to wick their drenched clothes to ice where skin did not touch to warm them, and snow had settled on their clothes.

Soon they found themselves at the doorstep of a farmstead, some miles outside the town.

"I am Caleb Knolls, and these are my friends. I apologize for our intrusion onto your land, sir. We are in dire need of shelter and warmth."

"We'll not have a word of it. You turn back to the city, now." The crouched and haggard farmhand who had leered cautiously at them from the window on their approach, upon cracking the door had for them a pitchfork at the ready and a household full of others just behind him. The man shook it at them. "I got a boy and our fastest horse ready to let the town guard know all about you. I heard about the massacre in town." he threatened.

"Sir, if I may." said Argent. His cloak was now red and white. "I am a lord of Ormond, William Mathune, and these are my companions. We need a place to stead our horses, and we are not permitted into the city *because* of said massacre. Any help we could get..."

He was silenced by the man's chuckle. "You're a Mathune? Then, I'm the lord saint Lowelyn, and these are my companions: the Lord of Autumn, the Emperor of Histban, and King Tersus of Ragandmond." he said, amidst the egging hoots and chuckles found within. "Now scram!"

"...Is that really Lowelyn?" Delaney's tiny voice whispered to Tirlag.

The man behind him stood up, holding a shillelagh. Argent simply straightened his cloak collar. "Perhaps you do not believe me, but I would not want you to be you if you were wrong about me telling you I were me."

The man puzzled at the kuon for a moment, then his brow furrowed. "Are you threatening me? 'Highborn cannot intrude upon or seize their citizen's lands or possessions.' It's in the Code of Kain."

He had turned around, seeming to gaze upon his 'entourage', but sure to let the man get full view of the wolf emblem that was now emblazoned on his back. He spun back. "False. If you heard that it was for one family to get advantage over another." He began to speak in a strange tongue. Adimus had heard it a few times before from the reeve at the Meet. It was ancient Daldistan.

The man's eyes glazed over. He elaborated once he was finished. "As you can see by the phrasing the provision which allows such protections are subject to the caveat that the nation not be under a state of strife, both civilly or abroad. Now, I could argue that at its utmost the nation has been in strife since the king passed and every member of the court would side with me. I could state precedent if you'd like, but I would at least posit that the killings which upended the civil order of the town--if only just for the night--were grounds enough to warrant the enforcement of the Law of Abetment, <u>requiring</u> your assistance."

"Milord--. My humble apologies." He looked back to his posse for approval. "Come in, please." one tried to stammer a protest inside. The old man dismissed it, "Lord or lawyer, trouble either way."

"We can?" Caleb cut in. "Perhaps he'd like your bed, or perhaps your wife to keep him warm?"

Adimus gritted his teeth, wanting to run up and warn him that the same look was on the man's face as when he addressed Pembrooke.

"No need for that. I am a benevolent and merciful lord." William bowed to the man at the door. "I chose to elucidate you instead of having my men come with the irons, didn't I?" The bard seemed either unphased or unaware of the swordsman's judgment. Argent looked sideways at him. "We will take the barn. I thank you." Caleb answered for him. Argent let him, but not without shooting the swordsman a glib glower as he fled the stairs.

The barn was full of sheep--and their droppings--the old man having not the energy or wherewithal to brave the cold to clean it out as often as he chose. As he showed them he showed open regret, and insisted that they stay inside, but Caleb would not have it.

They were to sleep in the cramped hay loft, their horses amongst the livestock. Argent tried to protest a few times, but was ignored. Alfred sat on the quiet, the spear across his lap. Gazing off into a black corner. The swordsman sharpened his blade by the lantern light. Though he showed no outward menace, Adimus wasn't the only one that felt unease—he could do to all of them what he'd done to the others, quite easily, and from his countenance and his interactions with the noble Mathune may well be tempted to.

"Are you in shock?" Tirlag nudged him, bringing him to. Alfred was touching the spear again.

"What does it say to you?" Argent said from the darkness.

"I can't Read it. It's a Sublimated item. The *most* Sublimated item, having full Votiveness."

"Votiveness?" Asked Adimus.

" 'Free will' would be a good analogy for the layman."

"You mean this thing has a will?" Tirlag said ominously.

"Of sorts. Votiveness is a quality which must be sequestered in order to Work Magic, Reading included."

"So...you <u>can't</u> Read it?" Tirlag scratched her head.

Argent questioned. "I thought I heard you say something in the caves. That you were certain that Lowelyn wasn't the last to touch it."

"I've told you before, it was a lie, to get him to talk. He obviously knew the Spear was down there. <u>Somehow</u>." He reversed the accusation.

Caleb cut in. "I will tell you how, though you wouldn't hear it."

Argent knew immediately at whom the blade was pointed. "You jest! This wasn't me, on either account if that's what you're insinuating! Truth be told it is quite serendipitous that you just so happened to arrive to save the day. Pembroke and Dougall are related, what shadow games does <u>your</u> charge play?!"

The man's eyes narrowed but he said nothing.

"How chummy is Mathune and Bran these days?" Said Tirlag. She meant it facetiously, he knew. Said it to get a rise out of him. He didn't bite.

Caleb's attention wavered when he looked down at the carnal ichor that issued from it. "Is it common for items of Magic to do that?"

The Sumseer helped Alara to adjust and change the linens that they had to keep upon it. "It most certainly is not." Alfred echoed the absurdity.

"Uncanny, to be sure." he replied. "No doubt a relic of the Tuatha. So, have you folks any plans for the Spear yourselves?" he casually segued, eyeing his sword for any chips as he did. "What is your next move?"

It was at least good to hear that the man recognized them as the owners; it meant that if his bluster about honor and honesty weren't all a show they might survive the night.

"You know," Tirlag started. "We should take it to Madreg." said Tirlag.

"That city in the cursed wasteland?" Said Argent.

"And have it lost at sea? Or in the hands of some pirate or jin robber?" Said Alara.

His eyes shot to the sailor. "In the absence of a better choice that seems reasonable." Caleb replied.

"I wasn't aware he had a say." Argent jeered.

"I have been there." he explained in appeal. "It's where I met my master, in fact. Not as bad as they say, and far from the reach of squabbling warlords. The patrons of the city may be a problem, but Cadifor has contacts there who would be willing to put pressure on them to stay back."

"Of course he does." Said Mathune.

Tirlag pressed the advantage. "I've got connections there too, they could arrange an escrow for the Spear. It's the end of the season, my mother and father are there right now. This needn't be in our hands. Take the greatest sum we can get and leave it to the whims of fate who gets the crown, be rid of the cursed thing as quickly as possible, I say."

"I do not wish the fate of my country to be sold off to the highest bidder." William tried to protest.

"I wasn't aware you had such a sense of patriotism, Mathune." Caleb slurred his name.

Alfred shook his head, ignoring them both. "It's far too dangerous. I trust you know the route, but this isn't just another black market good." said Alfred. "I don't think we could keep it safe from whoever might try and take it."

"What's more, like she says, it is the end of the season." Said Argent. "As I understand it, the pass through the Tidal Marsh becomes nigh impassable after the Nehmset. I don't think we could make it there before then, it's too late in the year."

There were a few moments of silence. Then Adimus spoke. "I think we should let it be known that the Spear is found as soon as possible. The ones who'll want it will come either way."

Everyone looked at him, as if perhaps he'd said the wrong thing. Maybe it was his imagination, but it made him slink, especially when Tirlag rebutted. "Why would we do that?" she said, now that her stake was on the line. "It would put a target on our backs."

"Thieves strike under cover of darkness for a reason." Alfred agreed. "Bring it to light."

He was kind of shocked he had something to say, much less that he'd spoken up.

"A good sentiment. Draw your enemies out and confront them on your terms. What was your name again, young sir?"

"Adimus, sir."

"I like him."

"Very good. I will send word tomorrow." Argent rubbed his hands together giddy with excitement.

"I don't like *him*." he pointed at the bard.

He looked genuinely hurt. "That is commerce, Sir Knolls. There is nothing shameful to it."

"You are Mathune. Your clan is naught but intrigue and turmoil." the swordsman's eyes narrowed "I had respect for your art until I saw its duplicitousness up close. You hide your face or flaunt your name with equal depravity, however and whenever it may suit you."

"Are you talking about what I did for us back there?" the bard scoffed. "If that man didn't want to take us in for the night we would have been in trouble back there."

"We cannot choose for him whether he wishes to do so."

"Why, he <u>did</u> choose. Because of me. Elsewise we would be out there freezing, possibly dying. He's a good chap for choosing as he did." he smiled.

"Words deceive. Distort. Manipulate." said the swordsman.

"Politics and swordplay are selfsame, Servant Knolls: full of feints and flourishes." he replied. "Likewise, in both, one false move can get you killed. Therefore my words need be as polished as your blade, my strikes and parries just as well thought out and my footwork just as deft. At either rate, I agree with the Watcher. It <u>would</u> help us leverage a better deal to have the clan's bid for the Spear made public. At any rate, if anyone would care to hear my recommendation might I suggest we keep safe in Ederton until such provisions are met?"

"Ederton is controlled by the Merchant Lords of the north," said Alara. "Avoiding them is the exact reason we came through Ormond and Balfour to begin with!"

"It is a Free City. Beyond the reach of the clans." he shrugged. "With lots of 'swordsman' like myself there, that could help you cut through the morass of all this politics." he mimed slashing the air.

"Ederton?" Caleb spat. "You'll put it in reach of every other country. It will end up in the hands of some Jin robber or the Imperial Magustrate before we could blink."

"I didn't think someone as…" Argent glanced down at his sword, "culturally sensitive as you would harbor such fears."

"I have heard of this place. It is a very safe city, protected by the Merchant Lords of the north." echoed Laina.

"If Madreg is off limits, Ederton should be too." snapped Tirlag.

"Ederton is a stone's throw from here." William pointed. "Not ten leagues through a literally cursed swamp or on some Named boat passage in the Treadless Sea." Argent plead. "And *I* know some people there. People who will see to its safety."

"What sane person would think any of that to be safe? I have been to Ederton. You couldn't keep the spear a secret parading it through a simple village, you cannot hope to conceal it in a city with that many people."

"It's that or Hewnyleigh. Right into the lion's den." Argent shrugged.

"We will summon Torrin to the city. He has a few contacts there as well, as I understand it."

"You said that rather definitively. It's your decision, then?" asked Alara.

Alfred nodded in the dark.

"You wish your enemies drawn into the light?" Caleb stood. "There he is." he pointed at the bard. Theswordsman looked at Alfred, "Whatever his play, you'll not know it until he tips his hand. Then it will be too late."

"I do not doubt it. But Ederton does seem the most logical stage for our next move. Torrin is a nobleman of Torant. He will bring his presence to bear on this, undoubtedly. That should at least keep any blade-bearing to a minimum, figurative or otherwise." he glowered at the bard.

With that Argent stomped off defeated to play his flute and write sheet music until the small hours of the night, while Caleb sat quietly stropping his blade.

The following day Adimus awoke to the sound of chopping firewood. He peeked outside and there Caleb stood, swinging the axe. He'd find that he'd been up since well before dawn choring for the old man in thanks.

Argent himself had everything packed for the company and ready to go at the crow of the first cock as well, not to be shown up.

The snow was deep, to be fair, and if their need for travel was not so dire they would have stayed, but they trudged on.

Aethan made little complaint of the snow as it was. He was slightly furrier and stouter than the others, who took coaxing, especially Argent's who fought with him all morning.

"Want a ride, master Seer? I wish to stretch my legs." Caleb offered the Seer.

His horse, a black stallion, no doubt a war horse, was well mannered, and knew to keep to the road, as the wizard (with a little help from Adimus to get astride it) was unaccustomed to riding, still had little trouble handling him.

"And you, lady Cait Shii." he asked Alara.

"Thank you." she took the opportunity immediately. "Quite gracious of you."

"You're most welcome." He took her hand to help her up.

Adimus and Laina rode Aethan. After they had settled, the horses drifted near to each other, and Laina, catching the man's sideways glance of fascination addressed, "You have questions."

"What?"

"About yesterday."

Alfred tried to conceal his eagerness, bating his response a moment. "I do." he admitted. "I am curious. More than curious, how you Wield with no need of Implements or knowledge of the Great Works."

"I have said to you: I do nothing. It is by the Grace of my goddess that I am granted my power."

"But you speak the Gladr, same as I, when you do it. What words do you know and how do you study?"

"Gladr? I know not of which you speak."

"The words you spoke. And Dhuun. You speak the language of All Creation. You Invoked. Quite well I might add. It must have taken many years to speak it fluently--I just don't understand."

"The Tongue of Flames. Sacred words. They are the Grace of my goddess. I do not speak them, I am but an instrument."

"You are not conscious of the words that come from your mouth?" he questioned. Regretfully, she nodded.

"I've heard that word before, Graces." Alara butted in, trotting up. "They are granted to lesser Fae by greater: the Vatra, Pans, the Four Sovereigns, the Partholonians and the like. It is the power of the Covenant, of the Geas they place upon us. They tempt the likes of us to their cause with such powers in exchange for swearing fealty to the Seelie Court."

Laina stuck her nose in the air. "You are not the first to say this here." Adimus was sure she was talking about Tolten. "My goddess is not some Fae. The Law was set forth from the moment of creation, it has always been--what purposes a tiny stream can serve, so too can a great reservoir. But it does not make them equal." And then she was silent.

"What you used was a *quite* advanced method of Thaumaturgy, far beyond my own ability." he admitted. "And you did it effortlessly." he stifled his astonishment as best he could. "...Do you think you could teach me?"

"There is no vocation, only dedication. A reverence for the divine. I am gifted with my power by my deeds in her name." She smiled, bowing her head.

"And with all due respect, though I've not the power of a Seer to hasten it, my judgment of your character--and I'm sure you would agree--would be accurate if I were to say that you are not one to bow your head."

"I could. I could do it..." he said.

"I could teach what prayers to speak, but you would not understand their meaning. I could show you the rituals to undertake, but their importance would hold no weight. I could share with you the prohibitions of our order from of old, required to purify the body and mind, but their significance would be lost to you."

"What do you mean by this, Magus?" Argent asked. "Is it a difference of tradition too vast to traverse? Something that it would be too difficult for a southlander to understand in his culture?"

"No..." Said Laina.

Caleb's voice startled them. "There are no such barriers that cannot be overcome with time, patience, and the effort of understanding." Perhaps it was Adimus's empathy with the Seer, but he could not help but feel the swordsman held a strange gleam in his eye, as if perhaps he understood, and only sought for elaboration to watch the Seer squirm. "Customs and traditions may be different, even the fundamental qualities of what some call decent or moral, but these are illusions brought by ignorance, a distorted reflection in the water." he professed. "Those waters are deep and mirky to those who stir it with bumbling feet, but much gold lies within its depths still."

They weren't sure what he meant personally, but Adimus caught a glimpse at the man looking down at his sword proudly after he said it.

"Then what is it? Am I not worthy of it? Not <u>pure</u> enough to learn it?"

She said nothing.

Alfred took a long moment, his face melted into a bivvy of expressions as he began to process what she'd said. He concealed it by taking a moment to clean the fog from his glasses, this perhaps embarrassment, then anger, then a flit of regret, then it was gone. He spoke nothing more of it.

"Argent. You, Argent, should know Magic." said Alfred. "Legend says you bards once wielded the greatest power. It was said your kind were founded when Tersus banned the Three Traditions. Your order went into hiding, concealing your Cunning in song and verse. What secrets do you keep?" He said.

Argent nodded, trying his hardest to ignore the tension in the air. "Our founders were slain, and they themselves were scattered to the four winds." he shook his head solemnly, "We were all hunted by the Order of Jasmine, and by the time of the fall of the Gray Cities only rumors remained. I am a but mute poet. The Wanderer, they called him, the Parthelonian who taught your kind. Simple words can be a powerful thing." he further confided, looking around to reassert confidence. "There is Magic in them. The Tuatha say that when the eldest brother invented names he brought Magic to the world." Argent shot him a glance.

The Seer answered. "Artur Bowen was one of your founders, one of the ones to whom the

Wanderer spoke." he said. "I did grow up a stone's throw from Hewnyleigh..." he added as to not seem presumptuous.

"A name defines. Binds." Argent clarified. "It says everything something is, but also, more crucially, what it isn't. We understand One by its relation to the Other: we understand white only by its contrast to black. The implicit *informs* the explicit; the notes you don't play are just as important as the ones you do." He looked at his, sincerely, and shrugged. "But alas, my friend, I too am lost to such things. I myself wouldn't mind to learn sometime. But I chase one legend at a time, Seer. One legend at a time." he patted him on the shoulder assurantly.

"That sounds like the Calcinative Quality."

"Hmm?" Argent started to question, then he threw up a fist, ordering all to stop.

On a fence post and in some trees were crows, gawking and japing at them.

He jumped down and drew near. He spoke. "Good morning." Adimus thought he heard him say. *"We mean you no harm."* he bowed.

The creatures, as expected, did not much more than what a bird might do. William reached into his pack and produced what was left of his ration of bread. *"Messengers to the gods, heralds of the ancestors, I bring you gifts."* he tore it up and placed it before them. *"I offer my humble obeisances to you in this, my hour of need."* He spoke in fluent Dhuun. He pulled out his sheet music book and begin tearing strips from it.

Over the next few minutes he would promise in hush tones to each of them warm welcomes and food for the favor of their courier services, that they take the messages he tied to them in turn. A few gave gestures which apparently signaled to him refusal, which he graciously passed over.

He described to them places that sounded not unlike rookeries in far-flung cities, and as he finished each flew in their instructed directions. "Let it be known to all clans, houses, guilds and orders, kingdoms far and wide, Hyu'man, Fae, Urisk, and Div: Sleg Lugus, the Spear of Fate, is found!"

The silence that held after they scattered spoke volumes to their astonishment, and Argent's humble handling of it, nonchalantly hopping back on his horse and get back in march like nothing at all had just happened, did more than any strut ever could.

"How do they know these things and you do not?" Tirlag chuckled, nudging Alfred in the ribs...

Alfred glowered on.

"I am a mute poet."

"A mute poet?"

I am a mute poet

I fumble the bungle of care chosen words. I speak softly, slowly, short and unsure

for only within doth true music stir

I am a mute poet

who refrains in futility, who rhymes in vain,

whose silver-glass eyes reflects his disdain

whose actions in shadows speak plainer than day

I am a mute poet

spewing painful, tasteless, ineloquence

my hooks then are knives in quiet quatrains

my voice then unheard speaks verses arcane

in moonlit stoccatas of soul, iron, and flame

I am a mute poet.

<u>Chapter 24</u>
Ederton

It was a large, grommeted waxed canvas Tirlag had packed, one they identified as an old mizzen sail, faced away from the road as to prevent the occasional horse and rider or small caravan–intrusions met with the cautious gripping of weapons, from splashing out the meager fire.

It had been a two week journey to Ederton over the Via Victimus, the great highway built in the days when the kingdom was one. There, roadside, between two large rocks, they camped. It was rainy again, and so, a stone's throw from the city, under a makeshift lean-to, they sat.

"So, what does everyone want out of this endeavor? What is it that you hope the spear to bring you?" Caleb finally spoke, being there last one might think if to add cheer to the morosely huddled lot.

He still spoke of it. Had the gall to speak of it. He and the others had only just stopped, but whether it was their proximity to the city or boredom they entertained it.

"The aspirations of Torrin Krasad is to accrue as much wealth as he can, to outshine even the merchant lords of the north. In his heart of hearts I think he also wishes to see Brigden win independence, to stand on its own two legs."

Alfred spoke simply when looked to,"A new life."

Tirlag stood. "To know. If there is ever such a thing as enough liquor." She giggled, stooping over her pack to retrieve one of the bottles of celebratory rum she'd been hoarding since their first trip to Keara: the boy supposed she now reasoned it safe to drink without fear of running dry.

Adimus spoke up of his own volition. "That its home have ears to hear our problem, a stern head and shoulders enough to heed it, and the courage to do something about it." It was an absent muttering, his main attention on his drawing. He realized as it did that it made him sound like an old man, and suddenly was granted a measure of insight on what embittered sentiment made Luloch talk so.

Caleb chuckled a knowing chuckle. "What about you, Lady Magus?"

It took Laina a moment to realize he was addressing her. "For myself? I had no desire, but if given some I will take the riches back to my people, and give it to the devotees of Ananya as offering to her."

Caleb pointed to Delaney with an inquisitive look, sure to receive a nod from the others before speaking up. "Delaney? The reward is yours as well. What do you wish to see done?"

"I just want to return to my masters back home."

Tirlag gave a dejected sigh.

Caleb's brow curled. "You have masters, little one?"

"Uh-huh."

"No. No she doesn't." Snapped Tirlag."We bought her freedom. Paid dearly for it, because <u>this</u> one wanted to do it the right way instead of just slitting her captor's throats in their beds!" He motioned at the wizard.

Delaney huffed. "You hired me. It's how I look at it. If I'm free, then I'm free to go anywhere I want, even back to them."

"They kept you in a pig-pen! They browned you until you were pliant, servile to their every want!"

"Browned?" Asked Laina.

"You would weep if you saw it." Her eyes were fire.

"That was before you met us." Delaney pleaded, looking at the ground "I was able to come and go as I pleased when we met. It's _how_ we met."

"Delaney I, I saw your Chatteling Cap, brownie! They tried to sell it to me, lock, key, and chin strap! I should have bought it to shake at you when you're being a bloody puterelle like you are!" He looked at them, "I was just going to steal her away into the night, but that know-it-all over here thought that making it official would help her in the transition."

"You are bonded to them…" Caleb observed.

"I can't help how I feel. They were nice in the end." She echoed, the last bit scurrying away in defeat.

Caleb rebutted. "Because you followed their every command to please them."

"Thank you. I'm glad someone else sees It." Tirlag nodded, offering him a drink. He passed.

"That's how all Hyu'man interactions work!" Delaney defended yet again. "None of them ever do nice things just because they're nice!"

"If a truer thing has been said, I have not heard it." Alfred concurred.

There was a long silence at that. Finally Caleb started again, "You, William." He asked Argent; it was the most jovial question the man had ever put to him. "What would you see done with the spear?"

The bard stared into the fire. "Well…" he said meaningfully. "None can avail it." he shrugged in defeat "I…didn't believe it when I first heard it. Surely it was a flourish in a bard's tale, a flowery device of poetry to say such things that, 'when its wielder wishes any being to perish, there is naught they can do but die.' But now that I have seen it…" he leered at it, as if it were a snake that might jump up and bite him. "It should be destroyed, likely. But I know that will not be the case. I can only see to it that he who gains it is merciful and just."

"Let us hope so." Said Caleb, driving the man into a slump as he affirmed what he had just said.

Adimus kept his head down, scribbling, shutting the rest of the world out.

Tirlag peered over his shoulder after a few moments, when she thought he wasn't looking, taking in the myriad patterns he drew with his wooden stylus. "That's not bad." the impressiveness of his hand finally forced her to say. "You can design the insets for my crown." she mused. She watched for a few more minutes. "Where did you learn that?"

He was always quite good at it--not shutting the world out, but sketching. It was a hobby that occupied his mind far before he knew of things like what the wizard taught. Especially nowadays it reminded him of home.

Adimus entertained her, "I always admired the patterns with which the people of the south personalized their things: delicate knotwork patterns on belts and sporrans and wallets, filigree on hilts and scabbards, illumination on the framing of book pages and covers. I always emulated them whenever I could, drawing them with charcoal and paper. Usually." He snorted. "Wouldn't doubt it if my grandpa got this tablet for me just so he'd stop finding them on his furniture or on all the walls and floors." he'd wager the distraction it presented loosened him, otherwise he didn't know why he spoke so openly.

"You miss them." Delaney verbalized.

Tirlag jested, sloshing her bottle. "It was probably the paper that did it. Expensive buggers, reams of parchment. Especially good ones."

"I bet." he replied.

"I stand corrected. I have heard truer words." chuckled Alfred, inordinately amused at it..

"What do you know about buying paper?" Delaney scowled.

"I..why? Are you going to be offended, knowing I chopped up your little friends to doodle on?"

"No more than you wearing leather offends you--I'm not a tree any more so than you are a cow." she said. "Well...perhaps even more so not a tree." she shot a smug grin.

Tirlag growled. "Anyway. Cartography." she was flustered now. "Here, let me see it." He handed it over; he'd only just started on a fresh one.

He watched over the course of the next hour or so as she drew trees and mountains, little coasts with waves on them, houses signifying villages and the like. She labeled them with a swishy font. *The Pangorian Mountains. Isle du Duende. Brigden. Puerto Salvat. Madari.*

"Madari is where I was born." Alara was watching. "You missed the bay south of Pingaree and Tintimber. That little outcrop."

"Oh yes. Blasted little place. We almost ran aground there. Ol' Crom only knows we would've been in trouble then."

"Smuggling Bruana weapons, were we?" The Cait Shii tisked.

"Coffee."

"Ooh." The cat winced.

"Show them Incurica Noian." came Laina.

It was where she was from, Adimus knew that much. "It's too high on the map, love. Won't fit." she replied. The priestess slumped at hearing it.

"Your calligraphy is atrocious, milady. For shame." tisked Caleb.

"You can read it, right? Then it's served its purpose."

"Here, let me see it." Adimus rummaged through the leather folder and pulled out a spade-shaped stylus. "Did you make these? They remind me of a brush set I once had."

"Niall helped me with them." He said. He suddenly realized they would have no idea who he was talking about. "He used to whittle shillelagh. I modeled them after his tools..."

"You know," the man smiled. "calligraphy and swordsmanship are intrinsically linked." Caleb made a rather embarrassing face when he drew, they'd found, absently sticking his tongue out.

"Why is everything about swords?" Argent mocked.

Caleb ignored him. "My master started teaching me swordplay by first teaching me how to write." Finally he finished. "Here. Notice the minimal strokes. The sureness of the linework as it's done in one brazen motion."

" 'Brazen'! " Laina erupted in a giggle, covering her face to hide her offense.

"Why, it is brazen. One encounter, one chance, one stroke, one kill. Same goes for penmanship."

"You covered up my mountain!" She smacked him with it when he handed it back.

"Sorry."

she told Adimus.

"Now there's a thumb-print." Adimus frowned.

Argent grabbed it next. At first he eyed it with a mock scrutiny, but the rise quickly melted into surprise, "I at first sought to chide you, oafish coxcomb that you are, but I must say you would put the scribes at Bowen to shame." Argent commented. "Also he is quite right: words can be swords as well. An expression of one's intent: that _is_ art, whether with a brush or a blade." The swordsman took it for the backhanded compliment it was.

The Patient Sea. Pingaree Island. Thane. He had incorporated some of the swirls the boy had started making.

When they were finished they lingered upon it for a while, and when the night was done he put it away.

* * * * *

It had been years since he'd seen it. At first it wasn't so bad. Like Hewnyleigh, its claustrophobic streets and jetted thoroughfares provided insulation from the true nature of its unthinkable architecture and the sheer number of people who lived here.

It was the central hub for all trade in the southlands. Freed in the heyday of the secession by a handful of vested interests, it served as the singular safe place of meeting for the north and the south.

One familiar with the ways of Free City would know that all of the shops would be open by the dawn's light; which if one were familiar with that fact they would also know that this meant the streets would be a writhing wall of chaos.

Making a soothing click of the tongue (which didn't seem to work at all), he guided Aethan his way through the roaming livestock. Finally passing the ramparted gate that loosely marked the beginning of it, he breathed a sigh of anticipation.

Immediately his senses were bombarded with noises and smells: breath and offal and flowers and perfumes, and all manner of scent in between in a nauseating rainbow, accompanied by a cacophony of criers peddlers, hagglers and swindlers, yelling shopkeepers and barking officers. "Still know this place like the back of my hand." William sighed contentedly; he had apparently missed it.

They had hoped to reach Ederton before the morning bell sounded, but once again he'd expected no less of late, and as their luck would all have it the bizarre of Red Row was in full swing by the time he passed through the Trade Bridge, the causeway which marked the beginning of the mercantile district. It was an hour's journey from the first gate to that bridge. Hastily wading through streets, zig-zagging between the mobs flooding Peddler's Pass, what at first was an object of their amusement all too quickly became pure frustration. Argent made shortcuts through the large pavilions to evade the hectic hassle of the crowds, feverishly trying to navigate, taking Adimus along as a spotter to trounce the vendor's merchandise and get cursed at.

The bridge spanned the great river Nalanen. It had been the only barrier between the north and south on this side. The bridge had been built in the old days of the Great Kingdom, much like the Ruined Road, but unlike it the bridge was much better intact, standing well in defiance of the nature it had conquered.

Adimus remembered being ushered in much less courteously when he was with Luloch, the gatehouse guards groping and probing every purse and bag but with Argent they asked little, and what little they did pry he disarmed with fast talk and levity. On each weapon's hilt they placed a waxen seal, stamped with the mark of a winged dragon, along with a receipt sealed with the same to be presented upon their leaving, which showed an inventory of each of the weapons that they may be checked for breakage of the seal on leaving.

There beyond all the streets were red brick paved, no doubt to keep ruts and the like to a minimum. The streets were very clean on this side--the people of the north always did well to keep it this way. Adimus saw several people in the throng that while he was younger just thought looked strange or foreign, but he could now see that they had the same auburn skin as Laina. They were Shambayan.
This was where they did business in the south, after all.

They passed the coliseum, still open for its day trading on the floors. Argent took them to a crowded, much more sophisticated alehouse: The Rose in The Rushes. There, players gathered playing Shadows, puffing on Nic pipes and drinking tea.

"Argent!" A man, himself holding a hand full of cards and enjoying some sort of large communal pipe hopped up to greet him.

His complexion was dark, darker than even Laina's, ebony even--he'd never before seen the likes of it. He wore strange dress: wispy pantaloons and hose, and a cinched black and gold pleated doublet that sheared his chest, forcing it to puff like a posturing peacock.

"Wyatt!" He embraced him. "How are you--what are you doing here? I thought I'd never see you again!"

"Fellows! This is Wyatt of Aquataine!" He shook hands with all the men and kissed the hands of all the women, "Wyatt is a courtier. A jack-of-knaves for the noble families in Torant."

"Another bard." Caleb scoffed.

The man looked at Argent. "I've come with my lady Foxwell, from the west."

"Where is she?" he glanced excitedly.

"She's been staying at your great uncle's in town."

"My what?"

"Your uncle. Who lives here."

"I wasn't aware I had an uncle who lives here."

"Reis, Reis Valkeir?" he said.

Argent shook his head in denial. "Must be my father's side of the family."

"Valkeir? Wasn't that the name of that bloke from the auction?" Tirlag chimed in.

"The strange one?"

Argent simply shrugged.

"Really? Could've swore he even said he'd met you." Wyatt gave him a discerning eye.

"Hmm." Was all the Whispermonger addressed it.

"At any rate, what brings you all the way over the mountains?"

Suddenly his face sobered. "Issues of international consequence, I'm afraid."

He sat them down, scarpering the people with whom he'd been playing cards. He pulled up a second table to accommodate them, and ordered them drinks and supper on a tab.

Adimus missed a large portion of the conversation. Quite a bit of it he couldn't understand anyway: somesuch about people and houses and goings on outside the realm; rumors and gossip true to his title.

The smell of the food had spirited him away.

"...Wait. Countess?"

"How long have you been in these backwaters, Whispermonger?" Wyatt laughed. "The

Lord Protector has been *very* generous to the Foxwells since he took power." He paused to take in his reaction. He patted him on the shoulder "You're a royal now, gov! Now spare some favor for a few games?" he slapped him on the shoulder.

Adimus was salivating before they had even brought out the dishes. It would be the first time in weeks he'd eaten something that wasn't pack rations.

It resembled mess foods and tavern fare at first, grilled vegetables and unidentifiable meat on skewers, spiced with mixes of pungent herbs. It was served with flatbreads and small and varied dishes of colored sauces for dipping, all to ensure one's hands didn't get sullied, and an ice cold cup of brandywine. He quickly learned it was to quell the fires in his mouth; Adimus had tasted horseradish, sassafras, mint, other strange aberrations which confiscated his sense of taste, but these dishes lingered, leaving him salivating and sweating from the thrill of it, and worse, wanting more. In a moment of conversational lull he'd found himself snarfing uncomfortably loudly.

"So what's this about 'international consequence'?'"

"Well, you know that Privy Council pow wow they have at La Rochelle every few years? The Countessa caught wind from an emissary of clan Dwyer, who heard it from the Caseys that one of your lords are trying to give up the keys to the Steward's Charge up to the Lapidaries."

"Wait. Steward's Charge?" Alfred interjected, cleaning the steam fog from his glasses. "You mean the Cache of Kainden?"

He glanced sideways at him, and his eyes locked on his now gloved hands--he'd taken them off to shake. He noticeably clammed up.

Argent quickly redoubled. "Oh, pay him no mind, he's not a Sum Seer." he jumped. "Well, he's not an *imperial* Sum Seer."

"I was taught by a master Thaumaturgist and All'khemist who lived within these borders."

"The art of psychometry is the Lapidaries' lifeblood. It isn't simply 'taught'." he gave critical eye.

"My teacher was a rogue. And a scoundrel." The last comment was apparently meant for himself alone.

"There's no such thing."

"You call this man a liar?" said Caleb, ready to more than show that he was willing to break his peace bond.

"You see this coin?" he pulled it from out of nowhere, slapping it on the table. It was a rectangular white piece of opal. It was a *bone*, an opal, the highest denomination--Adimus had never even seen one up close before. "I was given a receipt for this coin as long as my arm, signed by the Order of Jasmine in Malstat, that showed every hand that had been placed on it since it was dug out of the ground during the War of the Ransom Queen! True or no, alls I'm saying is that if they can keep tabs on a simple stone they can keep tabs on him." He leaned back in his chair crossing his legs, comfy with his point. "I'll tell you all about it. Later. In private." he looked at Alfred. "Cheers." He turned up his drink. "At any rate, that's the very least of it. William is with her, delivering a Duende to him."

"You don't say?" Adimus, nor, judging from their faces, anyone else, knew of which they spoke, just the bard looked genuinely shocked, even concerned.

"What do you think it is?"

"A summons from The Summer King."

"...Do you really think so?" he rocked in his chair uncomfortably.

"You think *we* have connections?" he snorted. "Your uncle puts all us to shame."

The rest of the lodging was in silence, until a young lady marched through the door.

"Cousin!" Argent ran to her as well. A man almost cut him off--or rather, cut him down, Adimus noticed, until he noticed the lady's sentiment towards the man.

"You have handlers now, I see." he glanced up at the two men, seemingly embarrassed at his obliviousness and lack of discretion.

She too wore a bodice which seemed to cinch her unnaturally. Her hair was done in extravagant golden curls, worn high to dangle and crown her powdered face. Flowery perfume wafted from her, that overpowered even the spicy bouquet of their meal.

She curtsied. Tirlag's eyes rolled. The two men, upon seeing Wyatt, took their leave (apparently they felt her safe at his presence).

William Mathune stood. "Everyone, meet Annelise Foxwell. My cousin."

Chapter 25
An Earned Respite

Aside from the watering hole back home (of which he steered well clear when the likes of anyone but his family came about), Adimus had never been acquainted with the notion of communal bathing.

He was, of course, derided as being prudish and backward when presented with the idea, but it didn't take much coaxing, as it was the one thing he'd craved more than food: a bath--and this wasn't some typical roadside stewhouse. It was up the High Road, the road which circled back around and over the river again, and overlooked the entire city from above. It was gated, like the Trade Bridge was, albeit by a different class of citizen, who let others pass only at the graces of the merchant lords.

Argent explained to them that the building was once a cathedral dedicated to the Great King Tersus, and was repurposed by the people; what they really sat on were once pews of a sort, and all the trappings of the bath were built around it.

The evening's lingering light beamed through meticulously set stained glass windows depicting gods and goddesses and all manner of divine scenery within. Three large statues of angelic maidens pouring water from great vessels provided the water for some half dozen pools there. Some were roiling hot and some simply cool, the hot ones piped in from heating houses outside that were said to glow and roar like forges after nightfall. Gentle stone stairs and seating allowed for leisure in each.

Adimus was suddenly even more self-conscious, that his gawking wouldn't be taken the wrong way when he approached. Stone idols still lingered amongst the newer fixtures, and, unlike the temple at the Ruined Road, Adimus recognized them. All, in fact; they were all from the abbey back home, and none were uncounted. There was Cernnunnos again, and Taranis. Joining them was Teutates, the keeper of the clans and patron of the Watchers, and Maponos, master of music and inventor of instruments, whose trills move the heart of even earth and sea. Epona, the first horse, birthed from sea foam was there, as well the Sisters of the Cauldron. In fact, the only one who seemed to be missing was Crom himself.

Adimus felt queasy before, and even more so now, more than a bit averse to disrobing and frolicing and cavorting before the deities. Had he known he may have been able to say no from the outset, and would've had more the reason for justifying it besides just 'being a prude'. He felt cornered, and after all their haranguing about it (even from Luloch, who didn't even come), all he felt he could do was shake his head and whisper a sincere prayer for forgiveness.

The establishment offered laundering services as well--all of their clothes were to be washed and dried in the furnace houses below. He was so excited with the prospect that he gave no thought to the fact until after that once he passed the small curtained foyer to have all his effect replaced with a paltry wash rag, there was no escape.

Adimus was shocked to find that the word 'communal' was precisely what it meant. He froze upon seeing it, and was the last in, even being passed by the likes of the normally timid Alfred.

The heat did feel good, he had to admit, when he finally settled in, ringing out the chill of weeks in the cold, and lowland sensibilities still kept the genders segregated for the most part, and there sat a thick fog of steam, heady with the bubbly scents of perfumes and soaps. It formed a hazy partition of sorts, forcing one to strain to make out any detail beyond its veil– a gesture which was immediately obvious and, he would hope, frowned upon by couth folk, of which he at first only hoped (but doubted) the ones he had come to call his companions were. Alas, only he and Caleb seemed to abide such unspoken rules as keeping their eyes to themselves (and presumably Alfred, who sat across from them, though he'd conspicuously worn his glasses, and continued to do so even though they fogged up incessantly).

Not all of the figures were Hyu'man, he'd noticed. A place beyond the empty spot that others dare-not or would-never-be caught dead occupying were inhabited with several manners of "others". He spied one would drifted too near toward them, and saw that he had a muzzle and fur, and a tail. They were Cessairians, and not of the ilk who gave rise to his own Kind, the Hyu'mans. They were Dhuun Shii, beast folk, like Alara was.

William, upon seeing, gestured back to the pool. Then he turned in astonishment. "Gents, there's a Tuatha here!"

It wasn't difficult to spot her, as Tuatha appeared to be Hyu'man for the most part, and she was the only one among them who appeared as Hyu'man. For the most part.

Adimus's eyes <u>were</u> bidden to look this time.

Whether it was the true alien nature of the transcendental creature that did not understand shame or simply a manner of (un)natural unalloyed confidence, she lounged, half-laying, half-sitting, on the knee of her maiden statue, reclining her leg unabashed, her foot propped on the figure's lifted arm. None with her seemed to mind it, and her nonchalant demeanor and exuberance in conversation put her host at ease as she chattered away with them, playing in the water pouring from the large chalice it held. Indeed, she commanded their attention, and they all gathered around her as one might some royal or celebrity.

Her ears were long and pointed, just as the stories had said, a trait that they "willed", to differentiate themselves from the cessairian Hyu'manii with but a simple glance. There were other odd characteristics that others had spoken of, that to his observation he simply did not see in her: the whispering wind that was said to hang about them, which stirred the air and disturbed their hair and not others, their shadow which could move independently of them, fangs, claws, wings, slitted eyes, the occasional horn; none of these he saw in her, though he could not make out much detail, though the one about their physical beauty being beyond compare, this one he could observe even from afar.

A garson brought a bottle of primrose wine around, and offered him a glass. The boy had only ever taken such drinks when his father allowed it: at special ceremonies and celebrations when tradition warranted that it was socially acceptable for one to allow a young man to do so. He knew it was a drink that calmed the nerves, and what's more it was chilled; he deemed that it was indeed warranted.

"Get this man another!" Argent cried, when he'd all but finished the drink.

The maiden statues that poured their water were the Sisters. The one beneath which they sat was the Aaronwyn. She herself had many names. Aaranrhod or the Aaronwyn was one of them, and the name 'Menkara' (Menkh Aara) was derived in days of old from the name for her worshippers. Don was still another, used by the Tuatha and the Cessairians, but still greater yet was the name Morigna or the Morrigan, the Great Queen after which the entire realm was named.

She held the Divine Sacrament, the severed head of the younger brother of the first man, the first sacrifice to the gods. The water for their bath poured from its orifices amidst jeers of disgust and derisive comments from many of his attendees. Adimus thought to try and vindicate her, to explain the grand story in the Numitorum of the first sacrifice and its necessity and the symbolism of it all, but decided to remain silent—the less attention he could draw to himself in this instance, the better.

The water poured from the head into their pool but drained in the men's, supplied evenly between the two pools through a large clay culvert, which Argent insisted he used as an echo chamber, obnoxiously hooting and chirping at the girls every few minutes. He could hear Laina and Tirlag's voices giggling and him casually going on with Miss Foxwell and her acquaintances as he stood beside and well clear of it. He couldn't tell if it was vapor or sweat that now beaded on his head. Before long, a lady sauntered right into their view, kneeling to get a bucket of water. Adimus turned his head out of respect of course, though she seemed to pay him no mind, not so much as making eye contact.

He averted his gaze when she saw them looking, then those same eyes widened when they were verbally acknowledged.

Then the worst happened.   "You. Yoo-hoo! You there! Jin!" Her voice called. The voice came not from Laina and Tirlag's pool. It was the Tuatha.

A few moments later she called something out in what Adimus could only perceive as another tongue, most likely the language of the Veiled Lands. Caleb immediately turned his head. The boy suddenly found blame in the swordsman--it was his dastardly stupidity after all which had singled them out. Not a single belonging lay about the floors above the pews upon which they walked, not a single article of clothing or coin or even glass, save that Named sword, which he'd ardently fought to keep with him and within arm's reach, and was allowed to do so only after miss Foxwell deem it alright.

"He is not Kyogodejin. He is Ormondian." Argent started to tease, that was, until Caleb answered her back in kind using the same tongue.

Caleb's eyes glazed over. It was almost unreadable to Adimus. Not embarrassment, not even shock...it was of a great steeling, as of the sort of face he made right before combat.

"Apologies." she cried. You carry a Kata Blade, I figured no Servant of the Blade would give one up to a southlander while he still drew breath, and I doubted any of the moorfolk could win it from one. You must be quite a man. What is your name?"

"Caleb Knolls, miss."

"Caleb, can you be a dear and bring me a pale of hot water? My soap seems to fight lathering."

With that he got up and fetched one of the nearby empty buckets and filled it, defensively shooting hateful glares at his judging peers.

He disappeared into the mists beyond. He did not take the sword with him.

"How did you come by that blade?" They heard her say.

"Tetsuyo Aritoshi, a sage smith and skilled swordsman of the Iron Warlord's court, was my master. It is my inheritance."

"I am sorry for your loss." her voice sounded genuinely empathetic. Then she gallivanted the exchange sideways. "So, are you a xenophile, or do you simply hate your own country?" A few in her court giggled, though most acted strangely engrossed, as if it were simply the natural course of the conversation and no insult was meant of it.

In either case, he didn't hesitate, "My master once said that a culture is simply a collection of ideas and traditions, and that those we most often share are the good ones. The bad ones must be eschewed, like dross in the crucible."

"Good ones. Like what?" She said after a few moments. Adimus could hear the ringing of her rag and the sloshing of the water as she cleaned herself.

"Values such as duty, steadfastness, charity. These we must refine."

She was silent until she finished. He patiently waited. She handed him the bucket, picked up a wine glass and eyed him. They could hear the smile in her voice. "There are also other, less desirable qualities that we all share as well. Malice, fear, ignorance…desire. How do you sift the good ones from the bad ones?"

"A swordsmith can tell the quality of the steel by its color in the forge." Was all he answered.

"And what colors do you have, Caleb Knolls?" He drew near to him.

"Red, right now!" Argent whooped. He ignored her. She shot him a smile.

"What of those that give one their identity? Traditions that bind families, communities? Make one different?"

"Do they bring us together? Or keep us apart? Each must be judged in this manner." he simply replied.

"…Us?" She looked him up and down and smiled.

The noble warrior shrunk. "I-I purely meant in a general sense."

With that she laughed in spite of herself. "May your fires ever burn bright, Caleb Knolls." She raised her glass to him.

When he returned it was in silence.

Argent nudged the boy on the shoulder as if to say 'watch this'. "Whew, this heat is getting to me. You mind if we move?" Said the jokester.

"… I'm fine." Said Caleb.

Argent smiled. "Must be the drink getting to me."

"Where did you have in mind?" Alfred, of all people asked.

He nodded toward the empty one. "That pool over there is a fair bit more tepid."

The one at which he pointed went right past the Cessairians, right past the Tuatha.

The bard took a moment to gauge his reaction. Finally Caleb replied. "If we must." Argent hid his shock, and before he knew it they all stood up to migrate.

"Come on, my boy." He motioned.

Adimus <u>had</u> slowly worked his way more and more out of the pool trying to keep cool, only to bobble back down when he felt self-conscious about exposing too much; it actually was hot, and he <u>was</u> right.

But, "I'm fine." the Grigor folded his arms. "You--You go on."

So they did, climbing out and along the catwalk in full view of the women and into the one adjacent to
the Tuatha.

Then it suddenly dawned on him, when another person sat down in the pool across from him: regret. Would that it were that there might be less eyes upon him if he'd left with the group, as only now he realized that sitting all alone caused him to draw even more attention.

Maybe I should move. He thought to himself, but the thought of now being the sole object before the scrutinizing eyes of the females careened him straight into panic. He suddenly felt hot.

Flushed. He panted, he tried to gather some semblance of composure. He felt numb. He felt faint. Then he felt...nothing.

* * * * *

"Adimus! Adimus!!!" First thing he felt next was the cold stone of the floor beneath his head. They all stood over him in their towels, jeering. He felt the lingering airiness about himself end as all too late Argent tossed him a cloth shield for his shame as well.

"Are you alright?" Argent asked.

He looked at all the eyes on them. "...Roll me back in so I can finish drowning."

They'd been finishing up by the time it had happened, and by the time Adimus recovered, they were all outside.

Atop the dam they gazed down at the city, witnessing the tiny lamplights that filled the city like thousands of tiny stars. The sight was distracting, thankfully. It hadn't been over, as upon trying to get his clothes back on he managed to roll an ankle on the wet floor and bounce his head off the pristine tile. He could feel the headache he would have later once his senses sharpened again, sure, but the sharpness of his ordeal cut through the haze regardless. The Tuatha had come out as well, dressed in a silken gown, her entourage staying back at the entrance while he alone looked on. They had the faces and figures of a weasel, a monkey, a rat, and Adimus passed them when he emerged, who jeered and snickered and whispered undoubtedly at him with their strange words.

"How did they all get lit so quickly?" Laina asked when he silently walked up.

"Khemetastry." Argent explained, still fopping his hair dry. "They need no wick and no oil. An invisible vapor is piped into them in much the same way as water to these bath houses. As I understand it. Ederton, like Madreg, and a few of the other high cities enjoy these marvels."

"It was given as gratuity by Par'Avoux for your cooperation during the Secession War." Alara added. "Though like the Pistil and the Bruana, this one and the Clockwork City were both commissioned by-and are maintained by-them, that the means by which the devices function are kept secret."

"Madreg, the Clockwork city." added Tirlag. "I've seen it. Quite a thing to behold."

"A highly secretive little guild, the Esotericists." Said Alara, who stayed outside for the whole ordeal, and still twitched and cringed unnaturally at the thought of getting wet. "They are the ones who give us our Pistils, and the Bruana that powers them."

"Not quite a guild; a political party." Argent corrected. "Though they hide it well. No blame to you for not knowing. But yes, secrecy is their platform, that these secrets be kept from those who may use it for ill."

"That doesn't seem right." Caleb commented. "These conveniences would seem to benefit all. Running water, for one, is life giving. I could see the use in having fire on command as well."

"That makes sense now." Explained Alara. "A lot of my compatriots back on the island where I stayed talked about cooperating with those who willingly divulged the secrets of these Implements."

"The Esotericists claim knowledge far greater than Bruana weapons that are heretofore undisclosed to all but the highest echelons of their seat. They warn of the dangers of such knowledge and claim to keep it as a mercy." He continued.

"It is hypocrisy, and a tool to empower some and enslave others."

"What about that sword of yours, Caleb?" said the bard, "Stronger than bronze or even iron. Yet you wish its secret divulged to everybody.

"It's a dangerous thought: What is to be withheld, what is to be permitted: it's a nuanced conversation to be sure, but these people would call you a radical just for implying it."

"My skill with a blade is limited by the quality of that blade. The same could be said of whole nations in regard to those secrets. I know the greatness of my country, I only seek to give it the will to achieve it."

"Pardon, but if I may." The lady, the Tuatha, not helping but overhear, had slunk up behind them. Argent gave her a confused glance. "That sounds like Imperial thinking to me. Should everyone have access to a Pistil? How about a Vesican Harp, or the ability to have the Seven Thunders called down upon us, that they can lay waste to the whole realm? It's what happened to the lands your people fled from!" She asked the swordsman. "There is always a line. You'd have us all knowing and profaning the Name of the Numinous just like the Dao Vaen priests did! The Histban Empire thinks much the same, though that they should have the secrets and not the ones they conquer."

"Dao Va is a myth." Tirlag huffed.

"It isn't." Caleb said quietly. "That is cowardice." he now addressed the lady. "I plan to give my enemies swords as well, that our wills be known to one another. "

She looked at him again, up and down with those judging eyes. "What of those whose will is peace?" she replied.

He had no retort. That ended the conversation. She smiled, and gracefully strode up to the man and spoke something only meant for his ears. "I must go, but we may discuss this at length another time, Caleb, if you'd like. I'm sure you've much to say." she looked into his eyes for approval, which, despite all the eyes on him, showed enough on his face to prompt her satisfaction. "I will send word to lady Foxwell."

She never glanced back, when without so much as a gesture her people followed her as she departed from them. Neither did he, for fear of any save those ahead of him seeing the shock on his face.

Chapter 26
Curious Sights

Wyatt sat at the bar, nursing a lonely drink at a lonely seat, the echoing sounds of cleaning servers the only sounds in the air. Argent came to greet him, and address his long face, to which he replied that he'd "lost it all to a 'Roni."

The rest of the evening had been quiet, the crowded halls of the Rose in the Rushes having turned out, the sparse patrons mostly keeping to themselves. The most noisy of the bunch were a congregation of regal-looking men in white and red robes. All around them were ornately carved wooden cases. Adimus watched them intently. They were Jin.

One of the cases on the table was open, and the Watcher could see that they were full of jade, lapis, and turquoise coins, neatly stacked. Standing near, inconspicuously, was a man with a sword similar to Caleb's, albeit a bit shorter than his. Argent entered the room, and seeing his forlorn friend, without hesitation he approached the men.

"Ministers of the Mark, greetings." he bowed to them. "My friend here would like a deck of Shadows, please." he said, handing him a string of coins.

The man who took his money (which from what the boy saw was a fair bit of scratch) pulled from his case a tied hempen bag with an almost disgusted look on his face, and after counting handed him his change. "Here." He tossed it to Wyatt, whose face lit up.

"I wasn't serious the other day. You didn't have to--." he started, but his friend just winked.

It had all been the quiet was simply the calm before the storm, Adimus would find, a lull between supper in which none were allowed to gamble and most of the main dishes had been served.

A small quartet arrived to play courtly music on string. Argent apparently also knew them, but they'd no time to linger, as when a man--a Jin in a powdered wig wearing regal-looking fare much akin to Wyatt's, came out and said something angry sounding to them in his native tongue they immediately went about tuning up, and gave the bard not so much as another glance. Then the closing bell sounded, and the first of the guests began to pour in.

Adimus sat and watched the games for some time that night, for lack of being able to summon up the nerve to return to the hostel room where the others were, with their discerning eyes and memories of the other night.

From what he gathered from Argent's choppy explanations between playing the game there were six suits, each corresponding to the value of the coins, though only three of them were needed to play at any one time. Though the real name for the game was some Jin word that he (and presumably others) could neither remember nor pronounce, in the vernacular the decks were named after the highest suit contained therein. One might play a game of Shadows (unlucky onyx) for leisure, Leaves (jade) if they felt like losing their life's savings, while richer folk played higher games still.

It was like a battle, with colorful statements describing play: *The Lady of Beasts rides upon the Field of Iron*. Some had faces on them, others were pipped cards depicting coins such as 'four of shadows'. Sometimes the coins were in bunches called Fans, such as a 'fan of iron', or sometimes in stacks called myriads, as in 'two myriad of stripes'. The winner won the Field and also took his winning card, and the owner of the deck required an ante from the others of some of their own cards to play. It wasn't money they gambled with, but the cards themselves it seemed, though plenty of people paid winners who would have their cards out of pocket in order to keep them.

Adimus watched until the nightshade smoke literally smoked him out of the room. It was like being at uncle Anwell's house.

Wyatt's luck turned. He paid the minstrel back and then some, and the following day he accompanied, eager to treat them all to the fruits of his winnings.

The next day had been all meticulously planned out by the Seer, but even he had been invited to breakfast, to indulge in quail egg-garnished meat pies or griddle cakes and milk-frothed coffee at an eclectic bistro at the High Market.

Only Caleb and Argent hadn't attended.

He showed them Saint Adrana's amphitheater, and the rose gardens of the Merchant Lords. He accompanied them as a keen guide and middle man, ushering them to the necessary esoteric corner shops and eccentric collectors who facilitated the 'liquidating' of their haul.

He helped Adimus sell the armor Adimus had come across—worth more to a museum than to a warrior, the boy found. Though the sword was worth more, the boy had decided to do it as a souvenir.

The Serpentanium bracelet would go to the Esotericists, who gave a meager finder's fee for it. It was a product of All'khemy, albeit old All'khemy, but was illegal to possess by their measure just the same, and Alfred would not risk the attention that might accompany trying to sell it on the black market, though Wyatt insisted that he 'knew a fella'.

The golden orb they had kept. Tirlag insisted; no one could tell them what it was or what it did, and none of the ones they'd spoken of treated it as more than a bauble, but she was convinced. "It's a Sublime item, I know it. We just have to find someone who knows what they're talking about." She encouraged Adimus. "And your cut will be all the higher for it." She added.

Wyatt was sure to be finished with it in time for the games to begin, however, and afterwards, they found themselves back at the Rose.

Inside they found Argent sitting all by himself.

He said nothing when they came in, greeting with the raising of a glass and a short and insincere grin.

"Good evening." Alfred obviously had caught on to his mood but didn't directly acknowledge it.

"So how was everything? Do you like the city?"

"A two-ton bronze monster from the age of the Great Kingdom isn't trying to cut our heads off--I'd say it was refreshing." Tirlag answered him.

"Yes. There were no bath houses today either." Adimus tried to add some levity to his incident, though he couldn't hide his actual embarrassment at what had happened enough to deliver with the gusto that brought smiles like the bard did--he learned in that moment that self-deprecating humor had to be sincere to work, not only sincere, but forgiving of the trespass--not liking yourself just wasn't enough. As such, he vowed to hang his hat of it, and eschew any care that his punchline hadn't landed.

"Heehee!" Delaney gave a delayed chuckle when she'd finally got it.

Though, in this moment, Argent's eyes darted like a lizard, and sweat that he tried to hide with a turned head beaded on his brow. Argent himself, old trickster he so often was, did poorly to hide his face behind such layers this time, so much so that Tirlag was bidden to ask. "What's got up your skirt?"

"--Before you say anything, know that it was for the best."

They had met Caleb not a stone's throw from the Rose, holding a jovial conversation with some Veiled Landers and Aos Shii, a few of which Adimus recognized from yesterday. At seeing them he had nonchalantly rejoined them.

Now he pushed to the front, though he said nothing--now that was a face he could read.

"What do you mean?" Laina tried as delicately to push it along as possible, as suddenly it appeared he had a strange fright.

"The Spear is safe. I will say that. You must trust me."

"Where is it?!" the swordsman roared. Apparently Alfred's assumption about the swordsman was wrong.

"I thought he was watching the Spear and you were watching him!" Tirlag exclaimed.

"I was...I have my own things to do!"

Alfred adjusted his glasses, observant of the unwelcomed eyes. "Maybe we should adjourn to our rooms." he glanced over his shoulder at the other scattered patrons.

The Seer's voice was calm and collected, but when he entered the room and saw it missing from its hiding place Adimus had to catch him like a fainting damsel.

"Let me explain." he quickly threw up his hands, and glanced over their shoulders to ensure that Delaney was shutting the door. "It's quite safe! I've given it to my uncle for study. Well, my cousin, gave it."

"Your cousin?" said Alfred.

"For study!?" Caleb's eye twitched.

"What is the meaning of this?" Asked Laina.

He frantically darted between the accusing eyes. "He is a holder of a parliament seat in the Kingless Council. They discharge the duties of the King No More. But this is beside the point: he is a powerful Magus in his own right, and true to the tales he is a Cessair, and as such a well trusted friend of the Seelie Court."

"Was Wyatt's hospitality just a plot?" Laina asked.

"You didn't even know of this uncle until yesterday." said Alara, slitted eyes narrowing, tail whipping.

"Come. I can take you there. You'll see."

It took no coaxing.

"You'd better."

They left swiftly. He tried yammering on several more times en route, "He is meeting with them very soon. I would have their allegiance with him acting as an ambassador."

"For us, hopefully?" Deleney chirped.

The road through the Red Row, the main merchant district, and on through the terrace that marked the residential plots was a tedious walk, burning away what little daylight remained, until there, at nearly dusk, following the bard as he himself fumbled to find its location, they stopped.

Adimus rubbed the itch from his eyes that tickled his brain with the thought that perhaps what he saw was a figment brought on by exhaustion. The tall, slender brick building that sat on the end of the Red Row, sandwiched between a curious cobbler and a haughty hatter, with an apple tree that grew on the street side reached into the back yard, depositing the sweetest apples he'd ever had. Inside were wonders greater still...he vividly remembered the place from his youth.

It was *The Ashen Curio*, home of Reis Valkeir.

"*...He* is your uncle?"

Argent just laughed and shrugged.

William galloped up the shallow run of stairs and rapped on the door. It opened a crack and blue eyes looked him up and down intently. A female voice came. "Yes? We're closed for the evening."

"Hello. William Mathune. May we come in?"

She cracked the door ever more so slightly. "Mathune?" The words twisted on her lips as if they were foreign. She swung open the door, face wearing an unwelcoming scowl. "William?!"

"...Charleze." he greeted.

"Alfred?!" her countenance diminished when his name left her lips.

"How...serendipitous." Alfred's face ran pale with the shock and puzzlement he tried to contain.

Then there was a peck on a window, and Adimus too almost fainted. "Dyrshul?!"

A moment later she burst past the gatekeeper and through the door. "Adi!" She leapt off the stairs and into his arms.

"What? How!?"

Charleze swung the door wide at the approach of the old man behind it. "Fate and fair weather, my boy, fate and fair weather." Luloch Buckroy beamed, and met to embrace him.

They were promptly filed in after that, where Adimus was welcomed by his father as well. "Adi! My boy!"

They were promptly filed in after that, where Adimus was welcomed by his father as well. "Father, we found Gae Bolg! We found the Spear of Fate!!" he exclaimed. He felt a slap on the side of the head from Tirlag telling him to keep quiet but he didn't care. Luloch took a hug from Laina as they came in. It felt like it had been so long since then, so long a journey since it had all begun, that it took his look of confused astonishment on his face to remind him that he hadn't a clue what the boy was talking about.

In the den to their left stood Annaliese, waiting to greet them.

"What a happy accident." a voice came from the right, what would be the study.

There he stood, the Reis Valkeir Adimus knew, no diplomat and statesmen, no hero of the Secession War, just the endlessly curious, warm, charming gem of an old man.

He stood before them introduced himself, though they most all recognized him, and their manic presentation cheapened any exchange.

Alfred finally addressed him. "You must excuse us, Mister–, *Lord* Valkeir, our compatriot did not disclose this decision with us." He glowered sideways at the bard.

It was only after it had been made known that the tension finally broke. Adimus could smell it in the other room before he heard it, and heard it before he saw it, clued in by the dripping sound resounding inside a mop bucket.

"The gods are eager enough to show their wrath to our Kind as it is without me inviting it by trying to pilfer one of the Treasures..."

Adimus felt a hand grab his. It was Dyrshul. He was quite familiar with the gesture—he'd used it many times himself, the signal saying *"I'm stealing you from this horrible adult situation."*

He took the others into the room, the small study to the right of the show room. But Adimus was not about to make its dour presence dull their reunion. It was Dytshul he followed.

She took him back into the vast room in the place's center. He looked around in wonder. "For a while I thought this place wasn't real. Imagined, like my dreams."

She didn't have to have it explained to her, she knew what he meant; more than once she had to be the one to snap him out of it, out of delirium and back into reality, when, like the spear, into this sacred space the dreams had bled.

The unassuming house seemed incomprehensibly bigger on the inside. Having more than enough money to live in the residential district away from all the chaos, the owner chose to live in its heart. Forgone were weeping arched trellises of wisteria and cobblestone walks of red winter roses; here he lived, overlooking the madness. And lovely it was. The smell of sandalwood and tea leaves filled his nostrils. The paint had been changed, and a couple of rooms perhaps added, sure, but it was the same. Old statues of pewter, tribal masks of painted wood, clay pots, expensive silverware, Longnight tree decorations, coat racks of canes and brooms and colorful parasols and swords, perfume bottles, ruby-lensed spectacles, monocles of quartz, crystal wine glasses, tapestries and tartans of lowborn houses, old maps, cabinets of coins and collectables; The Ashen Curio was, first and foremost, an antique shop. Some might even recount a great deal of it as junk: the whiskey barrel full of old shoes still sat in the corner, covered with layers of dust so thick that he'd wager that one of them was there when last he came. But then there was more than just the mundane here, he knew.

"The cabinet spider. He was real too? And the eyeball that moves?"

"...Yeah."

He gulped.

A few were missing, even fewer moved, but he knew these items not because they were labeled (though most were), but because his mind reeled with wonder in his youth, of them when enthusiastically inquired about each, over and over again, and every adult told was forced to entertain.

Onyx coins of the Empire of the Oni Shogunate, used to barter severed heads. Wooden dice imprinted with runes, which the Druids used for fortune telling….the musk of a Seelie Stoat of the Kind.

A Karanashi mummy, on display for everyone to see, upright standing as if prideful of the jewel-adorned lid of his sarcophagus; though both Nin-Keth III and the lid were bathed in such opulence, the funerary preparation which preserved his body was perhaps the greatest gift he would receive in his lifetime, as it staved away the curse of unlife that had destroyed his people. Adimus hoped.

Upon one wall was the massive cast skin of Arcos bin Zhubrator, a dragon of the age before the Great Kingdom, accompanied by a choice selection of scales kept in the coin-cabinet below it (with the spider).

A golden scarf hung on the wall beside it, said to be crafted by Otherworldly silkworms who did the bidding of maidens in their secluded forest village in the Veiled Lands through use of a secret song. Sunsilk, as this material was called, was impervious to cut or tear. This one was worn by a servant of the dethroned Iron Warlord of the Unicorn Clan, and it had saved his neck, literally.

A taxidermied mounting of one of the creatures whom the vouxites call Kalkatoroi. These ox-like beasts were plated with natural armor, and it was said that the generals of the Blossom Bride rode them into battle. What was worse, it was said that their breath could melt iron and turn a man to stone.

A Toran waystone covered in runes. It was massive, the size of one of Anwell's pumpkins, the language written on it was said to be that of the Giants, the Jantiliak.

Various implements of war adorned the walls. A curved scythe-like polearm belonging to the cynocephali, a dog-headed kith of the Cessairians, distant cousins to the likes of Alara's people. A blade of pure glass as long as a man's forearm, razor sharp, said to come from the Land of the White Sands, a world beyond, directly beneath the sun.

A baker's dozen of the cunning throwing weapons used in the Veiled Lands. Some were like a simple dagger, but some looked like pinwheels or six-pointed estoiles. He remembered being warned never to touch them, as some were etched with magical words called dweomer, meant to curse the receiver of such a nasty gift, while others were said to contain poison so potent it could still kill ten men no matter how long it sat there.

...Like so many of the other strange things in his mind, he thought he had dreamed it all—but for this, he found himself elated that this was not the case.

Chapter 27
Moving On

The house was two stories, with a landing above that overlooked the floor and served as a solar for reading. This upper level spanned both the gallery and the library, which, though bifurcated by a wall, both shared a vaulted glass dome at its top.

He could hear the muffled conversation ringing into the room. They treated with him, and discuss at great length a great many things, about their motivations and goals, the political climate, about the spear: that its origins were unknown, about the nature of its mysterious bleeding (of which Reis was surreally dismissive), about what their next move should be--but Adimus wasn't much listening. Finally, after circling the room he rounded on the den where Luloch and Bearach and Charleze sat.

"Come, sit."

He parked himself on the old green sofa, sitting the decorative pillow on the floor beside him, admiring . For the question had been begged "Why are you all here?"

"Tolten." Was all Bearach said. It was as the utterance of his name dwelt upon them, souring this room too. He elaborated anyway. It was all he really had to say.

"He's lost his mind, and he's found a few in the town that already have a hard time finding theirs to join him."

"What do you mean?"

"He's got half the village in his pocket. He wants to invoke the traditions of the order."

The boy's jaw felt like it was made of lead "You mean...?"

Luloch simply. "He wanted to start with your sister." Luloch nodded.

Images erupted in his mind at what that meant. Old folk used to tell stories that you could see the old marks at certain banks of Loch Sul, where the waterline used to sit before the bones of the dead rose it.

"Monster!" Adimus was overwhelmed. "Name him! *His* guts will spill on that altar before he lays a finger on her."

Luloch appeared taken aback at the proclamation, perhaps upon seeing a side of his grandson heretofore unseen, but Bearach just beamed. "Aye, boy. I know it. And us too. But I figure it safe here for the time being. We've appealed to Pembroke, told him where to find us. They'll suss this out. "

"...So they believe in the Night of the Shades enough to call for our blood but not enough to actually help us?"

Then a gnawing skepticism overcame him. "...You just recently spoke to Thadeus. Did he know at that time that Dyrshul was in danger?"

"What do you mean?"

"...Nothing." Adimus unleashed a stare of ire across the antechamber into the room where William Mathune sat. He remembered what the bard had told him when they had left, that he had made sure none of this had happened. It was a lie.

In the due course of the evening when they pried about Gae Bolg, and Adimus would be more than happy to oblige in telling them all about it.

"Well, right after we left, we visited this strange temple and I was bitten by a Church

Grimm." he started.

Bearach gasped. "You what now?!"

"But I was okay." He explained, before he had to elaborate even more than he cared to (it still gave him nightmares, apparently). "Laina saved me..." He glanced over unconsciously at her. "She is a Magus, the Seer says."

They each looked at each other, as if confirming something amongst themselves. "Well I suppose so. Makes sense. Eichgun told us much the same. And the town. Laina may not be able to return with us." Luloch plainly said.

It stopped him in his tracks.

Charleze leaned in. She'd seen him, though appearing to ask everyone he couldn't help but feel she addressed only him. "Would you like some tea?"

He nodded.

He imagined she was trying to comfort but it had made it worse, as now he was off kilter, self-conscious again.

"Did you meet with any lords in Hewnyleigh?" Bearach asked while she was gone. "Were you able to appeal to anyone about...you know?"

"No..." he slumped.

"I figured. All these nobles seem to care about is squabbling amongst themselves, they care little for the plights of folk like us. Except for this one. No worries, I believe Mister Valkeir will soon have it all in hand. He's has some associates what are on the Kingless Council."

Adimus suddenly remembered Alfred's question from the other day. "Grandfather, I meant to ask. How did you and grandfather come by meeting this lord anyway?"

"He's a friend of a friend, is all." The old man tersely replied.

"But, he's a Magus, isn't he? *And* a noble lord. How could you and he have met? Did he visit Hewnyleigh?"

"I've many a varied acquaintance." his grandpa continued to evade.

"Anyway," Bearach changed the subject, "tell us about this mighty adventure I hear whispers of in the other room."

Adimus remained curious, but still couldn't pass up the chance to tell them "Well, you see, the Seer and the Torrin fellow had these letters, which led us to an old fortress..." he started again. "Oh, Dyrshul! We met Killmoulises."

"Killmouli." Charleze interrupted. She immediately lowered her head when they looked up at her. "Sorry."

"Well go, on boy, in order now!" Luloch scolded, playfully frustrated.

He started about the pledging and the ancient forest, and their encounter with the Huldrafolk.

In the lull of the conversation the sound of his regaling them carried, and before too long a curious head popped up from around the corner, listening from beyond the threshold of the door, then another. Then another. Then another. Soon, all of them stood, listening to him go on about the flooded Fortress and the Labori.

The old man followed, sitting very comfortably in his chair across from the boy, one leg crossed over the other, while the boy grew more nervous and insular, until finally, seized up like he knew he would.

"I've heard tales of the Labori." Said Bearach. "Legends say they were brought to life to serve the Great King, and serve him still in places."

"I've seen them." said Annaliese, "In the Labyrinth City, toiling away at the final orders they were given to build a tomb for Githa before they could no longer be told to stop." She lowered her head, her interjection making her embarrassed when the room grew quiet. "All true." She sipped.

Reis rescued the conversation. "It is serendipitous that one of them would guard the resting place of the Spear." he said. "The blood which issues from it is the foundation for the Magic which gives them life."

"What do you mean? Uncle." He still tried to feign association with the strange man, but Adimus too was on to him now.

"It has myriad qualities that make it altogether transcendent of the law of All'Khemy."

"That's impossible." Alfred simply said.

Charleze stifled a giggle she realized to be inappropriate.

"Beg pardon?" The old man smiled.

"Nothing is beyond the purview of understanding given time. All'khemy is the whole, nothing can 'transcendant' of it."

"Of course. Of course..." The man quickly dissipated the argument. "I only meant that it is both a substance of fixed state, yet paradoxically seems to retain its ability to be Worked in its entirety, precipitating no Form when Calcinated."

"That's--that's impossible." Alfred affirmed again.

Everyone else's eyes glazed over, but Adimus leaned forward. "You mean it is both in a Coagulant state like gold, but is infinitely Dissolute, like Cold Iron?" His reading lessons had paid off somewhat. He only truly understood what the thing he read meant. Nonetheless, Alfred's face welled up with pride.

"Your pupil understands. Why do you not?" said Reis.

Charleze raised a brow, he saw. Adimus leaned over to Dyrshul while the other adults continued talking and pridefully whispered. "I'm his pupil." Laina hushed him and snapped him back to attention, albeit with a bemused grin.

"You teach him well, I see." Said Charleze.

"Yes. And I'm sure he keeps him from dabbling and trying to jump ahead in his understanding too." It was an obvious jab from Reis, as it caused her eyes to suddenly not find a place in the room in which to rest, though no one seemed to know the context. He continued with Alfred. "I scarcely believe you didn't notice the power within the blood. What, with your Reading."

"Psychometry cannot sense such things as Calcinative Quality. And I haven't had a chance to perform Works with the Spear."

"Psychometry can indeed be used to ascertain Calcinatives: Reading gives you knowledge about an object, what you do with that knowledge is up to you. Applying the truths of The Aurum Agri it is plain."

"Truths? The Aurum Agri is a misunderstanding at best, and Fae elitism at worst." Adimus could tell Alfred felt more than a little antagonized. "Vague, mystical, unhelpful in the slightest; One of many empty models to acquiesce to the Tuathan cultural worldview or for Sourcers to hold over the head of the Cyances in boast."

The old man didn't address it. "So, where in town are you staying, young Mathune?"

"The Rose in the Rushes." His nephew replied off-guard, choking down a gulp of tea.

"You mean that den of cheats on the edge of town?" he guffawed. He adjusted in his chair that he could reach the side table where his tea sat. "I shall send for someone to collect your effects. Charleze, turn down the beds in the guest room."

"Milord, I wouldn't wish to intrude--." Argent started.

"Neither of us shall be comfortable not sharing each other's company; the Spear is not safe there, and neither shall you trust me with it. As you shouldn't, William, now if you don't mind you can join her in removing the furniture and making the preparations, as long as my comfort is your concern." he glowered at him from under his bushy eyebrows. He removed the scowl from his face, perhaps realizing it was harsh. "After we finish, of course." Adimus didn't know the circumstances by which Luloch had met this man, but was not surprised that they were somehow friends.

"If I may ask..." Tirlag butted in. Her empathic friend was already tensing up. "Why are we going to do what you say?"

Laina sucked in her lips in shock. Caleb sat on the edge of his seat. Alfred took a sip of tea to hide his smile.

"Well my dear, I was under the impression that you needed me. It was, after all, what Annaleise has beseeched, on behalf of William here. Is that not the case?" He again lounged as if not a care in the world weighed on his mind.

"If you may, we, the Company ought to discuss this in private." Argent smiled.

"Of course." He said, and with a spry spring he hopped out of the chair. "Charleze." he said.

"Let us go and get to Madam Ghiana's before the bell sounds. I've a craving for those toffee peanuts." He smiled. On hearing it Adimus found himself guarding his scalding tea from spilling all over him when Dryshul started to leap up, but there was no need. Charleze, already passing for the door, gave her a warm smile and patted her on the head, "A slice of strawberry cake." she mused, before the girl beamed a thank you. "Your grace." she mockingly bowed in tease to her cousin Annaleise, ushering the rueful countess out the door.

"Adimus...?"

"Potato candy. Or a fried pie." He quickly replied.

Alfred shot a judging look.

When they all left there was a silence. They each looked at the other. Finally Argent broke the ice. "So, Keeper Bearach how have you been?"

Bearach blinked. Alfred dispelled the nonsense. "Mister Buckroy," he addressed Luloch. "Do you trust these people?"

Luloch nodded. "I do."

He only half heard, as he, having gotten so far down into his tea, looked down at it perplexed after having taken off his glove to examine it.

Argent spoke up. "This man has sworn an oath to see the kingship restored. I say we entrust him with the task."

Alara, whom most had forgotten was there, piped up. "It's not like he's some Fae under a Geas. Hyu'manii swear oaths and break them all the time. No offense." She added at the end, but Tirlag turned around, her face full of disgust just the same. "Just ask the divorce lawyer next time you're in Hewnyleigh." the cat jeered, showing her teeth.

"She's right." Said Delaney. "Those bad men in Keara swore an oath too."

Tirlag, having literally felt the sting of the Gnemedian's point, could say nothing. She turned around again. "Then I say we do this the proper way: a vote."

Caleb looked around, reading the room. "Sounds equitable."

Alfred, again lost in thought, this time on his knees, on the floor, caressing the other tea cups with his bare hands answered, snapping to. "Agreed."

"Very well, then." Argent huffed in begrudgement.

There was silence again, as all waited for another with enough heart to lead. Finally Alara stepped forward. "All in favor of allowing the Spear to reside here and allow Reis Valkeir to aid us in its proper acquisition...show of hands?"

Argent, Alfred, Laina, and Delaney (despite Tirlag's glare) raised their hands.

"...Brother?" Dyshul whispered. Adimus looked at the ground, arms folded. He could see the bard's eyes on him.

"It is a tie." Laina announced.

"What do we do?" Delaney asked.

Alfred gave the seemingly obvious answer. "We wait for Torrin. He is a founding member of the company. He has a vote."

"I thought Alara was voting as his proxy." Argent argued. "She is not a member of this company, any more than Regil. Or the horses for that matter." He sneered. "No offense." He punctuated the less than jovial jab.

"Is this the first time he hasn't gotten his way?" Caleb seemed more than pleased at the outcome.

Argent threw up his hands in defeat. "Very well," he stood. "Pack up the Spear, we'll be back in our inn room before they get back through the door."

Laina spoke. "It is only right that we formally decline, at least. And thank them for their hospitality."

"Well, either we take the spear or stay close and guard it." Alfred reasoned. "There isn't much compromise to be had."

"It would be safe to leave it if we left the swordsman here to ensure its safety."

"I will do so with my life." Caleb replied.

"And if anything goes amiss there will be plenty of witnesses." Said Alfred.

"I say it should be Adimus." He said. "He'll naturally be wishing to stay here, and it seems I've fallen out of his graces of late." Argent gave him an unreadable look. "Not that you should listen to the one you mistrust."

"We do not distrust you. It is the only way to be fair." Laina plead. But he didn't reply.

There was a long silence.

"For all this talk of 'company' they certainly don't seem to enjoy it." Luloch jested to his grandson.

"Oh, especially when it comes to one another's." Tirlag interjected with a wry grin.

"Well. Since we are to be parted, it would seem. There is something you should know." He addressed Alfred, who had been rooting around the room touching everything. Pensively he sat down beside the Bard.

"It seems that someone in power is looking to expand said power. Using the Lapidaries." Argent glanced back over his shoulder and Alfred were huddled in the small waiting room at the door.

"Why does this concern me? I told you, I'm not one of them--."

"Clan Ward." He cut him off.

"...What?"

He shrugged deviously, "I mean, I don't think it is of major import, the Lapidaries are an innocuous organization. Like the Esotericists. They are people of principle." He explained. "But these Named Ormandian warlords…"

"They won't see it that way." he let the Seer finish the revelation.

"Who knows. I would simply have you know, though Wyatt would disagree. It's the chief reason my cousin is here, to keep tabs on the movement of these merchant lords. Make sure they aren't conspiring against the Kingless Council."

Alfred didn't really give a reply, just an approving nod of thanks before he continued going about his routine, even checking chair legs and the like.

The rest waited, saying nothing more to one another, awkwardly huttled in the stranger's den until he'd returned with the others.

Charleze pranced through the door with a lollypop of her own enjoyment, and a dainty paper bag which she handed to Dyrshul. "Thank you!" she squealed.

Reis paced up to Luloch and haphazardly tossed him a small bag. "Oh, would you stop it!" He tried to protest. 'Thank you." It was licorice, Adimus could smell it from where he sat and it churned his stomach. He always had to deliver it himself into the old codgers hands when miss Lathern made it. He hated the stuff.

"I think we are to take our leave, uncle."

"That is a shame. I meet with the king with the council in a few weeks and the Seelie Court midsummer. I'd hoped their guidance would've helped."

"…The Fae Court?" said Alara.

"Oh yes. At The Sanguin Sabbath. It's a peculiar year for astronomical events. Wouldn't you agree, Luloch?" He turned to the old man. "I suppose it's for the better, I've so much to plan anyway. At any rate, here." He handed him a paper bag. "They're scones. Should stay warm through your trek across town." He says warmly. "Take care."

Adimus began to stand, but Dyshul jumped up and shoved him back onto the sofa. "Mister Valkeir, can Adimus stay with us?" She asked, but he didn't acknowledge it. She had to directly get his attention before he replied.

"Why, of course, my dear."

The boy figured that in much the same way his worries were trivial (who had seen him naked lately) so too was this, given larger matters at hand.

"Uncle, I think I shall stay too. If you would allow it." Said Argent, shooting a conniving grin at the swordsman, who returned one of discontent in kind. "What's more--and forgive my impertinence for so asking, but I would like to accompany you to these events to act as the Company's ambassador. That is, if you would allow it so." he added.

"Good. Good." Was all Reis Valkier replied.

"We will be going along as well." Said Luloch. Adimus gave a questioning look at this, to which he replied cryptically. "Many things have come to light since you've been gone." He didn't have to explain it to the boy, he already knew. *Dyrshul. This has to do with Dyrshul.*

They were beginning to be funneled out the door, each giving 'goodbyes' and 'pleasure meeting you's'.

"Here." Tirlag handed him the orb from her belt pouch. "Make yourself useful. See if you can weasel some answers out for us." she shook a finger at him, hiding as best she could the trust she'd placed in the boy. "Keep it safe here. You hear me?"

Adimus was only half listening, and quickly binding it in the plaid he'd just taken off scurried to place it in the corner of the showroom; he was honed in on the hushed exchange between Alfred and Argent.

"What game are you playing at? What is the meaning of this?"

"No games." Suddenly he raised his voice. "I have to keep an eye on Knolls. *'What's good for the goose',* after all..." he shrugged when his answer didn't seem to add up in the Sum Seer's eyes. "Why? Going to miss me?" He snorted. Alfred didn't think it funny. Argent wasted not another moment. He whipped off his cloak. "Here." He put it in the hands of the unexpecting man. "No tricks, no nonsense." he said. "Take it." He draped it around the wizard's shoulders.

It was all that the shocked wizard said to him. "I promise the spear will not be moved again unless you will it so--you're going to find yourself trusting my intentions. " He looked over at the boy. "Even if you cannot trust my actions." And he left it at that.

Chapter 28
Imposition

"How are you coming along, lad? Can't sleep?" Bearach's exasperated breath shown as a rolling cloud in the cold air.

It was early, and a mist the dawn was too fragile to dispel hung about the garden. He hadn't beaten his father though, who was eager to get to the fresh logs the timberman he dropped off the day before.

Adimus picked up the axe that his father had sat down to catch it. "I'm fine."

"Good. Good." He watched his son put a plunky log on the stump. "...Your shield arm well enough for that?"

"Let's see." He swung true.

He shot the man a pompous grin in play, but the man's face showed mirth.

"Lady Akima told me about that wound."

"Laina?" He had to verbalize it, as it took him a moment to realize he was talking about her. "You never called any of the other women in town 'lady'; maybe Tolten's right about you. Mister Valkeir has a collection of wedding rings. I could have Dyrshul play dress up with her to find out her size."

The man wore a half-grin through his beard of frost and saw dust, but Adimus realized he wasn't having any of it. "Seems like you were a bit worse off than that glib gob of yours put on."

The boy awkwardly chopped another piece. He gathered himself with a sigh. "It was scary, I'm not going to lie." Suddenly it was uncomfortable. His thoughts turned dark. The words brought him back to it. "I thought I was going to die. Or worse."

"There's a fate worse than death?"

"Nothingness. The Utterdeath that the touch of the Sluagh brings."

"Ah." He let out a phlegmy scoff of dismissal, "That's nothin'." now he was being glib, or so he thought. "Now, dishonor. Far worse. Allowing the touch of immorality idly." He tisked. "Even if there is a thereafter, how can a man live with himself, forever in shame?"

"...I take it she spoke to you at length."

He paused. "You were about to wage war on a holy man, for Dyrshul's sake, the other day. Where was your shame then?"

It was as scary as facing the Barghest.

"Excuse me father, for speaking against you, but propriety be Named, what Tolten does is wrong."

"But, boy, how can ye say that? It is what the Old Way demands."

"It's what the Pardoner demands. You'd have her given up?"

"I didn't say that."

"Then what is it you mean?"

"He is a member of the circle. He has the Magic of the Seven Veils to confirm his rectitude. His sense of right and wrong is surely keener than yours. Yet you say you will fight."

"It is plainer than the blinding day that he only seeks to bring hurt and pain to us."

"Self-evident. That's what I've heard those bookworms say. Self-evident." He was, of course, talking about grandpa and Reis. His face softened. "Adimus, you are becoming a fine man."

The boy's face twisted in confusion.

"What in Lyr's name makes you jump to that conclusion?"

"You've been tossing around with too many o' them muck-spouts, for sure!" He shook his head, using his foot to pry his blade from a knotty piece of wood when the boy got it stuck. "But still, you've learned more than your mouth puts on. That it's not your decision whether it is right or wrong. Nor is it his. Nor is the decision that it was better to live than die by the bite of that Black Shuck on the Ruined Road. The only dishonor is in not doing what it is within you to do. Yearn. Seek wisdom, then use it to uphold the utmost, in whatever you do. A man can do no more than this. Act in this way and you never lose your honor, nor should you have anything to lament. And if the Gaze falls upon you you'll never be found wanting." He took the axe from the boy and hoisted a particularly plunky log onto the stump.

"Is that a lesson Tolten taught?"

"No. But if this were untrue I wouldn't mind to face oblivion. It's impossible for a man to outthink himself, to outdo the best he can, innit? And if Ol' Crom is a just god, or if he's a god at all, he'd know it." He swung hard and true. "It's self-evident…"

* * * * *

It was a cozy abode, despite lacking the amenities and luxuries to be found even among the surrounding houses. Unlike the Rose in the Rushes, it was <u>not</u> heated by Khemetastry, and they had only a single horse stall, and a meager yard to put it in. There was no carriage and driver on call, no gardeners or groundskeepers, and the lot behind them encroached on their back yard only inches from the fence line. Still he had never enjoyed such luxury; the house was always warm, and Reis and his niece had food ready for him.

This time he had beaten her. It wasn't by choice, of course, his dreams were more pernicious of late. But she must have gotten up only moments before he, as she was fully brushed and robed and ready to go.

"Good morning." he said.

Charleze, crawling on her hands and knees and covered in dust brushed her hair out of her face. "Good morning. And no. You don't need to--."

"How can I help?"

It was a sensation he had always struggled to shake, even at his grandfather's house, that despite being invited as a guest the boy felt a great feeling of imposition, as if they were doing some service for him that he could not repay. Try as he may to shrug off this guilt, it behooved him to try his best to help out around the house. He'd come to find that his father felt much the same, restlessly awakening before the sun to undertake all manner of projects: fixing wobbly tables, thatching the roof (and on a particularly icy day at that), organizing the pantries, cleaning out the single horse stall (Charleze had a pony), or splitting the aforementioned wood for the fireplace.

Charleze always let him sleep though (when he could), despite his protestations otherwise, and every morning she politely fought him when he offered.

She'd even tried to drive him off. The first day he asked, she gave him the worst of it (he figured, at least), forcing him to feed a mouse to the spider in the coin shelf.

The glass enclosure served as a terrarium for the awful thing, which spun webs that sang like harpsichord strings when disturbed, who itself talked, belching a "thank you" when, with all the caution he might give a Barghest if he ever saw one again, he threw the mouse in and slammed the

217

door.

Charleze assured him that, despite what his uncle said, the creature wasn't <u>actually</u> sapient, and that it was just a trick they'd taught it, as the creature could mimic the sounds of any animal for the purposes of luring prey, usually small children.

Even after this, after tending his other chores (namely tending to Aethan, whom the crew had dropped off to save money on stabling) there the boy was.

"What can I do for you today?"

With a playful sigh of frustration she turned back around, and a moment later produced a large case, scooting it toward him. "You can catch." It was full enough for her to perhaps not even pick up on her own. He shouldered it as she lowered it down to him by one handle.

She climbed down before him, and wiping her hands off on the hems of her purple robe, she glanced about conspicuously.

"Is it safe?" She asked.

Adimus glanced down the banister, then to the cracked bedroom where Argent usually lay, where surprisingly found him missing.

Adimus gave the all clear, and with a word and a gesture the apprentice invoked a Spell. This one he'd seen her use before, used to separate the dirt from her. Like a snake shedding she contorted and shimmied and grabbing it pulled it free from her, rolling it into a tiny ball which she put in her pocket; he was admittedly a bit jealous of the trick.

That was one of them, one of several such 'shortcuts' that she could use on the house as well, as long as she didn't get caught by her uncle--she wasn't allowed to use Spells unsupervised anymore, she told him. She could conjure pure water to drink, or to fill buckets. Summon an unseen pair of hands to hold things or perform simple tasks for her without supervision. Adimus was loathe to be her accomplice, but reasoned to himself that whatever hospitality made him feel a trespasser might also grant him immunity.

She boasted that her family was heir to a much greater power in the days of the Great Kingdom, that it had diminished by magnitudes; that the power to call upon the help of celestial creatures with the use of True Names, to create flame with the will, to conjure storms, to create stone from air were the least of those. But she was forbidden by Reis to do them, and that all the scrubbing and chopping and carrying were to be upon upon back and brow.

She opened the case. It took him a few moments to realize that it was not just junk and knick knacks as usual, but her own personal effects.

Immediately an aroma roiled up his nostrils. It was a quite pleasant one, one that sent his mind reeling with thoughts of the sandalwood, champa flower, of the jasmine incense that Laina often burned. Though they looked nothing alike, she reminded him of her somehow, though he couldn't place it; something of the exotic that he had perhaps unduly categorized in the same place in his mind where he placed other mysterious females.

Inside, rolled in a decorative cloth, were a few candles, some books and vials of oil. A few of them, the perpetrators, having broken inside. "Here it is." she twisted her face at it, picking it up and letting it drip.

She took the cloth and used it as a place to lay it. "Maybe I shouldn't have waited so long." she confided. I hope I can separate the ink from the oil." She was speaking of her 'shortcut'. "

He heard the approach of someone. "Later." she whispered.

It was her uncle, stirring. "Charleze, my dear." he yelled up from the base of the stairs. "Can you come down and put a kettle on?"

"At the expense of sounding impertinent," Adimus asked, (it was a new word he'd learned only a few nights ago), "You say you do these things because your uncle is frail?"

"Yes." she guardedly addressed. "Why?"

Adimus winced at the disrespectful undertone of his own wording, he tried as gingerly as he could to redouble. He at once wondering if all women, save his sister, tied his tongue in a knot when he spoke. "So, I hear the place we are to meet the fae in the summer is the Endless Forest. In the cursed wood."

"Beyond it. At a Crossroads."

Suddenly his dream stirred in his mind, bidding him to steer the conversation. "Crossroads? What's a Crossroads?"

Charleze guffawed. "That Alfred...He did not teach you much." she waved her hand, a vain attempt to dispel her own slight. "A Crossroads: a place between this world and the Otherworld whereupon one may cross. Beyond the Curtain, the mist." she explained. "Now, what were you saying?"

It took Adimus a few moments to process all of her words. "Lord Valkeir. Is he in sound enough health for the journey?"

She crossed her arms. "Firstly, I do these things for him out of respect. I am quite thankful for his kind heart." she told him. "He's just a bit cross right now because of a misunderstanding he and I had." she quickly came to his defense, standing. "Secondly, self-awareness and keenness of intellect, rather than vigor or stamina, are the qualities needed to traverse the Forest of the Exiled. You'll see." she responded with a warm smile when he appeared now even more confused. And with that she hurried down. Dyrshul had apparently awoken to the resounding 'thud' of the case, as now she stood in the doorway to their chambers, stretching and rubbing her eyes.
"You are going, aren't you?" She asked.

Adimus shrugged. "I'm not sure..."

"Your grandfather is going."

"...Hmm."

"Where will you be going after *that*?" she nodded toward the downstairs. The thing intruded on his mind again."Will you be staying with us? After that?"

"What makes you say that?" Suddenly a flash of insight lit in the boy's mind. "You know I...I don't know. Possibly." it came out a little more excitedly than he would've liked.

"You may need to go with your other Pledgers." she herself shrugged, thinning aloud. "Alfred may need you."

Just then there was a rap at the door.

Charleze ignored it at first. Then it came again. "Is no one going to answer it?" she snarled.

Adimus jumped up when she started too. "I'll get it." he said, then trotted down the stairs. She followed if only to mutter in protest that he ought not have to.

Caleb was already halfway there, coming out of the den where he'd apparently slept with the Spear in arm's reach but Adimus made it there first. He swung open the door. It was William.

His clothes were dingy, his hair wild and tangled with neglect, with a visible bruise puffing out one side of it. Of his eyes one was sunken with exhaustion, the other one was black, and both looked at the ground.

Despite her being shorter and much more scrawny, Adimus found himself reeling from her push "Stand aside. You're letting the draft in!" Angrily she slammed the door in his face. She turned around and crossed her arms, eyes closed, pouting in outrage.

"Cousin." His muffled cry resounded on the door. "I'm sorry. Let me in."

"You're not, and you never have been. For shame, William Mathune! You were invited into our house, yet you show no decency to abide by a decent hour. Show some couth for once. Some gratitude! Like Adimus here." She smiled at the young Watchkeep. "You can sleep out there!"

"Want me to kill him, madam?" Caleb joked, probably. "I'll kill him."

"Charleze…" finally Reis scolded, and with a roll of the eyes she let him in.

Argent gave a judgemental glare to the boy as he passed; despite being sheepish about being called out, Adimus fought the feeling of superiority welling up in his chest. The smell of alcohol followed the Bard in.

"Gracious, child! What happened?" Reis came.

William wandered in behind his cousin, scratching his head and perhaps showing a little bit more embarrassment.

Adimus began to linger, until. "Come on." Charleze motioned him, taking his hand to drag him away.

They met Dyrshul halfway down the stairs. "What's that noise?" she said, wiping her eyes.

"A mongrel dog scratching at the door is all. Good morning, Dyrshul."

"Oh. Hello Carlie. Good morning, big brother."

They finished helping Charleze to clean out the old luggage, which they had found was her own personal want, as she needed a place to store her effects for the journey. Charleze sat cross legged on the floor, digging through it--the unpacking quickly devolved into the showing of souvenirs and Dyrshul playing dress-up with the hats and jewelry therein.

William announced himself with his shambling footsteps up the stairs. He stopped to look at them all.

"We're not going to a ball or to promenade. You need to pack like it."

Charleze simply glowered at him.

"It'll be your trip here all over again. Suit yourself, when it comes down to it I'm not carrying it. Maybe Adimus can be the gentlemen." he grinned. She threw a piece of the rubbage at him to get him to go away.

"Is he going with us?" She sounded giddy, but it could've been the boy's imagination.

"It will be his choice in the end. He's his own man, right Grigor?" He gave a snide snarl at her then looked at him. "But if you want my advice I can tell you're probably better off facing huldra and labori again, they've more of a heart." He cupped his mouth to her, "And aren't quite so heavy."

At that she threw a shoe at him and he scarpered behind the door.

"Why are you at each other's throats so much?" Asked Dyrshul, apparently Adimus wasn't the only one that had noticed.

She didn't look up. "Never you mind." she replied, then in a lower tone she muttered, half to herself. "Just know Alfred is doing the right thing. Just never tell him I said that." she mused, sniffing a small veil of unlabelled liquid, then curiously tucking it in the bosom of the gown under her robe. Adimus could only shake his head in bewilderment.

"So you know Alfred too? I heard you when we first came…" those time the prying came from Adimus.

"Uh-huh." She said flippantly. "He and I go way back." trying on a white sun-hat and looking at herself through a hand mirror she'd found.

"Really? Did you get training from that Teacher man he talks about?" he asked. "I thought you'd only just met him at the auction."

She burst out laughing, but never explained why.

"Did he used to be your boyfriend?" Asked Dyrshul. Adimus gave her a warning scowl.

Still she didn't answer that either. Instead she opened a small tiered jewelry box and began fondling ear rings.

She plucked a few sets of them from the selection. "Which is your favorite, Adimus?" She held up several of them in succession.

"You should do this one!" Dyrshul nabbed one from the box, a dangly silver and turquoise affair with the end of a peacock feather as its centerpiece. The ones she chose were a little less modest and bold to the other ones as Dyrshul pointed out.

She turned from her, seeking his approval.

Adimus curled an eyebrow at her persistence. "Well, *that* one would make an excellent bait for fly fishing." He looked at a few of them critically. "This one." He pointed to a set of polished knotwork-embossed copper hoops.

"...Really?" She actually looked a little disgusted by his choice. "Noted." Was all she said, closing it.

They both followed her downstairs to the small stove, and Adimus helped get it started, plunking the wood into it.

The kitchen was tiny, and spread out all along the back wall of the house. There was a coal and wood oven indoors, but also a secondary hut with thick clay wall and an oven directly outside, the oven opened on both sides so that the heat could be allowed in during the winter and relegated to just that room in the winter. It also seemed to be a little more than a typical bread oven. Caleb questioned bellows and the deep bed for coals and the sturdy way it was made. "You could forge iron in this."

There was a dumbwaiter also, that Adimus imagined might go down to a cellar where wood was kept to feed it, but he wasn't sure, nor had he as of yet seen such a place.

She had put the kettle on and set the cups and the pots and the tea basket out and she retired back upstairs to finish.

"Come on." Dyrshul said. Without a word Dyrshul swung onto the ladder and headed up where he knew her brother would follow.

The task of cleaning the attic had gone on for several days now, culminating in sweeping and dusting and mopping. Adimus was sure to bring the buckets of water, and take over when she was noticeably too exasperated to fight him back.

The attic itself had a lark, and most of the clutter Charleze had been sorting was shoveled under it. It was yesterday when they'd found the window, atop a small run of stairs above it.

Stand upon it, looking out at the city, the thought weighed on him more now, once a looming apparition unidentified in his mind, but manifest and given a face when Charleze had posed the question: *where was he going next?*

Chapter 29
Strangers

He was standing in a green field with high grass, the warm wind whipping it in gentle waves.

Dusk had just fallen, taming the sweltering day into a warm comforting breeze. He stood with a young lady with long, pointed ears, her long hair and flowing gown whipping in the wind. Her eyes were a strange violet.

"You see?" She pointed up at the brightest of them, the blue orb Nemh, the Moon of Seasons, swollen in midsummer glory among the others that haloed the tower that climbed the sky. The thought began to erupt from his mind. *I knew it was real.* But as one does in dreams, so enchanted, it slipped from his mind as he submerged himself back into the moment.

It was the Moon he had always remembered, or so he thought, until that moment. "A city!"

She nodded. "You can only see it from a Crossroads like this."

He gazed upon the tiny structures of crystal in amazement.

A Crossroads in a field beside my Mom's house. Mom's house? He looked about, at the shadowy woods beyond the field, where he'd spent his whole childhood, and where he'd found her. It wasn't the same woods he remembered for some reason, but again, as one does in a dream he played along, which wasn't hard when he looked at her.

The moons were bright, illuminating her haunting features, and when he looked at her, she giggled and smiled, and rested her head on his shoulder.

Then he heard a noise, It set him on edge, and he reached for a sword at his side-- monsters were common, especially nowadays. Then he identified it: the grinding of rubber turning off pavement and onto gravel, and saw the lights turning in, shining onto them.

"What is that!?"

"Probably just Tristan."

"A carriage?!" She marveled. "What manner of beast pulls it?"

He started to answer, but in a moment of self-awareness found it hard to articulate.

It <u>was</u> Tristan, he saw, when he hopped out.

"Adimus? With a girl?" He said. He jumped out.

Tristan knew well who she was, he was just giving him lip.

It was somehow a relief to see his jovial face, his wild black hair and his signature yellow bandana he'd worn since they were kids. He reached into the back seat, they could hear the clanking of glass.

He pulled out a couple of bottles, whacking the caps off using his metal door for leverage. "Guess who closed the sale on the shop today?" He strode up and handed them a drink. It was cold in his hand. With a congratulatory drink they clinked glasses and each took a swig of Baron's, the tuathan girl, Selean, hesitantly; it was her first time. It was fizzy and sweet, refreshing in the warm breeze.

Selean still looked at the strange chariot in bewilderment. Tristan saw that she was noticeably distraught by it.

"What is that? How does it function?"

"Where have you been keeping her Adimus? You haven't taken her on a ride to see the famous Larubian lights at night?" He tisked. "Come on." He ran back and got in.

She looked back at Adimus with bated breath.

Then Adimus's eyes locked onto what sat beyond the verge of the wood. A pair of yellow orbs, piercing the darkness. The boy opened his mouth to shout but nothing came out. The creature caught his gaze, and the following second Tristan honked his horn to gleefully spook the girl and it leapt from the bushes, this gangrel, hunched, wolf-like form. It stood and was taller and broader than any man. It showed its lupine fangs with a snarled just before it charged. Tristan swung the door open to help, and cried something in vain. It was on them before anyone could do anything. Adimus jumped in front of the girl and reached for his sword, but it wouldn't unsheath. He winced and opened his eyes, and realized he had been asleep all along. He awoke in bed.

It was still in the early morning, the sun had not yet risen, and everyone else was still asleep. It was during these times he would practice the exercise. He kept telling himself that it was a productive way to pass the time, but in truth it was the most powerful soporific he had access to-- and he, now being "a proper man" at the conclusion of his harrowing ordeals, had been given free and open access to his father's stash of whiskey.

Eventually, he came to begrudgingly accept that he wasn't going to sleep again. When his father awoke he would join him in chopping wood (the noise of his axe was actually the only way he knew that he wasn't already awake.)

It was in this hushed halflight of a lazy sun just beginning to peek that he heard the clink of a cup in the next room. He knew it wasn't his father. (he could hear his snore roaring in the baseboards even though he slept on a separate floor than him) *Grandpa. Or Reis.* He thought to himself. *Old people always get up at the crack of dawn.* He was surprised to see himself wrong; scurrying past his open door still in her nightgown, was Charleze.

It explained a lot about how he would always awake to see her doing chores, feeling as if he had slept in. *She wakes up before dawn.* She'd gone to her room to get something, apparently, and when she brushed back across the threshold of his room again, she saw that he was awake. Embarrassed, she tried to hide with her arms that she was in her nightgown and moved along quickly.

He sat for a few more moments, but found he could no longer concentrate for whatever reason. Finally he got up, rinsed his mouth out with water, and went out the foyer.

The banister overlooking the vestibule of the front door formed a balcony with a skylight overhead whereby one could look downstairs. Here in the sunlight there was a clear spot with a nice rug, and a nook for reading (it seemed like the whole house catered to the facilitation of such spots) with some cushy little stairs and dainty pillows. There she sat, the wisp of a candle she'd just blown out still wafting in the air.

"Good morning." she said. Not looking up from her book.

"...Morning."

She sat in one of the chairs, cross-legged reading a book.

Seeing that she in fact was not doing chores, he politely tried to tip-toe past her, though he wasn't sure where he was going.

"...That coin. What is it?" she startled him.

"Hmm?"

She shut the book, keeping her place with her finger, and looked up at him. "I've seen you holding it several times now. What's its significance to you?"

"Oh that. It's nothing." He found he was being evasive to save himself interaction. He normally would permit this. "I mean, it's part of an exercise Alfred gave me."

"Exercise?" she obviously didn't expect that answer.

"For psychometry. He seems to think I can learn it."

"Interesting." She reopened the book to continue, but then stopped again, obviously bothered. "What does he have you do in this exercise?"

He leaned against the rail, trying his hardest to feign confidence that he understood it at all. "He told me it's to train my mind. I concentrate on it for long periods of time. Every time I get distracted, I am to pull my attention back to it." He was loathe to admit.

"And how has that worked out? Any progress?"

He sighed, relenting to his honestly. "Not so far." He hid his slump.

"Doing that is not going to teach you Psychometry." She said off-handedly. She lifted the book to her face again.

Though she lifted the book to her face only to add weight to the answer to her begged question when he asked. "...What do you mean?"

"He's teaching you to focus your attention, it <u>does</u> make for a good starting point, I suppose. But he hasn't just imparted it to you straight off? It would've been easier for your sanity than inundating you with <u>that</u> measure of boredom would've."

"I...I guess not."

"He's keeping it from you. I wonder why..." she thought aloud. She opened and lifted the book with a shrug. "I'm sure he has his reasons." He started to leave, but then she slapped the book shut completely. "I can't believe he'd lie to his pupil though. For shame. Maybe he didn't teach you as well as I thought."

"What do you mean?"

"Maybe he's just an old fashioned teacher. I shouldn't judge. Reis is much the same. Vague. Overly Mystical. Unhelpful in the slightest." She enthusiastically slammed her book shut again. "Here. Stand up. I'm going to teach you an exercise too. Seithr exercises."

"What?" He said, but she was already standing.

He sat down with her on the rug facing her when she commanded.

"Can you do this?" She splayed her hands, that her fingers were grouped as twos and separated from one another.

Adimus's leered curiously, trying to hide his smirk of amusement. He struggled with it, but after a little effort was able.

"How about this one?" She did the opposite, with her middle finger and ring finger together and the others splayed.

Again, he struggled, but was able to do that as well.

"Now this." She switched back and forth the two positions in rapid succession.

This time Adimus couldn't help but chuckle. "What does this do?"

Charleze shushed him back to seriousness, though she herself was hiding her facetiousness until she could no more. "Nothing. Nothing at all, it's just fun." She snorted. "Now stand up."

"Now, follow my movements, <u>and repeat after me</u>."

He followed her feet. Slowly, deliberately, ensuring the boy followed her every movement, she spread her arms wide and then slowly rotated one down to the floor, and the other to the sky. "No, your feet should be like this at first. Right toes facing right, left foot forward. Like this. Now lower yourself at the knees. The knees. The knees, honey! For thrice sake you have the coordination of a drunken sloth. It's okay..." Much the same she corrected him on the placement of his legs, hips, the alignment of his shoulders to his neck, the fluidity of the motion, and how he held his hands in the bizarre configuration she demanded. Then his breathing. They started from the very beginning several times until she was satisfied. Then, when he had it perfect she progressed to a different motion, this one both hands forward. When he'd gotten that she showed how it flowed back to the starting position.

"This is called Rajata's Wheel." She introduced it. She began again, and again she adjusted him. Then again. Less and less she had to correct him. They slowly danced through the movements until eventually they had worked up a sweat, and feeling she could no longer keep her breath herself she stopped.

The next day he was woken up when a dainty pillow bounced off his chest. He lurched up.

"Shhh." The girl stood peeking into the room.

Quietly, he would obey her gesture to come and join her, each morning, at the crack of dawn, to do it again before their chores for the day.

"What does this do? Is this just exercise?"

"It's a mnemonic device."

"Hmmm?"

"...Don't worry about it."

Then the next day came. Then the next. Then the next. Each time they did the same movements.

"...Are there other exercises?" Adimus expressed his frustration in the midst of a particularly long session.

"Of course. Many." She tried to resist panting, controlling her breath.

"Why don't you teach me another one?"

"Maybe. Eventually."

They went on a few more minutes.

"Why don't you show me how to Read?"

"Breathe. Concentrate on the movements."

"...You have to admit it's frustrating. Did your master put you through this too?"

"...Are you going to concentrate or not?"

They finished. That time she left without saying a word.

The next day they began. "...I'm sorry." he said.

"Shhh. Breathe. Concentrate."

"Oh, right. Sorry."

"Ugh." They went one for a few moments until they'd worked up a sweat. This time she interrupted. "I made you something."

"Oh?"

William, to the astonishment of all, bright eyed and bushy tailed, fully dressed in fine clothes, popped from his room. A voice from below cut them short. "Charleze, my dear, would you put a large pot on to boil? We're having multiple people over."

Adimus gave a start despite himself that someone else had awoken so soon--he, for no reason he could explain, found himself having a sensation as if he'd gotten caught with his hand in a cookie jar.

She let out a groan loud even to ensure it audibly resounded down the banister to her interlocutor. "Must I?" She bemoaned. "And who?

But he answered with, "Uncle says so." Before slamming the door. Charleze immediately glanced around for something to throw, and, finding nothing in reach relented.

She turned to look back at Adimus, hiding the embarrassment of the light in her eyes by ensuring they didn't make contact with his. "Excuse me." She brushed past him, leaving for her room. She spun around before closing the door, as if forgetting something. "What I got you. It's on the table there." She pointed. "You can continue without me." She closed the door. A moment more and she opened it again. "Don't open it until tonight, when you're alone." and said ominously, then shut the door again.

William's eyebrows bristled with curiosity. Mischievously he slinked up. Adimus's eyes narrowed, and he framed up in anticipation, but the Bard was too quick, knocking over one of the chairs to block his pursuer and buying enough time to grab it. "What's this, eh?" He held it up.

He shot a mean glare that Adimus had a hard time reading as serious, given his proclivity for buffoonery, but he did get that weird feeling in his throat again; like he had both hands in the cookie jar.

"It's nothing. A gift. She gave me."

"My cousin is writing you love letters."

"That's not--it's educational, I'm sure."

"With this wax seal? Ensconcing...what is that? A sprig of lavender?" Adimus tried to stop him but he pulled it open. "And scented with her perfume no less. You must be right, because I am finding myself quite elucidated." He sat back in the chair, crossing his legs to enjoy whatever was on the paper.

Adimus just stood there, mouth parched for spit or words. The Bard's face grew more and more cross. He gave him a sideways glower still holding the paper. "...Are you sweet on her?"

"No... I mean. No!"

He tried to give him a judgemental look but couldn't, when the dam of his absurdity could take no more and broke along with his facade, that spilled over into a fit of roaring cackles. He wiped a tear from his eye and stood. "Very well. Very well. If that's what it takes, if that is the price to be in your good graces again, Adimus Buckroy, I gladly pay it." he handed it to him, but not before tickling his nose with it, ensuring he got a whiff.

He hopped over the chair, kicking it back up into its standing position as he did, before skipping down the stairs.

Adimus stood, staring at the letter. There was a knock at the door. His ears focused on the sound as Charleze opened it. *Alfred!*

There were many other familiar voices, but he heard his voice first. It seemed almost foreign to him, though it had only been a few weeks. He hurried to the balustrade and peeked down. Argent was at the door to greet him. *What had I not been told?*

The first thing he noticed was that while they were coming, Caleb was going. It took him a minute to recognize: his wild matte of scarlet hair was combed and pinned back, and he wore a strange garb, a layered, folded short robe tucked into a pleated trouser-like skirt. He sat at the small bench in front of the door, putting on some new wooden sandals.

Adimus started slowly down the stairs, trying to listen in, and then was spotted by Alara. "Hello there, curious one."

He announced himself shortly thereafter. Laina, hiding just beneath him where he could not see greeted him with a hug, then someone he did not expect came blasting through the doorway. "...Watcher?"

"Regil!" He shook his already reaching hand.

"How goes it, my boy?" Thadeus Pembrooke stood in the opposite hallways, nursing a cup of tea with a spoon.

"Lord Pembroke!" He beamed.

"Glad to see you and your family are well." he said. "No doubt your pa has told you about the matters going on back at the village."

He waited for him to respond. "...Yyeah?"

He chuckled. "Well, I came to tell him it's all in hand. He'll be reprimanded by the high lords now, likely to find himself in Cairnfang." He didn't need to elaborate upon whom he spoke. "At any rate, as soon as I convene with Lord Valkeir here on behalf of the Princes we can all head home and put all of this behind us."

"That's great!" Adimus exclaimed.

"...Well, if my service is no more needed, Mister Juminion, I will take my leave." the bard nodded.

"Of course. Thank you for all you have done for us so far." nodded the seer. If the comment were somehow to become self-aware and able to manifest itself as a tangible thing it would've become a hand to slap him.

With that Caleb left.

He gave a passing hollow smile and was finished with his exchange, now he was in the way. The boy struggled to peek over Rigel's burly shoulder and into the room beyond, where Alfred, Torrin, and Reis sat.

Now he could hear Torrin Krasad. "I hope I'm not imposing, milord, I only wished to come and see it for myself."

"Not at all. Not at all. I, having seen it, can hardly believe my own eyes."

Torrin's eyes never left the thing as he nestled into the chair. Beaming, his smile ear to ear, noticed the boy and addressed "Adimus." Torrin with a nod and a chuckle when he drew near. "...Are you ready to have the first king in an age?"

"I don't really think anyone present is, so far." Reis answered for him, curling his mustache.

Torrin leaned and plucked a decorative pillow that he'd been sitting on with a strain, and spent a moment wondering what to do with it. "It is a weighty decision to be sure. For more than just Ormondians. Whose hand shall hold the Kainspear when the uhh..." he glanced around as if they themselves might be present. "Histban comes knocking at the door?"

"Do you really think they shall come?" Alfred asked.

"Conquest of all the three kingdoms of old is the aim of Xyraxus of Petra, make no mistake." Reis looked around him. "To gather the relics of the Thrice Slain King and establish his kingdom here for himself. This very town will be the Empire's staging ground for invasion before it is over, mark my words." he said gravely. "You, Merchant Lord, should know."

Torrin stared soberly at the Spear. "...I've seen the Golden City for myself, quite a sight to behold. They say of him that he's the Thrice Slain King Returned. The King Once and Future."

"Backwater prophecies. Heh. Almost as destructive as backwater deities. Wouldn't you say, Luloch?" said Reis. The old man concurred, and the Lord continued. "That is what I've been-- ever so delicately--trying to emphasize to my nephew and this Eastward Endeavor: The Spear is found. Now an heir can be named. One mistake here will affect all of us, your kingdom, mine, *and*

Ormond. Personal grudges, superficial preference or even who pays your bill must be set by the wayside." he clanged his tea on the table. "I'm not to get in the way of these Pledgers, or step on traditions, mind you. I only seek to give knowledge and guidance, that they may make an informed decision."

"That is understandable." Torrin nodded. "I must say, when I heard that one of the Kingless Council had decided to meddle with us, I was prepared to contact the Steward Princes myself, but when I heard it was you my fears were allayed. I hope that I may be of service to that end in whatever way I can."

"You've heard of this man?" Argent peeked over Adimus's shoulder at the merchant, having seemingly appeared out of nowhere.

"My father mentioned him in passing. The man who garnered peace between Torant and Kessellon, who now serves the Kingless Council to see the same done.

"I'm flattered. Thought I had gotten away from all of that by coming here. Should have changed my name." he chortled.

"At any rate. If he can get the nobility and that brigand who sits upon the Alkonost to get along, he no doubt shall be able to usher in a great kingship--and negotiate the proper remuneration for our company." He announced to any who would listen, "Just let me know how I can help."

Alfred rocked back in his chair, perching his fingers against one another in the air, hiding whatever bode upon his mind with feigned platitudes where applicable.

Adimus didn't want to approach him, but he had much lay on his mind as well. But the question from the other day still nagged at him. He had only just mustered enough courage to confront the man with it, when Argent grabbed him by the shoulder. "You have the money you got a few weeks ago when you were with Wyatt? Am I right."

Adimus's mouth twisted, skeptically. "Yes?"

"Good. Torrin has agreed to award us, for 'exemplary service to the Company." He jingled the necklace of coins, before gleefully putting it around his neck as one might crown a king. "It's yours. Don't spend it all now," he warned. "You'll need a pinch to pay for some new clothes before too long. I'll not have you going to see the Fae in tattered tartans."

"Oh, Adimus." At that Alfred leaned forward. At that his attention had returned. "You'll be staying." He avoided eye contact, when he said it, doubtless feeling imposing himself. "We're leaving at around the same time as they. After the holidays, after the Salt Fair."

A dozen things flashed through his mind he ached to give in reply. "I rescind my allegiance to this Company." was one "No. I am a Grigor, I'm returning home." was another. But he said nothing.

Then Argent cut in, "Alfred. He has fulfilled the terms of the charter, but has not set out to perform his charge. Allow him his leave. If he cannot find aid among the people of Ormond, perhaps he must look outside them."

The Faeth's eyes narrowed. If it wasn't from the mouth of Mathune then its logic would've been unassailable perhaps. "Our Watcher is a man of his word. 'Unto the duration of the work.' Our work is not done. His assistance is still required."

The boy hung his head, "So it is."

* * * * *

It didn't seem real. He knew it sounded strange to think. He'd had his share of bloody noses, so recognized well that coppery smell. It stained well enough, getting on the linens upon which the bucket sat to prevent just that from happening to the rug beneath it. But, though he was no expert as far as things went, he'd visited butcheries before, and was acquainted with the harsh, sometimes vomit-inducing smells that accompanied the vocation. The blood that issued from the spear never clotted, never rotted, went rancid...never even grew cold. Somehow, this made it even more unsavory, and though the boy wasn't particularly squeamish, the warmth that wafted up to his hand when he gripped the handle and the noise it made, a frothy slosh, like Bessie's milking pale did, made his stomach churn.

On the count of three he shifted, and Charleze was there to catch the next drop from its horsetail. She also collected the ripened berries from its haft, just like last time, tossing them into the bucket along with the gory mess.

"Follow me."

Reis had helped her do it the first time, but Reis and Luloch and Dyrshul had gone out to scour the High Market and spend some money, and this room was the chore of the day.

Slowly, delicately, he waddled it to the door beneath the stairs.

He had recounted the door as a coat closet in his youth, but he'd come to find that it was some manner of cellar. When she placed her key into it a frigid wind blew it open. It had to be a cellar of some depth, as not only this, but concerns of flooding had been brought to the old man's attention in light of the Salt Faire's approach.

He could only guess, as he was not permitted to see it, until.

She nabbed an old oil lamp by the door and lit it. "Come."

Water trickled in through the stonework, furrowing into puddles that quicked his socks (Charleze was barefoot). Several rooms they passed, the dank smell cued him in: a root cellar. Then another, stockpiled with bottles. Wine. Then the wind came and nipped away all sense of smell. At the end of the hall was a door. It rattled at their approach, and an icy glow shone in its cracks. "Watch your step." she warned, just as Adimus almost slid into a split. Here the water clung to the walls. Fumbling for the key again she unlocked it, then the cold iron gate that lay behind it. It was as if the depths of winter itself sat behind them.

What Adimus saw he could not believe, nor could he quite comprehend.

He couldn't look at it directly, every time his eyes laid upon it it was as if they fled away. His heart seized in panic, though he could not know why. The entity frozen in the ice had definite features, this he knew. Adimus drew nearer it in astonishment: its head was like that of a man, but sat atop the haunches of a bull. But, the head was turned around completely backward from what it should have been were it creature of proper, reasonable shape; this it wasn't, and the horn-racked man-like bearded visage that sat atop the neck saw down its back at them. Accompanying it was a grotesque set of bird-like wings, adorned with what Adimus could only understand to be two massive piercing eyes that peered out from within their folds.

It made him feel sick. "What is this?"

"Fresh shaved ice, year round." she replied. "Never you mind it. Give me the bucket." She snapped her fingers.

Adimus stared at it, hardly aware that she placed the bucket in a corner of the room along with the others, nor that they had not frozen.

Adimus stepped forward and reached out to touch the ice. When he did he lept back; it wasn't ice, ice as he knew it. He looked at the water on his hand, then reached out again. It was as if the heat of his hand melted it. Not only this, but liquefied it, liquified it so swiftly it was as if it weren't even there.

"Stop that!" Charleze scolded. The worry on her face snapped him to, and before he knew it he was shooed out of the mysterious room and ordered back upstairs. "Name you, Adimus Buckroy, as often as I hear you told not to touch anything, I swear!" After a moment her face softened a little in spite of herself. "You're pure of heart. If it melts at your touch. That's what that means. So it's good to know. But at any rate, back upstairs now." she scolded. "I'll...be along." she softened.

She huffed at being scolded like a child by...her. Which made him feel all the more sheepish when he realized that he was pouting like one too.

He turned to go back to the den, suddenly his eyes were drawn to the front entrance. Customers frequented the Curio so seldomly that Adimus almost forgot that it was a shop and not a home. What was more, the tiny bell that usually alerted their coming had somehow evaded his senses.

So it was a shock that one stood at the doorway. A Tuatha no less.

"Hello."

Most often customers bought nothing, only drawn by the rumors of such a place or happening upon it whilst shopping the strip of Red Row. Often they gawked at the Kalkotaur, or the mummy, or the gigantic beast pelt in the den that served as a fireplace rug.

He was in the midst of taking off this garrish canary yellow cloak and hanging it on a peg.

"That's not for coats. Sorry. It's part of the merchandise Master Valkeir trades."

"Oh...?"

He looked puzzled. He glanced at the boy. "Sorry." He shrugged, putting it back on. It was the first time Adimus had actually caught a glimpse of the Fair Folk in full light What they said was true about their hair, that it moved as if underwater, the brunette quaff of his own drifting and flowing unnaturally. His ears were pointed, just as he was said. His long nails and pronounced canine teeth gave him a feral presence that somehow countermanded his mannerly countenance.

"...These are all for sale?"

"Yes."

"....Old clothes?"

Adimus dare not entertain criticizing his host. "Master Valkeir sells many things." It came out in a dignified tone despite sounding moronic.

"Who?"

"Reis Valkeir. The owner of the establishment."

At that the man chuckled. Adimus scratched his head.

He defaulted to the script he'd heard from Charleze. "Welcome to the Ashen Curio. Are you looking for anything in particular today?"

"Alfred Juminion III."

Adimus gulped.

"Is he here?"

The Watcher blinked. "No. There's no one here by that name."

"Presently?...Are you playing a game with me, Seelie?"

Suddenly Adimus did not feel safe. The man's stride, like his hair, was unnatural as it moved, in this instance toward him.

"I...don't know anyone by that name."

"Oh, so you aren't a Sworn, you are just a bad liar." He reached a long fingernail and touched the coin under the boy's shirt.

Adimus's blood froze.

"May I help you?" Charleze appeared.

He glanced around.

"Do I know you?" the man twisted his head like a curious puppy.

"Perhaps. We are well known in our circles. Are you a collector too?"

"Of sorts." He gave a puzzling smile.

He glanced around at the glass tables displaying their strange, strange wares. "Have any Espun-tail caps?"

"What? No!"

"Fauth seeds? Greenman husks?"

"We don't really deal in those sorts of things."

"Well, what do you deal in?"

"Antiques."

"Antiques? Intriguing." he nodded, leaving both to judge whether it was sarcasm. Regardless, with that he again began to peruse.

An awkward silence befell them, a stiffness for Adimus, almost as if freezing before a predator.

Several minutes passed. Charleze quietly put her hand behind her back; they were soiled with blood.

The Tuathan tapped on the glass cabinet. He'd seen the hand-sized red spider nestled in its corner and was somehow intrigued rather than revolt. When it responded with a "Hello." He burst into teary laughter, the warmth of which through the menace.

He marched around the room looking over everything. He gave a second glance into the study, realizing that the swordsman who sat there glowering was not part of the decor.

"...I know it's not part of the showroom, but the Pardwolf pelt in the back? Just there?" he gave an inquisitive shake of the hand.

"Not for sale either, sorry."

"Poor fellow." he tisked.

"Uncle says he'll forgive him someday, though."

"Ah." he put a knowing finger to his nose and they shared a grin. Adimus scratched his head as if tickling his brain might let him know what they were talking about.

"...The Agrathian Harp Spider, is he for sale?"

"It's a she. And no." She crossed her arms, then becoming self-conscious of the blood she hid her hands with the gesture.

He meandered for a few more moments. Finally, in one of the many shelves in one of the many cabinets he happened upon a bobble.

"What is that?" he pointed.

Finally, something he didn't know.

Charleze produced the key and handed it to Adimus, whose hands were clean. Nervously he unlocked it for him.

The man nabbed it before Adimus could, his curiosity overwhelming his manners.

He held it to the light. The thing he described was a sculpture which contained a landscape, but the single tree it depicted was, in fact, made of woven hair, and the rocks were sanded molars and the ground was a bronze cast of the outstretched palm of the deceased. Adimus had seen it, in fact, one uncannily identical to it a time before.

"It's a memento mori. A funerary object." she explained. "The idea is to grieve the death of a loved one by commemorating their death with the creation of something beautiful. It was a practice of the Pangor Tor people that died out in the late 1600s."

"It is. It is beautiful. Sadly beautiful. How much?"

"We accept trade or coin."

He produced a half-melted white candle "Burned whereby Anne Rosetta completed The Gray Cities."

"It's a pretty painting. But a nominal feat of Votive Work, surely. Skill and creativity have little effect on the Airs. And Works have even less effect on candles."

"But passion does. Have you seen it?

"It's what you <u>intend</u> to do with them that really matters."

"I do have intentions for it: I'm giving it to you for this, which in turn makes me very happy."

"You have nothing else to offer?" Again her arms crossed.

He looked around one more time. Adimus could swear his eyes more than drifted over the spear. "You have quite the hoard. I know not what you may need to complete it. I'm fresh out of Cauldron Chalices, and I left the Kingstone at home..."

"Currency would suffice." She masked professional salesmanship with a superficial grin.

"I'll tell you what." he said, reaching into his cloak. From it he produced a small stack of jade. He passed it to the boy. From it he produced a single coin. The glint of gold was unmistakable. He flipped the priceless thing into the air and before she could think she caught it.

He saw her hands, and though it too could have been in the Watcher's imagination, he could also swear that he held a knowing gaze. "Good?"

She glanced at it for just a moment. "Amicable."

With that he let out another guffaw, and began to turn, "Thank you very much."

He tossed it into the air a few times, then shoved it into his pocket, which seemed more than big enough to fit it.

He meandered a little more, giving what would see a final once over. Then he stopped dead. He had marveled over the mummy, and the dragon's coat, but this face still was a stranger to them, held in a twisted grin of heretofore un-illicted genuine curiosity.

Until the man reached out his hand Adimus had forgotten about the orb wrapped in his plaid. Until then, the room was still. Suddenly the wind howled. The wind from beneath the fortress. This one was different. Suddenly they were bored down upon, as if caught in a hurricane, meant only for them.

Nothing in the room would be disturbed, except they, so Adimus thought, but snidely the man caught the Goldsilk scarf, which had also whirled into the air like a kite blown in a tempest.

Charleze was slung against the wall, Adimus ground his heel and pushed.

The man's hair whipped wildly. He closed his hand, then just as suddenly the wind stopped. "Haha."

Charleze warned because she didn't know. "There is no use of Magics here!"

Caleb ran into the room, hand on sword. "What in Lyr's name...?!"

"Apologies." He threw his hand up in the air. He looked down at the backpack. "I don't suppose anything would entice you to trade for that. And I wouldn't blame you."

Hesitantly Caleb returned to his post, grumbling under his breath.

Adimus weighed tipping his hand versus actually being able to finally find out what the thing was. "No."

"Too bad. Oh, well. Thank you both for coming."

Charleze blinked. "You were the one who came here..."

"Oh right." he gave a hamfisted wave and made for the door. "Have a nice...day." he bid, glancing at something in his pocket as he said it, a gesture which would prompt a maddening search from Charleze as he did inventory to make sure he hadn't lifted anything.

* * * * *

Alfred stared down at the mysterious swath of cloth, again mesmerized.

Transmuted items like the cloak were always more difficult to Read, but he had become quite good at it, as he'd done nothing in the week that had passed save precisely that. In fact, he patiently awaited his next encounter with the Spear of Fate, as he was confident that his exposure to such an item had granted him the insight needed to Read it.

Indeed, he could see the past centuries of the cloak's past quite clearly now, dating back to the times of the Great Kingdom and beyond. It was once on the back of King Randall, who used it to escape during the Sacking of Brousse in the 1600's. He saw the faces of the Jin raiders of the Oni Shogunate and strolled the ramparts of the Alkonost in his mind in one of his more daring trances, reliving events that happened some four centuries ago as if they were the here and now. It was thrilling in and of itself--the history of the thing, and a decent distraction from the fact that ate as his mind every time he touched it, only making the experience slightly more worth it than not, for though still he could not see beyond its creation, beyond the origin of it--it was of the few limitations on Sublime items, he'd found, as these items were not wholly what they were before they had been made perfect, from his study how could tell resoundingly this: his Teacher had never laid hands on it.

This Sublime Raiment, the Casting Cloak, had been used for the past few generations as a simple tool of performance; an actor would don the cloak to take on the features of the character he or she needed to portray. When the hood was placed on the head, it could conjure from the memory of its wearer the features of anyone he or she could imagine...but this cloak was no mere prop, in truth it was an heirloom from the times of the Great Kingdom; But it was made by a powerful Magus for his grandchild. But it was fashioned from the pelt of some great fae beast. And most telling, it possessed many magnificent qualities and had much more to it than that which the Bard was even aware of, many powers within it to be mastered that William himself could neither perceive nor have the ability to control.

He did have time to study the cloak in other ways as well.

Alfred had tried the exercises himself. He could change the colors and designs on the cloak at a whim, that was easy enough. It would answer these requests and keep them without need for concentration until it was removed.

The more familiar he was with someone, the easier it was to take on their features. The 'reality' of this semblance however, was variable he'd found, and much harder to pin down, tied to some more ephemeral quality of the mind, one which Alfred could not quite place; sometimes he appeared to be someone but it was a mere illusion that he could reach through and feel his own wider face and duller features, while others the features were solid and could be touched, but shifted and morphed when he lost concentration in the slightest.

With a little practice the repertoire of roles that could be depicted could be expanded. This he knew from Adimus's story, that William had impersonated a member of the opposite sex, an old woman, a feat he could not manage himself.

He found it easy enough on the surface to take on the appearance of others, at least in the most superficial way, as his discipline demanded such acuity of memory.

When the hood was taken down whatever was upon his face, no matter how distorted or unnatural-looking, stayed, keeping one from having to concentrate, but without a mirror to ensure fidelity one had to be absolutely confident in the final product before doing so if they wanted to be convincing.

Alfred's consternation had grown to crescendo, then died into a listless boredom. He sat on his bunk with the mirror from the vanity that he had dismounted to put in front of him for more comfort.

He sat upon his bunk in his room in the Rose in the Rushes, before a mirror he had dismounted from the vanity.

"Are you done with it?" Tirlag asked.

"Yeah." he answered, and with needing an explanation to why the question was posed he handed it over.

"Hehe."

"I want to try it again next." Laina called.

Tirlag was fairly good at it, he'd observed, better than he, at least. What she seemed to enjoy most often doing with it was imitating the pretty faces of other women she'd seen before, makeup and all. She could pull off a convincing rendition of Laina, though the complexion was always a little too light, and could conjure up a ghost of Analise and even the Tuathan maiden from the bathhouse, replete with the ears.

Laina, on the other hand, could perform arguably greater feats. With it she could take on unnatural and fantastical forms: people with furry antler-wearing deer-like semblances, the face of a monkey, various demonic visages. She said they were all creatures from the stories of their people.

"I cannot oblige, sweetie. Wyatt is out there and I'm too bene-bousie for what steady hand's needed for makeup."

"It doesn't leave this room without me." Alfred said soberly.

Tirlag clutched it to her chest. "You don't trust me?"

Alfred didn't answer.

Laina guffawed. "Bene-bousie? Ha! I have never heard this one. I have always pictured you using something like 'high-sailing'."

"High sailing." she sighed. "I do so miss the ocean. You'd love it. The ocean spray is like being anointed by The Goddess herself." he said. But she nodded, eyeing her with sincerity. "Aye, but those eyes. Those eyes are like that ocean. Steady like the timber of a sure ship under my feet are his arms and chest, surely." she batted his eyes.

"...And what of his mast?" Laina smirked and they both giggled.

"Ugh!" Alara grumbled.

Alfred too ignored the childishness. "It doesn't leave this room."

"What's wrong, love?" asked Tirlag, noticing him being ever more drole and humorless than he typically was.

Laina ran his fingers through his hair. "He feels guilty now." she professed.

"Ever do you share more insight than a Seer's touch can tell." Tirlag replied when he still gave no response she pressed. "He now sees that William could be trusted after all."

Alara's voice came from her bunk. "Morally perhaps." she stretched and yawned with her mouth of gaping teeth, and stretched her long black arms. "He means well, perhaps, but it doesn't mean he knows what's best."

"I'm sorry." Laina at least acknowledged that she'd awoken her.

"The common room's just out there." Tirlag whined again.

"Tirlag, we can't just prance around the common room with a Sublime item in a city like this. Do you want us to get stabbed?" said Laina.

The cat's tail flicked with frustration "...Was that rhetorical?"

"What do you even do here at night anyway?" Tirlag asked.

"Linger. Fight the urge to taste the warmth of the entrails of those who don't let me sleep." She curled up in a sheet.

"Leave her be. She is in the midst of doing important work for me. I'm sorry Alara."

Laina crinkled her brow in confusion, but Tirlag was already busy making faces in the mirror.

"Have you found out anything more?" asked Laina.

Alfred sighed. "Perhaps." he started, halting to discern the level of actual interest Laina had and whether it was worth saying. He found himself spilling it just the same, if only that thinking it out using words could help. "Of what Analise spoke. This much was true of its previous owner; it rightfully belonged to William Mathune. I feel almost certain."

"Why would you say that?"

"Just impressions. I would hate to admit it, because I don't believe in such things, but his acquisition of it was anything but the hands of the gods placing the cloak back on the Named shoulders of its rightful heir. This cloak seemed intrinsically tied to the family line of Mathune. Somehow." he thought out loud now. "Teacher was at the very least a close friend of this family, if not a direct relation to William himself."

"Why can't you detect him?"

Again he hesitated, this time out of guarded pride. "I think he knew of a way to hide his presence. Something he never showed me--some trick."

"Did it exhibit those powers when your master wore it?"

"I never saw him use them, no. But he had no reason to."

"Couldn't it be possible that it was a look-alike?"

"No. A cloak of such high Sublimation, that held the same color, the same runic writing. Impossible."

"You know what that means, then?" answered Tirlag, he was surprised that she actually was listening.

Alfred looked back blankly.

"Did you ever see him without the cloak? It's obvious."

"Your master's face was a cheat."

"Perhaps."

He nodded. "There was no doubt that many other Seers of days past had touched the cloak. I suspected that its red and gold appearance, the one it takes when its taken off and took and no one wishs it to take on another, is some sort of residual memory imparted to the cloak using some talent with Psycholometry with which I am truly unfamiliar, a command to hide its true form to instead resemble the colors of House Mathune."

"Nnnn…" Alara growled, lurching up angrily and stomping out of the room.

"We move in within the week." Alfred reminded her, causing her to slow only slightly.

"Laina, I will need you to gather the others, probably. Tell Adimus that we are leaving."

"I…I don't think that he wants to come with us."

"What do you mean?"

"He wishes to go home. And I can't help but agree with him. This has been hard for him, and I don't suppose there's much need for him from here on."

"You are concerned for him. So you must know that we are not out of danger." he said. "That is nonsense. Where he goes is no longer his choice. He is a member of this company, he will leave with us. I will speak to Luloch myself if need be, or something like that." he left it at that. "At any rate, it needs to be done before the 5th of Crea; I will require your assistance on that day."

"What are you talking about?" asked Tirlag, half-concerned. "What are you planning…?"

Chapter 30
The Salt Fair

She looked down at the papers sprawled across the floor. "When were you born?"
Adimus's brow curled. "Huh?"

The attic was strewn with them now, various open books, used candles and quills, board games, stacked pages, maps...it had arguably become more of a cluttered mess since they had cleared it..

She asked again, more sternly. "When were you born?"

The boy gave a more questioning look, she explained before he could protest further.

"We have to determine your Nature as best we can. This is the best way our tradition has found." She stood, dusting off the rather pretty looking dress she wore today, and looked up at him seriously. "Your date of birth..."

"I don't know."

She eyed him critically and blinked. "...You don't know your birthday?"

"Nope."

Charleze slammed the book. "Was no one around that day?" she held back her frustration.

"I was adopted. I'm sure you've been told."

"I heard."

He leaned away from her, looking down at the papers. On it were confusing circular glyphs, and charts and symbols. "What is all this?"

She put her hands on her hips and paced for a few moments, then hurriedly put the book back. "Come here." she said. "Closer." she pursed her hands on her hips when he didn't comply as she'd liked. "Look into my eyes." She gazed up at him, unblinking. "It's the Cypher of Heimdahl. It's a star map, written in the script of the giants." She placed her hands on his face. "Hold still." she gave a disarming chuckle through her grin. "Breathe."

Adimus was uncomfortable with such things in the most comfortable of times, but here in the cold, bright, room, in hiding with a female he found such particularly nerve wracking, though he would be remiss to fail admission as to how nice it felt. They were there a long moment. "Charleze, what are you doing?" he asked.

"Xanthic Isometry. I'm Reading your Mercurial Quintessence in the Aurum Agri."

"I...never mind."

Finally she let out a phlegmy groan. "I give up."

"Aurum Agri? Alfred says that thing you just described isn't real." he said matter of factly.

"Alfred is a myopic, trite little skeptic who's about to bite off more than the jaws of his comprehension can chew." Adimus's eyes widened involuntarily at the sudden outburst, though he'd admit he'd said it just to get a rise

Adimus looked down at the chart. "Giants. You mean the Formerians?"

She didn't look up, involved in the reading. "...Tell me, what do you know of them?"

"The village elder told me that the corpses of their fallen were used to make the mountains and rivers. That their blood makes the ground fertile. We pay them eternal homage by keeping the traditions of Illea, the Old Way."

"Typical Southlander answer." She huffed. She paused long enough to flip through a nearby book and find a page she was working on. "The Formerians were locked away beneath the earth in the beginning of time, later slain by the Triumvirate and their army of descendants, the last falling at the hands of his own grandson in the Second Battle of Mag Tuired…Figurative or literal, doesn't matter, we stand upon their shoulders either way." She presented them. "These charts are a dialogue, a history, a metaphor, and a reality. Upon them every star is shown. It shows time as it is, therefore its continuation gives hints of the future, of how the way the World unfolds, from now unto the Epochellipse of the Final Day. It's a guide to us, incomplete--not in itself but in our understanding of it, but with even a cursory reading of it with the Numitorum practitioners may approximate their own Natures as well as others, even discern True Names from among this map of all fates."

"Numitorum?" He knew the word well. "The Binding Book! That is the literature of Illea."

"Adimus…" it came out a preface, practiced recitation and carefully placed recitation of his name to soften the question for which she had rehearsed the wording more than once. "Is it true that the people of Macmearion worship He of the Baleful Eye?"

"It is."

"Ole' Crom…" she mused to herself. "I see you sometimes, performing your ritual." She pursed her hands on her hips. "It's barbaric."

"Calling a culture you don't understand 'barbaric' is barbaric, wouldn't you say?"

"But it's a fact: Balor The Black is a loathsome god to worship."

Adimus thought to a time he might have been offended, but for a reason he couldn't place he wasn't this time. "I…can't really speak to his character. He is the protector of the valley." He started. "A snake is a dangerous thing, yet when one is poised to strike, you give it a wide berth and pray to what force you will that it won't bite you." he repeated what he'd heard Tolten say so many times. "And you always assume fangs." he amended.

He was somehow both offended and ashamed that now her quick wit and judgment had fallen upon him.

"Is Crom the force or the snake in this analogy? Fear is one thing, but respect? Truly?" She questioned. He didn't know. If it were anyone else, anyone else in the world at all, he might have responded with less understanding and more scathing indignity. "He defeated and imprisoned Sluagh Gora. Imprisoned the King of Shades." he defended.

"He enslaved the Goddess and the whole of the Param in his place! For a thousand years! But not before slaying Many Shapes, and when the Goddess cursed him for it he tried to kill his own grandchild to escape his fate! Is this even the same book as the one I read?!"

"Parthos flooded the world! And destroyed mankind." he argued back. "That thing with the Nameless Boy was…a metaphor."

"A metaphor?!" she snorted.

He continued, only slightly intimidated. "A metaphor. For our transition to worshiping the Fae as gods." he scowled. "They are not gods." he matter-of-factly proclaimed. "They come from the Otherworld. But the Formerians were here before, and Crom became their king."

"Nevermind that it makes no sense if Many Shapes <u>made</u> him to begin with, he demands blood! Your sister's blood, in fact." At that Adimus said nothing. "Respect implies adoration, especially when one speaks about where to place faith." she crossed her arms, then very solemnly added. "Adoration leads to emulation, Adimus. As one believes, so then they are. What qualities of this creature do *you* find admirable? Which do you wish to emulate?"

Adimus had only been repeating the apologetics he'd heard in witnessings, when elders espoused these proclamations of righteousness in faith. On its face he had not much to say.

"What is the god that fits this worldview of yours that you pray to? Hmm?" he then snapped. "What manner of contrivance? Which god is yours, then? Or are you like Alfred <u>and don't have one</u>?" Adimus grew to a whisper in the last word, at knowing having said what he oughtn't.

"Oh, Alfred." She chuckled, as she always seemed to whenever his name was mentioned. "Failure to name your god doesn't mean you don't have one…" she playfully bopped the boy's nose with her finger. "Unthought about gods are always the most pernicious ones, Adimus." she snickered to herself for a moment, then looked at him with sincerity. Her voice calmed, sure to be filled with empathy again. "You hate them, don't you, then? The Fae we associate with? Like that man earlier today? Even after having gotten to know them? Like that Alara?" she lambasted.

"I.." Adimus couldn't bear to share this position, the one that wasn't his. Of this he could regurgitate the words of his elders no longer. "I, after having traveled with them, after what I have seen, heard what I have heard, I…."

He shrugged, again at a loss.

"It's alright, Adimus. It's okay to grow." For some reason her tone had changed at least to him, the tone she used when she taught him.

"Of the ones I've met, not all were bad. I say they should each be judged on their individual merits." he affirmed to himself with a nod.

"You should use such reason and discretion with your choice of faith as well. Colloquial ideas never survive the scrutiny of the well traveled. Provincial gods are no exception." She said using a mirror she had been playing with to fix her hair. "…He's watching right now, isn't he? He of the Baleful Eye. He can even hear your thoughts, they say." She goaded. "Even you, Adimus, by all accounts should be on the altar, if not for just not being an outsider for simply having this conversation."

Suddenly the shame flooded upon him again. "…I know."

"You're forbidden from even entertaining the idea that you are wrong…" she shook her head, and locked sullen eyes with his.

Then William's voice came from. "Are we ready? We've a lot to see!"

* * * * *

The weather change started weeks before.

The Salt Fair came in the heart of winter, just before Longnight, every seven years. The seasonal metamorphosis which took place would lull the unwary into a false sense of security. For everyone not natives to the shores of the Nalanen valley it would seem like spring. Flowers bloomed out of season, grass greened and grew, leaves sprouted from trees—even nature seemed tricked by the peculiar event.

Adimus and Dyrshul watched the merchants who tempted fate by trying to get one last sale in as they now scurried for safety with all their wares from the encroaching water. This wasn't rain water, however, as the aforementioned weather had been fair, nor snow melt. The Salt Fair, as it was explained to him, was a time when the river Nalanen swelled. Every three years, around this time--for a reason none seemed to understand--the river changed its direction, backwashing.

During these times heady ocean water that inundated harbors, overpoured the levy, and turned several of the lowlaying burroughs into sea marshes. Preparations were already being made, the sealing of the small irrigation canals that sprawled from the river to serve as sewage, the careful evacuation of several lesser slums and wards sitting on unfortunate real estate.

They watched as the river crept up to the doorsteps of the folk across the street. This was just the beginning of the deluge, in the following week it would build to crescendo, waterlogging all but where they stood. The across the way sat on saddle-stones of course, deftly straddling the waters, the practicality of their small yards and large stilted porches now evident.

It was bittersweet, for with the backwash came fair weather, and thereafter almost always a coldsnap, and blanketing snows thereafter. Thadeus would depart in mere days, then, at the completion of the fair, return, and they would depart for home. And for the Night of the Shades.

The weeks had surely crept up on him, now he knew their time together was almost over.

When he looked up Charleze was standing there. Her hair was neatly groomed with a green bow in it, and her eyes were accented and her lips stained. She had the smell of that perfume about her, and she nursed a shawl and a small purse. "Don't think this has won me over." She huffed at William, sure to drive the point home with Adimus present.

Before he could protest, the encouraging eyes of Reis and his grandfather were upon him. "Aren't they coming with us?" he asked in vain, and with several gentle shoves he was out the door, without so much as a goodbye to anyone.

Soon, they stood outside on the red brick road, where crowds of people walked, and before the boy could get his bearings he was forced to follow.

Adimus always knew he hadn't the feet for the big city. He could run up rocky hills, climb trees one hand over another and the like, but the type of agility needed to sidestep and pirouette through crowds he knew always escaped him. But this wasn't it. He moved with purpose, and for not but a haphazard and impatient glance backwards to ensure they were behind him neither he nor Charleze could keep up.

"Could you slow down, you trouncing tramp? I'm not wearing the shoes to keep up with your nonsense!"

Hawkers and madmen both capitalized on the good weather and traffic, even more aggressively haranguing passersby who dared set foot in the Red Row where they were forced to detour.

A portion of traffic that would use these arteries of the city to travel, compounding the problem until the streets were flooded too, with not water, but people. Small boats and skiffs heretofore never seen on the banks of the river now ferried people across.

They slowly wound their way up the high road that overlooked the gardens of Red Row and the gatehouse of the river's northern side, which was completely underwater.

Argent peeked out over the railing, then with a nod he bade them both to come, then he himself stepped away. "Adimus? Charleze?" his inflection was concerned. "Who is he with?"

Peddler's Park was one such, whose green grass would suddenly see itself mired with the intrusive swell. The first days were always a mess, as silt and sediment washed over everything in sight, they explained. Merchants packed their tents in anticipation, the day before clearing a path for the invaders, always crowding in and fighting in these streets for prime real estate. But on the subsequent days something miraculous occurred.

It was here with which Caleb stood with the enchanted Tuathan maiden.

"So this proposition *had* all been a ruse after all." Charleze glowered over her shoulder.

They stood alongside a curb that served as a bank in this instance, him guiding her hand at swinging a fishing rod. Even as they arrived she was already celebrating with him the catching of an interesting multi-colored saltwater fish, enthralled and giggling as they took it off the line to throw it back.

Adimus gazed down at the clear water.

Finally, Argent paced up and peered down himself.

"That is a tidal perch," the bard sneered. "a rare fish that spawns during this week and this one alone, spending their entire lifetime waiting for this moment to swim upstream to find their mate. The lucky dog happened upon it by accident."

"The fish, or the moment?" Adimus grinned.

"Bah." The Bard dismissed. "I thought he was conspiring with his Jin friends or reporting to his lord or something, or at least had been lured into the den of the Cessairians to be torn apart for disagreeing with their Dame, not...courting."

"Do I detect an indignant tamber in your tone, William? Why, is that jealousy?" Charleze couldn't help but chide. "Here you are wasting your time when you could be out with...Tirlag? Is that her name?" she giggled.

He spun around and gave the both of them this strange sincere smile, then meandered off for a bit. Charleze leaned over the balcony, and her face beamed. Adimus too was spellbound.

The red brick roads dwelt below the deluge, and it was as if the waking walking world were somehow intruded upon by the ocean, yet was glad for it. Schools of fish swirled over submarine grass that showed green beneath the still pools of brine. Spring lilies and tulips protruded its surface, their leaves caught it bouncing beams of refracted sunlight.

"Come along, little lords and ladies, we've still much to see." he beckoned, and with that ushered them down the stairs close to where Caleb and the Tuatha were. There it was apparent where he had gone, as he waved them toward the gondola.

Adimus gulped. He had never been on the water before. It was a fight to bolster himself to climb into the shaky thing. Thankfully Charleze was seated first in the back and William stood with his back turned to her, that neither were witness to the myriad expressions of concern, worry, and ultimate terror that flashed on his face. The riffman did see, and even lifted from his seat to snatch him if need be.

Finally he sat beside her, and William basked at the bow while they floated down the great river, slowly watching the footbound folk scurry. They passed over the Trade Bridge, the guard tower's parapet a roost for seagulls. Finally they made their way to the High Market at the ride's end, where the rest of the day would proceed.

He did, in fact, take the boy to be fitted with new shoes, and to get a haircut, and to peruse colognes while he himself. If chaperoned Charleze to the shops. If that weren't enough of an ordeal the bard insisted on paying himself, giving the boy a handful of coins when he did.

After harrowing hours of this the boy stood along the road, apprehensively awaiting their return like a puppy dog awaiting his master at the door. It was mid-afternoon by the time they did, and it did not occur in the manner he had anticipated.

He stood and watched across the street as people gathered awaiting a ferry that came every hour that took people that did not want to walk the two hour journey on foot through the crowded High Road back to the residential burroughs. He was now awaiting his third time seeing it.

He heard a voice. "Adi!" then saw a waving arm. It was Dyrshul.

She held a rather large lollipop which she embarrassingly held up to his face until he tried. "Adimus! We saw the porpoises!"

"Por-what?"

"And seals. And a whale!"

There in the throng with them was his father, grandfather, Reis and Laina.

"We went on a boat ride to this place. It was all swallowed up with water, so we had to sit on the caps of the crenellation. There was a carnival boat there!"

"Adimus!" Laina came up, equally beaming and giddy, raring to say something, but she was stopped in her tracks. She examined him from a step back to examine him with an approving nod. "You smell nice."

He stumbled through the complement. "Uh, Thanks."

"The amphitheatre became a marina for just one day. You should have been there." He then saw that she, her father, grandfather and Reis all stood nearby. She looked down at him.

"That's incredible."

"We can still visit, if you want. I'd gladly see it again."

Dyrshul raised her hand amidst slurping "Ooh, ooh can I go?"

"Nay, child," Luloch cut in. "He's got much to do if he's to come with us now that it's safe."

He gave a confused look, Bearach's booming voice answered. "Ha! That's right. Thadeus came all this way to tell us that Torrin and his ilk are all Cairnfang-bound. called for their crimes against the Code of Kain."

"That's good to hear." He'd meant the sentiment, but it somehow came out flat.

"...Adimus. You're going back with them?" asked Laina.

Now he looked even more confused.

"You'll always have a place prepared for you at the Beat, Lady Laina, should you ever wish to come and visit. And if not you're welcome at the Buckroy's."

Adimus stretched his head, and pulled at his braid. "Are you not?"

"I meant to tell you." She looked at the ground, floundering to make eye contact.

"It is her time to complete her pilgrimage." Luloch confessed, with the care and sympathy in his tone that he could tell she was trying to convey.

The boarding bell rang. "Laina, the ferry!" Dyrshul tugged on her sleeve, the others were already heading on.

He watched as they departed off into the distance.

Argent grabbed his arm. "Come along." Was all he said, at a near jogging pace.

"Hi." Charleze stopped for just a moment to catch her breath and greet him. Straightening herself she commented. "Well, don't you clean up nice?" He chuckled, and probably blushed.

She herself had a new dress, dark violet and silky, along with some jewelry. She wore a long set of sleeves like the ones he'd seen Laina praying with, but these were teal and transparent, secured in such a way that neglected her shoulders to weave into the open back of her garment.

"What this time?" he tried to ask her, but she was intent on finding him in the crowd.

Her fingernails were lacquered, and her eyes and cheeks were pigmented and her lips glossy and stained. Finally they met up with him when he darted into an alley. There they came to a wall leading to the next terrace.

"Here, give us a boost, my boy." He said, standing expectantly against the cobblestone wall.

Adimus hesitantly approached him, and begrudgingly helped him at whatever it was he was trying to achieve. At his prompting the boy cupped his hands around the heel of the joker's boot and heaved him up the wall, where he grabbed the ledge of the terrace.

"Perhaps. Surely I can still invoke this minor Grace." She was speaking to herself.

He felt Charleze grab his hand, and reflexively jerked despite his conscious objection to doing so. She stepped forward with him, then stepped up onto the wall.

The boy stood there mesmerized by the way she stood there, her feet cleaving to the masonry as if it now were the ground, not even the hem of her dress betraying that it was not so. Beckoning by taking his other hand he questioningly placed a foot on the stone, and was shocked to find that the world moved for him.

His legs were shaky, for several reasons.

"Don't tell uncle." She looked at him and giggled. She paraded up the wall to her hanging cousin, whom upon several moments, too intent on what he spied to notice, whispered.

"Why didn't you tell me you could do that!?"

Her response was only a shrug. "This is nothing, on the right day I can fly. Remind me to take you. What are you looking for?" She asked.

Adimus tried to lean forward and peak. He absently sought to relinquish Charleze's hand in his nervousness, feeling the awkward pangs of imposition again. She squeezed it. "It'll stop working." she warned.

"...Alfred?"

He peered down now at what stood on the corresponding street, and standing there with Alara was the wizard.

Alfred stood in his signature closed eyed meditation, his hand pressed against the wall.

They were standing in the periphery of the brick wall of the city.

Then his eyes suddenly popped open and his eyes focused on their direction.

Fearing discovery, Argent let go. Slowly Adimus and Charleze came back down the real world.

The Whispermonger hopped up from where he'd tumbled to the ground, dusting himself off quickly before darting back into the mouth of the busy street. They followed him down to the end of the High Market, only able to keep up because he continually spun around, peering over the heads of those behind them, doubtless half-expecting to see a black Cait Shii or glowering pair of glasses.

"What was he doing?" The boy huffed, finally.

"The wrong thing, obviously." Answered Argent, finally passing Red Row, the Ashen Curio in sight. He spun around and shot them both a roguish glance,"You can stop holding hands now, you know."

Chapter 31
Of Magic

"Aspen wood is used to control the wind, and can even be used in flight. It is said that a broom of aspen with bristles of rowan or willow, if used to sweep every day for a full year, ending each chore with focus on intent, will allow the user to fly for one night to their heart's desire."

She wasn't making sense. This is what she explained well enough, until she undid the clasp on the attic windowsill and insisted that he follow her to sit on its edge, the blustery cold and snow pouring in.

"What are you doing?!"
But of course she said nothing, giving but a beckoning nod and grin.

"Well, it's Longnight's eve, for starters!" he'd yammered, a sentiment that carried with it the subtext of a dozen objections that he needn't begin to explain.

"There's an implement of great power that calls to me this night." She said, voice more blustery than the frigid draft of the snowstorm battering the shutters. "But I need someone to help me carry it, and to keep watch in case the Faeries grow angry and try and try and eat us." Adimus blinked.

"Watcher." was all she said, shouldering his belt and sheathed sword, and tucking his great kilt under her arm. "Come and watch."

Adimus glanced down over the bower, to the long fall to the ice-covered bricks below that awaited him.

With a gulp he slowly worked one leg in, then the other, until they both sat, legs out.

The snow and wind that battered at them had been a cozy sight in the

She giggled at his nervousness.

She, already sitting, pulled the propped broom in between them.

"I've never done this one before." she sounded more giddy than nervous. She held the broom with one hand, and with the other she traced a strange motion and sign with her hands, and from her mouth came a jumble of words that he could only swear he knew the meaning of.

"You'll have to hop on quickly." Was all the warning she gave, and with a leap she straddled the broom and dropped from the edge.

"Charleze!" he reached for her, grabbed her robe, but it never pulled back.

She turned. "Quickly." And, numb with disbelief, before he could think, he did, conjuring his muscle memory, and mounted the broom just as he would Aethan.

He'd no time to get used to the sensation, that while he did sit upon the thing it seemed almost not to be there. Instead, every limb was supported and eased; it was as if he himself were underwater, suspended with no need for effort. Even at this, the Watcher's knuckles were white from his death-grip on the tiny thing, when, for without warning, per the analogy analogy he now felt like he was rising to the surface after a quick dive. It was the only warning it gave that it was about to steal him away into the heavens, high above the icy city, leaving his heart, his stomach and his breath behind.

Charleze cackled. Brisk air engulfed them as they displaced it in the seemingly endlessly fall into the sky. Finally, a stable, whipping wind battering him told him that they had righted. "Turn your head if you are to vomit." After a few moments she handed him his kilt, which he swattled about himself like a newborn.

Adimus was no stranger to heights and lofty views. He'd been to the peak of Brasil Tor that overlooked the whole valley of Ormond. He'd climbed the highest tree in Brian Redsmith's wood on a dare. But there was no comparison, nor words to describe the sensation. Far above, the way the lamplit city twinkled was as of a starry night projected against drifting clouds in a gale, and fled just as quickly.

 In minutes they had traversed the city and were looking into rolling hills. These were the ones they had followed into the city, that took days to struggle in tarry on foot.

Now, the Blackthorn was a most dangerous tree. It was said to hold within it the spirit of winter, as evinced by its flourishing leaves and berries which ripened only within its frigid depths. This much Adimus had heard from Luloch. What he was never told was in their harvesting.

The parts of this tree, its berries, its branches, its thorns, were good for Working Magic, but whosoever harvested from it should surely die, for the host of the Unseen protected it, cursing with dire Fate any trespassers who dare disturb its boughs.

"...Olentzoro would slit our throats if we saw him. That's what we were told." Charleze chuckled, snipping leaves with scissors.

"That's gruesome! Cinder Teg simply spanked us with hawthorn switches."

"I always heard the Teg ate children. Whole."

Adimus wiped his nose on his sleeve. "Only the bad ones."

"Well. Let's really hope this doesn't count, huh?" she said, thinking to herself. "Valley-bound Isha can see through reflections, just don't pass any mirrors on the way back to bed. We'll be fine."

"Wait. Are...are they real?"

She shrugged.

It was deep in the night, only hours before morning, when they had landed. Others still slept, on Longnight, children slept.

What few (not even Luloch) knew was that the creatures who guarded the blackthorn were worshippers of the trifold goddess of fortune, whose sabbath came at the exalting full moon of Longnight's eve. So Charleze had told him. They had only until that dawn to collect.

 "How much longer?" The Grigor asked impatiently. He clasped his Cold Iron blade close to his body, under the folds of his plaide. He hoped that ole' Teg, the faeries, all of it were just stories.

The snow had shoved off (either that or they had outrun the clouds themselves), and so it was that the yellow moon held high and full in the sky, the blue moon behind it a pale sliver, the fingers of winter that clasped it like a pearl in the black.

With her siangham (hand sickle) she sheared the boughs of the bush, briar and berry and branch, separating them into piles.

Handling it was its own danger, Adimus knew that much all too well. He'd caught a few stingers from a blackthorn before, and would've gotten an infection were it not for Luloch's poultices.

"Hush." She said, sitting on her knees meticulously stacking the most unspoiled leaves into bundles and tieing them with twine.

"So what is all this used for, anyway?" He softened after realizing that his harshness was wrought of worry.

"Many things."

He rolled his eyes at the answer, so she obliged in giving a slightly more precise one: "Certain plants Work well with other items to cultivate the Quality. They are Familiar with them. What's more, plants—especially the sacred trees of the Ogham, have a high amount of Calcinates of their own, all while conversely possessing a Votiveness that is easily sequestered."

"...Oh."

He stood for a long while, as the witch harvested and processed her take. The dreary and the cold dwelt on him, and in it a black reminder: it would be the fated night all too soon. And in the hush he decided to ask, "You seem to know a lot about this Fae stuff. Charleze, do you know anything about the Winter Queen?"

He had been thinking about it for a while, what the bard had said to the Unavailed Cadifor of Dougall. Adimus knew many stories of the Fae Folk; The Account of the Invasions, which chronicled their arrival (and those of others), the quarrel between Bres of the Golden Crown and Nuada of the Silver Hand, the Great War of the Four Noble Houses of the Tuatha, the Betrayal of Lugh. But in these stories he had never revealed such a name; he had meant to ask him himself, after the whole Spear business, but he'd not the heart or head to ask him anymore.

Suddenly she looked back. Her answer was terse and concise, almost rehearsed. "*My arms are withered and thin, my hair once golden is grey. 'Tis winter my reign doth begin, youth's summer has faded away...*The Cailleach, she was called, Beira. One the Formerians."

"--Cailleach!" He interjected. "I know that name from my prayers!"

" Well, the first queen was, at least. See, when the house of Semias inter-married with the enemy to force a truce, it became a title, bestowed upon those chosen from the lineage."

"I have heard that some of the Tuatha made peace with the Formerians, that they even had children together. Like King Bres of the Tuatha."

"Correct." Was all she said.

"Well, I mean, but..." Adimus clodded his foot on the ground. He didn't know the correct question to ask. "What does she do?"

She looked at him and blinked. "I don't know what you mean. Do?" She half scoffed. There was a lingering pause before she decided to indulge him again. "She _is_ one of the Four Sovereigns."

"And what is that?"

"Each are bound to discharge the duties of their seat, regardless of their affiliation with the Seelie Court. It escapes me what was hers..." she shrugged. "See, I only know from my recent study in preparation for meeting the Erlking and his court. I know she is the Lady of the Longdead, Mother of Bones."

"Does that have to do with the Sluagh?"

Again, she shrugged. "Some say the Sluagh are the most ancient of beings, so old their names have been forgotten. The Cailleach is the oldest of the Formerians. It would make sense."

Suddenly it felt a lot colder.

That had held the silence until she was finished. He noticed her wearing that perfume again when the wind blew. "There." she said finally, dusting off her hands.

She wore on her head a barrette of wood that Adimus had made for her, with a knotwork pattern of his own making, painted green and red as to resemble holly leaves and berries, lacquered to a glossy shine. He was glad that it had turned out so well, as he'd never actually done more than simple whittling. He'd made two of them, of course: one for Charleze and one for his sister (though he'd be embarrassed to admit to his sister that hers was just for practice). It was a trinket, a bauble, never to match the pretty diadems and barretts in her collection; he knew she'd never wear it in earnest, save to feign appreciation for it and spare his feelings.

He'd gotten the copper tools from the money he'd saved. He also made gifts for the others with it, hand made pipe boxes for Reis and pawpaw, and a new brooch for his pa which he had also bought, made of fancy braided copper as well clasp his kilt instead of pinning it (he always hated having to put holes in the plaid).

Her knees and the hem of her dress were muddy now. He'd wished he'd offered her something to kneel on.

Helping her to her feet, the Grigor used his kilt, reversing its tail to make a big pocket in front of him to hold their loot. With that, finally, she picked up the broom, and shaking off the snow from the bristles invited him on.

* * * * *

Only hours before, they were all here. It had been weeks since he'd seen them, but they'd shown, and he had been ready. For Laina he bought incense, imported from her home land, for Caleb he bought bricks of tea, for Alfred some candles and for Tirlag and Delaney some funny looking matching bangles he thought suited them.

His present sat in the back. Together they had bought him a backpack. A proper one, with leather and fancy brass toggles and many straps to distribute its weight for easier carrying. What's more, each of them had placed for him something to ease the burden of travel: a hatchet from Regil, a copper dipper from Delaney ("for that food stuff Breathers like him ate"), a set of spices in tiny vials from Laina, a sturdy new rope from Alara, and a lantern, much like his own, from Alfred, along with a quill, some ink and a little vellum; better than any of these gifts individually was the sentiment that they all warmly inferred. They also went together to buy him a short bow and a quiver of arrows. *If only they knew how bad a shot I was.*

He followed her upstairs, where he gave up the items in his kilt. Then with a "Good night." he passed her to go to bed.

Morning was well on its way when she quietly produced the key that unlocked the door. It was Reis's key ring, he recognized it.

Luloch lay still conked on the sofa in the den, Dyrshul across his lap. Even Caleb was still out, leaning upright against the wall by the window of the study as he always did, sleeping upright, the butt of his sword sheath on the ground, handle beside his cheek. Presents lay unwrapped and strewn about the floor of the den.

She gave him only enough time to take his boots and plaid off, and stealthily warm himself in front of the fire. Before she returned. "Adimus, do you still have that bronze sword?"

"Umm, yes."

She took him upstairs and waited for him to dig it out for his effects. "Good." she inspected it briefly. Then she produced the key ring again. "Follow me."

The locked room was in proper dishevelment, and covered in thick cobwebs.

When she opened it, motes of heady dust stirred in the sleepy beams of the sunlight caught through the wide windows. They overlooked the backyard, and on more than one occasion he'd stared up at it wondering what could be in it. This was the atelier in which Charleze had worked and studied. It resided in the west wing of the house, in a high ceiling room with a glass dome much like the library, save that it was on the second floor.

It was telling that she only waited until Reis had left on one of his walkabouts that she had approached Adimus with the hushed invitation.

"I think he ought to be too busy today for me to get into *much* trouble." she ushered him in, and quietly shut the door behind him, relocking it.

Adimus nervously put his hands behind his back, realizing when he held them together how cold and sweaty they were.

Upon the floor several circles and patterns were drawn in chalk. Upon the shelves were old and tattered tomes, much worse for wear than the ones in the library; books of references for whatever took place here. Jars of creature parts, pickled or dried and pulverized, khemetic materials with complex names and all manner of odd and seemingly disparate things served as bookstops. Here he saw where the dumbwaiter from the kitchen led, beside an old kiln turned crucible.

There were several tables also. Upon most sat retorts and beakers tinged with the smoky residues of a thousand uses. The one she guided him to, however, was covered in papers adorned with strange lettering. Upon it was an astrolabe, a sextant, a telescope, and a compass.

On it was the Numitorum.

"What's with this?"

"We will study its mysteries."

"But I've read this book already."

"You perhaps have read, but do not understand." She went to one of the shelves, and took down this immense book. "This book clarifies many mystic revelations."

The boy groaned. "No more. 'Read this book, now this book. Again. Now breathe. Do these stretches, make this pose. Stare at this thing for an hour. Two hours. When do I get to learn Psychometry?' "

"Hush." she scolded. Her demeanor lightened, no doubt empathizing. "You have to read nothing more." she explained. "Thankfully, *I've* read it for you. We'll know in a moment."

"Know what?"

"Your Nature."

She started pacing around the room, seemingly nervous. Then she spun. "In fact, we're going to learn the best way: through application. Come now, let's get started." she snapped her fingers and rubbed her hands. She laid the sword on the table.

"It will now be complete, sanctified, its deficits and capacities uncovered." She boasted. "Its past unveiled by sacred sight betrayed by memory, its Fate sealed by careful Work evinced by vow. It shall be, now, a Votive Item, an Implement of Magic."

"Wait. Magic?!"

Charleze stared blankly.

"I thought we were doing...-! You're going to teach me Magic?! I-I can't."

"--Well, this is technically Thaumaturgy, the first steps of All'khemy, one of the most crucial parts of our Tradition. Magic is a lay term. Actual Magic--and Sourcery for that matter, are very different."

"It's all Magic, and it's all forbidden."

She completely ignored him. She stepped forward, presenting the sword on the table. "Should be easy; most don't know this, but copper is the eldest of metals. It can be used as a stand-in for the proper energies needed for Fermentation. And of tin it is said that it is the metal of potential, said to be only less mercurial than quicksilver; it is great for novices, an easy way to cut corners if the Work is too tedious, dangerous or beyond them. Depends on the airs and elves, of course." She dismissed his protest, putting the blade in his hands. "Here, let me strip that patina away for you." She said with effortless motion she performed the motions which stripped the hardened finish from it in a shower of blinding sparks. "Now *that* was Sourcery." She giggled, sounding the bronze sword against the table and making it hum like a tuning fork. "The Grace of Purity, same as I use to pluck away dirt."

He couldn't help but muse "Now, if ever I wanted one it would be that one. But I-"

"We'll perhaps bargain for it later." she went on, letting the comment linger, as he looked down into her large, giddy eyes. She produced one of the berries, and, whispering a few words to it, began rubbing it upon its edge, breaking its skin so that its juice covered it dripping as blood. "This sword has power all on its own." she continued. "With All'khemy we could tap into it, and through following the steps of the Great Work make it Sublimated, idealized. Perhaps listen to the whispers of Those Below or the Those Within to find the process of its transformation...there are many a great and legendary sword recounted in epics that are forged this way, made perfect, whether through an All'khemist's crucible, or the Work wrought of the great deeds of its wielder."

"Like Gram." Adimus trailed off.

"But this one is not destined for that."

She tossed it at him haphazardly--had it been sharp he'd have cut himself. She produced a second vial, this one from a pocket in her robe.

"What's that?"

She gave a curious grin. "A catalyst." with an unreadable grin she opened it and dappled some of its contents onto herself.

"Turn around." she said, he did. "Hold it out." she said, he did. "Deep breath, remember deep breath." His heart was racing, even more now than from his flight above the clouds. "Now say the words."

"...Words?"

"The ones we say in the exercise."

"I don't know what you mean."

"I know. It'll come to you. Remember, I said 'repeat after me' when I first showed you. What do I make you repeat? What do we say? It's the same as on the paper, you know, the note I gave you."

"I, I didn't read the note you gave me." He was ashamed that he'd never gotten a chance to read it. He remembered it, stuffed under his bed, but every time he'd come perchance to read it...

"Yes, yes you did." She snickered. "I've watched you read it, several times. Concentrate, like you do on the coin."

She silently came up behind him, draping her arms over his and leading him in the motions he had practiced so many times before. It startled him. He could feel the sweat pooling in his hands again, now getting on the pommel of the sword. "Breathe. See the words in your mind." It took a long moment for him to calm down, to deaden that flickering side of himself and focus on the task at hand. He breathed in through his nostrils. He could smell her perfume. Then it came to him.

He tried to picture the words again in his mind, and what the letter had said. He <u>had</u> read it.

"They are so complex." He <u>had</u> read the words. He could see it. Somehow, those words, whatever they were, had eluded him. But the words were there. He struggled between flashes of conscious effort to keep it from fading altogether. "Hard to grasp...like sand through my fingers."

"You do not have to grasp them right now. Just speak them."

She spread his arms out. *Rajata's Wheel.* He closed his eyes and felt his body move. There had been words there, and he had just spoken them.

Nothing happened at first. Standing in amazement of this revelation it had caught him off guard. Then a bristle touched his skin, tingled the tip of his nose. He'd mistaken it for a draft, this sensation that put his hairs on end, it was only immediately upon this dismissal that it made itself known.

He could see his breath now. The room grew cold. He had just been standing on the snowy plains for hours, flown miles in the sky on a frigid night. This was somehow colder. It cut right through him like a shard of ice pulled from the tops of Blade Peak in the midnight of the deepest storm.

"From the moving of the stars from night to dazzling day, to that which lies behind the eyes that observes it, what appears to be presses against what truly is. All things are Form and Nature, and all that appears and disappears is in the interplay of this force; it is the vital energy that imparts consciousness and intelligence to gross matter, it is time itself, and intention, and most importantly it is the power invoked in Spells...that which burns...the Calcinative Quality."

A frigid wind picked up, generated from nothing, nowhere. The sword hummed like a tuning fork. Pages of open books clung fervently to their spines for fear of being stolen by it. Windows fogged, and gnarls of rimey frost dotted their frames. It billowed in the baseboards, threw quills from their inkpots, rattled the door like it was trying to escape. The whole room felt its countenance. It was as the opening of a door in a blizzard. It roared in their ears and turned their clothes into kites.

"Consciousness, your being, experience and the inescapable Fate of all things? The charge, the pull, within the difference between Form and Nature, the One and the Other, the cosmos a giant crucible egg of Forms being transmuted by each other until they reach their final destinies."

It all became too much. It wasn't stopping. He panicked to silence it, prying the sword from his own hand, which had grown itself so frigid that it clung to him as if it had more to say; it stuck the tip down into the wood. He turned and glanced at Charleze, wide eyed. "Good." she giggled. "Very good. Haha!" Her clapping echoed in the hollow chamber, lingering amongst the snowflakes that had begun to fill the air.

She walked over to the book, and after having to find her place in it again uncorked a bottle of ink and began to jot down a few notes. She kept looking up at him, doing what appeared to be musing on what as he stood there. Adimus just stood there, feeling as if he were being examined like some sort of laboratory rat.

"*I* started with fire." She finally said, not taking her eyes off the book. "*That* was a mistake. But it took me *many* tries."

"I did it in just one." It was a storm of guilt, pride, astonishment, exhilaration. So many feelings welled up inside of him in that moment.

Charleze crossed her arms. "Such a modest pupil. It's not all candles and quicksilver from here, you know. The execution of the Spell changes based on the Natures of the object in question, and the correct adjustments must be made to harness the calcinatives. What's more, you simply unleashed the power, with the right application you can refine it, as well as harness more of it at a time. You could conjure a full on blizzard, freeze an opponent, or just chill a beverage."

"...I see." Adimus consciously hid the blankness that befell his eyes.

"You were just lucky--" she started to say.

"--Charleze. Thank you." he looked down at the sword, then back up at her. "Show me more."

But she'd started writing again and was only thinking aloud. "Could be a quirk. Maybe your Nature has an affinity for undines or something. At any rate, it will take more testing before we can safely proceed with more precise applications. You can keep that one, too. Now that we know that it works nominally well for you. As your Nature is uncovered we can begin the work of finding out the best way to fine tune the Spell for maximum effect."

"I thought I was going to learn the way of the Faeth."

"Invocations are dangerous, but..." she sighed. "As I promised I will do it for you. From me."

Adimus raised a brow, but before he could say anything she produced the earring. "This shall be your first Raiment." She spoke in those words, the ones he'd heard Laina and Argent speak, that he understood and had no idea how.

She spoke in the strange tongue, the one Laina and Argent used, the one all could comprehend. *"This is the covenant promised by the Dragonfather to the Seers of Alu Serrusu, keepers of Urta's foretelling, the carving of the living words of Am Carrig. I invoke the Weeping Eye, and pass the knowledge it imparts from my own being as he did to they, and thus they to me."*

Just then there was a voice. "...Adi?" It was Dyrshul.

Charleze put a finger to her lips. "We'll talk later. Go play."

He waited until it had sounded like she'd went downstairs before sneaking out. "Dyrshul? Up here."

He felt a little emasculated at the suggestion, he had to admit. And he tried to not to make the mood it left him in sully his interaction. "...you brought that with you!?" He cackled. She was wearing the paper mache face mask.

"Haha, yup. Come down, I want to show you my Longnight stuff."

He dragged his feet upon reaching the bottom.

They were beginning to pack.

Her enthusiasm belied a naivety that they were leaving, either that or she didn't feel the same as he.

"I want to show you some of the great souvenirs I got from this place."

"Look at this one. This is Madreg. See? There's Merris's clock tower. If you shake it it looks like its snowing."

She pulled out a box. "It's a sewing kit. Charleze bought it for me. She's really good at sewing, she taught me a few things."

She jangled through a sack of stuff. "And I got this. Reis bought it for me." It was a large folded scrap of paper shoved in a leather folder. She unfolded it. "There was a man on the roadside who did portraits from memory." she explained, handing it to him to show him.

The parchment felt rough in his hands, as if he could feel every fiber of it. He'd never seen such a thing, or given much thought to how paper must be made. It was a strange thought. He could imagine how it was pulped, pressed. In his mind was a strange device with a screw that pulped the paper into blocks, and dried and peeled with another. It was vividly there in his mind. The boy blinked, taken aback by it. "Are you okay?" Dyrshul said, seeing that he was noticeably disturbed.

The image was there, intruding upon him. He closed his eyes in a wince, but this made it worse. It was there. The man that turned the press, he had long blonde hair, braided.

He looked at the page, and could see the strokes of the charcoal, number them all, smell the air surrounding the laying of its lines. His lips forced out a plea, a pinch, a test, that he knew it wasn't all his imagination.

"Jory."

She gasped. "You know about Jory?"

Just then he saw Charleze round the stairs. She'd grabbed her sewing kit. "Forgot this part." she said, and coldly, without warning, plunged the needle into his ear.

"Ow."

Chapter 32
Assumed Fangs

After the first time he did not perform the Slaking, he perhaps felt worse. For that it was that engaging with his faith in light of his transgression, his fear or apprehension, guilt or simple longing to sin which had driven him not to he did not know, but every day following it became easier, not to think about, not to dwell on.

He had Worked Magic. After all, what the Bugbear had said was perhaps correct, and if that were the case, of what benefit was it to pretend it was not so? This thought bit at him, perhaps even more now.

He spent the evening playing checkers with Dyrshul just the same, with a festering despondency on him still.

Dyrshul was understandably upset about their leavetaking. After all, it was once in a lifetime event, one only vaguely alluded to and glossed over in Hyu'man tales of legend because even the mortal tellers weren't privy to what it actually entailed. So it was that her visitation with the Fae was quashed.

"It is too dangerous for one so young."

If the family were one of the sort to perhaps offer to placate the broken heart of a child, Adimus knew, it would have been done, but as it was this one--and not for lack of the fierce love that spurned such acts. Nothing would be offered, he knew, for it was the understanding of Buckroys--and perhaps all too many families of the south, that such mollycoddling softened the character, and the weakness wrought of such concessions was more dangerous than the fates that such difficult decisions aimed to keep them from.

The girl subduely abided, wiping away her tears. "I'm sorry, Dyrshul." was all Luloch could say.

"You keep a close eye on her, now." Said Luloch, handing him a generous helping of coins. "And make sure she gets plenty of those eclairs." he smiled and patted her head.

"Aye. You should be the one taking heed." said Bearach. He eyed the bard "You watch them well." he warned.

"He'll have to catch me." the old man said, rapping his cane against the back of the boy's leg making him trip, before cackling and saundering off with Reis.

"Goodbye, Adimus." Adimus dismissed the strange finality of the tone as the awkward hiccup of having to have an intimate exchange in a public conversation. He was glad the bard wasn't here to make it worse.

"He'll be along." Reis assured.

"Where is William?" Charleze asked.

"Oh, William. He's further on."

Before he knew it he was watching them march off into the distance.

* * * * *

Evening came. Caleb was downstairs, meditating. Adimus had just seen him. Dad was asleep, and the boy had talked the swordsman into playing the Royal Game with Dyrshul and him. He figured it would cheer her up and wind her down. And it did. They shared a laugh, and tea-- which the swordsman was already quite fond of before being exposed to the volume of consumption the old men were used to. He'd only just taken the pieces back upstairs to tidy up, so it was disconcerting, when from the top of the stairs, upon answering the rap at the door he heard such a change in the tone of voice.

"What is the meaning of this?"

Cracking the door, he peered at the wizard behind it.

"Caleb." Alfred greeted him.

Caleb's surprise allowed him to gain ground in. "We are leaving. Get the Spear." he took a few steps inside "I believe you." He threw his hands up to fend off his glare, William Mathune cannot be trusted. We will meet up with him after we make our decision."

The expectation, most obviously, was that the man expected the swordsman, without so much as a word, to follow him, and it showed on his face when he hunched forward and stopped. "That is not what you said to him." the swordsman said.

"Please don't make this hard, Sir Knolls." the wizard plead.

With that he swung the door wide. "I will allow you to see the Spear, but it will not leave this spot until William returns."

Adimus started at the touch of his father, who'd stirred in the ruckus. He held his hand axe in caution, along with an unsure look. When the boy tried to ask him what to do he stifled him with a finger, and locked his gaze onward.

"Adimus. You remember that time we came across the bear?"

Once, they had stumbled upon a bear, and, too close to judge whether it were wiser to back away and possibly flee or knock an arrow and pray, his father froze, and waited to see what the bear decided was best for him.

"Hairier and grizzlier than any bear, this one will be. Best grab your sword. I'll get Dyrshul ready. Take heed."

The boy didn't question. Adimus hurried past him to the bedroom, leaving the man to head to the attic and to hos sister. But this time Bearach grabbed him by the arm as he went past, with a grip tighter than he ever had when he played at sticks. "And you be ready too, Adi. You may need to call whether to strike first or flee this time. I'll stand with you either way."

Those words had the opposite effect. Suddenly the boy's legs were stuck in cement.

The bear hadn't seen them, and that day they were able to ease their way, step by step, away from the situation, and though it seemed that neither the swordsman or the Seer had noticed Adimus and his father, it wouldn't be the same outcome today.

The conversation had continued on with them

"You...you hate William. Now you're defending him? I don't understand." said the Seer.

"One of your morality never will. *I* made a vow. And I shall keep it."

"The Spear rightfully belongs to us. Does it not? You said it yourself..."

"I did...But William is in your charge--party to your charter, and you ought to act like it!" Adimus felt the slap of his sword and belt against his chest. Surprised, he wheeled one last glance at his father, instead of appearing cross at his son's apprehension, gave a proud, steeling, nod.

"I..." Alfred stammered. "You, you said yourself that he meant to do ill. Is your word worth more than doing the wrong thing?"

Caleb hesitated. "Now move!" The pure logic of the Sum Seer forced the man to relent, and the Seer used the opening to brush past him.

He met him again at the threshold of the room where the spear was kept.

"This is not right, wizard!" Caleb still protested, palms whitened from clenching.

"I myself cannot wait to have the treacherous thing rid of." Alfred replied, already starting to wrap it in its bandages. "Come on, we are hitting the road at nightfall." Alfred then said. "I will make sure he gets his share." he comforted.

"You will not take it anywhere until he returns. That was my oath." His eyes narrowed, and he gripped his sword in its sheath. "Come no further."
Caleb's eyes grew dull. It was as the day they met him.

"You great big liar! You know you want to stay here to smoochy smooch with that old Tuathan lady!"

His indignance showed plainly on his face. "I...I never! I may not know what is the correct choice, but you dare dishonor me?! You have until the count of three." He put his hand on the hilt of his sword. "One..."

At that the figment of Alfred dissipated, the cloak crumpling to the ground. Standing there as the Gnemedian.

"Delaney?!" Adimus exclaimed, someday against his will. He was spotted now. Caleb shot him a quick glance, one of shared disgust. Suddenly Adimus felt like he was picking sides, and all he said was a name. "Please don't kill me! Please don't kill me!" She panted.

"What manner of Sourcery..." he began to curse the little urisk, then a thought came that grew his lividity far more. "The wizard would not face me in person?"

Against his best interest he slowly descended the stairs toward them. He didn't know what he was going to do, but he'd decided if he had to protect Delaney, he would.

"No, no. That's not it at all. At least, I don't think..." It would seem she hadn't given it much thought herself. "He sent me so we could try and get the Spear from you."

He grumbled. "I do suppose his sword is not as sharp as Mathune's in that regard. So, he sent you to deliver the killing blow."

The urisk scratched her leafy head. "I'm not trying to kill you, I'm supposed to talk to you..." she drifted off, scratching her head in thought, oblivious to the concept of metaphor. "Adimus!" She said finally. Tell him he's wrong! You know more than most that he's no good. That man has lied to us at every turn!" She started counting on her fingers, "He acted like he didn't even know the Reis man, hid that he knew how to do Magic, pretended that he wasn't a noble, twice, told Adimus that his family was safe when they weren't, then got him bit by that black dog thing! Now Alfred says that Argent knows Alfred's mentor, who he says is a bad man!"

"...You memorized those, didn't you?" Said Caleb.

"Mmm-hmm." She nodded. Adimus almost snickered.

"I still think it is wrong to break my word." He relaxed the grip on his blade.

Adimus tried to interject, to argue or make a move. He meant to disagree with her, he wished to share Caleb's sentiment. He said nothing.

"You *think* it is wrong, but you *feel* that it isn't." she said. "No one is looking, no one is going to judge you. Your loyalty is to Cadifor, not some crook! And *I* feel that being true to yourself is more important than being true to your word."

"Then you are as deceitful as him. Either to others...or to yourself." He started to turn back to where he sat. "This is the leader of your company's strategy? It was a good one; you can read my emotions. You are a weapon to most, but not to me. You have failed as his representative, little one." He folded his arms in the most modest way one could, "I mean as I say as I do. How I *feel* about my station matters none at all."

"I know. But even that is how you feel: like emotions don't matter. You don't understand how I can wish to be returned to my keepers though I was a slave. It is because I was happy!"

"You were happy? Ignorance! This simply shows the perversion that feelings bring, twisting a simple matter of right and wrong..."

"Yet here you are, standing in the way of a decision that's not even in your power to make, for naught but want of courtship with some Tuathan...trollop!"

"Tread lightly, child of Gnemed, of what you say about either of us."

"Or you'll grow angry and kill me?"

He gave a seething huff, then closed his eyes and breathed. "I'm done with these games now, away with you. Go tell your new master that you have lost."

"But I haven't."

"Yes, yes you have!"

"I told you I came to talk to you, not to convince you of anything." She giggled.
Adimus saw the black figure only a second before Caleb spun to see it himself, see the black tail of Alara dart out the window.

The spear was gone.

"Drat!" Caleb dashed past Delaney and out the door, followed by the urisk a second later.
An unfamiliar silence struck the Ashen Curio. Adimus spun.

"Father!" He looked back lost. "What should I do?"

"Go!"

"To whom?"

"I can't tell you lad, but, mercy upon my heart, not to us!"

"...What?" It took him a moment to come to bear the weight of what the man said. The silence grew deeper.

"Your fate is bound to the Spear. Do, Adimus, what it is in you to do!"

Adimus snapped to. He gave a stern but solemn nod.

The Grigor made his way outside just in time to see Caleb's bright red ponytail wagging in agitation as he ran through the fog away from him. He struggled to catch up, and seeing him dart into an alley he saw the opportunity for a shortcut. He climbed the apple tree over the fence, and undoing the double hitch and latch on the gate hopped on the back of Aethan.

At first he thought it a mistake, riding bareback untrained through the frosty streets. He almost tumbled off his bitless horse when meet head-on a walking couple and a man steering a donkey and cart. Aethan snarled in disapproval at the boy's white-knuckle grip on his mane. But with the quick shake of his head to dust off any hesitation, as soon as he was able he spurned the horse to a gallop. It paid off, as seeing the man and cutting through a back alley he encountered the swordsman broadside. "Wait!"

The swordsman spun in surprise, but the expression was quickly overtaken. "You would oppose me as well?"

The Watcher had made his decision, and vocaling it dispelled any unsurity. "No. But I won't have anyone hurt. Put the sword away and I will help you."

Adimus fought to settle the gelding. Caleb raised a brow. Then, as if suddenly self-aware (and perhaps a little ashamed) he straightened, and sheathed the blade, and, much more dexterous than the Watcher, who had to climb the stall to mount Aethan with one-up from the alley wall he lept stride him.

Just as he did his eyes went vagrant, and Adimus and Aethan followed them to see the snowy footprints; footprints across the rooftops. They dashed. They fled towards them, flowing as they bound deftly from house to house and ended. Gone. A carriage passed, and the shadows shifted, the horse reared unsafely. Adimus threw himself forward to keep him from toppling. A figure on his periphery that darted like a bolting prey animal. A black tail and a spear. They pursued.

The Servant was proficient in the throwing of the daggers his master had made, which he carried in his coat, but with a quick huff of regret he unsheathed his small sword, and pulled the wooden sheath from his belt. It landed perfectly, catching the shins of the fleeing culprit, clattering on the pavement along with their face.

The horse atrode up, towering fearsomely over the Cait Shii. "It's over.", only to see again the face of urisk, morphing from the lithy cat to her diminutive self again.

"You fell for it twice!" She laughed.

Caleb let out a low growl.

"There!"

Caleb's eyes shot up to see the black tail disappear only around the next corner. "Observant as your name suggests, Watcher." They followed.

Alara ran, this time in sight, fled, now through Red Row, to find themselves at the very edge of the city. Outermost wall of solid brickwork and granite it had been, lent of the outermost burrough, sturdy enough to act as a retaining wall for the waters of the Salt Fair; a mass of brick with a core of granite. Not today, for words of Magic had riven them, the words of Alfred Juminion.

The breach in it was a perfectly round hole, like a hollow bubble, as if the wall were hot glass and wizard himself a glazier, his will the parison into which he blew.

There, Laina and Tirlag stood, and Alfred nonchalantly on the other side, his hand touching the wall to maintain the Spell.

Alara, and even Delaney was there; they hadn't realized until then that Cait Shii had led him through a longer route to allow the little accomplice's escape.

The Sum Seer said, not so much as looking up. "This spot is equidistant from the only exits this side of the river. You'll not be able to make it out of the city in time to pursue."

Adimus slowed his pace as he caught up, caught by the realization of where they stood. He came to the terrace, and the wall. "You were solving for its Votiveness." Adimus realized out loud.

"I can see you have been training. Yes, Adimus. And apparently you were spying to ascertain mine."

Caleb turned his feet and lowered his posture and gripped the blade of the small sword (still brandished) close to his chest, raring to charge.

"The Touch of the Fir Domnan requires intense concentration, Caleb Knolls. To allow the Spell to end and the stone to return from the Isthmus to its earthly home while you're still inside it would take literally <u>less</u> than a thought."

"You bluff."

"He'll do it!" Delaney blusterously squeaked.

"I'm not sure what will happen, but it will be your own doing." Alfred bolstered it.

"Alfred, why are you doing this?!" The Watcher called.

The Faeth gave no answer.

"Damn you, meddling wizard! And you, Delaney!" Caleb relented, his posture loosening into drooped shoulders.

"Run, tell your master that the Spear belongs to the Endeavor, and none else."

Then the urisks voice came. "They could come with us."

"...What?" Alfred said, as calmly as he possibly could.

"Yeah! He keeps his word even when it's dumb to."

A long moment passed.

"What of Adimus?" Asked Laina. Delaney answered, "I felt his feelings. His resentment for the bard isn't so deep that he thinks us right, but he wants to come with us just the same, because he's..."

"Curious." Alara answered for her.

"....Give me your word, Caleb, that you will harm none of us. Swear on your honor." The Seer spoke. "Come with us and be a part of the fate of Gae Bolg, your country, the World. Or go home."

"I agree to your terms."

Caleb tucked the scabbard back into his sash, and, wiping the blade, sheathed it, sighed, and began to walk through.

"Ah-choo!!" Tirlag's fortuitous sneeze erupted.

They were left in the darkness.

Seconds later, Alara appeared on the wall unfurling a rope from her arm.

Caleb shook his head wryly, replacing his sword. "Well, Adimus..." he said.

But the Grigor's face was reply enough, a twist of regret mixed with mournful resolve. What's more it spoke for him, as with a final bow of his head in respect he spun Aethan.

"I would like to stay and fight with you all...I just don't have it in me. Goodbye, Caleb."

With that he turned off into the darkness.

Chapter 33
Frozen in Flight

In places ornate detail shown; where a vision hewn in the metal by the hands of a god skillful enough to knit bones and flesh and blood from unliving stone--there, Crom Cruach, Balros, The Black King stood.

Alfred could feel the sweltering of his blood, the quickening and blistering of his skin...the smell of his own burning flesh, even now, from the first time he'd touched it. It was then, still in the ancient forest with more remorse than regret, that he'd decided to forego teaching the boy any further, and ultimately abandon his pupil and the bard outright.

He let go of the Spear, his hand covered in the blood it incessantly spilled.

It was not without purpose. Reflecting on the vision, the words of the bard echoed in his mind: *And so the god plucked the giants from the earth and with his blood gave them life.* A riddle whose answer was as another riddle, it seemed.

What's more, what was more painful than even the frostbite and squelching burns of past sight was that the bard knew of the treachery.

The Spear bore a new memory, of the Bard holding the Spear and speaking aloud.

"How are you fairing?" the bard would warmly cant. *"Hopefully not freezing those valuable little digits off."*

Always, he continued. "Well, just meaning to say, that I have enjoyed our time together, for what it's worth. I'm glad I met you, that you chose to take me with you, just wished you to know that, Alfred. I know you did what you felt needed to be done." he would smile. " I do not fault you for it. It is all a man can do, what he thinks to be right, but It only begs the question: will the one you choose as king think he was doing the right thing as well?..."

* * * * *

The foggy breath of watchers-by were as the billowing of greedy dragons as they trespassed through the downtown districts of Hewnyleigh, taking full advantage of the morning mist from the evaporated snow that still hung low in the air.

Alfred shivered, and not from the cold.

They hadn't rested, opting instead to push through before the morning bells could sound. It seemed all the more suspicious in retrospect, but they had made headway through the main thoroughfare, past the Bowen Library and the Ravenhound Hall where they'd stayed, openly stopping only to buy new linens, discarding the old gory ones in a discrete ditch.

They made it all the way to the south gate before they were probed, and then only with cursory questions thanks to Caleb.

The Princely Stewards had spirited themselves back to Kainden to make preparations for winter. This much the swordsman had learned from his lord's page, who also ominously told them that they had received William's word: *The Spear of Fate had been found.*

Well outside the city they collected themselves, at the all-so-familiar wagon ready to receive them.

Torrin arranged the reception of provisions from the hall to be discreetly dropped at the edge of town, whereupon they would undertake the treadless path back toward the Blade Mountains and the Ruined Road. Adaire, of course, was Pembrooke's domain, so they would have to bypass it entirely, relying on Delaney's skills at wayfaring offroad and ability to work with the horses.

The evenings grew brighter despite the weather getting darker in the claustrophobic canyons and basins a stone's throw from the town.

Then the snow began.

At first it was an amusing reason to huddle under the canvas of the wagon and drink, perhaps nursing a small fire outside the hutch, more for the cooking of meats than warmth, but soon it was a stifling all consuming concern that had all but halted them in their tracks.

The days had quickly turned into processing wood, tending said horses, clearing paths, and generally trying not to perish in the cold. The snow fell in a heavy, wet blanket that turned bushes and trees into mere lumps on a gentle plain, thigh deep in spots, and impassable even on hard ground, which, thanks to their bed for off-road travel they were not.

Caleb protested, half-heartedly, that the chopping of the wood was illegal, as this was the land of Thadeus, Lord of Adaire, but by that night was helping gather enough timber to weather the looming cold.

Torrin paced in the trail left by the wagon, lost in thought. He'd spearheaded the effort to get warm, but when it came time for someone else to take a turn handling the responsibility he never volunteered to take it back.

Regil chopped wood with his ax with frostbitten fingers and weary palms that held on for dear life.

Alfred wiped the freezing sweat from his brow and sat down on the stump Regil had used for the past two days, numb from the cold. The snow kept coming. They'd had had to circle the hill to find a path up it, for in the mud that had struggled, and didn't want to risk a snow drift or further injury to the horses, what's more, there were trees here that might provide cover, but in the disorienting blizzard he himself wasn't even sure from which direction they'd come. But now, even the tracks the wagon had left coming here were now buried. Yet another problem he hoped others had answers for now.

Alfred sat alone nowadays, braving the bitterness for solemnity and the ability to think.

The spear sat at his side, left to bleed in the snow for a short while, eschewing the risk of not attracting predators for practicality's sake. Torrin had sheepishly asked the others why they thought it was so, that a spear could bleed, as if there were some unspoken explanation that was all too obvious, only to learn that everyone else was just as perplexed. Warm blood at that, trickling out and slowly melting a path that left a scarlet river in its wake.

It was a gamble, a desperate play to be sure, a fool's errand to march for Kainden and confront the Princely Stewards head on. No other road remained. Still, even knowing this, Alfred lamented the decision he'd made, branding himself as rash, in the end.

He heard someone approaching. It was Laina, there to replace him in the snow veil. Her warm hands gifted him a small bowl of stew, melted snow and jerky--more broth than anything else, before filling her arms with the firewood and heading back toward the wagon.

Laina sat out too, carrying wood for the fire where she was cooking, insulating herself from the tensions inside.

"This is the rest of it." Laina said. It was tinged with a restrained rancor.

She'd quietly voiced her opinion to him, in counsel, after everyone else, and despite bearing the wisdom born from having literally been from a band of nomads who traveled all their lives she was dismissed just the same. But she took it all in stride. "Either Alfred is mad with hubris," she said. "Or he truly believes that we are now in more danger than we ever faced on that mountain."

Now she definitely seemed to regret it. It wouldn't be long now before they would be cooking boots to survive. There was still plenty of wine that could take off the chill in a pinch, freight acquisitioned by Torrin for the trip back, plus a bit for celebration, but all knew the dangers of such things and the dulling of senses it brought.

They all still argued, even now. As though it mattered. Despite the decision having already been made. Caleb had insisted that they take asylum in the Ravenhound Halls, and await a counsel of lords, that they should turn back once the weather had grown cold; it was the halls of his master after all, and he was a safe and honorable man just like he. He had suggested in a passive and mannerly kind of way, understanding full and well his station in the matter: that he held no stake or right to protest whatever the decision, Torrin on the other hand...Alfred had thought that the best course of action was to rough it and hope for the best. Not his most insightful decision; now their once plentiful larder dwindled along with their hopes, but said he Torrin knew better, that he'd toughed winters in the south being a merchant and held practical knowledge of the subject surpassing the bookworm's perceived omnipotence. But starvation and death was but another puzzle and distraction Alfred could not abide.

Heading back to the caravan, he sipped at the burning hot liquid before it grew cold again. He fought the urge to pour it in his soft boots. His feet were numb, especially on his right where a hole had been worn in his woolen sock. He would ask Laina to don them were he not so embarrassed by the smell--he'd been forced to wear them for nearly a week on end, and they were dirty to begin with—he'd not had a decent bath since Ederton.

Inside, the others huddled in the wagon, the canvas battened shut, the cold fumes of the outside on the noses of anyone who unsealed it. He would muster up the courage to head into the breach again, wedging himself between Tirlag and Regil.

"This is all we have." Tirlag echoed Laina's words.

"I guess we'll have to eat the bird before too long." Regil half-joked.

"The other breathers can have the choice cuts from <u>your</u> flanks if you so much as think about it!" Delaney, who had Finora (they didn't lock the cage any more). "She's cold..." she said between baby-talking it.

"Tirlag...You'll take care of her for me, won't you?"

It was a strange question, and elicited an equally muddled response without much thought. "Fine."

They had at the very least forbade her from feeding it any more bread. So she sat and fed it as she always did, the little bit of seeds that she'd been sure to buy when sure was given money to buy supplies in Ederton, singing quietly to it in that strange harmony she always did, then giving her a particularly large seed she began a melody he'ed never heard before. Alfred couldn't understand the words to it whatever it was, but it was the single most beautiful thing he'd ever heard, upon the final note, when finished, a glow issued from her mouth, a soft golden mist which she breathed into the duck's nostrils, who after doing so her curled up comfortably and went immediately to sleep on her lap. She patted her on the head, and herself, almost as if unable to stop it, nestled into the corner of the wagon herself. She withdrew. Alfred had never seen it happen to this extent or this up close. With a few assuring words to Tirlag her feet, her hair, even her hands unraveled into tiny rootlets that clung like a web to the inside corner of the wagon where she slept, creeping into the floor and ribs of the wagon. Tirlag tried to hide it, but she herself seemed a little concerned, and from that moment never left her side.

Alara, who'd remained outside until now, peeked her head in. He gave Alfred a strange look.

"What is it?"

"Just seeing what all the...merriment was about."

Regil and Alara had been taking turns scouting in the evening time, if only at short distance, to look for both danger and help.

She returned a few minutes later with the Spear of Fate. "Torrin? Torrin."

"Yes, lieutenant?"

"I need you to hold this for me." She plunged the Spear into the midst of them, the thing invading their space uncomfortably, especially after learning its deadliness. Blood trickled on the floor.

"Regil, can you get that?"

"No." The Cait Shii insisted, it came perhaps a little harshly. "Regil and Laina need to untie the horses. We'll need to take them down into the valley before it gets too dark. It'll be a windy night tonight." Again he thrust the Spear toward him. Torrin looked at it in disgust.

"Alright, alright." the man finally relented.

He'd even forgotten the bandages. "The bandages need changed. I'll bring them to you in a few moments. Thank you."

But he didn't come back.

They wait an uncomfortable amount of time before they finally decided to do something.

Regil and Alara stood not a dozen paces outside.

Torrin strode up, at first fascinated, then his eyes grew to worry. "Alara!"

"A scout." Alfred started when her voice came from overhead. They gazed up to see Alara scanning the horizon.

"What...? " said Tirlag standing.

Then they both froze, gazing off into the distance.

A dozen fires like yellow stars across the dark blue valley not but a few miles off.

"An army. That's an army." Said Tirlag.

"An army." Alfred echoed. He gazed out at the horizon, as his eyes adjusted to the sight he could see hundreds of tiny shapes in the firelight. "Well, what?" He wasn't even sure how to stammer it out. "Whose army?"

"Alfred!" Torrin's call was even louder this time. "There is nothing to be done."

Coming from Alfred it was damnation, but it was true. They could not run. They could not hide. They'd been through every plan and contingency.

"It could not involve us." Argent reasoned. "You of all people should know that the nobility often squabble and fued. I mean your--" Alfred's cold glance stifled him, which swiftly softened when the bard apologized. "Sorry."

"It's fine." he said. "And I know." he consoled him. "It is all we can hope for. Settle down and hope they pass." he cleaned the fog from his spectacles, which now fogged in the cold since they'd doused their fire.

"At dawn we gather the horses and scatter."

"Scatter??" "Split up!?" "What?!" they protested. Alfred simply dismissed them all with a wave and continued.

"Caleb and I will head north, and meet with the nobles at Ravenhound. We should've brought this to light all the sooner it seems. Torrin and Laina will remain here, as they are less likely to be harmed if captured. Regil and Alara will make for Kainden as his envoys, and Tirlag with him to head to Marron.

"I'm staying here with Delaney."

He rubbed his eyes in consternation. "Torrin will ensure her safety. If asked, she is his property."

"Good plan, I'll see that it's held to." She responded.

"Then say hello to your brother for me." He snapped.

"Laina should take the Ruined Road back home. Adaire isn't far from here, seek aid from the Pembrokes."

"...Who has the Spear?" Caleb then asks.

"I have no idea." He simply said, shaking his head. There was a dejected silence.

He continued, thinking aloud, "We will obviously leave tracks. All of us. They may head back to the city, or if they are from the nobility they may have a force already waiting there to ambush us, so we cannot risk carrying it. We cannot, of course, leave it here for them to find. They may expect us to head for Kainden or cross over the border with it. They could pursue any or all of us with equal probability."

"Or none of us." The bard was hopeful.

"Well, we could draw straws." Regil suggested.

They all looked dumbfounded at first. "If it's all an even risk." He defended his point when it was met with raised brows.

"I suppose so." Said Alfred, causing even more of them.

The wind cut through the wagons. They nestled the horses downwind against the canvas in the hopes it might ease their discomfort. The night was clear and cloudless, but as anyone in the southlands can tell you these were the worst nights of winter.

Icicles clung to Adimus's nose from simply watering the horses with the last remnant of warmth for the night: the pot of melted snow. He regretted dabbing at the hot water himself to warm his hands, as it all but instantly seemed to freeze to them. The morbid thought of warming his hands with the spear's blood crossed his mind--it was always warm, roiling a sickly stream from where it issued, cutting crimson pools in the snow. The thought of it made him shudder. It would be a welcome event for him to see the vile thing go. At this point, standing in the open frost, even after all it had taken to obtain it he was ready to be rid of the obviously evil thing, to leave it to evil men with their evil schemes where it rightly belonged.

He tucked his cloak with as much care as he covered his handle to carry the boiling pot handle; the wind scalded him.

Inside they all winced when he opened the flap, muttering curses when he took a moment to clear the snow caked to his boots amidst the agonizing draft.

Alara sat beside the opening, her eyes piercing the halflight of the circle moons, her ears pursed like taught tripwires ready upon the slightest sign of approach. He pulled off his boots, more quietly than what was necessary; he knew none of them could sleep. They would be leaving before the sun rose, and praying for a miracle. In fact, the weather was all that kept them from leaving now. In a few hours they would take horses, and scatter in all directions, and what's more determined by lottery which of them would carry the Spear of Fate. Barring any problems they would meet in Kainden on the next Moon, just before the festival of Longnight.

He sat criss-cross down beside Laina; it felt good to curl his toes under his legs in spite of it all.

She edged up against him and she held him. She was warm. He knew there was nothing of it but the motherly way she cared for her, or most people, no matter how he felt about it. She was always that way, and everyone else always was as he was: awestruck. She was unapproachable. Most could do nothing but observe, but be frozen in the moment until it passes and nothing's left, like watching a sunset.

He couldn't believe that in this moment he had fallen asleep, and his mind was tossed into a fit of confused panic upon being awoken by the jab of a spear. He fumbled for his sword glaring sideways hoping his eyes might adjust enough to even know what he was swinging at.

Two men stood, quietly, one with a short spear, the other with a sword.

"You, on your feet. Aaat! Don't even try it!"

Alara, her face twisted half in terror and half in defeat, stood hands up by the door, and was the first of them ushered out, the other one muttering to keep her at spear length.

Alfred bumped into Argent, who glanced back over his shoulder. "How did--?" he didn't have to finish the question.

"The same charm Alfred used on the Orc, it would seem." he uttered. "Poor Alara." At first he thought the sentiment to be aimed at her failure, but then he remembered Adaire, and the way people treated the Fae, and the remark became much more ominous, watching her stand there with more spears and arrows pointed at her than the others combined.

Torchlight danced outside, and when the boy made his way to his feet he could hear a gruff man's voice.

A stout man, his face obscured by a helmet that enclosed his eyes and thick, bushy, red facial hair stood before them, snarling.

Tirlag fumbled for the bird cage when one of the guards pulled at her and it swung open. "Let me go, shitehook!" She kicked at him, but three guards piled on her. And over the next few moments Tirlag silently concentrated on watching as Penelope the duck hired out of the carriage, waddled around for a few steps, and flew away; it was about as helpless as everyone else felt at this situation whose control had been wrested from them.

Alfred was already outside, trying his hardest to utter some concise word of protest with three spears at his neck to no avail.

Torrin and Regil were being spirited into horses. Alara and Argent led away, their hands bound with rope.

Weylan Pembrooke hovered over them. "Now you'll listen, Sumseer." The word was slathered with abhorrence. "Perhaps your gift of soothsaying lapses, as you seem quite ignorant to what will happen if you do not tell me!" Laina locked eyes with him, watery moats they were. It filled his heart with dread and sorrow. No knowing smirks, no careful puzzling that lead to a way out this time. The Sumseer slumped when Pembrooke said with a sadistic glee. "Can you foresee which one of them will die first, or will it only be after, when you can feel the anguish of their last moments on my blade?"

"Give me mine, and we shall see who is the better, Pembrooke." Caleb spat.

"You are but a commoner and knave at any rate, you've no right to address me, much less demand a duel, Caleb Knolls!"

Caleb's eyes made the blaze about them seem like shelter. Finally, before his men he relented. "It is lamentable that it ended like this, if only that I could prove your better, but alas, we've not the time."

With a nod the man motioned several men into the wagon to begin searching.

In the shadows one of them emerged. It was Ross Ward.

"I do not think that necessary." He smiled over them, perhaps expecting some manner of thankful glance in return for his mercy. "The spear's magic makes it impervious, it even withstood the gaze of the Baleful Eye. Burn it out." He pointed at the wagon.

"Nooo!!" Tirlag yelled, and was struck silent by a man's gauntlet and unconsciousness.

"One of our companions is in there, still." Alfred spat out as calmly yet as quickly as he could.

"Oh?" The man took his time to say.

"Delaney, of the Mealae." Caleb nodded. He struggled to stand "I demand that rules of our forefathers be upheld. She is my charge, as is all these others." His sentence was hardly finished before the guard behind him kicked him to the ground.

"A hob, you say?" it came out as a chuckle.

A few moments elapsed. One of the men opened the flap and shrugged and shook his head. They didn't see her.

Like the bewildering statement of Delaney to Tirlag, like the morning fog in Hewnyleigh, like the veil of snow that masked all direction, the next several moments were like a muffled muted haze in the Faeth's mind. He was inwardly as surprised by his detachment from it, that in his helplessness he was unable to do anything but stand and watch as the wagon went up in flames.

Tirlag was beaten unconscious--he was at least thankful for that--at least she wouldn't die, he knew she'd have fought to the death otherwise. Caleb wailed at the sight of the oriflammes, for they wore proudly the blazon of the perpetrator, the eye among thorns, his liege.

Chapter 34
Homecoming

Winter was finishing up. The largest of the snows had come and gone, surely, in the weeks intervening the end of the Salt Fair and the arrival of Thadeus.

The long journey home seemed trivial now. He'd traveled it several times in his life now. What's more, the trail that led through the plains to the hills directly to Adaire was easily only half of the time he'd traveled.

The thought had well occurred to Adimus, *why can't we just skip this Darkest Night thing?* But it seemed out of the question now. Niall had picked up the slack for them in their absence, Luloch explained, offering to house-sit in their absence, but Niall was getting old, and still had his own land to tend to. Though they made good time, he was anxious to arrive punctually; Bessie and the chickens needed tended to by young-backed folk, and the first crops needed to be sowed or they would be in more danger than any Fae could hope to muster against them.

Besides, Niall's house would need building, and the Adimus personally would prefer to not have to do it in the summer heat. All too soon they would be home. Everything would be as it had been, and he could put this whole ordeal behind him, if Sluagh Oiche would let them. *Shadespawn. He wished his grandpa was just mad.*

They would arrive at Adaire, then take Pardone's Pass back to the village. They did so in the late evening, passing through the dripping cave that bypassed the mountain of Sul Tor, still the old man fussed. "Pick up our pace, or we'll end up stricken roadside in the cold when the Night comes." the old man fussed.

Adimus glanced up at the moons, visible in the darkening daylight, one now setting, another but a sliver of a crescent shone: the night <u>was</u> coming.

But, they had passed Adaire, with Thadeus going back home. Dyrshul snoozed in the back of the small cart they'd purchased (she was the only one who was small enough to do so, and used this to her full advantage) and so, with the comment Adimus reckoned it was a good a prompt as any. "Pawpaw. What can you tell us about her? Tell us about the Winter Queen?"

"Not much. Not much." The man said. He obfuscated his reason for stopping dead in his tracks by adjusting his pack, but it was obvious it was the question that had done it. "What can you tell me about the Winter Queen. Have you learned anything of it in your travels, my boy?"

Adimus twisted his face. "She is The Grand Hag. Mother of Bones. The Veiled One who made the first mountains, and the first giants to rule from them."

"Mmm." The old man nodded and continued his determined gait.

"Bearach told me of what vexes you, boy. The words of that beast, the bugbear. Hmm?" At this the boy said nothing.

Of course he told him.

He braced himself. It was always some manner of quip or strange saying, some platitude to give solace, just like the old man often did when talking about the dreams. It was always comforting, of course, but he didn't think there was anything that could help with this.

Instead the man piped up. "The Cailleach is the stewardess of winter, but also the Shepherd of the Deer, the maker of mountains is also the benefactor of valleys of black soil and fish-laden ponds. She is the godmother and savior of the Nameless Boy."

"I thought she was evil? <u>The Mother of Bones</u>." the boy answered.

"Once, once she was beautiful. The lords of the Tuatha believed that the mixing of their bloodlines with her had led to the most beautiful beings upon which eyes could be set, and hers was apparent in her youth, they say. Not always a hag. Yes. Once she was beautiful. Always they are, I'm told, in the beginning. Wild and pure and free she once was, with hair of rowan and eyes like the sea...not all that is dreadful is an evil, boy. There is only nature, and she is a part of it. Remember, nothing is unnatural."

"Then why do you fear her? Why all this?"

"Fearing fate is natural too, my boy." he finally replied, trudging on heavily with his cane. "But you keep your legs steady, your shoulders straight, head high just the same. You, of all people, ought to know that."

It had seemed a much easier journey than the Ruined Road so far, even when downhill, and faster too. In fact, Adimus had bet that they had never crossed paths with them the first time because of this, and was found to be correct: Luloch and the others had left the same evening, cutting far and through the woods around the parish while Tolten was distracted by an invitation to the Beat for a chance to preach to the whole village at a celebratory feast and to the crossroads before the parish, which led beside the lake and up the hill to the Beat. This time though, they weren't sure they'd be so lucky.

A foreboding loomed upon the building as they passed it in the long light of the evening. Deep shadows swallowed the once welcoming entrance to the cloister and beyond. *Empty.* At least he could heave a sigh of relief for that.

They crested the hill where Adimus so often began his watch. He expected to see the lone tavern in the distance, across a long hill, green even in the depths of winter, windows aglow with the soft lights of hearth and chandelier, and on the hill just above it, their house.

"What in Lyr's name...?"

White tents dotted the landscape, from the hill, to the beat, to Brian's to the square. All of it was occupied. With tents. With fires. With horses. Mud. People.

"What is all this–?" Adimus started to say, but was drawn where his house lay. Barren of trees, the hill was it was, even his favorite oak.

"The gods bless us." Grandpa looked on in astonishment.

"If you say so." Said Bearch.

They tried to flag someone down, get someone's attention, but all of them were stern-faced, absorbed in their ordered activities. Then he saw the oriflamme : An eye among thorns. "...Lord Dougall?"

"Do what, boy?"

"Lord Dougall." he spoke up for the old man. "He heeded our call!"

"...Then this is your doing?"

"For what its worth." He sounded almost ashamed.

"Hah! My boy! My boy!" he beamed, to his surprise. "You must have the guile of a Bowen Bard and the cunning of Toranti Espun. Bless you!"

Niall ran out to greet them when they neared their house.

"Buckroys!"

It looked strange though, so lonely and barren. It was wrong; it didn't seem like their home any longer. It was as if he were still on the road, having not yet arrived, one of his fever dreams again where everything was wrong.

"How goes it? The Wanderer fared you well, I see." He embraced Luloch. "Adimus. Bearch. Dyrshul." He greeted in turn.

"Fine. We're fine." Luloch dismissed the platitude, "What's going on here?"

"There's more to tell than would take to freeze our noses off. Come in, come in. As if I have te invite you into your own home."

Inside, the place still seemed the same.

"Never mind the clutter..." He addressed the wood shavings and his tools.

"Never _you_ mind." Luloch dismissed the man. "You've done more than well."

"Well except for all the trees." Adimus commented.

"It's the reeve's command." He started before fumbling with the hospitalities again.

"Glad to see he's taking it seriously." Bearach remarked.

"He did as soon as Cadifor expressed such concern he said he'd come personally."

"He's coming? Here?"

On the hearth was a bubbling stew, which he kindly insisted on sharing with them (despite it obviously being meant for just him.)

"He wants to see you as soon as you settle in a bit, that McConell."

Luloch was just beginning to remove his boots. "Great. Very Well." he said, with forced cheer. "If these weary bones don't have enough tired in them to carry my mouth up there to give thanks, I should surely like to."

"He actually means Adimus, Lu." he corrected.

Adimus raised a brow. "I am tired, so I know you must be. You stay, rest. I'll give him more than enough thanks for all of us." the boy responded.

The men in the encampment surrounding the Beat hustled even by moonlight. It was a crowd Adimus was unacquainted with quantifying in number. There were dozens of them, perhaps hundreds.

He came before the Green Beat. Many a day he had day-dreams of its comforts.

The porch was full of men, yelling, cursing, drinking, eating. He had but approached it before he realized that he was standing in a queue, when a rowdy group of soldiers crammed in behind him.

It had become a cafeteria and mess hall to feed an army. He waited for what seemed like an hour, eventually taking a seat on the stairs, before he made it through the door.

There, he saw a familiar face. "...Maev?"

"Adi!" The frazzled, baggy-eyed girl started upon seeing him, dropping an empty tankard to the ground with a clatter that garnered more attention than any could tell she wanted. "Adi!" she hustled to him and gave an awkward curtsy. "I'm glad to see you're well." But her eyes were empty, untouched by the smile she gave.

"I'm looking for the general."

"He is upstairs speaking to the Pardoner."

Suddenly Adimus's teeth felt like they wouldn't came apart. "The Pardoner? The Pardoner's here."

"Yes. Upstairs." Maev's eyes spoke for him. They never broke contact. *They said "run".* Adimus staired for a long time at the top of the stairs. A dozen scenarios played out through his mind. In several he weighed the ramifications of what slaying the man might entail, but he felt guilt for considering it even in fancy.

He didn't remember climbing the stairs, only the face he knew he had to try and hide when, rounding the corner, he came face-to-face with the man.

The hearth roared, and would have actually felt quite nice, but in the cramped room with his captors it was an inferno.

"She fled the county to escape--"

"You, Blaise! To escape you!"

He paused only to take a sharp breath, a means of composing himself, to quell a marked nervousness, of a conviction which he knew overstepped. "Then, Lord Cadifor, let the sword answer for them. Put them to the question!"

He smiled at Adimus, then the old gnarled man let out a snort ruffled his mustache "It would be an insult to my ancestors to tarry the Slayer of Coarthanach with such a petty request." He turned to leave. "That is my final word." and with that he turned to leave. Seeing Adimus, he said. "Grigor Adimus, I don't know what game your family plays or what that named bard chooses to conceal, but if I find that there is more to this than you tell it will be you who shall see the gallows." And then he left.

His mouth was dry and his head rattling now before he even came in. He pressed on.

"You wished to see me."

He was a mouse before a lion.

"Another time." He gave Tolten an unreadable glance sideways. "The hour grows late. You'd best get some rest in your home, safe and secure."

With that he brushed past the boy. He meant to follow, but in Tolten spoke. It was the commanding tone he'd known from his youth. "Adimus."

"Pardoner Tolten." He tried to keep the greeting short, and his face free of outrage.

"Come in. Have a seat."

He tried to scramble for an excuse—he'd left the kettle on, his dog had died, he was trying not to get arrested for murder.

Tolten settled back into his chair. "...Would you like a drink? You've been far and abroad, and performed many a deed, Cadifor has told me. Enough to be considered what he would call a man." he finally said.

"No thank you."

The man shrugged, and Tolten uncorked a bottle of deep sanguine liquid from the table and poured it into a brass goblet. Adimus rang his hands on his clothes to remove the sweat.

He smelled the cork. "Beetwine brandy." he proclaimed with an exuberant smile on his face. He snuffed a sip before recorking it.

"You know, it took me a very, very, long time, Adimus, to accept that Maev had a talent which warranted _her_ being called away from me, from us." he gazed down into the drink, swilling it. "I mean, of course, we brewed lambics and wine, as is the tradition of our order, our culture." he was sure to slather the last word with undue importance. "It was her charge, and she was apprenticed by the monk before her. It was a duty performed joyfully, an act of devotion." he gazed down at it with an uneasy eye. "Ever did it overshadow her studies. During the hours of reflection when others were doing recitations she was filling tuns and lautering her mixes for wort. Her prayer books were marred with dates and ratios and temperatures."

"At first one would assume that an eye drawn toward such worldly things would be an eye astray from the godly, from the divine." he said. "When she left, I almost called for her excommunication from the order." Adimus didn't know what he was talking about, but the imagery it evoked didn't require it. "Then I tasted this wine…" he smiled. "And it came to me. That pull to do that which you cannot help but do is the expression of the Wheels of the Great Mystery. This is the nectar of devotion…At least this is what I tell myself." he finished the goblet and sat it down. "All is as willed. Perhaps I shall have to suffer you as such as well, Adimus." he said dryly. "I know not what manner of favor you hold with him, as I have divined you hold no Spell over him, but I must quietly abide it, and rationalize to myself as best I can why fate sees fit that it is as such."

"…I am not sure what you mean."

"My original postulation was that Bearach's lover was Fae." he said non-chalantly. "That <u>would</u> make sense. But it would exclude you."

He sat the glass on the table. Lent forward and eyed him. "Who are you, Adimus?" he said. "You are not faekind. And if I can be frank, aren't any such kindred I'd seen before besides full-blooded Cessair like myself.."

It was a side of Tolten need never seen before, like a wild dog that had been chained and house broken. Adimus smiled "I think you've had too much nectar of devotion, Pardoner." Tolten didn't seem amused. "I told you, I lived on the streets of Ederton with my mother, until Bearach found us."

"Your mother. Hah. What was her name?"

"Tanya. I hear my father tell."

"A good Shambayan name. Must've done all manner of study to conjure that one. Probably got it from that harlot." Adimus didn't have to ask of whom he spoke. "Tell me about her."

He'd rehearsed this one so often it almost didn't seem a lie. "You've heard this before, Pardoner. She was an indentured servant of a Merchant Lord. We stayed in a barracks in one of his towers, with the other slaves. I told you I don't remember much…" he always added that part to ensure he didn't have to go into much detail.

"Uh-huh."

Adimus hid his panic. Perhaps he should've taken that drink after all. He would bolster the position with details"…My father was a guard in the merchant's service. So I heard. One of the Angh'Becna. Died of the Thanic Plague before the lord could find out about me."

"You are right. I must have heard this fantasy out of you more than a dozen times now." he said. "Know this: Thadues had a lawyer there collecting registries of all of the Sworn who came through the gates at the Nalanen, and there was no such person. Ever. The only ones who corroborate this farce is the ones what curate it. " Tolten was careful to watch his suspect carefully when he said it, looking for any crack in the boy's expression.

Adimus rubbed his hands on his pants vigorously. "I wish I could help you more."

"Well. Don't you think it could be possible that your mother knew one of the Gentle Folk, in her time as a servant?"

It seemed to have disarmed him. If there was one thing he ever learned from his interactions with the dubious on his outing it was to double down. Adimus was silent for a few moments, partly for effect, partly to hide his surprise that it had worked, but mostly to commit to the earth any regrets about the yarn he was about to spin. "I do remember a man. Come to think of it."

"Really?"

"I think so."

"Tell me about him."

He thought to be ostentatious in his description, or even describe what Fae he had encountered, the customer from the Curio perhaps, or even Malcolm Bran "He looked like any other man, though. Bronze hair, and blue eyes. He would only come around sometimes, and he always kept to himself."

The worse on he went the worse he felt. It was that he held much reverence for what the Pardoner believed, not any more--he reckoned that just like Laina believed what she did because of where she'd come from, it was much the same here in Balfour, it was that the Pardoner, after all, was simply trying to protect everyone, everything he knew, and he more than once had questioned if what he told the man was selfish. *I wonder what I would believe if I knew where I actually did come from?*

"Aye. Could shed some light on it. Ambros says that he saw you touched by a Shade on the Ruined Road." It came out matter of factly, he peered down from under spectacles. He felt as a child who stole a cookie and was now being asked if he had just to see what he'd say. "And that you acted injured at first, but by the time you had reached Hewnyleigh there was no sign of such."

The boy's stomach churned. He took a sharp breath. "Ambros was misinformed about the situation." he replied. "We did see a Shade. A Church Grimm, the bard called it?" he tried to deflect with sympathy. "I'd never seen such things before. I..." he lowered his head. "lost my composure. Frightened, I spent days afterwards in a state of shock. Laina's kind words finally brought me out of it. She said it was unbecoming of a man of the mound, of a Watcher." He wondered if the last part was a bit too much.

"I've cross-examined other accounts in the village. Eichgun was a hard one to crack, but after explaining the direness of the situation with your sister to him--"

"Dyrshul!?" he said "What does this have to do with her?" His facade finally broke. It perhaps was telling that Adimus didn't seem to question what it was that Eichgun did or didn't know about Laina, but he didn't care.

The Pardoner smirked for a moment, perhaps revealing too much himself. "Truly, it is impressive, these powers such demoniac spirits impart to those who share covenant with it." his eyes narrowed. "Our tradition warns of pacts with the fae, who prop themselves up as gods and bestow their Graces." he spoke with a surety that Adimus knew was bluster itself, but could do nothing to stop it. "<u>You</u> were not accomplice to the events of Elloien, but no doubt your abetting of that faerie-minded trollop played a part in bringing that evil to our doorstep, like leaving a door open for robbers. And believe this: when this is settled I will have my day with you, and she will answer to me next."

"You think Dyrshul did this." he gave his thoughts words.

Tolten shifted uneasily in his seat. He'd never thought about it, but he could probably kill him with his bare hands just as easily. But again, guilt and doubt struck him.

"Shepherd. I beg you, see the truth: she has nothing to do with this."

"I know the truth of Dyrshul Buckroy, <u>and</u> your friend's heathen goddess! It is no longer a suspicion, it is a fact. <u>She</u> is a Changling."

"She isn't...-!" Adimus stood forebodingly. But, just like the stairs, he didn't remember being on his feet, and he had forgotten his face again, for whatever ghastly visage of rage he wore reflected as the surprise on the shepard's face. He forced himself into his seat again.

But the man just grinned. "And of you, boy. Have you lost your way as well in your travels? You are home, what have you brought with you?"

"Scrutiny and reason." The statement held neither malice nor disingenuinity.

"What these tales of fancy has brought you, all, no less." he took a sip from his goblet.

"You've forsaken the Slaking, I hear." At that Adimus was taken aback. *How could he know?*

"If Balros is just, he will understand."

"The King in Gold and Black is justice!" His words were the thesis statement of a thousand sermons, all of which Adimus had heard. "How dare you presume upon him the wants of your own heart!" he lurched aright, even without his cane. At that the pardoner's eyes lit up with a glow he'd never seen before, and the twisted words that fell from his mouth were just as foreign, but as they were spoken, the seat upon which he sat grew hot. Its varnished curled, and its planks cracked and blackened.

"Behold the powers of the Cunning Veils!" There was no hiss, no smoke from the quenching, and the chair was even cool afterwards, when, with the clutching of his hand, the stoking embers ready to burst into flames, were snuffed. "Doubt the truth now! Haha!"

Adimus glanced back at him. And he did. "Those words, pardoner. Where did you learn them? Where did you learn to harness the Calcinative Quality...?"

The man didn't dignify the statement with an answer. "You've studied the ways forbidden in your scripture too as well, in the meantime. It is a shame, Adimus, indeed.

"Thaumaturgy is the power of the gods, usurped by men. Your ole' pa is a fool. No. My power comes to me that I may lead men aright! It is granted to me so that others may behold its fury, and know it is but a spark of the power of the Baleful Eye!"

The boy was forced to jump out of the seat, at which point the flame extinguished itself, leaving only a black char and a whiff of ash that it had ever been there. The Pardoner spoke. "I don't know where you Buckroys went or what they were doing, what manner of foul discourse and faerie talk you've heard, or how you managed to get in our general's good graces, but mark my words: I will find out." he accused, leaning back in his chair. He popped the cork again, and slammed the bottle on the table when he was done pouring. He began again, matter of factly. "I am told to be still while their hounds sniff Dyrshul out, that I am of more value here in providing my blessings of the Veils and sanctifying Dougall's men than chasing the child, who is no doubt on her way to report our numbers and strengths to the enemy."

The shock and confusion was plain on his face, a confession he did not mean to give, as it at least did show the Pardoner that he knew nothing of it.

"...Shepherd. Is there anything I can do to help?" he could no longer make eye contact with the man.

"He said you would be useful should the Shades make themselves known. I petitioned for the confiscation of your sword to be placed in more experienced hands, but I have been superseded by Sir McDougall." He sounded more than disappointed. "You will be needed at the fore, Watcher, your position protects you. Anwell is going to lead us in what we'll need to do to prepare for this Darkest Night, but two days hence, child. Stand by until then."

"Very well. I thank you." He said almost before he could finish, and was almost out the door before that.

There he calmly left the stairs and crossed the common room until the large double doors of the inn were shut behind him.

When he came to the yard he realized it was night. It was beginning to snow again. The porch had cleared out, and even the camp was quiet.

In fact, the outside of the Green Beat was only occupied by a handful of soldiers of rank. They gawked and gathered around the great Orc warrior and Cadifor, who stood with them, regaling and assuring them.

He gave the boy a sideways glance as he emerged, watching the Grigor climb the hill into darkness.

Finally, the boy made his way back to the house.

The candles were already out; they had all went to bed. *It must be exceptionally late.*

That would not do. He would wake them, tell them they were in danger.

He was nestled in on his favorite chair, asleep sitting up. Bearch was laid out along the rug, and Niall on a stool at his work bench.

"Grandpa!" he ran through the door. "You have to wake up!" He didn't care how much Luloch protested, how much he talked about his "fate". He would drag them by the ear fighting back down that mountain.

"Huh?" he started and looked around disoriented until his eyes fell on the boy.

"We have to go. Tolten is here. Lord Pembroke lied."

Suddenly his eyes sobered. "Damnation! It was a trap." rasping the tiredness from himself he slung the blanket off and looked about. Immediately he dispersed, gathering his cane and bags. "We'll get you packed, and Dyrshul. I'll answer him."

Bearch jumped up and took his wood axe from the mantle.

Luloch put on his belt. "Shut that door, we'll get you out the back."

"I didn't leave it open."

The old man was addressing the draft in the room.

It was cold in the house, far colder than for which the warm fire Niall let would allot. Suddenly Adimus went into a panic. He ran for the back door. It was unbarred, and left standing. Tiny footprint led out into the snow.

"Dyrshul! Dyshul!!"

They would yell for his sister, for Dyrshul, but she was gone.

Chapter 35
Crossroads

Night was well in swiftly, and the snow poured from the hollow sky, still he trudged, driven by a fire hotter than the flame of a forge, a fire that availed the numb of any cold and burned away the weariness in his muscles.

Even after the turn of years had metamorphosed him from a boy into a young man, even after it too had all completely changed, grown up with trees grown from seed and blanketed with snow, his feet lead him back. The meeting spot was the beginning of it, the place where they had gathered just before the goblyns attacked. There, in an overgrown copse just past the looming rock was the basin where...where they'd came from, where his first memories had began.

Sure enough he'd found the small marks of her boot sole. And the hurried stalking of a large wolf.

"Oh no..." he muttered aloud.

He followed them around a tree, up atop a rock. Broken twigs and displaced snow choreographed handholds. She'd jumped off, then up a nearby tree. All the tree climbing they'd done in youth had paid off, it seemed. He breathed a sigh of relief. The wolf's tracks veered from here, saundering off back into the wood, no sign of struggle. Adimus hopped up into the tree himself--it was much easier for him, but would've been a great leap for her, even being chased but a wolf. In the distance he could see her tracks continued. This time there was a different set of prints with her. A rabbit. She'd followed it; even in such evident peril her playful curiosity and whimsy had gotten the best of her. Around another tree. Over a hill. Under the roots of an old tree. Then they stopped, and there was blood. Splattered all around the disturbed snow, crimson red blood, melting in the snow with its vital warmth. Mud and torn turf from shuffling feet, struggling to hold ground in battle. Adimus collapsed to his knees, with an uncontrollable press of sorrow welling, forcing its way out of his eyes he wept.

The snow and the darkened sky made only the growl and bark of hounds made them known.

"There he is!" A man then called.

At first he thought it was the wolves coming for him, but when he heard the cry and saw the figures he knew it was much worse. The three figures were haloed by the firelight.

"Adimus Buckroy! I found you!"

It was Tolten. "Where are you going? To inform your dark masters of us, no doubt!"

"You!" He lept to his feet again. "I was looking for my sister, who you drove away!" He hardly mustered an answer. It wouldn't matter anyhow, for either one of them.

"For your weakness of heart you are bound for the abyss, to sleep in the depths of the Soundless Sea forever. May the Baleful Eye burn the spark of you out! I Name you, Adimus Buckroy, enemy of the Old Way! For all time, may your food and drink bracken and wither upon your lips and give you no sustenance. May every seed you sow grow copper brambles! May the smoke of every fire you warm yourself beside choke and sicken you!"

A fear apprehended him, an arresting terror. The boy felt as if he'd swallowed his heart. The words he spoke were no stranger to him. These words were a curse, an edict of damnation, kept in the Numitorum for only the worst of heretics and blasphemers. The shepherd had just Named him.

He heard the sound of chains, only this time it was not some monster that came for him, but far worse--his kinsmen. "Take him but don't harm him, he'll be needed for the Weeping." He ordered, and Brian the Blacksmith stepped forward. The shorter one behind him was a monk with a bow pointed at him drawn taught, one of Tolten's friars. All of them, so intent on their quarry, cautiously surrounded him like some snake or other dangerous animal that none wanted to get too close to.

The worst came though was when Brian drew near. The man had numbed himself to apathy; whether out of fear of reproach at questioning the Pardoner or because truly in his heart to him wasn't just the boy from the village anymore, his countenance was as colder than the snow that fell around him. He saw the shackles. These looked different from the other ones, forged from the blacksmith's hand just for him, and if he had to guess they were Cold Iron.

The Grigor found himself paralyzed. The thought that this man, his friend, was coming to kill him, overwhelmed him.

This was it. The words of the boggart came to him again.

Brian's glare was intense, so much so that neither he nor they noticed when one of the nearby trees lurched to life.

As it unfurled itself from its distinct position which made it appear as such, Adimus immediately recognized it.

Brian was a big man to begin with, hardened from years of wringing his hammer, but his ribs still gave way beneath the force of its massive heel, his final heaving breath pressed from his lungs in a meek rasping sigh before they filled with his blood.

The monk in a panic had unleashed his arrow at the thing, which sounded with the 'thunk'' as one might expect an arrow striking a tree might, and did about as much damage. This drew its ire, and it picked him up like a rag doll, crushing the abbot with his bare hands.

A speedy hare had lept from between the beasts legs, that when Tolten uttered a prayer and tried to run from it became a man with a dark look in his eye. With much the same cold, numb, dutiful countenance the blacksmith had shown earlier as he dispatched him with a dagger.

Before Adimus could process it he stood in the carnage, he himself numb and then he perhaps knew that it wasn't the fear or the hatred that caused that look, at least in him, but the disbelief at what manner of end was demanded of the world that thirsted for such carnage.

"Adimus." the voice spoke. The boy struggled to unblur his vision, and there, standing in the wake of pawprints was Malkin.

He had to mention it a few times before the boy snapped to. "Bounder?"

"Bounder." the pooka smiled. "So it was you." In his grief the boy disregarded his strange use of tense. He clasped at his abdomen guarding a wound, one that was apparently nursing in the hollow of the tree.

Adimus looked down at it.

"Do not." he tried to dispel his concern. "I'm fine." he huffed, obviously not. "And so is she."

"Dyrshul?" it came out as a gasp.

"Tentatively." he explained. His flippant assessment of the situation was lost on the boy. "She was taken. By the Unseelie."

"..."

"The Court of the Uncouth." explained Malkin, the boy still said nothing. "I tried to save her, but their numbers were too great. They had an Unslaked with them. A Werewolf."

"Werewolf?" he thought back to the dream. It was the creature from it, he knew it without even pondering it. He had heard the word before, from Laina, but had never given it thought.

The boy took a few moments to gather himself. He stood "Well, we have to tell Luloch." He absently espoused, glancing back at Brian, Luloch and the other.

"No! She's safer with the Sluagh than you are, going back to town right now. She ran for a reason. We haven't the time neither. The Winter Queen conjures another storm."

Adimus looked around at the gathering clouds, trying to wrap his head around the concept of such a Magic.

"What do they intend to do with her?" He finally said.

He went over to the corpse of the monk, and picked up his bow and arrows. "Awful things. Dreadful things. The Unslaked seek innocent blood, and the blood of an Immortal is particularly desirable. Here."

An Immortal. A Fae.

He handed them to the boy, who took it, though looking at it like it was a snake "Despisers of Flesh and Form" the Unslaked...the Sluagh will only tear her apart if she's lucky."

He scratched his head, then looked up at the pummeling snow. "Damn this blanketing blizzard! It blockades intrusion into the Otherworld. "

"Otherworld?"

"Yes, it's where our quarry lies." He reached out and opened his cloak, snatching his waterskin without his permission and taking a small drink. He took a few swigs and handed it back to him. A cold wind picked up. "Keep this warm, and follow me."

They walked not too far from where they were, to a rocky outcropping that was familiar to boy.

Inside was a hollow hutch, a small cave. He and Dyrshul had played there a few times, probably against their better judgment. He remembered her finding bleached animal bones and the like back then. Now that he was older, he realized it was probably dug out by some small animals, like a coyote or a fox, only a few yards deep, but back then it was a thrilling and dangerous place; just far enough from the house to be a safe thrill to explore. But what was in there today was far stranger than any fancies a young brother and sister at play might have had. The plant creature reached in, and pulled out, once again, a red-haired lady.

It was Oinde. *They killed her.*

The body sat swaddled, bound in clothing and blankets, in the fetal position, encased in a cocoon of vines and brambles. Bounder knelt down and felt her face, and touched her lips. "Cover the head next time. I don't know if it made it." he said solemnly. Those lips, red when Adimus last saw her, were now brushed lifeless blue. The barrette still adorned her head.

"Well, go on." bounder said, and the giant sat down. "You can leave it here if that's the case. We'll need stealth for this undertaking.", then with the same knife (only hastily cleaned) he cut the foliage that held her. Her pale figure, nude, collapsed onto the ground like a rag doll, one of her eyes partly open, milky and glazed, the snow collecting on her hair and body.

Then, the tree creature, plopping down to sit in the same fold-legged position sat before her, and began to chant in a low, grumbling tone. Its voice seemed to make multiple melodious harmonious sounds, all harmonizing with themselves. He wondered if all Animaflora could make such sounds.

Then the thought fled, replaced by pure astonishment. He watched as slowly the maiden rose and opened her eyes. She stared at the creature blankly, as if hearing, listening to instructions.

When its final chord struck, its final breath left its Form, as the expulsion of a glowing golden mist.

Like smoke it danced in the air, wafted around by a wind all its own that defied the blustering blizzard. The maiden heaved a breath of life, one as if she had been startled or strangled, then another, each time taking it in the mist and exhaling none of it. Soon she would stretch her arms and move about as if waking from a long sleep. Slowly color started returning to her.

"...Well?" Bounder came.

"I don't know either." she nonchalantly replied "Can't hardly feel the fingers". She looked at them, nearly purple, hopping to her feet, stretching her arms.

"Can you wield a sword?" he said.

She walked over to the boy, "Hello again." and, locking eyes with him, pulled the sword from his sheath. She raised her eyebrows at him. Adimus averted his gaze. He could smell her perfume.

She twirled it in a myriad of skillful flourishes the likes which he'd never seen, she then mirrored with her other hand, tossing it deftly in the air tip over pommel when she did.

"I think it will do." She said, putting it back into his sheath for him.

He introduced "This is Oinde. Oinde, Adimus."

She gave a facetious curtsy, lifting the hems of her non-existent dress. "We've met." she grinned.

"...Will you put some clothes on before the boy faints?"

"He weathered that kind of bloodshed and hasn't fainted yet--*Sir* Adimus is no boy." She smiled. She turned around and started sifting through the clothes. "It is a bit cold." she shrugged. "It makes it easier to prepare what I need to wear for the evening's activities." She explained to the pooka, tossing aside a fairly expensive looking gown and a few more outfits before sliding on a pair of breeches. He noticed the hollow spot in her back, the spot fastidiously covered by her hair that day.

"...And turn your lure off." Bounder added. "It kind of defeats the purpose when they can smell you a mile off."

"Sorry."

"You're a huldra." Adimus observed.

She didn't dignify him with an answer, only a sideways glance while she put on her belt with multiple sheathed knives. She topped it off with a leather cuirass, lambraces, scarf and cloak, and put her hair back with a pin she kept in her cheek. Bounder handed her the late friar's accouterments and led on.

The path they walked was all too familiar. The trail along the edge of the Sul Tor basin–in a half hour's time they would be standing before Luloch's rock. "They'll be watching the lake." he said off-handedly. "Oinde, make sure all is well." He said after they had walked swift and clear of the sight of their battle. Adimus watched in astonishment as with a nod she flat-foot leapt to the top of the nearest tree with the deftness of a cat, barely even disturbing the snow. She came back down "Nothing yet." She said eerily.

But she had missed what was right before them, veiled by the snow.

Adimus stared down the valley. A foggy mist puffed from its nostrils. It called out in its own tongue first, then in daldistan, the common tongue, "Embraleigh smells you, shadowman! Sluagh! You will not escape my blade! Defeating me will be your only chance. Do not make me hunt you. I am tired. If Embraleigh must run to find you," she huffed. "death will be slow for you."

Shadowman?

Adimus gripped his sword, but by the time he had had, the creature spotted him.

With a fell battlecry she charged.

"Wait, I'm no shade!" He stumbled backwards, just barely un-shouldering his shield, much less glance back to want his compatriots. All he could do was squeal. "Shadetouched! Shadetouched!"

"You lie!" She swung.

His last run-in with an axe of that size was still fresh in his memory. He dashed any thought of trying to block it, and his hesitancy may have now almost cost him his life instead. He ducked under the blade and it drove him on all fours. "I'm just a simple boy! Just looking for his sister, please!"

"Boy?" The orc froze. "A Hyu'man boy, a Cessair boy...!"

So did Adimus, awaiting the next strike. But the creature simply stroke its chin. "Bres spoke of a boy...But. You could be a trick of Tethra! A Sluagh, shaped like a boy." She brandished her weapon again.

"Shadetouched, I was shadetouched. By a shuck. A big dog. He muttered. "Maybe it's that you smell." She looked him up and down.

Adimus yammered "But, but I'm well now. Someone fixed me." trying to sound as convincing as he could, which served difficult even though he was telling the truth. When no swing came the boy slowly stood, throwing up his hands to demonstrate his harmlessness. He left his shield-strap cradled in his elbow just the same.

"Fixed? No, Now I know you lie!" She shook her head. "Only my maker and his children have that Magic. Only he heals the Cold Flame."

The statement robbed the eloquence from the boy. "No! I swear!"

But again, the beast stopped. "You...swear?" Suddenly she did stop.

"That...dangerous thing for Fae to say." She stepped back and looked at him judgingly, her face twisted with indecision. "Embraleigh will take to Caddy For, make him see if you tell the truth." She said finally.

"Caddy...Cadifor? McDougall? You know Cadifor, you're with him?" The boy stammered.

She nodded. "You come now, or I kill." She raised her axe over her head.

"Hah! You're her! You're the Warrior at the Crossroads! The legends are true, you've come to help us!"

"I have no problem at all facing Gram for you, but I..."

Just then a voice rang in his head. It was Oinde's voice. *"Do not tell her of us, she will kill us."* Adimus tried to finish his sentence, but found himself not only breathless but literally unable to think. It was a foreign feeling, one he wished to never feel again, it was as if his own thoughts were being thought for him against his will, being wrested from his own will and made to sound out the words to him. Then it continued, in an instant no more than the silence between his words. *"We haven't the time for this. Tell her that Madam Gwyndol calls for her."*

"But I...came to tell you that Madam Gwyndol calls for you." the boy tried to hide the upward inflection at the end, as if it were a question.

"Oh, oh!" she immediately turned. "Gwyndol must want more wood for the fires. I must go." it turned and clodded off, turning only a second to mutter an apology, "...Sorry."

The rest of the trip was unobstructed. Finally, when the rock was in sight, the pooka broke a few sizable limbs from a dead tree, and speaking a few words and performing a gesture the water wringed from them; it was a trick Adimus had seen Alfred do before, albeit with the aid of his staff. Then cupping his hand he pronounced another Spell, this one combusting the dried wood.

He scooped the snow from the smooth divet in it beside where he'd built the for then took again the boy's water. "The hour is late, the night shall be even colder." He poured the water. Then with the touch of his index finger the pool gleamed with an ethereal light. "We have only until this fire goes out and this water freezes. Follow me."

And with that he transmogrified back into the form of the hare, and jumping into the pool, was gone.

The pool never stirred, nor revealed anything beneath its surface, not even the presence of the pooka who'd just jumped in. Dozens of thoughts stirred in the boy's mind, the least of which was his grandfather's sentiment for the place. He looked down at it, gulped and took a deep breath. *The Otherworld.*

He imagined he'd sink into the pool, like some bottomless lake, but all that came of it was a strange dizziness, and a feeling like deja vu at first, then suddenly it was like the world turned upside down, shook as of a child dumping a out toy box, peeling his feet from the ground as it was shaken, prevailing over what pitiful force held him to it to begin with.

He found himself standing on perfectly smooth hard ground. It was not slippery, nor did it give at all. It still seemed snowy, but hard somehow, as if standing on the unshaken base of Dyrshul's snow globe. Replacing the bright cloudy day was a sky full of wispy flickering shafts of light: whites and blacks and blues. Then he looked up and there were no trees, no hills. He struggled a gasp, but drew no breath. What he found himself standing on was a vast mirror-like plane, and above him, beyond these shafts was an unfathomable void.

Then he blinked. Something was very wrong. He screamed, but it didn't seem to carry, for had he known it there was nowhere upon which the sound to echo. A world had flashed before his closed eyes. It was the world he'd left behind; behind his eyelids he could see the world where they had stood.

It took a longer time than he was comfortable with to attune himself with the concept, and Bounder and Oinde both seemed to grow impatient. After a moment he wrested his sanity and fought on.

He eventually was able to envision, by virtue of this new sense, that he'd fallen off the rock, tumbled from it and landed here. He could feel the tingling of the snow tickling his skin and the numbness of the cold when he closed his eyes as well now, as if he straddle the worlds and when they shut he was physically there, but the sensation faded like waking from a dream upon opening.

In this new place he could see, hovering in the air, the portal whence they'd come, the surface of the water within the bowl, like a shiny mirror reflecting into the "real" world.

Bounder beckoned him, and he tried his best to follow, as did Oinde, slinking up behind him with deadly grace. The surfaces had cracks in it where a white light showed through the snow. He could make out the outlines of the shapes of trees, as if pressing up at him as against fogged glass, and as he trekked on he saw patches where the snow had receded, in them he could see the shadows of the trees scattering upon the surface of the world, as if being cast from below him by a light that was not the sun, a light within the world. The colors above him stirred in this place, matching what he would've seen in the real world--it was as if this world tore colors and shapes apart, and he now found himself wandering somewhere between them.

He found himself closing his eyes more and more to quell his nausea, but it didn't help, as he soon realized the world behind his eyes was actually different in small and horrifying ways from the one he knew.

Clouds seemed different, and trees, and colors sometimes were out of hue, skewing ever so slightly. Sometimes shadows made deep pits, and some objects sat beyond the periphery of his vision, taunting him, as he found that certain things he couldn't focus on no matter how hard he tried. Sometimes there would be a tree in full bloom, untouched by the weather, or dead and rotted, oozing a black ichor--he found one ablaze with blue fire. Sometimes creatures moved between the shapes, shadowy blurs hiding when he looked, or even more disconcertingly not so: brazenly standing in the open staring at him where he could not stare back.

Then Bounder disappeared again, but before he could see where he had gone the colors and shapes merged, he came to a spot in the wood wholly different. Abruptly there was no snow. Now he stood in a meadow of tall grass.

The sky cleared, a deep indigo filled with the brightest stars. The field glowed as if an unseen noonday sun beat upon it. Haloing the distance on all sides was a ring of light, as if a sun for each hour sat just beyond the horizon; a warm breeze threw pollen and petals from flowers he'd never seen before, or did even now, as his gaze was drawn to the effulgent expanse above him, more stars than he could count, alien stars, upon a sky wider than the breadth of any horizon to be seen with mortal eyes.

Before him now were several shapes.

They said something in a melodic-sounding foreign tongue. Their voices seemed sharper and more imminent, all the more disorienting, as if they were rather somehow trapped in a small room together than standing below the open sky. They repeated in daldistan so the boy could understand. "Halt, trespasser!" Adimus's gaze shot down to the woman with the short spear poised to strike, and at her compatriot's nocked arrows. Then to her pointed ears.

His hands went up almost reflexively. "I'm-I'm no harm!" The bungle of words came out. They spoke amongst themselves. *These were the Unseelie. The Unoathed.* He wished Bounder had given him warning, but it was too late.

After a hesitant moment, a long-eared lady with flowing sunny hair stepped forward. "What is your Name traveler?" She continued in the language the boy knew, fluently and void of accent.

"My name is Adimus. I'm here for Dyrshul." He thought to ready himself to draw a sword, but it would be no use; He'd be dead before it left his sheath. *I hope Bounder has a plan.* He suddenly regretted being so truthful.

"Adimus? Adimus?!" She chortled. Others laughed, not only the bows but many more unseen.

"Hyu'manii!" One of them jeered. It came out like a slur. She smiled a right grin with strangely bestial-looking teeth, looking at her men like an audience.

"Perhaps.' She waved her hand as if to stave them from running him through. "Tell me how you found your way here, traveler."

The boy took a moment, that the silence add heft to his statement. "Why should I?" He answered. "If I tell you what you need to know you'll have no reason to let me live." It was a bluff that had worked with the Bogeyman. "Can't have us all finding this place, can you?...My sister, is she here?"

It had been in the hunch that all Fae bluffed and blustered, leveraged motives, hiding and revealing what need be when it best suited them. *Maybe Argent is Fae.* Adimus dismissed the thought. "She's all I want, surrender her and I'll leave peacefully, and call off my men." He pressed on, seeing the man's surprise. He'd also watched the bard enough to know to double down when someone called your bluff. Laina had a saying for this: 'when eating poison, might as well lick the plate'. "If not, then prepare for war."

Some of the heads raised, curious to see what might happen. Some of them were animals. "Curious." Also a thing Fae often said, apparently. "Sister, you say? He is missing a sister." She announced to them loudly, as if it were the punchline to a joke he did not understand, then with no warning, same jovial grin on her face, she drew a sword. She was quick, Adimus thought, but, in this instance, having any sentiment at all about it was good; it meant he wasn't dead. The woman may well have run him through, but instead he touched the knife to his cheek.

It was the same way he'd been tested before. "I'm not one of you." He replied, batting the cold iron blade away flippantly.

She shrugged. She answered the crowd in that language, and with a sated expression sheathed her blade, proudly turning her back to the boy. Adimus grasped for the topic he was perhaps not privy to. "This one <u>is</u> Hyu'man."

Adimus drew a few deep breaths to fight the struggle enough to be able to speak a full sentence without sounding obviously afraid, "Release her, and I'll send my men away." There was a pause that he mistook for delegation, before she spun abruptly and backhanded him to the ground.

The flowers broke his fall, but gave him no room to back away or stumble to his feet when she strode forward again. "You dare speak falsely in the Lay Lands, Hyu'man? Unoathed swine!" She looked back at her audience. He gazed at the back of her hand in disgust, and drew a cloth from her tunic to wipe it. "What army is this that you bring to this world?!" she inquired. "What machinations does the Queen of Frosts leverage to muster your kind to do her bidding?!"

It hadn't worked quite as well as he'd hoped. "...Queen of Frosts?"

"She is a Changling, the one you call Dyrshul." She sneered. "A spy of your leige."

"What...*my* liege? I have no liege! I know not which you speak."

"Indeed. Is that why you brought them with you?" she spun to meet the eyes of tge man in the violet cloak, whom with a word summoned pink lightning from his fingertips.

Bounder stood from his hiding place in the brush, wincing in pain when it connected.

"They are lying!" Bounder cried. "Kill them! Quick! Save her!"

The lady spun back, and when the boy revealed even the slightest inclination to draw his blade, with a move that the boy couldn't even process in his mind he was on the ground, the Cold Iron sword within the Fae's hands. She then looked at the pooka. "Lykil! Draw your weapon." she paced toward him. The cloaked man relented, and he and the guard step forward. Adimus climbed to his feet.

Bounder appeared to fight to change back in his animal Form, contorting as he tried, but found that he could not, the tendrils of lightning squeezing around him like tightening ropes. Before he knew it he found himself being forced backwards by her advance, and when he'd tripped and fallen in the grass she clasped the sword carefully by the leather handle and plunged the sword into his throat.

When she jerked it clean the sound was as clear thunder, the ringing of bells, the breaking of stained glass. Light swallowed the boy's eyes through cracks that covered Bounder's flesh, then all was left was the ringing of the Cold Iron blade and a smoldering husk, cracked like a porcelain teapot, smoke pouring from his dead, doll-like eyes.

Adimus was like a frozen fawn at the sight. He tried to move his legs but they wouldn't budge. It was as the Bogeyman, but somehow worse now, far worse, for the thought that had smoldered in him now ignited at the sight engulfing his mind so wholly that it was as if there were no outside anymore in which his legs could run. *Even Immortals die.*

"RRraagh!!!" he heard Oinde's voice come, a monstrous trumpeting cacophony of voices all screaming in rage. She'd managed to make her way past the guards and toward the cage, but blew her cover when she stood. She picked up the nearest guard to her with one hand and used it as a shield to catch the arrows of the other. hmHer face unnaturally contorted with rage, and she threw still another guard with enough force to bear him and the one behind him to the ground. She moved toward the lady Tuatha but was blockaded by half a dozen pooka, themselves hidden in the grass, and who transmogrified into a wall of men carrying spears and swords and shields.

Several strikes landed on the Huldra when they clashed, but she relented none at all, snapping a spear haft with her bare hand, and simply pulling down the shield of another and driving a dagger through his chest with such force his legs buckled, the blows resounding off her with the hollow 'thunk'

Adimus drew his ski dhu, his boot dagger. The man was somewhat preoccupied with the spectacle; he could strike now, but now, unsure, could not bring himself to.

Then with the lifting of his staff the violet cloaked one summoned forth a serpentine gout of flame. It railed into Oinde, blowing her head over heels, her feet coming off the ground.

Trees and flowers lay singed, and they gathered cautiously, but almost immediately she lurched to her feet.

The incendiary scorched her porcelain visage, licking her hair charred and scarring her with deep cracks and furrows, inside of which embers still burned. It left half of her face blackened and marred, and when her bloodshot eyes fell on them she let out a feral hiss almost like that of a cat, and bounding leap cleared over them and springing into a sprint. She fled the guards, who pursued her into the periphery.

The woman with the blade turned his attention back to the boy.

Adimus's mouth ran dry, his hands trembled with a mournful dread. He reached for his Ski Dhu.

"Adimus." He heard the familiar voice call out. The purple man lowered the hood of his cloak, which went from violet to bright red. Standing before him was Alfred.

"You know this one?" she said, coming back for the boy.

"A sibling, most likely. Harmless."

Then he came, striding up with another pointed-ear Kindred, this one clad in looked familiar. *The Valeyard.*

Then he saw her. "Dyrshul!" The man stepped away to let Adimus in, and much to his comfort let him run to her in his arms long before it dawned on him what he'd seen on his approach.

"Wings?" A thought he verbalized it as it erupted from his mind, as if it forced its way out.

"I...don't know what is happening to me."

His arms brushed feathers and it startled him and he meant to jerk away. That he noticed. She was different. Quite different. In fact, for a few moments he wasn't sure if it were even her. Her ears were pointed, her eyes were now golden where once they were brown, even her facial features had morphed into someone who would have been unmistakably alien to him. His mind had tricked him somehow, he felt. It was a trap; some bit of Fae Magic that had cheated his mind, like Alfred and the Orc beneath the flooded fortress. Maybe she was some fell creature of the Sluagh, a Dearg Dhul, a vampyre drinking his blood, maybe he had never left the woods at all...

"It's me, Adi." she assured, grasping him tighter. "I promise." she fumbled for her pocket to show him the handful of change she'd given him two days before he'd left, so trivial a thing.

"Draw here by the Longing..." the woman tisked, striding up beside him. "Your attachment to her is unfortunate, Hyu'man. She has won your heart, just like the other ones." she looked upon the girl like some venomous creature, "I pity your loss. And hers I suppose." He allowed but a moment more before with another wave of his hand two gilded guards crossed spears between them and she was pulled away by the goading of the Valeyard's knife at her neck.

"Your friend is Unseelie." Said the Valeyard. "A spy, no doubt."

"Spy?"

"And what of this one?" He pointed at the boy with his own sword.

"He is safe." Was all Alfred said, and the Valeyard handed Adimus back the dire blade, leaving him holding it awkwardly while the boy dried his eyes.

"Want to bet on that, Alfred? How are you here?! Where is everyone?! Or did you have some Spell to jettison them too at the first opportunity?"

He shrugged off the afront. "Spacial Bilocation. You wouldn't understand. Yet. You needn't hurt your head with such things right now." The Valeyard gripped the wizard's arm with a worried look. "It's alright." Alfred answered him. "He doesn't understand the gravity of it all yet." The man that stepped into his view was the yellow cloak tuathan from his time at the Curio. "...I think he means 'why do your words hold such weight in the Kindly Court.' " he bantered at the seer.

Alfred took a deep breath as if to start a long winded explanation. "Uh... that perhaps is even more complicated."

"You will address the prince as his majesty when spoken too, seer." The Valeyard scolded.

"It's quite alright." The caped man assured with the wave of his hand. "He's more couth than I have wrath, though ever so little. Am I right?" He gave the sum seer an endearing smile.

"I understand he has no memory. Would it not be possible for him to be some Div or Stoneblooded, given the circumstances?" The woman said.

"What do you mean?" The yellow caped one asked.

"The Shakar Dahm may well have erased his memories and put him here."

"...But why? What good's a soldier with no memory of his objective?" Said the Valeyard

Alfred raised the boy's hand, showing the place where his blood was taken "I think maybe Lykil thought the same."

"Bounder's True Name." A new one, this one clad in a yellow cloak, playfully whispered into the boy.

"Milord," the Valeyard bowed to him, to which this 'lord' patted him on the head. "Good. So he's not a Devil. Does he see the Otherworld or the Isthmus when he closes his eyes?" he inquired...

"Well?"

"Well?"

Adimus had to point at himself to determine if someone was actually at last talking to him. "You mean the flat place or the..."

"The Realm Reposed. The one like yours, but full of nightmare-y stuff ."

"The Huntress, Adimus." He appeared to be introducing her, and he had no idea how the man knew his name. "She kills the nightmare-y stuff, among other things."

"Well?" The one called 'The Huntress' asked impatiently.

"I mean, closed. But..."

"See? He is from the One World. Or at least has been there long enough to consider it home." the warrior woman said.

"What is the meaning of all of this?! What is going on?!" he felt he had to say it or this would go on forever.

He was talking to Alfred again, but the prince replied, calmly, disregarding it as the outburst it was. "I myself do not know. And this troubles me, Adimus." The man in yellow said. "I know well the hearts of others, much more puzzled and complex hearts, labyrinthian with aeons more of scheming than yours or some simple yearling like hers but..." he ensured she'd been taken away. "I am running out of patience, which says much for one who endures such as I."

"What are you going to do with her?"

"Torture her with a thousand deaths if it would tell me what I wanted to know, but alas, Hyu'man--." The Huntress blustered, but was implored to silence by the simple raising of the yellow one's hand.

"She herself knows nothing." Adimus pleaded. The Grigor's face softened. He looked up at the prince in yellow. "What more can Fae Magic read that I could not tell you about her?" he flashed a smile of fondness, "She likes butter, and the sound of rain. To draw...her favorite color is green, and she wants to raise horses when she grows up."

"You lie, sir." she said. "She came here to Balfour only a few years ago."

"I meant..." he glanced at Alfred. "As long back as I can remember."

"Remember?" the Huntress's long ears perked.

"I mean," Perhaps it was the utter shock of seeing her as she was, or out of desperation, to potentially save all whom he loved--anything but his own self interest. "I don't remember."

The man's ears perked up. "Remember what?"

"Well, much of anything. From my childhood." he said.

"Intriguing." he said. "She told me as much, that you were both found only a few years back, wandering the forest with no memory as to where you've been or how you'd gotten there. Here, rest and be well Adimus, we've much to discuss."

The grove, they explained to him, was a haven from outside intrusion 'both physical and otherwise', they said. Bounder knew where it was, but anyone else wandering around out in the Isthmus as they called it, would have to blindly stumble upon it. They were Tuatha, and this Otherworld was their home before they came to the One World.

He'd heard the name in bedtime stories of course: those who came to the shores upon flying ships, burned them and refused to leave. Who took on Hyu'man Form as to not appear monstrous to them, marking themselves by their ears that they could identify their kin at a glance.

The yellow clad one was the Prince of Spring, who appeared as a man with long brown hair in wavy curls that seemed to move and sway unnaturally as if he were perhaps caught in a breeze that never touched anyone else's. He had pale skin and thin lips, his ears were tall and pointed, much like those of a wolf, or a cat, but still seeming Hyu'man; there were others who moved about the camp had more bestial features, the occasional pair of slitted eyes, antlers or a tail, but by and in large they appeared Hyu'man save for them. He was a sovereign of sorts that sat with them, in a large pavilion-like tent that appeared to be comprised of various seem together garments--gowns, dresses and like, actively being erected by creatures whom he'd mistaken for Lanternbeetles but were in fact Kindred of diminutive size, buzzing about on butterfly wings actively tending it with sewing needles that to them looked like swords.

"Much thanks, little ones." The Huntress told them when they were through, and he handed to them what appeared to be Hyu'man teeth as payment, sure to give them one each before they departed.

Inside, a pile of old things, a few ragged stuffed animals, a wagon wheel, and a busted copper pot sat ablaze, but the fire never touched them.

"So, Bounder was a spy? For who?"

"Yes, Adimus, for the Unseelie." The Valeyard answered. It was so strange how they knew and used his name with such ease.

"You are right. Again." Said Alfred. "Whoever she is, she's playing the long game, to be sure."

The Prince sat quietly, splaying his fingers together in thought.

"Fae do tend to," the Valeyard continued. "But I've never encountered one able to muster such complex schemes as these before. It would seem that Fate itself were on her side, pulling all the necessary strings to ensure the seemingly serendipitous events come to pass." The Valeyard stroked his goatee. "I've never seen Cunning like this before."

"For you to say that is troubling." The Huntress grimly said.

"I tell you, this could well be some wild chase. A diversion." the Prince said. "I can tell you with certainty that this has nothing to do with this Balfour. I've personally eavesdropped on its goings on for months now, and neither hushed whisper nor dream betrays them."

"So he's not a Devil..." The Valeyard observed. "One would think that would make things less complicated."

"He has strange visions, flashes. Though even you can't make sense of them from what I'm told of it. It could be some place outside the Realm of the Real for all we know."

"What am I?" He'd finally caught up to the conversation. It silenced the chatter. Only his seething breath could be heard. The Prince shot Alfred a wry smile that the boy caught. "Alfred. You tell me now. You don't want to tell me about you, that's fine. Tell me about me." The burn in his eyes even put the Valeyard at unease. "You Read me, when we first met. You brought me along with you, through all of this, as a curiosity, as your...little experiment!" He tore the coin from his neck. "If I'd been *here* this wouldn't have happened, so you tell me now!"

"Look what you've done." The Prince snickered; another joke that only he seemed to get.

"Adimus..." he took a long time to formulate his words, and the grave look on his face as he did bid the boy allow it "Whatever happens here I want you to remember, it could not be helped. There was never anything that could have been done."

He picked up the coin with his bare hand, and when he did shot him a curious, almost satisfied look.

"What do you mean?"

"She is to be given to the Queen, in exchange for your safety, and the safety of the village."

"Untrue." Said the Alfred. "We should fight for her. The Hyu'man king Cadifor is with them, with an army."

"Ah, now see? The Summer King has clearly overreacted. We didn't you and your Isha, much less the Named Wild Hunt! I can go home, he can have his Huntress back—she's quite busy this time of year I hear, and let us be on our way."

"Let us not be hasty." spoke the Valeyard, throwing up a hand. "He took the spear from you," he jabbed at Alfred "by force, if I remember."

"Once." was all he answered.

Adimus raised a brow at the revelation.

"This fight shall test his mettle, and if he survives then perhaps he is deserving of it, and deserving of the aid of our majesty." Said the Huntress.

"<u>Your</u> majesty." The Prince sneered. "The Nis could care less. I'm here because Many Names himself called on me. <u>That is all</u>."

"Well enough, I suppose." The faeth smiled.

The Prince gave a nod and stood. Then a big, mischievous grin fell on his face. It was like the day he saw him in the Curio.

"Are you ready to learn the ways of the Immortals?"

Adimus could not, with any part of himself, answer.

The prince pivoted. "...Can you use that bow?" He relieved him of it, and looked it over, somewhat impressed at its make.

"No..."

"Your legs and mouth, are they yours?"

"I...suppose?" The boy gave Alfred a confused look.

"Yet you use them deftly to walk and talk just the same, with such proficiency you don't even think about it. So will it be with this bow and horse." He pointed at the Huntress. "See it done."

The Valeyard looked at the Prince questioningly, and started to say something, but relented. "Huntress. You ride this evening to hunt the Questing Beast. Take <u>him</u> with you."

Alfred took a deep defeated sigh. He looked up at the boy once more, who gulped.

"Milord?" The Valeyard's shock rattled his voice. "Do you think that wise, to show this boy, this Cessair, what even your Nis are not privy to know."

"What it means, to be forever." The prince gave the boy a piercing stare.

The Huntress objected. "Never has a Hyu'man joined in the Wild Hunt. Never has—"

"--it been ordered around by the prince of goblyns and lost souls. Pray it is the least he asks." Was all the man in yellow said, then with the most teeth he'd ever seen in a grin and a finger wiggling gesture of dismissal the man was gone.

"Prepare yourself, young Adimus. We ride now."

Chapter 36

Blood and Stone

...A hand clasping a scepter, a free arm gripping hilt of whip, a hooved foot...a feathered wing; of what the sculptor had in mind to fashion no sane mind could tell, as elsewhile primordial ores and virgin unworked stone encumbered and concealed the otherwise perfect form; the sin of the being who struck down its maker before it had even finished being made that marred its flesh for all time.

His muted face was without a mouth or nose, nor any other defining feature save for a single sunken orifice where a right eye would be.

Crows buzzed around it like flies now, this semblance in mute repose of the once great king, its crevices serving as a rookery still where in ages past they feasted upon the carrion offered to the living idol. On its head was a crown fashioned of the antlers of a dozen cervine animals and the skulls of the greatest of men.

His immensity was difficult to grasp, as one might see a stormcloud from afar yet have no means to fathom its enormity, yet not be untouched by its shadow...such thoughts sending the mind into fits of vertigo and abyssal despair as it attempts to reconcile one's own smallness in contrast. He towered above, silent in the void of distance. Then the gaze of the dead, eyeless thing fell upon him, like the shining of a black sun, through time, through thought and fantasy, through him.

* * * * *

Alfred awoke in a cold sweat. He could still feel the sweltering of his blood, the quickening and blistering of his skin. The smell of his own burning flesh, even now, from the first and only time he had tried to Read the Spear of Fate. Wiping the sweat from his brow, Alfred Juminion stretched and peeked between the bars of the cage. He could hear the men accompanying him, the horses of the cavalrymen, the banter of the footmen, the clinking of their mail, and knew that they had grown heartily in number even over the past few days.
It was all hammered together by an experienced Shamabayan wainright, and purchased from the merchant lord who owned it.

The pants of the driver were dark blue, with a thirty-eight inch waistline, and the front left wheel or the carriage had been replaced recently, with a different type of wood than the rest of it. Maple perhaps. More importantly, it was built to transport dangerous criminals, notably those skilled in alchemy and thaumaturgy, that was not only ironclad but contained several layers of sublimated elements that were difficult to Solve, including pulvis solaris, greatly inhibiting any attempts to explosively Dissolve the walls or transmute.
It was the first day that the snow didn't turn everything into an indiscernible white blob, and from the craggy red rocks he spied from the barred windows he would wager a guess that they had made it to the base of the mountains of Ormond.
It had been several days since their capture, and one since the days he saw the snow-capped

houses of Adaire.

When the carriage stopped the door swung open "I was told to check on you. They said you were making a racket." said the shield maiden of whom he had been her charge.

"Just a dream."

She raised a concerned eyebrow, then slammed it in what he imagined (real or not) was a playful manner.

Her name was Gwyndol, Gwyn for short.

It wasn't the way he'd always imagined a prisoner being cared for. He had been treated well enough, enough to make him wonder why they had bothered keeping him at all. He was fed food he would be none surprised to find out were from Cadifor's personal larder, both at morning and night, and provided with enough blankets and clothing to work through the cold with little discomfort. And Gwyndol helped.

He'd not often that of things of that sort, but she was beautiful to look upon, with silky scarlet hair and piercing emerald eyes, on first sight she thought she looked familiar, but he didn't think he could forget a face like that, not just beautiful from a primitive notion of symmetries and the like, but for the expressions and sentiments it held. Flirty, mysterious, authentic, none were like it (though with a back to his wall Tirlag and Laina were pretty close).

He shook the thought from his head, the fogginess of wakefulness already starting to tear at him.

He'd felt that they'd stopped. He heard the jostling of the door as it was being unlocked. It was the first time that it hadn't been during one of these feedings. Bewildered, thoughts flitted in his mind. *What it could be? Questioning? Torture?* The terror-gripping thought suddenly erupted in him. *Execution?* Maybe the good treatment was a mercy to ease their final days.

He was motioned out, not being bothered to hear what the guard had said.

The light was blinding. After a few moments of eyes adjusting he could see the wagons and carriages whereupon Alfred and the others had been kept, but could not see them through the hoards of soldiers and militiamen which overflowed the small vale.

"The King wishes you to observe the majesty of the gift you have bestowed upon the Land of the Steward Princes."

He handed the spear with great pomp and grace to Caleb Knolls, who with a bow took it from him. And carried with him a bowl of blood. Anyone standing nearby could hear the grinding of the wizard's teeth. The words he spoke were the language of All Creation, which all heard, and understood.

"I bind thee in covenant with these bloods three. Of Many Shapes, life he gave thee,
of Sreng the Slayer of the 300 bold, who molded you warrior in the kiln of old.
Last I give this, the Matchless Gift to the stone, to gods sweeter than honey, I give blood mine own.
These, by your creator's you shall have the body to move, and by your makers a Purpose to prove,
and by mine you shall do as my will and act, now Harken, Quicken, Awaken from this dream of black!
Warrior! Orculli! Gird thine arm for conflict, nerve thy heart to meet, to serve in profit or ruin, death, glory, victory, defeat!"

Nothing happened at first. Silence. Deathly silence. Then, as if the ground itself beneath their feet answered, the earth trembled, sending a cascade of rocks from the shelves above, and from the beast a red glow issued, as of the smoldering of a crucible of molten iron, and the stone without--but the impure dross--chipped and flaked away, as in the next minutes the eyes of the face of the statue, frozen in grimace for millenium fell upon the old man and showing dismay, and it's mouth spoke its first words.

"Tethra!! Tethra!? Argh! Light, Blinding! You summon the very day! Black Magic, Dark Magic!" Then she looked down.

"Good day." Cadifor's voice was calm and commanding.

"Wha?! Humph. Escaped. Mmm." The beast searched its head. "Me lose. Again. But it is alright. I learn. I learn. That makes me mighty, this, they say of me." She seemed to say to herself, turned to look at him almost as an afterthought.

"You speak our tongue." He said in disbelief.

"Yes. I can speak with the little Hyu'mans, the Shakar's drink teaches me." She looked around at all of them. "You are big little army. Ha! You are Bres, then!"

"No. No, I know not of what you speak. I am the one that gave you life."

"You?"

She looked about, then down.

"A Cessair cannot Return the Blood to the Stone."

"Hyu'man only in appearance, my lady. I am Cadifor, the Unavailed Knight, Chosen of Slaine."

"Un...availed? Ha! What that mean?"

"I can die neither by age or ailment, and have never been bested in battle."

"I am this word too! Un-availed. tThat is what makes me mighty, this, they say of me."

"Well met, Lady Emberleigh of the Orculli. We are very much alike, it seems."

"The one who sent me said that he was Immortal too. He died. All of you, too soon. Die too soon...no time to miss being dead. But you <u>are</u> different. I smell Blood From Stone on you. You are old, you tell truth."

"Blood From the Stone? You speak of The God of Many Shapes." Cadifor nodded in understanding, as did the beast. "The Gift was given to me as well. If only for a brief moment. But it has blessed me all these years. Bathed in the waters of Slaine, have I. Risen from death was I. I bathed in it, and from the moment its waters touched my lips, I have neither aged nor grown frail."

"Slaine? Many died at Slaine to save the Cessair. Honorable Cessair. Mighty Cessair. But Emberleigh is not some bull-brained Domnan! Cessair problems are cessair problems!" she pointed to her chest with her thumb. "This one does as she wills. You are not Bres, I will wait for him." she huffed, and with that she sat down.

"Nay. I have awakened you today, and you shall follow me into battle, to my aid!"

The creature's belly shook with laughter. "Bahaha! You are not immortal, the Great Well makes you like me! You will still die when I tear your head off!" the great beast's tail whipped with frustration.

"I know of your kind as a cause of it, Emberleigh, I know of the Bolg! You are right, they are not like the immortals. The shores of Mag Mell do not wash away your tears with the bliss of an after, nor do you face a fate for your folly in any life beyond this one." His face grew stern. "You are like myself but for this blood. The blood is the life: once it is gone, sleep forever, dreamless and dark, is all that awaits you elsewise."

"Bahaha!"

"You laugh? Is this not said of your people? Your people even say it of us! We were made from the great tree and given life in much the same way, by the blood spilled of the gods! Therefore there was nothing for you before you were, and thereafter there is nothing! Only a ceaseless black!"

But the laugh grew. The entire chasm reverberated with her snorting jeer. "You no understand at all!"

"Even now, the last Fir Bolg journeys to find the Greatest Grace, the blood that was spilt and spoiled. The blood of Many Shapes is spent. Never again shall this be done!" he turned the bowl upside down and spilt the last settling drops of it on the ground. "This does not vex you, move you to act?!"

Finally the rumble ceased, the beast wiped a tear from her eye, and her face grew as fierce as it had been frozen for so long. "Then I must go now. Find Tethra. Slay Tethra. Then others will say that Embraleigh unavailed like you." She got up, and turned to leave, and when he did he pushed the spear to bar her path.

The creature's eyes lit up.

"Yes. Behold." He shook the spear at her.

"Murdering thief..." Tirlag began to speak up, but Alfred's eye of warning stopped him, but none cared or heeded much for the outburst, least of all her.

"Follow me, giant, for only I have the saving Grace. Defend me and your victories will be ever sweet. Serve me and death will never touch you!"

"The Seventh Shard! Horn of Anunda!" It muttered what seemed as a curse. "Hofou's Head, you have it! A Hyu'man has it!" With that she crumpled to her knees, prostrating. "Oh mighty of the cessair, holder of Velskanda, the blade that slew the Lord of Beasts! Immortals meet their end with your venoms, scepter of Three Kindly Folk. It yours! I will follow, it is my Purpose!"

He nodded. "Very well. Now stand tall, Orculli, steel thyself, for you are immortal same as I: in name only. No second chances, no life beyond this breath. Now use it to serve!"

Alfred and the others, before they were loaded back into them, gave glances and gestures of goodwill to one another. What lay in store for them none among them could tell, nor did they know if they would ever be seen together again. He saw Tirlag's sullen eyes, and Alara's graven concern; for him, the nightmare did not end at waking, and free air did not vanquish his solace.

Thereupon, at the departing of the wagons, they would be carried south. *To Kainden.*

Chapter 37

A Lament for the Questing Beast

"These men search for the Questing Beast, for only its flesh will quell, the quivering pits of their stomachs, burning like the fires of Hell." And though it was not the sport of the day it was always on their minds, and the sentiment would be echoed by her and they in kind.

Its cunning but matched by its swiftness and its preposterous shape: a leopard's skin, cervine flanks, its head and neck a snake. And might one think it be insane, so mad a sight to see, then try to catch one; its elusiveness surpasses these all three.

The Hunt rode 'cross the Isthmus fair, no care they did abide, each careful trot a horse's gallop, each gallop a horse's ride. The boy felt sick to the think of it--he'd long lost track of time, he pondered a night to allow such feats, but no answer would oblige.

"You there." She told the old man, with speed that would amaze "Are you lost, child? Come hither." he didn't escape her gaze. He protested, as one might, but just the same he joined the strange procession of peoples and creatures whose choice they had purloined.

"Some will plead," she explained "or lure with song and dance, or promises of wealth untold, or whispers of romantic, but if that fails it falls on us who march in column and row. Beware the Wild Hunt my boy, or into the ranks you'll go."

One laid dead by an old dirt road resting in his grave. "Dig him up and shake him off, his debt is yet unpaid." And so he marched with the rest of them, another restless Dead, though they would have to lead him, for they could not find his head.

Goblyns, Tuatha, Sanziana, changeling children too, even the elusive Leprechaun of whom they'd nabbed a few. None escaped the Huntress, of her reputation it is said, that even though it preceded her, she'd caught it before it had fled.

Even then the Questing Beast still could not be found, whose confounding tracks befuddled, whose scent confused her hounds.

A mujina, a badger man, a marlu, kangaroo, a shigaag skunk, and many more boggarts they caught 'fore they were through; A wayward stoat out for a smoke had barely lit her match, her pipe in paw she took a draw and before she exhaled was snatched. The furry fir durrig, a cautious rat who hid in a house in Adaire, had fortuitously gone out to fetch a drink, and was surprised to find them there. Swiftly they sprang out from the well, dragging him below. This one they carried, kicking and screaming, on a spit for show.

A busy Maythe of the gnemedian race recorded their names in kind, to report to the court of the Gentle Folk that they had done their time, for the Fae forbid such writing, but for such urisks it is fine; 'tis better sometimes to jot it down than wax of it in rhyme, but of these deeds performed this night, not of this it's said, of the Huntress's ride, her merry crew, this army that she'd fed. For when they'd thought they'd caught them and were taking them to the shore, that is when the Questing Beast let out his taunting roar. And laughing in play he bounced away escaping—or so he'd thought, but caught the doom of the flying arrow the boy had shot.

The boy then stood aback, abashed, when the beast cried out; he was noticeably disheartened when its voice did shout.

"Oh, the horror, oh, the pain, have mercy you have won! I perish today, dead forever, by this deed you've done!"

They butchered the meats and near the beach and a great blaze they did start, choice cuts were fed to the soldiers, and to the champion went the heart.

They held a mighty feast of him, as on his flesh they supped, and when they'd finally finished, its skin and bones they dumped.

There was a somber air about that no one could deny, for outwardly the boy stood proud, yet in his heart he cried.

That's when I, the Prince of Spring, saw his forlorn face, and showed him that those we captured now trode with helpless haste,

To Mag Mell, the lands beyond, its milky sea of brine; for as the year tires a thing transpires, only time to time.

"The Seelie send their psychopomps to collect their own, an act that is a courtesy; it is dangerous to go alone.

Like the drive of a dying thing, its need to find seclusion, ever so often we the Fae will Long for this conclusion,

To find that thing which lies beyond where shade and light reside, to seek the shores of Hy Brasil, so we may come to die...

And just then the boy's lamenting sorrow did subside, as right before him the Questing Beast stood and was revived,

"Well, that was fun." It chuckled, shaking off the sand, and with a hop it bounded off "Now catch me if you can!"

I bowed and gave a smile and continuing dismissed all the Cunning others, bearing new faces and Gifts,

"Our bodies churn away to dust as we seek these lands, then one akin to the one who died emerges from the sands.

Elders say we come from here, this vast and starry shore, and claim to us that it has happened many times before...

Tuatha state it as a fact, 'often I've came and went', but then I say to their dismay that it's irrelevant;

one's own birth is past approach, as is one's death for sure—I've no idea if I've <u>ever</u> been here, much less times before;

it is only what happens between these times to which I can attest, 'twould be fruitless to speculate or to anything profess.

But here, before this world so wide and this small thing called time, on the shores of what transcends the written, sung, or rhymed, let me tell you this my boy: when standing on this spot before its breadth and majesty...I say I doubt it not."

Chapter 38
The Darkest Night

It started with the scouting of the quarry by glazen-eyed dullahans, emerging from whatever esoteric caverns in the Crossroads of Dusk that served as their road, tossing their ghoulish heads above the treelines in grotesque pageantry. Drums sounded down into the valley, raucous and jubilant, yipps and howls and gibberish cries echoed in the hills of Balfour: The Darkest Night had come.

The ones with bodies arranged them in column and row. Arrayed upon the fields were gaunt skeletal figures with bows. Meatier ones served as infantry, corpses upon which frigid rime clung as armor, their faces frozen in permafrost grimace. Goblyns, the Forms of twisted changeling babes, cackled and blew their trumpets. Boggarts, Kindred scarred with the traits of ferocious beasts: badgers, tigers, snakes, rats, lurked in the shadows, poised to strike and skirmish against the weak. Cloaked figures hovered in the treelines, each held aloft by a dozen burning candles, their flames uplifting them with the grace of some esoteric craft, pulled along by Yeth, the Headless Hounds of the Rathlands.

Their cavalry were the Dai'ari. Sharp of ear and of fang, the shadetouched hoards of the Deep, eyes black as inkpots from the corruption that devoured but never availed their eternal sparks of immortality, their skin pale as the snow atop which their dark steeds danced. They sat atop threshwraiths, skeletal horse-like creatures from the dream dunes beyond the Obsidian City, barded with the feathers of crows and metals worked to resemble beaks. Most remained on the ground, their flails and arming swords and lances ready for the carnage, while some scoured in the skies, pulled by chariots, their antlered silhouettes seen in the mist as they circled overhead.

Worse though than they were the assembly of the Sluagh. Death Shades or Shadow Men they were called, They at first hid their numbers and encroached in stealth. Now they flirted with the bonfires, brazenly flitting across the undisturbed snow all about the camp like sharks ready to frenzy, clamoring for the sounding horn, as they were bidden only with the strongest binding Magic to be free in the land of the living for just one night.

All of the forest, every tree and shrub Adimus and Dyrshul had played around in their youth had been shorn to prevent their concealment, and to build the immense bonfires that would serve as the village's only defense against the unliving hordes. Cadifor's men stood abreast between them in groups of six, a dozen of such perhaps, including in its ranks the fit to fight denizens of Balfour: Bearach, Eichgun. Had he the time he'd admitted he would have the hamlet evacuated to a more defensible place, or abandoned altogether; even for those courageous as the lords of Ormond, when the Damned made war such concessions were small prices to pay.

Cadifor himself would take up arms and fight with the cavalry, donning his family's plated mail and riding a heavy horse, leaving bare instructions to Reeve McConelly, with his newly elected page Gavin to route messages and instruction signalers in changes to tactics.

They had trained in the intervening weeks, drilling and conditioning the useful and able of them, and from their makeshift redoubt, the Green Beat, reinstated as a stronghold like times of old, would survey the field from the safety of archers and longspears.

Each unit had men amongst their pikemen who wielded a long brand, a blazing wooden pole covered in oil-soaked linens, and footmen bearing polished bronze round shields to reflect the light. Where fortunate there was one true weapon of Cold Iron, or of Silver, as the ranks of the Unseelie may be hindered by either according to their kith. They all stood shakily, their fearful breaths misting in the cold, mocked by the stillness of the unmoving assembly of their host.

Standing at the fore was the Orculli warrior, Embraleigh, who herself was a beacon to bolster and rally behind. Each side clammored and postured, ready for the fight to come.

Then the final horn came forth, that horn of which none in the mortal ranks would know its doom, wrested from the head of some great Devil with which they had quarreled and defeated. For unbeknowst to the mortals even Devils were of this world, and despite being tempters and deceivers and corrupters of the hearts of men still shunned the nothingness. Then the horn blew its bellowing cry and the multitudes rallied and were upon them.

The Sluagh were deployed first, as the horn was yet blowing, not from the command of any tactical mind, but out of a failure to wrest and keep control of them.

"Burn like the eye of the morning!" The Orculli Embraleigh had blessed the blazing bonfires, spilling a drop of her blood on them, chanting prayers in Bolg over them. Whether it was all in their imaginations or the sealing of some Spell upon them the bonfires glew as white hot beacons for them--the men who fought between them were safe, their shadows never touching, which concealed their shadows behind them, and left a gap that whenever overstepped it could be solved with a brand. At first, the men were bolstered at how easily these creatures were thwarted by simple flame; their alien bodies cast upon the ground burned like oil when touched directly, quickly flitting out of existence in a wisp of putrid smoke, but then the first of them were touched. The first of them were left contorted in pain and terror, their voices utterances fading into supernatural silence; the first of them excuded a black issue through unseen cuts and through orifices, through eyes and mouths, and then the the gruesome black ichor that remained swallowed the first of them up into nothingness, leaving only their shadow, only to them challenge those whip remained.

Then the hoards engaged. Their ferocity was unmatched. They fought with no heed, none of that that would cause a mortal to hesitate, that which caused the boy's legs to shake. And the men, having been accustomed to such concessions, at least enough to catch one's breath, found themselves routing against the endless onslaught.

Calcinations of Spellfire crackled from the ether, lighting the site in the eldritch glow of colors. The smell of cinders from the blazing fires mingled in the crisp air with the smell of rotting flesh and hot blood.

Cadifor's companion, the Orculli giant, glowed as if ablaze in the moonslight, and no Shade dared draw near, and many of the frozen Damned she slew herself, her axe head felling great swaths as of the reaping of a scythe.

But the Shades were swifter than shadows, and Cadifor found himself stretched to keep the shields steady and the skirmishers fiery, and the great giant grew more hesitant as even meager stretches drew the Greatest Grace from her veins.

Cadifor spoke. "Give them your worst, men! Fear not Death, fear dishonor, for far worse it is! The halls of Hy Brasil recount not the lives of cowards. But to stand today and face this hoard, when the Mistress churns our lives to dust and sieves the dross in her cauldron what gold she shall find! Fight, Men of the Mounds, fight!"

And when he's spoken these words, Cadifor, Slayer of Corthanach, wielder of Gram, harkened still.

The bursting blinding light, as if all the fires burned their fuel all in a single go, burning and banishing the darkness, and to his bewildering astonishment he watched as the men threw down their polished shields as if they burned, and when they did they became glowing pools of light from which shadows emerged, one after the other.

Large and small, short or tall, Hyu'man or beast, they all fell in.

"Your virtue is proven, Cadifor." The voice of the Valeyard came. "The Prince of Spring sends his aid."

Rejuvenated, his resolve renewed, Cadifor rallied his men to the banner of the thorn-entangle eye.

* * * * *

The Fae Kind, hosts of Tuatha and Shii, beat their armor and clattered their shields with the same fever that seemed to infect their foes, meeting them with every bit of ferocity one who knew that they could not truly die might have.

Cavalry of the clans of Pembroke formed ranks and rode. Where before they were hampered, now they could meet their enemies.

Eichgun Lathern held them steady as best he could, but still more of them had come, and when a spooked horse carrying what was naught but an empty suit of armor braced astride by a war saddle rolled through their midst his men began to panic and rout, and Eichgun, caught alone was run upon by a rider on a threshbeast.

"Eichgun!" The boy's voice came, all too late. The lance wheeled him from his horse, bearing him to the ground. There was no hope for him.

The Dai'Ari warrior turned with a preternatural quickness that in the Deep this beast was known for. The Dai'ari's gaze fell upon Adimus, his eyes like black pearls, his black hair writhing in the night air. It hissed and stuck out its long tongue in an intimidating show, but snapped to alertness when an arrow skirted past him.

"Damn!" The boy spat.

Aethan wasn't a war horse, far from it. He steered with his legs, wheeling him around while he nocked another arrow in his short bow. This one hit dead on, then the next, then by the third the rider had slumped and he would only need to lead Aethan aside.

When he looked around, like a scattering raindrop, the chaos had broken into small skirmishes.

Then he saw the bright yellow cloak, and accompanying the Prince was Bearch, Luloch and Alfred.

"Adimus, you're with us." He said, but Adimus was already making his way off his horse to greet them.

They hesitated, this one's shivering vacant stare shone plainly across his blood splayed face and his father, wet with sweat even in the frost, but on drawing close they shared warm sentiments in the depths of the dread all the brighter still.

Horns sounded, and the units shifted and re-arranged to meet one another. Massive creatures of ice breached the palisades around the Green Beat, the hole filled with shields and pikes to buttress against them. Embraleigh faced down the beast in a wrestling match.

Skirmishers were sent after the archers to find where they perched, and the cavalry to pincer them. Cadifor rode hard on his horse to wheel around behind the wall, the hooves of his great barded horses stamping at them, and Gram singing in the winter wind. The Huntress and several of her choice bowmen straddled the ramparts and rained down upon them. Finally the dispersed.

Cadifor the Unavailed cried out. "You see now, men! Reward comes to the virtuous! The steadfast! The dutiful! Blessed be the children of Many Shapes, fair!" he cried to his men. "Now strike!" he cried, and led the charge back into the fray.

Just then a figure appeared from the darkness.

It strode through the debris and corpses left before it with a practiced swiftness and calm, removed from the chaos, somehow above it, at home dwelling in its depths. Adimus was no stranger now to the attitude that some immortal kindred seemed to hold, the seeming effect of the weary numbness brought on by age and experience that bred such jaded apathy and aloofness in the midst of even incomprehensible such carnage, but the sight of it on the face of someone he had trusted with a heart, someone he knew (or thought he had) disturbed him just the same. Her milk and charcoal face was streaked with the blood of the men she'd felled. Her wild curls of red dusted with snowflakes that no longer melted. With unparched lips Oinde let out a craven roar, and the sound that issued was that of a pride of wolf roaring in unison.

"Gwyndol!" Cadifor's voice shook, then became steel-hard. "Another betraying kinsmen! Fiend of the Blossom Bride! Perish!" His eyes were just as fierce.

She gave not even a wince at the boy's arrow in her back, which smoked and smoldered with a Magic which ignited her flesh like kindling. Adimus took a few steps forward and drew again. The Huntress moved to intercept, but Cadifor waved her stay her hand. Then Oinde charged.

He hurled his lancea at her, but like every other projectile it did little; the boy knew, beneath the deceiving bark which comprised her supple skin was wood and sinew like the hardest iron.

Gram sung feebly against her flesh as her twin blades came for his guts and he swatted at them, but like a lioness she pounced, with her weight reeling him backwards with enough force to rend the saddleback, and she and he tumbled from his horse.

Dashed to the ground, she straddled him, and pinning his shield against him she wedged one of the rondells beneath his gorget. Then it was over.

Adimus would arrive too late, he would find him a few moments later, his shield riven, his bones crushed, along with the hopes of all the men upon the field.

"O life that ebbs like the sea

I am weary and old, I am weary and old

Oh how can I happy be

All alone in the dark and cold

I'm the old Beira again

My mantle no longer is green

I think of my beauty with pain

And days when another was Queen.

My arms are withered and thin, my hair once golden is grey

Tis winter my reign doth begin

Youth's summer has faded away

Youth's summer and autumn have fled

I am weary and old, I am weary and old

Every flower must fade and fall dead

When the winds blow cold

When the winds blow cold."

Chapter 39

The Bonemother's Heir

That it was the axe of Embraleigh that bore down upon her, a creature full double her size that gave her pause. The low, scything sweep sent her hurling backwards, removing her from the ground.

She quickly redoubled back to her feet just the same. She looked down. The blow was enough to leave a great gash across her chest.

Just as it took many strokes from a woodman's axe, not just one to fell a mighty tree, her face twisted more in anger than pain. With her free hand she scraped from the wound a black ichor. She smoothed it onto the blade and with a menacing grin, before wheeling toward the great warrior. "Not even the Blood of Parthos can evade my venoms, orc!" she spat.

The springing speed of her woody sinew was like a striking snake, firing her at Embraleigh, allowing her to evade the orc's weapon with ease.

Before the warrior could respond the huldra had landed on the orculli, burying the rondall deep into her arm.

"Gggrraaahhh!" Embraleigh gnashed and growled. She grabbed her about her slender waist, and, hefting her up over the shoulder hurled her with all her might. Oinde tumbled heel over head several times, bounced like a stone skimmed across the pond, each time slamming a divot into the hard ground. She skidded to a stop on her feet, facing her opponent.

Just then an arrow caught her. She looked down at it and twisted her face. "Lord Adimus." she mocked in her feigned fawn voice. "And I thought we were getting on so well."

The Grigor stepped up beside the orc, and gave a stern nod of acknowledgement when she looked down at him.

Oinde started pacing forward again.

"Stop!" a booming voice. Came from the ranks of the unseelie. The huldra, looking most disappointed, took a step back. Just then a signal horn sounded, and as if its roar stirred the very wind, a blustering torrent cut through them, and snow began to blanket the battlesight once more, and in blinding haze of snowflakes she was gone.

* * * * *

The furthermost footmen hadn't seen him until he had drifted past; his horse had blended in with the blizzard and its footfalls were as silent as snowflakes.

His scale was of the finest of unslaked iron, Lunarium, made only by All'khemy, and was fashioned to appear as the feathers of a crow, familiar to him in Nature as to not harm his Form. His pauldrons and shoulders bore real feathers, and the armet of his beaked helmet held long plumes, as if perhaps in the Deep one might find a bird of carrion that flaunted such feathers with the flamboyance of a peacock or bird of paradise. His steed left no tracks, and bore an oriflamme which failed to waver in the buffeting chill, bearing a blazon that had not been seen by Hyu'man eyes since the Epochellipse: a crow perched astride a black chain on a chevron of red, haloed with blue roses. He carried with him a shield, marked with much the same in escutcheon, with a sheathed sword and a fluted lance which he held in rest.

"The raven knight." Adimus was helpless to stop the words leaving his lips.

Surely, it was that the host of them knew the dread that then lay upon them, for they had sent forth their messenger before even all of his men had heard it said.

The voice which emerged from him transcended the rattle of all the men assembled and the crackle of the fires and even the armament which encased his face, to make it so he spoke plainly and intimately beside each of them.

"Cessair of the Lathnim, I will treat with your living leaders. Bring them forth. I will not ask again."

The prince glanced over at Adimus, then hid his face conspicuously before sidling off into the crowd.

"You know <u>my</u> Name, Warden." Bellowed the Huntress. "Treat with me."

"Hacklebaroness! A fool's errand it is for the Erlking to meddle with the affairs of the Unseelie Court. What has the sun to say to the dead of night, when its time is well over and its rays could never reach?"

"It would ask, fittingly: what affairs does the slumbering damned have in the world above the mounds?"

At that the messenger said nothing. The Huntress pressed, "We have uncovered your agents, the family of Bran and their plot to gain the Kainspear, to rule the Hyu'man kingdom of Ormond.

"Be still your tongue, Huntmaster. Lest the true incompetence of the Seelie Court be demonstrated to its greatest foe." His horse reacted to his grip on the reins, though impatience never touched his voice. *"We know not of which you speak."*

The Huntress huffed, and as if she herself struggled with it, sheathed her blade. "Emough. The hero of Slaine has fallen. I will speak in his stead, such that it is." SheSay your peace."

The messenger straightened. *"Very well. I am Malacasta, Champion of the Rozen Court, High Warden of Tantlyn, Chancellor and Retainer of Beira, Matron of Frost, and her inheritors. Hear now the edict put forth by the Keeper of the False Flame, her majesty:"* his gaze was unblinking as it fell upon them each. *"return to us the heir who was stolen, and deliver to us her captor, the one you call Luloch. Do this and your plight shall cease. Do this and your mortal lives shall be spared. Do it not, and not even death will save you from us. You have one hour."*

"Luloch? Luloch Buckroy?"

"Who is that?"

"Is he from your village?"

"Here." The Prince of Spring popped up again. With him were the Buckroys, all but Dyrshul. "Right here. Are we ready folks?" he put his hands together. The Huntress fell in with them. The great stone warrior sat cross-legged in the snow. He turned to the wounded Embraleigh. "Orculli, would you fain to be our escort? Can you yet swing that axe should things turn sour?" Slowly she lifted herself to. She gave an odd chuckle "If Embraleigh has time. Embraleigh is dying." "Oh. Unfortunate."

"No. Not problem." She nodded and heaved herself to her feet.

"We'll be done well before it's time to pop off, for sure. Thank you." He said as she joined them.

The crowd parted around them. Adimus caught the gaze of several of his neighbors among them, heavy with judgment and scorn.

Nothing was ever going to be the same, this Adimus knew, and he lamented his inability to accept that he had somehow always known this.

They began their long ascension of slope, treading the barren remnants of the forest clearing.

In a hushed tone, the prince began to speak. "She is to...abdicate, Adimus. The Queen. The one whom you call Dyrshul is the sole and rightful heir to the throne." He seemed to be trying to explain, for what it was worth. It sounded solemn.

"You mortals may yet be spared, by this man's graces." he motioned at the prince. *"By making these things as they should be."*

The Prince froze in his tracks.

Malacasta turned. *"Your words betray you, Sovereign of the Dawn. Yes. I know it is you. All Tuatha have this Gift, not just the Sworn. Many faces you have changed, but the winds hide no secrets, and upon it the voice speaks to me, the voice of the Prince of Spring."*

The Tuathan prince shrank, as if now he was the child caught with his hand in the cookie jar.

"...As they should be?" echoed Adimus. "Grandpa, what's this all about?"

"Follow me."

The snow had ceased, and the clouds parted a little, casting a lurid light across the yards of bodies and the bulk of the Queen's armies.

They were led through the rabble. Nissies and Shades and all manner nameless horrid beast parted and yielded to the knight and his party and their journey up, up the mountain. "The Winter Queen is, by necessity, actually quite goodly and pure." The Prince explained unconvincingly to him. It came out like a hasty lesson, a casual and unaesthetic attempt to bring up to speed others who were already far behind, one which left much to be desired, but he pressed on, "Her court is the realm of the Damned; those Immortals too vile to be given new life. And so she sentences the Ardfrost upon them."

"Ardfrost?" said Adimus. He'd heard Alfred use the word before.

He answered. "The amulet she bears is Brisengamen, the First Shard, and within it is carried the darkest evil in the Two Worlds, the False Flame, and, some say, the dread being to whom it belonged, imprisoned within by a Spell spoken at the beginning of time."

"Some say? How many people were there at the beginning of time to confirm that?" Luloch, the old curmudgeon's wit only ever outdone by his lip.

"Well, just one before, and many after." It was a confusing answer. "And enough that their memory of the ordeal is fuzzy, I suppose."

"I know a Spell that can invoke it, is all." said Alfred, noticing the boy's acknowledgement.

"The Ardfrost is its indirect power felt upon this world, as is the power Shades wield; the foul muted radiance of what lies within it."

"You act as if you know this Prince and this man." Bearach questioned the boy; he apparently didn't even recognize Alfred.

"It's a long story." his son answered.

A creature hopped out of a tree and landed before them. *The Werewolf.* Adimus's his blood ran cold. The one from the dream. Those eyes, now made real. He jumped and drew his blade. *Not this time.* But this beast of dread from his nightmares, this werewolf, threw up his hands.

"There you are." Said the Prince. "Brindle, how are we?"

"Fair, considering." He snarled.

"You!' said Luloch in wonder. "You're the...thing from my dreams!" He deliriously prattled to Bearach. "He's the one who told me about Sluagh Oiche."

The strange creature bowed.

"Oh, we've met." said Adimus.

"It is a Gift unique to their Kind. And quite useful for espionage." The Prince explained. "Adimus, meet Brindle, a mole who is a dog." he joked.

"We've met." Brindle gave a toothy grin.

"What are you? A werewolf?"

"I should be asking you the same thing. What was that thing? The machine in your dream that made the noise."

"A car." He didn't know how or why or what is was he'd just said, much less how he knew it.

The Prince cut the tension with a laugh. "Let me guess, the old 'scare them awake' bit, Eh? Did you get caught peeping?"

Brindle scratched his head awkwardly. The Prince turned his head more seriously.

"I am of the Cynocephali, the Cuar Shii. Werewolves are a myth."

"A Dreamspeaker." Merris elaborated.

"With a bit more truth in it than others." the Prince said. He quickly changed the subject to something more grim, "You didn't get caught by them too, did you?" he gestured toward the hoard. He seemed unphased that Malacasta heard him.

"No. But this will cost you dearly, King of the Nis. My men have been taxed to their limit, and several more put in a pinch trying to suss out this Mother business."

"You can pull the teeth of every slain man and Fae if it helps.'

"I'm not after gormling plunder, Prince, I want my due."

"We'll talk when this is over." He was disinterested in the conversation now, pulling a strange device on a chain from his pocket and gazing at it.

After a few moments, Adimus felt a tug on his cloak. It was Bearach, who pulled him until they were sure they'd fallen behind. "Is *he* goodly?" he shot eyes at the back of the Prince's head. "What's his plan, eh? Dyrshul. He's not really going to...?"

But Adimus couldn't answer. "I trust him. I think."

"I'll not stand idly by, your friend or no." he whispered. "If anything happens to her--."

"--It'll only be your father's fault. " Brindle caught them off guard hearing them far from what they'd thought was earshot--they'd underestimated his senses.

"My fault?" said Bearach.

"Not <u>your</u> father." The Cuarn Shii's cold eyes locked onto the boy's. "HIs." His stare fell on Bearach. They each looked over its shoulder at Luloch. "It's true." the wolf chided.

They began to question, but they had found themselves in company.

The seat upon which she rested sat atop a royal palanquin, lifted and hauled by creatures Adimus would recognize as Labori, save they were made from ice tinged with swirls of blood.

She would have been beautiful in her day, a raven-haired, blue eyed, milken skinned maiden beyond compare, but the old queen, her face was scorched by rime, her ebony hair imprisoned in glacial scales that crawled skyward to hang in the air a solid mass. She sat haggardly in her chair, not so much as moving when they approached.

The Queen of Winter sat upon slopes of the broken mountain, whose name was forgotten, upon her palanquin.

She had an attendant with her, comely and sparsely clothed, who muttered comforting platitudes to her and soothing sentiments as adjusted a linen shroud which covered all but her highness's head, concealing what appeared some terrible growth on the sovereign's back. When they drew close the attendant hid her face with a folding fan, her pipped tail darting flirtily to and fro in the wind.

She stepped aside at his simple stern gaze, showing that he'd gotten the queen's attention.

"Hail and long live the Matron of Frosts, greater and fairest and wisest of the Four Sovereigns! Whose fire even now banishes the Flame, whose inner light avails the deepest shadows! Long be your reign…"

The Huntress glowered at him. "You besmirch the name of the Summer King, kowtowing and placating this Unseelie menace! Enough with the games and politics, she's come to fight!"

"Hacklebaroness Gowdan. It has been long years." The Queen greeted in kind.

"You will hold your tongue," she begged the Huntress. "I meant every word." He turned to the queen of monsters. "Holda. My Holda. Where has the fire that burned away the sadness of this dreary world gone?"

"Prince of cowards, prince of misfits, to whom do I owe the pleasure? "

He answered. "You have changed. As if you can't already see that. I've come to help you."

"You are a meddler and interloper, with naught but your own machinations in mind. I see through you, Prince of Rags! "

"I *want* to help. Believe in me."

"Like you did when you talked me into becoming a martyr for the Fae Court?"

His sentimental face grew cross. "Martyr?" He sneered. "Perhaps it is your vainglory that causes you so much pain of late. Do not act like you haven't enjoyed the power that comes with being the Keeper of the Ardfrost."

"You pass judgment?! On me?!"

"I'm trying. To be your guide once more. I pray your heart is not too hard to listen."

"Only so that I may leave this place and get back to work on your behalf! You trivialize how much I have sacrificed!" her voice grew shrill. "I was perfect, you said! It is why you chose me. Now look, gaze upon what your 'guidance' has wrought!" she said, and casting off the shroud they could see the malignancy in full: she was frozen to the throne. Around her neck was the amulet, Brisengaman, and radiating out from it was a single growth of ice, like a corkscrew, which penetrated her chest and through the other side of her back, pinning her there.

"It has taken an age to muster the courage to speak these words, but let it be known that <u>sins of others should not be the burden of the innocent</u>. One should not be made to suffer for their benefit. I've not come for the child, Prince. I've come to be free of this fate."

"Free of this fate?" the Prince mocked.

"I have served this post for lifetimes, lived until this thing has all but devoured me, this sliver of ice is in my heart for you!" And with that she reached out her hand to her attendant, and we and with wincing tugging lurch the ice shattered and she climbed to her feet. "I deserve recompense!" Her face softened "Take this pain from me I beg of you! End my torment, it is all I want."

"The power that allows you to keep the Shard safe is waning, and your courtly council is a wolf waiting in the wing to strike." he gave an assessment. "You are tired. I understand that more than most. But others don't need to suffer because you falter in your duties."

"We all fail, eventually, but only I have the honor of being Damned because of it." She said to him.

"You know the lesson of the Kingstone. You know what to do to drive away this madness."

It was then, standing that her eyes fell upon the old beleaguered man.

"Luloch!"

All of them, Adimus shot a confused look, save for the Prince. "I have waited a lifetime to gaze into those eyes one last time."

"It was a mistake. All. A mistake." she said. "...It is lamentable. Luloch. Dyrshul is not of this world, give her to us. It is where she rightly belongs. Relinquish her and this Darkest Night will end."

The old man came forward, his eyes teary before the suffering queen. "..."

The Prince cut in. "You allow it to haunt you instead of taking it for what it was. It most certainly wasn't a mistake at the time. Those days of sunsets and promises."

"What would you know? You know nothing of us!" She hissed.

"Oh, Brigit, I know much. And so did you once. Of love! All I need do is look at Dyrshul, born from it. So pure."

The Matron of Frosts's eye lit up "So it isn't just a suspicion. She can wield the Ardfrost! Your game is exposed, Prince. That's why you are here: to leverage, to bargain with her life. If you are finished dispensing your honeyed words from that silver-spoon tongue of yours now we can discuss our terms." she guffawed, throwing the shroud back over herself.

He smirked, revealing nothing. "Tell me what it is *you* wish to gain from this."

But the old man barred him with his shillelagh "No! Name you, creature, I'll not have you bargaining with the life of my daughter!"

"*Your* daughter?" said Adimus. He looked up or Bearch, who couldn't bring himself to lock gaze with the boy.

"Relief. Relief is all I want, dear prince. Plain and simple."

"Relief." he snorted once again. "Grant it to me. Use the Spear."

"No Geas binds you, my queen. It has been a long time since you took Brisengamen, and your memory fails you. The Spear would not grant you release. The true power that binds you no Grace or Cunning or Work of Thaumaturgy can undo."

"What is it then, what have you done to me? What power do you invoke?"

"Me? None. The power is yours. And only you wield it."

"Of what do you speak, Prince? Tell me!"

"Geases and oaths but cheapen it. And words betray it even more so."

"Enough with your riddles!"

"And you, Queen of the Sleeping City, wield it effortlessly. That is what I loved about you. It would be no other way, from the day I called upon you."

But Luloch answered her. "You told me what it meant, this burden, dear Holda, my Brigit. That it would kill you. That it would hurt. I wished not a moment for you to leave me, but I knew, for you there could be no other path." Then his face grew stern. "The way you spoke of the thing 'round your neck back then...you said you were doing a great thing, a great thing. And that you buy it gladly, even unto taking your leave to be gone from my sight forever." his face grew hot. "Only now you wish to cast it away and return, after I am so long in years? For shame! For shame!"

She reached her hand out and said, perhaps a little too insincerely. "I would return to you, my love, if you would but not interfere, intercede in what needs to be, for the sake of this realm. I *do* falter, even now. Stumble for you. My courage wavers, my hands tremble at this terrible weight. A shame, yes, but at least I have the sight to see now, that this weight was light compared to grief that dries my senses now. Dries them until all is numb." She looked again to the prince. "I would return to him, and be together once more, just a man and a woman."

"But you would give dear Dyrshul over to the same pain? What kind of mother does that?!" Luloch again spoke. "Never. Just let it be." he plead. "You can escape this fate he speaks of, even now. Know that it cannot cling to you forever. Let her go as well." he begged with hands together.

She turned her nose up. "I find no fault in this, prince of the dawn. I feel no remorse in asking for but a taste of freedom after all these years."

"Then what is it you seek? Here you are, coming out from beneath the mounds to trample all that which you once loved. That time is over. You cannot go back, only forward. You were told when you took this post how it would end, how it must end. Always. There are no exceptions for you or anyone else."

"I demand an appeal by the Court. To be taken to the Spear and have it all undone. To have my wounds cleaned with the Cauldron Chalice." her steely gaze locked with his.

"It <u>has</u> been found, you know, the Spear." he said. "This is the beginning of it all."

He nodded. "Of course I do.. Pimonia has willed this so. Haven't you, my dear?"

The lady stepped forward and curtsied.

"You trust this fiend? She is the advocate for them, A Forgotten herself!"

"Ahem. Call me a fiend, a Forgotten even if you will, but I am a <u>he</u>."

"Apologies, even a demon deserves the dignity of appropriate address." He shrugged. He tisked, "But Highness, you would stoop so low as to entertain his ideas…"

"More than entertain…" Pimonia began.

"Give us the words." the Queen insisted.

With his staff the Prince shoved Pimonia aside. "The Chalice does not come when called for the likes of you! Besides, it is indisposed for the moment as it were."

"Then we shall resume the unpleasantries." she clapped. "Sound the horns again." Delighted, he began to obey.

"--Wait!" the Prince said. Her attendant stood expectantly.

"Very well. Very well…" he lowered his head in defeat. "Call off your guard and have them return to your city in the dark and I shall summon it, the Great Grail, and you shall drink your fill. And then the Spear. Call off your forces."

She smiled a wry, triumphant grin from ear to ear, and with a motion canceled her helper's command. The prince turned around and looked at the dark knight with a smile.

"Malacasta, Steward of the Queen of Frosts, make this promise: leave this field of battle, and set no foot in the mortal lands again until it is time again to choose a Queen."

"I swear it."

There was something about that voice that sounded eager, excited even, that while the Queen, in her throes of victory, that though she herself did not hear it, made everyone else's blood run cold. The drums began to sound the signal to withdraw.

The Prince drew a little closer at that, and spoke to the Raven Knight in a little more hushed a tone. "There will be turmoil amongst the Unseelie. If you're not careful..."

"We must move the Eye of Beira."

"Agreed. The risk of bringing about the doom of the Forgotten is too high. It will go to Bres."

"I shall see it done." The knight resounded.

"Now, go and fetch Dyshul." he looked to the huntress.

"Now hold on!" Bearach protested. "You *are* giving her to them! What are you?! Who are you to make this decision for her?!"

"She is the lamb who will give herself regardless of what the Golden Ram or the Ewe Mother say." he gave Adimus a wink. "Ask her yourself." he gestured.

Bearach loosed his axe from his hip, but stopped when he felt her hand stay his.

He never gave mind to her appearance now, as Adimus had, embracing her fiercely, heedlessly, without so much as a word.

Luloch, resigned, stood behind her.

He started to ask, then the Queen's shrill shriek cut through all of them.

"What?!" The Queen cried. "What is happening to me!?"

Her skin grew white, her lips turned blue, with her icicle nails she clawed at her breast. "Why is this happening to me? I am goodly, I am pure!"

"I am sorry." the prince bowed. "Farewell my Queen. You shall have a room all your own in the Tower of Tears."

Frost glazed her crystalline form, and in an instance it was done, as with such force the shiver of ice grew that it sheared the veils upon her in twain.

The Queen slunk lifeless, impaled by the shiver, the icy fog rimming her empty eyes.

"What just happened?" the dread-stricken boy asked.

The Prince of Spring, sullen, shook his head. "In the great castle of ice at the end of the world there is a tower made from the piled bones of the queens of old; only when that tower reaches to the clouds will it be known...that never a true good deed was done under threat of pain or expectation of reward."

* * * * *

Dyrshul reached out to the Shard, and when she did her hand parted the steel-hard ice, just like the Prince of Spring said it would. In fact, since the moment the Queen had died, arctic winds blew, turning the already frigid night into a deadly blizzard that would dwarf even the threat of a standing army, rendering the singular goal of every man to seek shelter. *Would have been.*

Dyrshul stood barefoot in the snow, the cold touching not even her breath. She looked down at the Shard, gazing into it with unnerved disbelief at what she saw there. The Prince of Spring strode up beside her. "The Ardfrost clings to clingy souls, but yours is free. The darkness of the False Flame is not brighter than your light. Always remember that."

A tear rolled off her cheek, freezing as it fell, and she closed her hand around it, and the last snowflake fell, and suddenly the night was still. Malacasta, the golems, the whole army-- even the insolent Pimonia knelt.

"All Hail the Bonemother! All hail, Queen of Frosts."

"All hail! All Hail!"

Luloch, defeated, shrunken, came to her. "I have tried to, in vain, to keep you. But I cannot save you from Fate." He wiped tears from under his glasses. "It is a lesson hard learned from a pitiful old man. Just the same, remember your home, dear Dyrshul. And your happy memories. Coveting and mourning them is a fool's game. Do not turn back or you too shall freeze." She hugged them, and shared warm sentiments.

Adimus came to her. "Dyrshul…I'm sorry." Adimus felt strange again, drowsy now, as if in the delirium of his dreams again. He wasn't quite sure what he had just said.

She embraced him. "Adi, I forgive you. Don't worry. We'll meet again, I'm sure. I'll invite you."

It was a platitude, he'd thought. He hadn't expected what she replied. "What do you mean? You're not making sense. Dyrshul, you're going to live in the Deep beneath the mounds." what he left unspoken was apparent.

"You saved me once. You can do it again."

"What do you-?" he started a reply.

"Don't you remember. I know."

Pimonia looked at him. "You are the only missing piece of this puzzle." he relented. "How is it that you, a mere boy, with no skill, no prowess, no Magic or Cunning, were able to enter the court of the Winter Queen and abduct her?"

He was speechless. "..."

"I, for one, give him my thanks." Said the Prince. "Without knowing the true delights of the world one can never find purity of heart. You have been endeared upon hers for all time." he smiled at Pimonia, and put a finger to his nose. "You almost won, Forgotten."

Pimonia sneered at him. Then the demon's eyes narrowed, locking with the boy's. "Having trouble remembering? How are your dreams at night?" he jeered. "This is only the beginning."

In those eyes he found all the fear and dread of the boggart's words. It paralyzed him to inaction. Only now could he articulate it.

The boy stood in tears, in wordless stricken tears. Fearful, apprehensive of what lie ahead of him, of what truths his heart yet concealed.
The Prince of Spring stood aside, until the rabble became restless, then he gave a nod to Malacasta. "Come, Highness, it is time."

Then one by one they departed into the reflection of the lake, until naught but the cracks of dawn shown upon its finish.

Luloch cried a sob that would not cease, and Bearach, mustering a strength greater than any seen this night, fought for composure, until he'd gathered enough of it to lead his father from the slope and the cold.
Adimus simply stood, in the waste of the breathless morning until they had all but gone.
Finally, the orc Embraleigh strode before them, then as if just she might have been imposing, she waited for everyone to look at her, "I die now."

Some gasped, some bowed their head. Adimus simply looked at her and replied soberly "...Okay."

"Why do you have to be so heartless?" Brindle snapped.

But it was Embraleigh spoke to the Grigor, "...Want to a make good pose this time, not like last time." She grumbled at him. "More dignified."

Adimus walked up to her. He looked at the ground. "Are you afraid?"

Emberleigh guffawed. "Of course! The last one was embarrassing. Embraleigh will look fierce this time. Embraleigh is fierce."

"Of—Of dying, I think he means." Brindle corrected, listening intently himself.

"...Afraid to die?" This time she sounded even more amused. "Bahaha! You sound like that old man. Unavailed." She puffed up her chest. "No. Never afraid. I am blood from the stone. Smaller people think this is hard, to get blood from a stone, but they not know the one who made me—for him...it is easy. I understand this, that makes me mighty, this is what they say of me."

Then, gripping her ax and contorting into a terrifying scowl her face froze, and she was the stone warrior again.

Alfred came to him, and placed a hand on his shoulder.

Adimus allowed it.

It was the first time they had talked since he had lashed out in anger, but Alfred seemed reserved nonetheless. "Are you alright?" he asked.

"It was the Spear, that gave her life, you know, the spear we saved." He was prattling, as he always did, "It's a shame it will wind up in the hands of a tyrant now. You thought Tolten Blaise was mad, wait until you see Ross Ward..."

Adimus absently nodded, staring down at the snowscape over the hill. But the wheels of his mind were turning. "Alfred. What he, what Pimonia was saying...about my dreams. Are my dreams real? Am I truly who I am in them?"

"Your dreams are of you, from you. Of course: you are always who you dream."

He dismissed the enigmatic way the man answered. "What...what if I don't want it to be. If I do not want to dream for fear of awakening, opening the eyes of someone who is not me? It would be...like death."

It was a non sequitur to everyone but himself, he'd thought, and expected anything but his response. "It is appropriate to grieve. And to be afraid." the Seer nodded, placing a hand on the statue now before them. He locked gazes with the boy. "The answers will be coming soon. Soon, but not yet. But. Adimus, if you learn one thing from me, one single lesson, if I would have you know <u>one thing</u>, may it be this: <u>it will not help.</u>" He came close, and looked upon him meaningfully. "Trust me. Neither wondering what may have been or knowing what truly has been will ever help you remember."

"Remember? Where I'm really from?"

The Sum Seer smiled and shook his head. "No. Who you really are."

As the last of the fell army departed beyond the veil a grave look befell the wizard. He locked gaze with the prince in unspoken conversation. The prince shook his head and threw up his hands.

"If we don't do it now, he'll find out at a more inopportune time. This memory is the lynchpin. It, this," he flourished his hands to the surrounding and the ground beneath them. "This is the Fetch Life."

"We are finished here, I suppose." Said Brindle, he began to gather the others to guide them down the mountain.

Alfred paced up, and looked at Adimus, then back to the Prince.

"...What?"

"To remember will be to forget." the Prince replied.

Alfred snarled, then steeled him. "Adimus." He said now with surety. "Focus your Sight." The boy hesitantly nodded. The Wizard gave a deep sigh.

"Calm your breath. Focus." He handed him his ring. "Try to Read it."

They stood there for a long moment. Adimus's feet were cold and wet from snow. His nose ran, his throat was getting raw, but he shut it all out, just as Alfred had taught him.

"I...can't. It's sublimated. It takes practice, Charleze said." he finally said. Then Alfred took the ring from him.

"Of course not." He said. "But. Now, all that effort, all that intent, turn it inwards." he said. "See...yourself. Your body is the object, the Form, what you really are is the Nature. Gaze into the in between."

With this the Grigor closed his eyes, and then...was gone.

Epilogue

Adimus found himself standing before the great pillar of crystal.

He looked down at his hand. He stood in glazed bewilderment, struck in a haze of delirium.

"...Adimus?"

The girl's voice never registered to him.

Everything seemed so unfamilar, so new. Still more strange, more alien, is how wrong that notion seemed.

It bothered him and he'd no idea why, as if for but a brief moment he had mistaken a mirror's reflection as reality and everything cast upon it as false.

"Adimus!"

His mind strained to breaking trying to comprehend what had just happened. Then to remember what happened. Then to remember what he was trying to remember, "Years in a single breath...Lia Faile." He muttered to himself what he had been told only moments before. He looked again at his hand. His hand.

"Adimus Urie'arun Cadmon Zeran!" she called one last time.

He glanced behind him, only because of the noise the girl was making.

"Well?" Selean stared at him, her hands pursed on her hips. She blew her golden hair out of her face in frustration. She remained as strangely calm and nonchalant as ever with the royal guard descending on them--then again Selean was not a normal person, and her intentions and temperance was often not either.

He gasped and snapped to at a second rattle of the door, no doubt a battering ram.

"No." He answered absently. He tried to remember what he'd just been asked, and found himself longing for it, having been asked it so many years ago. He heaved, suddenly beginning only now to grasp where he was, what he was doing, and how much trouble they were now in.

All the royal guard of the Citadel of the Chalice Spire would soon be upon them. The roar of the Nephilim Guard in their suits of Deep Armor could be heard outside. Thankfully for them they'd built the Citadel precisely to prevent such a thing as a break in--and they were right to do so, he could see that now.

That strange man on the other end could tell them its truth, the truth behind this stone. Perhaps...

A stone that granted wishes. That made kings. That was what the Virians of old had said of it. But now he knew different. That was simply what it was always perceived as.

But he knew now that there was always a difference between what something is perceived as and what something truly is. *The nice girl with the black hair had taught me that. The one in the shop. What was her name?*

He looked up at the thing, casting shadows and scattering refractions gleamed through the broken vaulted glass bright as the noonday sun above them.

The Stone of Kings. He gazed at his reflection in it. It was still the same as he remembered, but when he looked down the clothing he wore was altogether different. Now he wore a sash of red clasped with gold and a baggy dhoti, and a silvery polished cuirass. His hair was different, now shorn close.

The dream had indeed been surreal, no less vivid, with its own seemingly nonsensical rules that still chirped in his mind, and as one does in such a dream he'd bought into its narrative while there, not so much as questioning it at the time; but now he stood across the breach, and had to adjust accordingly.

Glossary

Adaire- (ah-DARE) Small town in the valley east of Balfour, hometown of clan Pembroke.

Adranan- (ADD-rah-nan) capital of Menkara.

Akima, Laina- (LAY-nah AH-KI-mah) One of Adimus's friends from Balfour, and now one of the current members of the Eastward Endeavor crew. She is Mansii and a priestess of their goddess Ananya, and a practitioner of the Magica.

Alara- (ah-LA-rah) One of the Cait Shii, she was imprisoned in Torant's island penal colony along with Baron Krasad. When Krasad was to be freed, he pulled strings to free her as well in exchange for her servitude in order to help him find the Spear of Fate. Full name: Alara Pisici de la Plag la Nord.

Albrastricano- (ahl-bras-tra-KAHN-o) Literally, 'Silver Wolf'. Often depicted as a villain in children's tales, he is also found in far more serious stories, such as the legendarium which details the rise of the king of Kessellon.

Alfred- (AL-fred) One of the founders of Eastward Endeavor. An astute practitioner of Psychometry, he was instrumental in discovering the true location of Gae Bolg, and was this approached by Torrin von Krasad. Though called Sum Seer for lack of everyone's experience in those who can use psychometry who aren't of the order, he is also a practitioner of Thaumaturgy, and carries with him a Vesican Harp and a Sublimated ring with strange powers, both of which he got from Teacher.

Alkaiser- (AHL-kah-zar) Malkin's talking raven friend.

All Creation- the entirety of existence, encompassing both the One World and the Other World.

All'khemy-(ALL-kehm-ee) a process which seeks to find harmony between a substance's Form and Nature, bringing it to Sublime (perfected) state.

All'khemist Wand- a khemetic weapon which uses Bruana to propel its ammunition; a pistol.

Alkonost, the (AHL-koh-nost)- the seat and throne of The Great King, said to have once belonged to the King Once and Future.

Am Carrig- (ahm KAI-rigg) name of prison which the Sluagh used to trap the Goddess.

Animaflora- Ambulant (often monstrous) flora created during the War of the Leaves. Urisks are catagory of Animaflora.

Ang Becna- (AHNG-bek-na) literally 'The Brotherhood of the Dragon'. The holy protectors of the Merchant lords.

Anwyn- (AHN-win) the language of shadows, unable to be directly understood, and forgotten quickly.

Dhuun- the language of the gods, able to be understood by all creatures of the One World.

Casting Cloak- the marvelous morphing cloak, able to change itself and its wearer to appear any way the wearer chooses.

Ardfrost- a force which freezes materials as would a fire burn it. Understood to be an emanation of the power of the False Flame.

Argent- Name of the bards of Bowen, member of the Eastward Endeavor crew. Argent is a pseudonym, his real name is William Mathune.

Argetlam- (ARE-get-lahm) Preferred name for Nuada, as his True Name is considered sacred. Literally 'silver hand'.

Aurum Agri- 'the golden field', a reservoir of Calcinative power (not well understood by the other traditions) to which Xanthic practitioners (sourcerers) and Fae lay claim.

Balfour (BAHL-four) small village where the story begins, located on a break in the Barrier Mountains along the Ruined Road.

Balros-(BAHL-ross) King of the Baleful Eye. High King of the Formerians, whose eye destroys all who gaze upon it.

Beastmen- slur. The Dhunn Shii tribes of the Maritian Veldt.

Bhuvastra Sudre- (BHUV-astra SOOD-rah) the ancient name for a Heraldrix. See entry.

Black King, the- One of the many names of Balros of the Baleful eye. He is also sometimes called The King in Gold and Black.

Blaise, Tolten- (TOLE-ten BLACE) the Pardoner of Balfour.

Blossom Bride- Once the wife of the Nameless Boy, who betrayed him and attempted to murder him, and when she failed she waged war against the goodly Fae.

Bolg- (BOLG) a race of hooved giants of various types, said to have been carved from stone by Many Shapes and brought to life with his blood. There are six tribes of them according to the stories told to Adimus: The Fir Bolg, The Fir Domnan, The Orculli, The Glastig, the Fir Galeon, and the ones to be known as the Formerians.

Bran- (BRAHN) One of the clans of Ormond. They were once tasked with diplomatic matters and trade (namely because the task required the use of coin of found elsewhere), they used to be keepers of the archives along with Mathune. They were ousted and ostricized when it was found that the widowed matron of the clan had married into a family of Fae, that along with their ties to the royal family of Kessellon cast suspicion of their motives. Her offspring, such as Malcolm Bran, is a Pooka.

Bran, Malkin- (MAHL-kihn) a hare pooka from clan Bran. He is a fellow Pledger.

Breather- slur. Used by Gnemedians to describe non-Gnemedian Kindred, usually Hyu'man.

Brian- local blacksmith in the village of Balfour.

Brousse-(BROSE) the Labyrinth City, capital of Kessellon.

Bruana- (BROO-ah-nah) literally 'the seed of fire', a highly flammable/explosive khemetic material often used in weapon-making by the Voux.

Buckroy, Adimus- (A-dihm-us buck-ROY) a Grigor from Balfour who gets swept up in the journey to find the Spear of Fate.

Buckroy, Anwell- (ANN-well) uncle (?) of Adimus, known as a jokester and local the spinner of tall tales.

Buckroy, Bearch- (BARE-rick) father (?) of Adimus. Leader of the Grigors.

Buckroy, Dyrshul- (DEER-shul) sister (?) of Adimus. Shares a gap in memory like him. Suspected to be a changeling.

Buckroy, Luloch-(LOW-luck) grandfather (?) of Adimus.

Bugbear- a Fae creature who thrives on fear, and seems to most often come about as a Sprite as consequence of the use of Magic (Wielding); An Effigy Wraith, Bogeyman or Boggart.

Butcher- Toranti slang for a Histban Imperial soldier.

Cairnfang- (KARN-fang) a prison apparently guarded by Barghests, used as a prison for Fae and enemies of the clans alike.

Cait Shii- a Dhuun Shii with the qualities of a cat. See Dhuun Shii.

Calcination-(cal-sin-A-shun) The burning of the Calcinative Quality. Also, the first of seven stages in All'Khemy, which utilizes the Calcinative Quality as a catalyst for the other stages.

Calcinative Quality- (CAL-sin-a-tiv) a measure of the deficit between Form and Nature in an object or entity. This power is harnessed in the Three Traditions to Work the power that laymen call Magic.

Calling up the Named One- Expression: to make a ruckus

Candles and Quicksilver- Idiom used by wizards for something that is easy; 'a breeze'.

Casey- One of the clans of Ormond. Set to being in charge of settling internal conflict among the clans, they were disenfranchised, deemed as untrustworthy due to their closeness with the throne before the war and rumors of madness that ran in their bloodline. They have since found a place working as sellswords for the clans, though they still claim to maintain a sense of fairness, and will not act upon the clans directly.
They were also in charge of the breeding of war horses, having descended from royal knights of Rinehelm.

Cauldron Chalice, the- The Cauldron of All Wants. One of the four treasures of the four great cities of the Tuatha.

Changling- a Fae that appears indistinguishable from a Hyu'man. Many people believe they are used as spies.

Cinter Teg- one of several 'hearth spirits' in folklore who delivers presents to children of Longnight. There is also Olentzero and the Yule Lads, all of which are bound by the mysterious Vatra of Generosity.

Claimh Solais- the Sword of the Sun. One of the four treasures of the four great cities of the Tuatha.

Crom Cruach- (crom CROO-ik) The name the people of the hills give to Balros of the Baleful Eye.

Crossroads- a point of conjunction where the One World and Otherworld can meet.

Cyance- (science) a series of systems pertaining to the interactions of bodies in the physical world, including the Physica (study of the interaction of forces) and Khemetastry (study of the interaction of substances). These systems, as well as the standardized methods which came from them are a byproduct of Thaumaturgy and All'khemy, methods of Wielding which utilize the Essence inherent in a substance.

Daldista- the old name for the people who lived to the west who would one day found the Great Kingdom of Kessellon.

Deep, the- a vast cavernous world beneath the surface of the One World. The Rathlands and the Worldheart is located in the Deep.

Delaney- (dill-A-nee) Gnemedian that follows the Eastward Endeavor. Member of the Meleae Sept, she was chosen by the crew for her ability to bind with animals.

Dhuun- (DOON) the language of All Creation. Anyone make

Dhuun Shii- (DOON-shee) A Cessairian. A subrace of Fae with heavy animal-like traits. They are many and varied, but some more common than others.

Dominion- the power of Fae, gods, and spirits to grant power to be Wielded in the One World by those bound to them in covenant.

Dougall- One of the clans of Ormond. In charge of the land military to be mustered against foreign invaders. Normally not a task for one clan, they are heavily hand-cuffed in the number of conscripts and ability to rally. Talks of their very cordial relationship with Pembroke has been a point of concern for many years.

Dragonfather- the name of the being Invoked to awaken the powers of Seeing.

Dwarf Dream- expression. An inspired dream, sometimes (but not always) referring to dreamed interactions with entities.

Dweomer- 'dwarf-words'. Intricate markings on a subject which helps with the process of making the subject Familiar or Votive .

Dwyer- (DWEER)One of the clans of Ormond. Law-makers and record-keepers of the clans, nowadays they deal more in trade and bookkeeping for commerce, chartering ships and the like, dealing more in inventory manifests than writing sweeping law based on the words of Kain. Along with Ward, they took on some of the responsibilities that Bran had. They own the Bowen Archives jointly with Mathune in Bran's stead. They also have taken up the mantle and responsibility of horse breeding and control, with mixed results.

Dwyer mule- expression. Something that seems great but isn't; a bad deal or investment (as the mule can never breed). The act of cheating somebody is 'giving them a Dwyer Mule'. Origin: clan Dwyer used to give mules to the common folk in lieu of other much needed goods (which they were reported to have in abundance), encouraging them to farm with them instead. Dwyer mules are infamous for being frail and scrawny, and possibly more of them have been eaten than used.

Eastward Endeavor- an adventuring company founded by Alfred Juminion III and Torrin Von Krasad of Milliard, chartered with the sole mission of finding Gae Bolg.

Ederton- a Free City of trade in northern Menkara in the border of Kesselon and the Veldtlands. It is the gateway to the northern countries of Shambaya, and is, in part, under mild occupation by the accompaniment of the Merchant Lords due to their heavy presence.

Elaith- (eel-Al-eth) Malcolm's talking cat friend.

Endless Forest, the- a great forest that blankets all of the south, Bespelled with a power which confuses any who do not know its ways to become hopelessly lost within it. Also called the Forest of Exile, the Tuatha treat it as their homeland, and move freely within it.

Epochellipse- A world-shaping catastrophic event, as documented by the Bolg. In their astrology they count three, with four intervening ages, the final of which concluding with the annihilation of the One World.

Erlking- Another name for the Summer King literally 'high king'.

Essence- The name for the Wielded form of the energy found in Calcinative quality.

Eziadeus- (ez-AI-ah-dus) lair of the Shade King, first made to be a prison.

Faeth- old word for a seer or soothesayer.
Whispermonger- usually derogatory, a term coined for bards during the sucession.

False Flame- One of the fell powers able to be Wielded by the King of Shades and his host.

Familiar- an object or living thing whose Nature is likened to one's own. Such subjects are always Votive.

Favor- a turquoise coin, the second lowest denomination.

Fencebush- a mildly toxic thorny shrub native to the Pangor Vale. Used by shepherds and cattle owners to sequester and gate their livestock.

Flaith- (FLAYTH) One of the lower titles given to the Nine types of celestial spirits.

For Thrice Sake- A harsh expletive interjection. Unknown origin, possibly having to do with the sacred number three. Could be a reference to the Thice Slain King, the King Once and Future.

Forgotten, the- featured in the prologue, the demonic generals of the Shade King and his host who were sealed away, in part by the efforts of the Winter Queen.

Foxwell, Annalise- (anna-LEESE) A duchess from Torant, who is Argent's cousin.

Gae Bolga- (gaia BOLG-ah) the Spear of Fate. One of the four treasures of the four great cities of the Tuatha.

Galdr- (GALD-er) the words, usually in Anwyn, used in Spells or Working Magic.

Geas- (GYASS) a binding Spell which compels or forbids an action or series of actions, leveraged using a subject's True Name.

Githa- The queen of Kesselon who was overthrown during the Sucession War. Called the Bloody Queen for her insurrection against the Tala, she was rumored to be quite insane by her fall.

Gnemedian- (nih-MED-ee-in) a race of plant-like beings with empathic powers, product of the War of the Leaves.

Gnosis, the- the empathic power exhibited by Gnemedians. It manifests in different ways depending on a Gnemedians Sept.

Gordona- (gore-DOH-nah) The Flooded Fortress. An outpost built by the Daldistans, led by Lowylln Mac Dougall during the Secession War. The final resting place of the Spear of Fate.

Grace- power granted to a worshipper of a god, of a servant of a powerful Fae.

Great Kingdom, the- An expansive empire from near-antiquity that spanned the entire continent. They are responsible for the common language, calendar system, and several religious and cultural commonalities among the people. It was ruled by the lineage of Mathendon, said to have divine descent from Many Names and the Goddess.

Great Work, the- a seven-fold series of processes which leads to a ultimate Sublimation of a material. Thaumaturgy also uses it, but is typically only concerned with the first few steps.

Grigor- (GREE-gur) the ceremonial title of the position of night watchman in the rural village of Balfour.

Heraldrix- a special garden once used by practitioners of the Traditions. Nowadays worn for fashion.

Hewnyleigh- (HAWN-ah-lee) Cultural center of the kingdoms, located equidistant between Menkara and Ormond and their exilliary cities. Home to the Bowen Archives and their college, and Cairnfang prison.

Hob- Slur. Used by Hyu'mans to describe Gnemedians.

Hyu'man- one the Kind that are commonfolk and natives of the One World. Etymology unclear, possibly meaning 'of Man'.
Kindred- having a Form that is Hyu'man-like (arms, legs, walks upright); humanoid.

Jin- Slang. A person from Kyogode (short for Kyogodejin)

Kainden- capital of Ormond.

Kata Blade- the exotic swords employed by the Servants of the Blade, a special warrior caste found in Kyogode.

Kessellon- The Great Kingdom, founded by Mathendon II after the Epochellipse and the fall of the Kingdom of Agrathea, ruled by the King Once and Future.

Khemetastry- (khem-the study, codification and utilization of the interaction between mundane substances.

Killimoulus- A Fae of diminutive size. Typically live underground. Their heads are comprised entirely of a nose with two beady eyes. Pllural Killimouli (Charleze insists).

Kind- one's familial type, race or species.

King with No Name, the Parable of the- A tale recounting the last king of Lathnia, who had stretched his rule so thin that he could no longer hold it, until he encountered a Tuathan (Kain) who set about mentoring him in the ways of statesmanship and law. The king concludes that he must divide his kingdom and rule jointly with someone, but Kain declines. By the end the kingdom is on the verge of collapse, that is when the Nameless Boy, child of Kain comes forward and declares a contest for the warring clans fighting over the kingdom, that whosoever could find his father's spear, Gae Bolg, would be the king of this new land (Ormond) allotted by the mandate. The search for the spear continued into the modern era as such, the prior kingdom (Menkara) having fallen. The lesson of the parable drives home the validity of the need to divide the kingdom because the clansmen embarking on the quest don't even know the old king's name.

Knolls, Caleb- A swordsman and bodyguard to Cadifor McDougal. Though he is a southlander, he practices many of the cultural axioms of tge Veiled Landers, and even carries a Kata Blade. He has aspirations of passing on his master's teaching, including their means of iron manufacture, and kinda the Endeavor on fulfilling their purpose.

Krasad, Torrin- a baron from Torant. Like the rest of his family, he lived life exiled to an island penal colony for conspiracy against the crown during the Secession War. Newly pardoned, he received a series of clues he believed might lead him to the famed Spear of Fate, and thus founded the Eastward Endeavor company.

Labori- giants if stone or metal given life by the Dominion of the blood line of Mathendon, heirs to the Great Kingdom Kesselon.

Lantern Beetle- a large, banana-sized bio-luminescent beetle that inhabits the Pangor Vale.

Lathern, Eichgun- a Grigor along with Adimus and Bearach. Was injured by the Bugbear.

Lathnia- one of the three ancient kingdoms of old. The Lathnians lived in peace with the Tuatha, whom consider them the most fair if the Cessair (humans)

Lia Faile- the Stone of Kings. One of the four treasures of the four great cities of the Tuatha.

Lithaugury- the full de-Naturing of a subject precipitated by the backlash of the misunderstanding the subject's Nature. The result is usually petrification, as all Votiveness is wrested.

Lord Protector, the- The current ruler of Kessellon, who (for the most part) holds the favor of the noble houses to the west and discharges the duties of the king for the now-much-smaller nation.

Lyr- Many Faces. One of the trinity. Revered as god of the underworld and afterlife, he holds a mystical cauldron that grants rebirth. As a god of death and the underworld, he is often cursed, his name invoked in expressions of vulgar speech (though it is still frowned upon).

Madreg- the Clockwork City. A port city built on the edge of the Menkaran Wetlands, home to several marvels if modern Khemetastry heretofore unseen most other southlanders.

Maecmarion- the county wherein Balfour is located. Owned and maintained by the Pembroke family.

Magica, the- Working as it relates specifically to Graces, the invoking of true names, and Spells. Named for a tradition that no longer officially exists, the practitioners of which are called Magi (Magus, singular).

Magic- a common misnomer referring to the act of Wielding. It is thought to stem from the pervasiveness of Workers of the Magica before the Epochellipse; the word is sometimes mistakenly used both by laymen and the experienced for describing any type of use of the Quality. (ex: 'Working Magic' can refer to work in Cyance, Xanthos, or the Magica.)

Mansii- the name for the nomadic people of the Veldtlands. Their stories say they came from a land across the ocean.

Mariti- the name of the territory in which the Veldtlands lie. Named after a once flowering fallen city of the Karanashii who used to live there.

Mathendon II- the first king of Kessellon. Said to have been once friend and advisor to the King Once and Future,

Mathien- Many Names. Said to be the inventor of names and thus the creator of all the Traditions and methods of Wielding and Working (magic).

Mathune- One of the clans of Ormond, tasked with stateship and diplomacy abroad, as well as being fonts of cultural knowledge and representatives of domestic interests. Renowned as bards, and inheritors of the Casting Cloak, Nathan is a member of this clan.

Mathune, Nathan- see Argent.

Mathune, William- well known cousin of Argent.

Mayasma- Phantasmal mist found in the Otherworld that is not entirely a physical substance.

Mcdougal, Cadifor- hero of clan Dougall whom some say is immortal. He possesses the Sublime sword Gram, which has the power to compel the truth from others.

McConell, Cayden- the reeve of Balfour.

McCayden, Tirlag- One of the members of the Eastward Endeavor crew. She was a Roni smuggler before finding Alfred and joining.

Mealae- The Gnemedian Sept to which Delaney belongs, having to do with her ability to emphatically bond with animals, including Hyu'mans. Called the Slave Sept by many.

Meav- former acolyte turned inkeeper and bartender of the Green Beat.

Menkara- the second of the kingdoms that was once the kingdom of Lathnia, located in the adjacent northern region of Ormond. They also lay claim to the cursed eastern wetlands. Ruled by the Council of the Kingship, a governing body of elected officials from the peasentry who govern instead of a king.

Mergence- the Gnemedian reproductive act, described as being quite different to those of the Breathers.

Migdal Bevelle- the great tower and fortress at the center of the world from which Balros of the Baleful Eye ruled. It is unclear whether he built it, or whether it belonged to the Sluagh before his time.

Mist- the Curtain, the Crossroads.

Moon (timekeeping)- a 28 days period, as marked by the cadence of the Moon of Omens. There are nine in the calendar year used by the Great Kingdom.

Moon of Days- Named Macha. The largest (by measure of perceived size.) Red in color, it blots out the stationary sun and causes the day and night cycle in the One World. It skews in its orbit slightly throughout the calendar year, causing more night hours in the winter, less in the summer, that combined with the Moon of Seasons is understood by most to cause the changing seasons.

Moon of Omens- Named Baev. The smallest (by measure of size in the sky) Yellow-tinged in color, it moves in a precession of 28 days and its placement and phase at time of birth in relation to other moons and constellations is important in Heimdallan astrology.

Moon of Seasons- Named Nemh. A blue moon that rises and sets in half years cycles. Harbinger of the tide and warm weather.

Named- mild expletive. A curse uttered at a person or subject expressing the wish to have one's name known to all.

Nameless Boy- A figure in Tuathan myth who slew Balros of the Baleful Eye. In the Parable of the Nameless King he is depicted as the son of Kain, and a holder of the Spear of Fate.

Niall- a wooler and avid whittler from Balfour. His home was burned by the bugbear and goblyns.

Nic- short for *nicotia*, a form of nightshade enjoyed by the people of the southlands, usually either smoked or chewed.

Nis- also called the third court, composed mostly of goblyns and the Dhuun Shii, they are those who are neutral, undecided, or simply ignorant of the Seelie and Unseelie.

Nissie- A nis. Used as colloquial slang for monsterous Fae, especially goblyns, though most are unaware of its origin as a reference to a de facto political affiliation. Possibly originally Nis Shii.

Nuada- name of the king of the Tuatha.

Numinous, the- the Godhead, existing as one before the Catalystum. Viewed as the primordial being or force which gave rise to the gods.

Orc- Orculli. If the tribe of the Bolg having pig-like features. They live underground or beneaths the waves of the seas of the One World.

Ormond- One of the two kingdoms into which Lathnia was split during the events of the founding of the Kainden Codex. It was promised to the Fae known as Kain, but he refused. It is ruled jointly by the Steward Princes.

Old Ways- a reformist religion returning to the ways of the Daldistans and the practice of Illea, the worship of the primordial deities who existed before the coming of Parthos and his kim. Started by the Order of Jasmine.

One, the- a metaphysical notion in which all things are represented as pairs of opposites. Often associated with the soul, Nature, and the feminine power.

Order of Jasmine- A knightly order tasked with enforcing the state religion of the Great Kingdom, binding (or often simply slaying) Fae, and dispersing practitioners of the Traditions.

Other, the- the second constituent part of the metaphysical notion in which all things are represented as pairs of opposites.

One World, the- the name of the physical world.

Otherworld, the- the mystic elsewhere beyond the Mist wherein the Fae reside.

P'aravoux- A nation to the north known for their technological progress in the fields of Khemetastry and the Physica. During the Sucession War they aided the Torant, allowing them controlled use of their Bruana weapons and other devices, vengeance for the political incident the century before in which Kessellon consolidated their power and and usurped it for his own, destroying their democracy (known as the War of the Ransom Queen).

Pardoner- a ceremonial office within the priesthood of the Old Ways which acts as the head priest of a community.

Parthos- Many Shapes. Father of the Partholonians, honored as Lathnian gods and revered by the Tuatha for their divinity. His eye is the sun, which warms the world. Also gave life to the Bolg with his blood and skill at All'khemy.

Partholonians, the- often regarded as gods, they are the forefathers of the Fae culture, as well as (according them) responsible for the creation of the world nowadays.

Pembroke- One of the clans of Ormond. In charge of dealing with and discharging the executive duties of the counties, including collecting taxes and law enforcement.

Pembroke, Weylan- a catchpole from the city of Adaire, hailing from the clan of the same name.

Pembroke, Thadeus- Count of Meacmarion. Patron of clan Pembroke.

Physica- the study, codification and utilization of physical forces and their interaction with both each other and objects in the physical world.

Pistil- see Allkhemist Wand.

Pledger- one having been sworn in the Pledging to find Gae Bolg.

Pledging, the- a yearly event in which adventurers seek Gae Bolg, endorsed and sponsored by the clans of Ormond.

Pooka- a type of Kindred Fae that can shapechange into an animal.

Princely Provinces- a name for the combined lands of Ormond and Menkara that used to be one kingdom.

Puck- the vernacular language of Fae, which borrows heavily from Dhuun amongst other influences.

Rathlands- Land of the Mounds, where the Formerians are said to slumber and where Fae are sent to be punished.

Red Cap- a monsterous Gnemedian. Once ingesting food, a Gnemedian lose its ability to gain sustenence from sunlight and water through their heads and they lose their empathic abilities, becoming carnivorous, cannibalistic, and debased of intellect. Their name originates from the practice of watering their skulls with blood.

Rinehelm- small province in Kesellon host to a city by the same name. They breed horses, and keep close wraps on their provisioning.

Ruined Road, the- road us by Kessellon and the Daldistans until it fell into disuse and disrepair.

Secession War- A multi-sided conflict which saw the dissolving of the Great Kingdom. Its cause was manifold, and every nation seems to have their own reasons for it happening, from the southlander sentiment that the monarch's reach became too long (for them mirroring the parable of the King with No Name) to the failing monetary system, to the religion reformationist and rumors of madness within the royal line.

Seithr- the movements in Thaumaturgy taught to practitioners involved in Working Magic. Typically seen as a feminine practice by practitioners who rely on staves or wands to achieve the Gladr.

Sept- the manner in which the Gnemedians organize, having something to do with the way in which their Gnosis manifests. Not to be confused with family, which relates to the species of Gnemedian, there are nine such Septs.

Shepard- a general title given within the priests of the Old Ways.

Shade- a Sluagh.

Shamba'ala- An ancient city, home of the Mansii, depicted in their stories (the Sojourn Cycle) as a holy place and seat of power for the Numinous.

Silver Hand!- expletive expressing shock or disbelief. Typically used in the region of Marron and Gorn Eilean. Referring to the tale of Argetlam and the shocked response of the Formerian kings at his new hand.

Sluagh- (SLOO-ah), a category of various incorporeal Fae creatures who exist in the one world and steal the souls of the living. They usually live in the Deep.

Sluagh Gora- (SLOO-ah gor-RAH)- The Tuatha name for the King of the Forgotten; The Shade King.

Solaristine- one of Arcane Alloys, metals made artificially using All'khemy, along with Serpentanium, Lunaris, and Auric Calcium (Orichalcum)

Sourcery- Wielding performed by Xanthic practitioners using the Aurum Agri.

Spear of Fate- see Gae Bolg.

Spell- a specific application of Wielded words and their subsequent effects. Cognate from the verb 'to spell'.

Stripes- slang for a tiger eye piece, the lowest denomination of coin. Though its namesake would suggest it, it is made from myriad lesser stones, essentially any common ones that aren't used for other coins.

Sublime (object)- an object that has undergone Sublimation having been transmuted into its idealized form, making its Form and Nature the same. Such items often have Otherworldly (magical) properties.

Sum Seer- a position given to member of the Order of Lapidaries who was in charge of ensuring the authenticity of coin.

Summer King- The Sovereign of the Seasons, the Erlking, leader of the Seelie Fae.

Tala- a confederacy comprised of wild bands of Nis Shii who inhabit the Maritian Veldt.

Teacher- Alfred's instructor. He never revealed his name to him, resulting in several to postulate that he was Fae. Though Alfred points out that advanced Wielders often carry superstitions about revealing their names (although he learned this from Teacher himself).

Tersus- one of the kings of Kessellon. He demanded worship as a demigod, and founded his own state religion harkening back to the beliefs of Daldistan occultists who worshipped the Formerians. Also founded the Order of Jasmine.

Thaumaturgy- a method of Wielding and Working magic which utilizes the Calcinative qualities found in inorganic substances.

Those Below- mysterious entities referred to in All'khemical texts who, at the behest of a practitioner, reveal (usually through cryptic dreams) the processes by which a subject can be made Votive.

Those Within- mysterious entities referred to in All'khemical texts who, through the study of their Familial Nature, help the practitioner in the understanding of the processes by which a subject can be made Votive.

Traditions, the- The methods of Wielding and Working, of which there are three: Cyance, Xanthos, and the Magica.

Tripura- an event during the last Epochellipse, where Parthos brought down three of the four cities of the Tuatha to ensure the destruction of Migdal Bevelle.

Triumvirate- the trinity of gods who acted as catalyst for the birth of the world, rescuing the primordial Goddess from her icy prison, Am Carrig (or Formerians, depending on who you ask). They Parthos of Many Shapes, Lyr of Many Faces, and Mathien of Many Names.

True Name- a primordial word in the language of Dhuun that is both describes and directly corresponds to a specific Natures, including currently existing entities, in the One World. Spoken into existence by Mathien of Many Names, True Names are the fundamentals of Magic, used to bind, control, manipulate, and alter Form and Nature alike, as Names themselves bind and constrict, defining not only what something is but what it is not. According to the Tuatha, Name,

Form and Nature form the Trinity of Being that are intrinsically linked (selfsame).

Tuatha- the most common of the Fae folk, making up the bulk of the Seelie court. They are said to have arrived from the Otherworld long ago, and have decided to set up residence here.

Urisk- The greater category of Animaflora which have Kindred shapes, of which Gnemedians make up the bulk.

Veldtlands, the- The Maritian Veldt, a colossal expanse of tropical savanna inhabited by the Beast Men that divides the northern and southern countries.

Vesican Harp-an apparatus resembling a staff capable of invoking Magic.

Votive- the state of an object (or in the case of Magic and Sourcery, living being) whose Nature has been accurately approximated. This is done by sequestering the subject's Fate, and is done using various means, including the use of True Names, Geases, and rituals which make the subject Familiar to the Worker.

Votive Principle, The- an algorithmic model used in Thaumaturgy and All'khemy which solves for Calcination; its methods verify the statement, 'the more Votive an object is, the easier it is to Work.'

Vouxite- From P'aravoux.

Voux- of the P'aravoux.

Veiled Lands, the- A country (rather a conglomerate of warring city states) that exists on the other side of the impenetrable Endless Forest. Named Kyogode, and held together namely by the Iron Warlord. A narrow valley found in Kessellon that lead to the western reaches of their provinces (lands disputed to belong to the Great Kingdom) used to be the only entrance point, but this passage was shut off by the hostile warlords of the Oni Shogunate that held it and saw Kessellon as a threat, and it was only in recent years with the use the Vouxite ships to pierce the Treadless Sea that meaningful contact with them had been made and free trade and interaction could be fostered.

Ward- One of the clans of Ormond. Now tasked with being treasurers and keepers of the country's wealth. A clan of well-known reformists, even rumored to be related to members of the Order of Jasmine.

Valkeir , Reis- estranged uncle to Argent and an acquaintance of Luloch, whom he helped to formulate their alibi regarding the children (Adimus and Dyshul), and gave them room and board in Ederton. He is a member of the Kingly Council, and was also a known diplomat and statesman who during the secession facilitated the transition of power for the Lord Protector.

Verhousse, Charleze- estranged cousin of Argent. Reis is her uncle.

War of the Leaves, The- A conflict between the Seelie Court and the Blossom Bride that shaped the world during the Second Epochellipse.

Watcher Knows Why- used to show that you are annoyed because you do not know something, or because you think that something is unreasonable.

Weeping Eye- An obscure power (or perhaps object) possessed by the Dragonfather, which is Invoked to awaken the mystic sight of a Sum Seer.

Weeping, the- The ritualistic of hyu'man sacrifice practiced by the hill folk of Macmearion in the days of old.

Wielding- the act of utilizing the Calcinative power in Spell Casting.

Winter Queen- a powerful Fae mentioned to be the ruler of a vast underground kingdom.

Working- the act of Calcinating a subject to attain a desired effect.

Worldheart- Mentioned in passing, it is home to the Winter Queen.

Xanthos- the Golden Order, practitioners of Sourcery. Fae are most often thought to be the bulk of their practitioners.